FEAR NOTHING

G·K
Hall
&Cº

*Also by Dean Koontz
in Large Print:*

Mr. Murder
Dragon Tears
Hideaway
Cold Fire
The Bad Place
Midnight
Lightning
Watchers
The Key to Midnight
Winter Moon

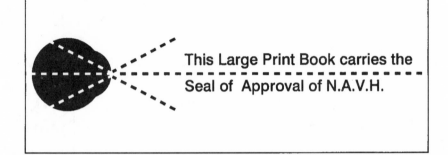

This Large Print Book carries the
Seal of Approval of N.A.V.H.

FEAR NOTHING

DEAN KOONTZ

G.K. Hall & Co.
Thorndike, Maine

Published in 1998 by arrangement with Bantam Books, a division of Bantam Doubleday Dell Publishing Group, Inc.

G.K. Hall Large Print Core Series.

The text of this Large Print edition is unabridged.
Other aspects of the book may vary from the original edition.

Set in 16 pt. Plantin by Minnie B. Raven.

Printed in the United States on permanent paper.

Library of Congress Cataloging in Publication Data

Koontz, Dean R. (Dean Ray), 1945–
    Fear nothing / Dean Koontz.
        p.   (large print)   cm.
    ISBN 0-7838-8358-7 (lg. print : hc : alk. paper)
    1. Large type books.   I. Title.
    [PS3561.O55F4   1998b]
    813′.54—dc21   97-50197

To Robert Gottlieb
for whose vision, genius, dedication,
and friendship I am daily grateful.

We have a weight to carry
and a distance we must go.
We have a weight to carry,
a destination we can't know.
We have a weight to carry
and can put it down nowhere.
We *are* the weight we carry
from there to here to there.

— *The Book of Counted Sorrows*

ONE

TWILIGHT TIME

1

On the desk in my candlelit study, the telephone rang, and I knew that a terrible change was coming.

I am not psychic. I do not see signs and portents in the sky. To my eye, the lines in my palm reveal nothing about my future, and I don't have a Gypsy's ability to discern the patterns of fate in wet tea leaves.

My father had been dying for days, however, and after spending the previous night at his bedside, blotting the sweat from his brow and listening to his labored breathing, I knew that he couldn't hold on much longer. I dreaded losing him and being, for the first time in my twenty-eight years, alone.

I am an only son, an only child, and my mother passed away two years ago. Her death had been a shock, but at least she had not been forced to endure a lingering illness.

Last night just before dawn, exhausted, I had returned home to sleep. But I had not slept much or well.

Now I leaned forward in my chair and willed the phone to fall silent, but it would not.

The dog also knew what the ringing meant. He padded out of the shadows into the candleglow, and stared sorrowfully at me.

Unlike others of his kind, he will hold any man's or woman's gaze as long as he is interested. Animals usually stare directly at us only briefly — then look away as though unnerved by something they see in human eyes. Perhaps Orson sees what other dogs see, and perhaps he, too, is disturbed by it, but he is not intimidated.

He is a strange dog. But he is my dog, my steadfast friend, and I love him.

On the seventh ring, I surrendered to the inevitable and answered the phone.

The caller was a nurse at Mercy Hospital. I spoke to her without looking away from Orson.

My father was quickly fading. The nurse suggested that I come to his bedside without delay.

As I put down the phone, Orson approached my chair and rested his burly black head in my lap. He whimpered softly and nuzzled my hand. He did not wag his tail.

For a moment I was numb, unable to think or act. The silence of the house, as deep as water in an oceanic abyss, was a crushing, immobilizing pressure. Then I phoned Sasha Goodall to ask her to drive me to the hospital.

Usually she slept from noon until eight o'clock. She spun music in the dark, from midnight until six o'clock in the morning, on KBAY, the only radio station in Moonlight Bay. At a few minutes past five on this March evening, she was most likely sleeping, and I regretted the need to wake her.

Like sad-eyed Orson, however, Sasha was my friend, to whom I could always turn. And she was a far better driver than the dog.

She answered on the second ring, with no trace of sleepiness in her voice. Before I could tell her what had happened, she said, "Chris, I'm so sorry," as though she had been waiting for this call and as if in the ringing of her phone she had heard the same ominous note that Orson and I had heard in mine.

I bit my lip and refused to consider what was coming. As long as Dad was alive, hope remained that his doctors were wrong. Even at the eleventh hour, the cancer might go into remission.

I believe in the possibility of miracles.

After all, in spite of my condition, I have lived more than twenty-eight years, which is a miracle of sorts — although some other people, seeing my life from outside, might think it a curse.

I believe in the possibility of miracles, but more to the point, I believe in our *need* for them.

"I'll be there in five minutes," Sasha promised.

At night I could walk to the hospital, but at this hour I would be too much of a spectacle and in too great a danger if I tried to make the trip on foot.

"No," I said. "Drive carefully. I'll probably take ten minutes or more to get ready."

"Love you, Snowman."

"Love you," I replied.

I replaced the cap on the pen with which I had been writing when the call had come from the hospital, and I put it aside with the yellow legal-size tablet.

Using a long-handled brass snuffer, I extinguished the three fat candles. Thin, sinuous ghosts of smoke writhed in the shadows.

11

Now, an hour before twilight, the sun was low in the sky but still dangerous. It glimmered threateningly at the edges of the pleated shades that covered all the windows.

Anticipating my intentions, as usual, Orson was already out of the room, padding across the upstairs hall.

He is a ninety-pound Labrador mix, as black as a witch's cat. Through the layered shadows of our house, he roams all but invisibly, his presence betrayed only by the thump of his big paws on the area rugs and by the click of his claws on the hardwood floors.

In my bedroom, across the hall from the study, I didn't bother to switch on the dimmer-controlled, frosted-glass ceiling fixture. The indirect, sour-yellow light of the westering sun, pressing at the edges of the window shades, was sufficient for me.

My eyes are better adapted to gloom than are those of most people. Although I am, figuratively speaking, a brother to the owl, I don't have a special gift of nocturnal sight, nothing as romantic or as thrilling as a paranormal talent. Simply this: Lifelong habituation to darkness has sharpened my night vision.

Orson leaped onto the footstool and then curled on the armchair to watch me as I girded myself for the sunlit world.

From a pullman drawer in the adjoining bathroom, I withdrew a squeeze bottle of lotion that included a sunscreen with a rating of fifty. I applied it generously to my face, ears, and neck.

The lotion had a faint coconut scent, an

12

aroma that I associate with palm trees in sunshine, tropical skies, ocean vistas spangled with noontime light, and other things that will be forever beyond my experience. This, for me, is the fragrance of desire and denial and hopeless yearning, the succulent perfume of the unattainable.

Sometimes I dream that I am walking on a Caribbean beach in a rain of sunshine, and the white sand under my feet seems to be a cushion of pure radiance. The warmth of the sun on my skin is more erotic than a lover's touch. In the dream, I am not merely bathed in the light but pierced by it. When I wake, I am bereft.

Now the lotion, although smelling of the tropical sun, was cool on my face and neck. I also worked it into my hands and wrists.

The bathroom featured a single window at which the shade was currently raised, but the space remained meagerly illuminated because the glass was frosted and because the incoming sunlight was filtered through the graceful limbs of a metrosideros. The silhouettes of leaves fluttered on the pane.

In the mirror above the sink, my reflection was little more than a shadow. Even if I switched on the light, I would not have had a clear look at myself, because the single bulb in the overhead fixture was of low wattage and had a peach tint.

Only rarely have I seen my face in full light.

Sasha says that I remind her of James Dean, more as he was in *East of Eden* than in *Rebel Without a Cause*.

I myself don't perceive the resemblance. The

hair is the same, yes, and the pale blue eyes. But he looked so wounded, and I do not see myself that way.

I am not James Dean. I am no one but me, Christopher Snow, and I can live with that.

Finished with the lotion, I returned to the bedroom. Orson raised his head from the armchair to savor the coconut scent.

I was already wearing athletic socks, Nikes, blue jeans, and a black T-shirt. I quickly pulled on a black denim shirt with long sleeves and buttoned it at the neck.

Orson trailed me downstairs to the foyer. Because the porch was deep with a low ceiling, and because two massive California live oaks stood in the yard, no direct sun could reach the sidelights flanking the front door; consequently, they were not covered with curtains or blinds. The leaded panes — geometric mosaics of clear, green, red, and amber glass — glowed softly like jewels.

I took a zippered, black leather jacket from the coat closet. I would be out after dark, and even following a mild March day, the central coast of California can turn chilly when the sun goes down.

From the closet shelf, I snatched a navy-blue, billed cap and pulled it on, tugging it low on my head. Across the front, above the visor, in ruby-red embroidered letters, were the words *Mystery Train.*

One night during the previous autumn, I had found the cap in Fort Wyvern, the abandoned military base inland from Moonlight Bay. It had been the only object in a cool, dry, concrete-walled room three stories underground.

Although I had no idea to what the embroidered words might refer, I had kept the cap because it intrigued me.

As I turned toward the front door, Orson whined beseechingly.

I stooped and petted him. "I'm sure Dad would like to see you one last time, fella. I know he would. But there's no place for you in a hospital."

His direct, coal-black eyes glimmered. I could have sworn that his gaze brimmed with grief and sympathy. Maybe that was because I was looking at him through repressed tears of my own.

My friend Bobby Halloway says that I tend to anthropomorphize animals, ascribing to them human attributes and attitudes which they do not, in fact, possess.

Perhaps this is because animals, unlike some people, have always accepted me for what I am. The four-legged citizens of Moonlight Bay seem to possess a more complex understanding of life — as well as more kindness — than at least some of my neighbors.

Bobby tells me that anthropomorphizing animals, regardless of my experiences with them, is a sign of immaturity. I tell Bobby to go copulate with himself.

I comforted Orson, stroking his glossy coat and scratching behind his ears. He was curiously tense. Twice he cocked his head to listen intently to sounds I could not hear — as if he sensed a threat looming, something even worse than the loss of my father.

At that time, I had not yet seen anything suspicious about Dad's impending death. Cancer was only fate, not murder — unless you wanted to try bringing criminal charges against God.

That I had lost both parents within two years, that my mother had died when she was only fifty-two, that my father was only fifty-six as he lay on his deathbed . . . well, all this just seemed to be my poor luck — which had been with me, literally, since my conception.

Later, I would have reason to recall Orson's tension — and good reason to wonder if he had sensed the tidal wave of trouble washing toward us.

Bobby Halloway would surely sneer at this and say that I am doing worse than anthropomorphizing the mutt, that now I am ascribing *super*human attributes to him. I would have to agree — and then tell Bobby to go copulate *vigorously* with himself.

Anyway, I petted and scratched and generally comforted Orson until a horn sounded in the street and then, almost at once, sounded again in the driveway.

Sasha had arrived.

In spite of the sunscreen on my neck, I turned up the collar of my jacket for additional protection.

From the Stickley-style foyer table under a print of Maxfield Parrish's *Daybreak*, I grabbed a pair of wraparound sunglasses.

With my hand on the hammered-copper doorknob, I turned to Orson once more. "We'll be all right."

In fact, I didn't know quite how we could go

on without my father. He was our link to the world of light and to the people of the day.

More than that, he loved me as no one left on earth could love me, as only a parent could love a damaged child. He understood me as perhaps no one would ever understand me again.

"We'll be all right," I repeated.

The dog regarded me solemnly and chuffed once, almost pityingly, as if he knew that I was lying.

I opened the front door, and as I went outside, I put on the wraparound sunglasses. The special lenses were totally UV-proof.

My eyes are my point of greatest vulnerability. I can take no risk whatsoever with them.

Sasha's green Ford Explorer was in the driveway, with the engine running, and she was behind the wheel.

I closed the house door and locked it. Orson had made no attempt to slip out at my heels.

A breeze had sprung up from the west: an onshore flow with the faint, astringent scent of the sea. The leaves of the oaks whispered as if transmitting secrets branch to branch.

My chest grew so tight that my lungs felt constricted, as was always the case when I was required to venture outside in daylight. This symptom was entirely psychological but nonetheless affecting.

Going down the porch steps and along the flagstone walk to the driveway, I felt weighed down. Perhaps this was how a deep-sea diver might feel in a pressure suit with a kingdom of water overhead.

2

When I got into the Explorer, Sasha Goodall said quietly, "Hey, Snowman."

"Hey."

I buckled my safety harness as Sasha shifted into reverse.

From under the bill of my cap, I peered at the house as we backed away from it, wondering how it would appear to me when next I saw it. I felt that when my father left this world, all of the things that had belonged to him would look shabbier and diminished because they would no longer be touched by his spirit.

It is a Craftsman-period structure, in the Greene and Greene tradition: ledger stone set with a minimum of mortar, cedar siding silvered by weather and time, entirely modern in its lines but not in the least artificial or insubstantial, fully of the earth and formidable. After the recent winter rains, the crisp lines of the slate roof were softened by a green coverlet of lichen.

As we reversed into the street, I thought that I saw the shade nudged aside at one of the living-room windows, at the back of the deep porch, and Orson's face at the pane, his paws on the sill.

As she drove away from the house, Sasha said, "How long since you've been out in this?"

"Daylight? A little over nine years."

"A novena to the darkness."

She was also a songwriter.

I said, "Damn it, Goodall, don't wax poetic on me."

"What happened nine years ago?"

"Appendicitis."

"Ah. That time when you almost died."

"Only death brings me out in daylight."

She said, "At least you got a sexy scar from it."

"You think so?"

"I like to kiss it, don't I?"

"I've wondered about that."

"Actually, it scares me, that scar," she said. "You might have died."

"Didn't."

"I kiss it like I'm saying a little prayer of thanks. That you're here with me."

"Or maybe you're sexually aroused by deformity."

"Asshole."

"Your mother never taught you language like that."

"It was the nuns in parochial school."

I said, "You know what I like?"

"We've been together almost two years. Yeah, I think I know what you like."

"I like that you never cut me any slack."

"Why should I?" she asked.

"Exactly."

Even in my armor of cloth and lotion, behind the shades that shielded my sensitive eyes from ultraviolet rays, I was unnerved by the day around and above me. I felt eggshell-fragile in its vise grip.

Sasha was aware of my uneasiness but pretended not to notice. To take my mind off both the threat and the boundless beauty of the sunlit world, she did what she does so well — which is be Sasha.

"Where will you be later?" she asked. "When it's over."

"*If* it's over. They could be wrong."

"Where will you be when I'm on the air?"

"After midnight . . . probably Bobby's place."

"Make sure he turns on his radio."

"Are you taking requests tonight?" I asked.

"You don't have to call in. I'll know what you need."

At the next corner, she swung the Explorer right, onto Ocean Avenue. She drove uphill, away from the sea.

Fronting the shops and restaurants beyond the deep sidewalks, eighty-foot stone pines spread wings of branches across the street. The pavement was feathered with shadow and sunshine.

Moonlight Bay, home to twelve thousand people, rises from the harbor and flatlands into gentle serried hills. In most California travel guides, our town is called the Jewel of the Central Coast, partly because the chamber of commerce schemes relentlessly to have this sobriquet widely used.

The town has earned the name, however, for many reasons, not least of which is our wealth of trees. Majestic oaks with hundred-year crowns. Pines, cedars, phoenix palms. Deep eucalyptus groves. My favorites are the clusters of lacy *melaleuca luminaria* draped with stoles of

20

ermine blossoms in the spring.

As a result of our relationship, Sasha had applied protective film to the Explorer windows. Nevertheless, the view was shockingly brighter than that to which I was accustomed.

I slid my glasses down my nose and peered over the frames.

The pine needles stitched an elaborate dark embroidery on a wondrous purple-blue, late-afternoon sky bright with mystery, and a reflection of this pattern flickered across the windshield.

I quickly pushed my glasses back in place, not merely to protect my eyes but because suddenly I was ashamed for taking such delight in this rare daytime journey even as my father lay dying.

Judiciously speeding, never braking to a full stop at those intersections without traffic, Sasha said, "I'll go in with you."

"That's not necessary."

Sasha's intense dislike of doctors and nurses and all things medical bordered on a phobia. Most of the time she was convinced that she would live forever; she had great faith in the power of vitamins, minerals, antioxidants, positive thinking, and mind-body healing techniques. A visit to any hospital, however, temporarily shook her conviction that she would avoid the fate of all flesh.

"Really," she said, "I should be with you. I love your dad."

Her outer calm was belied by a quiver in her voice, and I was touched by her willingness to go, just for me, where she most loathed to go.

I said, "I want to be alone with him, this little time we have."

"Truly?"

"Truly. Listen, I forgot to leave dinner out for Orson. Could you go back to the house and take care of that?"

"Yeah," she said, relieved to have a task. "Poor Orson. He and your dad were real buddies."

"I swear he knows."

"Sure. Animals know things."

"Especially Orson."

From Ocean Avenue, she turned left onto Pacific View. Mercy Hospital was two blocks away.

She said, "He'll be okay."

"He doesn't show it much, but he's already grieving in his way."

"I'll give him lots of hugs and cuddles."

"Dad was his link to the day."

"I'll be his link now," she promised.

"He can't live exclusively in the dark."

"He's got me, and I'm never going anywhere."

"Aren't you?" I asked.

"He'll be okay."

We weren't really talking about the dog anymore.

The hospital is a three-story California Mediterranean structure built in another age when that term did not bring to mind uninspired tract-house architecture and cheap construction. The deeply set windows feature patinaed bronze frames. Ground-floor rooms are shaded by loggias with arches and limestone columns.

Some of the columns are entwined by the woody vines of ancient bougainvillea that blanket the loggia roofs. This day, even with spring a couple of weeks away, cascades of crimson and radiant purple flowers overhung the eaves.

For a daring few seconds, I pulled my sunglasses down my nose and marveled at the sun-splashed celebration of color.

Sasha stopped at a side entrance.

As I freed myself from the safety harness, she put one hand on my arm and squeezed lightly. "Call my cellular number when you want me to come back."

"It'll be after sunset by the time I leave. I'll walk."

"If that's what you want."

"I do."

Again I drew the glasses down my nose, this time to see Sasha Goodall as I had never seen her. In candlelight, her gray eyes are deep but clear — as they are here in the day world, too. Her thick mahogany hair, in candlelight, is as lustrous as wine in crystal — but markedly more lustrous under the stroking hand of the sun. Her creamy, rose-petal skin is flecked with faint freckles, the patterns of which I know as well as I know the constellations in every quadrant of the night sky, season by season.

With one finger, Sasha pushed my sunglasses back into place. "Don't be foolish."

I'm human. Foolish is what we *are.*

If I were to go blind, however, her face would be a sight to sustain me in the lasting blackness.

I leaned across the console and kissed her.

"You smell like coconut," she said.

"I try."

23

I kissed her again.

"You shouldn't be out in this any longer," she said firmly.

The sun, half an hour above the sea, was orange and intense, a perpetual thermonuclear holocaust ninety-three million miles removed. In places, the Pacific was molten copper.

"Go, coconut boy. Away with you."

Shrouded like the Elephant Man, I got out of the Explorer and hurried to the hospital, tucking my hands in the pockets of my leather jacket.

I glanced back once. Sasha was watching. She gave me a thumbs-up sign.

3

When I stepped into the hospital, Angela Ferry-man was waiting in the corridor. She was a third-floor nurse on the evening shift, and she had come downstairs to greet me.

Angela was a sweet-tempered, pretty woman in her late forties: painfully thin and curiously pale-eyed, as though her dedication to nursing was so ferocious that, by the harsh terms of a devilish bargain, she must give the very substance of herself to ensure her patients' recoveries. Her wrists seemed too fragile for the work she did, and she moved so lightly and quickly that it was possible to believe that her bones were as hollow as those of birds.

She switched off the overhead fluorescent panels in the corridor ceiling. Then she hugged me.

When I had suffered the illnesses of childhood and adolescence — mumps, flu, chicken pox — but couldn't be safely treated outside our house, Angela had been the visiting nurse who stopped in daily to check on me. Her fierce, bony hugs were as essential to the conduct of her work as were tongue depressors, thermometers, and syringes.

Nevertheless, this hug frightened more than comforted me, and I said, "Is he?"

"It's all right, Chris. He's still holding on. Holding on just for you, I think."

I went to the emergency stairs nearby. As the

stairwell door eased shut behind me, I was aware of Angela switching on the ground-floor corridor lights once more.

The stairwell was not dangerously well-lighted. Even so, I climbed quickly and didn't remove my sunglasses.

At the head of the stairs, in the third-floor corridor, Seth Cleveland was waiting. He is my father's doctor, and one of mine. Although tall, with shoulders that seem round and massive enough to wedge in one of the hospital loggia arches, he manages never to be looming over you. He moves with the grace of a much smaller man, and his voice is that of a gentle fairy-tale bear.

"We're medicating him for pain," Dr. Cleveland said, turning off the fluorescent panels overhead, "so he's drifting in and out. But each time he comes around, he asks for you."

Removing my glasses at last and tucking them in my shirt pocket, I hurried along the wide corridor, past rooms where patients with all manner of maladies, in all stages of illness, either lay insensate or sat before bed trays that held their dinners. Those who saw the corridor lights go off were aware of the reason, and they paused in their eating to stare at me as I passed their open doors.

In Moonlight Bay, I am a reluctant celebrity. Of the twelve thousand full-time residents and the nearly three thousand students at Ashdon College, a private liberal-arts institution that sits on the highest land in town, I am perhaps the only one whose name is known to all. Because of my nocturnal life, however, not every one of my fellow townspeople has seen me.

As I moved along the hall, most of the nurses and nurses' aides spoke my name or reached out to touch me.

I think they felt close to me not because there was anything especially winning about my personality, not because they loved my father — as, indeed, everyone who knew him loved him — but because they were devoted healers and because I was the ultimate object of their heartfelt desire to nurture and make well. I have been in need of healing all my life, but I am beyond their — or anyone's — power to cure.

My father was in a semiprivate room. At the moment no patient occupied the second bed.

I hesitated on the threshold. Then with a deep breath that did not fortify me, I went inside, closing the door behind me.

The slats of the venetian blinds were tightly shut. At the periphery of each blind, the glossy white window casings glowed orange with the distilled sunlight of the day's last half hour.

On the bed nearest the entrance, my father was a shadowy shape. I heard his shallow breathing. When I spoke, he didn't answer.

He was monitored solely by an electrocardiograph. In order not to disturb him, the audio signal had been silenced; his heartbeat was traced only by a spiking green line of light on a cathode-ray tube.

His pulse was rapid and weak. As I watched, it went through a brief period of arrhythmia, alarming me, before stabilizing again.

In the lower of the two drawers in his night-stand were a butane lighter and a pair of three-inch-diameter bayberry candles in glass cups. The medical staff pretended to be unaware of the presence of these items.

I put the candles on the nightstand.

Because of my limitations, I am granted this dispensation from hospital rules. Otherwise, I would have to sit in utter darkness.

In violation of fire laws, I thumbed the lighter and touched the flame to one wick. Then to the other.

Perhaps my strange celebrity wins me license also. You cannot overestimate the power of celebrity in modern America.

In the flutter of soothing light, my father's face resolved out of the darkness. His eyes were closed. He was breathing through his open mouth.

At his direction, no heroic efforts were being taken to sustain his life. His breathing was not even assisted by an inhalator.

I took off my jacket and the Mystery Train cap, putting them on a chair provided for visitors.

Standing at his bed, on the side more distant from the candles, I took one of his hands in one of mine. His skin was cool, as thin as parchment. Bony hands. His fingernails were yellow, cracked, as they had never been before.

His name was Steven Snow, and he was a great man. He had never won a war, never made a law, never composed a symphony, never written a famous novel as in his youth he had hoped to do, but he was greater than any general, politician, composer, or prize-winning novelist who had ever lived.

He was great because he was kind. He was great because he was humble, gentle, full of laughter. He had been married to my mother for thirty years, and during that long span of temptation, he had remained faithful to her. His love for her had been so luminous that our house, by necessity dimly lighted in most rooms, was bright in all the ways that mattered. A professor of literature at Ashdon — where Mom had been a professor in the science department — Dad was so beloved by his students that many remained in touch with him decades after leaving his classroom.

Although my affliction had severely circumscribed his life virtually from the day that I was born, when he himself was twenty-eight, he had never once made me feel that he regretted fathering me or that I was anything less than an unmitigated joy and a source of undiluted pride to him. He lived with dignity and without complaint, and he never failed to celebrate what was *right* with the world.

Once he had been robust and handsome. Now his body was shrunken and his face was haggard, gray. He looked much older than his fifty-six years. The cancer had spread from his liver to his lymphatic system, then to other organs, until he was riddled with it. In the struggle to survive, he had lost much of his thick white hair.

On the cardiac monitor, the green line began

to spike and trough erratically. I watched it with dread.

Dad's hand closed weakly on mine.

When I looked at him again, his sapphire-blue eyes were open and focused on me, as riveting as ever.

"Water?" I asked, because he was always thirsty lately, parched.

"No, I'm all right," he replied, although he sounded dry. His voice was barely louder than a whisper.

I could think of nothing to say.

All my life, our house was filled with conversation. My dad and mom and I talked about novels, old movies, the follies of politicians, poetry, music, history, science, religion, art, and about owls and deer mice and raccoons and bats and fiddler crabs and other creatures that shared the night with me. Our discourse ranged from serious colloquies about the human condition to frothy gossip about neighbors. In the Snow family, no program of physical exercise, regardless of how strenuous, was considered to be adequate if it didn't include a daily workout of the tongue.

Yet now, when I most desperately needed to open my heart to my father, I was speechless.

He smiled as if he understood my plight and appreciated the irony of it.

Then his smile faded. His drawn and sallow face grew even more gaunt. He was worn so thin, in fact, that when a draft guttered the candle flames, his face appeared to be hardly more substantial than a reflection floating on the surface of a pond.

30

As the flickery light stabilized, I thought that Dad seemed to be in agony, but when he spoke, his voice revealed sorrow and regret rather than pain: "I'm sorry, Chris. So damn sorry."

"You've nothing to be sorry about," I assured him, wondering if he was lucid or speaking through a haze of fever and drugs.

"Sorry about the inheritance, son."

"I'll be okay. I can take care of myself."

"Not money. There'll be enough of that," he said, his whispery voice fading further. His words slipped from his pale lips almost as silently as the liquid of an egg from a cracked shell. "The other inheritance . . . from your mother and me. The XP."

"Dad, no. You couldn't have known."

His eyes closed again. Words as thin and transparent as raw egg white: "I'm so sorry. . . ."

"You gave me *life*," I said.

His hand had gone limp in mine.

For an instant I thought that he was dead. My heart fell stone-through-water in my chest.

But the beat traced in green light by the electrocardiograph showed that he had merely lost consciousness again.

"Dad, you gave me life," I repeated, distraught that he couldn't hear me.

My dad and mom had each unknowingly carried a recessive gene that appears in only one in two hundred thousand people. The odds against two such people meeting, falling in love, and having children are millions to one. Even then, both must pass the gene to their offspring for calamity to strike, and there is only one chance in four that they will do so.

With me, my folks hit the jackpot. I have xeroderma pigmentosum — XP for short — a rare and frequently fatal genetic disorder.

XP victims are acutely vulnerable to cancers of the skin and eyes. Even brief exposure to sun — indeed, to any ultraviolet rays, including those from incandescent and fluorescent lights — could be disastrous for me.

All human beings incur sunlight damage to the DNA — the genetic material — in their cells, inviting melanoma and other malignancies. Healthy people possess a natural repair system: enzymes that strip out the damaged segments of the nucleotide strands and replace them with un-damaged DNA.

In those with XP, however, the enzymes don't function; the repair is not made. Ultraviolet-in-duced cancers develop easily, quickly — and me-tastasize unchecked.

The United States, with a population exceed-ing two hundred and seventy million, is home to more than eighty thousand dwarfs. Ninety thousand of our countrymen stand over seven feet tall. Our nation boasts four million million-aires, and ten thousand more will achieve that happy status during the current year. In any twelve months, perhaps a thousand of our citi-zens will be struck by lightning.

Fewer than a thousand Americans have XP, and fewer than a hundred are born with it each year.

The number is small in part because the affliction is so rare. The size of this XP population is also limited by the fact that many of us do not live long.

Most physicians familiar with xeroderma pigmentosum would have expected me to die in childhood. Few would have bet that I could survive adolescence. None would have risked serious money on the proposition that I would still be thriving at twenty-eight.

A handful of XPers (my word for us) are older than I am, a few significantly older, though most if not all of them have suffered progressive neurological problems associated with their disorder. Tremors of the head or the hands. Hearing loss. Slurred speech. Even mental impairment.

Except for my need to guard against the light, I am as normal and whole as anyone. I am not an albino. My eyes have color. My skin is pigmented. Although certainly I am far paler than a California beach boy, I'm not ghost-white. In the candlelit rooms and the night world that I inhabit, I can even appear, curiously, to have a dusky complexion.

Every day that I remain in my current condition is a precious gift, and I believe that I use my time as well and as fully as it can be used. I relish life. I find delight where anyone would expect it — but also where few would think to look.

In 23 B.C., the poet Horace said, "Seize the day, put no trust in the morrow!"

I seize the *night* and ride it as though it were a great black stallion.

Most of my friends say that I am the happiest person they know. Happiness was mine to choose or reject, and I embraced it.

Without my particular parents, however, I might not have been granted this choice. My mother and father radically altered their lives to shield me aggressively from damaging light, and until I was old enough to understand my predicament, they were required to be relentlessly, exhaustingly vigilant. Their selfless diligence contributed incalculably to my survival. Furthermore, they gave me the love — and the love of life — that made it impossible for me to choose depression, despair, and a reclusive existence.

My mother died suddenly. Although I know that she understood the profound depth of my feeling for her, I wish that I had been able to express it to her adequately on that last day of her life.

Sometimes, out in the night, on the dark beach, when the sky is clear and the vault of stars makes me feel simultaneously mortal and invincible, when the wind is still and even the sea is hushed as it breaks upon the shore, I tell my mother what she meant to me. But I don't know that she hears.

Now my father — still with me, if only tenuously — did not hear me when I said, "You gave me life." And I was afraid that he would take his leave before I could tell him all the things that I'd been given no last chance to tell my mother.

His hand remained cool and limp. I held it anyway, as if to anchor him to this world until

I could say good-bye properly.

At the edges of the venetian blinds, the window frames and casings smoldered from orange to fiery red as the sun met the sea.

There is only one circumstance under which I will ever view a sunset directly. If I should develop cancer of the eyes, then before I succumb to it or go blind, I will one late afternoon go down to the sea and stand facing those distant Asian empires where I will never walk. On the brink of dusk, I'll remove my sunglasses and watch the dying of the light.

I'll have to squint. Bright light pains my eyes. Its effect is so total and swift that I can virtually feel the developing burn.

As the blood-red light at the periphery of the blinds deepened to purple, my father's hand tightened on mine.

I looked down, saw that his eyes were open, and tried to tell him all that was in my heart.

"I know," he whispered.

When I was unable to stop saying what didn't need to be said, Dad found an unexpected reserve of strength and squeezed my hand so hard that I halted in my speech.

Into my shaky silence, he said, "Remember . . ."

I could barely hear him. I leaned over the bed railing to put my left ear close to his lips.

Faintly, yet projecting a resolve that resonated with anger and defiance, he gave me his final words of guidance: "Fear nothing, Chris. Fear nothing."

Then he was gone. The luminous tracery of the electrocardiogram skipped, skipped again, and went flatline.

The only moving lights were the candle flames, dancing on the black wicks.

I could not immediately let go of his slack hand. I kissed his forehead, his rough cheek.

No light any longer leaked past the edges of the blinds. The world had rotated into the darkness that welcomed me.

The door opened. Again, they had extinguished the nearest banks of fluorescent panels, and the only light in the corridor came from other rooms along its length.

Nearly as tall as the doorway, Dr. Cleveland entered the room and came gravely to the foot of the bed.

With sandpiper-quick steps, Angela Ferryman followed him, one sharp-knuckled fist held to her breast. Her shoulders were hunched, her posture defensive, as if her patient's death were a physical blow.

The EKG machine beside the bed was equipped with a telemetry device that sent Dad's heartbeat to a monitor at the nurses' station down the hall. They had known the moment that he slipped away.

They didn't come with syringes full of epinephrine or with a portable defibrillator to shock his heart back into action. As Dad had wanted, there would be no heroic measures.

Dr. Cleveland's features were not designed for solemn occasions. He resembled a beardless Santa Claus with merry eyes and plump rosy cheeks. He strove for a dour expression of grief and sympathy, but he managed only to look puzzled.

His feelings were evident, however, in his soft voice. "Are you okay, Chris?"

"Hanging in there," I said.

4

From the hospital room, I telephoned Sandy
Kirk at Kirk's Funeral Home, with whom my
father himself had made arrangements weeks
ago. In accordance with Dad's wishes, he was
to be cremated.

Two orderlies, young men with chopped hair
and feeble mustaches, arrived to move the body
to a cold-holding room in the basement.

They asked if I wanted to wait down there
with it until the mortician's van arrived. I said
that I didn't.

This was not my father, only his body. My
father had gone elsewhere.

I opted not to pull the sheet back for one last
look at Dad's sallow face. This wasn't how I
wanted to remember him.

The orderlies moved the body onto a gurney.
They seemed awkward in the conduct of their
business, at which they ought to have been practiced, and they glanced at me surreptitiously
while they worked, as if they felt inexplicably
guilty about what they were doing.

Maybe those who transport the dead never become entirely easy with their work. How reassuring it would be to believe as much, for such
awkwardness might mean that people are not as
indifferent to the fate of others as they sometimes seem to be.

More likely, these two were merely curious,

sneaking glances at me. I am, after all, the only citizen of Moonlight Bay to have been featured in a major article in *Time* magazine.

And I am the one who lives by night and shrinks from the sight of the sun. Vampire! Ghoul! Filthy wacko pervert! Hide your children!

To be fair, the vast majority of people are understanding and kind. A poisonous minority, however, are rumormongers who believe anything about me that they hear — and who embellish all gossip with the self-righteousness of spectators at a Salem witch trial.

If these two young men were of the latter type, they must have been disappointed to see that I looked remarkably normal. No grave-pale face. No blood-red eyes. No fangs. I wasn't even having a snack of spiders and worms. How boring of me.

The wheels on the gurney creaked as the orderlies departed with the body. Even after the door swung shut, I could hear the receding *squeak-squeak-squeak.*

Alone in the room, by candlelight, I took Dad's overnight bag from the narrow closet. It held only the clothes that he had been wearing when he'd checked into the hospital for the last time.

The top nightstand drawer contained his watch, his wallet, and four paperback books. I put them in the suitcase.

I pocketed the butane lighter but left the candles behind. I never wanted to smell bayberry again. The scent now had intolerable associations for me.

Because I gathered up Dad's few belongings with such efficiency, I felt that I was admirably in control of myself.

In fact, the loss of him had left me numb. Snuffing the candles by pinching the flames between thumb and forefinger, I didn't feel the heat or smell the charred wicks.

When I stepped into the corridor with the suitcase, a nurse switched off the overhead fluorescents once more. I walked directly to the stairs that I had climbed earlier.

Elevators were of no use to me because their ceiling lights couldn't be turned off independently of their lift mechanisms. During the brief ride down from the third floor, my sunscreen lotion would be sufficient protection; however, I wasn't prepared to risk getting stuck between floors for an extended period.

Without remembering to put on my sunglasses, I quickly descended the dimly lighted concrete stairs — and to my surprise, I didn't stop at the ground floor. Driven by a compulsion that I didn't immediately understand, moving faster than before, the suitcase thumping against my leg, I continued to the basement, where they had taken my father.

The numbness in my heart became a chill. Spiraling outward from that icy throb, a series of shudders worked through me.

Abruptly I was overcome by the conviction that I'd relinquished my father's body without fulfilling some solemn duty, although I was not able to think what it was that I ought to have done.

My heart was pounding so hard that I could hear it — like the drumbeat of an approaching funeral cortege but in double time. My throat swelled half shut, and I could swallow my suddenly sour saliva only with effort.

At the bottom of the stairwell was a steel fire door under a red emergency-exit sign. In some confusion, I halted and hesitated with one hand on the push bar.

Then I remembered the obligation that I had almost failed to meet. Ever the romantic, Dad had wanted to be cremated with his favorite photograph of my mother, and he had charged me with making sure that it was sent with him to the mortuary.

The photo was in his wallet. The wallet was in the suitcase that I carried.

Impulsively I pushed open the door and stepped into a basement hallway. The concrete walls were painted glossy white. From silvery parabolic diffusers overhead, torrents of fluorescent light splashed the corridor.

I should have reeled backward across the threshold or, at least, searched for the light switch. Instead, I hurried recklessly forward, letting the heavy door sigh shut behind me, keeping my head down, counting on the sunscreen and my cap visor to protect my face.

I jammed my left hand into a jacket pocket. My right hand was clenched around the handle of the suitcase, exposed.

The amount of light bombarding me during a race along a hundred-foot corridor would not be sufficient, in itself, to trigger a raging skin cancer or tumors of the eyes. I was acutely aware, however, that the damage sustained by the DNA in my skin cells was cumulative because my body could not repair it. A measured minute of exposure each day for two months would have the same catastrophic effect as a one-hour burn sustained in a suicidal session of sunworship.

My parents had impressed upon me, from a young age, that the consequences of a single irresponsible act might appear negligible or even nonexistent but that inevitable horrors would ensue from *habitual* irresponsibility.

Even with my head tucked down and my cap visor blocking a direct view of the egg-crate fluorescent panels, I had to squint against the glare that ricocheted off the white walls. I should have put on my sunglasses, but I was only seconds from the end of the hallway.

The gray-and-red-marbled vinyl flooring looked like day-old raw meat. A mild dizziness overcame me, inspired by the vileness of the pattern in the tile and by the fearsome glare.

I passed storage and machinery rooms.

The basement appeared to be deserted.

The door at the farther end of the corridor became the door at the nearer end. I stepped into a small subterranean garage.

This was not the public parking lot, which lay above ground. Nearby were only a panel truck with the hospital name on the side and a paramedics' van.

More distant was a black Cadillac hearse from Kirk's Funeral Home. I was relieved that Sandy Kirk had not already collected the body and departed. I still had time to put the photo of my mother between Dad's folded hands.

Parked beside the gleaming hearse was a Ford van similar to the paramedics' vehicle except that it was not fitted with the standard emergency beacons. Both the hearse and the van were facing away from me, just inside the big roll-up door, which was open to the night.

Otherwise, the space was empty, so delivery trucks could pull inside to off-load food, linens, and medical supplies to the freight elevator. At the moment, no deliveries were being made.

The concrete walls were not painted here, and the fluorescent fixtures overhead were fewer and farther apart than in the corridor that I had just left. Nevertheless, this was still not a safe place for me, and I moved quickly toward the hearse and the white van.

The corner of the basement immediately to the left of the roll-up garage door and past those two waiting vehicles was occupied by a room that I knew well. It was the cold-holding chamber, where the dead were kept until they could be transported to mortuaries.

One terrible January night two years ago, by candlelight, my father and I had waited miserably in cold-holding more than half an hour with the body of my mother. We could not bear to leave her there alone.

Dad would have followed her from the hospital to the mortuary and into the crematorium furnace that night — if not for his inability to abandon me. A poet and a scientist, but such similar souls.

She had been brought from the scene of the accident by ambulance and rushed from the emergency room to surgery. She died three minutes after reaching the operating table, without regaining consciousness, even before the full extent of her injuries could be determined.

Now the insulated door to the cold-holding chamber stood open, and as I approached it, I heard men arguing inside. In spite of their anger, they kept their voices low; an emotional note of strenuous disagreement was matched by a tone of urgency and secrecy.

Their circumspection rather than their anger brought me to a stop just before I reached the doorway. In spite of the deadly fluorescent light, I stood for a moment in indecision.

From beyond the door came a voice I recognized. Sandy Kirk said, "So who is this guy I'll be cremating?"

Another man said, "Nobody. Just a vagrant."

"You should have brought him to my place, not here," Sandy complained. "And what happens when he's missed?"

A third man spoke, and I recognized his voice as that of one of the two orderlies who had collected my father's body from the room upstairs: "Can we for God's sake just move this along?"

Suddenly certain that it was dangerous to be encumbered, I set the suitcase against the wall, freeing both hands.

A man appeared in the doorway, but he didn't see me because he was backing across the threshold, pulling a gurney.

The hearse was eight feet away. Before I was

spotted, I slipped to it, crouching by the rear door through which cadavers were loaded.

Peering around the fender, I could still see the entrance to the cold-holding chamber. The man backing out of that room was a stranger: late twenties, six feet, massively built, with a thick neck and a shaved head. He was wearing work shoes, blue jeans, a red-plaid flannel shirt — and one pearl earring.

After he drew the gurney completely across the threshold, he swung it around toward the hearse, ready to push instead of pull.

On the gurney was a corpse in an opaque, zippered vinyl bag. In the cold-holding chamber two years ago, my mother was transferred into a similar bag before being released to the mortician.

Following the stone-bald stranger into the garage, Sandy Kirk gripped the gurney with one hand. Blocking a wheel with his left foot, he asked again, "What happens when he's missed?"

The bald man frowned and cocked his head. The pearl in his earlobe was luminous. "I told you, he was a vagrant. Everything he owned is in his backpack."

"So?"

"He disappears — who's to notice or care?"

Sandy was thirty-two and so good-looking that even his grisly occupation gave no pause to the women who pursued him. Although he was charming and less self-consciously dignified than many in his profession, he made me uneasy. His handsome features seemed to be a mask behind which was not another face but an emptiness —

not as though he were a different and less morally motivated man than he pretended to be, but as though he were no man at all.

Sandy said, "What about his hospital records?"

"He didn't die here," the bald man said. "I picked him up earlier, out on the state highway. He was hitchhiking."

I had never voiced my troubling perception of Sandy Kirk to anyone: not to my parents, not to Bobby Halloway, not to Sasha, not even to Orson. So many thoughtless people have made unkind assumptions about me, based on my appearance and my affinity for the night, that I am reluctant to join the club of cruelty and speak ill of anyone without ample reason.

Sandy's father, Frank, had been a fine and well-liked man, and Sandy had never done anything to indicate that he was less admirable than his dad. Until now.

To the man with the gurney, Sandy said, "I'm taking a big risk."

"You're untouchable."

"I wonder."

"Wonder on your own time," said the bald man, and he rolled the gurney over Sandy's blocking foot.

Sandy cursed and scuttled out of the way, and the man with the gurney came directly toward me. The wheels squeaked — as had the wheels of the gurney on which they had taken away my father.

Still crouching, I slipped around the back of the hearse, between it and the white Ford van.

A quick glance revealed that no company or institution name adorned the side of the van.

The squeaking gurney was rapidly drawing nearer.

Instinctively, I knew I was in considerable jeopardy. I had caught them in some scheme that I didn't understand but that clearly involved illegalities. They would especially want to keep it secret from me, of all people.

I dropped facedown on the floor and slid under the hearse, out of sight and also out of the fluorescent glare, into shadows as cool and smooth as silk. My hiding place was barely spacious enough to accommodate me, and when I hunched my back, it pressed against the drive train.

I was facing the rear of the vehicle. I watched the gurney roll past the hearse and continue to the van.

When I turned my head to the right, I saw the threshold of the cold-holding chamber only eight feet beyond the Cadillac. I had an even closer view of Sandy's highly polished black shoes and the cuffs of his navy-blue suit pants as he stood looking after the bald man with the gurney.

Behind Sandy, against the wall, was my father's small suitcase. There had been nowhere nearby to conceal it, and if I had kept it with me, I wouldn't have been able to move quickly enough or slip noiselessly under the hearse.

Apparently no one had noticed the suitcase yet. Maybe they would continue to overlook it.

The two orderlies — whom I could identify

by their white shoes and white pants — rolled a second gurney out of the holding room. The wheels on this one did not squeak.

The first gurney, pushed by the bald man, reached the back of the white van. I heard him open the rear cargo doors on that vehicle.

One of the orderlies said to the other, "I better get upstairs before someone starts wondering what's taking me so long." He walked away, toward the far end of the garage.

The collapsible legs on the first gurney folded up with a hard clatter as the bald man shoved it into the back of his van.

Sandy opened the rear door on the hearse as the remaining orderly arrived with the second gurney. On this one, evidently, was another opaque vinyl bag containing the body of the nameless vagrant.

A sense of unreality overcame me — that I should find myself in these strange circumstances. I could almost believe that I had somehow fallen into a dream without first falling into sleep.

The cargo-hold doors on the van slammed shut. Turning my head to the left, I watched the bald man's shoes as he approached the driver's door.

The orderly would wait here to close the big roll-up after the two vehicles departed. If I stayed under the hearse, I would be discovered when Sandy drove away.

I didn't know which of the two orderlies had remained behind, but it didn't matter. I was relatively confident that I could get the better of either of the young men who had wheeled my father away from his deathbed.

If Sandy Kirk glanced at his rear-view mirror as he drove out of the garage, however, he might see me. Then I would have to contend with both him and the orderly.

The engine of the van turned over.

As Sandy and the orderly shoved the gurney into the back of the hearse, I eeled out from under that vehicle. My cap was knocked off. I snatched it up and, without daring to glance toward the rear of the hearse, crabbed eight feet to the open door of the cold-holding chamber.

Inside this bleak room, I scrambled to my feet and hid behind the door, pressing my back to the concrete wall.

No one in the garage cried out in alarm. Evidently I had not been seen.

I realized that I was holding my breath. I let it out with a long hiss between clenched teeth.

My light-stung eyes were watering. I blotted them on the backs of my hands.

Two walls were occupied by over-and-under rows of stainless-steel morgue drawers in which the air was even colder than in the holding chamber itself, where the temperature was low enough to make me shiver. Two cushionless wooden chairs stood to one side. The flooring was white porcelain tile with tight grout joints for easy cleaning if a body bag sprang a leak.

Again, there were overhead fluorescent tubes, too many of them, and I tugged my Mystery Train cap far down on my brow. Surprisingly, the sunglasses in my shirt pocket had not been broken. I shielded my eyes.

A percentage of ultraviolet radiation penetrates even a highly rated sunscreen. I had sustained more exposure to hard light in the past hour than during the entire previous year. Like the hoofbeats of a fearsome black horse, the perils of cumulative exposure thundered through my mind.

From beyond the open door, the van's engine roared. The roar swiftly receded, fading to a grumble, and the grumble became a dying murmur.

The Cadillac hearse followed the van into the night. The big motorized garage door rolled down and met the sill with a solid blow that echoed through the hospital's subterranean realms, and in its wake, the echo shook a trembling silence out of the concrete walls.

I tensed, balling my hands into fists.

Although he was surely still in the garage, the orderly made no sound. I imagined him, head cocked with curiosity, staring at my father's suitcase.

A minute ago I had been sure that I could overpower this man. Now my confidence ebbed. Physically, I was more than his equal — but he might possess a ruthlessness that I did not.

I didn't hear him approaching. He was on the other side of the open door, inches from me, and I became aware of him only because the rubber soles of his shoes squeaked on the porcelain tile when he crossed the threshold.

If he came all the way inside, a confrontation was inevitable. My nerves were coiled as tight as clockwork mainsprings.

After a disconcertingly long hesitation, the orderly switched off the lights. He pulled the door shut as he backed out of the room.

I heard him insert a key in the lock. The dead bolt snapped into place with a sound like the hammer of a heavy-caliber revolver driving the firing pin into an empty chamber.

I doubted that any corpses occupied the chilled morgue drawers. Mercy Hospital — in quiet Moonlight Bay — doesn't crank out the dead at the frenetic pace with which the big institutions process them in the violence-ridden cities.

Even if breathless sleepers were nestled in all these stainless-steel bunks, however, I wasn't nervous about being with them. I will one day be as dead as any resident of a graveyard — no doubt sooner than will other men of my age. The dead are merely the countrymen of my future.

I *did* dread the light, and now the perfect darkness of this cool windowless room was, to me, like quenching water to a man dying of thirst. For a minute or longer I relished the absolute blackness that bathed my skin, my eyes.

Reluctant to move, I remained beside the door, my back against the wall. I half expected the orderly to return at any moment.

Finally I took off my sunglasses and slipped them into my shirt pocket again.

Although I stood in blackness, through my mind spun bright pinwheels of anxious speculation.

My father's body was in the white van. Bound for a destination that I could not guess. In the custody of people whose motivations were utterly incomprehensible to me.

I couldn't imagine any logical reason for this bizarre corpse swap — except that the cause of Dad's death must not have been as straightforward as cancer. Yet if my father's poor dead bones could somehow incriminate someone, why wouldn't the guilty party let Sandy Kirk's crematorium destroy the evidence?

Apparently they needed his body.

For what?

A cold dew had formed inside my clenched fists, and the back of my neck was damp.

The more I thought about the scene that I had witnessed in the garage, the less comfortable I felt in this lightless way station for the dead. These peculiar events stirred primitive fears so deep in my mind that I could not even discern their shape as they swam and circled in the murk.

A murdered hitchhiker would be cremated in my father's place. But why kill a harmless vagrant for this purpose? Sandy could have filled the bronze memorial urn with ordinary wood ashes, and I would have been convinced that they were human. Besides, it was unlikely in the extreme that I would ever pry open the sealed urn once I received it — unlikelier still that I would submit the powdery contents for laboratory testing to determine their composition and true source.

My thoughts seemed tangled in a tightly

woven mesh. I couldn't thrash loose.

Shakily, I withdrew the lighter from my pocket. I hesitated, listening for furtive sounds on the far side of the locked door, and then I struck a flame.

I would not have been surprised to see an alabaster corpse silently risen from its steel sarcophagus, standing before me, face greasy with death and glimmering in the butane lambency, eyes wide but blind, mouth working to impart secrets but producing not even a whisper. No cadaver confronted me, but serpents of light and shadow slipped from the fluttering flame and purled across the steel panels, imparting an illusion of movement to the drawers, so that each receptacle appeared to be inching outward.

Turning to the door, I discovered that to prevent anyone from being accidentally locked in the cold-holding room, the dead bolt could be disengaged from within. On this side, no key was required; the lock could be operated with a simple thumbturn.

I eased the dead bolt out of the striker plate as quietly as possible. The doorknob creaked softly.

The silent garage was apparently deserted, but I remained alert. Someone could be concealed behind one of the supporting columns, the paramedics' van, or the panel truck.

Squinting against the dry rain of fluorescent light, I saw to my dismay that my father's suitcase was gone. The orderly must have taken it.

I did not want to cross the hospital basement to the stairs by which I had descended. The risk of encountering one or both of the orderlies was too great.

Until they opened the suitcase and examined the contents, they might not realize whose property it was. When they found my father's wallet with his ID, they would know I had been here, and they would be concerned about what, if anything, I might have heard and seen.

A hitchhiker had been killed not because he had known anything about their activities, not because he could incriminate them, but merely because they needed a body to cremate for reasons that still escaped me. With those who posed a genuine threat to them, they would be merciless.

I pressed the button that operated the wide roll-up. The motor hummed, the chain drive jerked taut overhead, and that big segmented door ascended with a frightful clatter. I glanced nervously around the garage, expecting to see an assailant break from cover and rush toward me.

When the door was more than halfway open, I stopped it with a second tap of the button and then brought it down again with a third. As it descended, I slipped under the door and into the night.

Tall pole lamps shed a brass-cold, muddy yellow light on the driveway that sloped up from the subterranean garage. At the top of the drive, the parking lot was also cast in this sullen radiance, which was like the frigid glow that might illuminate an anteroom to some precinct of Hell where punishment involved an eternity of ice rather than fire.

As much as possible, I moved through land-scape zones, in the nightshade of camphor trees and pines.

I fled across the narrow street into a residential neighborhood of quaint Spanish bungalows. Into an alleyway without streetlamps. Past the backs of houses bright with windows. Beyond the windows were rooms where strange lives, full of infinite possibility and blissful ordinariness, were lived beyond my reach and almost beyond my comprehension.

Frequently, I feel weightless in the night, and this was one of those times. I ran as silently as the owl flies, gliding on shadows.

This sunless world had welcomed and nurtured me for twenty-eight years, had been always a place of peace and comfort to me. But now for the first time in my life, I was plagued by the feeling that some predatory creature was pursuing me through the darkness.

Resisting the urge to look over my shoulder, I picked up my pace and sprinted-raced-streaked-*flew* through the narrow backstreets and darkways of Moonlight Bay.

TWO

THE EVENING

5

I have seen photographs of California pepper trees in sunlight. When brightly limned, they are lacy, graceful, green dreams of trees.

At night, the pepper acquires a different character from the one that it reveals in daylight. It appears to hang its head, letting its long branches droop to conceal a face drawn with care or grief.

These trees flanked the long driveway to Kirk's Funeral Home, which stood on a three-acre knoll at the northeast edge of town, inland of Highway 1 and reached by an overpass. They waited like lines of mourners, paying their respects.

As I climbed the private lane, on which low mushroom-shaped landscape lamps cast rings of light, the trees stirred in a breeze. The friction between wind and leaves was a whispery lamentation.

No cars were parked along the mortuary approach, which meant that no viewings were in progress.

I myself travel through Moonlight Bay only on foot or on my bicycle. There is no point in learning to drive a car. I couldn't use it by day, and by night I would have to wear sunglasses to spare myself the sting of oncoming headlights. Cops tend to frown on night driving with shades, no matter how cool you look.

The full moon had risen.

I like the moon. It illuminates without scorching. It burnishes what is beautiful and grants concealment to what is not.

At the broad crown of the hill, the blacktop looped back on itself to form a spacious turnaround with a small grassy circle at its center. In the circle was a cast-concrete reproduction of Michelangelo's *Pietà*.

The body of the dead Christ, cradled on his mother's lap, was luminous with reflected moonlight. The Virgin also glowed faintly. In sunshine, this crude replica must surely look unspeakably tacky.

Faced with terrible loss, however, most mourners find comfort in assurances of universal design and meaning, even when as clumsily expressed as in this reproduction. One thing I love about people is their ability to be lifted so high by the smallest drafts of hope.

I stopped under the portico of the funeral home, hesitating because I couldn't assess the danger into which I was about to leap.

The massive two-story Georgian house — red brick with white wood trim — would have been the loveliest house in town, were the town not Moonlight Bay. A spaceship from another galaxy, perched here, would have looked no more alien to our coastline than did Kirk's handsome pile. This house needed elms, not pepper trees, drear heavens rather than the clear skies of California, and periodic lashings with rains far colder than those that would drench it here.

The second floor, where Sandy lived, was dark.

The viewing rooms were on the ground floor. Through beveled, leaded panes that flanked the front door, I saw a weak light at the back of the house.

I rang the bell.

A man entered the far end of the hallway and approached the door. Although he was only a silhouette, I recognized Sandy Kirk by his easy walk. He moved with a grace that enhanced his good looks.

He reached the foyer and switched on both the interior lights and the porch lights. When he opened the door, he seemed surprised to see me squinting at him from under the bill of my cap.

"Christopher?"

"Evening, Mr. Kirk."

"I'm so very sorry about your father. He was a wonderful man."

"Yes. Yes, he was."

"We've already collected him from the hospital. We're treating him just like family, Christopher, with the utmost respect — you can be sure of that. I took his course in twentieth-century poetry at Ashdon. Did you know that?"

"Yes, of course."

"From him I learned to love Eliot and Pound. Auden and Plath. Beckett and Ashbery. Robert Bly. Yeats. All of them. Couldn't tolerate poetry when I started the course — couldn't live without it by the end."

"Wallace Stevens. Donald Justice. Louise Glück. They were his personal favorites."

Sandy smiled and nodded. Then: "Oh, excuse me, I forgot."

Out of consideration for my condition, he extinguished both the foyer and porch lights.

Standing on the dark threshold, he said, "This must be terrible for you, but at least he isn't suffering anymore."

Sandy's eyes were green, but in the pale landscape lighting, they looked as smooth-black as certain beetles' shells.

Studying his eyes, I said, "Could I see him?"

"What — your father?"

"I didn't turn the sheet back from his face before they took him out of his room. Didn't have the heart for it, didn't think I needed to. Now . . . I'd really like just one last look."

Sandy Kirk's eyes were like a placid night sea. Below the unremarkable surface were great teeming depths.

His voice remained that of a compassionate courtier to the bereaved. "Oh, Christopher . . . I'm sorry, but the process has begun."

"You've already put him in the furnace?"

Having grown up in a business conducted with a richness of euphemisms, Sandy winced at my bluntness. "The deceased is in the cremator, yes."

"Wasn't that terribly quick?"

"In our work, there's no wisdom in delay. If only I'd known you were coming . . ."

I wondered if his beetle-shell eyes would be able to meet mine so boldly if there had been enough light for me to see their true green color.

Into my silence, he said, "Christopher, I'm so distressed by this, seeing you in this pain, knowing I could have helped."

In my odd life, I have had much experience of some things and little of others. Although I am a foreigner to the day, I know the night as no one else can know it. Although I have been the object on which ignorant fools have sometimes spent their cruelty, most of my understanding of the human heart comes from my relationships with my parents and with those good friends who, like me, live primarily between sunset and dawn; consequently, I have seldom encountered hurtful deception.

I was embarrassed by Sandy's deceit, as though it shamed not merely him but also me, and I couldn't meet his obsidian stare any longer. I lowered my head and gazed at the porch floor.

Mistaking my embarrassment for tongue-binding grief, he stepped onto the porch and put one hand on my shoulder.

I managed not to recoil.

"My business is comforting folks, Christopher, and I'm good at it. But truthfully — I have no words that make sense of death or make it easier to bear."

I wanted to kick his ass.

"I'll be okay," I said, realizing that I had to get away from him before I did something rash.

"What I hear myself saying to most folks is all the platitudes you'd never find in the poetry your dad loved, so I'm not going to repeat them to you, not to you of all people."

Keeping my head down, nodding, I eased backward, out from under his hand. "Thanks, Mr. Kirk. I'm sorry to've bothered you."

"You didn't bother me. Of course you didn't. I only wish you'd called ahead. I'd have been able to . . . delay."

"Not your fault. It's all right. Really."

Having backed off the stepless brick porch onto the blacktop under the portico, I turned away from Sandy.

Retreating once more to that doorway between two darknesses, he said, "Have you given any thought to the service — when you want to hold it, how you want it conducted?"

"No. No, not yet. I'll let you know tomorrow."

As I walked away, Sandy said, "Christopher, are you all right?"

Facing him from a little distance this time, I spoke in a numb, inflectionless voice that was only half calculated: "Yeah. I'm all right. I'll be okay. Thanks, Mr. Kirk."

"I wish you had called ahead."

Shrugging, I jammed my hands in my jacket pockets, turned from the house once more, and walked past the *Pietà*.

Flecks of mica were in the mix from which the replica had been poured, and the big moon glimmered in those tiny chips, so that tears appeared to shimmer on the cheeks of Our Lady of Cast Concrete.

I resisted the urge to glance back at the undertaker. I was certain he was still watching me.

I continued down the lane between the forlorn, whispering trees. The temperature had fallen only into the low sixties. The onshore breeze was pure after its journey across thou-

64

sands of miles of ocean, bearing nothing but the faintest whiff of brine.

Long after the slope of the driveway had taken me out of Sandy's line of sight, I looked back. I could see just the steeply pitched roof and chimneys, somber forms against the star-salted sky.

I moved off the blacktop onto grass, and I headed uphill again, this time in the sheltering shadows of foliage. The pepper trees braided the moon in their long tresses.

6

The funeral-home turnaround came into sight again. The *Pietà*. The portico.

Sandy had gone inside. The front door was closed.

Staying on the lawn, using trees and shrubs for cover, I circled to the back of the house. A deep porch stepped down to a seventy-foot lap pool, an enormous brick patio, and formal rose gardens — none of which could be seen from the public rooms of the funeral home.

A town the size of ours welcomes nearly two hundred newborns each year while losing a hundred citizens to death. There were only two funeral homes, and Kirk's probably received over 70 percent of this business — plus half that from the smaller towns in the county. Death was a good living for Sandy.

The view from the patio must have been breathtaking in daylight: unpopulated hills rising in gentle folds as far to the east as the eye could see, graced by scattered oaks with gnarled black trunks. Now the shrouded hills lay like sleeping giants under pale sheets.

When I saw no one at the lighted rear windows, I quickly crossed the patio. The moon, white as a rose petal, floated on the inky waters of the swimming pool.

The house adjoined a spacious L-shaped garage, which embraced a motor court that could be entered only from the front. The garage accommodated two hearses and Sandy's personal vehicles — but also, at the end of the wing farthest from the residence, the crematorium.

I slipped around the corner of the garage, along the back of the second arm of the L, where immense eucalyptus trees blocked most of the moonlight. The air was redolent of their medicinal fragrance, and a carpet of dead leaves crunched underfoot.

No corner of Moonlight Bay is unknown to me — especially not this one. Most of my nights have been spent in the exploration of our special town, which has resulted in some macabre discoveries.

Ahead, on my left, frosty light marked the crematorium window. I approached it with the conviction — correct, as it turned out — that I was about to see something stranger and far worse than what Bobby Halloway and I had seen on an October night when we were thirteen. . . .

A decade and a half ago, I'd had as morbid a streak as any boy my age, was as fascinated as all boys are by the mystery and lurid glamour of death. Bobby Halloway and I, friends even then, thought it was daring to prowl the undertaker's property in search of the repulsive, the ghoulish, the shocking.

I can't recall what we expected — or hoped — to find. A collection of human skulls? A porch swing made of bones? A secret laboratory where the deceptively normal-looking Frank Kirk and his deceptively normal-looking son Sandy called down lightning bolts from storm clouds to re-animate our dead neighbors and use them as slaves to do the cooking and housecleaning?

Perhaps we expected to stumble upon a shrine to the evil gods Cthulhu and Yog-Sothoth in some sinister bramble-festooned end of the rose garden. Bobby and I were reading a lot of H. P. Lovecraft in those days.

Bobby says we were a couple of weird kids. I say we were weird, for sure, but neither more nor less weird than other boys.

Bobby says maybe so, but the other boys gradually grew out of their weirdness while we've grown further into ours.

I don't agree with Bobby on this one. I don't believe that I'm any more weird than anyone else I've ever met. In fact, I'm a damn sight less weird than some.

Which is true of Bobby, too. But because he treasures his weirdness, he wants me to believe in and treasure mine.

He *insists* on his weirdness. He says that by acknowledging and embracing our weirdness, we are in greater harmony with nature — because nature is deeply weird.

Anyway, one October night, behind the fu-neral-home garage, Bobby Halloway and I found the crematorium window. We were attracted to it by an eldritch light that throbbed against the glass.

Because the window was set high, we were not tall enough to peer inside. With the stealth of commandos scouting an enemy encampment, we snatched a teak bench from the patio and carried it behind the garage, where we positioned it under the glimmering window.

Side by side on the bench, we were able to reconnoiter the scene together. The interior of the window was covered by a Levolor blind; but someone had forgotten to close the slats, giving us a clear view of Frank Kirk and an assistant at work.

One remove from the room, the light was not bright enough to cause me harm. At least that was what I told myself as I pressed my nose to the pane.

Even though I had learned to be a singularly cautious boy, I was nonetheless a boy and, therefore, in love with adventure and camaraderie, so I might knowingly have risked blindness to share that moment with Bobby Halloway.

On a stainless-steel gurney near the window was the body of an elderly man. It was cloaked in a sheet, with only the ravaged face exposed. His yellow-white hair, matted and tangled, made him look as though he had died in a high wind. Judging by his waxy gray skin, sunken cheeks, and severely cracked lips, however, he had succumbed not to a storm but to a prolonged illness.

If Bobby and I had been acquainted with the man in life, we didn't recognize him in this ashen and emaciated condition. If he'd been someone we knew even casually, he would have been no less grisly but perhaps less an object of boyish fascination and dark delight.

To us, because we were just thirteen and proud of it, the most compelling and remarkable and wonderful thing about the cadaver was also, of course, the grossest thing about it. One eye was closed, but the other was wide open and staring, occluded by a bright red starburst hemorrhage.

How that eye mesmerized us.

As death-blind as the painted eye of a doll, it nevertheless saw through us to the core.

Sometimes in a silent rapture of dread and sometimes whispering urgently to each other like a pair of deranged sportscasters doing color commentary, we watched as Frank and his assistant readied the cremator in one corner of the chamber. The room must have been warm, for the men slipped off their ties and rolled up their shirtsleeves, and tiny drops of perspiration wove beaded veils on their faces.

Outside, the October night was mild. Yet Bobby and I shivered and compared gooseflesh and wondered that our breath didn't plume from us in white wintry clouds.

The morticians folded the sheet back from the cadaver, and we boys gasped at the horrors of advanced age and murderous disease. But we gasped with the same sweet thrill of terror that we had felt while gleefully watching videos like *Night of the Living Dead.*

As the corpse was moved into a cardboard case and eased into the blue flames of the cremator, I clutched Bobby's arm, and he clamped one damp hand to the back of my neck, and we held fast to each other, as though a supernatural magnetic power might pull us inexorably forward, shattering the window, and sweep us into the room, into the fire with the dead man.

Frank Kirk shut the cremator.

Even through the closed window, the clank of the furnace door was loud enough, final enough, to echo in the hollows of our bones.

Later, after we had returned the teak bench to the patio and had fled the undertaker's property, we repaired to the bleachers at the football field behind the high school. With no game in progress, that place was unlighted and safe for me. We guzzled Cokes and munched potato chips that Bobby had gotten en route at a 7-Eleven.

"That was cool, that was so cool," Bobby declared excitedly.

"It was the coolest thing ever," I agreed.

"Cooler than Ned's cards."

Ned was a friend who had moved to San Francisco with his parents just that previous August. He had obtained a deck of playing cards — how, he would never reveal — that featured color photographs of really hot-looking nude women, fifty-two different beauties.

"Definitely cooler than the cards," I agreed. "Cooler than when that humongous tanker truck overturned and blew up out on the highway."

"Jeez, yeah, megadegrees cooler than that. Cooler than when Zach Blenheim got chewed up by that pit bull and had to have twenty-eight stitches in his arm."

"Unquestionably quantum arctics cooler than that," I confirmed.

"His eye!" Bobby said, remembering the starburst hemorrhage.

"Oh, God, his *eye!*"

"Gag-o-rama!"

We swilled down Cokes and talked and laughed more than we had ever laughed before in one night.

What amazing creatures we are when we're thirteen.

There on the athletic-field bleachers, I knew that this macabre adventure had tied a knot in our friendship that nothing and no one would ever loosen. By then we had been friends for two years; but during this night, our friendship became stronger, more complex than it had been at the start of the evening. We had shared a powerfully formative experience — and we sensed that this event was more profound than it seemed to be on the surface, more profound than boys our age could grasp. In my eyes, Bobby had acquired a new mystique, as I had acquired in his eyes, because we had done this daring thing.

Subsequently, I would discover that this moment was merely prelude. Our *real* bonding came the second week of December — when we saw something infinitely more disturbing than the corpse with the blood-red eye.

Now, fifteen years later, I would have thought that I was too old for these adventures and too ridden by conscience to prowl other people's property as casually as thirteen-year-old boys seem able to do. Yet here I was, treading cautiously on layers of dead eucalyptus leaves, putting my face to the fateful window one more time.

The Levolor blind, though yellowed with age, appeared to be the same one through which Bobby and I had peered so long ago. The slats were adjusted at an angle, but the gaps between them were wide enough to allow a view of the entire crematorium — into which I was tall enough to see without the aid of a patio bench.

Sandy Kirk and an assistant were at work near the Power Pak II Cremation System. They wore surgeons' masks, latex gloves, and disposable plastic aprons.

On the gurney near the window was one of the opaque vinyl body bags, unzipped, split like a ripe pod, with a dead man nestled inside. Evidently this was the hitchhiker who would be cremated in my father's name.

He was about five ten, a hundred sixty pounds. Because of the beating that he had taken, I could not estimate his age. His face was grotesquely battered.

At first I thought that his eyes were hidden by black crusts of blood. Then I realized that both eyes were gone. I was staring into empty sockets.

I thought of the old man with the starburst hemorrhage and how fearsome he had seemed to Bobby and me. That was nothing compared to this. That had been only nature's impersonal work, while this was human viciousness.

During that long-ago October and November, Bobby Halloway and I periodically returned to the crematorium window. Creeping through the darkness, trying not to trip in the ground ivy, we saturated our lungs with air redolent of the surrounding eucalyptuses, a scent that to this day I identify with death.

During those two months, Frank Kirk conducted fourteen funerals, but only three of those deceased were cremated. The others were embalmed for traditional burials.

Bobby and I lamented that the embalming room offered no windows for our use. That sanctum sanctorum — "where they do the wet work," as Bobby put it — was in the basement, secure against ghoulish spies like us.

Secretly, I was relieved that our snooping would be restricted to Frank Kirk's dry work. I believe that Bobby was relieved as well, although he pretended to be sorely disappointed.

On the positive side, I suppose, Frank performed most embalmings during the day while restricting cremations to the night hours. This made it possible for me to be in attendance.

Although the hulking cremator — cruder than the Power Pak II that Sandy uses these days — disposed of human remains at a very high temperature and featured emission-control devices, thin smoke escaped the chimney. Frank conducted only nocturnal cremations out of respect for bereaved family members or friends who might, in daylight, glance at the hilltop mortuary from lower in town and see the last of their loved ones slipping skyward in wispy gray curls.

Conveniently for us, Bobby's father, Anson, was the editor in chief of the *Moonlight Bay Gazette*. Bobby used his connections and his familiarity with the newspaper offices to get us the most current information about deaths by accident and by natural causes.

We always knew when Frank Kirk had a fresh one, but we couldn't be sure whether he was going to embalm it or cremate it. Immediately after sunset, we would ride our bikes to the vicinity of the mortuary and then creep onto the property, waiting at the crematorium window either until the action began or until we had to admit at last that this one was not going to be a burning.

Mr. Garth, the sixty-year-old president of the First National Bank, died of a heart attack in late October. We watched him go into the fire.

In November, a carpenter named Henry Aimes fell off a roof and broke his neck. Although Aimes was cremated, Bobby and I saw nothing of the process, because Frank Kirk or his assistant remembered to close the slats on the Levolor blind.

The blinds were open the second week in December, however, when we returned for the cremation of Rebecca Acquilain. She was married to Tom Acquilain, a math teacher at the junior high school where Bobby attended classes but I did not. Mrs. Acquilain, the town librarian, was only thirty, the mother of a five-year-old boy named Devlin.

Lying on the gurney, swathed in a sheet from the neck down, Mrs. Acquilain was so beautiful that her face was not merely a vision upon our eyes but a weight upon our chests. We could not breathe.

We had realized, I suppose, that she was a pretty woman, but we had never mooned over her. She was the librarian, after all, and someone's mother, while we were thirteen and inclined not to notice beauty that was as quiet as starlight dropping from the sky and as clear as rainwater. The kind of woman who appeared nude on playing cards had the flash that drew our eyes. Until now, we had often looked at Mrs. Acquilain but had never *seen* her.

Death had not ravaged her, for she had died quickly. A flaw in a cerebral artery wall, no doubt with her from birth but never suspected, swelled and burst in the course of one afternoon. She was gone in hours.

As she lay on the mortuary gurney, her eyes were closed. Her features were relaxed. She seemed to be sleeping; in fact, her mouth was curved slightly, as though she were having a pleasant dream.

When the two morticians removed the sheet to convey Mrs. Acquilain into the cardboard case and then into the cremator, Bobby and I saw that she was slim, exquisitely proportioned, lovely beyond the power of words to describe. This was a beauty exceeding mere eroticism, and we didn't look at her with morbid desire but with awe.

She looked so young.

She looked immortal.

The morticians conveyed her to the furnace with what seemed to be unusual gentleness and respect. When the door was closed behind the dead woman, Frank Kirk stripped off his latex gloves and blotted the back of one hand against his left eye and then his right. It was not perspiration that he wiped away.

During other cremations, Frank and his assistant had chatted almost continuously, though we could not quite hear what they said. This night, they spoke hardly at all.

Bobby and I were silent, too.

We returned the bench to the patio. We crept off Frank Kirk's property.

After retrieving our bicycles, we rode through Moonlight Bay by way of its darkest streets.

We went to the beach.

At this hour, in this season, the broad strand was deserted. Behind us, as gorgeous as phoenix feathers, nesting on the hills and fluttering through a wealth of trees, were the town lights. In front of us lay the inky wash of the vast Pacific.

The surf was gentle. Widely spaced, low breakers slid to shore, lazily spilling their phosphorescent crests, which peeled from right to left like a white rind off the dark meat of the sea.

Sitting in the sand, watching the surf, I kept thinking how near we were to Christmas. Two weeks away. I didn't want to think about Christmas, but it twinkled and jingled through my mind.

I don't know what Bobby was thinking. I didn't ask. I didn't want to talk. Neither did he.

I brooded about what Christmas would be like for little Devlin Acquilain without his mother. Maybe he was too young to understand what death meant.

Tom Acquilain, her husband, knew what death meant, sure enough. Nevertheless, he would probably put up a Christmas tree for Devlin.

How would he find the strength to hang the tinsel on the boughs?

Speaking for the first time since we had seen the sheet unfolded from the woman's body, Bobby said simply, "Let's go swimming."

Although the day had been mild, this was December, and it wasn't a year when El Niño — the warm current out of the southern hemisphere — ran close to shore. The water temperature was inhospitable, and the air was slightly chilly.

As Bobby undressed, he folded his clothes and, to keep the sand out of them, neatly piled them on a tangled blanket of kelp that had washed ashore earlier in the day and been dried by the sun. I folded my clothes beside his.

Naked, we waded into the black water and then swam out against the tide. We went too far from shore.

We turned north and swam parallel to the coast. Easy strokes. Minimal kicking. Expertly riding the ebb and flow of the waves. We swam a dangerous distance.

We were both superb swimmers — though reckless now.

Usually a swimmer finds cold water less discomfiting after being in it awhile; as the body temperature drops, the difference between skin and water temperatures becomes much less perceptible. Furthermore, exertion creates the impression of heat. A reassuring but false sense of warmth can arise, which is perilous.

This water, however, grew colder as fast as our body temperatures dropped. We reached no comfort point, false or otherwise.

Having swum too far north, we should have made for shore. If we'd had any common sense, we would have walked back to the mound of dry kelp where we'd left our clothes.

Instead, we merely paused, treading water, sucking in deep shuddery breaths cold enough to sluice the precious heat out of our throats. Then as one, without a word, we turned south to swim back the way we had come, still too far from shore.

My limbs grew heavy. Faint but frightening cramps twisted through my stomach. The pounding of my riptide heart seemed hard enough to push me deep under the surface.

Although the incoming swells were as gentle as they had been when we first entered the water, they felt meaner. They bit with teeth of cold white foam.

We swam side by side, careful not to lose sight of each other. The winter sky offered no comfort, the lights of town were as distant as stars, and the sea was hostile. All we had was our friendship, but we knew that in a crisis, either of us would die trying to save the other.

When we returned to our starting point, we barely had the strength to walk out of the surf. Exhausted, nauseated, paler than the sand, shivering violently, we spat out the astringent taste of the sea.

We were so bitterly cold that we could no longer imagine the heat of the crematorium furnace. Even after we had dressed, we were still freezing, and that was good.

We walked our bicycles off the sand, across the grassy park that bordered the beach, to the nearest street.

As he climbed on his bike, Bobby said, "Shit."

"Yeah," I said.

We cycled to our separate homes.

We went straight to bed as though ill. We slept. We dreamed. Life went on.

We never returned to the crematorium window.

We never spoke again of Mrs. Acquilain.

All these years later, either Bobby or I would still give his life to save the other — and without hesitation.

How strange this world is: Those things that we can so readily touch, those things so real to the senses — the sweet architecture of a woman's body, one's own flesh and bone, the cold sea and the gleam of stars — are far less real than things we cannot touch or taste or smell or see. Bicycles and the boys who ride them are less real than what we feel in our minds and hearts, less substantial than friendship and love and loneliness, all of which long outlast the world.

On this March night far down the time stream from boyhood, the crematorium window and the scene beyond it were more real than I would have wished. Someone had brutally beaten the hitchhiker to death — and then had cut out his eyes.

Even if the murder and the substitution of this corpse for the body of my father made sense when all the facts were known, why take the eyes? Could there possibly be a logical reason for sending this pitiable man eyeless into the all-consuming fire of the cremator?

Or had someone disfigured the hitchhiker sheerly for the deep, dirty thrill of it?

I thought of the hulking man with the shaved head and the single pearl earring. His broad blunt face. His huntsman's eyes, black and steady. His cold-iron voice with its rusty rasp.

It was possible to imagine such a man taking pleasure from the pain of another, carving flesh in the carefree manner of any country gentleman lazily whittling a twig.

Indeed, in the strange new world that had come into existence during my experience in the hospital basement, it was easy to imagine that Sandy Kirk himself had disfigured the body: Sandy, as good-looking and slick as any *GQ* model; Sandy, whose dear father had wept at the burning of Rebecca Acquilain. Perhaps the eyes had been offered up at the base of the shrine in the far and thorny corner of the rose garden that Bobby and I had never been able to find.

In the crematorium, as Sandy and his assistant rolled the gurney toward the furnace, the telephone rang.

Guiltily, I flinched from the window as though I had triggered an alarm.

When I leaned close to the glass again, I saw Sandy pull down his surgical mask and lift the

81

handset from the wall phone. The tone of his voice indicated confusion, then alarm, then anger, but through the dual-pane window, I was not able to hear what he was saying.

Sandy slammed down the telephone handset almost hard enough to knock the box off the wall. Whoever had been on the other end of the line had gotten a good ear cleaning.

As he stripped out of his latex gloves, Sandy spoke urgently to his assistant. I thought I heard him speak my name — and not with either admiration or affection.

The assistant, Jesse Pinn, was a lean-faced whippet of a man with red hair and russet eyes and a thin mouth that seemed pinched in anticipation of the taste of a chased-down rabbit. Pinn started to zip the body bag shut over the corpse of the hitchhiker.

Sandy's suit jacket was hung on one of a series of wall pegs to the right of the door. When he lifted it off the peg, I was astonished to see that under the coat hung a shoulder holster sagging with the weight of a handgun.

Seeing Pinn fumbling with the body bag, Sandy spoke sharply to him — and gestured at the window.

As Pinn hurried directly toward me, I jerked back from the pane. He closed the half-open slats on the blind.

I doubted that I had been seen.

On the other hand, keeping in mind that I am an optimist on such a deep level that it's a subatomic condition with me, I decided that on this one occasion, I would be wise to listen to a more pessimistic instinct and not linger. I hurried between the garage wall and the eucalyptus grove, through the death-scented air, toward the backyard.

The drifted leaves crunched as hard as snail shells underfoot. Fortunately, I was given cover by the soughing of the breeze through the branches overhead.

The wind was full of the hollow susurrant sound of the sea over which it had so long traveled, and it masked my movements.

It would also cloak the footsteps of anyone stalking me.

I was certain that the telephone call had been from one of the orderlies at the hospital. They had examined the contents of the suitcase, found my father's wallet, and deduced that I must have been in the garage to witness the body swap.

With this information, Sandy had realized that my appearance at his front door had not been as innocent as it had seemed. He and Jesse Pinn would come outside to see if I was still lurking on the property.

I reached the backyard. The manicured lawn looked broader and more open than I remembered it.

The full moon was no brighter than it had been minutes earlier, but every hard surface that had previously absorbed this languid light now reflected and amplified it. An eerie silver radiance suffused the night, denying me concealment.

I dared not attempt to cross the broad brick patio. In fact I decided to stay well clear of the house and the driveway. Leaving via the same route by which I had arrived would be too risky.

I raced across the lawn to the acre of rose gardens at the back of the property. Before me lay descending terraces with extensive rows of trellises standing at angles to one another, numerous tunnel-like arbors, and a maze of meandering pathways.

Spring along our mellow coast doesn't delay its debut to match the date celebrating it on the calendar, and already the roses were blooming. The red and other darkly colored flowers appeared to be black in the moonlight, roses for a sinister altar, but there were enormous white blooms, too, as big as babies' heads, nodding to the lullaby of the breeze.

Men's voices arose behind me. They were worn thin and tattered by the worrying wind.

Crouching behind a tall trellis, I looked back through the open squares between the white lattice crossings. Gingerly I pushed aside looping trailers with wicked thorns.

Near the garage, two flashlight beams chased shadows out of shrubbery, sent phantoms leaping up through tree limbs, dazzled across windows.

Sandy Kirk was behind one of the flashlights and was no doubt toting the handgun that I had glimpsed. Jesse Pinn might also have a weapon.

There was once a time when morticians and their assistants didn't pack heat. Until this evening I had assumed I was still living in that era.

I was startled to see a third flashlight beam appear at the far corner of the house. Then a fourth. Then a fifth.

A sixth.

I had no clue as to who these new searchers might be or where they could have come from so quickly. They spread out to form a line and advanced purposefully across the yard, across the patio, past the swimming pool, toward the rose garden, probing with the flashlights, menacing figures as featureless as demons in a dream.

7

The faceless pursuers and the thwarting mazes that trouble us in sleep were now reality.

The gardens stepped in five broad terraces down a hillside. In spite of these plateaus and the gentleness of the slopes between them, I was gathering too much speed as I descended, and I was afraid that I would stumble, fall, and break a leg.

Rising on all sides, the arbors and fanciful trellises began to resemble gutted ruins. In the lower levels, they were overgrown with thorny trailers that clawed the lattice and seemed to writhe with animal life as I fled past them.

The night had fallen into a waking nightmare.

My heart pounded so fiercely that the stars reeled.

I felt as though the vault of the sky were sliding toward me, gaining momentum like an avalanche.

Plunging to the end of the gardens, I sensed as much as saw the looming wrought-iron fence: seven feet high, its glossy black paint glimmering with moonlight. I dug my heels into the soft earth and braked, jarring against the sturdy pickets but not hard enough to hurt myself.

I hadn't made much noise, either. The spear-point verticals were solidly welded to the horizontal rails; instead of clattering from my impact, the fence briefly thrummed.

I sagged against the ironwork.

A bitter taste plagued me. My mouth was so dry that I couldn't spit.

My right temple stung. I raised a hand to my face. Three thorns prickled my skin. I plucked them out.

During my flight downhill, I must have been lashed by a trailing rose brier, although I didn't recall encountering it.

Maybe because I was breathing harder and faster, the sweet fragrance of roses became too sweet, sharpened into a half-rotten stench. I could smell my sunscreen again, too, almost as strongly as when it had been freshly applied — but with a sour taint now — because my perspiration had revitalized the scent of the lotion.

I was overcome by the absurd yet unshakable conviction that the six searchers could sniff me out, as though they were hounds. I was safe for the moment only because I was downwind of them.

Clutching the fence, out of which the thrumming had passed into my hands and bones, I glanced uphill. The search party was moving from the highest terrace to the second.

Six scythes of light slashed through the roses. Portions of the lattice structures, when briefly backlit and distorted by those bright sweeping swords, loomed like the bones of slain dragons.

The gardens presented the searchers with more possible hiding places to probe than did the open lawn above. Yet they were moving faster than before.

I scaled the fence and swung over the top,

wary of snaring my jacket or a leg of my jeans on the spear-point pickets. Beyond lay open land: shadowed vales, steadily rising ranks of moonlit hills, widely scattered and barely discernible black oaks.

The wild grass, lush from the recent winter rains, was knee-high when I dropped into it from the fence. I could smell the green juice bursting from the blades crushed beneath my shoes.

Certain that Sandy and his associates would survey the entire perimeter of the property, I bounded downhill, away from the funeral home. I was eager to get beyond the reach of their flashlights before they arrived at the fence.

I was heading farther from town, which wasn't good. I wouldn't find help in the wilderness. Every step eastward was a step into isolation, and in isolation I was as vulnerable as anyone, more vulnerable than most.

Some luck was with me because of the season. If the searing heat of summer had already been upon us, the high grass would have been as golden as wheat and as dry as paper. My progress would have been marked by a swath of trampled stalks.

I was hopeful that the still-verdant meadow would be resilient enough to spring shut behind me, for the most part concealing the fact that I had passed this way. Nevertheless, an observant searcher would most likely be able to track me.

Approximately two hundred feet beyond the fence, at the bottom of the slope, the meadow gave way to denser brush. A barrier of tough, five-foot-high prairie cordgrass was mixed with what might have been goatsbeard and massive clumps of aureola.

I hurriedly pushed through this growth into a ten-foot-wide natural drainage swale. Little grew here because an epoch of storm runoff had exposed a spine of bedrock under the hills. With no rain in over two weeks, this rocky course was dry.

I paused to catch my breath. Leaning back into the brush, I parted the tall cordgrass to see how far down into the rose gardens the searchers had descended.

Four of them were already climbing the fence. Their flashlight beams slashed at the sky, stuttered across the pickets, and stabbed randomly at the ground as they clambered up and over the iron.

They were unnervingly quick and agile.

Were all of them, like Sandy Kirk, carrying weapons?

Considering their animal-keen instinct, speed, and persistence, perhaps they wouldn't need weapons. If they caught me, maybe they would tear me apart with their hands.

I wondered if they would take my eyes.

The drainage channel — and the wider declivity in which it lay — ran uphill to the northeast and downhill to the southwest. As I was already at the extreme northeast end of town, I could find no help if I went uphill.

I headed southwest, following the brush-flanked swale, intending to return to well-populated territory as quickly as possible.

In the shallowly cupped channel ahead of me,

the moon-burnished bedrock glowed softly like the milky ice on a winter pond, dwindling into obscurity. The embracing curtains of high, silvery cordgrass appeared to be stiff with frost.

Suppressing all fear of falling on loose stones or of snapping an ankle in a natural borehole, I gave myself to the night, allowing the darkness to push me as wind pushes a sailing ship. I sprinted down the gradual slope with no sensation of feet striking ground, as though I actually were *skating* across the frozen rock.

Within two hundred yards, I came to a place where hills folded into one another, resulting in a branching of the hollow. With barely any decrease in speed, I chose the right-hand course because it would lead more directly back into Moonlight Bay.

I had gone only a short distance past that intersection when I saw lights approaching. A hundred yards ahead, the hollow turned out of sight to the left, around a sweeping curve of grassy hillside. The source of the questing beams lay beyond that bend, but I could see that they must be flashlights.

None of the men from the funeral home could have gotten out of the rose gardens and ahead of me so quickly. These were additional searchers.

They were attempting to trap me in a pincer maneuver. I felt as though I were being pursued by an army, by platoons that had sprung sorcerously from the ground itself.

I came to a complete halt.

I considered stepping off the bare rock, into

concealment behind the man-high prairie grass and other dense brush that still bracketed the drainage swale. No matter how little I disturbed this vegetation, however, I was nearly certain to leave signs of my passage that would be obvious to these trackers. They would burst through the brush and capture me or gun me down as I scrambled up the open hillside.

At the bend ahead, the flashlight beams swelled brighter. Sprays of tall prairie grass flared like beautifully chased forms on a sterling platter.

I retreated to the Y in the hollow and took the left-hand branch that I'd forgone a minute earlier. Within six or seven hundred feet, I came to another Y, wanted to go to the right — toward town — was afraid I'd be playing into their assumptions, and took the left-hand branch instead, although it would lead me deeper into the unpopulated hills.

From somewhere above and off to the west arose the grumble of an engine, distant at first but then suddenly nearer. The engine noise was so powerful that I thought it came from an aircraft making a low pass. This wasn't the stuttering clatter of a helicopter, but more like the roar of a fixed-wing plane.

Then a dazzling light swept the hilltops to the left and right of me, passing directly across the hollow, sixty to eighty feet over my head. The beam was so bright, so intense, that it seemed to have weight and texture, like a white-hot gush of some molten substance.

A high-powered searchlight. It arced away and

reflected off distant ridges to the east and north.

Where did they get this sophisticated ordnance on such short notice?

Was Sandy Kirk the grand kleagle of an anti-government militia headquartered in secret bunkers jammed with weapons and ammo, deep under the funeral home? No, that didn't ring true. Such things were merely the stuff of real life these days, the current events of a society in freefall — while this felt *uncanny*. This was territory through which the wild rushing river of the evening news had not yet swept.

I had to know what was happening up there on higher ground. If I didn't reconnoiter, I would be no better than a dumb rat in a laboratory maze.

I thrashed through the brush to the right of the swale, crossed the sloping floor of the hollow, and then climbed the long hillside, because the searchlight seemed to have originated in that direction. As I ascended, the beam seared the land above again — indeed, blazing in from the northwest as I'd thought — and then scorched past a third time, brightly illuminating the brow of the hill toward which I was making my way.

After crawling the penultimate ten yards on my hands and knees, I wriggled the final ten on my belly. At the crest, I coiled into an outcropping of weather-scored rocks that provided a measure of cover, and I cautiously raised my head.

A black Hummer — or maybe a Humvee, the original military version of the vehicle before it had been gentrified for sale to civilians — stood one hilltop away from mine, immediately lee-ward of a giant oak. Even poorly revealed by the backwash of its own lights, the Hummer pre-sented an unmistakable profile: a boxy, hulking, four-wheel-drive wagon perched on giant tires, capable of crossing virtually any terrain.

I now saw two searchlights: Both were hand-held, one by the driver and one by his front-seat passenger, and each had a lens the size of a salad plate. Considering their candlepower, they could have been operated only off the Hummer engine.

The driver extinguished his light and put the Hummer in gear. The big wagon sped out from under the spreading limbs of the oak and shot across the high meadow as though it were cruis-ing a freeway, putting its tailgate toward me. It vanished over the far edge, soon reappeared out of a hollow, and rapidly ascended a more distant slope, effortlessly conquering these coastal hills.

The men on foot, with flashlights and perhaps handguns, were keeping to the hollows. In an attempt to prevent me from using the high ground, to force me down where the searchers might find me, the Hummer was patrolling the hilltops.

"Who *are* you people?" I muttered.

Searchlights slashed out from the Hummer, raking farther hills, illuminating a sea of grass in an indecisive breeze that ebbed and flowed. Wave after wave broke across the rising land and lapped against the trunks of the island oaks.

Then the big wagon was on the move again, rollicking over less hospitable terrain. Headlights bobbling, one searchlight swinging wildly, along a crest, into a hollow and out again, it motored east and south to another vantage point.

I wondered how visible this activity might be from the streets of Moonlight Bay on the lower hills and the flatlands, closer to the ocean. Possibly only a few townspeople happened to be outside and looking up at an angle that revealed enough commotion to engage their curiosity.

Those who glimpsed the searchlights might assume that teenagers or college boys in an ordinary four-by-four were spotting coastal elk or deer: an illegal but bloodless sport of which most people are tolerant.

Soon the Hummer would arc back toward me. Judging by the pattern of its search, it might arrive on this very hill in two more moves.

I retreated down the slope, into the hollow from which I had climbed: exactly where they wanted me. I had no better choice.

Heretofore, I had been confident that I would escape. Now my confidence was ebbing.

8

I pushed through the prairie grass into the drainage swale and continued in the direction that I had been headed before the searchlights had drawn me uphill. After only a few steps, I halted, startled by something with radiant green eyes that waited on the trail in front of me.

Coyote.

Wolflike but smaller, with a narrower muzzle than that of a wolf, these rangy creatures could nonetheless be dangerous. As civilization encroached on them, they were quite literally murder on family pets even in the supposedly safe backyards of residential neighborhoods near the open hills. In fact, from time to time you heard of a coyote savaging and dragging off a child if the prey was young and small enough. Although they attacked adult humans only rarely, I wouldn't care to rely on their restraint or on my superior size if I was to encounter a pack — or even a pair — of them on their home ground.

My night vision was still recovering from the dazzle of the searchlights, and a tense moment passed before I perceived that these hot green eyes were too closely set to be those of a coyote. Furthermore, unless this beast was in a full pounce posture with its chest pressed to the ground, its baleful stare was directed at me from too low a position to be that of a coyote.

As my vision readjusted to nightshade and

moonlight, I saw that nothing more threatening than a cat stood before me. Not a cougar, which would have been far worse than a coyote and reason for genuine terror, but a mere house cat: pale gray or light beige, impossible to tell which in this gloom.

Most cats are not stupid. Even in the obsessive pursuit of field mice or little desert lizards, they will not venture deeply into coyote country.

Indeed, as I got a clearer view of it, the particular creature before me seemed more than usually quick and alert. It sat erect, head cocked quizzically, ears pricked, studying me intensely.

As I took a step toward it, the cat rose onto all fours. When I advanced another step, the cat spun away from me and dashed along the moon-silvered path, vanishing into the darkness.

Elsewhere in the night, the Hummer was on the move again. Its shriek and snarl rapidly grew louder.

I picked up my pace.

By the time I had gone a hundred yards, the Hummer was no longer roaring but idling somewhere nearby, its engine noise like a slow deep panting. Overhead, the predatory gaze of the lights swept the night for prey.

Upon reaching the next branching of the hollow, I discovered the cat waiting for me. It sat at the point of division, committed to neither trail.

When I moved toward the left-hand path, the cat scurried to the right. It halted after several steps — and turned its lantern eyes on me.

The cat must have been acutely aware of the

searchers all around us, not just of the noisy Hummer but of the men on foot. With its sharp senses, it might even perceive pheromones of aggression streaming from them, violence pending. It would want to avoid these people as much as I did. Given the chance, I would be better off choosing an escape route according to the animal's instincts rather than according to my own.

The idling engine of the Hummer suddenly thundered. The hard peals echoed back and forth through the hollows, so that the vehicle seemed to be simultaneously approaching and racing away. With this storm of sound, indecision flooded me, and for a moment I floundered in it.

Then I decided to go the way of the cat.

As I turned from the left-hand trail, the Hummer roared over the hilltop on the eastern flank of the hollow into which I had almost proceeded. For an instant it hung, suspended, as though weightless in a clock-stopped gap in time, headlights like twin wires leading a circus tightrope walker into midair, one searchlight stabbing straight up at the black tent of the sky. Time snapped across that empty synapse and flowed again: The Hummer tipped forward, and the front wheels crashed onto the hillside, and the rear wheels crossed the crest, and gouts of earth and grass spewed out from under its tires as it charged downhill.

A man whooped with delight, and another laughed. They were reveling in the hunt.

As the big wagon descended only fifty yards ahead of me, the hand-held searchlight swept the hollow.

I threw myself to the ground and rolled for cover. The rocky swale was hell on bones, and I felt my sunglasses crack apart in my shirt pocket.

As I scrambled to my feet, a beam as bright as an oak-cleaving thunderbolt sizzled across the ground on which I had been standing. Wincing at the glare, squinting, I saw the searchlight quiver and then sweep away to the south. The Hummer was not coming up the hollow toward me.

I might have stayed where I was, at the intersection of the trails, with the narrower point of the hill at my back, until the Hummer moved out of the vicinity, rather than risk encountering it in the next hollow. When four flashlights winked far back on the trail that I had followed to this point, however, I ceased to have the luxury of hesitation. I was beyond the reach of these men's lights, but they were approaching at a trot, and I was in imminent danger of discovery.

When I rounded the point of the hill and entered the hollow to the west of it, the cat was still there, as though waiting for me. Presenting its tail to me, it scampered away, though not so fast that I lost sight of it.

I was grateful for the stone under me, in which I could not leave betraying footprints — and then I realized that only fragments of my broken sunglasses remained in my shirt pocket. As I ran, I fingered my pocket and felt one bent stem and a jagged piece of one lens. The rest must have scattered on the ground where I had fallen, at the fork in the trail.

The four searchers were sure to spot the broken frames. They would divide their forces, two men to each hollow, and they would come after me harder and faster than ever, energized by this evidence that they were closing on their quarry.

On the far side of this hill, out of the vale where I had barely escaped the searchlight, the Hummer began to climb again. The shriek of its engine rose in pitch, swelled in volume.

If the driver paused on this grassy hilltop to survey the night once more, I would run undetected beneath him and away. If instead he raced across the hill and into this new hollow, I might be caught in his headlights or pinned by a searchlight beam.

The cat ran, and I ran.

As it sloped down between dark hills, the hollow grew wider than any that I had traveled previously, and the rocky swale in the center widened, too. Along the verge of the stone path, the tall cordgrass and the other brush bristled thicker than elsewhere, evidently watered by a greater volume of storm runoff, but the vegetation was too far to either side to cast even a faint dappling of moonshadows over me, and I felt dangerously exposed. Furthermore, this broad declivity, unlike those before it, ran as straight as a city street, with no bends to shield me from those who might enter it in my wake.

On the highlands, the Hummer seemed to have come to a halt once more. Its grumble drained away in the sluicing breeze, and the only engine sounds were mine: the rasp and wheeze of breathing, heartbeat like a pounding piston.

The cat was potentially fleeter than I — wind on four feet; it could have vanished in seconds. For a couple of minutes, however, it paced me, staying a constant fifteen feet ahead, pale gray or pale beige, a mere ghost of a cat in the moon-glow, occasionally glancing back with eyes as eerie as séance candles.

Just when I began to think that this creature was purposefully leading me out of harm's way, just as I began to indulge in one of those orgies of anthropomorphizing that make Bobby Halloway's brain itch, the cat sped away from me. If that dry rocky wash had been filled with a storm gush, the tumbling water could not have outrun this feline, and in two seconds, three at most, it disappeared into the night ahead.

A minute later, I found the cat at the terminus of the channel. We were in the dead end of a blind hollow, with exposed grassy hills rising steeply on three sides. They were so steep, in fact, that I could not scale them quickly enough to elude the two searchers who were surely pursuing on foot. Boxed in. Trapped.

Driftwood, tangled balls of dead weeds and grass, and silt were mounded at the end of the wash. I half expected the cat to give me an evil Cheshire grin, white teeth gleaming in the gloom. Instead, it scampered to the pile of debris and slinked-wriggled into one of many small gaps, disappearing again.

This *was* a wash. Therefore the runoff had to go somewhere when it reached this point.

Hastily I climbed the nine-foot-long, three-foot-high slope of packed debris, which sagged and rattled and crunched but held beneath me. It was all drifted against a grid of steel bars, which served as a vertical grate across the mouth of a culvert set into the side of the hill.

Beyond the grate was a six-foot-diameter concrete drain between anchoring concrete buttresses. It was apparently part of a flood-control project that carried storm water out of the hills, under the Pacific Coast Highway, into drains beneath the streets of Moonlight Bay, and finally to the sea.

A couple of times each winter, maintenance crews would clear the trash away from the grate to prevent water flow from being completely impeded. Clearly, they had not been here recently.

Inside the culvert, the cat meowed. Magnified, its voice echoed with a new sepulchral tone along the concrete tunnel.

The openings in the steel-bar grid were four-inch squares, wide enough to admit the supple cat but not wide enough for me. The grate extended the width of the opening, from buttress to buttress, but it didn't reach all the way to the top.

I swung legs-first and backward through the two-foot-high gap between the top of the grate and the curved ceiling of the drain. I was grateful that the grid had a headrail, for otherwise I would have been poked and gouged painfully by the exposed tops of the vertical bars.

Leaving the stars and the moon behind, I stood with my back to the grate, peering into absolute blackness. I had to hunch only slightly to keep from bumping my head against the ceiling.

The smell of damp concrete and moldering grass, not entirely unpleasant, wafted from below.

I eased forward, sliding my feet. The smooth floor of the culvert had only a slight pitch. After just a few yards, I stopped, afraid I would blunder into a sudden drop-off and wind up dead or broken-backed at the bottom.

I withdrew the butane lighter from a pocket of my jeans, but I was reluctant to strike a flame. The light flickering along the curved walls of the culvert would be visible from outside.

The cat called again, and its radiant eyes were all that I could see ahead. Guessing at the distance between us, judging by the angle at which I looked down upon the animal, I deduced that the floor of the huge culvert continued at an increased — but not drastic — slope.

I proceeded cautiously toward the lambent eyes. When I drew close to the creature, it turned away, and I halted at the loss of its twin beacons.

Seconds later it spoke again. Its green gaze reappeared and fixed unblinking on me.

Edging forward once more, I marveled at this odd experience. All that I had witnessed since sundown — the theft of my father's body, the battered and eyeless corpse in the crematorium, the pursuit from the mortuary — was incredible, to say the least, but for sheer strangeness, nothing equaled the behavior of this small descendant of tigers.

Or maybe I was making a lot more of the moment than it deserved, attributing to this simple house cat an awareness of my plight that it didn't actually possess.

Maybe.

Blindly, I came to another mound of debris smaller than the first. Unlike the previous heap, this one was damp. The flotsam squished beneath my shoes, and a sharper stench rose from it.

I clambered forward, cautiously groping at the darkness in front of me, and I discovered that the debris was packed against another steel-bar grate. Whatever trash managed to wash over the top of the first grate was caught here.

After climbing this barrier and crossing safely to the other side, I risked using the lighter. I cupped my hand around the flame to contain and direct the glow as much as possible.

The cat's eyes blazed bright: gold now, flecked with green. We stared at each other for a long moment, and then my guide — if that's what it was — whipped around and sprinted out of sight, down into the drain.

Using the lighter to find my way, keeping the flame low to conserve butane, I descended through the heart of the coastal hills, passing smaller tributary culverts that opened into this main line. I arrived at a spillway of wide concrete steps on which were puddles of stagnant water and a thin carpet of hardy gray-black fungus that probably thrived only during the four-month rainy season. The scummy steps were treacherous, but for the safety of maintenance crews, a steel handrail was bolted to one wall, hung now with a drab tinsel of dead grass deposited by the most recent flood.

As I descended, I listened for the sounds of pursuit, voices in the tunnel behind me, but all I heard were my own stealthy noises. Either the searchers had decided that I hadn't escaped by way of the culvert — or they had hesitated so long before following me into the drain that I had gotten well ahead of them.

At the bottom of the spillway, on the last two broad steps, I almost plunged into what I thought at first were the pale, rounded caps of large mushrooms, clusters of vile-looking fungi growing here in the lightless damp, no doubt poisonous in the extreme.

Clutching the railing, I eased past sprouting forms on the slippery concrete, reluctant to touch them even with one of my shoes. Standing in the next length of sloping tunnel, I turned to examine this peculiar find.

When I cranked up the flame on the lighter, I discovered that before me lay not mushrooms but a collection of skulls. The fragile skulls of birds. The elongated skulls of lizards. The larger skulls of what might have been cats, dogs, raccoons, porcupines, rabbits, squirrels. . . .

Not a scrap of flesh adhered to any of these death's-heads, as if they had been boiled clean: white and yellow-white in the butane light, scores of them, perhaps a hundred. No leg bones, no rib cages, just skulls. They were arranged neatly side by side in three rows — two on the bottom step and one on the second from the bottom — facing out, as though, even with their empty eye sockets, they were here to bear witness to something.

I had no idea what to make of this. I saw no satanic markings on the culvert walls, no indications of macabre ceremonies of any kind, yet the display had an undeniably symbolic purpose. The extent of the collection indicated obsession, and the cruelty implicit in so much killing and decapitation was chilling.

Recalling the fascination with death that had gripped me and Bobby Halloway when we were thirteen, I wondered if some kid, far weirder than we ever were, had done this grisly work. Criminologists claim that by the age of three or four, most serial killers begin torturing and killing insects, progressing to small animals during childhood and adolescence, and finally graduating to people. Maybe in these catacombs, a particularly vicious young murderer was practicing for his life's work.

In the middle of the third and highest row of these bony visages rested a gleaming skull that was markedly different from all the others. It appeared to be human. Small but human. Like the skull of an infant.

"Dear God."

My voice whispered back to me along the concrete walls.

More than ever, I felt as though I were in a dreamscape, where even such things as concrete and bone were no more solid than smoke. Nevertheless, I did not reach out to touch the small human skull — or any of the others, for that matter. However unreal they might seem, I knew that they would be cold, slick, and too solid to the touch.

Anxious to avoid encountering whoever had acquired this grim collection, I continued downward through the drain.

I expected the cat with the enigmatic eyes to reappear, pale paws meeting concrete with feather-on-feather silence, but either it remained out of sight ahead of me or it had detoured into one of the tributary lines.

Sections of sloped concrete pipe alternated with more spillways, and just as I was beginning to worry that the lighter didn't contain enough fuel to see me to safety, a circle of dim gray light appeared and gradually brightened ahead. I hurried toward it and found that no grate barred the lower end of the tunnel, which led into an open drainage channel of mortar-set river rock.

I was in familiar territory at last, the northern flats of town. A couple of blocks from the sea. Half a block from the high school.

After the dank culvert, the night air smelled not merely fresh but sweet. The high points of the polished sky glittered diamond-white.

9

According to the digital light board on the Wells Fargo Bank building, the time was 7:56 P.M., which meant that my father had been dead less than three hours, though days seemed to have passed since I'd lost him. The same sign set the temperature at sixty degrees, but the night seemed colder to me.

Around the corner from the bank and down the block, the Tidy Time Laundromat was flooded with fluorescent light. Currently no customers were doing their laundry.

With the dollar bill ready in my hand, with my eyes squinted to slits, I went inside, into the flowery fragrance of soap powders and the chemical keenness of bleach, my head lowered to maximize the protection provided by the bill of my cap. I ran straight to the change machine, fed it, snatched up the four quarters that it spat into the tray, and fled.

Two blocks away, outside the post office, stood a pay phone with winglike sound shields. Above the phone, mounted on the wall of the building, was a security light behind a wire cage.

When I hung my hat on the cage, shadows fell.

I figured that Manuel Ramirez would still be at home. When I phoned him, his mother, Rosalina, said that he had been gone for hours.

He was working a double shift because another officer had called in sick. This evening he was on desk duty; later, after midnight, he would be on patrol.

I punched in the main number of the Moonlight Bay Police and asked the operator if I could speak to Officer Ramirez.

Manuel, in my judgment the best cop in town, is three inches shorter than I am, thirty pounds heavier, twelve years older, and a Mexican American. He loves baseball; I never follow sports because I have an acute sense of time slipping away and a reluctance to use my precious hours in too many passive activities. Manuel prefers country music; I like rock. He is a staunch Republican; I have no interest in politics. In movies, his guilty pleasure is Abbott and Costello; mine is the immortal Jackie Chan. We are friends.

"Chris, I heard about your dad," Manuel said when he came on the line. "I don't know what to say."

"Neither do I, really."

"No, there never is anything to say, is there?"

"Not that matters."

"You going to be okay?"

To my surprise, I couldn't speak. My terrible loss seemed suddenly to be a surgeon's needle that stitched shut my throat and sewed my tongue to the roof of my mouth.

Curiously, immediately after Dad's death, I'd been able to answer this same question from Dr. Cleveland without hesitation.

I felt closer to Manuel than to the physician.

Friendship thaws the nerves, making it possible for pain to be felt.

"You come over some evening when I'm off duty," Manuel said. "We'll drink some beer, eat some tamales, watch a couple of Jackie Chan movies."

In spite of baseball and country music, we have much in common, Manuel Ramirez and I. He works the graveyard shift, from midnight until eight in the morning, sometimes doubling on the swing shift when, as on this March evening, there is a personnel shortage. He likes the night as I do, but he also works it by necessity. Because the graveyard shift is less desirable than daytime duty, the pay is higher. More important, he is able to spend afternoons and evenings with his son, Toby, whom he cherishes. Sixteen years ago, Manuel's wife, Carmelita, died minutes after bringing Toby into the world. The boy is gentle, charming — and a victim of Down's syndrome. Manuel's mother moved into his house immediately after Carmelita's death and still helps to look after Toby. Manuel Ramirez knows about limitations. He feels the hand of fate every day of his life, in an age when most people no longer believe in purpose or destiny. We have much in common, Manuel Ramirez and I.

"Beer and Jackie Chan sound great," I agreed. "But who makes the tamales — you or your mother?"

"Oh, not *mi madre*, I promise."

Manuel is an exceptional cook, and his mother *thinks* that she is an exceptional cook. A comparison of their cooking provides a fearsomely illuminating example of the difference between a good deed and a good intention.

A car passed in the street behind me, and when I looked down, I saw my shadow pull at my unmoving feet, stretching from my left side around to my right, growing not merely longer but blacker on the concrete sidewalk, straining to tear loose of me and flee — but then snapping back to the left when the car passed.

"Manuel, there's something you can do for me, something more than tamales."

"You name it, Chris."

After a long hesitation, I said, "It involves my dad . . . his body."

Manuel matched my hesitation. His thoughtful silence was the equivalent of a cat's ears pricking with interest.

He heard more in my words than they appeared to convey. His tone was different when he spoke this time, still the voice of a friend but also the harder voice of a cop. "What's happened, Chris?"

"It's pretty weird."

"Weird?" he said, savoring the word as though it were an unexpected taste.

"I'd really rather not talk about it on the phone. If I come over to the station, can you meet me in the parking lot?"

I couldn't expect the police to switch off all their office lights and take my statement by the glow of candles.

Manuel said, "We're talking something criminal?"

"Deeply. And weird."

"Chief Stevenson's been working late today. He's still here but not for much longer. You think maybe I should ask him to wait?"

In my mind rose the eyeless face of the dead hitchhiker.

"Yeah," I said. "Yeah, Stevenson should hear this."

"Can you be here in ten minutes?"

"See you then."

I racked the telephone handset, snatched my cap off the light cage, turned to the street, and shielded my eyes with one hand as two more cars drove past. One was a late-model Saturn. The other was a Chevy pickup.

No white van. No hearse. No black Hummer.

I didn't actually fear that the search for me was still on. By now the hitchhiker would be charring in the furnace. With the evidence reduced to ashes, no obvious proof existed to support my bizarre story. Sandy Kirk, the orderlies, and all the nameless others would feel safe.

Indeed, any attempt to kill or abduct me would risk witnesses to *that* crime, who would then have to be dealt with, increasing the likelihood of still more witnesses. These mysterious conspirators were best served now by discretion rather than aggression — especially when their sole accuser was the town freak, who came out of his heavily curtained house only between dusk and dawn, who feared the sun, who lived by the grace of cloaks and veils and hoods and masks of lotion, who crawled even the night town under a carapace of cloth and chemicals.

Considering the outrageous nature of my ac-

111

cusations, few would find my story credible, but I was sure that Manuel would know I was telling the truth. I hoped the chief would believe me, too.

I stepped away from the telephone outside the post office and headed for the police station. It was only a couple of blocks away.

As I hurried through the night, I rehearsed what I would tell Manuel and his boss, Lewis Stevenson, who was a formidable figure for whom I wanted to be well prepared. Tall, broad-shouldered, athletic, Stevenson had a face noble enough to be stamped in profile on ancient Roman coins. Sometimes he seemed to be but an actor playing the role of dedicated police chief, although if it was a performance, then it was of award caliber. At fifty-two, he gave the impression — without appearing to try — that he was far wiser than his years, easily commanding respect and trust. There was something of the psychologist and something of the priest in him — qualities everyone in his position needed but few possessed. He was that rare person who enjoyed having power but did not abuse it, who exercised authority with good judgment and compassion, and he'd been chief of police for fourteen years without a hint of scandal, ineptitude, or inefficiency in his department.

Thus I came through lampless alleys lit by a moon riding higher in the sky than it had been earlier, came past fences and footpaths, past gardens and garbage cans, came mentally murmuring the words with which I hoped to tell a convincing story, came in two minutes instead of the ten that Manuel had suggested, came to the parking lot behind the municipal building and saw Chief Stevenson in a conspiratorial moment that stripped away all the fine qualities I'd projected onto him. Revealed now was a man who, regardless of his noble face, did not deserve to be honored by coins or by monuments or even by having his photograph hung in the station house next to those of the mayor, the governor, and the President of the United States.

Stevenson stood at the far end of the municipal building, near the back entrance to the police station, in a cascade of bluish light from a hooded security lamp above the door. The man with whom he conferred stood a few feet away, only half revealed in blue shadows.

I crossed the parking lot, heading toward them. They didn't see me coming because they were deeply engrossed in conversation. Furthermore, I was mostly screened from them as I passed among the street-department trucks and squad cars and water-department trucks and personal vehicles, while also staying as much as possible out of the direct light from the three tall pole lamps.

Just before I would have stepped into the open, Stevenson's visitor moved closer to the chief, shedding the shadows, and I halted in shock. I saw his shaved head, his hard face. Red-plaid flannel shirt, blue jeans, work shoes.

At this distance, I wasn't able to see his pearl earring.

I was flanked by two large vehicles, and I quickly retreated a few steps to shelter more completely in the oily darkness between them. One of the engines was still hot; it pinged and ticked as it cooled.

Although I could hear the voices of the two men, I could not make out their words. An on-shore breeze still romanced the trees and quarreled against all the works of man, and this ceaseless whisper and hiss screened the conversation from me.

I realized that the vehicle to my right, the one with the hot engine, was the white Ford van in which the bald man had driven away from Mercy Hospital earlier in the night. With my father's mortal remains.

I wondered if the keys might be in the ignition. I pressed my face to the window in the driver's door, but I couldn't see much of the interior.

If I could steal the van, I would most likely have possession of crucial proof that my story was true. Even if my father's body had been taken elsewhere and was no longer in this van, forensic evidence might remain — not least, some of the hitchhiker's blood.

I had no idea how to hot-wire an engine.

Hell, I didn't know how to *drive*.

And even if I discovered that I possessed a natural talent for the operation of motor vehicles that was the equivalent of Mozart's brilliance at musical composition, I wouldn't be able to drive twenty miles south along the coast or thirty miles north to another police jurisdiction. Not in the glare of oncoming headlights. Not without my precious sunglasses, which lay broken far away in the hills to the east.

Besides, if I opened the van door, the cab lights would wink on. The two men would notice.

They would come for me.

They would kill me.

The back door of the police station opened. Manuel Ramirez stepped outside.

Lewis Stevenson and his conspirator broke off their urgent conversation at once. From this distance, I wasn't able to discern whether Manuel knew the bald man, but he appeared to address only the chief.

I couldn't believe that Manuel — good son of Rosalina, mourning widower of Carmelita, loving father of Toby — would be a part of any business that involved murder and grave-robbing. We can never know many of the people in our lives, not truly *know* them, regardless of how deeply we believe that we see into them. Most of them are murky ponds, containing infinite layers of suspended particles, stirred by strange currents in their greatest depths. But I was willing to bet my life that Manuel's clearwater heart concealed no capacity for treachery.

I wasn't willing to bet *his* life, however, and if I called out to him to search the back of the white van with me, to impound the vehicle for an exhaustive forensics workup, I might be signing his death warrant as well as mine. In fact, I was sure of it.

Abruptly Stevenson and the bald man turned from Manuel to survey the parking lot. I knew then that he had told them about my telephone call.

I dropped into a crouch and shrank deeper into the gloom between the van and the water-department truck.

At the back of the van, I tried to read the license plate. Although usually I am plagued by too much light, this time I was hampered by too little.

Frantically, I traced the seven numbers and letters with my fingertips. I wasn't able to memorize them by braille reading, however, at least not quickly enough to avoid discovery.

I knew that the bald man, if not Stevenson, was coming to the van. Was already on the move. The bald man, the butcher, the trader in bodies, the thief of eyes.

Staying low, I retraced the route by which I had come through the ranks of parked trucks and cars, returning to the alley and then scurrying onward, using rows of trash cans as cover, all but crawling to a Dumpster and past it, to a corner and around, into the other alleyway, out of sight of the municipal building, rising to my full height now, running once more, as fleet as the cat, gliding like an owl, a creature of the night, wondering if I would find safe shelter before dawn or would still be afoot in the open to curl and blacken under the hot rising sun.

10

I assumed that I could safely go home but that
I might be foolish to linger there too long. I
wouldn't be overdue at the police station for another two minutes, and they would wait for me
at least ten minutes past the appointed time before Chief Stevenson realized that I must have
seen him with the man who had stolen my father's body.

Even then, they might not come to the house
in search of me. I was still not a serious threat
to them — and not likely to become one. I had
no proof of anything I'd seen.

Nevertheless, they seemed inclined to take extreme measures to prevent the exposure of their
inscrutable conspiracy. They might be loath to
leave even the smallest of loose ends — which
meant a knot in my neck.

I expected to find Orson in the foyer when I
unlocked the front door and stepped inside, but
he was not waiting for me. I called his name,
but he didn't appear; and if he had been approaching through the gloom, I would have
heard his big paws thumping on the floor.

He was probably in one of his dour moods.
For the most part, he is good-humored, playful,
and companionable, with enough energy in his
tail to sweep all the streets in Moonlight Bay.
From time to time, however, the world weighs
heavily on him, and then he lies as limp as a

rug, sad eyes open but fixed on some doggy memory or on some doggy vision beyond this world, making no sound other than an occasional attenuated sigh.

More rarely, I have found Orson in a state of what seems to be bleakest dejection. This ought to be a condition too profound for any dog to wear, although it fits him well.

He once sat before a mirrored closet door in my bedroom, staring at his reflection for nearly half an hour — an eternity to the dog mind, which generally experiences the world as a series of two-minute wonders and three-minute enthusiasms. I hadn't been able to tell what fascinated him in his image, although I ruled out both canine vanity and simple puzzlement; he seemed full of sorrow, all drooping ears and slumped shoulders and wagless tail. I swear, at times his eyes brimmed with tears that he was barely able to hold back.

"Orson?" I called.

The switch operating the staircase chandelier was fitted with a rheostat, as were most of the switches throughout the house. I dialed up the minimum light that I needed to climb the stairs.

Orson wasn't on the landing. He wasn't waiting in the second-floor hall.

In my room, I dialed a wan glow. Orson wasn't here, either.

I went directly to the nearest nightstand. From the top drawer I withdrew an envelope in which I kept a supply of knocking-around money. It contained only a hundred and eighty dollars, but this was better than nothing. Though I didn't know why I might need the cash, I intended to be prepared, so I transferred the entire sum to one of the pockets of my jeans.

As I slid shut the nightstand drawer, I noticed a dark object on the bedspread. When I picked it up, I was surprised that it was actually what it had appeared to be in the shadows: a pistol.

I had never seen this weapon before.

My father had never owned a gun.

Acting on instinct, I put down the pistol and used a corner of the bedspread to wipe my prints off it. I suspected that I was being set up to take a fall for something I had not done.

Although any television emits ultraviolet radiation, I've seen a lot of movies over the years, because I'm safe if I sit far enough from the screen. I know all the great stories of innocent men — from Cary Grant and James Stewart to Harrison Ford — relentlessly hounded for crimes they never committed and incarcerated on trumped-up evidence.

Stepping quickly into the adjacent bathroom, I switched on the low-watt bulb. No dead blonde in the bathtub.

No Orson, either.

In the bedroom once more, I stood very still and listened to the house. If other people were present, they were only ghosts drifting in ecto-plasmic silence.

I returned to the bed, hesitated, picked up the pistol, and fumbled with it until I ejected the magazine. It was fully loaded. I slammed the magazine back into the butt. Being inexperienced with handguns, I found the piece heavier

119

than I had expected: It weighed at least a pound and a half.

Next to where I'd found the gun, a white envelope lay on the cream-colored bedspread. I hadn't noticed it until now.

I withdrew a penlight from a nightstand drawer and focused the tight beam on the envelope. It was blank except for a professionally printed return address in the upper left corner: Thor's Gun Shop here in Moonlight Bay. The unsealed envelope, which bore neither a stamp nor a postmark, was slightly crumpled and stippled with curious indentations.

When I picked up the envelope, it was faintly damp in spots. The folded papers inside were dry.

I examined these documents in the beam of the penlight. I recognized my father's careful printing on the carbon copy of the standard application, on which he had attested to the local police that he had no criminal record or history of mental illness that would be grounds to deny him the right to own this firearm. Also included was a carbon copy of the original invoice for the weapon, indicating that it was a 9-millimeter Glock 17 and that my father had purchased it with a check.

The date on the invoice gave me a chill: January 18, two years ago. My father had bought the Glock just three days after my mother had been killed in the car crash on Highway 1. As though he thought he needed protection.

In the study across the hallway from the bedroom, my compact cellular phone was recharging. I unplugged it and clipped it to my belt, at my hip.

Orson was not in the study.

Earlier, Sasha had stopped by the house to feed him. Maybe she had taken him with her when she'd gone. If Orson had been as somber as he'd been when I'd left for the hospital — and especially if he had settled into an even blacker mood — Sasha might not have been able to leave the poor beast here alone, because as much compassion as blood flows through her veins.

Even if Orson had gone with Sasha, who had transferred the 9-millimeter Glock from my father's room to my bed? Not Sasha. She wouldn't have known the gun existed, and she wouldn't have prowled through my dad's belongings.

The desk phone was connected to an answering machine. Next to the blinking message light, the counter window showed two calls.

According to the machine's automatic time-and-date voice, the first call had come in only half an hour ago. It lasted nearly two minutes, although the caller spoke not a word.

Initially, he drew slow deep breaths and let them out almost as slowly, as though he possessed the magical power to inhale the myriad scents of my rooms even across a telephone line, and thereby discover if I was home or out. After a while, he began to hum as though he had forgotten that he was being recorded and was merely humming to himself in the manner of a daydreamer lost in thought, humming a tune that seemed to be improvised, with no coherent melody, spiraling and low, eerie and repetitive, like the song a madman might hear when he believes that angels of destruction, in choirs, are singing to him.

I was sure he was a stranger. I believed that I would have been able to recognize the voice of a friend even from nothing more than the humming. I was also sure that he had not reached a wrong number; somehow he was involved with the events following my father's death.

By the time the first caller disconnected, I discovered that I had tightened my hands into fists. I was holding useless air in my lungs. I exhaled a hot dry gust, inhaled a cool sweet draft, but could not yet unclench my hands.

The second call, which had come in only minutes before I had returned home, was from Angela Ferryman, the nurse who had been at my father's bedside. She didn't identify herself, but I recognized her thin yet musical voice: Through her message, it quickened like an increasingly restless bird hopping from picket point to picket point along a fence.

"Chris, I'd like to talk to you. *Have* to talk. As soon as it's convenient. Tonight. If you can, tonight. I'm in the car, on my way home now. You know where I live. Come see me. Don't call. I don't trust phones. Don't even like making this call. But I've got to see you. Come to the back door. No matter how late you get this, come anyway. I won't be asleep. Can't sleep."

I put a new message tape on the machine. I

hid the original cassette under the crumpled sheets of writing paper at the bottom of the wastebasket beside my desk.

These two brief tape recordings wouldn't convince a cop or a judge of anything. Nevertheless, they were the only scraps of evidence I possessed to indicate that something extraordinary was happening to me — something even more extraordinary than my birth into this tiny sunless caste. More extraordinary than surviving twenty-eight years unscathed by xeroderma pigmentosum.

I had been home less than ten minutes. Nevertheless, I was lingering too long.

As I searched for Orson, I more than half expected to hear a door being forced or glass breaking on the lower floor and then footsteps on the stairs. The house remained quiet, but this was a tremulous silence like the surface tension on a pond.

The dog wasn't moping in Dad's bedroom or bathroom. Not in the walk-in closet, either.

Second by second, I grew more worried about the mutt. Whoever had put the 9-millimeter Glock pistol on my bed might also have taken or harmed Orson.

In my room again, I located a spare pair of sunglasses in a bureau drawer. They were in a soft case with a Velcro seal, and I clipped the case in my shirt pocket.

I glanced at my wristwatch, on which the time was displayed by light-emitting diodes.

Quickly, I returned the invoice and the police

questionnaire to the envelope from Thor's Gun Shop. Whether it was more evidence or merely trash, I hid it between the mattress and box springs of my bed.

The date of purchase seemed significant. Suddenly *everything* seemed significant.

I kept the pistol. Maybe this was a setup, just like in the movies, but I felt safer with a weapon. I wished that I knew how to use it.

The pockets of my leather jacket were deep enough to conceal the gun. It hung in the right pocket not like a weight of dead steel but like a thing alive, like a torpid but not entirely dormant snake. When I moved, it seemed to writhe slowly: fat and sluggish, an oozing tangle of thick coils.

As I was about to go downstairs to search for Orson, I recalled a July night when I had watched him from my bedroom window as he sat in the backyard, his head tilted to lift his snout to the breeze, transfixed by something in the heavens, deep in one of his most puzzling moods. He had not been howling, and in any event the summer sky had been moonless; the sound he made was neither a whine nor a whimper but a mewling of singular and disturbing character.

Now I raised the blind at that same window and saw him in the yard below. He was busily digging a black hole in the moon-silvered lawn. This was peculiar, because he was a well-behaved dog and never a digger.

As I looked on, Orson abandoned the patch of earth at which he had been furiously clawing, moved a few feet to the right, and began to dig a new hole. A quality of frenzy marked his behavior.

"What's happened, boy?" I wondered, and in the yard below, the dog dug, dug, dug.

On my way downstairs, with the Glock coiling heavily in my jacket pocket, I remembered that July night when I had gone into the backyard to sit beside the mewling dog. . . .

His cries grew as thin as the whistle-hiss of a glassblower shaping a vase over a flame, so soft that they did not even disturb the nearest of our neighbors, yet there was such wretchedness in the sound that I was shaken by it. With those cries he shaped a misery darker than the darkest glass and stranger in form than anything a blower could blow.

He was uninjured and did not appear to be ill. For all I could tell, the sight of the stars themselves was the thing that filled him with torment. Yet if the vision of dogs is as poor as we are taught, they can't see the stars well or at all. And why should stars cause Orson such anguish, anyway, or the night that was no deeper than other nights before it? Nevertheless, he gazed skyward and made tortured sounds and didn't respond to my reassuring voice.

When I put a hand on his head and stroked his back, I felt hard shudders passing through him. He sprang to his feet and padded away, only to turn and stare at me from a distance, and I swear that for a while he hated me. He loved me as always; he was still my dog, after all, and could not escape loving me; but at the same time, he hated me intensely. In the warm July air, I could virtually feel the cold hatred radiating off him. He paced the yard, alternately staring at me — holding my gaze as only he among all dogs is able to hold it — and looking at the sky, now stiff and shaking with rage, now weak and mewling with what seemed despair.

When I'd told Bobby Halloway about this, he'd said that dogs are incapable of hating anyone or of feeling anything as complex as genuine despair, that their emotional lives are as simple as their intellectual lives. When I insisted on my interpretation, Bobby had said, "Listen, Snow, if you're going to keep coming here to bore my ass off with this New Age crap, why don't you just buy a shotgun and blow my brains out? That would be more merciful than the excruciatingly slow death you're dealing out now, bludgeoning me with your tedious little stories and your moronic philosophies. There are limits to human endurance, Saint Francis — even to mine."

I know what I know, however, and I know Orson hated me that July night, hated me and loved me. And I know that something in the sky tormented him and filled him with despair: the stars, the blackness, or perhaps something he imagined.

Can dogs imagine? Why not?

I know they dream. I've watched them sleep, seen their legs kick as they chase dream rabbits, heard them sigh and whimper, heard them growl at dream adversaries.

Orson's hatred that night did not make me fear him, but I feared *for* him. I knew his problem was not distemper or any physical ailment that might have made him dangerous to me, but was instead a malady of the soul.

Bobby raves brilliantly at the mention of souls in animals and splutters ultimately into a tremendously entertaining incoherence. I could sell tickets. I prefer to open a bottle of beer, lean back, and have the whole show to myself.

Anyway, throughout that long night, I sat in the yard, keeping Orson company even though he might not have wanted it. He glowered at me, remarked upon the vaulted sky with razor-thin cries, shuddered uncontrollably, circled the yard, circled and circled until near dawn, when at last he came to me, exhausted, and put his head in my lap and did not hate me anymore.

Just before sunrise, I went upstairs to my room, ready for bed hours earlier than usual, and Orson came with me. Most of the time, when he chooses to sleep to my schedule, he curls near my feet, but on this occasion he lay on his side with his back to me, and until he slept, I stroked his burly head and smoothed his fine black coat.

I myself slept not at all that day. I lay thinking about the hot summer morning beyond the blinded windows. The sky like an inverted blue porcelain bowl with birds in flight around its rim. Birds of the day, which I had seen only in pictures. And bees and butterflies. And shadows ink-pure and knife-sharp at the edges as they never can be in the night. Sweet sleep couldn't pour into me because I was filled to the brim with bitter yearning.

Now, nearly three years later, as I opened the kitchen door and stepped onto the back porch, I hoped that Orson wasn't in a despondent mood. This night, we had no time for therapy either for him or for me.

My bicycle was on the porch. I walked it down the steps and rolled it toward the busy dog.

In the southwest corner of the yard, he had dug half a dozen holes of various diameters and depths, and I had to be careful not to twist an ankle in one of them. Across that quadrant of the lawn were scattered ragged clumps of up-rooted grass and clods of earth torn loose by his claws.

"Orson?"

He did not respond. He didn't even pause in his frenzied digging.

Giving him a wide berth to avoid the spray of dirt that fanned out behind his excavating fore-paws, I went around the current hole to face him.

"Hey, pal," I said.

The dog kept his head down, his snout in the ground, sniffing inquisitively as he dug.

The breeze had died, and the full moon hung like a child's lost balloon in the highest branches of the melaleucas.

Overhead, nighthawks dived and soared and barrel-looped, crying *peent-peent-peent* as they harvested flying ants and early-spring moths from the air.

Watching Orson at work, I said, "Found any good bones lately?"

He stopped digging but still didn't acknowledge me. Urgently he sniffed the raw earth, the scent of which rose even to me.

"Who let you out here?"

Sasha might have brought him outside to toilet, but I was sure that she would have returned him to the house afterward.

"Sasha?" I asked nevertheless.

If Sasha were the one who had left him loose to wreak havoc on the landscaping, Orson was not going to rat on her. He wouldn't meet my eyes lest I read the truth in them.

Abandoning the hole he had just dug, he returned to a previous pit, sniffed it, and set to work again, seeking communion with dogs in China.

Maybe he knew that Dad was dead. Animals know things, as Sasha had noted earlier. Maybe this industrious digging was Orson's way of working off the nervous energy of grief.

I lowered my bicycle to the grass and hunkered down in front of the burrowing fiend. I gripped his collar and gently forced him to pay attention to me.

"What's wrong with you?"

His eyes had in them the darkness of the ravaged soil, not the brighter glimmering darkness of the starry sky. They were deep and unreadable.

"I've got places to go, pal," I told him. "I want you to come with me."

He whined and twisted his head to look at the

devastation all around him, as though to say that he was loath to leave this great work unfinished.

"Come morning, I'm going to stay at Sasha's place, and I don't want to leave you here alone."

His ears pricked, although not at the mention of Sasha's name or at anything I had said. He wrenched his powerful body around in my grip to look toward the house.

When I let go of his collar, he raced across the yard but then stopped well short of the back porch. He stood at attention, head raised high, utterly still, alert.

"What is it, fella?" I whispered.

From a distance of fifteen or twenty feet, even with the breeze dead and the night hushed, I could barely hear his low growl.

On my way out of the house, I had dialed the switches all the way off, leaving lightless rooms behind me. Blackness still filled the place, and I could see no ghostly face pressed to any of the panes.

Orson sensed someone, however, because he began to back away from the house. Suddenly he spun around with the agility of a cat and raced toward me.

I raised my bike off its side, onto its wheels.

Tail low but not tucked between his legs, ears flattened against his head, Orson shot past me to the back gate.

Trusting in the reliability of canine senses, I joined the dog at the gate without delay. The property is surrounded by a silvered cedar fence as tall as I am, and the gate is cedar, too. The gravity latch was cold under my fingers. Quietly

I slipped it open and silently cursed the squeaking hinges.

Beyond the gate is a hard-packed dirt footpath bordered by houses on one side and by a narrow grove of old red-gum eucalyptuses on the other. As we pushed through the gate, I half expected someone to be waiting for us, but the path was deserted.

To the south, beyond the eucalyptus grove, lies a golf course and then the Moonlight Bay Inn and Country Club. At this hour on a Friday night, viewed between the trunks of the tall trees, the golf course was as black and rolling as the sea, and the glittering amber windows of the distant inn were like the portals on a magnificent cruise ship forever bound for far Tahiti.

To the left, the footpath led uphill toward the heart of town, ultimately terminating in the graveyard adjacent to St. Bernadette's, the Catholic church. To the right, it led downhill toward the flats, the harbor, and the Pacific.

I shifted gears and cycled uphill, toward the graveyard, with the eucalyptus perfume reminding me of the light at a crematorium window and of a beautiful young mother lying dead upon a mortician's gurney, but with good Orson trotting alongside my bike and with the faint strains of dance music filtering across the golf course from the inn, and with a baby crying in one of our neighbors' houses to my left, but with the weight of the Glock pistol in my pocket and with nighthawks overhead snapping insects in their sharp beaks: the living and the dead all together in the trap of land and sky.

131

11

I wanted to talk to Angela Ferryman, because her message on my answering machine had seemed to promise revelations. I was in the mood for revelations.

First, however, I had to call Sasha, who was waiting to hear about my father.

I stopped in St. Bernadette's cemetery, one of my favorite places, a harbor of darkness in one of the more brightly lighted precincts of town. The trunks of six giant oaks rise like columns, supporting a ceiling formed by their interlocking crowns, and the quiet space below is laid out in aisles similar to those in any library; the gravestones are like rows of books bearing the names of those who have been blotted from the pages of life, who may be forgotten elsewhere but are remembered here.

Orson wandered, though not far from me, sniffing the spoor of the squirrels that, by day, gathered acorns off the graves. He was not a hunter tracking prey but a scholar satisfying his curiosity.

From my belt, I unclipped my cellular phone, switched it on, and keyed in Sasha Goodall's mobile number. She answered on the second ring.

"Dad's gone," I said, meaning more than she could know.

Earlier, in anticipation of Dad's death, Sasha had expressed her sorrow. Now her voice tightened slightly with grief so well controlled that only I could have heard it: "Did he . . . did he go easy at the end?"

"No pain."

"Was he conscious?"

"Yeah. We had a chance to say good-bye."

Fear nothing.

Sasha said, "Life stinks."

"It's just the rules," I said. "To get in the game, we have to agree to stop playing some-day."

"It still stinks. Are you at the hospital?"

"No. Out and about. Rambling. Working off some energy. Where're you?"

"In the Explorer. Going to Pinkie's Diner to grab breakfast and work on my notes for the show." She would be on the air in three and a half hours. "Or I could get takeout, and we could go eat somewhere together."

"I'm not really hungry," I said truthfully. "I'll see you later though."

"When?"

"You go home from work in the morning, I'll be there. I mean, if that's okay."

"That's perfect. Love you, Snowman."

"Love you," I replied.

"That's our little mantra."

"It's our truth."

I pushed *end* on the keypad, switched off the phone, and clipped it to my belt again.

When I cycled out of the cemetery, my four-legged companion followed but somewhat reluc-tantly at first. His head was full of squirrel mysteries.

I made my way to Angela Ferryman's house as far as possible by alleyways where I was not likely to encounter much traffic and on streets with widely spaced lampposts. When I had no choice but to pass under clusters of streetlamps, I pedaled hard.

Faithfully, Orson matched his pace to mine. He seemed happier than he had been earlier, now that he could trot at my side, blacker than any nightshadow that I could cast.

We encountered only four vehicles. Each time, I squinted and looked away from the headlights.

Angela lived on a high street in a charming Spanish bungalow that sheltered under magnolia trees not yet in bloom. No lights were on in the front rooms.

An unlocked side gate admitted me to an arbor-covered passage. The walls and arched ceiling of the arbor were entwined with star jasmine. In summer, sprays of the tiny five-petaled white flowers would be clustered so abundantly that the lattice would seem to be draped with multiple layers of lace. Even this early in the year, the hunter-green foliage was enlivened by those pinwheel-like blooms.

While I breathed deeply of the jasmine fragrance, savoring it, Orson sneezed twice.

I wheeled my bike out of the arbor and around to the back of the bungalow, where I leaned it against one of the redwood posts that supported the patio cover.

"Be vigilant," I told Orson. "Be big. Be bad."

He chuffed as though he understood his assignment. Maybe he *did* understand, no matter what Bobby Halloway and the Rationality Police would say.

Beyond the kitchen windows and the translucent curtains was a slow pulse of candlelight.

The door featured four small panes of glass. I rapped softly on one of them.

Angela Ferryman drew aside the curtain. Her quick nervous eyes pecked at me — and then at the patio beyond me to confirm that I had come alone.

With a conspiratorial demeanor, she ushered me inside, locking the door behind us. She adjusted the curtain until she was convinced that no gap existed through which anyone could peer in at us.

Though the kitchen was pleasantly warm, Angela was wearing not only a gray sweat suit but also a navy-blue wool cardigan over the sweats. The cable-knit cardigan might have belonged to her late husband; it hung to her knees, and the shoulder seams were halfway to her elbows. The sleeves had been rolled so often that the resultant cuffs were as thick as great iron manacles.

In this bulk of clothing, Angela appeared thinner and more diminutive than ever. Evidently she remained chilly; she was virtually colorless, shivering.

She hugged me. As always it was a fierce, sharp-boned, *strong* hug, though I sensed in her an uncharacteristic fatigue.

She sat at the polished-pine table and invited me to take the chair opposite hers.

I took off my cap and considered removing

my jacket as well. The kitchen was too warm. The pistol was in my pocket, however, and I was afraid it might fall out on the floor or knock against the chair as I pulled my arms from the coat sleeves. I didn't want to alarm Angela, and she was sure to be frightened by the gun.

In the center of the table were three votive candles in little ruby-red glass containers. Arteries of shimmering red light crawled across the polished pine.

A bottle of apricot brandy also stood on the table. Angela had provided me with a cordial glass, and I half filled it.

Her glass was full to the brim. This wasn't her first serving, either.

She held the glass in both hands, as if taking warmth from it, and when she raised it with both hands to her lips, she looked more waiflike than ever. In spite of her gauntness, she could have passed for thirty-five, nearly fifteen years younger than her true age. At this moment, in fact, she seemed almost childlike.

"From the time I was a little girl, all I ever really wanted to be was a nurse."

"And you're the best," I said sincerely.

She licked apricot brandy from her lips and stared into her glass. "My mother had rheumatoid arthritis. It progressed more quickly than usual. So fast. By the time I was six, she was in leg braces and using crutches. Shortly after my twelfth birthday, she was bedridden. She died when I was sixteen."

I could say nothing meaningful or helpful about that. No one could have. Any words, no matter how sincerely meant, would have tasted as false as vinegar is bitter.

Sure enough, she had something important to tell me, but she needed time to marshal all the words into orderly ranks and march them across the table at me. Because whatever she had to tell me — it scared her. Her fear was visible: brittle in her bones and waxy in her skin.

Slowly working her way to her true subject, she said, "I liked to bring my mother things when she couldn't get them easily herself. A glass of iced tea. A sandwich. Her medicine. A pillow for her chair. Anything. Later, it was a bedpan. And toward the end, fresh sheets when she was incontinent. I never minded that, either. She always smiled at me when I brought her things, smoothed my hair with her poor swollen hands. I couldn't heal her, or make it possible for her to run again or dance, couldn't relieve her pain or her fear, but I could *attend* her, make her comfortable, monitor her condition — and doing those things was more important to me than . . . than anything."

The apricot brandy was too sweet to be called brandy but not as sweet as I had expected. Indeed, it was potent. No amount of it could make me forget my parents, however, or Angela her mother.

"All I ever wanted to be was a nurse," she repeated. "And for a long time it was satisfying work. Scary and sad, too, when we lost a patient, but mostly rewarding." When she looked up from the brandy, her eyes were pried wide open by a memory. "God, I was so scared when you had appendicitis. I thought I was going to lose my little Chris."

"I was nineteen. Not too little."

"Honey, I've been your visiting nurse since you were diagnosed when you were a toddler. You'll always be a little boy to me."

I smiled. "I love you, too, Angela."

Sometimes I forget that the directness with which I express my best emotions is unusual, that it can startle people and — as in this case — move them more deeply than I expect.

Her eyes clouded with tears. To repress them, she bit her lip, but then she resorted to the apricot brandy.

Nine years ago, I'd had one of those cases of appendicitis in which the symptoms do not manifest until the condition is acute. After breakfast, I suffered mild indigestion. Before lunch, I was vomiting, red-faced, and gushing sweat. Stomach pain twisted me into the curled posture of a shrimp in the boiling oil of a deep fryer.

My life was put at risk because of the delay caused by the need for extraordinary preparations at Mercy Hospital. The surgeon was not, of course, amenable to the idea of cutting open my abdomen and conducting the procedure in a dark — or even dimly lighted — operating room. Yet protracted exposure to the bright lights of the surgery was certain to result in a severe burn to any skin not protected from the glare, risking melanoma but also inhibiting the healing of the incision. Covering everything below the point of incision — from my groin to my toes — was easy: a triple layer of cotton sheeting pinned to prevent it from slipping aside. Additional sheeting was used to improvise complex tenting over my head and upper body, designed to protect me from the light but also to allow the anesthesiologist to slip under from time to time, with a penlight, to take my blood pressure and my temperature, to adjust the gas mask, and to ensure that the electrodes from the electrocardiograph remained securely in place on my chest and wrists to permit continued monitoring of my heart. Their standard procedure required that my abdomen be draped except for a window of exposed skin at the site of the surgery, but in my case this rectangular window had to be reduced to the narrowest possible slit. With self-retaining retractors to keep the incision open and judicial use of tape to shield the skin to the very lip of the cut, they dared to slice me. My guts could take all the light that my doctors wanted to pour into them — but by the time they got that far, my appendix had burst. In spite of a meticulous cleanup, peritonitis ensued; an abscess developed and was swiftly followed by septic shock, requiring a second surgical procedure two days later.

After I recovered from septic shock and was no longer in danger of imminent death, I lived for months with the expectation that what I had endured might trigger one of the neurological problems related to XP. Generally these conditions develop after a burn or following long-term cumulative exposure to light — or for reasons not understood — but sometimes they apparently can be engendered by severe physical trauma or shock. Tremors of the head or the hands. Hearing loss. Slurred speech. Even mental impairment. I waited for the first signs of a progressive, irreversible neurological disorder — but they never came.

William Dean Howells, the great poet, wrote that death is at the bottom of everyone's cup. But there is still some sweet tea in mine.

And apricot brandy.

After taking another thick sip from her cordial glass, Angela said, "All I ever wanted was to be a nurse, but look at me now."

She wanted me to ask, and so I did: "What do you mean?"

Gazing at captive flames through a curve of ruby glass, she said, "Nursing is about life. I'm about death now."

I didn't know what she meant, but I waited.

"I've done terrible things," she said.

"I'm sure you haven't."

"I've seen others do terrible things, and I haven't tried to stop them. The guilt's the same."

"Could you have stopped them if you'd tried?"

She thought about that awhile. "No," she said, but she looked no less troubled.

"No one can carry the whole world on her shoulders."

"Some of us better try," she said.

I gave her time. The brandy was fine.

She said, "If I'm going to tell you, it has to be now. I don't have much time. I'm becoming."

"Becoming?"

"I feel it. I don't know who I'll be a month from now, or six months. Someone I won't like to be. Someone who terrifies me."

"I don't understand."

"I know."

"How can I help?" I asked.

"No one can help. Not you. Not me. Not God." Having shifted her gaze from the votive candles to the golden liquid in her glass, she spoke quietly but fiercely: "We're screwing it up, Chris, like we always do, but this is bigger than we've ever screwed up before. Because of pride, arrogance, envy . . . we're losing it, all of it. Oh, God, we're losing it, and already there's no way to turn back, to undo what's been done."

Although her voice was not slurred, I suspected that she had drunk more than one previous glass of apricot brandy. I tried to take comfort in the thought that drink had led her to exaggerate, that whatever looming catastrophe she perceived was not a hurricane but only a squall magnified by mild inebriation.

Nevertheless, she had succeeded in countering the warmth of the kitchen and the cordial. I no longer considered removing my jacket.

"I can't stop them," she said. "But I can stop keeping secrets for them. You deserve to know what happened to your mom and dad, Chris — even if pain comes with the knowledge. Your life's been hard enough, plenty hard, without this, too."

Truth is, I don't believe my life has been especially hard. It has been *different*. If I were to rage against this difference and spend my nights yearning for so-called normalcy, then I would surely make life as hard as granite and break myself on it. By embracing difference, by choosing to thrive on it, I lead a life no harder than most others and easier than some.

I didn't say a word of this to Angela. If she was motivated by pity to make these pending revelations, then I would compose my features into a mask of suffering and present myself as a figure of purest tragedy. I would be Macbeth. I would be mad Lear. I would be Schwarzenegger in *Terminator 2*, doomed to the vat of molten steel.

"You've got so many friends . . . but there're enemies you don't know about," Angela continued. "Dangerous bastards. And some of them are strange. . . . They're becoming."

That word again. *Becoming.*

When I rubbed the back of my neck, I discovered that the spiders I felt were imaginary.

She said, "If you're going to have a chance . . . any chance at all . . . you need to know the truth. I've been wondering where to begin, how to tell you. I think I should start with the monkey."

"The monkey?" I echoed, certain I had not heard her correctly.

"The monkey," she confirmed.

In this context, the word had an inescapable comic quality, and I wondered again about Angela's sobriety.

When at last she looked up from her glass, her eyes were desolate pools in which lay drowned some vital part of the Angela Ferryman whom I had known since childhood. Meeting her stare — its bleak gray sheen — I felt the nape of my neck shrink, and I no longer found any comic potential whatsoever in the word *monkey*.

12

"It was Christmas Eve four years ago," she said. "About an hour after sunset. I was here in the kitchen, baking cookies. Using both ovens. Chocolate-chip in one. Walnut-oatmeal in the other. The radio was on. Somebody like Johnny Mathis singing 'Silver Bells.' "

I closed my eyes to try to picture the kitchen on that Christmas Eve — but also to have an excuse to shut out Angela's haunted stare.

She said, "Rod was due home any minute, and we both were off work the entire holiday weekend."

Rod Ferryman had been her husband.

Over three and a half years ago, six months after the Christmas Eve of which Angela was speaking, Rod had committed suicide with a shotgun in the garage of this house. Friends and neighbors had been stunned, and Angela had been devastated. He was an outgoing man with a good sense of humor, easy to like, not depressive, with no apparent problems that could have driven him to take his own life.

"I'd decorated the Christmas tree earlier in the day," Angela said. "We were going to have a candlelight dinner, open some wine, then watch *It's a Wonderful Life*. We loved that movie. We had gifts to exchange, lots of little gifts. Christmas was our favorite time of year, and we were like kids about the gifts. . . ."

She fell silent.

When I dared to look, I saw that she had closed her eyes. Judging by her wrenched expression, her quicksilver memory had slipped from that Christmas night to the evening in the following June when she found her husband's body in the garage.

Candlelight flickered across her eyelids.

In time, she opened her eyes, but for a while they remained fixed on a faraway sight. She sipped her brandy.

"I was happy," she said. "The cookie smells. The Christmas music. And the florist had delivered a huge poinsettia from my sister, Bonnie. It was there on the end of the counter, so red and cheerful. I felt wonderful, really wonderful. It was the last time I ever felt wonderful — and the last time I ever will. So . . . I was spooning cookie batter onto a baking sheet when I heard this sound behind me, an odd little chirrup, and then something like a sigh, and when I turned, there was a monkey sitting right on this table."

"Good heavens."

"A rhesus monkey with these awful dark-yellow eyes. Not like their normal eyes. Strange."

"Rhesus? You recognized the species?"

"I paid for nursing school by working as a lab assistant for a scientist at UCLA. The rhesus is one of the most commonly used animals in experiments. I saw a lot of them."

"And suddenly one of them is sitting right here."

"There was a bowl of fruit on the table — apples and tangerines. The monkey was peeling

145

and eating one of the tangerines. Neat as you please, this big monkey placing the peelings in a tidy pile."

"Big?" I asked.

"You're probably thinking of an organ grinder's monkey, one of those tiny cute little things. Rhesuses aren't like that."

"How big?"

"Probably two feet tall. Maybe twenty-five pounds."

Such a monkey would seem enormous when encountered, unexpected, in the middle of a kitchen table.

I said, "You must have been pretty surprised."

"More than surprised. I was a little scared. I know how strong those buggers are for their size. Mostly they're peaceable, but once in a while you get one with a mean streak, and he's a real handful."

"Not the kind of monkey anyone would keep as a pet."

"God, no. Not anyone normal — at least not in my book. Well, I'll admit that rhesuses can be cute sometimes, with their pale little faces and that ruff of fur. But this one wasn't cute." Clearly, she could see it in her mind's eye. "No, not this one."

"So where did it come from?"

Instead of answering, Angela stiffened in her chair and cocked her head, listening intently to the house.

I couldn't hear anything out of the ordinary.

Apparently, neither did she. Yet when she spoke again, she did not relax. Her thin hands were locked clawlike on the cordial glass. "I couldn't figure how the thing got inside, into the house. December wasn't overly warm that year. No windows or doors were open."

"You didn't hear it enter the room?"

"No. I was making noise with the cookie sheets, the mixing bowls. Music on the radio. But the damn thing must've been sitting on the table a minute or two, anyway, because by the time I realized it was there, it had eaten half the tangerine."

Her gaze swept the kitchen, as though from the corner of her eye she had seen purposeful movement in the shadows at the periphery.

After steadying her nerves with brandy once more, she said, "Disgusting — a monkey right on the kitchen table, of all places."

Grimacing, she brushed one trembling hand across the polished pine, as though a few of the creature's hairs might still be clinging to the table four years after the incident.

"What did you do?" I pressed.

"I edged around the kitchen to the back door, opened it, hoping the monkey would run out."

"But it was enjoying the tangerine, feeling pretty comfortable where it was," I guessed.

"Yeah. It looked at the open door, then at me — and it actually seemed to laugh. This little tittering noise."

"I swear I've seen dogs laugh now and then. Monkeys probably do, too."

Angela shook her head. "Can't remember any of them laughing in the lab. Of course, considering what their lives were like . . . they didn't have much reason to be in high spirits."

She looked up uneasily at the ceiling, on which three small overlapping rings of light quivered like the smoldering eyes of an apparition: images of the trio of ruby-red glasses on the table.

Encouraging her to continue, I said, "It wouldn't go outside."

Instead of responding, she rose from her chair, stepped to the back door, and tested the dead bolt to be sure it was still engaged.

"Angela?"

Hushing me, she pulled aside the curtain to peer at the patio and the moonlit yard, pulled it aside with trembling caution and only an inch, as if she expected to discover a hideous face pressed to the far side of the pane, gazing in at her.

My cordial glass was empty. I picked up the bottle, hesitated, and then put it down without pouring more.

When Angela turned away from the door, she said, "It wasn't just a laugh, Chris. It was this frightening sound I could never adequately describe to you. It was an evil . . . an evil little cackle, a vicious edge to it. Oh, yes, I know what you're thinking — this was just an animal, just a monkey, so it couldn't be either good or evil. Maybe mean but not vicious, because animals *can* be bad-tempered, sure, but not consciously malevolent. That's what you're thinking. Well, I'm telling you, this one was more than just mean. This laugh was the coldest sound I've ever heard, the coldest and the ugliest — and evil."

"I'm still with you," I assured her.

Instead of returning to her chair from the door, she moved to the kitchen sink. Every square inch of glass in the windows above the sink was covered by the curtains, but she plucked at those panels of yellow fabric to make doubly sure we were fully screened from spying eyes.

Turning to stare at the table as though the monkey sat there even now, Angela said, "I got the broom, figuring I'd shoo the thing onto the floor and then toward the door. I mean, I didn't take a whack at it or anything, just brushed at it. You know?"

"Sure."

"But it wasn't intimidated," she said. "It *exploded* with rage. Threw down the half-eaten tangerine and grabbed the broom and tried to pull it away from me. When I wouldn't let go, it started to climb the broom straight toward my hands."

"Jesus."

"Nimble as anything. So *fast*. Teeth bared and screeching, spitting, coming straight at me, so I let go of the broom, and the monkey fell to the floor with it, and I backed up until I bumped into the refrigerator."

She bumped into the refrigerator again. The muffled clink of bottles came from the shelves within.

"It was on the floor, right in front of me. It knocked the broom aside. Chris, it was so *furious*. Fury out of proportion to anything that had happened. I hadn't hurt it, hadn't even touched it with the broom, but it wasn't going to take any crap from me."

"You said rhesuses are basically peaceable."

"Not this one. Lips skinned back from its teeth, screeching, running at me and then back and then at me again, hopping up and down, tearing at the air, glaring at me so hatefully, pounding the floor with its fists . . ."

Both of her sweater sleeves had partly unrolled, and she drew her hands into them, out of sight. This memory monkey was so vivid that apparently she half expected it to fling itself at her right here, right now, and bite off the tips of her fingers.

"It was like a troll," she said, "a gremlin, some wicked thing out of a storybook. Those dark-yellow eyes."

I could almost see them myself. Smoldering.

"And then suddenly, it leaps up the cabinets, onto the counter near me, all in a wink. It's right *there*" — she pointed — "beside the refrigerator, inches from me, at eye level when I turn my head. It hisses at me, a mean hiss, and its breath smells like tangerines. That's how close we are. I knew —"

She interrupted herself to listen to the house again. She turned her head to the left to look toward the open door to the unlighted dining room.

Her paranoia was contagious. And because of what had happened to me since sundown, I was vulnerable to the infection.

Tensing in my chair, I cocked my head to allow any sinister sound to fall into the upturned cup of my ear.

The three rings of reflected light shimmered soundlessly on the ceiling. The curtains hung silently at the windows.

After a while Angela said, "Its breath smelled like tangerines. It hissed and hissed. I knew it could kill me if it wanted, kill me somehow, even though it was only a monkey and hardly a fourth my weight. When it had been on the floor, maybe I could have drop-kicked the little son of a bitch, but now it was right in my face."

I had no difficulty imagining how frightened she had been. A seagull, protecting its nest on a seaside bluff, diving repeatedly out of the night sky with angry shrieks and a hard *burrrr* of wings, pecking at your head and snaring strands of hair, is a fraction the weight of the monkey that she'd described but nonetheless terrifying.

"I considered running for the open door," she said, "but I was afraid I would make it angrier. So I froze here. My back against the refrigerator. Eye to eye with the hateful thing. After a while, when it was sure I was intimidated, it jumped off the counter, shot across the kitchen, pushed the back door shut, climbed quick onto the table again, and picked up the unfinished tangerine."

I poured another shot of apricot brandy for myself after all.

"So I reached for the handle of this drawer here beside the fridge," she continued. "There's a tray of knives in it."

Keeping her attention on the table, as she had that Christmas Eve, Angela skinned back the cardigan sleeve and reached blindly for the drawer again, to show me which one contained the knives. Without taking a step to the side, she had to lean and stretch.

"I wasn't going to attack it, just get something I could defend myself with. But before I could put my hand on anything, the monkey leaped to its feet on the table, screaming at me again."

She groped for the drawer handle.

"It snatches an apple out of the bowl and throws it at me," she said, "really whales it at me. Hits me on the mouth. Splits my lip." She crossed her arms over her face as if she were even now under assault. "I try to protect myself. The monkey throws another apple, then a third, and it's shrieking hard enough to crack crystal if there were any around."

"Are you saying it knew what was in that drawer?"

Lowering her arms from the defensive posture, she said, "It had some intuitive sense what was in there, yeah."

"And you didn't try for the knife again?"

She shook her head. "The monkey moved like lightning. Seemed like it could be off that table and all over me even as I was pulling the drawer open, biting my hand before I could get a good grip on the handle of a knife. I didn't want to be bitten."

"Even if it wasn't foaming at the mouth, it might have been rabid," I agreed.

"Worse," she said cryptically, rolling up the cuffs of the cardigan sleeves again.

"Worse than rabies?" I asked.

"So I'm standing at the refrigerator, bleeding from the lip, scared, trying to figure what to do

152

next, and Rod comes home from work, comes through the back door there, whistling, and walks right into the middle of this weirdness. But he doesn't do anything you might expect. He's surprised — but not surprised. He's surprised to see the monkey here, yeah, but not surprised by the monkey itself. Seeing it *here,* that's what rattles him. Do you understand what I'm saying?"

"I think so."

"Rod — damn him — he knows this monkey. He doesn't say, *A monkey?* He doesn't say, *Where the hell did a monkey come from?* He says, *Oh, Jesus.* Just, *Oh, Jesus.* It's cool that night, there's a threat of rain, he's wearing a trench coat, and he takes a pistol out of one of his coat pockets — as if he was expecting something like this. I mean, yeah, he's coming home from work, and he's in uniform, but he doesn't wear a side-arm at the office. This is peacetime. He's not in a war zone, for God's sake. He's stationed right outside Moonlight Bay, at a desk job, pushing papers and claiming he's bored, just putting on weight and waiting for retirement, but suddenly he's got this pistol on him that I don't even know he's been carrying until I see it now."

Colonel Roderick Ferryman, an officer in the United States Army, had been stationed at Fort Wyvern, which had long been one of the big economic engines that powered the entire county. The base had been closed eighteen months ago and now stood abandoned, one of the many military facilities that, deemed superfluous, had been decommissioned following the

153

end of the Cold War.

Although I had known Angela — and to a far lesser extent, her husband — since childhood, I had never known what, exactly, Colonel Ferryman did in the Army.

Maybe Angela hadn't really known, either. Until he came home that Christmas Eve.

"Rod — he's holding the gun in his right hand, arm out straight and stiff, the muzzle trained square on the monkey, and he looks more scared than I am. He looks grim. Lips tight. All the color is gone from his face, just gone, he looks like bone. He glances at me, sees my lip starting to swell and blood all over my chin, and he doesn't even ask about that, looks right back at the monkey, afraid to take his eyes off it. The monkey's holding the last piece of tangerine but not eating now. It's staring very hard at the gun. Rod says, *Angie, go to the phone. I'm going to give you a number to call.*"

"Do you remember the number?" I asked.

"Doesn't matter. It's not in service these days. I recognized the exchange, 'cause it was the same first three digits as his office number on the base."

"He had you call Fort Wyvern."

"Yes. But the guy who answers — he doesn't identify himself or say which office he's in. He just says hello, and I tell him Colonel Ferryman is calling. Then Rod reaches for the phone with his left hand, the pistol still in his right. He tells the guy, *I just found the rhesus here at my house, in my kitchen.* He listens, keeping his eyes on the monkey, and then he says, *Hell if I know, but it's*

154

here, all right, and I need help to bag it."

"And the monkey's just watching all this?"

"When Rod hangs up the phone, the monkey raises its ugly little eyes from the gun, looks straight at him, a challenging and angry look, and then coughs out that damn sound, that awful little laugh that makes your skin crawl. Then it seems to lose interest in Rod and me, in the gun. It eats the last segment of the tangerine and starts to peel another one."

As I lifted the apricot brandy that I had poured but not yet touched, Angela returned to the table and picked up her half-empty glass. She surprised me by clinking her glass against mine.

"What're we toasting?" I asked.

"The end of the world."

"By fire or ice?"

"Nothing that easy," she said.

She was as serious as stone.

Her eyes seemed to be the color of the brushed stainless-steel drawer fronts in the cold-holding room at Mercy Hospital, and her stare was too direct until, mercifully, she shifted it from me to the cordial glass in her hand.

"When Rod hangs up the phone, he wants me to tell him what happened, so I do. He has a hundred questions, and he keeps asking about my bleeding lip, about whether the monkey touched me, bit me, as if he can't quite believe the business with the apple. But he won't answer any of my questions. He just says, *Angie, you don't want to know.* Of course I want to know, but I understand what he's telling me."

155

"Privileged information, military secrets."

"My husband had been involved in sensitive projects before, national-security matters, but I thought that was behind him. He said he couldn't talk about this. Not to me. Not to anyone outside the office. Not a word."

Angela continued to stare at her brandy, but I sipped mine. It didn't taste as pleasing as it had before. In fact, this time I detected an underlying bitterness, which reminded me that apricot pits were a source of cyanide.

Toasting the end of the world tends to focus the mind on the dark potential in all things, even in a humble fruit.

Asserting my incorrigible optimism, I took another long sip and concentrated on tasting only the flavor that had pleased me previously.

Angela said, "Not fifteen minutes pass before three guys respond to Rod's phone call. They must've driven in from Wyvern using an ambulance or something for cover, though there wasn't any siren. None of them are wearing uniforms, either. Two of them come around to the back, open the door, and step into the kitchen without knocking. The third guy must have picked the lock on the front door and come in that way, quiet as a ghost, because he steps into the dining-room doorway the same time as the other two come in the back. Rod's still got the pistol trained on the monkey — his arms shaking with fatigue — and all three of the others have tranquilizer-dart guns."

I thought of the quiet lamplit street out front, the charming architecture of this house, the pair of matched magnolia trees, the arbor hung with star jasmine. No one passing the place that night would have guessed at the strange drama playing out within these ordinary stucco walls.

"The monkey seems like he's expecting them," Angela said, "isn't concerned, doesn't try to get away. One of them shoots him with a dart. He bares his teeth and hisses but doesn't even try to pluck the needle out. He drops what's left of the second tangerine, struggles hard to swallow the bite he has in his mouth, then just curls up on the table, sighs, goes to sleep. They leave with the monkey, and Rod goes with them, and I never see the monkey again. Rod doesn't come back until three o'clock in the morning, until Christmas Eve is over, and we never do exchange gifts until late Christmas Day, and by then we're in Hell and nothing's ever going to be the same. No way out, and I know it."

Finally she tossed back her remaining brandy and put the glass down on the table so hard that it sounded like a gunshot.

Until this moment she had exhibited only fear and melancholy, both as deep as cancer in the bone. Now came anger from a still deeper source.

"I had to let them take their goddamn blood samples the day after Christmas."

"Who?"

"The project at Wyvern."

"Project?"

"And once a month ever since — their sample. Like my body isn't mine, like I've got to pay a

157

rent in blood just to be allowed to go on living in it."

"Wyvern has been closed a year and a half."

"Not all of it. Some things don't die. Can't die. No matter how much we wish them dead."

Although she was thin almost to the point of gauntness, Angela had always been pretty in her way. Porcelain skin, a graceful brow, high cheekbones, sculpted nose, a generous mouth that balanced the otherwise vertical lines of her face and paid out a wealth of smiles — these qualities, combined with her selfless heart, made her lovely in spite of the fact that her skull was too near the skin, her skeleton too ill-concealed beneath the illusion of immortality that the flesh provides. Now, however, her face was hard and cold and ugly, fiercely sharpened at every edge by the grinding wheel of anger.

"If I ever refuse to give them the monthly sample, they'll kill me. I'm sure of that. Or lock me away in some secret hospital out there where they can keep a closer watch on me."

"What's the sample for? What're they afraid of?"

She seemed about to tell me, but then she pressed her lips together.

"Angela?"

I gave a sample every month myself, for Dr. Cleveland, and often Angela drew it. In my case it was for an experimental procedure that might detect early indications of skin and eye cancers from subtle changes in blood chemistry. Although giving the samples was painless and for my own good, I resented the invasion, and I

158

could imagine how deeply I would resent it if it were compulsory rather than voluntary.

She said, "Maybe I shouldn't tell you. Even though you need to know to . . . to defend yourself. Telling you all of it is like lighting a fuse. Sooner or later, your whole world blows up."

"Was the monkey carrying a disease?"

"I wish it were a disease. Wouldn't that be nice? Maybe I'd be cured by now. Or dead. Dead would be better than what's coming."

She snatched up her empty cordial glass, made a fist around it, and for a moment I thought she would hurl it across the room.

"The monkey never bit me," she insisted, "never clawed me, never even touched me, for God's sake. But they won't believe me. I'm not sure even Rod believed me. They won't take any chances. They made me . . . *Rod* made me submit to sterilization."

Tears stood in her eyes, unshed but shimmering like the votive light in the red glass candleholders.

"I was forty-five years old then," she said, "and I'd never had a child, because I was *already* sterile. We'd tried so hard to have a baby — fertility doctors, hormone therapy, everything, everything — and nothing worked."

Oppressed by the suffering in Angela's voice, I was barely able to remain in my chair, looking passively up at her. I had the urge to stand, to put my arms around her. To be the nurse this time.

With a tremor of rage in her voice, she said, "And still the bastards made me have the surgery, *permanent* surgery, didn't just tie my tubes but removed my ovaries, cut me, cut out all hope." Her voice almost broke, but she was strong. "I was forty-five, and I'd given up hope anyway, or pretended to give it up. But to have it *cut* out of me . . . The humiliation of it, the hopelessness. They wouldn't even tell me *why*. Rod took me out to the base the day after Christmas, supposedly for an interview about the monkey, about its behavior. He wouldn't elaborate. Very mysterious. He took me into this place . . . this place out there that even most people on the base didn't know existed. They sedated me against my will, performed the surgery without my permission. And when it was all over, the sons of bitches *wouldn't even tell me why!*"

I pushed my chair away from the table and got to my feet. My shoulders ached, and my legs felt weak. I hadn't been expecting to hear a story of this weight.

Although I wanted to comfort her, I didn't attempt to approach Angela. The cordial glass was still sealed in the hard shell of her fist. Grinding anger had sharpened her once-pretty face into a collection of knives. I didn't think she would want me to touch her just then.

Instead, after standing awkwardly at the table for seconds that were interminable, not sure what to do, I went at last to the back door and double-checked the dead bolt to confirm that it was engaged.

"I know Rod loved me," she said, although the anger in her voice didn't soften. "It broke his heart, just broke him entirely, to do what he had to do. Broke his heart to cooperate with them, tricking me into surgery. He was never the same after that."

I turned and saw that her fist was cocked. The blades of her face were polished by candlelight.

"And if his superiors had understood how close Rod and I had always been, they would have known he couldn't go on keeping secrets from me, not when I'd suffered so much for them."

"Eventually he told you all of it," I guessed.

"Yes. And I forgave him, truly forgave him for what had been done to me, but he was still in despair. There was nothing I could do to nurse him out of it. So deep in despair . . . and so scared." Now her anger was veined with pity and with sorrow. "So scared he had no joy in anything anymore. Finally he killed himself . . . and when he was dead, there was nothing left to cut out of me."

She lowered her fist. She opened it. She stared at the cordial glass — and then carefully set it on the table.

"Angela, what was wrong with the monkey?" I asked.

She didn't reply.

Images of candle flames danced in her eyes. Her solemn face was like a stone shrine to a dead goddess.

I repeated the question: "What was wrong with the monkey?"

When at last Angela spoke, her voice was hardly louder than a whisper: "It wasn't a monkey."

161

I knew that I had heard her correctly, yet her words made no sense. "Not a monkey? But you said —"

"It appeared to be a monkey."

"Appeared?"

"And it was a monkey, of course."

Lost, I said nothing.

"Was and wasn't," she whispered. "And that's what was wrong with it."

She did not seem entirely rational. I began to wonder if her fantastic story had been more fantasy than truth — and if she knew the difference.

Turning away from the votive candles, she met my eyes. She was not ugly anymore, but she wasn't pretty again, either. Hers was a face of ashes and shadows. "Maybe I shouldn't have called you. I was emotional about your dad dying. I wasn't thinking clearly."

"You said I need to know . . . to defend myself."

She nodded. "You do. That's right. You need to know. You're hanging by such a thin thread. You need to know who hates you."

I held out my hand to her, but she didn't take it.

"Angela," I pleaded, "I want to know what really happened to my parents."

"They're dead. They're gone. I loved them, Chris, loved them as friends, but they're gone."

"I still need to know."

"If you're thinking that somebody has to pay for their deaths . . . then you have to realize that nobody ever will. Not in your lifetime. Not in anyone's. No matter how much of the truth you learn, no one will be made to pay. No matter what you try to do."

I found that I had drawn my hand back and had curled it into a fist on the table. After a silence, I said, "We'll see."

"I've quit my job at Mercy this evening." Revealing this sad news, she appeared to shrink, until she resembled a child in adult clothing, once more the girl who had brought iced tea, medicine, and pillows to her disabled mother. "I'm not a nurse anymore."

"What will you do?"

She didn't answer.

"It was all you ever wanted to be," I reminded her.

"Doesn't seem any point to it now. Bandaging wounds in a war is vital work. Bandaging wounds in the middle of Armageddon is foolish. Besides, I'm becoming. I'm becoming. Don't you see?"

In fact, I didn't see.

"I'm becoming. Another me. Another Angela. Someone I don't want to be. Something I don't dare think about."

I still didn't know what to make of her apocalyptic talk. Was it a rational response to the secrets of Wyvern or the result of the personal despair arising from the loss of her husband?

She said, "If you insist on knowing about this, then once you know, there's nothing to do but sit back, drink what pleases you most, and watch it all end."

"I insist anyway."

"Then I guess it's time for show-and-tell," Angela said with evident ambivalence. "But . . . oh, Chris, it's going to break your heart." Sadness elongated her features. "I think you need to know . . . but it's going to break your heart."

When she turned from me and crossed the kitchen, I began to follow her.

She stopped me. "I'll have to turn some lights on to get what I need. You better wait here, and I'll bring everything back."

I watched her navigate the dark dining room. In the living room, she switched on a single lamp, and from there she moved out of sight.

Restlessly, I circled this room to which I had been confined, my mind spinning as I prowled. The monkey was and was not a monkey, and its wrongness lay in this simultaneous wasness and notness. This would seem to make sense only in a Lewis Carroll world, with Alice at the bottom of a magical rabbit hole.

At the back door, I tried the dead bolt again. Locked.

I drew the curtain aside and surveyed the night. I could not see Orson.

Trees were stirring. The wind had returned.

Moonlight was on the move. Apparently, new weather was coming in from the Pacific. As the wind flung tattered clouds across the face of the moon, a silvery radiance appeared to ripple across the nightscape. In fact, what traveled were the dappling shadows of the clouds, and the movement of the light was but an illusion. Nevertheless, the backyard was transformed into a winter stream, and the light purled like water moving under ice.

From elsewhere in the house came a brief wordless cry. It was as thin and forlorn as Angela herself.

13

The cry was so short-lived and so hollow that it might have been no more real than the movement of the moonlight across the backyard, merely a ghost of sound haunting a room in my mind. Like the monkey, it possessed both a quality of wasness and notness.

As the door curtain slipped through my fingers and fell silently across the glass, however, a muffled thump sounded elsewhere in the house and shuddered through the walls.

The second cry was briefer and thinner than the first — but it was unmistakably a bleat of pain and terror.

Maybe she had merely fallen off a step stool and sprained her ankle. Maybe I'd heard only wind and birds in the eaves. Maybe the moon is made of cheese and the sky is a chocolate nonpareil with sugar stars.

I called loudly to Angela.

She didn't answer.

The house was not so large that she could have failed to hear me. Her silence was ominous.

Cursing under my breath, I drew the Glock from my jacket pocket. I held it in the candlelight, searching desperately for safeties.

I found only one switch that might be what I wanted. When I pressed it down, an intense beam of red light shot out of a smaller hole below the muzzle and painted a bright dot on the refrigerator door.

My dad, wanting a weapon that was user-friendly even to gentle professors of literature, had paid extra for laser sighting. Good man.

I didn't know much about handguns, but I knew some models of pistols featured "safe action" systems with only internal safety devices that disengaged as the trigger was pulled and, after firing, engaged again. Maybe this was one of those weapons. If not, then I would either find myself unable to get off a shot when confronted by an assailant — or, fumbling in panic, would shoot myself in the foot.

Although I wasn't trained for this work, there was no one but me to do the job. Admittedly, I thought about getting out of there, climbing on my bike, riding to safety, and placing an anonymous emergency call to the police. Thereafter, however, I would never be able to look at myself in a mirror — or even meet Orson's eyes.

I didn't like the way my hands were shaking, but I sure as hell couldn't pause for deep-breathing exercises or meditation.

As I crossed the kitchen to the open door at the dining room, I considered returning the pistol to my pocket and taking a knife from the cutlery drawer. Telling the story of the monkey, Angela had shown me where the blades were kept.

Reason prevailed. I was no more practiced with knives than I was expert with firearms.

Besides, using a knife, slashing and gouging at another human being, seemed to require a ruthlessness greater than that needed to pull a trigger. I figured I could do whatever was necessary if my life — or Angela's — was on the line, but I couldn't rule out the possibility that I was better suited to the comparatively dry business of shooting than to the up-close-and-personal wet work of evisceration. In a desperate confrontation, a flinch might be fatal.

As a thirteen-year-old boy, I had been able to look into the crematorium. Yet all these years later, I still wasn't ready to watch the grimmer show in an embalming chamber.

Swiftly crossing the dining room, I called out to Angela once more. Again, she failed to respond.

I wouldn't call her a third time. If indeed an intruder was in the house, I would only be revealing my position each time I shouted Angela's name.

In the living room, I didn't pause to switch off the lamp, but I stepped wide of it and averted my face.

Squinting in the stinging rain of foyer light, I glanced through the open door to the study. No one was in there.

The powder-room door was ajar. I pushed it all the way open. I didn't need to turn on a light to see that no one was in there, either.

Feeling naked without my cap, which I had left on the kitchen table, I switched off the ceiling fixture in the foyer. Blessed gloom fell.

I peered up at the landing where the shadowy stairs turned back and disappeared overhead. As far as I could tell, no lights were lit on the upper floor — which was fine with me. My dark-adapted eyes were my biggest advantage.

The cellular phone was clipped to my belt. As I started up the stairs, I considered calling the police.

After my failure to keep our appointment earlier in the evening, however, Lewis Stevenson might be looking for me. If so, then the chief himself would answer this call. Maybe the bald man with the earring would come along for the ride.

Manuel Ramirez couldn't assist me himself, because he was the duty officer this evening, restricted to the station. I didn't feel safe asking for any other officer. As far as I knew, Chief Stevenson might not be the only compromised cop in Moonlight Bay; perhaps every member of the force, except Manuel, was involved in this conspiracy. In fact, in spite of our friendship, I couldn't trust Manuel, either, not until I knew a lot more about this situation.

Climbing the stairs, I gripped the Glock with both hands, ready to press the laser-sighting switch if someone moved. I kept reminding myself that playing hero meant trying not to shoot Angela by mistake.

I turned at the landing and saw that the upper flight was darker than the lower. No ambient light from the living room reached this high. I ascended quickly and silently.

My heart was doing more than idling; it was revving nicely, but I was surprised that it wasn't racing. Only yesterday, I could not have imagined that I would be able to adapt so rapidly to the prospect of imminent violence. I was even beginning to recognize within myself a disconcerting *enthusiasm* for danger.

Four doors opened off the upstairs hall. Three were closed. The fourth — the door farthest from the stairs — was ajar, and from the room beyond came a soft light.

I disliked passing the three closed rooms without confirming that they were deserted. I would be leaving my back vulnerable.

Given my XP, however, and especially considering how quickly my eyes would sting and water when exposed to very bright light, I'd be able to search those spaces only with the pistol in my right hand and the penlight in my left. This would be awkward, time-consuming, and dangerous. Each time I stepped into a room, no matter how low I crouched and how fast I moved, the penlight would instantly pinpoint my location for any would-be assailant before I found him with the narrow beam.

My best hope was to play to my strengths, which meant using the darkness, blending with the shadows. Moving sideways along the hall, keeping a watch in both directions, I made no sound, and neither did anyone else in the house.

The second door on the left was open only a crack, and the narrow wedge of light revealed little of the room beyond. Using the gun barrel, I pushed the door inward.

The master bedroom. Cozy. The bed was neatly made. A gaily colored afghan draped one arm of an easy chair, and on the footstool waited a folded newspaper. On the bureau, a collection of antique perfume bottles sparkled.

One of the nightstand lamps was aglow. The bulb was not strong, and the pleated-fabric shade screened most of the rays.

Angela was nowhere to be seen.

A closet door stood open. Perhaps Angela had come upstairs to fetch something from there. I couldn't see anything but hanging clothes and shoe boxes.

The door to the adjacent bathroom was ajar, and the bathroom was dark. To anyone in there, looking out, I was a well-lit target.

I approached the bathroom as obliquely as possible, aiming the Glock at the black gap between the door and the jamb. When I pushed on the door, it opened without resistance.

The smell stopped me from crossing the threshold.

Because the glow of the nightstand lamp didn't illuminate much of the space before me, I fished the penlight from my pocket. The beam glistered across a red pool on a white tile floor. The walls were sprayed with arterial gouts.

Angela Ferryman was slumped on the floor, head bent backward over the rim of the toilet bowl. Her eyes were as wide, pale, and flat as those of a dead seagull that I had once found on the beach.

At a glance, I thought her throat appeared to have been slashed repeatedly with a half-sharp knife. I couldn't bear to look at her too closely or for too long.

The smell was not merely blood. Dying, she

had fouled herself. A draft bathed me in the stench.

A casement window was cranked all the way open. It wasn't a typically small bathroom window but large enough to have provided escape for the killer, who must have been liberally splashed with his victim's blood.

Perhaps Angela had left the window open. If there was a first-story porch roof under it, the killer could have entered as well as exited by this route.

Orson had not barked — but then this window was toward the front of the house, and the dog was at the back.

Angela's hands were at her sides, almost lost in the sleeves of the cardigan. She looked so innocent. She looked twelve.

All her life, she had given of herself to others. Now someone, unimpressed by her selfless giving, had cruelly taken all that was left.

Anguished, shaking uncontrollably, I turned away from the bathroom.

I hadn't approached Angela with questions. I hadn't brought her to this hideous end. She had called me, and although she had used her car phone, someone had known that she needed to be silenced permanently and quickly. Maybe these faceless conspirators decided that her despair made her dangerous. She had quit her job at the hospital. She felt that she had no reason to live. And she was terrified of *becoming*, whatever that meant. She was a woman with nothing to lose, beyond their control. They would have killed her even if I had not responded to her call.

Nevertheless, I was awash in guilt, drowning in cold currents, robbed of breath, and I stood gasping.

Nausea followed those currents, rippling like a fat slippery eel through my gut, swimming up my throat and almost surging into my mouth. I choked it down.

I needed to get out of here, yet I couldn't move. I was half crushed under a weight of terror and guilt.

My right arm hung at my side, pulled as straight as a plumb line by the weight of the gun. The penlight, clutched in my left hand, stitched jagged patterns on the wall.

I could not think clearly. My thoughts rolled thickly, like tangled masses of seaweed in a sludge tide.

On the nearer nightstand, the telephone rang.

I kept my distance from it. I had the queer feeling that this caller was the deep-breather who had left the message on my answering machine, that he would try to steal some vital aspect of me with his bloodhound inhalations, as if my very soul could be vacuumed out of me and drawn away across the open telephone line. I didn't want to hear his low, eerie, tuneless humming.

When at last the phone fell silent, my head had been somewhat cleared by the strident ringing. I clicked off the penlight, returned it to my pocket, raised the big pistol from my side — and realized that someone had switched on the light in the upstairs hall.

Because of the open window and the blood

smeared on the frame, I had assumed I was alone in the house with Angela's body. I was wrong. An intruder was still present — waiting between me and the stairs.

The killer couldn't have slipped out of the master bath by way of the bedroom; a messy trail of blood would have marked his passage across the cream-colored carpet. Yet why would he have escaped from the upstairs only to return immediately through a ground-floor door or window?

If, after fleeing, he had changed his mind about leaving a potential witness and had decided to come back to get me, he wouldn't have turned on the light to announce his presence. He would have preferred to take me by surprise.

Cautiously, squinting against the glare, I stepped into the hallway. It was deserted.

The three doors that had been closed when I had first come upstairs were now standing wide open. The rooms beyond them were forbiddingly bright.

14

Like blood out of a wound, silence welled from the bottom of the house into this upstairs hall. Then a sound rose, but it came from outside: the keening of the wind under the eaves.

A strange game seemed to be under way. I didn't know the rules. I didn't know the identity of my adversary. I was screwed.

Flicking a wall switch, I brought forth a soothing flow of shadows to the hall, which made the lights in the three open rooms seem brighter by comparison.

I wanted to run for the stairs. Get down, out, away. But I didn't dare leave unexplored rooms at my back this time. I'd end up like Angela, throat slashed from behind.

My best chance of staying alive was to remain calm. Think. Approach each door with caution. Inch my way out of the house. Make sure my back was protected every step of the way.

I squinted less, listened more, heard nothing, and moved to the doorway opposite the master bedroom. I didn't cross the threshold but remained in the shadows, using my left hand as a visor to shade my eyes from the harsh overhead light before me.

This might have been a son's or daughter's room if Angela had been able to have children. Instead, it contained a tool cabinet with many drawers, a bar stool with a back, and two high worktables placed to form an L. Here she spent time at her hobby: dollmaking.

A quick glance along the hallway. Still alone.

Keep moving. Don't be an easy target.

I pushed the hobby-room door all the way open. No one was hiding behind it.

I stepped briefly into the brightly lighted room, staying sideways to the hall to cover both spaces.

Angela was a fine dollmaker, as proved by the thirty dolls on the shelves of an open display cabinet at the far end of the hobby room. Her creations were attired in richly imagined, painstakingly realized costumes that Angela herself had sewn: cowboy and cowgirl outfits, sailor suits, party dresses with petticoats. . . . The wonder of the dolls, however, was their faces. She sculpted each head with patience and real talent, and she fired it in a kiln in the garage. Some were matt-finish bisque. Others were glazed. All were hand-painted with such attention to detail that their faces looked real.

Over the years, Angela had sold some of her dolls and had given many away. These remaining were evidently her favorites, with which she had been most reluctant to part. Even under the circumstances, alert for the approach of a psychopath with a half-sharp knife, I saw that each face was unique — as though Angela wasn't merely making dolls but was lovingly imagining the possible faces of the children whom she had never carried in her womb.

I switched off the ceiling fixture, leaving only a worktable lamp. In the sudden swelling of shadows, the dolls appeared to shift on the shelves, as if preparing to leap to the floor. Their painted eyes — some bright with points of reflected light and some with a fixed inky glare — seemed watchful and intent.

I had the heebie-jeebies. Big time.

The dolls were only dolls. They were no threat to me.

Back into the corridor, sweeping the Glock left, right, left again. No one.

Next along this side of the hall was a bathroom. Even with my eyes narrowed to slits to filter out the dazzle of porcelain and glass and mirrors and yellow ceramic tile, I could see into every corner. No one was waiting there.

As I reached inside to switch off the bathroom lights, a noise rose behind me. Back toward the master bedroom. A quick rapping like knuckles on wood. From the corner of my eye, I saw movement.

I spun toward the sound, bringing up the Glock in a two-hand grip again, as if I knew what the hell I was doing, imitating Willis and Stallone and Schwarzenegger and Eastwood and Cage from a hundred jump-run-shoot-chase movies, as if I actually believed that *they* knew what the hell they were doing. I expected to see a hulking figure, demented eyes, an upraised arm, an arcing knife, but I was still alone in the hallway.

The movement I'd seen was the master-bedroom door being pushed shut from the inside. In the diminishing wedge of light between the moving door and the jamb, a twisted shadow loomed, writhed, shrank. The door fell shut with a solid sound like the closing of a bank vault.

That room had been deserted when I left it, and no one had come past me since I'd stepped into the hallway. Only the murderer could be in there — and only if he'd returned through the bathroom window from a porch roof where he'd been when I'd discovered Angela's body.

If the killer was already in the master bedroom again, however, he couldn't also have slipped behind me, moments earlier, to turn on the second-floor lights. So there were two intruders. I was caught between them.

Go forward or back? Lousy choice. Deep shit either way, and me without rubber boots.

They would expect me to run for the stairs. But it was safer to do the unexpected, so without hesitation I rushed to the master-bedroom door. I didn't bother with the knob, kicked hard, sprung the latch, and pushed inside with the Glock in front of me, ready to squeeze off four or five shots at anything that moved.

I was alone.

The nightstand lamp was still lit.

No bloody footprints stained the carpet, so no one could have reentered the splattered bathroom from outside and then returned here by that route to close the hall door.

I checked the bathroom anyway. I left the penlight in my pocket this time, relying on an influx of faint light from the bedroom lamp, because I didn't need — or want — to see all the vivid details again. The casement window remained open. The smell was as repulsive as it had been

178

two minutes ago. The shape slumped against the toilet was Angela. Although she was mercifully veiled in gloom, I could see her mouth gaping as though in amazement, her wide eyes unblinking.

I turned away and glanced nervously at the open door to the hall. No one had followed me in here.

Baffled, I retreated to the middle of the bedroom.

The draft from the bathroom window was not strong enough to have blown the bedroom door shut. Besides, no draft had cast the twisted shadow that I had glimpsed.

Although the space under the bed might have been large enough to hide a man, he would have been uncomfortably compressed between the floor and the box springs, with frame slats banding his back. Anyway, no one could have squirmed into that hiding place before I'd kicked my way into the room.

I could see through the open door to the walk-in closet, which obviously did not harbor an intruder. I took a closer look anyway. The penlight revealed an attic access in the closet ceiling. Even if a fold-down ladder was fitted to the back of that trap door, no one could have been spider-quick enough to climb into the attic and pull the ladder after himself in the two or three seconds that I had taken to burst in from the hallway.

Two draped windows flanked the bed. Both proved to be locked from the inside.

He hadn't gone out that way, but maybe I

could. I wanted to avoid returning to the hall.

Keeping the bedroom door in view, I tried to open a window. It was painted shut. These were French windows with thick mullions, so I couldn't just break a pane and climb out.

My back was to the bathroom. Suddenly I felt as though spiders were twitching through the hollows of my spine. In my mind's eye, I saw Angela behind me, not lying by the toilet any longer but risen, red and dripping, eyes as bright and flat as silver coins. I expected to hear the wound bubbling in her throat as she tried to speak.

When I turned, tingling with dread, she was not behind me, but the hot breath of relief that erupted from me proved how seriously I'd been gripped by this fantastic expectation.

I was *still* gripped by it: I expected to hear her thrash to her feet in the bathroom. Already, my anguish over her death had been supplanted by fear for my own life. Angela was no longer a person to me. She was a thing, death itself, a monster, a fist-in-the-face reminder that we all perish and rot and turn to dust. I'm ashamed to say that I hated her a little because I'd felt obliged to come upstairs to help her, hated her for having put me in this vise, hated myself for hating her, my loving nurse, hated her for making me hate myself.

Sometimes there is no darker place than our own thoughts: the moonless midnight of the mind.

My hands were clammy. The butt of the pistol was slick with cold perspiration.

I stopped chasing ghosts and reluctantly returned to the upstairs hallway. A doll was waiting for me.

This was one of the largest from Angela's hobby-room shelves, nearly two feet high. It sat on the floor, legs splayed, facing me in the light that came through the open door from the only room that I hadn't yet explored, the one opposite the hall bath. Its arms were outstretched, and something hung across both its hands.

This was not good.

I know *not good* when I see it, and this was fully, totally, radically *not good.*

In the movies, a development like the appearance of this doll was inevitably followed by the dramatic entrance of a really big guy with a bad attitude. A really big guy wearing a cool hockey mask. Or a hood. He'd be carrying an even cooler chain saw or a compressed-air nail gun or, in an unplugged mood, an ax big enough to decapitate a T-Rex.

I glanced into the hobby room, which was still half illuminated by the worktable lamp. No intruder lurked there.

Move. To the hall bathroom. It was still deserted. I needed to use the facilities. Not a convenient time. Move.

Now to the doll, which was dressed in black sneakers, black jeans, and a black T-shirt. The object in its hands was a navy-blue cap with two words embroidered in ruby-red thread above the bill: *Mystery Train.*

For a moment I thought it was a cap like mine. Then I saw that it was my own, which

I'd left downstairs on the kitchen table.

Between glances at the head of the stairs and at the open door to the only room that I hadn't searched, expecting trouble from one source or the other, I plucked the cap from the small china hands. I pulled it on my head.

In the right light and circumstances, any doll can have an eerie or evil aspect. This was different, because not a single feature in this bisque face struck me as malevolent, yet the skin on the back of my neck creped like Halloween-party bunting.

What spooked me was not any strangeness about the doll but an uncanny familiarity: It had my face. It had been modeled after me.

I was simultaneously touched and creeped out. Angela had cared for me enough to sculpt my features meticulously, to memorialize me lovingly in one of her creations and keep it upon her shelves of favorites. Yet unexpectedly coming upon such an image of oneself wakes primitive fears — as if I might touch this fetish and instantly find my mind and soul trapped within it, while some malignant spirit, previously immobilized in the doll, came forth to establish itself in my flesh. Gleeful at its release, it would lurch into the night to crack virgins' skulls and eat the hearts of babies in my name.

In ordinary times — if such times exist — I am entertained by an unusually vivid imagination. Bobby Halloway calls it, with some mockery, "the three-hundred-ring circus of your mind." This is no doubt a quality I inherited from my mother and father, who were intelligent enough to know that little could be known, inquisitive enough never to stop learning, and perceptive enough to understand that all things and all events contain infinite possibilities. When I was a child, they read to me the verses of A. A. Milne and Beatrix Potter but also, certain that I was precocious, Donald Justice and Wallace Stevens. Thereafter, my imagination has always churned with images from lines of verse: from Timothy Tim's ten pink toes to fireflies twitching in the blood. In extraordinary times — such as this night of stolen cadavers — I am too imaginative for my own good, and in the three-hundred-ring circus of my mind, all the tigers wait to kill their trainers and all the clowns hide butcher knives and evil hearts under their baggy clothes.

Move.

One more room. Check it out, protect my back, then straight down the stairs.

Superstitiously avoiding contact with the doppelgänger doll, stepping wide of it, I went to the open door of the room opposite the hall bath. A guest bedroom, simply furnished.

Tucking my capped head down and squinting against the glare from the ceiling fixture, I saw no intruder. The bed had side rails and a footboard behind which the spread was tucked, so the space under it was revealed.

Instead of a closet, there were a long walnut bureau with banks of drawers and a massive armoire with a pair of side-by-side drawers below and two tall doors above. The space behind the armoire doors was large enough to conceal a grown man with or without a chain saw.

Another doll awaited me. This one was sitting in the center of the bed, arms outstretched like the arms of the Christopher Snow doll behind me, but in the shrouding brightness, I couldn't tell what it held in its pink hands.

I switched off the ceiling light. One nightstand lamp remained lit to guide me.

I backed into the guest room, prepared to respond with gunfire to anyone who appeared in the hall.

The armoire hulked at the edge of my vision. If the doors began to swing open, I wouldn't even need the laser sighting to chop holes in them with a few 9-millimeter rounds.

I bumped into the bed and turned from both the hall door and the armoire long enough to check out the doll. In each upturned hand was an eye. Not a hand-painted eye. Not a glass-button eye taken from the dollmaker's supply cabinet. A human eye.

The armoire doors hung unmoving on piano hinges.

Nothing but time moved in the hall.

I was as still as ashes in an urn, but life continued within me: My heart raced as it had never raced before, no longer merely revving nicely, but spinning with panic in its squirrel cage of ribs.

Once more I looked at the offering of eyes that filled those small china hands — bloodshot brown eyes, milky and moist, startling and startled in their lidless nakedness. I knew that one of the last things ever seen through them was a white van pulling to a stop in response to an upturned thumb. And then a man with a shaven head and one pearl earring.

Yet I was sure that I wasn't dealing with that same bald man here, now, in Angela's house. This game-playing wasn't his style, this taunting, this hide-and-seek. Quick, vicious, violent action was more to his taste.

Instead, I felt as though I had stumbled into a sanitarium for sociopathic youth, where psychotic children had savagely overthrown their keepers and, giddy with freedom, were now at play. I could almost hear their hidden laughter in other rooms: macabre silvery giggles stifled behind small cold hands.

I refused to open the armoire.

I had come up here to help Angela, but there was no helping her now or ever. All I wanted was to get downstairs, outside, onto my bicycle, and away.

As I started toward the door, the lights went out. Someone had thrown a breaker in a junction box.

This darkness was so bottomless that it didn't welcome even me. The windows were heavily draped, and the milk-pitcher moon couldn't find gaps through which to pour itself. All was blackness on blackness.

Blindly, I rushed toward the door. Then I angled to one side of it when I was overcome by the conviction that someone was in the hall and that I would encounter the thrust of a sharp blade at the threshold.

I stood with my back to the bedroom wall,

listening. I held my breath but was unable to quiet my heart, which clattered like horses' hooves on cobblestones, a runaway *parade* of horses, and I felt betrayed by my own body.

Nevertheless, over the thundering stampede of my heart, I heard the creak of the piano hinges. The armoire doors were coming open.

Jesus.

It was a prayer, not a curse. Or maybe both.

Holding the Glock in a two-hand grip again, I aimed toward where I thought the big armoire stood. Then I reconsidered and swung the muzzle three inches to the left. Only to swing it immediately back to the right.

I was disoriented in the absolute blackness. Although I was certain that I would hit the armoire, I couldn't be sure that I would put the round straight through the center of the space above the two drawers. The first shot had to count, because the muzzle flash would give away my position.

I couldn't risk pumping out rounds indiscriminately. Although a spray of bullets would probably waste the bastard, whoever he might be, there was a chance that I would only wound him — and a smaller but still very real chance that I would merely piss him off.

When the pistol magazine was empty — then what?

Then what?

I sidled to the hallway, risking an encounter there, but it didn't happen. As I crossed the threshold, I pulled the guest-room door shut behind me, putting it between me and whoever had come out of the armoire — assuming I hadn't imagined the creaking of the piano hinges.

The ground-floor lights were evidently on their own circuit. A glow rose through the stair-well at the end of the black hall.

Instead of waiting to see who, if anyone, would burst out of the guest room, I ran to the stairs.

I heard a door open behind me.

Gasping, descending two stairs at a time, I was almost to the landing when my head in miniature sailed past. It shattered against the wall in front of me.

Startled, I brought an arm up to shield my eyes. China shrapnel tattooed my face and chest.

My right heel landed on the bullnose edge of a step and skidded off. I nearly fell, pitched forward, slammed into the landing wall, but kept my balance.

On the landing, crunching shards of my glazed face underfoot, I whipped around to confront my assailant.

The decapitated body of the doll, appropriately attired in basic black, hurtled down. I ducked, and it passed over my head, thumping against the wall behind me.

When I looked up and covered the dark top of the stairs with the gun, there was no one to shoot — as if the doll had torn off its own head to throw at me and then had hurled itself into the stairwell.

The downstairs lights went out.

Through the forbidding blackness came the smell of something burning.

15

Groping in the impenetrable gloom, I finally found the handrail. I clutched at the smooth wood with one sweaty hand and started down the lower flight of stairs toward the foyer.

This darkness had a strange sinuosity, seemed to coil and writhe around me as I descended through it. Then I realized that it was the air, not the darkness, that I was feeling: serpentine currents of hot air swarming up the stairwell.

An instant later, tendrils and then tentacles and then a great pulsing mass of foul-smelling smoke poured into the stairwell from below, invisible but palpable, enveloping me as some giant sea anemone might envelop a diver. Coughing, choking, struggling to breathe, I reversed directions, hoping to escape through a second-floor window, although not through the master bathroom where Angela waited.

I returned to the landing and clambered up three or four steps of the second flight before halting. Through smoke-stung eyes flooded with tears — and through the pall of smoke itself — I saw a throbbing light above.

Fire.

Two fires had been set, one above and one below. Those unseen psychotic children were busy in their mad play, and there seemed to be so *many* of them. I was reminded of the veritable platoon of searchers that appeared to spring from the ground outside the mortuary, as though Sandy Kirk possessed the power to summon the dead from their graves.

Downward, once more and quickly, I plunged toward the only hope of nourishing air. I would find it, if anywhere, at the lowest point of the structure, because smoke and fumes rise while the blaze sucks in cooler air at its base in order to feed itself.

Each inhalation caused a spasm of coughing, increased my feeling of suffocation, and fed my panic, so I held my breath until I reached the foyer. There, I dropped to my knees, stretched out on the floor, and discovered that I could breathe. The air was hot and smelled sour, but all things being relative, I was more thrilled by it than I had ever been by the crisp air coming off the washboard of the Pacific.

I didn't lie there and surrender to an orgy of respiration. I hesitated just long enough to draw several deep breaths to clear my soiled lungs, and to work up enough saliva to spit some of the soot out of my mouth.

Then I raised my head to test the air and to learn how deep the precious safe zone might be. Not deep. Four to six inches. Nevertheless, this shallow pool ought to be enough to sustain me while I found my way out of the house.

Wherever the carpet was afire, of course, there would be no safe-air zone whatsoever.

The lights were still out, the smoke was blindingly thick, and I squirmed on my stomach, frantically heading toward where I believed I would find the front door, the nearest exit. The first thing I encountered in the murk was a sofa, judging by the feel of it, which meant that I had passed through the archway and into the living room, at least ninety degrees off the course I imagined I'd been following.

Now luminous orange pulses passed through the comparatively clear air near the floor, underlighting the curdled masses of smoke as if they were thunderheads looming over a plain. From my eye-to-the-carpet perspective, the beige nylon fibers stretched away like a vast flat field of dry grass, fitfully brightened by an electrical storm. This narrow, life-sustaining realm under the smoke seemed to be an alternate world into which I had fallen after stepping through a door between dimensions.

The ominous throbs of light were reflections of fire elsewhere in the room, but they didn't relieve the gloom enough to help me find the way out. The stroboscopic flickering only contributed to my confusion and scared the hell out of me.

As long as I couldn't see the blaze, I could pretend that it was in a distant corner of the house. Now I no longer had the refuge of pretense. Yet there was no advantage to glimpsing the reflected fire, because I wasn't able to tell if the flames were inches or feet from me, whether they were burning toward or away from me, so the light increased my anxiety without providing guidance.

Either I was suffering worse effects of smoke inhalation than I realized, including a distorted perception of time, or the fire was spreading with unusual swiftness. The arsonists had probably used an accelerant, maybe gasoline.

Determined to get back into the foyer and then to the front door, I sucked desperately at the increasingly acrid air near the floor and squirmed across the room, digging my elbows into the carpet to pull myself along, ricocheting off furniture, until I cracked my forehead solidly against the raised brick hearth of the fireplace. I was farther than ever from the foyer, and yet I couldn't picture myself crawling into the fireplace and up the chimney like Santa Claus on his way back to the sleigh.

I was dizzy. A headache split my skull on a diagonal from my left eyebrow to the part in my hair on the right. My eyes stung from the smoke and the salty sweat that poured into them. I wasn't choking again, but I was gagging on the pungent fumes that flavored even the clearer air near the floor, and I was beginning to think I might not survive.

Trying hard to remember where the fireplace was situated in relationship to the foyer arch, I squirmed along the raised hearth and then angled off into the room again.

It seemed absurd to me that I couldn't find my way out of this place. This wasn't a mansion, for God's sake, not a castle, merely a modest house with seven rooms, none of them large, and 2.5 baths, and not even the cleverest Realtor in the country could have described it in such a way as to give the impression that it had enough rattling-around space to satisfy the Prince of Wales and his retinue.

On the evening news, from time to time, you see stories about people dying in house fires, and you can never quite understand why they couldn't make it to a door or window, when one or the other was surely within a dozen steps. Unless they were, of course, drunk. Or wasted on drugs. Or foolish enough to rush back into the flames to rescue Fluffy, the kitten. Which may sound ungrateful of me after I myself was this same night rescued, in a sense, by a cat. But now I understood how people died in these circumstances: The smoke and the churning darkness were more disorienting than drugs or booze, and the longer you breathed the tainted air, the less nimble your mind became, until your thoughts rambled and even panic couldn't focus them.

When I had first climbed the stairs to see what had happened to Angela, I had been amazed at how calm and collected I was in spite of the threat of imminent violence. With a fat dollop of male pride as cloying as a cupful of mayonnaise, I had even sensed in my heart a disconcerting *enthusiasm* for danger.

What a difference ten minutes can make. Now that it was brutally apparent to me that I was never going to acquit myself in these situations with even half the aplomb of Batman, the romance of danger failed to stir me.

Suddenly, creeping out of the dismal blear, something brushed against me and nuzzled my neck, my chin: something *alive*. In the three-hundred-ring circus of my mind, I pictured Angela Ferryman on her belly, reanimated by some evil voodoo, slithering across the floor to meet me, and planting a cold-lipped, bloody kiss on my throat. The effects of oxygen deprivation were becoming so severe that even this hideous image was not sufficient to shock me into a clearer state of mind, and I reflexively squeezed off a shot.

Thank God, I fired entirely in the wrong direction, because even as the crack of the shot echoed through the living room, I recognized the cold nose at my throat and the warm tongue in my ear as those of my one and only dog, my faithful companion, my Orson.

"Hey, pal," I said, but it came out as a meaningless croak.

He licked my face. He had dog's breath, but I couldn't really blame him for that.

I blinked furiously to clear my vision, and red light pulsed through the room brighter than ever. Still, I got no better than a smeary impression of his furry face pressed to the floor in front of mine.

Then I realized that if he could get into the house and find me, he could show me the way out before we caught fire with a stink of burning denim and fur.

I gathered sufficient strength to rise shakily to my feet. That stubborn eel of nausea swam up my throat again, but as before I choked it down.

Squeezing my eyes shut, trying not to think about the wave of intense heat that abruptly broke over me, I reached down and gripped Orson's thick leather collar, which was easy to find because he was pressed against my legs.

Orson kept his snout close to the floor, where

he could breathe, but I had to hold my breath and ignore the nostril-tickling smoke as the dog led me through the house. He walked me into as few pieces of furniture as he could manage, and I have no suspicion whatever that he was amusing himself in the midst of such tragedy and terror. When I smacked my face into a door frame, I didn't knock out any teeth. Nevertheless, during that short journey, I thanked God repeatedly for testing me with XP rather than with blindness.

Just when I thought I might pass out if I didn't drop to the floor to get some air, I felt a cold draft on my face, and when I opened my eyes, I could see. We were in the kitchen, into which the fire had not yet reached. There was no smoke, either, because the breeze coming in the open back door drove it all into the dining room.

On the table were the votive candles in ruby-red holders, the cordial glasses, and the open bottle of apricot brandy. Blinking at this cozy tableau, I could half believe that the events of the past several minutes had been only a monstrous dream and that Angela, still lost in her dead husband's cardigan, would sit here with me once more, refill her glass, and finish her strange story.

My mouth was so dry and foul that I almost took the bottle of brandy with me. Bobby Halloway would have beer, however, and that would be better.

The dead bolt on the kitchen door was disengaged now. As clever as Orson might be, I doubted that he could have opened a locked door to reach me; for one thing, he didn't have a key. Evidently the killers had fled by this route.

Outside, wheezing to expel a few final traces of smoke from my lungs, I shoved the Glock in my jacket pocket. I nervously surveyed the back-yard for assailants as I blotted my damp hands on my jeans.

Like fishes schooling below the silvered sur-face of a pond, cloud shadows swam across the moonlit lawn.

Nothing else moved except the wind-shaken vegetation.

Grabbing my bicycle and wheeling it across the patio toward the arbor-covered passageway, I looked up at the house in astonishment, amazed that it was not entirely engulfed in flames. Instead, from the exterior, there were as yet only minor indications of the blaze growing from room to room inside: bright vines of flames twining up the draperies at two upstairs win-dows, white petals of smoke flowering from attic vent holes in the eaves.

Except for the bluster and grumble of the in-constant wind, the night was preternaturally si-lent. Moonlight Bay is no city, but it usually has a distinct night voice nonetheless: a few cars on the move, distant music from a cocktail lounge or a kid practicing guitar on a back porch, a barking dog, the whisking sound of the big brushes on the street-cleaning machine, voices of strollers, laughter from the high-school kids gathered outside the Millennium Arcade down on Embarcadero Way, now and then a melan-choly whistle as an Amtrak passenger train or a chain of freight cars approaches the Ocean Avenue crossing. . . . Not at this moment, however, and not on this night. We might as well have been in the deadest neighborhood of a ghost town deep in the Mojave Desert.

Apparently, the crack of the single gunshot that I had fired in the living room had not been loud enough out here to draw anyone's attention.

Under the lattice arch, through the sweet fragrance of jasmine, walking the bicycle, its wheel bearings clicking softly, my heart thudding not softly at all, I hurried after Orson to the front gate. He leaped up and pawed open the latch, a trick of his that I'd seen before. Together we followed the walkway to the street, moving quickly but not running.

We were in luck: no witnesses. No traffic was either approaching or receding along the street. No one was on foot, either.

If a neighbor saw me running from the house just as it went up in flames, Chief Stevenson might decide to use that as an excuse to come looking for me. To shoot me down when I resisted arrest. Whether I resisted or not.

I swung onto my bike, balancing it by keeping one foot on the pavement, and looked back at the house. The wind trembled the leaves of the huge magnolia trees, and through the branches, I could see fire lapping at several of the downstairs and upstairs windows.

Full of grief and excitement, curiosity and dread, sorrow and dark wonder, I raced along the pavement, heading for a street with fewer lamps. Panting loudly, Orson sprinted at my side.

We had gone nearly a block when I heard the windows begin to explode at the Ferryman house, blown out by the fierce heat.

16

Stars between branches, leaf-filtered moonlight, giant oaks, a nurturing darkness, the peace of gravestones — and, for one of us, the eternally intriguing scent of hidden squirrels: We were back in the cemetery adjacent to St. Bernadette's Catholic Church.

My bike was propped against a granite marker topped by the haloed head of a granite angel. I was sitting — sans halo — with my back against another stone that featured a cross at its summit.

Blocks away, sirens shrieked into sudden silence as fire-department vehicles arrived at the Ferryman residence.

I hadn't cycled all the way to Bobby Halloway's house, because I'd been hit by a persistent fit of coughing that hampered my ability to steer. Orson's gait had grown wobbly, too, as he expelled the stubborn scent of the fire with a series of violent sneezes.

Now, in the company of a crowd too dead to be offended, I hawked up thick soot-flavored phlegm and spat it among the gnarled surface roots of the nearest oak, with the hope that I wasn't killing this mighty tree that had survived two centuries of earthquakes, storms, fires, insects, disease, and — more recently — modern America's passion for erecting a minimall with doughnut shop on every street corner. The taste in my mouth could not have been much different if I had been eating charcoal briquettes in a broth of starter fluid.

Having been in the burning house a shorter time than his more reckless master, Orson recovered faster than I. Before I was half done hawking and spitting, he was padding back and forth among the nearest tombstones, diligently sniffing out arboreal bushy-tailed rodents.

Between spells of hacking and expectorating, I talked to Orson if he was in sight, and sometimes he lifted his noble black head and pretended to listen, occasionally wagging his tail to encourage me, though often he was unable to tear his attention away from squirrel spoor.

"What the hell happened in that house?" I asked. "Who killed her, why were they playing games with me, what was the point of all that business with the dolls, why didn't they just slit my throat and burn me with her?"

Orson shook his head, and I made a game of interpreting his response. He didn't know. Shook his head in bafflement. Clueless. He was clueless. He didn't know why they hadn't slit my throat.

"I don't think it was the Glock. I mean, there were more than one of them, at least two, probably three, so they could easily have overpowered me if they'd wanted. And though they slashed her throat, they must have been carrying guns of their own. I mean, these are serious bastards, vicious killers. They cut people's eyes out for the fun of it. They wouldn't be squeamish about carrying guns, so they wouldn't be intimidated by the Glock."

Orson cocked his head, considering the issue. *Maybe it was the Glock. Maybe it wasn't. Then again, maybe it was. Who knew? What's a Glock, anyway? And what's that smell? Such an amazing smell. Such a luxurious fragrance. Is that squirrel piss? Excuse me, Master Snow. Business. Business to attend to here.*

"I don't think they set the house afire to kill me. They didn't really care whether they killed me or not. If they cared, they would have made a more direct effort to get me. They set the fire to cover up Angela's murder. That was the reason, nothing more."

Sniff, sniff, sniff-sniff-sniff: out with the remaining bad air of the burning house, in with the revitalizing scent of squirrel, out with the bad, in with the good.

"God, she was such a good person, so giving," I said bitterly. "She didn't deserve to die like that, to die at all."

Orson paused in his sniffing but only briefly. *Human suffering. Terrible. Terrible thing. Misery, death, despair. But nothing to be done. Nothing to be done about it. Just the way of the world, the nature of human existence. Terrible. Come smell the squirrels with me, Master Snow. You'll feel better.*

A lump rose in my throat, not poignant grief but something more prosaic, so I hacked with tubercular violence and finally planted a black oyster among the tree roots.

"If Sasha were here," I said, "I wonder if right now I'd remind her so much of James Dean?"

My face felt greasy and tender. I wiped at it with a hand that also felt greasy.

Across the thin grass on the graves and across the polished surfaces of the granite markers, the moonshadows of wind-trembled leaves danced like cemetery fairies.

Even in this peculiar light, I could see that the palm of the hand I had put to my face was smeared with soot. "I must stink to high heaven."

Immediately, Orson lost interest in the squirrel spoor and came eagerly to me. He sniffed vigorously at my shoes, along my legs, across my chest, finally sticking his snout under my jacket and into my armpit.

Sometimes I suspect that Orson not only understands more than we expect a dog to understand, but that he has a sense of humor and a talent for sarcasm.

Forcibly withdrawing his snout from my armpit, holding his head in both hands, I said, "You're no rose yourself, pal. And what kind of guard dog are you, anyway? Maybe they were already in the house with Angela when I arrived, and she didn't know it. But how come you didn't bite them in the ass when they left the place? If they escaped by the kitchen door, they went right past you. Why didn't I find a bunch of bad guys rolling around on the backyard, clutching their butts and howling in pain?"

Orson's gaze held steady, his eyes deep. He was shocked by the question, the implied accusation. Shocked. He was a peaceful dog. A dog of peace, he was. A chaser of rubber balls, a licker of faces, a philosopher and boon companion. *Besides, Master Snow, the job was to prevent villains from entering the house, not to prevent them from leaving. Good riddance to villains. Who wants them around, anyway? Villains and fleas. Good riddance.*

As I sat nose-to-nose with Orson, staring into his eyes, a sense of the uncanny came over me — or perhaps it was a transient madness — and for a moment I imagined that I could read his *true* thoughts, which were markedly different from the dialogue that I invented for him. Different and unsettling.

I dropped my bracketing hands from his head, but he chose not to turn away from me or to lower his gaze.

I was unable to lower mine.

To express a word of this to Bobby Halloway would have been to elicit a recommendation of lobotomy: Nevertheless, I sensed that the dog feared for me. Pitied me because I was struggling so hard not to admit the true depth of my pain. Pitied me because I could not acknowledge how profoundly the prospect of being alone scared me. More than anything, however, he *feared* for me, as though he saw an oncoming juggernaut of which I was oblivious: a great white blazing wheel, as big as a mountain, that would grind me to dust and leave the dust burning in its wake.

"What, when, where?" I wondered.

Orson's stare was intense. Anubis, the dog-headed Egyptian god of tombs, weigher of the hearts of the dead, could not have stared more piercingly. This dog of mine was no Lassie, no carefree Disney pooch with strictly cute moves and an unlimited capacity for mischievous fun.

"Sometimes," I told him, "you spook me."

He blinked, shook his head, leaped away from me, and padded in circles among the tombstones, busily sniffing the grass and the fallen oak leaves, pretending to be just a dog again.

Maybe it wasn't Orson who had spooked me. Maybe I had spooked myself. Maybe his lustrous eyes had been mirrors in which I'd seen my own eyes; and in the reflections of my eyes, perhaps I had seen truths in my own heart that I was unwilling to look upon directly.

"That would be the Halloway interpretation," I said.

With sudden excitement, Orson pawed through a drift of fragrant leaves still damp from an afternoon watering by the sprinkler system, burrowed his snout among them as though engaged in a truffle hunt, chuffed, and beat the ground with his tail.

Squirrels. Squirrels had sex. Squirrels had sex, had sex right here. Squirrels. Right here. *Squirrel-heat-musk smell here, right here, Master Snow, here, come smell here, come smell, quick quick quick quick, come smell squirrel sex.*

"You confound me," I told him.

My mouth still tasted like the bottom of an ashtray, but I was no longer hacking up the phlegm of Satan. I should be able to steer to Bobby's place now.

Before fetching my bike, I rose onto my knees and turned to face the headstone against which I had been leaning. "How're things with you, Noah? Still resting in peace?"

I didn't have to use the penlight to read the engraving on the stone. I'd read it a thousand times before, and I'd spent hours pondering the name and the dates under it.

NOAH JOSEPH JAMES

June 5, 1888–July 2, 1984

Noah Joseph James, the man with three first names. It's not your name that amazes me; it's your singular longevity.

Ninety-six years of life.

Ninety-six springs, summers, autumns, winters.

Against daunting odds, I have thus far lived twenty-eight years. If Lady Fortune comes to me with both hands full, I might make thirty-eight. If the physicians prove to be bad prognosticators, if the laws of probability are suspended, if fate takes a holiday, perhaps I'll live to be forty-eight. Then I would have enjoyed one half the span of life granted to Noah Joseph James.

I don't know who he was, what he did with the better part of a century here on earth, whether he had one wife with whom to share his days or outlived three, whether the children whom he fathered became priests or serial killers, and I don't want to know. I've fantasized a rich and wondrous life for this man. I believe him to have been well traveled, to have been to Borneo and Brazil, to Mobile Bay during Jubilee and to New Orleans during Mardi Gras, to the sun-washed isles of Greece and to the secret land of Shangri-la high in the fastness of Tibet. I believe that he loved truly and was deeply loved in return, that he was a warrior and a poet, an adventurer and a scholar, a musician and an artist and a sailor who sailed all the seven seas, who boldly cast off what limitations — if any — were placed upon him. As long as he remains only a name to me and is otherwise a mystery, he can be whatever I want him to be, and I can vicariously experience his long, long life in the sun.

Softly I said, "Hey, Noah, I'll bet when you died back there in 1984, undertakers didn't carry guns."

I rose to my feet and stepped to the adjacent tombstone, where my bicycle was propped under the guardian gaze of the granite angel.

Orson let out a low growl. Abruptly he was tense, alert. His head was raised high, ears pricked. Although the light was poor, his tail seemed to be tucked between his legs.

I followed the direction of his coaly gaze and saw a tall, stoop-shouldered man stalking among the tombstones. Even in the softening shadows, he was a collection of angles and sharp edges, like a skeleton in a black suit, as if one of Noah's neighbors had climbed out of his casket to go visiting.

The man stopped in the very row of graves in which Orson and I stood, and he consulted a curious object in his left hand. It appeared to be the size of a cellular telephone, with an illuminated display screen.

He tapped on the instrument's keypad. The

eerie music of electronic notes carried briefly through the cemetery, but these were different from telephone tones.

Just as a scarf of cloud blew off the moon, the stranger brought the sour-apple-green screen closer to his face for a better look at whatever data it provided, and those two soft lights revealed enough for me to make an identification. I couldn't see the red of his hair or his russet eyes, but even in profile the whippet-lean face and thin lips were chillingly familiar: Jesse Pinn, assistant mortician.

He was not aware of Orson and me, though we stood only thirty or forty feet to his left.

We played at being granite. Orson wasn't growling anymore, even though the soughing of the breeze through the oaks would easily have masked his grumble.

Pinn raised his face from the hand-held device, glanced to his right, at St. Bernadette's, and then consulted the screen again. Finally he headed toward the church.

He remained unaware of us, although we were little more than thirty feet from him.

I looked at Orson.

He looked at me.

Squirrels forgotten, we followed Pinn.

17

The mortician hurried to the back of the church, never glancing over his shoulder. He descended a broad set of stone stairs that led to a basement door.

I followed closely to keep him in sight. Halting only ten feet from the head of the stairs and at an angle to them, I peered down at him.

If he turned and looked up, he would see me before I could move out of sight, but I was not overly concerned. He seemed so involved in the task at hand that the summons of celestial trumpets and the racket of the dead rising from their graves might not have drawn his attention.

He studied the mysterious device in his hand, switched it off, and tucked it into an inside coat pocket. From another pocket he extracted a second instrument, but the light was too poor to allow me to see what he held; unlike the first item, this one incorporated no luminous parts.

Even above the susurration of wind and oak leaves, I heard a series of clicks and rasping noises. These were followed by a hard snap, another snap, and then a third.

On the fourth snap, I thought I recognized the distinctive sound. A Lockaid lock-release gun. The device had a thin pick that you slipped into the key channel, under the pin tumblers. When you pulled the trigger, a flat steel spring jumped upward and lodged some of the pins at the sheer line.

A few years ago, Manuel Ramirez gave me a Lockaid demonstration. Lock-release guns were sold only to law-enforcement agencies, and the possession of one by a civilian was illegal.

Although Jesse Pinn could hang a consoling expression on his mug as convincingly as could Sandy Kirk, he incinerated murder victims in a crematorium furnace to assist in the cover-up of capital crimes, so he was not likely to be fazed by laws restricting Lockaid ownership. Maybe he had limits. Maybe, for instance, he wouldn't push a nun off a cliff for no reason whatsoever. Nevertheless, recalling Pinn's sharp face and the stiletto flicker of his red-brown eyes as he had approached the crematorium window earlier this evening, I wouldn't have put money on the nun at any odds.

The undertaker needed to fire the lock-release gun five times to clear all the pins and disengage the dead bolt. After cautiously trying the door, he returned the Lockaid to his pocket.

When he pushed the door inward, the windowless basement proved to be lighted. Silhouetted, he stood listening on the threshold for perhaps half a minute, his bony shoulders canted to the left and his half-hung head cocked to the right, wind-spiked hair bristling like straw; abruptly he jerked himself into a better posture, like a suddenly animated scarecrow pulling loose of its supporting cross, and he went inside, pushing the door only half shut behind him.

"Stay," I whispered to Orson.

I went down the stairs, and my ever-obedient dog followed me.

When I put one ear to the half-open door, I heard nothing from the basement.

Orson stuck his snout through the eighteen-inch gap, sniffing, and although I rapped him lightly on the top of the head, he didn't withdraw.

Leaning over the dog, I put my snout through the gap, too, not for a sniff but far enough inside to see what lay beyond. Squinting against the fluorescent glare, I saw a twenty-by-forty-foot room with concrete walls and ceiling, lined with equipment that served the church and the attached wing of Sunday-school rooms: five gas-fired furnaces, a big water heater, electric-service panels, and machinery that I didn't recognize.

Jesse Pinn was three-quarters of the way across this first room, approaching a closed door in the far wall, his back to me.

Stepping away from the door, I unclipped the glasses case from my shirt pocket. The Velcro closure peeled open with a sound that made me think of a snake breaking wind, though I don't know why, as I'd never in my life *heard* a snake breaking wind. My aforementioned flamboyant imagination had taken a scatological turn.

By the time I put on the glasses and peered inside again, Pinn had disappeared into the second basement room. That farther door stood half open as well, and light blazed beyond.

"It's a concrete floor in there," I whispered. "My Nikes won't make a sound, but your claws will tick. Stay."

I pressed open the door before me and eased into the basement.

Orson remained outside, at the foot of the stairs. Perhaps he was obedient this time because I'd given him a logical reason to be.

Or perhaps, because of something he had smelled, he knew that proceeding farther was ill-advised. Dogs have an olfactory sense thousands of times sharper than ours, bringing them more data than all human senses combined.

With the sunglasses, I was safe from the light, yet I could see more than well enough to navigate the room. I avoided the open center, staying close to the furnaces and the other equipment, where I could duck into a niche and hope to hide if I heard Jesse Pinn returning.

Time and sweat had by now diminished the effectiveness of the sunscreen on my face and hands, but I was counting on my layer of soot to protect me. My hands appeared to be sheathed in black silk gloves, and I assumed that my face was equally masked.

When I reached the inner door, I heard two distant voices, both male, one belonging to Pinn. They were muffled, and I couldn't understand what was being said.

I glanced at the outside door, where Orson peered in at me, one ear at attention and the other at ease.

Beyond the inner door was a long, narrow, largely empty room. Only a few of the overhead lights were aglow, suspended on chains between exposed water pipes and heating ducts, but I didn't remove my sunglasses.

At the end, this chamber proved to be part of an L-shaped space, and the next length, which opened to the right, was longer and wider than the first, although still dimly lighted. This second section was used as a storeroom, and seeking the voices, I crept past boxes of supplies, decorations for various holidays and celebrations, and file cabinets full of church records. Everywhere shadows gathered like convocations of robed and cowled monks, and I removed my sunglasses.

The voices grew louder as I proceeded, but the acoustics were terrible, and I still couldn't discern any words. Although he was not shouting, Pinn was angry, which I deduced from a low menace in his voice. The other man sounded as though he was trying to placate the undertaker.

A complete life-size crèche was arrayed across half the width of the room: not merely Joseph and the Holy Virgin at a cradle with the Christ child, but also the entire manger scene with wise men, camels, donkeys, lambs, and heralding angels. The stable was made of lumber, and the bales of hay were real; the people and animals were plaster over chicken wire and lath, their clothes and features painted by a gifted artist, protected by a waterproof lacquer that gave them a supernatural glow even in this poor light. Judging by the tools, paint, and other supplies at the periphery of the collection, repairs were being made, after which the crèche would be put under drop cloths until next Christmas.

Beginning to make out scattered words of

Pinn's conversation with the unknown man, I moved among the figures, some of which were taller than I am. The scene was disorienting because none of the elements was staged for display; none was in its proper relationship to the others. One of the wise men stood with his face in the bell of an angel's raised trumpet, and Joseph appeared to be engaged in a conversation with a camel. Baby Jesus lay unattended in His cradle, which stood on a bale of hay to one side. Mary sat with a beatific smile and an adoring gaze, but the object of her attention, rather than being her holy child, was a galvanized bucket. Another wise man seemed to be looking up a camel's butt.

I wended through this disorganized crèche, and near the end of it, I used a lute-playing angel for cover. I was in shadows, but peering past the curve of a half-furled wing, I saw Jesse Pinn in the light about twenty feet away, hectoring another man near the stairs that led up to the main floor of the church.

"You've been warned," Pinn said, raising his voice until it was almost a snarl. "How many *times* have you been warned?"

At first I could not see the other man, who was blocked by Pinn. He spoke quietly, evenly, and I could not hear what he said.

The undertaker reacted in disgust and began to pace agitatedly, combing one hand through his disarranged hair.

Now I saw that the second man was Father Tom Eliot, rector of St. Bernadette's.

"You fool, you stupid shit," Pinn said furiously,

bitterly. "You prattling, God-gushing *moron.*"

Father Tom was five feet eight, plump, with the expressive and rubbery face of a natural-born comedian. Although I wasn't a member of his — or any — church, I'd spoken with him on several occasions, and he seemed to be a singularly good-natured man with a self-deprecating sense of humor and an almost childlike enthusiasm for life. I had no trouble understanding why his parishioners adored him.

Pinn did not adore him. He raised one skeletal hand and pointed a bony finger at the priest: "You make me sick, you self-righteous son of a bitch."

Evidently Father Tom had decided to weather this outrageous verbal assault without response.

As he paced, Pinn chopped at the air with the sharp edge of one hand, as though struggling — with considerable frustration — to sculpt his words into a truth that the priest could understand. "We're not taking any more of your crap, no more of your interference. I'm not going to threaten to kick your teeth out myself, though I'd sure as hell enjoy doing it. Never liked to dance, you know, but I'd sure like to dance on your stupid *face.* But no threats like before, no, not this time, not ever again. I'm not even going to threaten to send *them* after you, because I think that would actually appeal to you. Father Eliot the martyr, suffering for God. Oh, you'd like that — wouldn't you? — being a martyr, suffering such a rotten death without complaint."

Father Tom stood with his head bowed, his

eyes downcast, his arms straight at his sides, as though waiting patiently for this storm to pass.

The priest's passivity inflamed Pinn. The mortician made a sharp-knuckled fist of his right hand and pounded it into the palm of his left, as if he needed to hear the hard snap of flesh on flesh, and now his voice was as rich with scorn as with fury. "You'd wake up some night, and they'd be all over you, or maybe they'd take you by surprise in the bell tower or in the sacristy when you're kneeling at the *prie-dieu,* and you'd surrender yourself to them in ecstasy, in a sick ecstasy, *reveling* in the pain, suffering for your God — that's the way you'd see it — suffering for your dead God, suffering your way straight into Heaven. You dumb bastard. You hopeless retard. You'd even pray for them, pray your heart out for them as they tore you to pieces. Wouldn't you, priest?"

To all of this, the chubby priest responded with lowered eyes and mute endurance.

Keeping my own silence required effort. I had questions for Jesse Pinn. Lots of questions.

Here, however, there was no crematory fire to which I could hold his feet to force answers out of him.

Pinn stopped pacing and loomed over Father Tom. "No more threats against you, priest. No point to it. Just gives you a thrill to think of suffering for the Lord. So this is what'll happen if you don't stay out of our way — we'll waste your sister. Pretty Laura."

Father Tom raised his head and met Pinn's eyes, but still he said nothing.

"I'll kill her myself," Pinn promised. "With this gun."

He withdrew a pistol from inside his suit coat, evidently from a shoulder holster. Even at a distance and in this poor light, I could see that the barrel was unusually long.

Defensively, I put my hand into my jacket pocket, on the butt of the Glock.

"Let her go," said the priest.

"We'll never let her go. She's too . . . interesting. Fact is," Pinn said, "before I kill Laura, I'll rape her. She's still a good-looking woman, even if she's getting strange."

Laura Eliot, who had been a friend and colleague of my mother's, was indeed a lovely woman. Although I hadn't seen her in a year, her face came readily to mind. Supposedly, she had obtained employment in San Diego when Ashdon eliminated her position. Dad and I had received a letter from Laura, and we'd been disappointed that she hadn't come around to say good-bye in person. Evidently that was a cover story and she was still in the area, being held against her will.

Finding his voice at last, Father Tom said, "God help you."

"I don't need help," Pinn said. "When I jam the gun in her mouth, just before I pull the trigger, I'll tell her that her brother says he'll see her soon, see her soon in Hell, and then I'll blow her brains out."

"God help me."

"What did you say, priest?" Pinn inquired mockingly.

Father Tom didn't answer.

"Did you say, 'God help me'?" Pinn taunted. " 'God help me'? Not very damn likely. After all, you aren't one of His anymore, are you?"

This curious statement caused Father Tom to lean back against the wall and cover his face with his hands. He might have been weeping; I couldn't be sure.

"Picture your lovely sister's face," said Pinn. "Now picture her bone structure twisting, distorting, and the top of her skull blowing out."

He fired the pistol at the ceiling. The barrel was long because it was fitted with a sound suppressor, and instead of a loud report, there was nothing but a noise like a fist hitting a pillow.

In the same instant and with a hard *clang,* the bullet struck the rectangular metal shade of the lamp suspended directly above the mortician. The fluorescent tube didn't shatter, but the lamp swung wildly on its long chains; an icy blade of light like a harvesting scythe cut bright arcs through the room.

In the rhythmic sweep of light, though Pinn himself did not at first move, his scarecrow shadow leaped at other shadows that flapped like blackbirds. Then he holstered the pistol under his coat.

As the chains of the swinging light fixture torqued, the links twisted against one another with enough friction to cause an eerie ringing, as if lizard-eyed altar boys in blood-soaked cassocks and surplices were ringing the unmelodious bells of a satanic mass.

The shrill music and the capering shadows

seemed to excite Jesse Pinn. An inhuman cry issued from him, primitive and psychotic, a caterwaul of the sort that sometimes wakes you in the night and leaves you wondering about the species of origin. As that spittle-rich sound sprayed from his lips, he hammered his fists into the priest's midsection, two hard punches.

Quickly stepping out from behind the lute-playing angel, I tried to draw the Glock, but it caught on the lining of my jacket pocket.

As Father Tom doubled over from the two blows, Pinn locked his hands and clubbed them against the back of the priest's neck.

Father Tom dropped to the floor, and I finally ripped the pistol out of my pocket.

Pinn kicked the priest in the ribs.

I raised the Glock, aimed at Pinn's back, and engaged the laser sighting. As the mortal red dot appeared between his shoulder blades, I was about to say *enough,* but the mortician relented and stepped away from the priest.

I kept my silence, but to Father Tom, Pinn said, "If you're not part of the solution, you're part of the problem. If you can't be part of the future, then get the hell out of the way."

That sounded like a parting line. I switched off the laser sighting and retreated behind the angel just as the undertaker turned away from Father Tom. He didn't see me.

To the singing of the chains, Jesse Pinn walked back the way he had come, and the jittery sound seemed to issue not from overhead but from within him, as though locusts were swarming in his blood. His shadow repeatedly darted ahead of him and then leaped behind until he passed beyond the arcing sword of light from the swinging fixture, became one with the darkness, and rounded the corner into the other arm of the L-shaped room.

I returned the Glock to my jacket pocket.

From the cover of the dysfunctional crèche, I watched Father Tom Eliot. He was lying at the foot of the stairs, in the fetal position, curled around his pain.

I considered going to him to determine if he was seriously hurt, and to learn what I could about the circumstances that lay behind the confrontation I had just witnessed, but I was reluctant to reveal myself. I stayed where I was.

Any enemy of Jesse Pinn's should be an ally of mine — but I could not be certain of Father Tom's goodwill. Although adversaries, the priest and the mortician were players in some mysterious underworld of which I had been utterly unaware until this very night, so each of them had more in common with the other than with me. I could easily imagine that, at the sight of me, Father Tom would scream for Jesse Pinn, and that the undertaker would fly back, black suit flapping, with the inhuman caterwaul vibrating between his thin lips.

Besides, Pinn and his crew evidently were holding the priest's sister somewhere. Possession of her gave them a lever and fulcrum with which to move Father Tom, while I had no leverage whatsoever.

The chilling music of the torquing chains gradually faded, and the sword of light described a steadily diminishing arc.

Without a protest, without even an involuntary groan, the priest drew himself to his knees, gathered himself to his feet. He was not able to stand fully erect. Hunched like an ape and no longer comic in any aspect of face or body, with one hand on the railing, he began to pull himself laboriously up the steep, creaking steps toward the church above.

When at last he reached the top, he would switch off the lights, and I would be left here below in a darkness that even St. Bernadette herself, miracle worker of Lourdes, would find daunting. Time to go.

Before retracing my path through the life-size figures of the crèche, I raised my eyes for the first time to the painted eyes of the lute-playing angel in front of me — and thought I saw a blue to match my own. I studied the rest of the lacquered-plaster features and, although the light was weak, I was sure that this angel and I shared a face.

This resemblance paralyzed me with confusion, and I struggled to understand how this Christopher Snow angel could have been here waiting for me. I have rarely seen my own face in brightness, but I know its reflection from the mirrors of my dimly lit rooms, and this was a similar light. This was unquestionably me: beatific as I am not, idealized, but me.

Since my experience in the hospital garage, every incident and object seemed to have significance. No longer could I entertain the possibility of coincidence. Everywhere I looked, the world oozed uncanniness.

This was, of course, the route to madness: viewing *all* of life as one elaborate conspiracy conducted by elite manipulators who see all and know all. The sane understand that human beings are incapable of sustaining conspiracies on a grand scale, because some of our most defining qualities as a species are inattention to detail, a tendency to panic, and an inability to keep our mouths shut. Cosmically speaking, we are barely able to tie our shoes. If there is, indeed, some secret order to the universe, it is not of our doing, and we are probably not even capable of apprehending it.

The priest was a third of the way up the stairs.

Stupefied, I studied the angel.

Many nights during the Christmas season, year after year, I had cycled along the street on which St. Bernadette's stood. The crèche had been arranged on the front lawn of the church, each figure in its proper place, none of the gift-bearing magi posing as a proctologist to camels — and this angel had not been there. Or I hadn't realized that it was there. The likely explanation, of course, was that the display was too brightly lighted for me to risk admiring it; the Christopher Snow angel had been part of the scene, but I had always turned my face from it, squinted my eyes.

The priest was halfway up the stairs and climbing faster.

Then I remembered that Angela Ferryman had attended Mass at St. Bernadette's. Undoubtedly, considering her dollmaking, she had been prevailed upon to lend her talent to the making of the crèche.

End of mystery.

I still couldn't understand why she would have assigned my face to an angel. If my features belonged anywhere in the manger scene, they should have been on the donkey. Clearly, her opinion of me had been higher than I warranted.

Unwanted, an image of Angela rose in my mind's eye: Angela as I had last seen her on the bathroom floor, her eyes fixed on some last sight farther away than Andromeda, head tilted backward into the toilet bowl, throat slashed.

Suddenly I was certain that I had missed an important detail when I'd found her poor torn body. Repulsed by the gouts of blood, gripped by grief, in a state of shock and fear, I had avoided looking long at her — just as, for years, I had avoided looking at the figures in the brightly lighted crèche outside the church. I had seen a vital clue, but it had not registered consciously. Now my subconscious taunted me with it.

As Father Tom reached the top of the steps, he broke into sobs. He sat on the landing and wept inconsolably.

I could not hold fast to a mental image of Angela's face. Later there would be time to confront and, reluctantly, explore that Grand Guignol memory.

From angel to camel to magi to Joseph to donkey to Holy Virgin to lamb to Lamb, I wove silently through the crèche, then past file cabinets and boxes of supplies, into the shorter and

221

narrower space where little was stored, and onward toward the door of the utilities room.

The sounds of the priest's anguish resonated off the concrete walls, fading until they were like the cries of some haunting entity barely able to make itself heard through the cold barrier between this world and the next.

Grimly, I recalled my father's wrenching grief in the cold-holding room at Mercy Hospital, on the night of my mother's death.

For reasons I don't entirely understand, I keep my own anguish private. When one of those wild cries threatens to arise, I bite hard until I chew the energy out of it and swallow it unspoken.

In my sleep I grind my teeth — no surprise — until I wake some nights with aching jaws. Perhaps I am fearful of giving voice in dreams to sentiments I choose not to express when awake.

On the way out of the church basement, I expected the undertaker — waxy and pale, with eyes like day-old blood blisters — to drop on me from above or to soar out of the shadows around my feet or to spring like an evil jack-in-the-box from a furnace door. He was not waiting anywhere along my route.

Outside, Orson came to me from among the tombstones, where he had hidden from Pinn. Judging by the dog's demeanor, the mortician was gone.

He stared at me with great curiosity — or I imagined that he did — and I said, "I don't really know what happened in there. I don't know what it meant."

He appeared dubious. He has a gift for looking dubious: the blunt face, the unwavering eyes.

"Truly," I insisted.

With Orson padding at my side, I returned to my bicycle. The granite angel guarding my transportation did not resemble me in the least.

The fretful wind had again subsided into a caressing breeze, and the oaks stood silent.

A shifting filigree of clouds was silver across the silver moon.

A large flock of chimney swifts swooped down from the church roof and alighted in the trees, and a few nightingales returned, too, as though the cemetery had not been sanctified until Pinn had departed it.

Holding my bike by the handlebars, I pondered the ranks of tombstones and said: " '. . . the dark grew solid around them, finally changing to earth.' That's Louise Glück, a great poet."

Orson chuffed as if in agreement.

"I don't know what's happening here, but I think a lot of people are going to die before this is over — and some of them are likely to be people we love. Maybe even me. Or you."

Orson's gaze was solemn.

I looked past the cemetery at the streets of my hometown, which were suddenly a lot scarier than any boneyard.

"Let's get a beer," I said.

I climbed on my bike, and Orson danced a dog dance across the graveyard grass, and for the time being, we left the dead behind.

THREE

MIDNIGHT HOUR

18

The cottage is the ideal residence for a board-head like Bobby. It stands on the southern horn of the bay, far out on the point, the sole structure within three-quarters of a mile. Point-break surf surrounds it.

From town, the lights of Bobby Halloway's house appear to be so far from the lights along the inner curve of the bay that tourists assume they are seeing a boat anchored in the channel beyond our sheltered waters. To longtime residents, the cottage is a landmark.

The place was constructed forty-five years ago, before many restrictions were placed on coastal building, and it never acquired neighbors because, in those days, there was an abundance of cheap land along the shore, where the wind and the weather were more accommodating than on the point, and where there were streets and convenient utility hookups. By the time the shore lots — then the hills behind them — filled up, regulations issued by the California Coastal Commission had made building on the bay horns impossible.

Long before the house came into Bobby's possession, a grandfather clause in the law preserved its existence. Bobby intended to die in this singular place, he said, shrouded in the sound of breaking surf — but not until well past the middle of the first century of the new millennium.

No paved or graveled road leads along the horn, only a wide rock track flanked by low dunes precariously held in place by tall, sparse shore grass.

The horns that embrace the bay are natural formations, curving peninsulas: They are the remnants of the rim of a massive extinct volcano. The bay itself is a volcanic crater layered with sand by thousands of years of tides. Near shore, the southern horn is three to four hundred feet wide, but it narrows to a hundred at the point.

When I was two-thirds of the way to Bobby's house, I had to get off my bike and walk it. Soft drifts of sand, less than a foot deep, sloped across the rock trail. They would pose no obstacle to Bobby's four-wheel-drive Jeep wagon, but they made pedaling difficult.

This walk was usually peaceful, encouraging meditation. Tonight the horn was serene, but it seemed as alien as a spine of rock on the moon, and I kept glancing back, expecting to see someone pursuing me.

The one-story cottage is of teak, with a cedar-shingle roof. Weathered to a lustrous silver-gray, the wood takes the caress of moonlight as a woman's body receives a lover's touch. Encircling three sides of the house is a deep porch furnished with rocking chairs and gliders.

There are no trees. The landscaping consists only of sand and wild shore grass. Anyway, the eye is impatient with the nearer view and favors the sky, the sea, and the shimmering lights of Moonlight Bay, which look more distant than three-quarters of a mile.

Buying time to settle my nerves, I leaned my bike against the front porch railing and walked past the cottage, to the end of the point. There, I stood with Orson at the top of a slope that dropped thirty feet to the beach.

The surf was so slow that you would have to work hard to catch a wave, and the ride wouldn't last long. It was almost a neap tide, though this was the fourth quarter of the moon. The surf was a little sloppy, too, because of the onshore wind, which was blustery enough to cause some chop out here, even though it was all but dead in town.

Offshore wind is best, smoothing the ocean surface. It blows spray from the crest of the waves, makes them hold up longer, and causes them to hollow out before they break.

Bobby and I have been surfing since we were eleven: him by day, both of us by night. Lots of surfers hit the waves by moonlight, fewer when the moon is down, but Bobby and I like it best in storm waves without even stars.

We were grommets together, totally annoying surf mongrels, but we graduated to surf nazis before we were fourteen, and we were mature boardheads by the time Bobby graduated high school and I took my equivalency degree for home education. Bobby is more than just a boardhead now; he's a surf mensch, and people all over the world turn to him to find out where the big waves will be breaking next.

God, I love the sea at night. It is darkness distilled into a liquid, and nowhere in this world do I feel more at home than in these black swells. The only light that ever arises in the ocean is from bioluminescent plankton, which become radiant when disturbed, and although they can make an entire wave glow an intense lime green, their brightness is friendly to my eyes. The night sea contains nothing from which I must hide or from which I must even look away.

By the time I walked back to the cottage, Bobby was standing in the open front door. Because of our friendship, all the lights in his house are on rheostats; now he had dimmed them to the level of candlelight.

I haven't a clue as to how he knew that I had arrived. Neither I nor Orson had made a sound. Bobby just always knows.

He was barefoot, even in March, but he was wearing jeans instead of swim trunks or shorts. His shirt was Hawaiian — he owns no other style — but he had made a concession to the season by wearing a long-sleeve, crewneck, white cotton sweater under the short-sleeve shirt, which featured bright quizzical parrots and lush palm fronds.

As I climbed the steps to the porch, Bobby gave me a shaka, the surfer hand signal that's easier to make than the sign they exchange on *Star Trek*, which is probably based on the shaka. Fold your middle three fingers to your palm, extend your thumb and little finger, and lazily waggle your hand. It means a lot of things — hello, what's up, hang loose, great ride — all friendly, and it will never be taken as an insult unless you wave it at someone who isn't a surfer, such as an L.A. gang member, in which case it might get you shot dead.

I was eager to tell him about everything that had transpired since sundown, but Bobby values a laid-back approach to life. If he were any more laid back, he'd be dead. Except when riding a wave, he values tranquility. Treasures it. If you're going to be a friend of Bobby Halloway's, you have to learn to accept his view of life: Nothing that happens farther than half a mile from the beach is of sufficient importance to worry about, and no event is solemn enough or stylish enough to justify the wearing of a necktie. He responds to languid conversation better than to chatter, to indirection better than to direct statements.

"Flow me a beer?" I asked.

Bobby said, "Corona, Heineken, Löwenbräu?"

"Corona for me."

Leading the way across the living room, Bobby said, "Is the one with the tail drinking tonight?"

"He'll have a Heinie."

"Light or dark?"

"Dark," I said.

"Must've been a rough night for dogs."

"Full-on gnarly."

The cottage consists of a large living room, an office where Bobby tracks waves worldwide, a bedroom, a kitchen, and one bath. The walls are well-oiled teak, dark and rich, the windows are big, the floors are slate, and the furniture is comfortable.

Ornamentation — other than the natural setting — is limited to eight astonishing watercolors by Pia Klick, a woman whom Bobby still loves, though she left him to spend time in Waimea Bay, on the north shore of Oahu. He wanted to go with her, but she said she needed to be alone in Waimea, which she calls her spiritual home; the harmony and beauty of the place are supposed to give her the peace of mind she requires in order to decide whether or not to live with her fate. I don't know what that means. Neither does Bobby. Pia said she'd be gone a month or two. That was almost three years ago. The swell at Waimea comes out of extremely deep water. The waves are high, wall-like. Pia says they are the green of translucent jade. Some days I dream of walking that shore and hearing the thunder of those breakers. Once a month, Bobby calls Pia or she calls him. Sometimes they talk for a few minutes, sometimes for hours. She isn't with another man, and she does love Bobby. Pia is one of the kindest, gentlest, smartest people I have ever known. I don't understand why she's doing this. Neither does Bobby. The days go by. He waits.

In the kitchen, Bobby plucked a bottle of Corona from the refrigerator and handed it to me.

I twisted off the cap and took a swallow. No lime, no salt, no pretension.

He opened a Heineken for Orson. "Half or all?"

I said, "It's a radical night." In spite of my dire news, I was deep in the tropical rhythms of Bobbyland.

He emptied the bottle into a deep, enameled-metal bowl on the floor, which he keeps for Orson. On the bowl he has painted ROSEBUD in block letters, a reference to the child's sled in Orson Welles's *Citizen Kane.*

I have no intention of inducing my canine companion to become an alcoholic. He doesn't get beer every day, and usually he splits a bottle with me. Nevertheless, he has his pleasures, and I don't intend to deny him what he enjoys. Considering his formidable body weight, he doesn't become inebriated on a single beer. Dare to give him two, however, and he redefines the term *party animal.*

As Orson noisily lapped up the Heineken, Bobby opened a Corona for himself and leaned against the refrigerator.

I leaned against the counter near the sink. There was a table with chairs, but in the kitchen, Bobby and I tend to be leaners.

We are alike in many ways. We're the same height, virtually the same weight, and the same body type. Although he has very dark brown hair and eyes so raven-black that they seem to have blue highlights, we have been mistaken for brothers.

We both have a collection of surf bumps, too, and as he leaned against the refrigerator, Bobby was absentmindedly using the bottom of one bare foot to rub the bumps on the top of the other. These are knotty calcium deposits that develop from constant pressure against a surfboard; you get them on your toes and the tops of your feet from paddling while in a prone position. We have them on our knees, as well, and

Bobby has them on his bottom ribs.

I am not tanned, of course, as Bobby is. He's beyond tanned. He's a maximum brown sun god, year round, and in summer he's well-buttered toast. He does the mambo with melanoma, and maybe one day we'll die of the same sun that he courts and I reject.

"There were some unreal zippers out there today," he said. "Six-footers, perfect shape."

"Looks way slow now."

"Yeah. Mellowed out around sunset."

We sucked at our beers. Orson happily licked his chops.

"So," Bobby said, "your dad died."

I nodded. Sasha must have called him.

"Good," he said.

"Yeah."

Bobby is not cruel or insensitive. He meant it was good that the suffering was over for my father.

Between us, we often say a lot with a few words. People have mistaken us for brothers not merely because we are the same height, weight, and body type.

"You got to the hospital in time. So it was cool."

"It was."

He didn't ask me how I was handling it. He knew.

"So after the hospital," he said, "you sang a couple numbers in a minstrel show."

I touched one sooty hand to my sooty face. "Someone killed Angela Ferryman, set her house on fire to cover it. I almost caught the great *onaula-loa* in the sky."

"Who's the someone?"

"Wish I knew. Same people stole Dad's body."

Bobby drank some beer and said nothing.

"They killed a drifter, swapped his body for Dad's. You might not want to know about this."

For a while, he weighed the wisdom of ignorance against the pull of curiosity. "I can always forget I heard it, if that seems smart."

Orson belched. Beer makes him gaseous.

When the dog wagged his tail and looked up beseechingly, Bobby said, "No more for you, fur face."

"I'm hungry," I said.

"You're filthy, too. Catch a shower, take some of my clothes. I'll throw together some clucking tacos."

"Thought I'd clean up with a swim."

"It's nipple out there."

"Feels about sixty degrees."

"I'm talking water temp. Believe me, the nip factor is high. Shower's better."

"Orson needs a makeover, too."

"Take him in the shower with you. There're plenty of towels."

"Very broly of you," I said. *Broly* meaning "brotherly."

"Yeah, I'm so Christian, I don't ride the waves anymore — I just walk on them."

After a few minutes in Bobbyland, I was relaxed and willing to ease into my news. Bobby's more than a beloved friend. He's a tranquilizer.

Suddenly he stood away from the refrigerator

235

and cocked his head, listening.

"Something?" I asked.

"Someone."

I hadn't heard anything but the steadily diminishing voice of the wind. With the windows closed and the surf so slow, I couldn't even hear the sea, but I noticed that Orson was alert, too.

Bobby headed out of the kitchen to see who the visitor might be, and I said, "Bro," and offered him the Glock.

He stared dubiously at the pistol, then at me. "Stay casual."

"That drifter. They cut out his eyes."

"Why?"

I shrugged. "Because they could?"

For a moment Bobby considered what I'd said. Then he took a key from a pocket of his jeans and unlocked a broom closet, which to the best of my recollection had never featured a lock before. From the narrow closet, he took a pistol-grip, pump-action shotgun.

"That's new," I said.

"Goon repellent."

This was not life as usual in Bobbyland. I couldn't resist: "Stay casual."

Orson and I followed Bobby across the living room and onto the front porch. The onshore flow smelled faintly of kelp.

The cottage faced north. No boats were on the bay — or at least none with running lights. To the east, the town twinkled along the shore and up the hills.

Surrounding the cottage, the end of the horn featured low dunes and shore grass frosted with moonlight. No one was in sight.

Orson moved to the top of the steps and stood rigid, his head raised and thrust forward, sniffing the air and catching a scent more interesting than kelp.

Relying perhaps on a sixth sense, Bobby didn't even look at the dog to confirm his own suspicion. "Stay here. If I flush anyone out, tell him he can't leave till we validate his parking ticket."

Barefoot, he descended the steps and crossed the dunes to look down the steep incline to the beach. Someone could have been lying on that slope, watching the cottage from concealment.

Bobby walked along the crest of the embankment, heading toward the point, studying the slope and the beach below, turning every few steps to survey the territory between him and the house. He held the shotgun ready in both hands and conducted the search with military methodicalness.

Obviously, he had been through this routine more than once before. He hadn't told me that he was being harassed by anyone or troubled by intruders. Ordinarily, if he was having a serious problem, he would have shared it with me.

I wondered what secret he was keeping.

19

Having turned away from the steps and pushed his snout between a pair of balusters at the east end of the porch, Orson was looking not west toward Bobby but back along the horn toward town. He growled deep in his throat.

I followed the direction of his gaze. Even in the fullness of the moon, which the snarled rags of cloud didn't currently obscure, I was unable to see anyone.

With the steadiness of a grumbling motor, the dog's low growl continued uninterrupted.

To the west, Bobby had reached the point, still moving along the crest of the embankment. Although I could see him, he was little more than a gray shape against the stark-black backdrop of sea and sky.

While I had been looking the other way, someone could have cut Bobby down so suddenly and violently that he had been unable to cry out, and I wouldn't have known. Now, rounding the point and beginning to approach the house along the southern flank of the horn, this blurry gray figure could have been anyone.

To the growling dog, I said, "You're spooking me."

Although I strained my eyes, I still couldn't discern anyone or any threat to the east, where Orson's attention remained fixed. The only movement was the flutter of the tall, sparse grass. The fading wind wasn't even strong enough to blow sand off the well-compacted dunes.

Orson stopped grumbling and thumped down the porch steps, as though in pursuit of quarry. Instead, he scampered into the sand only a few feet to the left of the steps, where he raised one hind leg and emptied his bladder.

When he returned to the porch, visible tremors were passing through his flanks. Looking eastward again, he didn't resume his growling; instead, he whined nervously.

This change in him disturbed me more than if he had begun to bark furiously.

I sidled across the porch to the western corner of the cottage, trying to watch the sandy front yard but also wanting to keep Bobby — if, indeed, it was Bobby — in sight as long as possible. Soon, however, still edging along the southern embankment, he disappeared behind the house.

When I realized that Orson had stopped whining, I turned toward him and discovered he was gone.

I thought he must have chased after something in the night, though it was remarkable that he had sprinted off so soundlessly. Anxiously moving back the way I had come, across the porch toward the steps, I couldn't see the dog anywhere out there among the moonlit dunes.

Then I found him at the open front door, peering out warily. He had retreated into the living room, just inside the threshold. His ears were flattened against his skull. His head was lowered. His hackles bristled as if he had sustained an electrical shock. He was neither growling nor whining, but tremors passed through his flanks.

Orson is many things — not least of all, strange — but he is not cowardly or stupid. Whatever he was retreating from must have been worthy of his fear.

"What's the problem, pal?"

Failing to acknowledge me with even as little as a quick glance, the dog continued to obsess on the barren landscape beyond the porch. Although he drew his black lips away from his teeth, no snarl came from him. Clearly he no longer harbored any aggressive intent; rather, his bared teeth appeared to express extreme distaste, repulsion.

As I turned to scan the night, I glimpsed movement from the corner of my eye: the fuzzy impression of a man running in a half crouch, passing the cottage from east to west, progressing swiftly with long fluid strides through the last rank of dunes that marked the top of the slope to the beach, about forty feet away from me.

I swung around, bringing up the Glock. The running man had either gone to ground or had been a phantom.

Briefly I wondered if it was Pinn. No. Orson would not have been fearful of Jesse Pinn or of any man like him.

I crossed the porch, descended the three wooden steps, and stood in the sand, taking a closer look at the surrounding dunes. Scattered sprays of tall grass undulated in the breeze. Some of the shore lights shimmered across the lapping waters of the bay. Nothing else moved.

Like a tattered bandage unraveling from the dry white face of a mummified pharaoh, a long narrow cloud wound away from the chin of the moon.

Perhaps the running man was merely a cloud shadow. Perhaps. But I didn't think so.

I glanced back toward the open door of the cottage. Orson had retreated farther from the threshold, deeper into the front room. For once, he was not at home in the night.

I didn't feel entirely at home, either.

Stars. Moon. Sand. Grass. And a feeling of being watched.

From the slope that dropped to the beach or from a shallow swale between dunes, through a screen of grass, someone was watching me. A gaze can have weight, and this one was coming at me like a series of waves, not like slow surf but like fully macking double overheads, hammering at me.

Now the dog wasn't the only one whose hackles rose.

Just when I began to worry that Bobby was taking a mortally long time, he appeared around the east end of the cottage. As he approached, sand pluming around his bare feet, he never looked at me but let his gaze travel ceaselessly from dune to dune.

I said, "Orson haired out."

"Don't believe it," Bobby said.

"Totally haired out. He's never done that before. He's pure guts, that dog."

"Well, if he did," Bobby said, "I don't blame him. Almost haired out myself."

"Someone's out there."

"More than one."

"Who?"

Bobby didn't reply. He adjusted his grip on the shotgun but continued to hold it at the ready while he studied the surrounding night.

"They've been here before," I guessed.

"Yeah."

"Why? What do they want?"

"I don't know."

"Who are they?" I asked again.

As before, he didn't answer.

"Bobby?" I pressed.

A great pale mass, a few hundred feet high, gradually resolved out of the darkness over the ocean to the west: A fog bank, revealed in lunar whitewash, extended far to the north and the south. Whether it came to land or hung offshore all night, the fog pushed a quieting pressure ahead of it. On silent wings, a formation of pelicans flew low over the peninsula and vanished across the black waters of the bay. As the remaining onshore breeze faded, the long grass drooped and was still, and I could better hear the slow surf breaking along the bay shore, although the sound was less a rumble than a lulling hushaby.

From out at the point, a cry as eerie as the call of a loon carved this deepening silence. An answering cry, equally sharp and chilling, arose from the dunes nearer the house.

I was reminded of those old Western movies in which the Indians call to one another in the night, imitating birds and coyotes, to coordinate their moves immediately before attacking the circled wagons of the homesteaders.

Bobby fired the shotgun into a nearby mound of sand, startling me so much that I nearly blew an aortic valve.

When echoes of the crash rebounded from the bay and receded again, when the last reverberations were absorbed by the vast pillow of fog in the west, I said, "Why'd you do that?"

Instead of answering me at once, Bobby chambered another shell and listened to the night.

I remembered Pinn firing the handgun into the ceiling of the church basement to punctuate the threat that he had leveled against Father Tom Eliot.

Finally, when no more loonlike cries arose, Bobby said, almost as if talking to himself, "Probably isn't necessary, but once in a while it doesn't hurt to float the idea of buckshot past them."

"Who? Who are you warning off?"

I had known him to be mysterious in the past, but never quite so enigmatic as this.

The dunes continued to command his attention, and another minute of mental hang time passed before Bobby suddenly looked at me as if he had forgotten that I was standing beside him. "Let's go inside. You scrub off the bad Denzel Washington disguise, and I'll slam together some killer tacos."

I knew better than to press the issue any further. He was being mysterious either to stoke my curiosity and enhance his treasured reputation for weirdness or because he had good reason to keep this secret even from me. In either case, he was in that special Bobby place, where he's as inaccessible as if he were on his board, halfway through a tube radical, in an insanely hollow wave.

As I followed him into the house, I was still aware of being watched. The attention of the unknown observer prickled my back, like hermit-crab tracks on a surf-smoothed beach. Before closing the front door, I scanned the night once more, but our visitors remained well hidden.

The bathroom is large and luxurious: an absolute-black granite floor, matching countertops, handsome teak cabinetry, and acres of beveled-edge mirrors. The huge shower stall can accommodate four people, which makes it ideal for dog grooming.

Corky Collins — who built Bobby's fine house long before Bobby's birth — was an unpretentious guy, but he indulged in amenities. Like the four-person, marble-lined spa in the corner diagonally across the room from the shower. Maybe Corky — whose name had been Toshiro Tagawa before he changed it — fantasized about orgies with three beach girls or maybe he just liked to be totally, awesomely clean.

As a young man — a prodigy fresh out of law school in 1941, at the age of only twenty-one

— Toshiro had been interred in Manzanar, the camp where loyal Japanese Americans remained imprisoned throughout World War II. Following the war, angered and humiliated, he became an activist, committed to securing justice for the oppressed. After five years, he lost faith in the possibility of equal justice and also came to believe that most of the oppressed, given a chance, would become enthusiastic oppressors in their own right.

He switched to personal-injury law. Because his learning curve was as steep as the huge monoliths macking in from a South Pacific typhoon, he rapidly became the most successful personal-injury attorney in the San Francisco area.

In another four years, having banked some serious cash, he walked away from his law practice. In 1956, at the age of thirty-six, he built this house on the southern horn of Moonlight Bay, bringing in underground power, water, and phone lines at considerable expense. With a dry sense of humor that prevented his cynicism from becoming bitterness, Toshiro Tagawa legally changed his name to Corky Collins on the day he moved into the cottage, and he dedicated every day of the rest of his life to the beach and the ocean.

He grew surf bumps on the tops of his toes and feet, below his kneecaps, and on his bottom ribs. Out of a desire to hear the unobstructed thunder of the waves, Corky didn't always use earplugs when he surfed, so he developed an exostosis; the channel to the inner ear constricts

when filled with cold water, and because of repeated abuse, a benign bony tumor narrows the
ear canal. By the time he was fifty, Corky was
intermittently deaf in his left ear. Every surfer
experiences faucet nose after a thrashing skim
session, when your sinuses empty explosively,
pouring forth all the seawater forced up your
nostrils during wipeouts; this grossness usually
happens when you're talking to an outrageously
fine girl who's wearing a bun-floss bikini. After
twenty years of epic hammering and subsequent
nostril Niagaras, Corky developed an exostosis
in his sinus passages, requiring surgery to alleviate headaches and to restore proper drainage.
On every anniversary of this operation, he had
thrown a Proper Drainage Party. From years of
exposure to the glaring sun and the salt water,
Corky was also afflicted with surfer's eye —
pterygium — a winglike thickening of the con-
junctiva over the white of the eye, eventually extending across the cornea. His vision gradually
deteriorated.

Nine years ago, he was spared ophthalmologi-
cal surgery when he was killed — not by melanoma, not by a shark, but by Big Mama herself,
the ocean. Though Corky was sixty-nine at the
time, he went out in monster storm waves,
twenty-foot behemoths, quakers, rolling thunder
that most surfers a third his age wouldn't have
tried, and according to witnesses, he was a party
of one, hooting with joy, repeatedly almost airborne, racing the lip, carving truly sacred rail
slashes, repeatedly getting barreled — until he
wiped out big time and was held down by a

breaking wave. Monsters that size can weigh thousands of tons, which is a lot of water, too much to struggle against, and even a strong swimmer can be held on the bottom half a minute or longer, maybe a lot longer, before he can get air. Worse, Corky surfaced at the wrong moment, just in time to be hammered deep by the next wave in the set, and he drowned in a two-wave hold-down.

Surfers from one end of California to the other shared the opinion that Corky Collins had led the perfect life and had died the perfect death. Exostosis of the ear, exostosis of the sinuses, pterygium in both eyes — none of that meant shit to Corky, and all of it was better than boredom or heart disease, better than a fat pension check that had to be earned by spending a lifetime in an office. Life was surf, death was surf, the power of nature vast and enfolding, and the heart stirred at the thought of Corky's enviably sweet passage through a world that was so much trouble for so many others.

Bobby inherited the cottage.

This development astonished Bobby. We had both known Corky Collins since we were eleven and first ventured to the end of the horn with board racks on our bikes. He was mentor to every surf rat who was ravenous for experience and eager to master the point break. He didn't act like the point was his, but everyone respected Corky as much as if he actually owned the beach from Santa Barbara all the way to Santa Cruz. He was impatient with any gyrospaz who ripped and slashed up a good wave, ruining it for everyone, and he had only disdain for freeway surfers and wish-wases of all types, but he was a friend and an inspiration to all of us who were in love with the sea and in sync with its rhythms. Corky had legions of friends and admirers, some of whom he had known for more than three decades, so we were baffled as to why he had bequeathed all his worldly possessions to Bobby, whom he had known only eight years.

As explanation, the executor of the estate presented to Bobby a letter from Corky that was a masterpiece of succinctness:

Bobby,
What most people find important, you do not. This is wisdom.
To what you believe is important, you are ready to give your mind, heart, and soul. This is grace.
We have only the sea, love, and time. God gave you the sea. By your own actions you will find love always. So I give you time.

Corky saw in Bobby someone who had an innate understanding, from boyhood, of those truths that Corky himself had not learned until he was thirty-seven. He wanted to honor and encourage that understanding. God bless him for it.

The summer following his freshman year at Ashdon College, when Bobby inherited, after taxes, the house and a modest sum of cash, he dropped out of school. This infuriated his parents. He was able to shrug off their fury, however, because the beach and the sea and the future were his.

Besides, his folks have been furious about one thing or another all their lives, and Bobby is inured to it. They own and edit the town newspaper, and they fancy themselves tireless crusaders for enlightened public policy, which means they think most citizens are either too selfish to do the right thing or too stupid to know what is best for them. They expected Bobby to share what they called their "passion for the great issues of our time," but Bobby wanted to escape from his family's loudly announced idealism — and from all the poorly concealed envy, rancor, and egotism that was a part of it. All Bobby wanted was peace. His folks wanted peace, too, for the entire planet, peace in every corner of Spaceship Earth, but they weren't capable of providing it within the walls of their own home.

With the cottage and the seed money to launch the business that now supported him, Bobby found peace.

The hands of every clock are shears, trimming us away scrap by scrap, and every timepiece with a digital readout blinks us toward implosion. Time is so precious that it can't be purchased. What Corky had given Bobby was not time, really, but the chance to live without clocks, without an awareness of clocks, which seems to make time pass more gently, with less shearing fury.

My parents tried to give the same thing to me. Because of my XP, however, I occasionally hear ticking. Maybe Bobby occasionally hears it, too.

249

Maybe there's no way any of us can entirely escape an awareness of clocks.

In fact, Orson's night of despair, when he had regarded the stars with such despondency and had refused all my efforts to comfort him, might have been caused by an awareness of his own days ticking away. We are told that the simple minds of animals are not capable of encompassing the concept of their own mortality. Yet every animal possesses a survival instinct and recognizes danger. If it struggles to survive, it understands death, no matter what the scientists and the philosophers might say.

This is not New Age sentimentalism. This is simply common sense.

Now, in Bobby's shower, as I scrubbed the soot off Orson, he continued to shiver. The water was warm. The shivers had nothing to do with the bath.

By the time I blotted the dog with several towels and fluffed him with a hair dryer that Pia Klick had left behind, his shakes had passed. While I dressed in a pair of Bobby's blue jeans and a long-sleeve, blue cotton sweater, Orson glanced at the frosted window a few times, as if leery of whoever might be out there in the night, but his confidence appeared to be returning.

With paper towels, I wiped off my leather jacket and my cap. They still smelled of smoke, the cap more than the jacket.

In the dim light, I could barely read the words above the bill: *Mystery Train.* I rubbed the ball of my thumb across the embroidered letters, recalling the windowless concrete room where I'd found the cap, in one of the more peculiar abandoned precincts of Fort Wyvern.

Angela Ferryman's words came back to me, her response to my statement that Wyvern had been closed for a year and a half: *Some things don't die. Can't die. No matter how much we wish them dead.*

I had another flashback to the bathroom at Angela's house: a mental image of her death-startled eyes and the silent surprised *oh* of her mouth. Again, I was gripped by the conviction that I had overlooked an important detail regarding the condition of her body, and as before, when I tried to summon a more vivid memory of her blood-spattered face, it grew not clearer in my mind but fuzzier.

We're screwing it up, Chris . . . bigger than we've ever screwed up before . . . and already there's no way . . . to undo what's been done.

The tacos — packed with shredded chicken, lettuce, cheese, and salsa — were delicious. We sat at the kitchen table to eat, instead of leaning over the sink, and we washed down the food with beer.

Although Sasha had fed him earlier, Orson cadged a few bits of chicken, but he couldn't charm me into giving him another Heineken.

Bobby had turned on the radio, and it was tuned to Sasha's show, which had just come on the air. Midnight had arrived. She didn't mention me or introduce the song with a dedication, but she played "Heart Shaped World" by Chris Isaak, because it's a favorite of mine.

Enormously condensing the events of the evening, I told Bobby about the incident in the hospital garage, the scene in Kirk's crematorium, and the platoon of faceless men who pursued me through the hills behind the funeral home.

Throughout all of this, he only said, "Tabasco?"

"What?"

"To hotten up the salsa."

"No," I said. "This is killer just the way it is."

He got a bottle of Tabasco sauce from the refrigerator and sprinkled it into his half-eaten first taco.

Now Sasha was playing "Two Hearts" by Chris Isaak.

For a while I repeatedly glanced through the window beside the table, wondering whether anyone outside was watching us. At first I didn't think Bobby shared my concern, but then I realized that from time to time, he glanced intently, though with seeming casualness, at the blackness out there.

"Lower the blind?" I suggested.

"No. They might think I cared."

We were pretending not to be intimidated.

"Who are they?"

He was silent, but I outwaited him, and at last he said, "I'm not sure."

That wasn't an honest answer, but I relented.

When I continued my story, rather than risk Bobby's scorn, I didn't mention the cat that led me to the culvert in the hills, but I described the skull collection arranged on the final two steps of the spillway. I told him about Chief

Stevenson talking to the bald guy with the earring and about finding the pistol on my bed.

"Bitchin' gun," he said, admiring the Glock.

"Dad opted for laser sighting."

"Sweet."

Sometimes Bobby is as self-possessed as a rock, so calm that you have to wonder if he is actually listening to you. As a boy, he was occasionally like this, but the older he has gotten, the more that this uncanny composure has settled over him. I had just brought him astonishing news of bizarre adventures, and he reacted as if he were listening to basketball scores.

Glancing at the darkness beyond the window, I wondered if anyone out there had me in a gun sight, maybe in the cross hairs of a night scope. Then I figured that if they had meant to shoot us, they would have cut us down when we were out in the dunes.

I told Bobby everything that had happened at Angela Ferryman's house.

He grimaced. "Apricot brandy."

"I didn't drink much."

He said, "Two glasses of that crap, you'll be talking to the seals," which was surfer lingo for vomiting.

By the time I had told him about Jesse Pinn terrorizing Father Tom at the church, we had gone through three tacos each. He built another pair and brought them to the table.

Sasha was playing "Graduation Day."

Bobby said, "It's a regular Chris Isaak festival."

"She's playing it for me."

"Yeah, I didn't figure Chris Isaak was at the station holding a gun to her head."

Neither of us said anything more until we finished the final round of tacos.

When at last Bobby asked a question, the only thing he wanted to know about was something that Angela had said: "So she told you it was a monkey and it wasn't."

"Her exact words, as I recall, were . . . 'It appeared to be a monkey. And it was a monkey. Was and wasn't. And that's what was wrong with it.' "

"She seem totally zipped up to you?"

"She was in distress, scared, way scared, but she wasn't kooked out. Besides, somebody killed her to shut her up, so there must have been something to what she said."

He nodded and drank some beer.

He was silent for so long that I finally said, "Now what?"

"You're asking me?"

"I wasn't talking to the dog," I said.

"Drop it," he said.

"What?"

"Forget about it, get on with life."

"I knew you'd say that," I admitted.

"Then why ask me?"

"Bobby, maybe my mom's death wasn't an accident."

"Sounds like more than a maybe."

"And maybe there was more to my dad's cancer than just cancer."

"So you're gonna hit the vengeance trail?"

"These people can't get away with murder."

"Sure they can. People get away with murder all the time."

"Well, they shouldn't."

"I didn't say they should. I only said they do."

"You know, Bobby, maybe life isn't just surf, sex, food, and beer."

"I never said it was. I only said it should be."

"Well," I said, studying the darkness beyond the window, "*I'm* not hairing out."

Bobby sighed and leaned back in his chair. "If you're waiting to catch a wave, and conditions are epic, really big smokers honing up the coast, and along comes a set of twenty-footers, and they're pushing your limit but you know you can stretch to handle them, yet you sit in the lineup, just being a buoy through the whole set, then you're hairing out. But say, instead, what comes along all of a sudden is a long set of thirty-footers, massive pumping mackers that are going to totally prosecute you, that are going to blast you off the board and hold you down and make you suck kelp and pray to Jesus. If your choice is to be snuffed or be a buoy, then you're not hairing out if you sit in the lineup and soak through the whole set. You're exhibiting mature judgment. Even a total surf rebel needs a little of that. And the dude who tries the wave even though he knows he's going over the falls, knows he's going to be totally quashed — well, he's an asshole."

I was touched by the length of his speech, because it meant that he was deeply worried about me.

"So," I said, "you're calling me an asshole."

"Not yet. Depends on what you do about this."

"So I'm an asshole waiting to happen."

"Let's just say that your asshole potential is off the Richter."

I shook my head. "Well, from where I sit, this doesn't look like a thirty-footer."

"Maybe a forty."

"It looks like a twenty max."

He rolled his eyes up into his head, as if to say that the only place he was going to see any common sense was inside his own skull. "From what Angela said, this all goes back to some project at Fort Wyvern."

"She went upstairs to get something she wanted to show me — some sort of proof, I guess, something her husband must have squirreled away. Whatever it was, it was destroyed in the fire."

"Fort Wyvern. The Army. The military."

"So?"

"We're talking about the government here," Bobby said. "Bro, the government isn't even a thirty-footer. It's a hundred. It's a tsunami."

"This is America."

"It used to be."

"I have a duty here."

"What duty?"

"A moral duty."

Beetling his brow, pinching the bridge of his nose with thumb and forefinger, as though listening to me had given him a headache, he said, "I guess if you turn on the evening news and hear there's a comet going to destroy the earth, you pull on your tights and cape and fly into outer space to deflect that sucker toward the other end of the galaxy."

"Unless the cape is at the dry cleaner."

"Asshole."

"Asshole."

20

"Look here," Bobby said. "Data coming down right now. This is from a British government weather satellite. Process it, and you can measure the height of any wave, anywhere in the world, to within a few centimeters."

He had not turned on any lights in his office. The oversize video displays at the various computer workstations provided enough illumination for him and more than enough for me. Colorful bar graphs, maps, enhanced satellite photos, and flow charts of dynamic weather situations moved on the screens.

I have not embraced the computer age and never will. With UV-proof sunglasses, I can't easily read what's on a video display, and I can't risk spending hours in front of even a filtered screen with all those UV rays pumping out at me. They are low-level emissions to you, but considering cumulative damage, a few hours at a computer would be a lightstorm to me. I do my writing by hand in legal tablets: the occasional article, the best-selling book that resulted in the long *Time* magazine article about me and XP.

This computer-packed room is the heart of Surfcast, Bobby's surf-forecasting service, which provides daily predictions by fax to subscribers all over the world, maintains a Web site, and has a 900 number for surf information. Four employees work out of offices in Moonlight Bay, networked with this room, but Bobby himself does the final data analysis and surf predictions.

Along the shores of the world's oceans, approximately six million surfers regularly ride the waves, and about five and a half million of these are content with waves that have faces — measured from trough to crest — of six or eight feet. Ocean swells hide their power below the surface, extending down as much as one thousand feet, and they are not waves until they shoal up and break to the shore; consequently, there was no way, until the late 1980s, to predict with any reliability even where and when six-foot humpers could be found. Surf junkies could spend days at the beach, waiting through surf that was mushy or soft or even flat, while a few hundred miles up or down the coast, plunging breakers were macking to shore, corduroy to the horizon. A significant percentage of those five and a half million boardheads would rather pay Bobby a few bucks to learn where the action will or won't be than rely strictly on the goodwill of Kahuna, the god of all surf.

A few bucks. The 900 number alone draws eight hundred thousand calls each year, at two dollars a pop. Ironically, Bobby the slacker and surf rebel has probably become the wealthiest person in Moonlight Bay — although no one realizes this and although he gives away most of it.

"Here," he said, dropping into a chair in front of one of the computers. "Before you rush off to save the world and get your brains blown out, think about this." As Orson cocked his head to watch the screen, Bobby hammered the keyboard, calling up new data.

Most of the remaining half million of those six million surfers sit out waves above, say, fifteen feet, and probably fewer than ten thousand can ride twenty-footers, but although these more awesomely skilled and ballsy types are fewer in number, a higher percentage of them want Bobby's forecasts. They live and die for the ride; to miss a session of epic monsters, especially in their neighborhood, would be nothing less than Shakespearean tragedy with sand.

"Sunday," Bobby said, still tapping the keyboard.

"This Sunday?"

"Two nights from now, you'll want to be here. Rather than be dead, I mean."

"Big surf coming?"

"It's gonna be sacred."

Perhaps three hundred or four hundred surfers on the planet have the experience, talent, and *cojones* to mount waves above twenty feet, and a handful of them pay Bobby well to track truly giant surf, even though it is treacherous and likely to kill them. A few of these maniacs are wealthy men who will fly anywhere in the world to challenge storm waves, thirty- and even forty-foot behemoths, into which they are frequently towed by a helper on a Jet Ski, because catching such huge monoliths in the usual fashion is difficult and often impossible. Worldwide, you can find well-formed, ride-worthy waves thirty feet and higher no more than thirty days a year, and often they come to shore in exotic places. Using maps, satellite photos, and weather data from numerous sources, Bobby can provide two- or three-day warnings, and his predictions are so trustworthy that these most demanding of all clients have never complained.

"There." Bobby pointed to a wave profile on the computer. Orson took a closer look at the screen as Bobby said, "Moonlight Bay, point-break surf. It's going to be classic Sunday afternoon, evening, all the way until Monday dawn — fully pumping mackers."

I blinked at the video display. "Am I seeing twelve-footers?"

"Ten to twelve feet, with a possibility of some sets as high as fourteen. They're hitting Hawaii soon . . . then us."

"That'll be *live*."

"Entirely live. Coming off a big, slow-moving storm north of Tahiti. There's going to be an offshore wind, too, so these monsters are going to give you more dry, insanely hollow barrels than you've seen in your dreams."

"Cool."

He swiveled in his chair to look up at me. "So what do you want to ride — the Sunday-night surf rolling out of Tahiti or the tsunami pipeline of death rolling out of Wyvern?"

"Both."

"Kamikaze," he said scornfully.

"Duck," I called him, with a smile — which is the same as saying *buoy*, meaning one who sits in the lineup and never has the guts to take a wave.

Orson turned his head from one of us to the other, back and forth, as if watching a tennis match.

"Geek," Bobby said.

"Decoy," I said, which is the same as saying *duck*.

"Asshole," he said, which has identical definitions in surfer lingo and standard English.

"I take it you're not with me on this."

Getting up from the chair, he said, "You can't go to the cops. You can't go to the FBI. They're all paid by the other side. What can you possibly hope to learn about some way-secret project at Wyvern?"

"I've already uncovered a little."

"Yeah, and the next thing you learn is the thing that'll get you killed. Listen, Chris, you aren't Sherlock Holmes or James Bond. At best, you're Nancy Drew."

"Nancy Drew had an unreal rate of case closure," I reminded him. "She nailed one hundred percent of the bastards she went after. I'd be honored to be considered the equal of a kick-ass crime fighter like Ms. Nancy Drew."

"Kamikaze."

"Duck."

"Geek."

"Decoy."

Laughing softly, shaking his head, scratching his beard stubble, Bobby said, "You make me sick."

"Likewise."

The telephone rang, and Bobby answered it. "Hey, gorgeous, I totally get off on the new format — all Chris Isaak, all the time. Play 'Dancin' ' for me, okay?" He passed the handset to me. "It's for you, Nancy."

I like Sasha's disc-jockey voice. It's only subtly different from her real-world voice, marginally deeper and softer and silkier, but the effect is profound. When I hear Sasha the deejay, I want to curl up in bed with her. I want to curl up in bed with her anyway, as often as possible, but when she's using her radio voice, I want to curl up in bed with her *urgently*. The voice comes over her from the moment she enters the studio, and it's with her even when she is off-mike, until she leaves work.

"This tune ends in about a minute, I've got to do some patter between cuts," she told me, "so I'll be quick. Somebody came around here at the station a little while ago, trying to get in touch with you. Says it's life or death."

"Who?"

"I can't use the name on the phone. Promised I wouldn't. When I said you were probably at Bobby's . . . this person didn't want to call you there or come there to see you."

"Why?"

"I don't know why exactly. But . . . this person was really nervous, Chris. 'I have been one acquainted with the night.' Do you know who I mean?"

I have been one acquainted with the night.

It was a line from a poem by Robert Frost.

My dad had instilled in me his passion for poetry. I had infected Sasha.

"Yes," I said. "I think I know who you mean."

"Wants to see you as soon as possible. Says it's life or death. What's going on, Chris?"

"Big surf coming in Sunday afternoon," I said.

"That's not what I mean."

"I know. Tell you the rest later."

"Big surf. Can I handle it?"

"Twelve-footers."

"I think I'll just Gidget-out and beach party."

"Love your voice," I said.

"Smooth as the bay."

She hung up, and so did I.

Although he had only heard my half of the conversation, Bobby relied on his uncanny intuition to figure out the tone and intent of Sasha's call. "What're you walking into?"

"Just Nancy stuff," I said. "You wouldn't be interested."

As Bobby and I led a still-uneasy Orson onto the front porch, the radio in the kitchen began to swing with "Dancin' " by Chris Isaak.

"Sasha is an awesome woman," Bobby said.

"Unreal," I agreed.

"You can't be with her if you're dead. She's not that kinky."

"Point taken."

"You have your sunglasses?"

I patted my shirt pocket. "Yeah."

"Did you use some of my sunscreen?"

"Yes, Mother."

"Geek."

I said, "I've been thinking. . . ."

"It's about time you started."

"I've been working on the new book."

"Finally got your lazy ass in gear."

"It's about friendship."

"Am I in it?"

"Amazingly, yes."

"You're not using my real name, are you?"

"I'm calling you Igor. The thing is . . . I'm afraid readers might not relate to what I have to say, because you and I — all my friends — we live such different lives."

Stopping at the head of the porch steps, regarding me with his patented look of scorn, Bobby said, "I thought you had to be smart to write books."

"It's not a federal law."

"Obviously not. Even the literary equivalent of a gyrospaz ought to know that every last one of us leads a different life."

"Yeah? Maria Cortez leads a different life?"

Maria is Manuel Ramirez's younger sister, twenty-eight like Bobby and me. She is a beautician, and her husband works as a car mechanic. They have two children, one cat, and a small tract house with a big mortgage.

Bobby said, "She doesn't live her life in the beauty shop, doing someone's hair — or in her house, vacuuming the carpet. She lives her life between her ears. There's a *world* inside her skull, and probably way stranger and more bitchin' than you or I, with our shallow brain pans, can imagine. Six billion of us walking the planet, six billion smaller worlds on the bigger one. Shoe salesmen and short-order cooks who look boring from the outside — some have weirder lives than you. Six billion stories, every one an epic, full of tragedy and triumph, good and evil, despair and hope. You and me — we aren't so special, bro."

I was briefly speechless. Then I fingered the sleeve of his parrot-and-palm-frond shirt and said, "I didn't realize you were such a philosopher."

He shrugged. "That little gem of wisdom? Hell, that was just something I got in a fortune cookie."

"Must've been a big honker of a cookie."

"Hey, it was a huge monolith, dude," he said, giving me a sly smile.

The great wall of moonlit fog loomed half a mile from the shore, no closer or farther away than it had been earlier. The night air was as still as that in the cold-holding room at Mercy Hospital.

As we descended the porch steps, no one shot at us. No one issued that loonlike cry, either.

They were still out there, however, hiding in the dunes or below the crest of the slope that fell to the beach. I could feel their attention like the dangerous energy pending release in the coils of a motionless, strike-poised rattlesnake.

Although Bobby had left his shotgun inside, he was vigilant. Surveying the night as he accompanied me to my bike, he began to reveal more interest in my story than he had admitted earlier: "This monkey Angela mentioned . . ."

"What about it?"

"What was it like?"

"Monkeylike."

"Like a chimpanzee, an orangutan, or what?"

266

Gripping the handlebars of my bicycle and turning it around to walk it through the soft sand, I said, "It was a rhesus monkey. Didn't I say?"

"How big?"

"She said two feet high, maybe twenty-five pounds."

Gazing across the dunes, he said, "I've seen a couple myself."

Surprised, leaning the bike against the porch railing again, I said, "Rhesus monkeys? Out here?"

"Some kind of monkeys, about that size."

There is, of course, no species of monkey native to California. The only primates in its woods and fields are human beings.

Bobby said, "Caught one looking in a window at me one night. Went outside, and it was gone."

"When was this?"

"Maybe three months ago."

Orson moved between us, as if for comfort.

I said, "You've seen them since?"

"Six or seven times. Always at night. They're secretive. But they're also bolder lately. They travel in a troop."

"Troop?"

"Wolves travel in a pack. Horses in a herd. With monkeys, it's called a troop."

"You've been doing research. How come you haven't told me about this?"

He was silent, watching the dunes.

I was watching them, too. "Is that what's out there now?"

"Maybe."

"How many in this troop?"

"Don't know. Maybe six or eight. Just a guess."

"You bought a shotgun. You think they're dangerous?"

"Maybe."

"Have you reported them to anyone? Like animal control?"

"No."

"Why not?"

Instead of answering me, he hesitated and then said, "Pia's driving me nuts."

Pia Klick. Out there in Waimea for a month or two, going on three years.

I didn't understand how Pia related to Bobby's failure to report the monkeys to animal-control officers, but I sensed that he would make the connection for me.

"She says she's discovered that she's the reincarnation of Kaha Huna," Bobby said.

Kaha Huna is the mythical Hawaiian goddess of surfing, who was never actually incarnate in the first place and, therefore, incapable of being *re*.

Considering that Pia was not a *kamaaina*, a native of Hawaii, but a *haole* who had been born in Oskaloosa, Kansas, and raised there until she left home at seventeen, she seemed an unlikely candidate to be a mythological *uber wahine*.

I said, "She lacks some credentials."

"She's dead-solid serious about this."

"Well, she's way pretty enough to be Kaha Huna. Or any other goddess, for that matter."

Standing beside Bobby, I couldn't see his eyes

too well, but his face was bleak. I had never seen him bleak before. I hadn't even realized that bleakness was an option for him.

Bobby said, "She's trying to decide whether being Kaha Huna requires her to be celibate."

"Ouch."

"She thinks she probably shouldn't ever live with an ordinary dude, meaning a mortal man. Somehow that would be a blasphemous rejection of her fate."

"Brutal," I said sympathetically.

"But it would be cool for her to shack up with the current reincarnation of Kahuna."

Kahuna is the mythical *god* of surfing. He is largely a creation of modern surfers who extrapolate his legend from the life of an ancient Hawaiian witch doctor.

I said, "And you aren't the reincarnation of Kahuna."

"I refuse to be."

From that response, I inferred that Pia was trying to convince him that he was, indeed, the god of surfing.

With audible misery and confusion, Bobby said, "She's so smart, so talented."

Pia had graduated *summa cum laude* from UCLA. She had paid her way through school by painting portraits; now her hyperrealist works sold for impressive prices, as quickly as she cared to produce them.

"How can she be so smart and talented," Bobby demanded, "and then . . . this?"

"Maybe you *are* Kahuna," I said.

"This isn't funny," he said, which was a striking statement, because to one degree or another, everything was funny to Bobby.

In the moonlight, the dune grass drooped, no blade so much as trembling in the now windless night. The soft rhythm of the surf, rising from the beach below, was like the murmured chanting of a distant, prayerful crowd.

This Pia business was fascinating, but understandably, I was more interested in the monkeys.

"These last few years," Bobby said, "with this New Age stuff from Pia . . . well, sometimes it's okay, but sometimes it's like spending days in radical churly-churly."

Churly-churly is badly churned-up surf heavy with sand and pea gravel, which smacks you in the face when you walk into it. This is not a pleasant surf condition.

"Sometimes," Bobby said, "when I get off the phone with her, I'm so messed up, missing her, wanting to be with her . . . I could almost convince myself she *is* Kaha Huna. She's so *sincere*. And she doesn't rave on about it, you know. It's this quiet thing with her, which makes it even more disturbing."

"I didn't know you got disturbed."

"I didn't know it, either." Sighing, scuffing at the sand with one bare foot, he began to make the connection between Pia and the monkeys: "When I saw the monkey at the window the first time, it was cool, made me laugh. I figured it was someone's pet that got loose . . . but the second time I saw more than one. And it was as weird as all this Kaha Huna shit, because they weren't behaving at all like monkeys."

270

"What do you mean?"

"Monkeys are playful, goofing around. These guys . . . they weren't playful. Purposeful, solemn, creepy little geeks. Watching me and studying the house, not out of curiosity but with some agenda."

"What agenda?"

Bobby shrugged. "They were so strange. . . ."

Words seemed to fail him, so I borrowed one from H. P. Lovecraft, for whose stories we'd had such enthusiasm when we were thirteen: "Eldritch."

"Yeah. They were eldritch to the max. I knew no one was going to believe me. I almost felt I was hallucinating. I grabbed a camera but couldn't get a picture. You know why?"

"Thumb over the lens?"

"They didn't want to be photographed. First sight of the camera, they ran for cover, and they're insanely fast." He glanced at me, reading my reaction, then looked to the dunes again. "They knew what the camera was."

I couldn't resist: "Hey, you're not anthropomorphizing them, are you? You know — ascribing human attributes and attitudes to animals?"

Ignoring me, he said, "After that night, I didn't put the camera away in the closet. I kept it on a kitchen counter, close at hand. If they showed up again, I figured I might get a snapshot before they realized what was happening. One night about six weeks ago, it was pumping eight-footers with a good offshore, barrel after barrel, so even though it was way nipple out there, I put on my wet suit and spent a couple

271

of hours totally tucked away. I didn't take the camera down to the beach with me."

"Why not?"

"I hadn't seen the damn monkeys in a week. I figured maybe I'd never see them again. Anyway, when I came back to the house, I stripped out of the neoprene, went into the kitchen, and got a beer. When I turned away from the fridge, there were monkeys at two windows, hanging on the frames outside, looking in at me. So I reached for my camera — and it was gone."

"You misplaced it."

"No. It's gone for good. I left the door unlocked when I went to the beach that night. I don't leave it unlocked anymore."

"You're telling me the monkeys took it?"

He said, "The next day I bought a disposable camera. Put it on the counter by the oven again. That night I left the lights on, locked up, and took my stick down to the beach."

"Good surf?"

"Slow. But I wanted to give them a chance. And they took it. While I was gone, they broke a pane, unlocked the window, and stole the disposable camera. Nothing else. Just the camera."

Now I knew why the shotgun was kept in a locked broom closet.

This cottage on the horn, without neighbors, had always appealed to me as a fine retreat. At night, when the surfers left, the sky and the sea formed a sphere in which the house stood like a diorama in one of those glass paperweights that fills with whirling snow when you shake it, though instead of a blizzard there were deep peace and a glorious solitude. Now, however, the nurturing solitude had become an unnerving isolation. Rather than offering a sense of peace, the night was thick and still with expectation.

"And they left me a warning," Bobby said.

I pictured a threatening note laboriously printed in crude block letters — WATCH YOUR ASS. Signed, THE MONKEYS.

They were too clever to leave a paper trail, however, and even more direct. Bobby said, "One of them crapped on my bed."

"Oh, nice."

"They're secretive, like I said. I've decided not even to try to photograph them. If I managed to get a flash shot of them some night . . . I think they'd be way pissed."

"You're afraid of them. I didn't know you got disturbed, and I didn't know you were ever afraid. I'm learning a lot about you tonight, bro."

He didn't admit to feeling fear.

"You bought the shotgun," I pressed.

"Because I think it's good to challenge them from time to time, good to show the little bastards that I'm territorial, and that this is, by God, my territory. But I'm not afraid, really. They're just monkeys."

"And then again — they're not."

Bobby said, "Some days I wonder if I've picked up some New Age virus over the telephone line from Pia, all the way from Waimea — and now while she's obsessed with being Kaha Huna, I'm obsessed with the monkeys of the new millennium. I suspect that's what the

273

tabloids would call them, don't you?"

"The millennium monkeys. Has a ring to it."

"That's why I haven't reported them. I'm not going to make myself a target of the press or anyone. I'm not going to be the geek who saw Bigfoot or extraterrestrials in a spaceship shaped like a four-slice toaster. Life wouldn't ever be the same for me after that, would it?"

"You'd be a freak like me."

"Exactly."

My awareness of being watched became more intense. I almost borrowed a trick from Orson, almost growled low in my throat.

The dog, still standing between Bobby and me, remained alert and quiet, his head raised and one ear pricked. He was no longer shaking, but he was clearly respectful of whatever was observing us from the surrounding night.

"Now that I've told you about Angela, you know the monkeys have something to do with what was going on out at Fort Wyvern," I said. "This isn't just a tabloid fantasy anymore. This is real, this is totally *live,* and we can do something about it."

"Still going on," he said.

"What?"

"From what Angela told you, Wyvern's not entirely shut down."

"But it was abandoned eighteen months ago. If there were still personnel staffing any operations at all out there, we'd know about it. Even if they lived on base, they'd come into town to shop, to go to a movie."

"You said Angela called this Armageddon. It's

the end of the world, she said."

"Yeah. So?"

"So maybe if you're busily working on a project to destroy the world, you don't have time to come into town for a movie. Anyway, like I said, this is a tsunami, Chris. This is the government. There's no way to surf these waters and survive."

I gripped the handlebars of my bike and stood it upright again. "In spite of these monkeys and what you've seen, you're going to just lay back?"

He nodded. "If I stay cool, it's possible they'll eventually go away. They're not here every night, anyway. Once or twice a week. If I wait them out . . . I might get my life back like it was."

"Yeah, but maybe Angela wasn't just smoking something. Maybe there's no chance, ever again, that anything will be like it was."

"Then why put on your tights and cape if it's a lost cause?"

"To XP-Man," I said with mock solemnity, "there are no lost causes."

"Kamikaze."

"Duck."

"Geek."

"Decoy," I said affectionately and walked the bicycle away from the house, through the soft sand.

Orson let out a thin whine of protest as we left the comparative safety of the cottage behind us, but he didn't try to hold back. He stayed close to me, sniffing the night air as we headed inland.

We'd gone about thirty feet when Bobby, kicking up small clouds of sand, sprinted in front of us and blocked the way. "You know what your problem is?"

I said, "My choice of friends?"

"Your problem is you want to make a mark on the world. You want to leave something behind that says, *I was here.*"

"I don't care about that."

"Bullshit."

"Watch your language. There's a dog present."

"That's why you write the articles, the books," he said. "To leave a mark."

"I write because I enjoy writing."

"You're always bitching about it."

"Because it's the hardest thing I've ever done, but it's also rewarding."

"You know why it's so hard? Because it's unnatural."

"Maybe to people who can't read and write."

"We're not here to leave a mark, bro. Monuments, legacies, marks — that's where we always go wrong. We're here to revel in the world, to soak in the awesomeness of it, to enjoy the ride."

"Orson, look, it's Philosopher Bob again."

"The world's maximum perfect as it is, beauty from horizon to horizon. Any mark any of us tries to leave — hell, it's only graffiti. Nothing can improve on the world we've been given. Any mark anyone leaves is no better than vandalism."

I said, "The music of Mozart."

"Vandalism," Bobby said.

"The art of Michelangelo."

"Graffiti."

"Renoir," I said.

"Graffiti."

"Bach, the Beatles."

"Aural graffiti," he said fiercely.

As he followed our conversation, Orson was getting whiplash.

"Matisse, Beethoven, Wallace Stevens, Shakespeare."

"Vandals, hooligans."

"Dick Dale," I said, dropping the sacred name of the King of the Surf Guitar, the father of all surf music.

Bobby blinked but said, "Graffiti."

"You are a sick man."

"I'm the healthiest person you know. Drop this insanely useless crusade, Chris."

"I must really be swimming in a school of slackers when a little curiosity is seen as a crusade."

"Live life. Soak it up. Enjoy. That's what you're here to do."

"I'm having fun in my own way," I assured him. "Don't worry — I'm just as big a bum and jerk-off as you are."

"You wish."

When I tried to walk the bike around him, he sidestepped into my path again.

"Okay," he said resignedly. "All right. But walk the bike with one hand and keep the Glock in the other until you're back on hard ground and can ride again. Then ride fast."

I patted my jacket pocket, which sagged with

the weight of the pistol. One round fired accidentally at Angela's. Nine left in the magazine. "But they're just monkeys," I said, echoing Bobby himself.

"And they're not."

Searching his dark eyes, I said, "You have something else that I should know?"

He chewed on his lower lip. Finally: "Maybe I am Kahuna."

"That's not what you were about to tell me."

"No, but it's not as fully nutball as what I was going to say." His gaze traveled over the dunes. "The leader of the troop . . . I've only glimpsed him at a distance, in the darkness, hardly more than a shadow. He's bigger than the rest."

"How big?"

His eyes met mine. "I think he's a dude about my size."

Earlier, as I had stood on the porch waiting for Bobby to return from his search of the beach scarp, I had glimpsed movement from the corner of my eye: the fuzzy impression of a man loping through the dunes with long fluid strides. When I'd swung around with the Glock, no one had been there.

"A man?" I said. "Running with the millennium monkeys, leading the troop? Our own Moonlight Bay Tarzan?"

"Well, I hope it's a man."

"And what's that supposed to mean?"

Breaking eye contact, Bobby shrugged. "I'm just saying there aren't only the monkeys I've seen. There's someone or something big out there with them."

I looked toward the lights of Moonlight Bay. "Feels like there's a clock ticking somewhere, a bomb clock, and the whole town's sitting on explosives."

"That's my point, bro. Stay out of the blast zone."

Holding the bike with one hand, I drew the Glock from my jacket pocket.

"As you go about your perilous and foolish adventures, XP-Man," Bobby said, "here's something to keep in mind."

"More boardhead wisdom."

"Whatever was going on out there at Wyvern — and might still be going on — a big troop of scientists must have been involved. Hugely educated dudes with foreheads higher than your whole face. Government and military types, too, and lots of them. The elite of the system. Movers and shakers. You know why they were part of this before it all went wrong?"

"Bills to pay, families to support?"

"Every last one of them wanted to leave his mark."

I said, "This isn't about ambition. I just want to know why my mom and dad had to die."

"Your head's as hard as an oyster shell."

"Yeah, but there's a pearl inside."

"It's not a pearl," he assured me. "It's a fossilized seagull dropping."

"You've got a way with words. You should write a book."

He squeezed out a sneer as thin as a shaving of lemon peel. "I'd rather screw a cactus."

"That's pretty much what it's like. But rewarding."

"This wave is going to put you through the rinse cycle and then down the drain."

"Maybe. But it'll be a totally cool ride. And aren't you the one who said we're here to enjoy the ride?"

Finally defeated, he stepped out of my way, raised his right hand, and made the shaka sign.

I held the bike with my gun hand long enough to make the *Star Trek* sign.

In response, he gave me the finger.

With Orson at my side, I walked the bike eastward through the sand, heading toward the rockier part of the peninsula. Before I'd gone far, I heard Bobby say something behind me, but I couldn't catch his words.

I stopped, turned, and saw him heading back toward the cottage. "What'd you say?"

"Here comes the fog," he repeated.

Looking beyond him, I saw towering white masses descending out of the west, an avalanche of churning vapor patinaed with moonlight. Like some silently toppling wall of doom in a dream.

The lights of town seemed to be a continent away.

FOUR

DEEP NIGHT

21

By the time Orson and I walked out of the dunes and reached the sandstone portion of the peninsula, thick clouds swaddled us. The fog bank was hundreds of feet deep, and though a pale dusting of moonlight sifted through the mist all the way to the ground, we were in a gray murk more blinding than a starless, moonless night would have been.

The lights of town were no longer visible.

The fog played tricks with sound. I could still hear the rough murmur of breaking surf, but it seemed to come from all four sides, as though I were on an island instead of a peninsula.

I wasn't confident about being able to ride my bicycle in that cloying gloom. Visibility continuously shifted between zero and a maximum of six feet. Although no trees or other obstacles lay along the curved horn, I could easily become disoriented and ride off the edge of the beach scarp; the bike would pitch forward, and when the front tire plowed into the soft sand of the slope below the scarp, I would come to a sudden halt and take a header off the bike to the beach, possibly breaking a limb or even my neck.

Besides, to build speed and to keep my balance, I would have to steer the bike with two hands, which meant pocketing the pistol. After my conversation with Bobby, I was loath to let go of the Glock. In the fog, something could close to within a few feet of me before I became aware of it, which wouldn't leave me time enough to tear the gun out of my jacket pocket and get off a shot.

I walked at a relatively brisk pace, wheeling the bicycle with my left hand, pretending I was carefree and confident, and Orson trotted slightly ahead of me. The dog was wary, no good at whistling in the graveyard either literally or figuratively. He turned his head ceaselessly from side to side.

The click of the wheel bearings and the tick of the drive chain betrayed my position. There was no way to quiet the bicycle short of picking it up and carrying it, which I could do with one arm but only for short distances.

The noise might not matter, anyway. The monkeys probably had acute animal senses that detected the most meager stimuli; in fact, they were no doubt able to track me by scent.

Orson would be able to smell them, too. In this nebulous night, his black form was barely visible, and I couldn't see if his hackles were raised, which would be a sure sign that the monkeys were nearby.

As I walked, I wondered what it was about these creatures that made them different from an ordinary rhesus.

In appearance, at least, the beast in Angela's kitchen had been a typical example of its species, even if it had been at the upper end of the size range for a rhesus. She'd said only that it had "awful dark-yellow eyes," but as far as I knew, that was well within the spectrum of eye colors for this group of primates. Bobby hadn't mentioned anything strange about the troop that was bedeviling him, other than their peculiar behavior and the unusual size of their shadowy leader: no misshapen craniums, no third eyes in their foreheads, no bolts in their necks to indicate that they had been stitched and stapled together in the secret laboratory of Dr. Victor Frankenstein's megalomaniacal great-great-great-great-granddaughter, Heather Frankenstein.

The project leaders at Fort Wyvern had been worried that the monkey in Angela's kitchen had either scratched or bitten her. Considering the scientists' fear, it was logical to infer that the beast had carried an infectious disease transmitted by blood, saliva, or other bodily fluids. This inference was supported by the physical examination to which she'd been subjected. For four years, they had also taken monthly blood samples from her, which meant that the disease had a potentially long incubation period.

Biological warfare. The leaders of every country on Earth denied making preparations for such a hateful conflict. Evoking the name of God, warning of the judgment of history, they solemnly signed fat treaties guaranteeing never to engage in this monstrous research and development. Meanwhile, each nation was busily brewing anthrax cocktails, packaging bubonic-plague aerosols, and engineering such a splendiferous collection of exotic new viruses and bacteria that no line at any unemployment office anywhere on the planet would ever contain a single out-of-work mad scientist.

Nevertheless, I couldn't understand why they would have forcibly subjected Angela to sterilization. No doubt certain diseases increase the chances that one's offspring will suffer birth defects. Judging by what Angela had told me, however, I didn't think that the people at Wyvern sterilized her out of a concern either for her or for any children that she might conceive. They appeared to have been motivated not by compassion but by fear swollen nearly to panic.

I had asked Angela if the monkey was carrying a disease. She had as much as denied it: *I wish it were a disease. Wouldn't that be nice? Maybe I'd be cured by now. Or dead. Dead would be better than what's coming.*

But if not a disease, what?

Suddenly the loonlike cry that we had heard earlier now pierced the night and fog again, jolting me out of my ruminations.

Orson twitched to a full stop. I halted, too, and the click-tick of the bicycle fell silent.

The cry seemed to issue from the west and south, and after only a brief moment, an answering call came, as best I could tell, from the north and east. We were being stalked.

Because sound traveled so deceptively through the mist, I was not able to judge how far from us the cries arose. I would have bet one lung that they were close.

The rhythmic, heartlike pulse of the surf throbbed through the night. I wondered which Chris Isaak song Sasha was spinning across the airwaves at that moment.

Orson began to move again, and so did I, a

little faster than before. We had nothing to gain by hesitating. We wouldn't be safe until we were off the lonely peninsula and back in town — and perhaps not even then.

When we had gone no more than thirty or forty feet, that eerie ululant cry rose again. It was answered, as before.

This time we kept moving.

My heart was racing, and it didn't slow when I reminded myself that these were only monkeys. Not predators. Eaters of fruits, berries, nuts. Members of a peaceable kingdom.

Suddenly, perversely, Angela's dead face flashed onto my memory screen. I realized what I had misinterpreted, in my shock and anguish, when I'd first found her body. Her throat appeared to have been slashed repeatedly with a half-sharp knife, because the wound was ragged. In fact, it hadn't been slashed: It had been bitten, torn, chewed. I could see the terrible wound more clearly now than I'd been willing to see it when standing on the threshold of the bathroom.

Furthermore, I half recalled other marks on her, wounds that I'd not had the stomach to consider at the time. Livid bite marks on her hands. Perhaps even one on her face.

Monkeys. But not ordinary monkeys.

The killers' actions in Angela's house — the business with the dolls, the game of hide-and-seek — had seemed like the play of demented children. More than one of these monkeys must have been in those rooms: small enough to hide in places where a man could not have been concealed, so inhumanly quick as to have seemed like ghosts.

Another cry arose in the murk and was answered by a low hooting from *two* other locations.

Orson and I kept moving briskly, but I resisted the urge to bolt. If I broke into a run, my haste might be interpreted — and rightly — as a sign of fear. To a predator, fear indicates weakness. If they perceived any weakness, they might attack.

I had the Glock, on which my grip was so tight that the weapon seemed to be welded to my hand. But I didn't know how many of these creatures might be in this troop: perhaps only three or four, perhaps ten, maybe even more. Considering that I had never fired a gun before — except once, earlier this evening, entirely by accident — I was not going to be able to cut down all of these beasts before they overwhelmed me.

Although I didn't want to give my fevered imagination such dark material with which to work, I couldn't help wondering what a rhesus monkey's teeth were like. All blunt bicuspids? No. Even herbivores — assuming that the rhesus was indeed herbivorous — needed to tear at the peel of a fruit, at husks, at shells. They were sure to have incisors, maybe even pointy eyeteeth, as did human beings. Although these particular specimens might have stalked Angela, the rhesus itself hadn't evolved as a predator; therefore, they wouldn't be equipped with fangs. Certain apes had fangs, though. Baboons had enormous, wicked teeth. Anyway, the biting power of the rhesus was moot, because regardless of the nature of their dental armaments, these particular specimens had been well enough equipped to kill Angela Ferryman savagely and quickly.

At first I heard or sensed, rather than saw, movement in the fog a few feet to my right. Then I glimpsed a dark, undefined shape close to the ground, coming at me swiftly and silently.

I twisted toward the movement. The creature brushed against my leg and vanished into the fog before I could see it clearly.

Orson growled but with restraint, as though to warn off something without quite challenging it to fight. He was facing the billowy wall of gray mist that scudded through the darkness on the other side of the bicycle, and I suspected that with light I would see not merely that his hackles were raised but that every hair on his back was standing stiffly on end.

I was looking low, toward the ground, half expecting to see the shining, dark-yellow gaze of which Angela had spoken. The shape that suddenly loomed in the fog was, instead, nearly as big as I am. Maybe bigger. Shadowy, amorphous, like a swooping angel of death hovering in a dream, it was more suggestion than substance, fearsome precisely because it remained mysterious. No baleful yellow eyes. No clear features. No distinct form. Man or ape, or neither: the leader of the troop, there and gone.

Orson and I had come to a halt again.

I turned my head slowly to survey the streaming murk around us, intent on picking up any helpful sound. But the troop moved as silently as the fog.

I felt as though I were a diver far beneath the sea, trapped in blinding currents rich with plankton and algae, having glimpsed a circling shark, waiting for it to reappear out of the gloom and bite me in half.

Something brushed against the back of my legs, plucked at my jeans, and it wasn't Orson because it made a wicked hissing sound. I kicked at it but didn't connect, and it vanished into the mist before I could get a look at it.

Orson yelped in surprise, as though he'd had an encounter of his own.

"Here, boy," I said urgently, and he came at once to my side.

I let go of the bicycle, which clattered to the sand. Gripping the pistol in both hands, I began to turn in a full circle, searching for something to shoot at.

Shrill, angry chittering arose. These seemed recognizably to be the voices of monkeys. At least half a dozen of them.

If I killed one, the others might flee in fear. Or they might react as the tangerine-eating monkey had reacted to the broom that Angela had brandished in her kitchen: with furious aggressiveness.

In any event, visibility was virtually zero, and I couldn't see their eyeshine or their shadows, so I dared not waste ammunition by firing blindly into the fog. When the Glock was empty, I would be easy prey.

As one, the chittering voices fell silent.

The dense, ceaselessly seething clouds now damped even the sound of the surf. I could hear Orson's panting and my own too-rapid breathing, nothing else.

The great black form of the troop leader swelled again through the vaporous gray shrouds. It swooped as if it were winged, although this appearance of flight was surely illusory.

Orson snarled, and I juked back, triggering the laser-sighting mechanism. A red dot rippled across the morphing face of the fog. The troop leader, no more defined than a fleeting shadow on a frost-crusted window, was swallowed entirely by the mist before I could pin the laser to its mercurial shape.

I recalled the collection of skulls on the concrete stairs of the spillway in the storm culvert. Maybe the collector wasn't some teenage sociopath in practice for his adult career. Maybe the skulls were trophies that had been gathered and arranged by the monkeys — which was a peculiar and disturbing notion.

An even more disturbing thought occurred to me: Maybe my skull and Orson's — stripped of all flesh, hollow-eyed and gleaming — would be added to the display.

Orson howled as a screeching monkey burst through the veils of mist and leaped onto his back. The dog twisted his head, snapping his teeth, trying to bite his unwanted rider, simultaneously trying to thrash it off.

We were so close that even in the meager light

and churning mist, I could see the yellow eyes. Radiant, cold, and fierce. Glaring up at me. I couldn't squeeze off a shot at the attacker without hitting Orson.

The monkey had hardly landed on Orson's back when it sprang off the dog. It slammed hard into me, twenty-five pounds of wiry muscle and bone, staggering me backward, clambering up my chest, using my leather jacket for purchase, and in the chaos I was unable to shoot it without a high risk of wounding myself.

For an instant, we were face-to-face, eye to murderous eye. The creature's teeth were bared, and it was hissing ferociously, breath pungent and repulsive. It was a monkey yet not a monkey, and the profoundly *alien* quality of its bold stare was terrifying.

It snatched my cap off my head, and I swatted at it with the barrel of the Glock. Clutching the hat, the monkey dropped to the ground. I kicked, and the kick connected, knocking the cap out of its hand. Squealing, the rhesus tumbled-scampered into the fog, out of sight.

Orson started after the beast, barking, all his fear forgotten. When I called him back, he did not obey.

Then the larger form of the troop leader appeared again, more fleetingly than before, a sinuous shape billowing like a flung cape, gone almost as soon as it appeared but lingering long enough to make Orson reconsider the wisdom of pursuing the rhesus that had tried to steal my cap.

"*Jesus,*" I said explosively as the dog whined

and backed away from the chase.

I snatched the cap off the ground but didn't return it to my head. Instead, I folded it and jammed it into an inside pocket of my jacket.

Shakily, I assured myself that I was okay, that I hadn't been bitten. If I'd been scratched, I didn't feel the sting of it, not on my hands or face. No, I hadn't been scratched. Thank God. If the monkey was carrying an infectious disease communicable only by contact with bodily fluids, I couldn't have caught it.

On the other hand, I'd smelled its fetid breath when we were face-to-face, breathed the very air that it exhaled. If this was an airborne contagion, I was already in possession of a one-way ticket to the cold-holding room.

In response to a tinny clatter behind me, I swung around and discovered that my fallen bicycle was being dragged into the fog by something I couldn't see. Flat on its side, combing sand with its spokes, the rear wheel was the only part of the bike still in sight, and it almost disappeared into the murk before I reached down with one hand and grabbed it.

The hidden bicycle thief and I engaged in a brief tug of war, which I handily won, suggesting that I was pitted against one or two rhesus monkeys and not against the much larger troop leader. I stood the bike on its wheels, leaned it against my body to keep it upright, and once more raised the Glock.

Orson returned to my side.

Nervously, he relieved himself again, shedding the last of his beer. I was half surprised that I hadn't wet my pants.

For a while I gasped noisily for breath, shaking so badly that even a two-hand grip on the pistol couldn't keep it from jigging up and down. Gradually I grew calmer. My heart worked less diligently to crack my ribs.

Like the hulls of ghost ships, gray walls of mist sailed past, an infinite flotilla, towing behind them an unnatural stillness. No chittering. No squeals or shrieks. No loonlike cries. No sigh of wind or sough of surf. I felt almost as though, without realizing it, I had been killed in the recent confrontation, as though I now stood in a chilly antechamber outside the corridor of life, waiting for a door to open into Judgment.

Finally it became apparent that the games were over for a while. Holding the Glock with only one hand, I began to walk the bicycle east along the horn. Orson padded at my side.

I was sure that the troop was still monitoring us, although from a greater distance than before. I saw no stalking shapes in the fog, but they were out there, all right.

Monkeys. But not monkeys. Apparently escaped from a laboratory at Wyvern.

The end of the world, Angela had said.

Not by fire.

Not by ice.

Something worse.

Monkeys. The end of the world by monkeys.

Apocalypse with primates.

Armageddon. The end, *fini*, omega, doomsday, close the door and turn out the lights forever.

This was totally, fully, way crazy. Every time I tried to get my mind around the facts and pull them into some intelligible order, I wiped out big time, got radically clamshelled by a huge wave of imponderables.

Bobby's attitude, his relentless determination to distance himself from the insoluble troubles of the modern world and be a champion slacker, had always struck me as a legitimate lifestyle choice. Now it seemed to be not merely legitimate but reasoned, logical, and wise.

Because I was not expected to survive to adulthood, my parents raised me to play, to have fun, to indulge my sense of wonder, to live as much as possible without worry and without fear, to live in the moment with little concern for the future: in short, to trust in God and to believe that I, like everyone, am here for a purpose; to be as grateful for my limitations as for my talents and blessings, because both are part of a design beyond my comprehension. They recognized the need for me to learn self-discipline, of course, and respect for others. But, in fact, those things come naturally when you truly believe that your life has a spiritual dimension and that you are a carefully designed element in the mysterious mosaic of life. Although there had appeared to be little chance that I would outlive both parents, Mom and Dad prepared for this eventuality when I was first diagnosed: They purchased a large second-to-die life-insurance policy, which would now provide handsomely for me even if I never earned another cent from my books and articles. Born for play and fun and wonder, destined never to have to hold a job, destined never to be burdened by the responsibilities that weigh down most people, I could give up my writing and become such a total surf bum that Bobby Halloway, by comparison, would appear to be a compulsive workaholic with no more capacity for fun than a cabbage. Furthermore, I could embrace absolute slackerhood with no guilt whatsoever, with no qualms or doubts, because I was raised to be what all humanity might have been if we hadn't violated the terms of the lease and been evicted from Eden. Like all who are born of man and woman, I live by the whims of fate: Because of my XP, I'm just more acutely aware of the machinations of fate than most people are, and this awareness is liberating.

Yet, as I walked my bicycle eastward along the peninsula, I persevered in my search for meaning in all that I'd seen and heard since sunset.

Before the troop had arrived to torment Orson and me, I'd been trying to pin down exactly what was different about these monkeys; now I returned to that riddle. Unlike ordinary rhesuses, these were bold rather than shy, brooding rather than lighthearted. The most obvious difference was that these monkeys were hot-tempered, vicious. Their potential for violence was not, however, the primary quality that separated them from other rhesuses; it was only a consequence of another, more profound difference that I recognized but that I was inexplicably reluctant to consider.

The curdled fog was as thick as ever, but

gradually it began to brighten. Smears of blurry light appeared in the murk: buildings and street-lamps along the shore.

Orson whined with delight — or just relief — at these signs of civilization, but we weren't any safer in town than out of it.

When we left the southern horn entirely and entered Embarcadero Way, I paused to take my cap from the jacket pocket in which I had tucked it. I put it on and gave the visor a tug. The Elephant Man adjusts his costume.

Orson peered up at me, cocked his head con-sideringly, and then chuffed as though in ap-proval. He was the Elephant Man's dog, after all, and as such, a measure of his own self-image was dependent upon the style and grace with which I comported myself.

Because of the streetlamps, visibility had in-creased to perhaps a hundred feet. Like the ghost tides of an ancient and long-dead sea, fog surged off the bay and into the streets; each fine drop of mist refracted the golden sodium-vapor light and translated it to the next drop.

If members of the troop still accompanied us, they would be forced to lurk at a greater distance here than they had on the barren peninsula, to avoid being seen. Like players in a recasting of Poe's "The Murders in the Rue Morgue," they would have to confine their skulking to parks, unilluminated alleyways, balconies, high ledges, parapets, and rooftops.

At this late hour, no pedestrians or motorists were in sight. The town appeared to have been abandoned.

I was overcome by the disturbing notion that these silent and empty streets foreshadowed a real, frightening desolation that would befall Moonlight Bay in the not-too-distant future. Our little burg was preparing to be a ghost town.

I climbed onto my bike and headed north on Embarcadero Way. The man who had contacted me through Sasha, at the radio station, was waiting on his boat at the marina.

As I pedaled along the deserted avenue, my mind returned to the millennium monkeys. I was sure that I had identified the most fundamental difference between ordinary rhesuses and this extraordinary troop that secretly roamed the night, but I was reluctant to accept my own conclusion, inevitable though it seemed: *These monkeys were smarter than ordinary monkeys.*

Way smarter, radically smarter.

They had understood the purpose of Bobby's camera, and they had stolen it. They filched his new camera, too.

They recognized my face among the faces of the thirty dolls in Angela's workroom, and they used that one to taunt me. Later, they set a fire to conceal Angela's murder.

The big brows at Fort Wyvern might have been engaged in secret bacteriological-warfare research, but that didn't explain why their laboratory monkeys were markedly smarter than any monkeys that had previously walked the earth.

Just how smart *was* "markedly smarter"? Maybe not smart enough to win a bundle on *Jeopardy!* Maybe not smart enough to teach poetry at the university level or to successfully manage a radio station or to track the patterns of surf worldwide, maybe not even smart enough to write a *New York Times* best-seller — but perhaps smart enough to be the most dangerous, uncontrollable pest humanity had ever known. Imagine what damage rats could do, how rapidly their numbers would grow, if they were even half as smart as human beings and could learn how to avoid all traps and poisons.

Were these monkeys truly escapees from a laboratory, loose in the world and cleverly eluding capture? If so, how did they get to be so intelligent in the first place? What did they want? What was their agenda? Why hadn't a massive effort been launched to track them down, round them up, and return them to better cages from which they could never break free?

Or were they tools being used by someone at Wyvern? The way the cops use trained police dogs. The way the Navy uses dolphins to search for enemy submarines and, in wartime — it is rumored — even to plant magnetic packages of explosives on the hulls of targeted boats.

A thousand other questions swarmed through my mind. All of them were equally crazy.

Depending on the answers, the ramifications of these monkeys' heightened intelligence could be earth-shattering. The possible consequences to human civilization were especially alarming when you considered the viciousness of these animals and their apparently innate hostility.

Angela's prediction of doom might not have been farfetched, might actually have been *less* pessimistic than my assessment of the situation would be when — if ever — I knew all the facts. Certainly, doom had come to Angela herself.

I also intuited that the monkeys were not the entire story. They were but one chapter of an epic. Other astonishments were awaiting discovery.

Compared to the project at Wyvern, Pandora's fabled box, from which had been unleashed all the evils that plague humanity — wars, pestilence, diseases, famines, floods — might prove to have held only a collection of petty nuisances.

In my haste to get to the marina, I was cycling too fast to allow Orson to keep pace with me. He was sprinting full throttle, ears flapping, panting hard, but falling steadily behind.

In truth, I was cranking the bike to the max not because I was in a hurry to reach the marina but because, unconsciously, I wanted to outrace the tidal wave of terror sweeping toward us. There was no escaping it, however, and no matter how furiously I pedaled, I could outrun nothing but my dog.

Recalling Dad's final words, I stopped pedaling and coasted until Orson was able to stay at my side without heroic effort.

Never leave a friend behind. Friends are all we have to get us through this life — and they are the only things from this world that we could hope to see in the next.

Besides, the best way to deal with a rising sea of trouble is to catch the wave at the zero break and ride it out, slide along the face straight into the cathedral, get totally Ziplocked in the green room, walk the board all the way through the barrel, hooting, showing no fear. That's not only cool: It's classic.

22

With a gentle and even tender sound, like flesh on flesh in a honeymoon bed, low waves slipped between the pilings and slapped against the sea wall. The damp air offered a faint and pleasant aromatic mélange of brine, fresh kelp, creosote, rusting iron, and other fragrances I couldn't quite identify.

The marina, tucked into the sheltered northeast corner of the bay, offers docking for fewer than three hundred vessels, only six of which are full-time residences for their owners. Although social life in Moonlight Bay does not center around boating, there is a long waiting list for any slip that becomes available.

I walked my bike toward the west end of the main pier, which ran parallel to shore. The tires swished and bumped softly across the dew-wet, uneven planks. Only one boat in the marina had lights in its windows at that hour. Dock lamps, though dim, showed me the way through the fog.

Because the fishing fleet ties up farther out along the northern horn of the bay, the comparatively sheltered marina is reserved for pleasure craft. There are sloops and ketches and yawls ranging from modest to impressive — although more of the former than the latter — motor yachts mostly of manageable length and price, a few Boston Whalers, and even two houseboats. The largest sailing yacht — in fact, the largest boat — docked here is currently *Sunset Dancer*, a sixty-foot Windship cutter. Of the motor yachts, the largest is *Nostromo*, a fifty-six-foot Bluewater coastal cruiser; and it was to this boat that I was headed.

At the west end of the pier, I took a ninety-degree turn onto a subsidiary pier that featured docking slips on both sides. The *Nostromo* was in the last berth on the right.

I have been one acquainted with the night.

That was the code Sasha had used to identify the man who had come to the radio station seeking me, who hadn't wanted his name used on the phone, and who had been reluctant to come to Bobby's house to talk with me. It was a line from a poem by Robert Frost, one that most eavesdroppers would be unlikely to recognize, and I had assumed that it referred to Roosevelt Frost, who owned the *Nostromo*.

As I leaned my bicycle against the dock railing near the gangway to Roosevelt's slip, tidal action caused the boats to wallow in their berths. They creaked and groaned like arthritic old men murmuring feeble complaints in their sleep.

I had never bothered to chain my bike when I left it unattended, because until this night Moonlight Bay had been a refuge from the crime that infected the modern world. By the time this weekend passed, our picturesque town might lead the country in murders, mutilations, and priest beatings, per capita, but we probably didn't have to worry about a dramatic increase in bicycle theft.

The gangway was steep because the tide was not high, and it was slippery with condensation. Orson descended as carefully as I did.

We were two-thirds of the way down to the port-side finger of the slip when a low voice, hardly more than a gruff whisper, seeming to originate magically from the fog directly over my head, demanded, *"Who goes there?"*

Startled, I almost fell, but I clutched the dripping gangway handrail and kept my feet under me.

The Bluewater 563 is a sleek, white, low-profile, double-deck cruiser with an upper helm station that is enclosed by a hard top and canvas walls. The only light aboard came from behind the curtained windows of the aft stateroom and the main cabin amidships, on the lower deck. The open upper deck and the helm station were dark and fog-wrapped, and I couldn't see who had spoken.

"Who goes there?" the man whispered again, no louder but with a harder edge to his voice.

I recognized the voice now as that of Roosevelt Frost.

Taking my cue from him, I whispered: "It's me, Chris Snow."

"Shield your eyes, son."

I made a visor of my hand and squinted as a flashlight blazed, pinning me where I stood on the gangway. It switched off almost at once, and Roosevelt said, still in a whisper, "Is that your dog with you?"

"Yes, sir."

"And nothing else?"

"I'm sorry?"

"Nothing else with you, no one else?"

"No, sir."

"Come aboard, then."

I could see him now, because he had moved closer to the railing on the open upper deck, aft of the helm station. I couldn't identify him even from this relatively short distance, however, because he was screened by the pea-soup fog, the night, and his own darkness.

Urging Orson to precede me, I boarded the boat through the gap in the port railing, and we quickly climbed the open steps to the upper deck.

When we got to the top, I saw that Roosevelt Frost was holding a shotgun. Pretty soon the National Rifle Association would move its headquarters to Moonlight Bay. He wasn't aiming the gun at me, but I was sure he'd been covering me with it until he had been able to identify me in the beam of the flashlight.

Even without the shotgun, he was a formidable figure. Six feet four. Neck like a dock piling. Shoulders as wide as a staysail boom. Deep chest. With a two-hand spread way bigger than the diameter of the average helm wheel. This was the guy who Ahab should have called to cold-cock Moby Dick. He had been a football star in the sixties and early seventies, when sportswriters routinely referred to him as the Sledgehammer. Though he was now sixty-three, a successful businessman who owned a men's clothing store, a minimall, and half-interest in the Moonlight Bay Inn and Country Club, he appeared capable of pulverizing any of the genetic-mutant, steroid-pumped behemoths who played some of the power positions on contemporary teams.

"Hello, dog," he murmured.

Orson chuffed.

"Hold this, son," Frost whispered, handing the shotgun to me.

A pair of curious-looking, high-tech binoculars hung on a strap around his neck. He brought them to his eyes and, from this top-deck vantage point overlooking surrounding craft, surveyed the pier along which I had recently approached the *Nostromo*.

"How can you see anything?" I wondered.

"Night-vision binoculars. They magnify available light eighteen thousand times."

"But the fog . . ."

He pressed a button on the glasses, and as a mechanism purred inside them, he said, "They also have an infrared mode, shows you only heat sources."

"Must be lots of heat sources around the marina."

"Not with boat engines off. Besides, I'm interested only in heat sources *on the move*."

"People."

"Maybe."

"Who?"

"Whoever might've been following you. Now hush, son."

I hushed. As Roosevelt patiently scanned the marina, I passed the next minute wondering about this former football star and local businessman who was not, after all, quite what he seemed.

I wasn't surprised, exactly. Since sundown, the people I'd encountered had revealed dimensions to their lives of which I had previously been unaware. Even Bobby had been keeping secrets: the shotgun in the broom closet, the troop of monkeys. When I considered Pia Klick's conviction that she was the reincarnation of Kaha Huna, which Bobby had been keeping to himself, I better understood his bitter, disputatious response to any view that he felt smacked of New Age thinking, including my occasional innocent comments about my strange dog. At least Orson, if no one else, had remained in character throughout the night — although, considering the way things were going, I wouldn't have been bowled over if suddenly he revealed an ability to stand on his hind paws and tap dance with mesmerizing showmanship.

"No one's trailing after you," said Roosevelt as he lowered the night glasses and took back his shotgun. "This way, son."

I followed him aft across the sun deck to an open hatch on the starboard side.

Roosevelt paused and looked back, over the top of my head, to the port railing where Orson still lingered. "Here now. Come along, dog."

The mutt hung behind, but not because he sensed anything lurking on the dock. As usual, he was curiously and uncharacteristically shy around Roosevelt.

Our host's hobby was "animal communication" — a quintessential New Age concept that had been fodder for most daytime television talk shows, although Roosevelt was discreet about his talent and employed it only at the request of neighbors and friends. The mere mention of animal communication had been able to start Bobby foaming at the mouth even long before Pia Klick had decided that she was the goddess of surfing in search of her Kahuna. Roosevelt claimed to be able to discern the anxieties and desires of troubled pets that were brought to him. He didn't charge for this service, but his lack of interest in money didn't convince Bobby: *Hell, Snow, I never said he was a charlatan trying to make a buck. He's well-meaning. But he just ran headfirst into a goalpost once too often.*

According to Roosevelt, the only animal with which he had never been able to communicate was my dog. He considered Orson a challenge, and he never missed an opportunity to try to chat him up. "Come here now, old pup."

With apparent reluctance, Orson finally accepted the invitation. His claws clicked on the deck.

Carrying the shotgun, Roosevelt Frost went through the open hatch and down a set of molded fiberglass stairs lit only by a faint pearly glow at the bottom. He ducked his head, hunched his huge shoulders, pulled his arms against his sides to make himself smaller, but nevertheless appeared at risk of becoming wedged in the tight stairway.

Orson hesitated, tucked his tail between his legs, but finally descended behind Roosevelt, and I went last. The steps led to a porch-style afterdeck overhung by the cantilevered sun deck.

Orson was reluctant to go into the stateroom,

which looked cozy and welcoming in the low light of a nightstand lamp. After Roosevelt and I stepped inside, however, Orson vigorously shook the condensed fog off his coat, spraying the entire afterdeck, and then followed us. I could almost believe that he'd hung back out of consideration, to avoid splattering us.

When Orson was inside, Roosevelt locked the door. He tested it to be sure it was secure. Then tested it again.

Beyond the aft stateroom, the main cabin included a galley with bleached-mahogany cabinets and matching faux-mahogany floor, a dining area, and a salon in one open and spacious floor plan. Out of respect for me, it was illuminated only by one downlight in a living-room display case full of football trophies and by two fat green candles standing in saucers on the dinette table.

The air was redolent of fresh-brewed coffee, and when Roosevelt offered a cup, I accepted.

"Sorry to hear about your dad," he said.

"Well, at least it's over."

He raised his eyebrows. "Is it really?"

"I mean, for him."

"But not for you. Not after what you've seen."

I frowned. "How do you know what I've seen?"

"The word's around," he said cryptically.

"What do you —"

He held up one hubcap-size hand. "We'll talk about it in a minute. That's why I asked you to come here. But I'm still trying to think through what I need to tell you. Let me get around to it in my own way, son."

Coffee served, the big man took off his nylon windbreaker, hung it on the back of one of the oversized chairs, and sat at the table. He indicated that I should sit catercorner to him, and with his foot, he pushed out another chair. "Here you go, dog," he said, offering the third seat to Orson.

Although this was standard procedure when we visited Roosevelt, Orson pretended incomprehension. He settled onto the floor in front of the refrigerator.

"That is unacceptable," Roosevelt quietly informed him.

Orson yawned.

With one foot, Roosevelt gently rattled the chair that he had pushed away from the table for the dog. "Be a good puppy."

Orson yawned more elaborately than before. He was overplaying his disinterest.

"If I have to, pup, I'll come over there, pick you up, and put you in this chair," Roosevelt said, "which will be an embarrassment to your master, who would like you to be a courteous guest."

He was smiling good-naturedly, and no slightest threatening tone darkened his voice. His broad face was that of a black Buddha, and his eyes were full of kindness and amusement.

"Be a good puppy," Roosevelt repeated.

Orson swept the floor with his tail, caught himself, and stopped wagging. He shyly shifted his stare from Roosevelt to me and cocked his head.

I shrugged.

Once more Roosevelt lightly rattled the offered chair with his foot.

Although Orson got up from the floor, he didn't immediately approach the table.

From a pocket of the nylon windbreaker that hung on his chair, Roosevelt extracted a dog biscuit shaped like a bone. He held it in the candle-light so that Orson could see it clearly. Between his big thumb and forefinger, the biscuit appeared to be almost as tiny as a trinket from a charm bracelet, but it was in fact a large treat. With ceremonial solemnity, Roosevelt placed it on the table in front of the seat that was reserved for the dog.

With wanting eyes, Orson followed the biscuit hand. He padded toward the table but stopped short of it. He was being more than usually standoffish.

From the windbreaker, Roosevelt extracted a second biscuit. He held it close to the candles, turning it as if it were an exquisite jewel shining in the flame, and then he put it on the table beside the first biscuit.

Although he whined with desire, Orson didn't come to the chair. He ducked his head shyly and then looked up from under his brow at our host. This was the only man into whose eyes Orson was sometimes reluctant to stare.

Roosevelt took a third biscuit from the wind-breaker pocket. Holding it under his broad and oft-broken nose, he inhaled deeply, lavishly, as if savoring the incomparable aroma of the bone-shaped treat.

Raising his head, Orson sniffed, too.

Roosevelt smiled slyly, winked at the dog — and then popped the biscuit into his mouth. He crunched it with enormous delight, rinsed it down with a swig of coffee, and let out a sigh of pleasure.

I was impressed. I had never seen him do this before. "What did that taste like?"

"Not bad. Sort of like shredded wheat. Want one?"

"No, sir. No, thank you," I said, content to sip my coffee.

Orson's ears were pricked; Roosevelt now had his undivided attention. If this towering, gentle-voiced, giant black human truly enjoyed the biscuits, there might be fewer for any canine who played too hard to get.

From the windbreaker draped on the back of his chair, Roosevelt withdrew another biscuit. He held this one under his nose, too, and inhaled so expansively that he was putting me in danger of oxygen deprivation. His eyelids drooped sensuously. A shiver of pretended pleasure swept him, almost swelled into a swoon, and he seemed about to fall into a biscuit-devouring frenzy.

Orson's anxiety was palpable. He sprang off the floor, into the chair across the table from mine, where Roosevelt wanted him, sat on his hindquarters, and craned his neck forward until his snout was only two inches from Roosevelt's nose. Together, they sniffed the endangered biscuit.

Instead of popping this one into his mouth, Roosevelt carefully placed it on the table beside the two that were already arranged in front of Orson's seat. "Good old pup."

I wasn't sure that I believed in Roosevelt Frost's supposed ability to communicate with animals, but in my opinion, he was indisputably a first-rate dog psychologist.

Orson sniffed the biscuits on the table.

"Ah, ah, ah," Roosevelt warned.

The dog looked up at his host.

"You mustn't eat them until I say you may," Roosevelt told him.

The dog licked his chops.

"So help me, pup, if you eat them without my permission," said Roosevelt, "there will never, ever, ever again be biscuits for you."

Orson issued a thin, pleading whine.

"I mean it, dog," Roosevelt said quietly but firmly. "I can't make you talk to me if you don't want to. But I can insist that you display a minimum of manners aboard my boat. You can't just come in here and wolf down the canapés as if you were some wild beast."

Orson gazed into Roosevelt's eyes as though trying to judge his commitment to this no-wolfing rule.

Roosevelt didn't blink.

Apparently convinced that this was no empty threat, the dog lowered his attention to the three biscuits. He gazed at them with such desperate longing that I thought I ought to try one of the damn things, after all.

"Good pup," said Roosevelt.

He picked up a remote-control device from the table and jabbed one of the buttons on it, although the tip of his finger seemed too large to press fewer than three buttons at once. Behind Orson, motorized tambour doors rolled up and out of sight on the top half of a built-in hutch, revealing two stacks of tightly packed electronic gear gleaming with light-emitting diodes.

Orson was interested enough to turn his head for a moment before resuming worship of the forbidden biscuits.

In the hutch, a large video monitor clicked on. The quartered screen showed murky views of the fog-shrouded marina and the bay on all four sides of the *Nostromo*.

"What's this?" I wondered.

"Security." Roosevelt put down the remote control. "Motion detectors and infrared sensors will pick up anyone approaching the boat and alert us at once. Then a telescopic lens automatically isolates and zooms in on the intruder before he gets here, so we'll know what we're dealing with."

"What *are* we dealing with?"

The man mountain took two slow, dainty sips of his coffee before he said, "You might already know too much about that."

"What do you mean? Who are you?"

"I'm nobody but who I am," he said. "Just old Rosie Frost. If you're thinking that maybe I'm one of the people behind all this, you're wrong."

"What people? Behind what?"

Looking at the four security-camera views on the quartered video monitor, he said, "With any luck, they're not even aware that I know about them."

"Who? People at Wyvern?"

He turned to me again. "They're not just at Wyvern anymore. Townspeople are in it now. I don't know how many. Maybe a couple of hundred, maybe five hundred, but probably not more than that, at least not yet. No doubt it's gradually spreading to others . . . and it's already beyond Moonlight Bay."

Frustrated, I said, "Are you *trying* to be inscrutable?"

"As much as I can, yes."

He got up, fetched the coffeepot, and without further comment freshened our cups. Evidently he intended to make me wait for morsels of information in much the way that poor Orson was being made to wait patiently for his snack.

The dog licked the tabletop around the three biscuits, but his tongue never touched the treats.

When Roosevelt returned to his chair, I said, "If you're not involved with these people, how do you know so much about them?"

"I don't know all that much."

"Apparently a lot more than I do."

"I know only what the animals tell me."

"What animals?"

"Well, not your dog, for sure."

Orson looked up from the biscuits.

"He's a regular sphinx," Roosevelt said.

Although I hadn't been aware of doing so, sometime soon after sunset, I had evidently walked through a magic looking-glass.

Deciding to play by the lunatic rules of this

new kingdom, I said, "So . . . aside from my phlegmatic dog, what do these animals tell you?"

"You shouldn't know all of it. Just enough so you realize it's best that you forget what you saw in the hospital garage and up at the funeral home."

I sat up straighter in my chair, as though pulled erect by my tightening scalp. "You *are* one of them."

"No. Relax, son. You're safe with me. How long have we been friends? More than two years now since you first came here with your dog. And I think you know you can trust me."

In fact, I was at least half convinced that I could still trust Roosevelt Frost, even though I was no longer as sure of my character judgment as I had once been.

"But if you don't forget what you saw," he continued, "if you try to contact authorities outside town, you'll endanger lives."

As my chest tightened around my heart, I said, "You just told me I could trust you, and now you're threatening me."

He looked wounded. "I'm your friend, son. I wouldn't threaten you. I'm only telling you —"

"Yeah. What the animals said."

"It's the people from Wyvern who want to keep a lid on this at any cost, not me. Anyway, you aren't *personally* in any danger even if you try to go to outside authorities, at least not at first. They won't touch you. Not you. You're revered."

This was one of the most baffling things that

he had said yet, and I blinked in confusion. "Re-vered?"

"Yes. They're in awe of you."

I realized that Orson was staring at me in-tently, temporarily having forgotten the three promised biscuits.

Roosevelt's statement was not merely baffling: It was downright wacky. "Why would anyone be in awe of me?" I demanded.

"Because of who you are."

My mind looped and spun and tumbled like a capering seagull. "Who am I?"

Roosevelt frowned and pulled thoughtfully at his face with one hand before finally saying, "Damned if I know. I'm only repeating what I've been told."

What the animals told you. The black Dr. Doo-little.

Some of Bobby's scorn was creeping into me.

"The point is," he said, "the Wyvern crowd won't kill you unless you give them no choice, unless it's absolutely the only way to shut you up."

"When you talked to Sasha earlier tonight, you told her this was a matter of life and death."

Roosevelt nodded solemnly. "And it is. For her and others. From what I hear, these bastards will try to control you by killing people you love until you agree to cease and desist, until you forget what you saw and just get on with your life."

"People I love?"

"Sasha. Bobby. Even Orson."

"They'll kill my friends to shut me up?"

"*Until* you shut up. One by one, they'll kill them one by one until you shut up to save those who are left."

I was willing to risk my own life to find out what had happened to my mother and father — and why — but I couldn't put the lives of my friends on the line. "This is monstrous. Killing innocent —"

"That's who you're dealing with."

My skull felt as though it would crack to relieve the pressure of my frustration: "Who *am* I dealing with? I need something more specific than just the people at Wyvern."

Roosevelt sipped his coffee and didn't answer.

Maybe he was my friend, and maybe the warning he'd given me would, if I heeded it, save Sasha's life or Bobby's, but I wanted to punch him. I might have done it, too, might have hammered him with a merciless series of blows if there had been any chance whatsoever that I wouldn't have broken my hands.

Orson had put one paw on the table, not with the intention of sweeping his biscuits to the floor and absconding with them but to balance himself as he leaned sideways in his chair to look past me. Something in the salon, beyond the galley and dining area, had drawn his attention.

When I turned in my chair to follow Orson's gaze, I saw a cat sitting on the arm of the sofa, backlit by the display case full of football trophies. It appeared to be pale gray. In the shadows that masked its face, its eyes glowed green and were flecked with gold.

It could have been the same cat that I had encountered in the hills behind Kirk's Funeral Home earlier in the night.

23

Like an Egyptian sculpture in a pharaoh's sepulcher, the cat sat motionless and seemed prepared to spend eternity on the arm of the sofa.

Although it was only a cat, I was uncomfortable with my back to the animal. I moved to the chair opposite Roosevelt Frost, from which I could see, to my right, the entire salon and the sofa at the far end of it.

"When did you get a cat?" I asked.

"It's not mine," Roosevelt said. "It's just visiting."

"I think I saw this cat earlier tonight."

"Yes, you did."

"That's what it told you, huh?" I said with a touch of Bobby's scorn.

"Mungojerrie and I had a talk, yes," Roosevelt confirmed.

"Who?"

Roosevelt gestured toward the cat on the sofa. "Mungojerrie." He spelled it for me.

The name was exotic yet curiously familiar. Being my father's son in more than blood and name, I needed only a moment to recognize the source. "It's one of the cats in *Old Possum's Book of Practical Cats*, the T. S. Eliot collection."

"Most of these cats like those names from Eliot's book."

"These cats?"

"These new cats like Mungojerrie here."

"New cats?" I asked, struggling to follow him.

Rather than explain what he meant by that term, Roosevelt said, "They prefer those names. Couldn't tell you why — or how they came by them. I know one named Rum Tum Tugger. Another is Rumpelteazer. Coricopat and Growltiger."

"Prefer? You make it sound almost as if they choose their own names."

"Almost," Roosevelt said.

I shook my head. "This is radically bizarre."

"After all these years of animal communication," Roosevelt said, "I sometimes still find it bizarre myself."

"Bobby Halloway thinks you were hit in the head once too often."

Roosevelt smiled. "He's not alone in that opinion. But I was a football player, you know, not a boxer. What do you think, Chris? Has half my brain turned to gristle?"

"No, sir," I admitted. "You're as sharp as anyone I've ever known."

"On the other hand, intelligence and flakiness aren't mutually exclusive, are they?"

"I've met too many of my parents' fellow academics to argue that one with you."

From the living room, Mungojerrie continued to watch us, and from his chair, Orson continued to monitor the cat not with typical canine antagonism but with considerable interest.

"I ever tell you how I got into this animal-communication thing?" Roosevelt wondered.

"No, sir. I never asked." Calling attention to such an eccentricity had seemed as impolite as mentioning a physical deformity, so I had always pretended to accept this aspect of Roosevelt as though it were not in the least remarkable.

"Well," he said, "about nine years ago I had this really great dog named Sloopy, black and tan, about half the size of your Orson. He was just a mutt, but he was special."

Orson had shifted his attention from the cat to Roosevelt.

"Sloopy had a terrific disposition. He was always a playful, good-tempered dog, not one bad day in him. Then his mood changed. Suddenly he became withdrawn, nervous, even depressed. He was ten years old, not nearly a pup anymore, so I took him to a vet, afraid I was going to hear the worst kind of diagnosis. But the vet couldn't find anything much wrong with him. Sloopy had a little arthritis, something an aging ex-linebacker with football knees can identify with, but he didn't have it bad enough to inhibit him much, and that was the only thing wrong. Yet week after week, he wallowed in his funk."

Mungojerrie was on the move. The cat had climbed from the arm to the back of the sofa and was stealthily approaching us.

"So one day," Roosevelt continued, "I read this human-interest story in the paper about this woman in Los Angeles who called herself a pet communicator. Name was Gloria Chan. She'd been on a lot of TV talk shows, counseled a lot of movie people on their pets' problems, and she'd written a book. The reporter's tone was smart-ass, made Gloria sound like your typical Hollywood flake. For all I knew, he probably had her pegged. You remember, after the football career was over, I did a few movies. Met a lot of celebrities, actors and rock stars and comedians. Producers and directors, too. Some of them were nice folks and some were even smart, but frankly a lot of them and a lot of the people who hung out with them *were* so bugshit crazy you wouldn't want to be around them unless you were carrying a major concealed weapon."

After creeping the length of the sofa, the cat descended to the nearer arm. It shrank into a crouch, muscles taut, head lowered and thrust forward, ears flattened against its skull, as if it was going to spring at us across the six feet between the sofa and the table.

Orson was alert, focused again on Mungojerrie, both Roosevelt and the biscuits forgotten.

"I had some business in L.A.," Roosevelt said, "so I took Sloopy with me. We went down by boat, cruised the coast. I didn't have the *Nostromo* then. I was driving this really sweet sixty-foot Chris-Craft Roamer. I docked her at Marina Del Rey, rented a car, took care of business for two days. I got Gloria's number through some friends in the film business, and she agreed to see me. She lived in the Palisades, and I drove out there with Sloopy late one morning."

On the sofa arm, the cat was still crouched to spring. Its muscles were coiled even tighter than before. Little gray panther.

Orson was rigid, as still as the cat. He made a high-pitched, thin, anxious sound and then was silent again.

Roosevelt said, "Gloria was fourth-generation

Chinese American. A petite, doll-like person. Beautiful, really beautiful. Delicate features, huge eyes. Like something a Chinese Michelangelo might have carved out of luminous amber jade. You expected her to have a little-girl voice, but she sounded like Lauren Bacall, this deep smoky voice coming from this tiny woman. Sloopy instantly liked her. Before I knew it, she's sitting with him in her lap, face-to-face with him and talking to him, petting him, and telling me what he's so moody about."

Mungojerrie leaped off the sofa arm, not to the dinette but to the deck, and then instantly sprang from the deck to the seat of the chair that I had abandoned when I had moved one place around the table to keep an eye on him.

Simultaneously, as the spry cat landed on the chair, Orson and I twitched.

Mungojerrie stood with his hind paws on the chair, forepaws on the table, staring intently at my dog.

Orson issued that brief, thin, anxious sound again — and didn't take his eyes off the cat.

Unconcerned about Mungojerrie, Roosevelt said, "Gloria told me that Sloopy was depressed mostly because I wasn't spending any time with him anymore. 'You're always out with Helen,' she said. 'And Sloopy knows Helen doesn't like him. He thinks you're going to have to choose between him and Helen, and he knows you'll have to choose her.' Now, son, I'm stunned to be hearing all this, because I was, in fact, dating a woman named Helen here in Moonlight Bay, but no way could Gloria Chan have known about her. And I *was* obsessed with Helen, spending most of my free time with her, and she didn't like dogs, which meant Sloopy always got left behind. I figured she would come around to liking Sloopy, 'cause even Hitler couldn't have helped having a soft spot in his heart for that mutt. But as it turned out, Helen was already turning as sour on me as she was on dogs, though I didn't know it yet."

Staring intently at Orson, Mungojerrie bared his fangs.

Orson pulled back in his chair, as if afraid the cat was going to launch itself at him.

"Then Gloria tells me a few other things bothering Sloopy, one of which was this Ford pickup I'd bought. His arthritis was mild, but the poor dog couldn't get in and out of the truck as easy as he could a car, and he was scared of breaking a bone."

Still baring his fangs, the cat hissed.

Orson flinched, and a brief keening sound of anxiety escaped him, like a burst of steam whistling out of a teakettle.

Evidently oblivious to this feline-canine drama, Roosevelt said, "Gloria and I had lunch and spent the whole afternoon talking about her work as an animal communicator. She told me she didn't have any special talent, that it wasn't any paranormal psychic nonsense, just a sensitivity to other species that we all have but that we've repressed. She said anyone could do it, that I could do it myself if I learned the techniques and spent enough time at it, which sounded preposterous to me."

Mungojerrie hissed again, somewhat more ferociously, and again Orson flinched, and then I swear the cat smiled or came as close to smiling as any cat can.

Stranger yet, Orson appeared to break into a wide grin — which requires no imagination to picture because all dogs are able to grin. He was panting happily, grinning at the smiling cat, as though their confrontation had been an amusing joke.

"I ask you, son, who wouldn't want to learn such a thing?" said Roosevelt.

"Who indeed?" I replied numbly.

"So Gloria taught me, and it took a frustratingly long time, months and months, but I eventually got as good at it as she was. The first big hurdle is believing you can actually do it. Putting aside your doubt, your cynicism, all your preconceived notions about what's possible and what isn't. Most of all, hardest of all, you have to stop worrying about looking foolish, 'cause fear of being humiliated really limits you. Lots of folks could never get past all that, and I'm sort of surprised that I got past it myself."

Shifting forward in his chair, Orson leaned over the table and bared his teeth at Mungojerrie.

The cat's eyes widened with fear.

Silently but threateningly, Orson gnashed his teeth.

Wistfulness filled Roosevelt's deep voice: "Sloopy died three years later. God, how I grieved for him. But what a fascinating and wonderful three years they were, being so in tune with him."

Teeth still bared, Orson growled softly at Mungojerrie, and the cat whimpered. Orson growled again, the cat bawled a pitiful meow of purest fear — and then both grinned.

"What the hell is going on here?" I wondered.

Orson and Mungojerrie seemed to be perplexed by the nervous tremor in my voice.

"They're just having fun," Roosevelt said.

I blinked at him.

In the candlelight, his face shone like darkly stained and highly polished teak.

"Having fun mocking their stereotypes," he explained.

I couldn't believe I was hearing him correctly. Considering how completely I must be misperceiving his words, I was going to need a high-pressure hose and a plumber's drain snake to clean out my ears. "Mocking their stereotypes?"

"Yes, that's right." He bobbed his head in confirmation. "Of course they wouldn't put it in those terms, but that's what they're doing. Dogs and cats are supposed to be mindlessly hostile. These guys are having fun mocking that expectation."

Now Roosevelt was grinning at me as stupidly as the dog and the cat were grinning at me. His lips were so dark red that they were virtually black, and his teeth were as big and white as sugar cubes.

"Sir," I told him, "I take back what I said earlier. After careful reconsideration, I've decided you're totally awesomely crazy, whacked-out to the max."

He bobbed his head again, continuing to grin at me. Suddenly, like the darkling beams of a black moon, lunacy rose in his face. He said, "You wouldn't have any damn trouble believing me if I were *white*," and as he snarled the final word, he slammed one massive fist into the table so hard that our coffee cups rattled in their saucers and nearly tipped over.

If I could have reeled backward while in a chair, I would have done so, because his accusation stunned me. I had never heard either of my parents use an ethnic slur or make a racist statement; I'd been raised without prejudice. Indeed, if there was an ultimate outcast in this world, it was *me*. I was a minority all to myself, a minority of one: the Nightcrawler, as certain bullies had called me when I was a little kid, before I'd ever met Bobby and had someone who would stand beside me. Though not an albino, though my skin was pigmented, I was stranger, in many people's eyes, than Bo Bo the Dog-Faced Boy. To some I was merely unclean, tainted, as if my genetic vulnerability to ultraviolet light could be passed to others with a sneeze, but some people feared and despised me more than they would fear or despise a three-eyed Toad Man in any carnival freak show from sea to shining sea, if only because I lived next door.

Half rising out of his chair, leaning across the table, shaking a fist as big as a cantaloupe, Roosevelt Frost spoke with a hatred that astonished and sickened me: "Racist! You mealy racist bastard!"

I could barely find my voice. "W-when did race ever matter to me? *How* could it ever matter to me?"

He looked as if he would reach across the table, tear me out of my chair, and strangle me until my tongue unraveled to my shoes. He bared his teeth and growled at me, growled like a dog, very much like a dog, suspiciously like a dog.

"What the hell is going on here?" I asked again, but this time I found myself asking the dog and cat.

Roosevelt growled at me again, and when I only gaped stupidly at him, he said, "Come on, son, if you can't call me a name, at least give me a little growl. Give me a little growl. Come on, son, you can do it."

Orson and Mungojerrie watched me expectantly.

Roosevelt growled once more, giving his snarl an interrogatory inflection at the end, and finally I growled back at him. He growled louder than before, and I growled louder, too.

Smiling broadly, he said, "Hostility. Dog and cat. Black and white. Just having a little fun mocking stereotypes."

As Roosevelt settled into his chair again, my bewilderment began to give way to a tremulous sense of the miraculous. I was aware of a looming revelation that would rock my life forever, expose dimensions of the world that I could not now imagine; but although I strained to grasp it, this understanding remained elusive, tantalizingly just beyond the limits of my reach.

I looked at Orson. Those inky, liquid eyes.

I looked at Mungojerrie.

The cat bared his teeth at me.

Orson bared his, too.

A faint cold fear thrilled through my veins, as the Bard of Avon would put it, not because I thought the dog and cat might bite me but because of what this amused baring of teeth implied. Not just fear shivered through me, either, but also a delicious chill of wonder and giddy excitement.

Although such an act would have been out of character for him, I actually wondered if Roosevelt Frost had spiked the coffee. Not with brandy. With hallucinogenics. I was simultaneously disoriented and clearer of mind than I'd ever been, as if I were in a heightened state of consciousness.

The cat hissed at me, and I hissed at the cat.

Orson growled at me, and I growled at him.

In the most astonishing moment of my life to this point, we sat around the dinette table, grinning men and beasts, and I was reminded of those cute but corny paintings that were popular for a few years: scenes of dogs playing poker. Only one of us was a dog, of course, and none of us had cards, so the painting in my mind's eye didn't seem to apply to this situation, and yet the longer I dwelled on it, the closer I came to revelation, to epiphany, to understanding all of the ramifications of what had happened at this table in the past few minutes —

— and then my train of thought was derailed by a beeping that arose from the electronic security equipment in the hutch beside the table.

As Roosevelt and I turned to look at the video monitor, the four views on the screen resolved into one. The automated system zoomed in on the intruder and revealed it in the eerie, enhanced light of a night-vision lens.

The visitor stood in the eddying fog at the aft end of the port finger of the boat slip in which the *Nostromo* was berthed. It looked as though it had stepped directly out of the Jurassic Period into our time: perhaps four feet tall, pterodactyl-like, with a long wicked beak.

My mind was so full of feverish speculations related to the cat and the dog — and I was so unnerved by the other events of the night — that I was prepared to see the uncanny in the ordinary, where it did not in fact exist. My heart raced. My mouth soured and went dry. If I hadn't been frozen by shock, I would have bolted to my feet, knocking my chair over. Given another five seconds, I still might have managed to make a fool of myself, but I was saved from mortification by Roosevelt. He was either by nature more deliberative than I was or he had lived so long with the uncanny that he was quick to differentiate genuine eldritch from faux eldritch.

"Blue heron," he said. "Doing a little night fishing."

I was as familiar with the great blue heron as with any bird that thrived in and around Moonlight Bay. Now that Roosevelt had named our visitor, I recognized it for what it was.

Cancel the call to Mr. Spielberg. There is no movie here.

In my defense, I would note that for all its elegant physiology and its undeniable grace, this heron has a fierce predatory aura and a cold reptilian gaze that identify it as a survivor of the age of dinosaurs.

The bird was poised at the very edge of the slip finger, peering intently into the water. Suddenly it bent forward, its head darted down, its beak stabbed into the bay, it snatched up a small fish, and it threw its head back, swallowing the catch. Some die that others may live.

Considering how hastily I had ascribed preternatural qualities to this ordinary heron, I began to wonder if I was attributing more significance to the recent episode with the cat and the dog than it deserved. Certainty gave way to doubt. The onrushing, macking wave of epiphany abruptly receded without breaking, and a churly-churly tide of confusion slopped over me again.

Drawing my attention from the video display, Roosevelt said, "In the years since Gloria Chan taught me interspecies communication, which is basically just being a cosmically good listener, my life has been immeasurably enriched."

"Cosmically good listener," I repeated, wondering if Bobby would still be able to execute one of his wonderfully entertaining riffs on a nutball phrase like that. Maybe his experiences with the monkeys had left him with a permanent deficit of both sarcasm and skepticism. I hoped not. Although change might be a fundamental principle of the universe, some things were meant to be timeless, including Bobby's insistence on a life that allowed only for things as basic as sand, surf, and sun.

"I've greatly enjoyed all the animals that have come to me over the years," Roosevelt said as drily as if he were a veterinarian reminiscing about a career in animal medicine. He reached out to Mungojerrie and stroked his head, scratched behind his ears. The cat leaned into the big man's hand and purred. "But these new cats I've been encountering the last two years or so . . . they open a far more exciting dimension of communication." He turned to Orson: "And I'm sure that you are every bit as interesting as the cats."

Panting, tongue lolling, Orson assumed an expression of perfect doggy vacuousness.

"Listen, dog, you have never fooled me," Roosevelt assured him. "And after your little game with the cat a moment ago, you might as well give up the act."

Ignoring Mungojerrie, Orson looked down at the three biscuits in front of him, on the table.

"You can pretend to be all dog appetite, pretend nothing's more important to you than those tasty treats, but I know differently."

Gaze locked on the biscuits, Orson whined longingly.

Roosevelt said, "It was you who brought Chris here the first time, old pup, so why did you come if not to talk?"

On Christmas Eve, more than two years ago, not a month before my mother died, Orson and I had been roaming the night, according to our usual habits. He had been only a year old then. As a puppy, he had been frisky and playful, but he had never been as hyper as most very young dogs. Nevertheless, at the age of one, he was not always able to control his curiosity and not always as well-behaved as he ultimately became. We were on the outdoor basketball court behind the high school, my dog and I, and I was shooting baskets. I was telling Orson that Michael Jordan should be *damn* glad that I'd been born with XP and was unable to compete under lights, when the mutt abruptly sprinted away from me. Repeatedly I called to him, but he only paused to glance back at me, then trotted away again. By the time I realized that he was not going to return, I didn't even have time to snug the ball into the net bag that was tied to the handlebars of my bicycle. I pedaled after the fugitive fur ball, and he led me on a wild chase: street to alley to street, through Quester Park, down to the marina, and ultimately along the docks to the *Nostromo*. Although he rarely barked, that night Orson flew into a barking frenzy as he leaped off the dock directly onto the porchlike afterdeck of the cruiser, and by the time I braked to a skidding halt on the damp dock planks, Roosevelt had come out of the boat to cuddle and calm the dog.

"You want to talk," Roosevelt told Orson now. "You originally came here wanting to talk, but I suspect you just don't trust me."

Orson kept his head down, his eyes on the biscuits.

"Even after two years, you half suspect maybe

334

I'm hooked up with the people at Wyvern, and you're not going to be anything but the most doggie of dogs until you're sure of me."

Sniffing the biscuits, once more licking the table around them, Orson seemed not even to be aware that anyone was speaking to him.

Turning his attention to me, Roosevelt said, "These new cats, they come from Wyvern. Some are first-generation, the original escapees, and some are second-generation who were born in freedom."

"Lab animals?" I asked.

"The first generation were, yes. They and their offspring are different from other cats. Different in lots of ways."

"Smarter," I said, remembering the behavior of the monkeys.

"You know more than I thought."

"It's been a busy night. How smart are they?"

"I don't know how to calibrate that," he said, and I could see that he was being evasive. "But they're smarter and different in other ways, too."

"Why? What was done to them out there?"

"I don't know," he said.

"How'd they get loose?"

"Your guess is as good as mine."

"Why haven't they been rounded up?"

"Beats me."

"No offense, sir, but you're a bad liar."

"Always have been," Roosevelt said with a smile. "Listen, son, I don't know everything, either. Only what the animals tell me. But it's not good for you to know even that much. The more you know, the more you'll want to know

— and you've got your dog and those friends to worry about."

"Sounds like a threat," I said without animosity.

When he shrugged his immense shoulders, there should have been a low thunder of displaced air. "If you think I've been co-opted by them at Wyvern, then it's a threat. If you believe I'm your friend, then it's advice."

Although I wanted to trust Roosevelt, I shared Orson's doubt. I found it hard to believe that this man was capable of treachery. But here on the weird side of the magical looking-glass, I had to assume that every face was a false face.

Edgy from the caffeine but with a craving for more, I took my cup to the coffeemaker and refilled it.

"What I *can* tell you," Roosevelt said, "is there were supposed to be dogs out at Fort Wyvern as well as cats."

"Orson didn't come from Wyvern."

"Where did he come from?"

I stood with my back against the refrigerator, sipping the hot coffee. "One of my mom's colleagues gave him to us. Their dog had a lot of puppies, and they needed to find homes for them."

"One of your mom's colleagues at the university?"

"Yeah. A professor at Ashdon."

Roosevelt Frost stared, unspeaking, and a terrible cloud of pity crossed his face.

"What?" I asked, and heard a quavery note in my voice that I did not like.

He opened his mouth to speak, thought better of it, and kept his silence. Suddenly he seemed to want to avoid my eyes. Now both he and Orson were studying the damn dog biscuits.

The cat had no interest in the biscuits. Instead, he watched me.

If another cat made of pure gold with eyes of jewels, standing silent guard for millennia in the most sacred room of a pyramid far beneath a sea of sand, had suddenly come to life before my eyes, it would not have seemed more mysterious than this cat with his steady, somehow ancient gaze.

To Roosevelt, I said, "You don't think that's where Orson came from? Not Wyvern? Why would my mother's colleague lie to her?"

He shook his head, as if he didn't know, but he knew all right.

I was frustrated by the way he fluctuated between making disclosures and guarding his secrets. I didn't understand his game, couldn't grasp why he was alternately forthcoming and closemouthed.

Under the gray cat's hieroglyphic gaze, in the draft-trembled candlelight, with the humid air thickened by mystery as manifest as incense, I said, "All you need to complete your act is a crystal ball, silver hoop earrings, a Gypsy headband, and a Romanian accent."

I couldn't get a rise out of him.

Returning to my chair at the table, I tried to use what little I knew to encourage him to believe that I knew even more. Maybe he would open up further if he thought some of his secrets weren't so secret, after all. "There weren't only cats and dogs in the labs at Wyvern. There were monkeys."

Roosevelt didn't reply, and he still avoided my eyes.

"You do know about the monkeys?" I asked.

"No," he said, but he glanced from the biscuits to the security-camera monitor in the hutch.

"I suspect it's because of the monkeys that you got a mooring outside the marina three months ago."

Realizing that he had betrayed his knowledge by looking at the monitor when I mentioned the monkeys, he returned his attention to the dog biscuits.

Only a hundred moorings were available in the bay waters beyond the marina, and they were nearly as prized as the dock slips, though it was a necessary inconvenience to travel to and from your moored boat in another craft. Roosevelt had subleased a space from Dieter Gessel, a fisherman whose trawler was docked farther out along the northern horn with the rest of the fishing fleet but who had kept a junk dinghy at the mooring against the day when he retired and acquired a pleasure boat. Rumor was that Roosevelt was paying five times what the lease was costing Dieter.

I had never before asked him about it because it wasn't any of my business unless he brought it up first.

Now I said, "Every night, you move the *Nostromo* from this slip out to the mooring, and you sleep there. Every night without fail — except tonight, while you're waiting here for me. Folks thought you were going to buy a second boat, something smaller and fun, just to play with. When you didn't, when you just went out there every night to bunk down, they figured — 'Well, okay, he's a little eccentric anyway, old Roosevelt, talking to people's pets and whatnot.' "

He remained silent.

He and Orson appeared to be so intensely and equally fascinated by those three dog biscuits that I could almost believe *either* of them might abruptly break discipline and gobble up the treats.

"After tonight," I said, "I think I know why you go out there to sleep. You figure it's safer. Because maybe monkeys don't swim well — or at least they don't enjoy it."

As if he hadn't heard me, he said, "Okay, dog, even if you won't talk to me, you can have your nibbles."

Orson risked eye-to-eye contact with his inquisitor, seeking confirmation.

"Go ahead," Roosevelt urged.

Orson looked dubiously at me, as if asking whether I thought Roosevelt's permission was a trick.

"He's the host," I said.

The dog snatched up the first biscuit and happily crunched it.

Finally turning his attention to me, with that unnerving pity still in his face and eyes, Roosevelt said, "The people behind the project at Wyvern . . . they might have had good intentions. Some of them, anyway. And I think some good things might've come from their work." He reached out to pet the cat again, which relaxed under his hand, though he never shifted his piercing eyes from me. "But there was also a dark side to this business. A very dark side. From what I've been told, the monkeys are only one manifestation of it."

"Only one?"

Roosevelt held my stare in silence for a long time, long enough for Orson to eat the second biscuit, and when at last he spoke, his voice was softer than ever: "There were more than just cats and dogs and monkeys in those labs."

I didn't know what he meant, but I said, "I suspect you aren't talking about guinea pigs or white mice."

His eyes shifted away from me, and he appeared to be staring at something far beyond the cabin of this boat. "Lot of change coming."

"They say change is good."

"Some is."

As Orson ate the third biscuit, Roosevelt rose from his chair. Picking up the cat, holding him against his chest, stroking him, he seemed to be considering whether I needed to — or should — know more.

When he finally spoke, he slid once again from a revelatory mood into a secretive one. "I'm tired, son. I should have been in bed hours ago. I was asked to warn you that your friends are in danger if you don't walk away from this, if you keep probing."

"The cat asked you to warn me."

"That's right."

As I got to my feet, I became more aware of the wallowing motion of the boat. For a moment I was stricken by a spell of vertigo, and I gripped the back of the chair to steady myself.

This physical symptom was matched by mental turmoil, as well, and my grip on reality seemed increasingly tenuous. I felt as if I were spinning along the upper rim of a whirlpool that would suck me down faster, faster, faster, until I went through the bottom of the funnel — my own version of Dorothy's tornado — and found myself not in Oz but in Waimea Bay, Hawaii, solemnly discussing the fine points of reincarnation with Pia Klick.

Aware of the extreme flakiness of the question, I nevertheless asked, "And the cat, Mungojerrie . . . he isn't in league with these people at Wyvern?"

"He escaped from them."

Licking his chops to be sure that no precious biscuit crumbs adhered to his lips or to the fur around his muzzle, Orson got off the dinette chair and came to my side.

To Roosevelt, I said, "Earlier tonight, I heard the Wyvern project described in apocalyptic terms . . . the end of the world."

"The world as we know it."

"You actually believe that?"

"It could play out that way, yes. But maybe when it all shakes down, there'll be more good changes than bad. The end of the world *as we know it* isn't necessarily the same as the end of the world."

"Tell that to the dinosaurs after the comet impact."

"I have my jumpy moments," he admitted.

"If you're frightened enough to go to the mooring to sleep every night and if you really believe that what they were doing at Wyvern was so dangerous, why don't you get out of Moonlight Bay?"

"I've considered it. But my businesses are here. My life's here. Besides, I wouldn't be escaping. I'd only be buying a little time. Ultimately, nowhere is safe."

"That's a bleak assessment."

"I guess so."

"Yet you don't seem depressed."

Carrying the cat, Roosevelt led us out of the main cabin and through the aft stateroom. "I've always been able to handle whatever the world threw at me, son, both the ups and the downs, as long as it was at least *interesting*. I've had the blessing of a full and varied life, and the only thing I really dread is boredom." We stepped out of the boat onto the afterdeck, into the clammy embrace of the fog. "Things are liable to get downright hairy here in the Jewel of the Central Coast, but whichever way it goes, for damn sure it won't be boring."

Roosevelt had more in common with Bobby Halloway than I would have thought.

"Well, sir . . . thank you for the advice. I guess." I sat on the coaming and swung off the boat to the dock a couple of feet below, and Orson leaped down to my side.

The big blue heron had departed earlier. The

fog eddied around me, the black water purled under the boat slip, and all else was as still as a dream of death.

I had taken only two steps toward the gangway when Roosevelt said, "Son?"

I stopped and looked back.

"The safety of your friends really is at stake here. But your happiness is on the line, too. Believe me, you don't want to know more about this. You've got enough problems . . . the way you have to live."

"I don't have any problems," I assured him. "Just different advantages and disadvantages from most people."

His skin was so black that he might have been a mirage in the fog, a trick of shadow. The cat, which he held, was invisible but for his eyes, which appeared to be disembodied, mysterious — bright green orbs floating in midair. "Just different advantages . . . do you really believe that?" he asked.

"Yes, sir," I said, although I wasn't sure whether I believed it because it was, in fact, the truth or because I had spent most of my life convincing myself that it was true. A lot of the time, reality is what you make it.

"I'll tell you one more thing," he said. "One more thing because it might convince you to let this go and get on with life."

I waited.

At last, with sorrow in his voice, he said, "The reason most of them don't want to harm you, the reason they'd rather try to control you by killing your friends, the reason most of them re-

vere you is because of who your mother was."

Fear, as death-white and cold as a Jerusalem cricket, crawled up the small of my back, and for a moment my lungs constricted so that I couldn't draw a breath — although I didn't know why Roosevelt's enigmatic statement should affect me so instantly and profoundly. Maybe I understood more than I thought I did. Maybe the truth was already waiting to be acknowledged in the canyons of the subconscious — or in the abyss of the heart.

When I could breathe, I said, "What do you mean?"

"If you think about it for a while," he said, "really think about it, maybe you'll realize that you have nothing to gain by pursuing this thing — and so much to lose. Knowledge seldom brings us peace, son. A hundred years ago, we didn't know about atomic structure or DNA or black holes — but are we any happier and more fulfilled now than people were then?"

As he spoke that final word, fog filled the space where he had stood on the afterdeck. A cabin door closed softly; with a louder sound, a dead bolt was engaged.

24

Around the creaking *Nostromo*, the fog seethed in slow motion. Nightmare creatures appeared to form out of the mist, loom, and then dissolve.

Inspired by Roosevelt Frost's final revelation, more fearful things than fog monsters took shape from the mists in my mind, but I was reluctant to concentrate on them and thereby impart to them a greater solidity. Maybe he was right. If I learned everything I wanted to know, I might wish I had remained ignorant of the truth.

Bobby says that truth is sweet but dangerous. He says people couldn't bear to go on living if they faced every cold truth about themselves.

In that case, I tell him, he'll never be suicidal.

As Orson preceded me up the gangway from the slip, I considered my options, trying to decide where to go and what to do next. There was a siren singing, and only I could hear her dangerous song; though I was afraid of wrecking on the rocks of truth, this hypnotic melody was one I couldn't resist.

When we reached the top of the gangway, I said to my dog, "So . . . anytime you want to start explaining all this to me, I'm ready to listen."

Even if Orson could have answered me, he didn't seem to be in a communicative mood.

My bicycle was still leaning against the dock railing. The rubber handlebar grips were cold and slick, wet with condensation.

Behind us, the *Nostromo*'s engines turned over. When I glanced back, I saw the running lights of the boat diffused and ringed by halos in the fog.

I couldn't make out Roosevelt at the upper helm station, but I knew he was there. Though only a few hours of darkness remained, he was moving his boat out to his mooring even in this low visibility.

As I walked my bike shoreward through the marina, among the gently rocking boats, I looked back a couple of times, to see if I could spot Mungojerrie in the dim wash of the dock lights. If he was following us, he was being discreet. I suspected that the cat was still aboard the *Nostromo*.

. . . the reason most of them revere you is because of who your mother was.

When we turned right onto the main dock pier and headed toward the entrance to the marina, a foul odor rose off the water. Evidently the tide had washed a dead squid or a man-of-war or a fish in among the pilings. The rotting corpse must have gotten caught above the water line on one of the jagged masses of barnacles that encrusted the concrete caissons. The stench became so ripe that the humid air seemed to be not merely scented but flavored with it, as repulsive as a broth from the devil's dinner table. I held my breath and kept my mouth tightly closed against the disgusting taste that had been imparted to the fog.

The grumble of the *Nostromo*'s engines had

faded as it cruised out to the mooring. Now the muffled rhythmic thumping that came across the water sounded not like engine noise at all but like the ominous beat of a leviathan's heart, as though a monster of the deep might surface in the marina, sinking all the boats, battering apart the dock, and plunging us into a cold wet grave.

When we reached the midpoint of the main pier, I looked back and saw neither the cat nor a more fearsome pursuer.

Nevertheless, I said to Orson, "Damn, but it's starting to *feel* like the end of the world."

He chuffed in agreement as we left the stench of death behind us and walked toward the glow of the quaint ship lanterns that were mounted on massive teak pilasters at the main pier entrance.

Moving out of an almost liquid gloom beside the marina office, Lewis Stevenson, the chief of police, still in uniform as I had seen him earlier in the night, crossed into the light. He said, "I'm in a mood here."

For an instant, as he stepped from the shadows, something about him was so peculiar that a chill bored like a corkscrew in my spine. Whatever I had seen — or thought I'd seen — passed in a blink, however, and I found myself shivering and keenly disturbed, overcome by an extraordinary perception of being in the presence of something unearthly and malevolent, without being able to identify the precise cause of this feeling.

Chief Stevenson was holding a formidable-looking pistol in his right hand. Although he was not in a shooting stance, his grip on the weapon wasn't casual. The muzzle was trained on Orson, who was two steps ahead of me, standing in the outer arc of the lantern light, while I remained in shadows.

"You want to guess what mood I'm in?" Stevenson asked, stopping no more than ten feet from us.

"Not good," I ventured.

"I'm in a mood not to be screwed with."

The chief didn't sound like himself. His voice was familiar, the timbre and the accent unchanged, but there was a hard note when before there had been quiet authority. Usually his speech flowed like a stream, and you found yourself almost floating on it, calm and warm and assured; but now the flow was fast and turbulent, cold and stinging.

"I don't feel good," he said. "I don't feel good at all. In fact, I feel like shit, and I don't have much patience for anything that makes me feel even worse. You understand me?"

Although I didn't understand him entirely, I nodded and said, "Yes. Yes, sir, I understand."

Orson was as still as cast iron, and his eyes never left the muzzle of the chief's pistol.

I was acutely aware that the marina was a desolate place at this hour. The office and the fueling station were not staffed after six o'clock. Only five boat owners, other than Roosevelt Frost, lived aboard their vessels, and they were no doubt sound asleep. The docks were no less lonely than the granite rows of eternal berths in St. Bernadette's cemetery.

The fog muffled our voices. No one was likely to hear our conversation and be drawn to it.

Keeping his attention on Orson but addressing me, Stevenson said, "I can't get what I need, because I don't even know what it *is* I need. Isn't that a bitch?"

I sensed that this was a man at risk of coming apart, perilously holding himself together. He had lost his noble aspect. Even his handsomeness was sliding away as the planes of his face were pulled toward a new configuration by what seemed to be rage and an equally powerful anxiety.

"You ever feel this emptiness, Snow? You ever feel an emptiness so bad, you've got to fill it or you'll die, but you don't know where the emptiness is or what in the name of God you're supposed to fill it *with?*"

Now I didn't understand him *at all*, but I didn't think that he was in a mood to explain himself, so I looked solemn and nodded sympathetically. "Yes, sir. I know the feeling."

His brow and cheeks were moist but not from the clammy air; he glistened with greasy sweat. His face was so supernaturally white that the mist seemed to pour from him, boiling coldly off his skin, as though he were the father of all fog. "Comes on you bad at night," he said.

"Yes, sir."

"Comes on you anytime, but worse at night." His face twisted with what might have been disgust. "What kind of damn dog is this, anyway?"

His gun arm stiffened, and I thought I saw his finger tighten on the trigger.

Orson bared his teeth but neither moved nor made a sound.

I quickly said, "He's just a Labrador mix. He's a good dog, wouldn't harm a cat."

His anger swelling for no apparent reason, Stevenson said, "Just a Labrador mix, huh? The hell he is. Nothing's *just* anything. Not here. Not now. Not anymore."

I considered reaching for the Glock in my jacket. I was holding my bike with my left hand. My right hand was free, and the pistol was in my right-hand pocket.

Even as distraught as Stevenson was, however, he was nonetheless a cop, and he was sure to respond with deadly professionalism to any threatening move I made. I didn't put much faith in Roosevelt's strange assurance that I was revered. Even if I let the bicycle fall over to distract him, Stevenson would shoot me dead before the Glock cleared my pocket.

Besides, I wasn't going to pull a gun on the chief of police unless I had no choice but to use it. And if I shot him, that would be the end of my life, a thwarting of the sun.

Abruptly Stevenson snapped his head up, looking away from Orson. He drew a deep breath, then several that were as quick and shallow as those of a hound following the spoor of its quarry. "What's that?"

He had a keener sense of smell than I did, because I only now realized that an almost imperceptible breeze had brought us a faint hint of the stench from the decomposing sea creature back under the main pier.

Although Stevenson was already acting strangely enough to make my scalp crinkle into faux corduroy, he grew markedly stranger. He tensed, hunched his shoulders, stretched his neck, and raised his face to the fog, as though savoring the putrescent scent. His eyes were feverish in his pale face, and he spoke not with the measured inquisitiveness of a cop but with an eager, nervous curiosity that seemed perverse: "What is that? You smell that? Something dead, isn't it?"

"Something back under the pier," I confirmed. "Some kind of fish, I guess."

"Dead. Dead and rotting. Something . . . It's got an edge to it, doesn't it?" He seemed about to lick his lips. "Yeah. Yeah. Sure does have an interesting edge to it."

Either he heard the eerie current crackling through his voice or he sensed my alarm, because he glanced worriedly at me and struggled to compose himself. It *was* a struggle. He was teetering on a crumbling ledge of emotion.

Finally the chief found his normal voice — or something that approximated it. "I need to talk to you, reach an understanding. Now. Tonight. Why don't you come with me, Snow."

"Come where?"

"My patrol car's out front."

"But my bicycle —"

"I'm not arresting you. Just a quick chat. Let's make sure we understand each other."

The last thing I wanted to do was get in a patrol car with Stevenson. If I refused, however, he might make his invitation more formal by taking me into custody.

Then, if I tried to resist arrest, if I climbed on my bicycle and pumped the pedals hard enough to make the crank axle smoke — where would I go? With dawn only a few hours away, I had no time to flee as far as the next town on this lonely stretch of coast. Even if I had ample time, XP limited my world to the boundaries of Moonlight Bay, where I could return home by sunrise or find an understanding friend to take me in and give me darkness.

"I'm in a mood here," Lewis Stevenson said again, through half-clenched teeth, the hardness returning to his voice. "I'm in a real mood. You coming with me?"

"Yes, sir. I'm cool with that."

Motioning with his pistol, he indicated that Orson and I were to precede him.

I walked my bike toward the end of the entrance pier, loath to have the chief behind me with the gun. I didn't need to be an animal communicator to know that Orson was nervous, too.

The pier planks ended in a concrete sidewalk flanked by flower beds full of ice plant, the blooms of which open wide in sunshine and close at night. In the low landscape lighting, snails were crossing the walkway, antennae glistening, leaving silvery trails of slime, some creeping from the right-hand bed of ice plant to the identical bed on the left, others laboriously making their way in the opposite direction, as if these humble mollusks shared humanity's restlessness and dissatisfaction with the terms of existence.

I weaved with the bike to avoid the snails, and

although Orson sniffed them in passing, he stepped over them.

From behind us rose the crunching of crushed shells, the squish of jellied bodies tramped underfoot. Stevenson was stepping on not only those snails directly in his path but on every hapless gastropod in sight. Some were dispatched with a quick snap, but he *stomped* on others, came down on them with such force that the slap of shoe sole against concrete rang like a hammer strike.

I didn't turn to look.

I was afraid of seeing the cruel glee that I remembered too well from the faces of the young bullies who had tormented me throughout childhood, before I'd been wise enough and big enough to fight back. Although that expression was unnerving when a child wore it, the same look — the beady eyes that seemed perfectly reptilian even without elliptical pupils, the hate-reddened cheeks, the bloodless lips drawn back in a sneer from spittle-shined teeth — would be immeasurably more disturbing on the face of an adult, especially when the adult had a gun in his hand and wore a badge.

Stevenson's black-and-white was parked at a red curb thirty feet to the left of the marina entrance, beyond the reach of the landscape lights, in deep night shade under the spreading limbs of an enormous Indian laurel.

I leaned my bike against the trunk of the tree, on which the fog hung like Spanish moss. At last I turned warily to the chief as he opened the back door on the passenger side of the patrol car.

Even in the murk, I recognized the expression on his face that I had dreaded seeing: the hatred, the irrational but unassuageable anger that makes some human beings more deadly than any other beast on the planet.

Never before had Stevenson disclosed this malevolent aspect of himself. He hadn't seemed capable of unkindness, let alone senseless hatred. If suddenly he had revealed that he wasn't the real Lewis Stevenson but an alien life-form mimicking the chief, I would have believed him.

Gesturing with the gun, Stevenson spoke to Orson: "Get in the car, fella."

"He'll be all right out here," I said.

"Get in," he urged the dog.

Orson peered suspiciously at the open car door and whined with distrust.

"He'll wait here," I said. "He never runs off."

"I want him in the car," Stevenson said icily. "There's a leash law in this town, Snow. We never enforce it with you. We always turn our heads, pretend not to see, because of . . . because a dog is exempted if he belongs to a disabled person."

I didn't antagonize Stevenson by rejecting the term *disabled*. Anyway, I was interested less in that one word than in the six words I was sure he had almost said before catching himself: *because of who your mother was.*

"But this time," he said, "I'm not going to sit here while the damn dog trots around loose, crapping on the sidewalk, flaunting that he isn't on a leash."

Although I could have noted the contradiction

between the fact that the dog of a disabled person was exempt from the leash law and the assertion that Orson was flaunting his leashlessness, I remained silent. I couldn't win any argument with Stevenson while he was in this hostile state.

"If he won't get in the car when I tell him to," Stevenson said, "*you* make him get in."

I hesitated, searching for a credible alternative to meek cooperation. Second by second, our situation seemed more perilous. I'd felt safer than this when we had been in the blinding fog on the peninsula, stalked by the troop.

"Get the goddamn dog in the goddamn car now!" Stevenson ordered, and the venom in this command was so potent that he could have killed snails without stepping on them, sheerly with his voice.

Because his gun was in his hand, I remained at a disadvantage, but I took some thin comfort from the fact that he apparently didn't know that I was armed. For the time being, I had no choice but to cooperate.

"In the car, pal," I told Orson, trying not to sound fearful, trying not to let my hammering heart pound a tremor into my voice.

Reluctantly the dog obeyed.

Lewis Stevenson slammed the rear door and then opened the front. "Now you, Snow."

I settled into the passenger seat while Stevenson walked around the black-and-white to the driver's side and got in behind the wheel. He pulled his door shut and told me to close mine, which I had hoped to avoid doing.

Usually I don't suffer from claustrophobia in tight spaces, but no coffin could have been more cramped than this patrol car. The fog pressing at the windows was as psychologically suffocating as a dream about premature burial.

The interior of the car seemed chillier and damper than the night outside. Stevenson started the engine in order to be able to switch on the heater.

The police radio crackled, and a dispatcher's static-filled voice croaked like frog song. Stevenson clicked it off.

Orson stood on the floor in front of the backseat, forepaws on the steel grid that separated him from us, peering worriedly through that security barrier. When the chief pressed a console button with the barrel of his gun, the power locks on the rear doors engaged with a hard sound no less final than the *thunk* of a guillotine blade.

I had hoped that Stevenson would holster his pistol when he got into the car, but he kept a grip on it. He rested the weapon on his leg, the muzzle pointed at the dashboard. In the dim green light from the instrument panel, I thought I saw that his forefinger was now curled around the trigger guard rather than around the trigger itself, but this didn't lessen his advantage to any appreciable degree.

For a moment he lowered his head and closed his eyes, as though praying or gathering his thoughts.

Fog condensed on the Indian laurel, and drops of water dripped from the points of the leaves, snapping with an unrhythmical *ponk-pank-ping* against the roof and hood of the car.

Casually, quietly, I tucked both hands into my jacket pockets. I closed my right hand around the Glock.

I told myself that, because of my overripe imagination, I was exaggerating the threat. Stevenson was in a foul mood, yes, and from what I had seen behind the police station, I knew that he was not the righteous arm of justice that he had long pretended to be. But this didn't mean that he had any violent intentions. He might, indeed, want only to talk, and having said his piece, he might turn us loose unharmed.

When at last Stevenson raised his head, his eyes were servings of bitter brew in cups of bone. As his gaze flowed to me, I was again chilled by an impression of inhuman malevolence, as I had been when he'd first stepped out of the gloom beside the marina office, but this time I knew why my harp-string nerves thrummed with fear. Briefly, at a certain angle, his liquid stare rippled with a yellow luminance similar to the eyeshine that many animals exhibit at night, a cold and mysterious inner light like nothing I had ever seen before in the eyes of man or woman.

25

The electric and electrifying radiance passed through Chief Stevenson's eyes so fleetingly, as he turned to face me, that on any night before this one, I might have dismissed the phenomenon as merely a queer reflection of the instrument-panel lights. But since sundown, I had seen monkeys that were not merely monkeys, a cat that was somehow more than a cat, and I had waded through mysteries that flowed like rivers along the streets of Moonlight Bay, and I had learned to expect significance in the seemingly insignificant.

His eyes were inky again, glimmerless. The anger in his voice was now an undertow, while the surface current was gray despair and grief. "It's all changed now, all changed, and no going back."

"What's changed?"

"I'm not who I used to be. I can hardly remember what I used to be like, the kind of man I was. It's lost."

I felt he was talking as much to himself as to me, grieving aloud for this loss of self that he imagined.

"I don't have anything to lose. Everything that matters has been taken from me. I'm a dead man walking, Snow. That's all I am. Can you imagine how that feels?"

"No."

"Because even you, with your shitty life, hiding from the day, coming out only at night like some slug crawling out from under a rock — even you have reasons to live."

Although the chief of police was an elected official in our town, Lewis Stevenson didn't seem to be concerned about winning my vote.

I wanted to tell him to go copulate with himself. But there is a difference between showing no fear and begging for a bullet in the head.

As he turned his face away from me to gaze at the white sludge of fog sliding thickly across the windshield, that cold fire throbbed in his eyes again, a briefer and fainter flicker than before yet more disturbing because it could no longer be dismissed as imaginary.

Lowering his voice as though afraid of being overheard, he said, "I have terrible nightmares, terrible, full of sex and blood."

I had not known exactly what to expect from this conversation; but revelations of personal torment would not have been high on my list of probable subjects.

"They started well over a year ago," he continued. "At first they came only once a week, but then with increasing frequency. And at the start, for a while, the women in the nightmares were no one I'd ever seen in life, just pure fantasy figures. They were like those dreams you have during puberty, silken girls so ripe and eager to surrender . . . except that in these dreams, I didn't just have sex with them. . . ."

His thoughts seemed to drift with the bilious fog into darker territory.

Only his profile was presented to me, dimly lit and glistening with sour sweat, yet I glimpsed a savagery that made me hope that he would not favor me with a full-face view.

Lowering his voice further still, he said, "In these dreams, I beat them, too, punch them in the face, punch and punch and *punch* them until there's nothing left of their faces, choke them until their tongues swell out of their mouths. . . ."

As he had begun to describe his nightmares, his voice had been marked by dread. Now, in addition to this fear, an unmistakable perverse excitement rose in him, evident not only in his husky voice but also in the new tension that gripped his body.

". . . and when they cry out in pain, I love their screams, the agony on their faces, the sight of their blood. So delicious. So *exciting*. I wake shivering with pleasure, swollen with need. And sometimes . . . though I'm fifty-two, for God's sake, I climax in my sleep or just as I'm waking."

Orson dropped away from the security grille and retreated to the backseat.

I wished that I, too, could put more distance between myself and Lewis Stevenson. The cramped patrol car seemed to close around us, as though it were being squashed in one of those salvage-yard hydraulic crushers.

"Then Louisa, my wife, began to appear in the dreams . . . and my two . . . my two daughters. Janine. Kyra. They're afraid of me in these dreams, and I give them every reason to be, because their terror excites me. I'm disgusted but

. . . but also thrilled at what I'm doing with them, to them. . . ."

The anger, the despair, and the perverse excitement were still to be detected in his voice, in his slow heavy breathing, in the hunch of his shoulders — and in the subtle but ghastly reconstruction of his face, obvious even in profile. But among those powerfully conflicted desires that were at war for control of his mind, there was also a desperate hope that he could avoid plunging into the abyss of madness and savagery on the brink of which he appeared to be so precariously balanced, and this hope was clearly expressed in the anguish that now became as evident in his voice and demeanor as were his anger, despair, and depraved need.

"The nightmares got so bad, the things I did in them so sick and filthy, so repulsive, that I was afraid to go to sleep. I'd stay awake until I was exhausted, until no amount of caffeine could keep me on my feet, until even an ice cube held against the back of my neck couldn't stop my burning eyes from slipping shut. Then when I finally slept, my dreams would be more intense than ever, as though exhaustion drove me into sounder sleep, into a deeper darkness inside me where worse monsters lived. Rutting and slaughter, ceaseless and vivid, the first dreams I ever had in color, such *intense* colors, and sounds as well, their pleading voices and my pitiless replies, their screams and weeping, their convulsions and death rattles when I tore their throats out with my teeth even as I thrust into them."

Lewis Stevenson seemed to see these hideous

images where I could see only the lazily churning fog, as if the windshield before him were a screen on which his demented fantasies were projected.

"And after a while . . . I no longer fought sleep. For a time, I just endured it. Then somewhere along the way — I can't remember the precise night — the dreams ceased to hold any terror for me and became *purely* enjoyable, when previously they inspired far more guilt than pleasure. Although at first I couldn't admit it to myself, I began to look forward to bedtime. These women were so precious to me when I was awake, but when I slept . . . then . . . *then* I thrilled at the chance to debase them, humiliate them, torture them in the most imaginative ways. I no longer woke in fear from these nightmares . . . but in a strange bliss. And I'd lie in the dark, wondering how much better it might feel to commit these atrocities for real than just to dream of them. Merely *thinking* about acting out my dreams, I became aware of this awesome *power* flowing into me, and I felt so free, utterly free, as never before. In fact, it seemed as if I'd lived my life in huge iron manacles, wrapped in chains, weighted down by blocks of stone. It seemed that giving in to these desires wouldn't be criminal, would have no moral dimension whatsoever. Neither right nor wrong. Neither good nor bad. But tremendously *liberating*."

Either the air in the patrol car was growing increasingly stale or I was sickened by the thought of inhaling the same vapors that the chief exhaled: I'm not sure which. My mouth

362

filled with a metallic taste, as if I had been sucking on a penny, my stomach cramped around a lump of something as cold as arctic rock, and my heart was sheathed in ice.

I couldn't understand why Stevenson would lay bare his troubled soul to me, but I had a premonition that these confessions were only a prelude to a hateful revelation that I would wish I'd never heard. I wanted to silence him before he sprang that ultimate secret on me, but I could see he was powerfully compelled to relate these horrific fantasies — perhaps because I was the first to whom he had dared to unburden himself. There was no way to shut him up short of killing him.

"Lately," he continued in a hungry whisper that would haunt *my* sleep for the rest of my life, "these dreams all focus on my granddaughter. Brandy. She's ten. A pretty girl. A very pretty girl. So slim and pretty. The things I do to her in dreams. Ah, the things I do. You can't imagine such merciless brutality. Such exquisitely vicious *inventiveness*. And when I wake up, I'm beyond exhilaration. Transcendent. In a *rapture*. I lie in bed, beside my wife, who sleeps on without guessing what strange thoughts obsess me, who can't possibly ever know, and I *thrum* with power, with the awareness that absolute freedom is available to me any time I want to seize it. Any time. Next week. Tomorrow. *Now*."

Overhead, the silent laurel spoke as, in quick succession, at least a double score of its pointed green tongues trembled with too great a weight of condensed fog. Each loosed its single watery note, and I twitched at the sudden rataplan of fat droplets beating on the car, half surprised that what streamed down the windshield and across the hood was not blood.

In my jacket pocket, I closed my right hand more tightly around the Glock. After what Stevenson had told me, I couldn't imagine any circumstances in which he could allow me to leave this car alive. I shifted slightly in my seat, the first of several small moves that shouldn't make him suspicious but would put me in a position to shoot him through my jacket, without having to draw the pistol from the pocket.

"Last week," the chief whispered, "Kyra and Brandy came over for dinner with us, and I had trouble taking my eyes off the girl. When I looked at her, in my mind's eye she was naked, as she is in the dreams. So slim. So fragile. Vulnerable. I became aroused by her vulnerability, by her tenderness, her weakness, and had to hide my condition from Kyra and Brandy. From Louisa. I wanted . . . wanted to . . . *needed* to . . ."

His sudden sobbing startled me: Waves of grief and despair swept through him once more, as they had washed through him when first he had begun to speak. His eerie needfulness, his obscene hunger, was drowned in this tide of misery and self-hatred.

"A part of me wants to kill myself," Stevenson said, "but only the smaller part, the smaller and weaker part, the fragment that's left of the man I used to be. This predator I've become will never kill himself. Never. He's too *alive*."

His left hand, clutched into a fist, rose to his open mouth, and he crammed it between his teeth, biting so fiercely on his clenched fingers that I wouldn't have been surprised if he had drawn his own blood; he was biting and choking back the most wretched sobs that I'd ever heard.

In this new person that Lewis Stevenson seemed to have become, there was none of the calm and steady bearing that had always made him such a credible figure of authority and justice. At least not tonight, not in this bleak mood that plagued him. Raw emotion appeared always to be flowing through him, one current or another, without any intervals of tranquil water, the tide always running, battering.

My fear of him subsided to make room for pity. I almost reached out to put a comforting hand on his shoulder, but I restrained myself because I sensed that the monster I'd been listening to a moment ago had not been vanquished or even chained.

Lowering his fist from his mouth, turning his head toward me, Stevenson revealed a face wrenched by such abysmal torment, by such agony of the heart and mind, that I had to look away.

He looked away, too, facing the windshield again, and as the laurel shed the scattershot distillate of fog, his sobs faded until he could speak. "Since last week, I've been making excuses to visit Kyra, to be around Brandy." A tremor distorted his words at first, but it quickly faded, replaced by the hungry voice of the soulless troll. "And sometimes, late at night, when this damn mood hits me, when I get to feeling so cold and hollow inside that I want to scream and never stop screaming, I think the way to fill the emptiness, the only way to stop this awful gnawing in my gut . . . is to do what makes me happy in the dreams. And I'm going to do it, too. Sooner or later, I'm going to do it. Sooner than later." The tide of emotion had now turned entirely from guilt and anguish to a quiet but demonic glee. "I'm going to do it and do it. I've been looking for girls Brandy's age, just nine or ten years old, as slim as she is, as pretty as she is. It'll be safer to start with someone who has no connection to me. Safer but no less satisfying. It's going to feel good. It's going to feel *so* good, the power, the destruction, throwing off all the shackles they make you live with, tearing down the walls, being totally free, totally free at last. I'm going to bite her, this girl, when I get her alone, I'm going to bite her and bite her. In the dreams I lick their skin, and it's got a salty taste, and then I bite them, and I can feel their screams vibrating in my teeth."

Even in the dim light, I could see the manic pulse throbbing in his temples. His jaw muscles bulged, and the corner of his mouth twitched with excitement. He seemed to be more animal than human — or something less than both.

My hand clutched the Glock so ferociously that my arm ached all the way to my shoulder. Abruptly I realized that my finger had tightened on the trigger and that I was in danger of unintentionally squeezing off a shot, though I had not yet fully adjusted my position to bring the muzzle toward Stevenson. With considerable effort, I managed to ease off the trigger.

"What made you like this?" I asked.

As he turned his head to me, the transient luminosity shimmered through his eyes again. His gaze, when the eyeshine passed, was dark and murderous. "A little delivery boy," he said cryptically. "Just a little delivery boy that wouldn't die."

"Why tell me about these dreams, about what you're going to do to some girl?"

"Because, you damn freak, I've got to give you an ultimatum, and I want you to understand how serious it is, how dangerous I am, how little I have to lose and how much I'll enjoy gutting you if it comes to that. There's others who won't touch you —"

"Because of who my mother was."

"So you know that much already?"

"But I don't know what it means. Who *was* my mother in all this?"

Instead of answering, Stevenson said, "There's others who won't touch you and who don't want me to touch you, either. But if I have to, I will. You keep pushing your nose into this, and I'll smash your skull open, scoop your brain out, and toss it in the bay for fish food. Think I won't?"

"I believe you," I said sincerely.

"With the book you wrote being a best-seller, you can maybe get certain media types to listen to you. If you make any calls trying to stir up trouble, I'll get my hands on that deejay bitch first. I'll turn her inside out in more ways than one."

His reference to Sasha infuriated me, but it also scared me so effectively that I held my silence.

Now it was clear that Roosevelt Frost's warning had indeed been only advice. *This* was the threat that Roosevelt, claiming to speak for the cat, had warned me to expect.

The pallor was gone from Stevenson's face, and he was flushed with color — as though, the moment that he had decided to surrender to his psychotic desires, the cold and empty spaces within him had been filled with fire.

He reached to the dashboard controls and he switched off the car heater.

Nothing was surer than that he would abduct a little girl before the next sunset.

I found the confidence to push for answers only because I had shifted sufficiently in my seat to bring the pocketed pistol to bear on him. "Where's my father's body?"

"At Fort Wyvern. There has to be an autopsy."

"Why?"

"You don't need to know. But to put an end to this stupid little crusade of yours, I'll at least tell you it *was* cancer that killed him. Cancer of a kind. There's no one for you to get even with, the way you were talking to Angela Ferryman."

"Why should I believe you?"

"Because I could kill you as easily as give you an answer — so why would I lie?"

"What's happening in Moonlight Bay?"

The chief cracked a grin the likes of which had seldom been seen beyond the walls of an asylum. As if the prospect of catastrophe were nourishment to him, he sat up straighter and appeared to fatten as he said, "This whole town's on a roller coaster straight to Hell, and it's going to be an *incredible* ride."

"That's no answer."

"It's all you'll get."

"Who killed my mother?"

"It was an accident."

"I thought so until tonight."

His wicked grin, thin as a razor slash, became a wider wound. "All right. One more thing if you insist. Your mother was killed, like you suspect."

My heart rolled, as heavy as a stone wheel. "Who killed her?"

"She did. She killed herself. Suicide. Cranked that Saturn of hers all the way up to a hundred and ran it head-on into the bridge abutment. There wasn't any mechanical failure. The accelerator didn't stick. That was all a cover story we concocted."

"You lying son of a bitch."

Slowly, slowly, Stevenson licked his lips, as if he found his smile to be sweet. "No lie, Snow. And you know what? If I'd known two years ago what was going to happen to me, how much everything was going to change, I'd have killed your old lady myself. Killed her because of the part she played in this. I'd have taken her somewhere, cut her heart out, filled the hole in her chest with salt, burned her at a stake — whatever you do to make sure a witch is dead. Because what difference is there between what she did and a witch's curse? Science or magic? What's it matter when the result is the same? But I didn't know what was coming then, and she did, so she saved me the trouble and took a high-speed header into eighteen-inch-thick concrete."

Oily nausea welled in me, because I could hear the truth in his voice as clearly as I had ever heard it spoken. I understood only a fraction of what he was saying, yet I understood too much.

He said, "You've got nothing to avenge, freak. No one killed your folks. In fact, one way you look at it, your old lady did them both — herself and your old man."

I closed my eyes. I couldn't bear to look at him, not merely because he took pleasure in the fact of my mother's death but because he clearly believed — with reason? — that there had been justice in it.

"Now what I want you to do is crawl back under your rock and stay there, live the rest of your days there. We won't allow you to blow this wide open. If the world finds out what's happened here, if the knowledge goes beyond those at Wyvern and us, outsiders will quarantine the whole county. They'll seal it off, kill every last one of us, burn every building to the ground, poison every bird and every coyote and every house cat — and then probably nuke the place a few times for good measure. And that would all be for nothing, anyway, because the plague has already spread far beyond this place, to the other end of the continent and beyond. We're the original source, and the effects are more obvious here and compounding faster, but now it'll go on spreading without us. So none of us are ready to die just so the scum-sucking politicians can claim to have taken action."

When I opened my eyes, I discovered that he'd raised his pistol and was covering me with it. The muzzle was less than two feet from my face. Now my only advantage was that he didn't know I was armed, and it was a useful advantage only if I was the first to pull the trigger.

Although I knew it was fruitless, I tried to argue with him — perhaps because arguing was the only way that I could distract myself from what he had revealed about my mother. "Listen, for God's sake, only a few minutes ago, you said you had nothing to live for, anyway. Whatever's happened here, maybe if we get help —"

"I was in a *mood*," he interrupted sharply. "Weren't you listening to me, freak? I told you I was in a mood. A seriously ugly mood. But now I'm in a different mood. A better mood. I'm in the mood to be all that I can be, to embrace what I'm becoming instead of trying to resist it. Change, little buddy. That's what it's all about, you know. Change, glorious change, everything changing, always and forever, change. This new world coming — it's going to be *dazzling*."

"But we can't —"

"If you did solve your mystery and tell the world, you'd just be signing your own death warrant. You'd be killing your sexy little deejay bitch and all your friends. Now get out of the car, get on your bike, and haul your skinny ass home. Bury whatever ashes Sandy Kirk chooses to give you. Then if you can't live with not knowing more, if you maybe picked up too much curiosity from a cat bite, go down to the beach for a few days and catch some sun, work up a really *bitchin'* tan."

I couldn't believe he was going to let me go.

Then he said, "The dog stays with me."

"No."

He gestured with his pistol. "Out."

"He's my dog."

"He's nobody's dog. And this isn't a debate."

"What do you want with him?"

"An object lesson."

"What?"

"Gonna take him down to the municipal garage. There's a wood-chipping machine parked there, to grind up tree limbs."

"No way."

"I'll put a bullet in the mutt's head —"

"No."

"— toss him in the chipper —"

"Let him out of the car now."

"— bag the slush that comes out the other end, and drop it by your house as a reminder."

Staring at Stevenson, I knew that he was not merely a changed man. He was not the same man at all. He was someone new. Someone who had been born out of the old Lewis Stevenson, like a butterfly from a chrysalis, except that this time the process was hideously reversed: the butterfly had gone into the chrysalis, and a worm had emerged. This nightmarish metamorphosis had been underway for some time but had culminated before my eyes. The last of the former chief was gone forever, and the person whom I now challenged eye to eye was driven entirely by need and desire, uninhibited by a conscience, no longer capable of sobbing as he had sobbed only minutes ago, and as deadly as anyone or anything on the face of the earth.

If he carried a laboratory-engineered infection that could induce such a change, would it pass now to me?

My heart fought itself, throwing hard punch after hard punch.

Although I had never imagined myself capable of killing another human being, I thought I was capable of wasting this man, because I'd be saving not only Orson but also untold girls and women whom he intended to welcome into his nightmare.

With more steel in my voice than I had expected, I said, "Let the dog out of the car *now*."

Incredulous, his face splitting with that familiar rattlesnake smile, he said, "Are you forgetting who's the cop? Huh, freak? You forgetting who's got the gun?"

If I fired the Glock, I might not kill the bastard instantly, even at such close range. Even if the first round stopped his heart in an instant, he might reflexively squeeze off a round that, from a distance of less than two feet, couldn't miss me.

He broke the impasse: "All right, okay, you want to *watch* while I do it?"

Incredibly, he half turned in his seat, thrust the barrel of his pistol through one of the inch-square gaps in the steel security grille, and fired at the dog.

The blast rocked the car, and Orson squealed.

"No!" I shouted.

As Stevenson jerked his gun out of the grille, I shot him. The slug punched a hole through my leather jacket and tore open his chest. He fired wildly into the ceiling. I shot him again, in the throat this time, and the window behind him shattered when the bullet passed out of the back of his neck.

26

I sat stunned, as if spellbound by a sorcerer, unable to move, unable even to blink, my heart hanging like an iron plumb bob in my chest, numb to emotion, unable to feel the pistol in my hand, unable to see anything whatsoever, not even the dead man whom I knew to be at the other end of the car seat, briefly blinded by shock, baffled and bound by blackness, temporarily deafened either by the gunfire or perhaps by a desperate desire not to hear even the inner voice of my conscience chattering about consequences.

The only sense that I still possessed was the sense of smell. The sulfurous-carbon stink of gunfire, the metallic aroma of blood, the acidic fumes of urine because Stevenson had fouled himself in his death throes, and the fragrance of my mother's rose-scented shampoo whirled over me at once, a storm of odor and malodor. All were real except the attar of roses, which was long forgotten but now summoned from memory with all its delicate nuances. *Extreme terror gives us back the gestures of our childhood,* said Chazal. The smell of that shampoo was my way, in my terror, of reaching out to my lost mother with the hope that her hand would close reassuringly around mine.

In a rush, sight, sound, and all sensation returned to me, jolting me almost as hard as the pair of 9-millimeter bullets had jolted Lewis Stevenson. I cried out and gasped for breath.

Shaking uncontrollably, I pressed the console button that the chief had pressed earlier. The electric locks on the back doors clicked when they disengaged.

I shoved open the door at my side, clambered out of the patrol car, and yanked open the rear door, frantically calling Orson's name, wondering how I could carry him to the veterinarian's office in time to save him if he was wounded, wondering how I was going to cope if he was dead. He couldn't be dead. He was no ordinary dog: He was Orson, my dog, strange and special, companion and friend, only with me for three years but now as essential a part of my dark world as was anyone else in it.

And he *wasn't* dead. He bounded out of the car with such relief that he nearly knocked me off my feet. His piercing squeal, in the wake of the gunshot, had been an expression of terror, not pain.

I dropped to my knees on the sidewalk, let the Glock slip out of my hand, and pulled the dog into my arms. I held him fiercely, stroking his head, smoothing his black coat, reveling in his panting, in the fast thudding of his heart, in the swish of his tail, reveling even in the dampish reek of him and in the stale-cereal smell of his biscuit-scented breath.

I didn't trust myself to speak. My voice was a keystone mortared in my throat. If I managed to break it loose, an entire dam might collapse, a babble of loss and longing might pour out of me, and all the unshed tears for my father and for Angela Ferryman might come in a flood.

I do not allow myself to cry. I would rather be a bone worn to dry splinters by the teeth of sorrow than a sponge wrung ceaselessly in its hands.

Besides, even if I could have trusted myself to speak, words weren't important here. Though he was certainly a special dog, Orson wasn't going to join me in spirited conversation — at least not if and until I shed enough of my encumbering reason to ask Roosevelt Frost to teach me animal communication.

When I was able to let go of Orson, I retrieved the Glock and rose to my feet to survey the marina parking lot. The fog concealed most of the few cars and recreational vehicles owned by the handful of people who lived on their boats. No one was in sight, and the night remained silent except for the idling car engine.

Apparently the sound of gunfire had been largely contained in the patrol car and suppressed by the fog. The nearest houses were outside the commercial marina district, two blocks away. If anyone aboard the boats had been awakened, they'd evidently assumed that those four muffled explosions had been nothing more than an engine backfiring or dream doors slamming between the sleeping and the waking worlds.

I wasn't in immediate danger of being caught, but I couldn't cycle away and expect to escape blame and punishment. I had killed the chief of police, and though he had no longer been the man whom Moonlight Bay had long known and admired, though he had metamorphosed from a conscientious servant of the people into someone lacking all the essential elements of humanity, I couldn't *prove* that this hero had become the very monster that he was sworn to oppose.

Forensic evidence would convict me. Because of the identity of the victim, first-rate police-lab technicians from both county and state offices would become involved, and when they processed the patrol car, they wouldn't miss anything.

I could never tolerate imprisonment in some narrow candlelit cell. Though my life is limited by the presence of light, no walls must enclose me between the sunset and the dawn. None ever will. The darkness of closed spaces is profoundly different from the darkness of the night; the night has no boundaries, and it offers endless mysteries, discoveries, wonders, opportunities for joy. Night is the flag of freedom under which I live, and I will live free or die.

I was sickened by the prospect of getting back into the patrol car with the dead man long enough to wipe down everything on which I might have left a fingerprint. It would be a futile exercise, anyway, because I'd surely overlook one critical surface.

Besides, a fingerprint wasn't likely to be the only evidence that I'd left behind. Hairs. A thread from my jeans. A few tiny fibers from my Mystery Train cap. Orson's hairs in the backseat, the marks of his claws on the upholstery.

And no doubt other things equally or more in-criminating.

I'd been damn lucky. No one had heard the shots. But by their nature, both luck and time run out, and although my watch contained a mi-crochip rather than a mainspring, I swore that I could hear it ticking.

Orson was nervous, too, vigorously sniffing the air for monkeys or another menace.

I hurried to the back of the patrol car and thumbed the button to release the trunk lid. It was locked, as I'd feared.

Tick, tick, tick.

Steeling myself, I returned to the open front door. I inhaled deeply, held my breath, and leaned inside.

Stevenson sat twisted in his seat, head tipped back against the doorpost. His mouth shaped a silent gasp of ecstasy, and his teeth were bloody, as though he had fulfilled his dreams, had been biting young girls.

Drawn by a meager cross-draft, entering through the shattered window, a scrim of fog floated toward me, as if it were steam rising off the still-warm blood that stained the front of the dead man's uniform.

I had to lean in farther than I hoped, one knee on the passenger seat, to switch off the engine.

Stevenson's black-olive eyes were open. No life or unnatural light glimmered in them, yet I half expected to see them blink, swim into focus, and fix on me.

Before the chief's clammy gray hand could reach out to clutch at me, I plucked the keys from the ignition, backed out of the car, and finally exhaled explosively.

In the trunk I found the large first-aid kit that I expected. From it, I extracted only a thick roll of gauze bandage and a pair of scissors.

While Orson patrolled the entire perimeter of the squad car, diligently sniffing the air, I un- rolled the gauze, doubling it again and again into a collection of five-foot loops before snipping it with the scissors. I twisted the strands tightly together, then tied a knot at the upper end, an- other in the middle, and a third at the lower end. After repeating this exercise, I joined the two multiple-strand lengths together with a final knot — and had a fuse approximately ten feet long.

Tick, tick, tick.

I coiled the fuse on the sidewalk, opened the fuel port on the side of the car, and removed the tank cap. Gasoline fumes wafted out of the neck of the tank.

At the trunk again, I replaced the scissors and what remained of the roll of gauze in the first-aid kit. I closed the kit and then the trunk.

The parking lot remained deserted. The only sounds were the drops of condensation plopping from the Indian laurel onto the squad car and the soft ceaseless padding of my worried dog's paws.

Although it meant another visit with Lewis Stevenson's corpse, I returned the keys to the ignition. I'd seen a few episodes from the most popular crime series on television, and I knew how easily even fiendishly clever criminals could be tripped up by an ingenious homicide detective. Or by a best-selling female mystery novelist who solves real murders as a hobby. Or a retired spinster schoolteacher. All this between the opening credits and the final commercial for a vaginal deodorant. I intended to give them — both the professionals and the meddlesome hobbyists — damned little with which to work.

The dead man croaked at me as a bubble of gas broke deep in his esophagus.

"Rolaids," I advised him, trying unsuccessfully to cheer myself.

I didn't see any of the four expended brass cartridges on the front seat. In spite of the platoons of amateur sleuths waiting to pounce, and regardless of whether having the brass might help them identify the murder weapon, I didn't have the nerve to search the floor, especially under Stevenson's legs.

Anyway, even if I found all the cartridges, there was still a bullet buried in his chest. If it wasn't too grossly distorted, this wad of lead would feature score marks that could be matched to the singularities of the bore of my pistol, but even the prospect of prison wasn't sufficient to make me take out my penknife and perform exploratory surgery to retrieve the incriminating slug.

If I'd been a different man than I am, with the stomach for such an impromptu autopsy, I wouldn't have risked it, anyway. Assuming that Stevenson's radical personality change — his newfound thirst for violence — was but one symptom of the weird disease he carried, and assuming that this illness could be spread by contact with infected tissues and bodily fluids, this type of grisly wet work was out of the question, which is also why I had been careful not to get any of his blood on me.

When the chief had been telling me about his dreams of rape and mutilation, I'd been sickened by the thought that I was breathing the same air that he'd used and exhaled. I doubted, however, that the microbe he carried was airborne. If it were *that* highly contagious, Moonlight Bay wouldn't be on a roller-coaster ride to Hell, as he had claimed the town was: It would long ago have arrived in the sulfurous Pit.

Tick, tick, tick.

According to the gauge on the instrument panel, the fuel tank was nearly full. Good. Perfect. Earlier in the night, at Angela's, the troop had taught me how to destroy evidence and possibly conceal a murder.

The fire should be so intense that the four brass cartridges, the sheet-metal body of the car, and even portions of the heavier frame would melt. Of the late Lewis Stevenson, little more than charred bones would remain, and the soft lead slug would effectively vanish. Certainly, none of my fingerprints, hairs, or clothes fibers would survive.

Another slug had passed through the chief's neck, pulverizing the window in the driver's door. It was now lying somewhere out in the parking lot or, with luck, was at rest deep in the ivy-covered slope that rose from the far end of the lot to the higher-situated Embarcadero Way, where it would be all but impossible to find.

Incriminating powder burns marred my jacket. I should have destroyed it. I couldn't. I loved that jacket. It was cool. The bullet hole in the pocket made it even cooler.

"Gotta give the spinster schoolteachers *some* chance," I muttered as I closed the front and back doors of the car.

The brief laugh that escaped me was so humorless and bleak that it scared me almost as much as the possibility of imprisonment.

I ejected the magazine from the Glock, took one cartridge from it, which left six, and then slapped it back into the pistol.

Orson whined impatiently and picked up one end of the gauze fuse in his mouth.

"Yeah, yeah, yeah," I said — and then gave him the double take that he deserved.

The mutt might have picked it up solely because he was curious about it, as dogs tend to be curious about everything.

Funny white coil. Like a snake, snake, snake . . . but not a snake. Interesting. Interesting. Master Snow's scent on it. Might be good to eat. Almost anything might be good to eat.

Just because Orson picked up the fuse and whined impatiently didn't necessarily mean that he understood the purpose of it or the nature of the entire scheme I'd concocted. His interest — and uncanny timing — might be purely coincidental.

Yeah. Sure. Like the purely coincidental eruption of fireworks every Independence Day.

Heart pounding, expecting to be discovered at

any moment, I took the twisted gauze fuse from Orson and carefully knotted the cartridge to one end of it.

He watched intently.

"Do you approve of the knot," I asked, "or would you like to tie one of your own?"

At the open fuel port, I lowered the cartridge into the tank. The weight of it pulled the fuse all the way down into the reservoir. Like a wick, the highly absorbent gauze would immediately begin to soak up the gasoline.

Orson ran nervously in a circle: *Hurry, hurry. Hurry quick. Quick, quick, quick, Master Snow.*

I left almost five feet of fuse out of the tank. It hung along the side of the patrol car and trailed onto the sidewalk.

After fetching my bicycle from where I'd leaned it against the trunk of the laurel, I stooped and ignited the end of the fuse with my butane lighter. Although the exposed length of gauze was not gasoline-soaked, it burned faster than I expected. Too fast.

I climbed onto my bike and pedaled as if all of Hell's lawyers and a few demons of this earth were baying at my heels, which they probably were. With Orson sprinting at my side, I shot across the parking lot to the ramped exit drive, onto Embarcadero Way, which was deserted, and then south past the shuttered restaurants and shops that lined the bay front.

The explosion came too soon, a solid *whump* that wasn't half as loud as I'd anticipated. Around and even ahead of me, orange light bloomed; the initial flare of the blast was refracted a considerable distance by the fog.

Recklessly, I squeezed the hand brake, slid through a hundred-and-eighty-degree turn, came to a halt with one foot on the blacktop, and looked back.

Little could be seen, no details: a core of hard yellow-white light surrounded by orange plumes, all softened by the deep, eddying mist.

The worst thing I saw wasn't in the night but inside my head: Lewis Stevenson's face bubbling, smoking, streaming hot clear grease like bacon in a frying pan.

"Dear God," I said in a voice that was so raspy and tremulous that I didn't recognize it.

Nevertheless, I could have done nothing else but light that fuse. Although the cops would know Stevenson had been killed, evidence of how it was done — and by whom — would now be obliterated.

I made the drive chain sing, leading my accomplice dog away from the harbor, through a spiraling maze of streets and alleyways, deeper into the murky, nautilus heart of Moonlight Bay. Even with the heavy Glock in one pocket, my unzipped leather jacket flapped as though it were a cape, and I fled unseen, avoiding light for more than one reason now, a shadow flowing liquidly through shadows, as though I were the fabled Phantom, escaped from the labyrinth underneath the opera house, now on wheels and hell-bent on terrorizing the world above ground.

Being able to entertain such a flamboyantly romantic image of myself in the immediate aftermath of murder doesn't speak well of me. In my defense, I can only say that by recasting these events as a grand adventure, with me in a dashing role, I was desperately trying to quell my fear and, more desperately still, struggling to suppress the memories of the shooting. I also needed to suppress the ghastly images of the burning body that my active imagination generated like an endless series of pop-up spooks leaping from the black walls of a funhouse.

Anyway, this shaky effort to romanticize the event lasted only until I reached the alleyway behind the Grand Theater, half a block south of Ocean Avenue, where a grime-encrusted security lamp made the fog appear to be brown and polluted. There, I swung off my bike, let it clatter to the pavement, leaned into a Dumpster, and brought up what little I had not digested of my midnight dinner with Bobby Halloway.

I had murdered a man.

Unquestionably, the victim had deserved to die. And sooner or later, relying on one excuse or another, Lewis Stevenson would have killed me, regardless of his coconspirators' inclination to grant special dispensation to me; arguably, I acted in self-defense. And to save Orson's life.

Nevertheless, I'd killed a human being; even these qualifying circumstances didn't alter the moral essence of the act. His vacant eyes, black with death, haunted me. His mouth, open in a silent scream, his bloodied teeth. Sights are readily recalled from memory; recollections of sounds and tastes and tactile sensations are far less easily evoked; and it is virtually impossible to experience a scent merely by willing it to rise from memory. Yet earlier I'd recalled the fragrance of my mother's shampoo, and now the metallic odor of Stevenson's fresh blood lingered so pungently that it kept me hanging on to the Dumpster as if I were at the railing of a yawing ship.

In fact, I was shaken not solely by having killed him but by having destroyed the corpse and all evidence with brisk efficiency and self-possession. Apparently I had a talent for the criminal life. I felt as though some of the darkness in which I'd lived for twenty-eight years had seeped into me and had coalesced in a previously unknown chamber of my heart.

Purged but feeling no better for it, I boarded the bicycle again and led Orson through a series of byways to Caldecott's Shell at the corner of San Rafael Avenue and Palm Street. The service station was closed. The only light inside came from a blue-neon wall clock in the sales office, and the only light outside was at the soft-drink vending machine.

I bought a can of Pepsi to cleanse the sour taste from my mouth. At the pump island, I opened the water faucet partway and waited while Orson drank his fill.

"What an awesomely lucky dog you are to have such a thoughtful master," I said. "Always tending to your thirst, your hunger, your grooming. Always ready to kill anyone who lifts a finger against you."

The searching look that he turned on me was disconcerting even in the gloom. Then he licked my hand.

"Gratitude acknowledged," I said.

He lapped at the running water again, finished, and shook his dripping snout.

Shutting off the faucet, I said, "Where *did* Mom get you?"

He met my eyes again.

"What secret was my mother keeping?"

His gaze was unwavering. He knew the answers to my questions. He just wasn't talking.

27

I suppose God really might be loafing around in St. Bernadette's Church, playing air guitar with a companion band of angels, or games of mental chess. He might be there in a dimension that we can't quite see, drawing blueprints for new universes in which such problems as hatred and ignorance and cancer and athlete's-foot fungus will have been eliminated in the planning stage. He might be drifting high above the polished-oak pews, as if in a swimming pool filled with clouds of spicy incense and humble prayer instead of water, silently bumping into the columns and the corners of the cathedral ceiling as He dreamily meditates, waiting for parishioners in need to come to Him with problems to be solved.

This night, however, I felt sure God was keeping His distance from the rectory adjoining the church, which gave me the creeps when I cycled past it. The architecture of the two-story stone house — like that of the church itself — was modified Norman, with enough of the French edge abraded to make it fit more comfortably in the softer climate of California. The overlapping black-slate tiles of the steep roof, wet with fog, were as armor-thick as the scales on the beetled brow of a dragon, and beyond the blank black eyes of window glass — including an oculus on each side of the front door — lay a soulless realm. The rectory had never appeared forbidding to me before, and I knew that I now viewed it with uneasiness only because of the scene I had witnessed between Jesse Pinn and Father Tom in the church basement.

I pedaled past both the rectory and the church, into the cemetery, under the oaks, and among the graves. Noah Joseph James, who'd had ninety-six years from birthday to deathbed, was just as silent as ever when I greeted him and parked my bike against his headstone.

I unclipped the cell phone from my belt and keyed in the number for the unlisted back line that went directly to the broadcasting booth at KBAY. I heard four rings before Sasha picked up, although no tone would have sounded in the booth; she would have been alerted to the incoming call solely by a flashing blue light on the wall that she faced when at her microphone. She answered it by pushing a hold button, and while I waited, I could hear her program over the phone line.

Orson began to sniff out squirrels again.

Shapes of fog drifted like lost spirits among the gravestones.

I listened to Sasha run a pair of twenty-second "doughnut" spots — which are not ads for doughnuts but commercials with recorded beginnings and endings that leave a hole for live material in the center. She followed these with some way smooth historical patter about Elton John, and then brought up "Japanese Hands" with a silky six-bar talk-over. Evidently the Chris Isaak festival had ended.

Taking me off hold, she said, "I'm doing back-to-back tracks, so you've got just over five minutes, baby."

"How'd you know it was me?"

"Only a handful of people have this number, and most of them are asleep at this hour. Besides, when it comes to you, I've got great intuition. The moment I saw the phone light flash, my nether parts started to tingle."

"Your nether parts?"

"My female nether parts. Can't wait to see you, Snowman."

"Seeing would be a good start. Listen, who else is working tonight?"

"Doogie Sassman." He was her production engineer, operating the board.

"Just the two of you there alone?" I worried.

"You're jealous all of a sudden? How sweet. But you don't have to worry. I don't measure up to Doogie's standards."

When Doogie wasn't parked in a command chair at an audio control panel, he spent most of his time with his massive legs wrapped around a Harley-Davidson. He was five feet eleven and weighed three hundred pounds. His wealth of untamed blond hair and his naturally wavy beard were so lush and silky that you had to resist the urge to pet him, and the colorful mural that covered virtually every inch of his arms and torso had put some tattooist's child through college. Yet Sasha wasn't entirely joking when she said that she didn't measure up to Doogie's standards. With the opposite sex, he had more bearish charm than Pooh to the tenth power. Since

I'd met him six years ago, each of the four women with whom he'd enjoyed a relationship had been stunning enough to attend the Academy Awards in blue jeans and a flannel shirt, sans makeup, and outshine every dazzling starlet at the ceremony.

Bobby says that Doogie Sassman (pick one) has sold his soul to the devil, is the secret master of the universe, has the most astonishingly proportioned genitalia in the history of the planet, or produces sexual pheromones that are more powerful than Earth's gravity.

I was glad Doogie was working the night, because I had no doubt that he was a lot tougher than any of the other engineers at KBAY.

"But I thought there'd be someone besides the two of you," I said.

Sasha knew I wasn't jealous of Doogie, and now she heard the concern in my voice. "You know how things have tightened up here since Fort Wyvern closed and we lost the military audience at night. We're barely making money on this airshift even with a skeleton staff. What's wrong, Chris?"

"You keep the station doors locked, don't you?"

"Yeah. All us late-night jocks and jockettes are required to watch *Play Misty for Me* and take it to heart."

"Even though it'll be after dawn when you leave, promise me you'll have Doogie or someone from the morning shift walk you out to your Explorer."

"Who's on the loose — Dracula?"

"Promise me."

"Chris, what the hell —"

"I'll tell you later. Just promise me," I insisted.

She sighed. "All right. But are you in some kind of trouble? Are you —"

"I'm all right, Sasha. Really. Don't worry. Just, damn it, promise me."

"I did promise —"

"You didn't use the word."

"Jesus. Okay, okay. I *promise.* Cross my heart and hope to die. But now I'm expecting a great story later, at least as spooky as the ones I used to hear around Girl Scout campfires. You'll be waiting for me at home?"

"Will you wear your old Girl Scout uniform?"

"The only part of it I could duplicate are the kneesocks."

"That's enough."

"You're stirred by that picture, huh?"

"Vibrating."

"You're a bad man, Christopher Snow."

"Yeah, I'm a killer."

"See you in a little while, killer."

We disconnected, and I clipped the cell phone to my belt once more.

For a moment I listened to the silent cemetery. Not a single nightingale performed, and even the chimney swifts had gone to bed. No doubt the worms were awake and laboring, but they always conduct their solemn work in a respectful hush.

To Orson, I said, "I find myself in need of some spiritual guidance. Let's pay a visit to Father Tom."

As I crossed the cemetery on foot and went behind the church, I drew the Glock from my jacket pocket. In a town where the chief of police dreamed of beating and torturing little girls and where undertakers carried handguns, I could not assume that the priest would be armed solely with the word of God.

The rectory had appeared dark from the street, but from the backyard I saw two lighted windows in a rear room on the second floor.

After the scene that I'd witnessed in the basement of the church, from the cover of the crèche, I wasn't surprised that the rector of St. Bernadette's was unable to sleep. Although it was nearly three o'clock in the morning, four hours since Jesse Pinn's visit, Father Tom was still reluctant to turn out the light.

"Make like a cat," I whispered to Orson.

We crept up a set of stone steps and then, as silently as possible, across the wooden floor of the back porch.

I tried the door, but it was locked. I had been hoping that a man of God would consider it a point of faith to trust in his Maker rather than in a dead bolt.

I didn't intend to knock or to go around to the front and ring the bell. With murder already under my belt, it seemed foolish to have qualms about engaging in criminal trespass. I hoped to avoid breaking and entering, however, because the sound of shattering glass would alert the priest.

Four double-hung windows faced onto the

porch. I tried them one by one, and the third was unlocked. I had to tuck the Glock in my jacket pocket again, because the wood of the window was swollen with moisture and moved stiffly in the frame; I needed both hands to raise the lower sash, pressing first on the horizontal muntin and then hooking my fingers under the bottom rail. It slid upward with sufficient rasping and squeaking to lend atmosphere to an entire Wes Craven film.

Orson chuffed as though scornful of my skills as a lawbreaker. Everyone's a critic.

I waited until I was confident that the noise had not been heard upstairs, and I slipped through the open window into a room as black as the interior of a witch's purse.

"Come on, pal," I whispered, for I didn't intend to leave him outside alone, without a gun of his own.

Orson sprang inside, and I slid the window shut as quietly as possible. I locked it, too. Although I didn't believe that we were currently being watched by members of the troop or by anyone else, I didn't want to make it easy for someone or something to follow us into the rectory.

A quick sweep with my penlight revealed a dining room. Two doors — one to my right, the other in the wall opposite the windows — led from the room.

Switching off the penlight, drawing the Glock again, I tried the nearer door, to the right. Beyond lay the kitchen. The radiant numerals of digital clocks on the two ovens and the microwave cast just enough light to enable me to cross to the pivot-hinged hall door without walking into the refrigerator or the cooking island.

The hallway led past dark rooms to a foyer lit only by a single small candle. On a three-legged, half-moon table against one wall was a shrine to the Holy Mother. A votive candle in a ruby-red glass fluttered fitfully in the half-inch of wax that remained.

In this inconstant pulse of light, the face on the porcelain figure of Mary was a portrait less of beatific grace than of sorrow. She appeared to know that the resident of the rectory was, these days, more a captive of fear than a captain of faith.

With Orson at my side, I climbed the two broad flights of stairs to the second floor. The felon freak and his four-legged familiar.

The upstairs hall was in the shape of an L, with the stairhead at the junction. The length to the left was dark. At the end of the hall directly ahead of me, a ladder had been unfolded from a ceiling trapdoor; a lamp must have been lit in a far corner of the attic, but only a ghostly glow stepped down the ladder treads.

Stronger light came from an open door on the right. I eased along the hall to the threshold, cautiously looked inside, and found Father Tom's starkly furnished bedroom, where a crucifix hung above the simple dark-pine bed. The priest was not here; he was evidently in the attic. The bedspread had been removed and the covers neatly folded back, but the sheets had not been disturbed.

Both nightstand lamps were lit, which made that area too bright for me, but I was more interested in the other end of the room, where a writing desk stood against the wall. Under a bronze desk lamp with a green glass shade lay an open book and a pen. The book appeared to be a journal or diary.

Behind me, Orson growled softly.

I turned and saw that he was at the bottom of the ladder, gazing up suspiciously at the dimly lighted attic beyond the open trapdoor. When he looked at me, I raised a finger to my lips, softly hushed him, and then motioned him to my side.

Instead of climbing like a circus dog to the top of the ladder, he came to me. For the time being, anyway, he still seemed to be enjoying the novelty of routine obedience.

I was certain that Father Tom would make enough noise descending from the attic to alert me long before his arrival. Nevertheless, I stationed Orson immediately inside the bedroom door, with a clear view of the ladder.

Averting my face from the light around the bed, crossing the room toward the writing desk, I glanced through the open door of the adjoining bathroom. No one was in there.

On the desk, in addition to the journal, was a decanter of what appeared to be Scotch. Beside the decanter was a double-shot glass more than half full of the golden liquid. The priest had been sipping it neat, no ice. Or maybe not just sipping.

I picked up the journal. Father Tom's handwriting was as tight and precise as machine-generated script. I stepped into the deepest shadows in the room, because my dark-adapted eyes needed little light by which to read, and I scanned the last paragraph on the page, which referred to his sister. He had broken off in mid sentence:

When the end comes, I might not be able to save myself. I know that I will not be able to save Laura, because already she is not fundamentally who she was. She is already gone. Little more than her physical shell remains — and perhaps even that is changed. Either God has somehow taken her soul home to His bosom while leaving her body inhabited by the entity into which she has evolved — or He has abandoned her. And will therefore abandon us all. I believe in the mercy of Christ. I believe in the mercy of Christ. I believe because I have nothing else to live for. And if I believe, then I must live by my faith and save whom I can. If I can't save myself or even Laura, I can at least rescue these pitiful creatures who come to me to be freed from torment and control. Jesse Pinn or those who give him orders may kill Laura, but she is not Laura anymore, Laura is long lost, and I can't let their threats stop my work. They may kill me, but until they do

Orson stood alertly at the open door, watching the hall.

I turned to the first page of the journal and

saw that the initial entry was dated January 1 of this year:

Laura has been held for more than nine months now, and I've given up all hope that I will ever see her again. And if I were given the chance to see her again, I might refuse, God forgive me, because I would be too afraid of facing what she might have become. Every night, I petition the Holy Mother to intercede with her Son to take Laura from the suffering of this world.

For a full understanding of his sister's situation and condition, I would have to find the previous volume or volumes of this journal, but I had no time to search for them.

Something thumped in the attic. I froze, staring at the ceiling, listening. At the doorway, Orson pricked one ear.

When half a minute passed without another sound, I turned my attention once more to the journal. With a sense of time running out, I searched hurriedly through the book, reading at random.

Much of the contents concerned the priest's theological doubts and agonies. He struggled daily to remind himself — to convince himself, to plead with himself to remember — that his faith had long sustained him and that he would be utterly lost if he could not hold fast to his faith in this crisis. These sections were grim and might have been fascinating reading for the portrait of a tortured psyche that they provided, but they revealed nothing about the facts of the Wyvern conspiracy that had infected Moonlight Bay. Consequently, I skimmed through them.

I found one page and then a few more on which Father Tom's neat handwriting deteriorated into a loose scrawl. These passages were incoherent, ranting and paranoid, and I assumed that they had been composed after he'd poured down enough Scotch to start speaking with a burr.

More disturbing was an entry dated February 5 — three pages on which the elegant penmanship was obsessively precise:

I believe in the mercy of Christ. I believe in the mercy of Christ. I believe in the mercy of Christ. I believe in the mercy of Christ. I believe in the mercy of Christ. . . .

Those seven words were repeated line after line, nearly two hundred times. Not a single one appeared to have been hastily penned; each sentence was so meticulously inscribed on the page that a rubber stamp and an ink pad could hardly have produced more uniform results. Scanning this entry, I could feel the desperation and terror that the priest had felt when he'd written it, as if his turbulent emotions had been infused into the paper with the ink, to radiate from it evermore.

I believe in the mercy of Christ.

I wondered what incident on the fifth of February had brought Father Tom to the edge of an emotional and spiritual abyss. What had he seen? I wondered if perhaps he had written this impassioned but despairing incantation after experiencing a nightmare similar to the dreams of rape and mutilation that had troubled — and ultimately delighted — Lewis Stevenson.

Continuing to page through the entries, I found an interesting observation dated the eleventh of February. It was buried in a long, tortured passage in which the priest argued with himself over the existence and nature of God, playing both skeptic and believer, and I would have skimmed over it if my eye had not been caught by the word *troop*.

> *This new troop, to whose freedom I have committed myself, gives me hope precisely because it is the antithesis of the original troop. There is no evil in these newest creatures, no thirst for violence, no rage —*

A forlorn cry from the attic called my attention away from the journal. This was a wordless wail of fear and pain, so eerie *and* so pathetic that dread reverberated like a gong note through my mind simultaneously with a chord of sympathy. The voice sounded like that of a child, perhaps three or four years old, lost and afraid and in extreme distress.

Orson was so affected by the cry that he quickly padded out of the bedroom, into the hallway.

The priest's journal was slightly too large to fit into one of my jacket pockets. I tucked it under the waistband of my jeans, against the small of my back.

When I followed the dog into the hall, I found him at the foot of the folding ladder again, gazing up at the pleated shadows and soft light that hung in the rectory attic. He turned his expressive eyes on me, and I knew that if he could speak, he would say, *We've got to do something.*

This peculiar dog not only harbors a fleet of mysteries, not only exhibits greater cleverness than any dog should possess, but often seems to have a well-defined sense of moral responsibility. Before the events of which I write herein, I had sometimes half-seriously wondered if reincarnation might be more than superstition, because I could envision Orson as a committed teacher or dedicated policeman or even as a wise little nun in a former life, now reborn in a downsized body, furry, with tail.

Of course, ponderings of this nature have long qualified me as a candidate for the Pia Klick Award for exceptional achievement in the field of airheaded speculation. Ironically, Orson's true origins as I would soon come to understand them, although not supernatural, would prove to be more astonishing than any scenario that I and Pia Klick, in fevered collaboration, could have imagined.

Now the cry issued from above a second time, and Orson was so affected that he let out a whine of distress too thin to carry into the attic. Even more than the first time, the wailing voice seemed to be that of a small child.

It was followed by another voice, too low for

the words to be distinct. Though I was sure that this must be Father Tom, I couldn't hear his tone well enough to tell if it was consoling or threatening.

28

If I'd trusted to instinct, I would have fled the rectory right then, gone directly home, brewed a pot of tea, spread lemon marmalade on a scone, popped a Jackie Chan movie on the TV, and spent the next couple of hours on the sofa, with an afghan over my lap and with my curiosity on hold.

Instead, because pride prevented me from admitting that I had a sense of moral responsibility less well-developed than that of my dog, I signaled Orson to stand aside and wait. Then I went up the ladder with the 9-millimeter Glock in my right hand and Father Tom's stolen journal riding uncomfortably against the small of my back.

Like a raven frantically beating its wings against a cage, dark images from Lewis Stevenson's descriptions of his sick dreams flapped through my mind. The chief had fantasized about girls as young as his granddaughter, but the cry that I'd just heard sounded as though it had come from a child much younger than ten. If the rector of St. Bernadette's was in the grip of the same dementia that had afflicted Stevenson, however, I had no reason to expect him to limit his prey to those ten or older.

Near the top of the ladder, one hand on the flimsy, collapsible railing, I turned my head to peer down along my flank and saw Orson staring up from the hallway. As instructed, he had not tried to climb after me.

He'd been solemnly obedient for the better part of an hour, having commented on my commands with not a single sarcastic chuff or rolling of the eyes. This restraint marked a personal best for him. In fact, it was a personal best by a margin of at least half an hour, an Olympic-caliber performance.

Expecting to take a kick in the head from an ecclesiastical boot, I climbed higher nonetheless, into the attic. Evidently I'd been sufficiently stealthy to avoid drawing Father Tom's attention, because he wasn't waiting to kick my sinus bones deep into my frontal lobe.

The trapdoor lay at the center of a small clear space that was surrounded, as far as I could discern, by a maze of cardboard cartons of various sizes, old furniture, and other objects that I couldn't identify — all stacked to a height of about six feet. The bare bulb directly over the trap was not lit, and the only light came from off to the left, in the southeast corner, toward the front of the house.

I eased into the vast attic in a crouch, though I could have stood erect. The steeply pitched Norman roof provided plenty of clearance between my head and the rafters. Although I wasn't concerned about walking face-first into a roof beam, I still believed there was a risk of being clubbed on the skull or shot between the eyes or stabbed in the heart by a crazed cleric, and I was intent on keeping as low a profile as possible. If I could have slithered on my belly like a snake, I wouldn't have been all the way up in a crouch.

The humid air smelled like time itself distilled and bottled: dust, the staleness of old cardboard, a lingering woody fragrance from the rough-sawn rafters, mildew spooring, and the faint stink of some small dead creature, perhaps a bird or mouse, festering in a lightless corner.

To the left of the trapdoor were two entrances into the maze, one approximately five feet wide, and the other no wider than three feet. Assuming that the roomier passage provided the most direct route across the cluttered attic and, therefore, was the one that the priest regularly used to go to and from his captive — if indeed there was a captive — I slipped quietly into the narrower aisle. I preferred to take Father Tom by surprise rather than encounter him accidentally at some turning in this labyrinth.

To both sides of me were boxes, some tied with twine, others festooned with peeling lengths of shipping tape that brushed like insectile feelers against my face. I moved slowly, feeling my way with one hand, because the shadows were confounding, and I dared not bump into anything and set off a clatter.

I reached a T intersection but didn't immediately step into it. I stood at the brink, listening for a moment, holding my breath, but heard nothing.

Cautiously I leaned out of the first passageway, looking right and left along this new corridor in the maze, which was also only three feet wide. To the left, the lamplight in the southeast corner was slightly brighter than before. To the right lay deep sable gloom that wouldn't yield its secrets even to my night-loving eyes, and I had the impression that a hostile inhabitant of this darkness was within arm's length, watching and set to spring.

Assuring myself that all trolls lived under bridges, that wicked gnomes lived in caves, that gremlins established housekeeping only in machinery, and that goblins — being demons — wouldn't dare to take up residence in a rectory, I stepped into the new passageway and turned left, putting my back to the impenetrable dark.

At once a squeal arose, so chilling that I swung around and thrust the pistol toward the blackness, certain that trolls, wicked gnomes, gremlins, goblins, ghosts, zombies, and several psychotic mutant altar boys were descending on me. Fortunately I didn't squeeze the trigger, because this transient madness passed, and I realized that the cry had arisen from the same direction as before: from the lighted area in the southeast corner.

This third wail, which had covered the noise that I'd made when turning to confront the imaginary horde, was from the same source as the first two, but here in the attic, it sounded different from how it had sounded when I'd been down in the second-floor hallway. For one thing, it didn't seem as much like the voice of a suffering child as it had earlier. More disconcerting: The weirdness factor was a lot higher, way off the top of the chart, as if several bars of theremin music had issued from a human throat.

I considered retracing my path to the ladder, but I was in too deep to turn back now. There was still a chance, however slim, that I was hearing a child in jeopardy.

Besides, if I retreated, my dog would know that I had haired out. He was one of my three closest friends in a world where only friends and family matter, and as I no longer had any family, I put enormous value on his high opinion of me.

The boxes on my left gave way to stacked wicker lawn chairs, a jumbled collection of thatched and lacquered baskets made of wicker and reed, a battered dresser with an oval mirror so grimy that I cast not even a shadowy reflection in it, unguessable items concealed by drop cloths, and then more boxes.

I turned a corner, and now I could hear Father Tom's voice. He was speaking softly, soothingly, but I couldn't make out a word of what he said.

I walked into a cobweb barrier, flinching as it clung to my face and brushed like phantom lips against my mouth. With my left hand I wiped the tattered strands from my cheeks and from the bill of my cap. The gossamer had a bitter-mushroom taste; grimacing, I tried to spit it out without making a sound.

Because I was hoping again for revelations, I was compelled to follow the priest's voice as irresistibly as I might have followed the music of a piper in Hamelin. All the while, I was struggling to repress the desire to sneeze, which was spawned by dust with a scent so musty that it must have come from the previous century.

After one more turn, I was in a last short

length of passageway. About six feet beyond the end of this narrow corridor of boxes was the steeply pitched underside of the roof at the east flank — the front — of the building. The rafters, braces, collar beams, and the underside of the roof sheathing, to which the slate was attached, were revealed by muddy-yellow light issuing from a source out of sight to the right.

Creeping to the end of the passage, I was acutely aware of the faint creaking of the floorboards under me. It was no louder or more suspicious than the ordinary settling noises in this high redoubt, but it was nonetheless potentially betraying.

Father Tom's voice grew clearer, although I could catch only one word in five or six.

Another voice rose, higher-pitched and tremulous. It resembled the voice of a very young child — and yet was nothing as ordinary as that. Not as musical as the speech of a child. Not half as innocent. I couldn't make out what, if anything, it was saying. The longer I listened, the eerier it became, until it made me pause — though I didn't dare pause for long.

My aisle terminated in a perimeter passage that extended along the eastern flank of the attic maze. I risked a peek into this long straight run.

To the left was darkness, but to the right was the southeast corner of the building, where I had expected to find the source of the light and the priest with his wailing captive. Instead, the lamp remained out of sight to the right of the corner, around one more turn, along the south wall.

I followed this six-foot-wide perimeter passage, half crouched by necessity now, for the wall to my left was actually the steeply sloped underside of the roof. To my right, I passed the dark mouth of another passageway between piles of boxes and old furniture — and then halted within two steps of the corner, with only the last wall of stored goods between me and the lamp.

Abruptly a squirming shadow leaped across the rafters and roof sheathing that formed the wall ahead of me: a fierce spiky thrashing of jagged limbs with a bulbous swelling at the center, so alien that I nearly shouted in alarm. I found myself holding the Glock in both hands.

Then I realized that the apparition before me was the distorted shadow of a spider suspended on a single silken thread. It must have been dangling so close to the source of the light that its image was projected, greatly enlarged, across the surfaces in front of me.

For a ruthless killer, I was far too jumpy. Maybe the caffeine-laden Pepsi, which I'd drunk to sweeten my vomit-soured breath, was to blame. Next time I killed someone and threw up, I'd have to use a caffeine-free beverage and lace it with Valium, in order to avoid tarnishing my image as an emotionless, efficient homicide machine.

Cool with the spider now, I also realized that I could at last hear the priest's voice clearly enough to understand his every word: ". . . hurts, yes, of course, it hurts very much. But now I've cut the transponder out of you, cut it out and crushed it, and they can't follow you anymore."

I flashed back to the memory of Jesse Pinn stalking through the cemetery earlier in the night, holding the peculiar instrument in his hand, listening to faint electronic tones and reading data on a small, glowing green screen. He'd evidently been tracking the signal from a surgically implanted transponder in this creature. A monkey, was it? Yet not a monkey?

"The incision wasn't very deep," the priest continued. "The transponder was just under the subcutaneous fat. I've sterilized the wound and sewn it up." He sighed. "I wish I knew how much you understand me, if at all."

In Father Tom's journal, he had referred to the members of a *new* troop that was less hostile and less violent than the first, and he had written that he was committed to their liberation. Why there should be a new troop, as opposed to an old one, or why they should be set loose in the world with transponders under their skin — even *how* these smarter monkeys of either troop could have come into existence in the first place — I couldn't fathom. But it was clear that the priest styled himself as a modern-day abolitionist fighting for the rights of the oppressed and that this rectory was a key stop on an underground railroad to freedom.

When he had confronted Father Tom in the church basement, Pinn must have believed that this current fugitive had already received superficial surgery and moved on, and that his hand-held tracker was picking up the signal from the transponder no longer embedded in the creature it was meant to identify. Instead, the fugitive was recuperating here in the attic.

The priest's mysterious visitor mewled softly, as if in pain, and the cleric replied with a sympathetic patter perilously close to baby talk.

Taking courage from the memory of how meekly the priest had responded to the undertaker, I crossed the remaining couple of feet to the final wall of boxes. I stood with my back to the end of the row, knees bent only slightly to accommodate the slope of the roof. From here, to see the priest and the creature with him, I needed only to lean to my right, turn my head, and look into the perimeter aisle along the south flank of the attic where the light and the voices originated.

I hesitated to reveal my presence only because I recalled some of the odder entries in the priest's diary: the ranting and paranoid passages that bordered on incoherence, the two hundred repetitions of *I believe in the mercy of Christ.* Perhaps he wasn't always as meek as he had been with Jesse Pinn.

Overlaying the odors of mildew and dust and old cardboard was a new medicinal scent composed of rubbing alcohol, iodine, and an astringent antiseptic cleanser.

Somewhere in the next aisle, the fat spider reeled itself up its filament, away from the lamplight, and the magnified arachnid shadow rapidly dwindled across the slanted ceiling, shrinking into a black dot and finally vanishing.

Father Tom spoke reassuringly to his patient: "I have antibiotic powder, capsules of various penicillin derivatives, but no effective painkiller.

I wish I did. But this world is about suffering, isn't it? This vale of tears. You'll be all right. You'll be just fine. I promise. God will look after you through me."

Whether the rector of St. Bernadette's was a saint or villain, one of the few rational people left in Moonlight Bay or way insane, I couldn't judge. I didn't have enough facts, didn't understand the context of his actions.

I was certain of only one thing: Even if Father Tom might be rational and doing the right thing, his head nevertheless contained enough loose wiring to make it unwise to let him hold the baby during a baptism.

"I've had some very basic medical training," the priest told his patient, "because for three years after seminary, I was called to a mission in Uganda."

I thought I heard the patient: a muttering that reminded me — but not quite — of the low cooing of pigeons blended with the more guttural purr of a cat.

"I'm sure you'll be all right," Father Tom continued. "But you really must stay here a few days so I can administer the antibiotics and monitor the healing of the wound. Do you understand me?" With a note of frustration and despair: "Do you understand me at all?"

As I was about to lean to the right and peer around the wall of boxes, the Other replied to the priest. *The Other:* That was how I thought of the fugitive when I heard it speaking from such close range, because this was a voice that I was not able to imagine as being either that of

413

a child or a monkey, or of anything else in *God's Big Book of Creation.*

I froze. My finger tightened on the trigger.

Certainly it sounded partly like a young child, a little girl, and partly like a monkey. It sounded partly like a lot of things, in fact, as though a highly creative Hollywood sound technician had been playing with a library of human and animal voices, mixing them through an audio console until he'd created the ultimate voice for an extraterrestrial.

The most affecting thing about the Other's speech was not the tonal range of it, not the pattern of inflections, and not even the earnestness and the emotion that clearly shaped it. Instead, what most jolted me was the perception that it had *meaning.* I was not listening merely to a babble of animal noises. This was not English, of course, not a word of it; and although I'm not multilingual, I'm certain it wasn't any foreign tongue, either, for it was not complex enough to be a true language. It was, however, a fluent series of exotic sounds crudely composed like words, a powerful but primitive *attempt* at language, with a small polysyllabic vocabulary, marked by urgent rhythms.

The Other seemed pathetically desperate to communicate. As I listened, I was surprised to find myself emotionally affected by the longing, loneliness, and anguish in its voice. These were not qualities that I imagined. They were as real as the boards beneath my feet, the stacked boxes against my back, and the heavy beating of my heart.

When the Other and the priest both fell silent, I wasn't able to look around the corner. I suspected that whatever the priest's visitor might look like, it would not pass for a real monkey, as did those members of the original troop that had been tormenting Bobby and that Orson and I had encountered on the southern horn of the bay. If it resembled a rhesus at all, the differences would be greater and surely more numerous than the baleful dark-yellow color of the other monkeys' eyes.

If I was afraid of what I might see, my fear had nothing whatsoever to do with the possible hideousness of this laboratory-born Other. My chest was so tight with emotion that I couldn't draw deep breaths, and my throat was so thick that I could swallow only with effort. What I feared was meeting the gaze of this entity and seeing my own isolation in its eyes, my own yearning to be normal, which I'd spent twenty-eight years denying with enough success to be happy with my fate. But my happiness, like everyone's, is fragile. I had heard a terrible longing in this creature's voice, and I felt that it was akin to the sharp longing around which I had ages ago formed a pearl of indifference and quiet resignation; I was afraid that if I met the Other's eyes, some resonance between us would shatter that pearl and leave me vulnerable once more.

I was shaking.

This is also why I cannot, dare not, *will* not express my pain or my grief when life wounds me or takes from me someone I love. Grief too easily leads to despair. In the fertile ground of despair, self-pity can sprout and thrive. I can't begin to indulge in self-pity, because by enumerating and dwelling upon my limitations, I will be digging a hole so deep that I'll never again be able to crawl out of it. I've got to be something of a cold bastard to survive, live with a chinkless shell around my heart at least when it comes to grieving for the dead. I'm able to express my love for the living, to embrace my friends without reservation, to give my heart without concern for how it might be abused. But on the day that my father dies, I must make jokes about death, about crematoriums, about life, about every damn thing, because I can't risk — *won't* risk — descending from grief to despair to self-pity and, finally, to the pit of inescapable rage and loneliness and self-hatred that is freakdom. I can't love the dead too much. No matter how desperately I want to remember them and hold them dear, I have to let them go — and quickly. I have to push them out of my heart even as they are cooling in their deathbeds. Likewise, I have to make jokes about being a killer, because if I think too long and too hard about what it really means to have murdered a man, even a monster like Lewis Stevenson, then I will begin to wonder if I am, in fact, the freak that those nasty little shitheads of my childhood insisted that I was: the Nightcrawler, Vampire Boy, Creepy Chris. I must not care too much about the dead, either those whom I loved or those whom I despised. I must not care too much about being alone. I must not care too much about what I cannot change. Like all of us in this storm between birth and death, I can wreak no great changes on the world, only small changes for the better, I hope, in the lives of those I love, which means that to live I must care not about what I am but about what I can become, not about the past but about the future, not even so much about myself as about the bright circle of friends who provide the only light in which I am able to flourish.

I was shaking as I contemplated turning the corner and facing the Other, in whose eyes I might see far too much of myself. I was clutching the Glock as if it were a talisman rather than a weapon, as though it were a crucifix with which I could ward off all that might destroy me, but I forced myself into action. I leaned to the right, turned my head — and saw no one.

This perimeter passage along the south side of the attic was wider than the one along the east flank, perhaps eight feet across; and on the plywood floor, tucked in against the eaves, was a narrow mattress and a tangle of blankets. The light came from a cone-shaped brass desk lamp plugged into a GFI receptacle that was mounted on an eave brace. Beside the mattress were a thermos, a plate of sliced fruit and buttered bread, a pail of water, bottles of medication and rubbing alcohol, the makings for bandages, a folded towel, and a damp washcloth spotted with blood.

The priest and his guest seemed to have vanished as if they had whispered an incantation.

Although immobilized by the emotional impact of the longing in the Other's voice, I could

417

not have been standing at the end of the box row for more than a minute, probably half a minute, after the creature had fallen silent. Yet neither Father Tom nor his visitor was in sight in the passageway ahead.

Silence ruled. I heard not a single footfall. Not any creak or pop or tick of wood that sounded more significant than the usual faint settling noises.

I actually looked up into the rafters toward the center of the space, overcome by the bizarre conviction that the missing pair had learned a trick from the clever spider and had drawn themselves up gossamer filaments, curling into tight black balls in the shadows overhead.

As long as I stayed close to the wall of boxes on my right side, I had sufficient headroom to stand erect. Soaring from the eaves to my left, the sharply pitched rafters cleared my head by six or eight inches. Nevertheless, I moved defensively in a modified crouch.

The lamp was not dangerously bright, and the brass cone focused the light away from me, so I moved to the mattress for a closer look at the items arrayed beside it. With the toe of one shoe, I disturbed the tangled blankets; although I'm not sure what I expected to find under them, what I did find was a lot of nothing.

I wasn't concerned that Father Tom would go downstairs and find Orson. For one thing, I didn't think he was finished with his work up here in the attic. Besides, my criminally experienced mutt would have the street savvy to duck for cover and lie low until escape was more feasible.

418

Suddenly, however, I realized that if the priest went below, he might fold away the ladder and close the trapdoor. I could force it open and release the ladder from above, but not without making almost as much racket as Satan and his conspirators had made when cast out of Heaven.

Rather than follow this passage to the next entrance to the maze and risk encountering the priest and the Other on the route they might have taken, I turned back the way I'd come, reminding myself to be light on my feet. The high-quality plyboard had few voids, and it was screwed rather than nailed to the floor joists, so I was virtually silent even in my haste.

When I turned the corner at the end of the row of boxes, plump Father Tom loomed from the shadows where I had stood listening only a minute or two ago. He was dressed neither for Mass nor bed, but was wearing a gray sweat suit and a sheen of sweat, as if he'd been fending off gluttonous urges by working out to an exercise video.

"You!" he said bitterly when he recognized me, as though I were not merely Christopher Snow but were the devil Baal and had stepped out of a conjurer's chalk pentagram without first asking permission or obtaining a lavatory pass.

The sweet-tempered, jovial, good-natured padre that I had known was evidently vacationing in Palm Springs, having given the keys of his parish to his evil twin. He poked me in the chest with the blunt end of a baseball bat, hard enough to hurt.

Because even XP-Man is subject to the laws

of physics, I was rocked backward by the blow, stumbled into the eaves, and cracked the back of my head against a rafter. I didn't see stars, not even a great character actor like M. Emmet Walsh or Rip Torn, but if not for the cushion provided by my James Dean thatch of hair, I might have gone out cold.

Poking me in the chest again with the baseball bat, Father Tom said, "You! You!"

Indeed, I was me, and I had never tried to claim otherwise, so I didn't know why he should be so incensed.

"You!" he said with a new rush of anger.

This time he rammed the damn bat into my stomach, which winded me but not as badly as it might have if I hadn't seen it coming. Just before the blow landed, I sucked in my stomach and tightened my abdominal muscles, and because I'd already thrown up what was left of Bobby's chicken tacos, the only consequence was a hot flash of pain from my groin to my breastbone, which I would have laughed off if I'd been wearing my armored spandex superhero uniform under my street clothes.

I pointed the Glock at him and wheezed threateningly, but he was either a man of God with no fear of death — or he was nuts. Gripping the bat with both hands to put even more power behind it, he poked it savagely at my stomach again, but I twisted to the side and dodged the blow, although unfortunately I mussed my hair on a rough-sawn rafter.

I was nonplussed to be in a fight with a priest. The encounter seemed more absurd than frightening — though it was plenty frightening enough to make my heart race and to make me worry that I'd have to return Bobby's jeans with urine stains.

"You! You!" he said more angrily than ever and seemingly with more surprise, too, as though my appearance in his dusty attic were so outrageous and improbable that his astonishment would grow at an ever-accelerating rate until his brain went nova.

He swung at me again. He would have missed this time even if I hadn't wrenched myself away from the bat. He was a priest, after all, not a ninja assassin. He was middle-aged and overweight, too.

The baseball bat smashed into one of the cardboard boxes with enough force to tear a hole in it and knock it out of the stack into the empty aisle beyond. Although woefully ignorant of even the basic principles of the martial arts and not gifted with the physique of a mighty warrior, the good father could not be faulted for a lack of enthusiasm.

I couldn't imagine shooting him, but I couldn't very well allow him to club me to death. I backed away from him, toward the lamp and the mattress in the wider aisle along the south side of the attic, hoping that he would recover his senses.

Instead, he came after me, swinging the bat from left to right, cutting the air with a *whoosh,* then immediately swinging it right to left, chanting *"You!"* between each swing.

His hair was disarranged and hanging over his

brow, and his face appeared to be contorted as much by terror as by rage. His nostrils dilated and quivered with each stentorian breath, and spittle flew from his mouth with each explosive repetition of the pronoun that seemed to constitute his entire vocabulary.

I was going to end up radically dead if I waited for Father Tom to recover his senses. If he even *had* senses left, the priest wasn't carrying them with him. They were put away somewhere, perhaps over in the church, locked up with a splinter of a saint's shinbone in the reliquary on the altar.

As he swung at me again, I searched for that animal eyeshine I'd seen in Lewis Stevenson, because a glimpse of that uncanny glow might justify meeting violence with violence. It would mean I was battling not a priest or an ordinary man, but something with one foot in the Twilight Zone. But I couldn't see a glimmer. Perhaps Father Tom was infected with the same disease that had corrupted the police chief's mind, but if so, he didn't seem as far gone as the cop.

Moving backward, attention on the baseball bat, I hooked the lamp cord with my foot. Proving myself a worthy victim for an aging, overweight priest, I fell flat on my back, drumming a nice paradiddle on the floor with the back of my skull.

The lamp fell over. Fortunately, it neither went out nor flung its light directly into my sensitive eyes.

I shook my foot out of the entangling cord

and scooted backward on my butt as Father Tom rushed in and hammered the floor with the bat.

He missed my legs by inches, punctuating the assault with that now-familiar accusation in the second-person singular: *"You!"*

"You!" I said somewhat hysterically, casting it right back at him as I continued to scoot out of his way.

I wondered where all these people were who supposedly revered me. I was more than ready to be revered a little, but Stevenson and Father Tom Eliot certainly didn't qualify for the Christopher Snow Admiration Society.

Although the priest was streaming sweat and panting, he was out to prove he had stamina. He approached in the stooped, hunch-shouldered, rolling lurch of a troll, as if he were on a work-release program from under the bridge to which he was usually committed. This cramped posture allowed him to raise the bat high over his head without cracking it against an overhanging rafter. He wanted to keep it high over his head because he clearly intended to play Babe Ruth with my skull and make my brains squirt out my ears.

Eyeshine or no eyeshine, I was going to have to blast the chubby little guy without delay. I couldn't scoot backward as fast as he could troll-walk toward me, and although I was a little hysterical — okay, *way* hysterical — I could figure the odds well enough to know that even the greediest bookie in Vegas wouldn't cover a bet on my survival. In my panic, hammered by terror and by a dangerously giddy sense of the absurd, I thought that the most humane course of action would be to shoot him in the gonads because he had taken a vow of celibacy, anyway.

Fortunately, I never had the opportunity to prove myself to be the expert marksman that such a perfectly placed shot would have required. I aimed in the general direction of his crotch, and my finger tightened on the trigger. No time to use the laser sighting. Before I could squeeze off a round, something monstrous growled in the passageway behind the priest, and a great dark snarling predator leaped on his back, causing him to scream and drop the baseball bat as he was driven to the attic floor.

For an instant, I was stunned that the Other should be so utterly unlike a rhesus and that it should attack Father Tom, its nurse and champion, rather than tear out *my* throat. But, of course, the great dark snarling predator was not the Other: It was Orson.

Standing on the priest's back, the dog bit at the sweat-suit collar. Fabric tore. He was snarling so viciously that I was afraid he'd actually maul Father Tom.

I called him off as I scrambled to my feet. The mutt obeyed at once, without inflicting a wound, not a fraction as bloodthirsty as he'd pretended to be.

The priest made no effort to get up. He lay with his head turned to one side, his face half covered with tousled, sweat-soaked hair. He was breathing hard and sobbing, and after every third or fourth breath, he said bitterly, "*You. . . .*"

Obviously he knew enough about what was happening at Fort Wyvern and in Moonlight Bay to answer many if not all of my most pressing questions. Yet I didn't want to talk to him. I *couldn't* talk to him.

The Other might not have left the rectory, might still be here in the shadowy cloisters of the attic. Although I didn't believe that it posed a serious danger to me and Orson, especially not when I had the Glock, I had not seen it and, therefore, couldn't dismiss it as a threat. I didn't want to stalk it — or be stalked by it — in this claustrophobic space.

Of course, the Other was merely an excuse to flee.

Those things that I truly feared were the answers Father Tom might give to my questions. I thought I was eager to hear them, but evidently I was not yet prepared for certain truths.

You.

He'd spoken that one word with seething hatred, with uncommonly dark emotion for a man of God but also for a man who was usually kind and gentle. He transformed the simple pronoun into a denunciation and a curse.

You.

Yet I'd done nothing to earn his enmity. I hadn't given life to the pitiable creatures that he had committed himself to freeing. I hadn't been a part of the program at Wyvern that had infected his sister and possibly him, as well. Which meant that he hated not me, as a person, but hated me because of who I was.

And who was I?

Who was I if not my mother's son?

According to Roosevelt Frost — and even Chief Stevenson — there were, indeed, those who revered me because I was my mother's son, though I'd yet to meet them. For the same lineage, I was hated.

Christopher Nicholas Snow, only child of Wisteria Jane (Milbury) Snow, whose own mother named her after a flower. Christopher born of Wisteria, come into this too-bright world near the beginning of the Disco Decade. Born in a time of tacky fashion trends and frivolous pursuits, when the country was eagerly winding down a war, and when the worst fear was mere nuclear holocaust.

What could my brilliant and loving mother possibly have done that would make me either revered or reviled?

Sprawled on the attic floor, racked by emotion, Father Tom Eliot knew the answer to that mystery and would almost certainly reveal it when he had regained his composure.

Instead of asking the question at the heart of all that had happened this night, I shakily apologized to the sobbing priest. "I'm sorry. I . . . I shouldn't have come here. God. Listen. I'm so sorry. Please forgive me. Please."

What had my mother done?

Don't ask.

Don't ask.

If he had started to answer my unspoken question, I would have clamped my hands to my ears.

I called Orson to my side and led him away from the priest, into the maze, proceeding as fast as I dared. The narrow passages twisted and branched until it seemed as though we were not in an attic at all but in a network of catacombs. In places the darkness was nearly blinding; but I'm the child of darkness, never thwarted by it. I brought us quickly to the open trapdoor.

Though Orson had climbed the ladder, he peered at the descending treads with trepidation and hesitated to find his way into the hall below. Even for a four-footed acrobat, going down a steep ladder was immeasurably more difficult than going up.

Because many of the boxes in the attic were large and because bulky furniture was also stored there, I knew that a second trap must exist, and that it must be larger than the first, with an associated sling-and-pulley system for raising and lowering heavy objects to and from the second floor. I didn't want to search for it, but I wasn't sure how I could safely climb backward down an attic ladder while carrying a ninety-pound dog.

From the farthest end of the vast room, the priest called out to me — "Christopher" — in a voice heavy with remorse. "Christopher, I'm lost."

He didn't mean that he was lost in his own maze. Nothing as simple as that, nothing as hopeful as that.

"Christopher, I'm lost. Forgive me. *I'm so lost.*"

From elsewhere in the gloom came the child-monkey-not-of-this-world voice that belonged to the Other: struggling toward language, desperate to be understood, charged with longing and loneliness, as bleak as any arctic ice field but also, worse, filled with a reckless hope that would surely never be rewarded.

This plaintive bleat was so unbearable that it drove Orson to try the ladder and may even have given him the balance to succeed. When he was only halfway to the bottom, he leaped over the remaining treads to the hallway floor.

The priest's journal had almost slipped out from under my belt and into the seat of my pants. As I descended the ladder, the book rubbed painfully against the base of my spine, and when I reached the bottom I clawed it from under my belt and held it in my left hand, as the Glock was still clamped fiercely in my right.

Together, Orson and I raced down through the rectory, past the shrine to the Blessed Virgin, where the guttering candle was extinguished by the draft of our passing. We fled along the lower hall, through the kitchen with its three green digital clocks, out the back door, across the porch, into the night and the fog, as if we were escaping from the House of Usher moments before it collapsed and sank into the deep dank tarn.

We passed the back of the church. Its formidable mass was a tsunami of stone, and while we were in its nightshadow, it seemed about to crest and crash and crush us.

I glanced back twice. The priest was not behind us. Neither was anything else.

Although I half expected my bicycle to be gone or damaged, it was propped against the headstone, where I had left it. No monkey business.

I didn't pause to say a word to Noah Joseph James. In a world as screwed up as ours, ninety-six years of life didn't seem as desirable as it had only hours ago.

After pocketing the pistol and tucking the journal inside my shirt, I ran beside my bike along an aisle between rows of graves, swinging aboard it while on the move. Bouncing off the curb into the street, leaning forward over the handlebars, pedaling furiously, I bored like an auger through the fog, leaving a temporary tunnel in the churning mist behind me.

Orson had no interest in the spoor of squirrels. He was as eager as I was to put distance between us and St. Bernadette's.

We had gone several blocks before I began to realize that escape wasn't possible. The inevitable dawn restricted me to the boundaries of Moonlight Bay, and the madness in St. Bernadette's rectory was to be found in every corner of the town.

More to the point, I was trying to run away from a threat that could never be escaped even if I could fly to the most remote island or mountaintop in the world. Wherever I went, I would carry with me the thing that I feared: the need to know. I wasn't frightened merely of the answers that I might receive when I asked questions about my mother. More fundamentally, I was afraid of the questions them-

429

selves, because the very nature of them, whether they were eventually answered or not, would change my life forever.

29

From a bench in the park at the corner of Palm Street and Grace Drive, Orson and I studied a sculpture of a steel scimitar balanced on a pair of tumbling dice carved from white marble, which were in turn balanced on a highly polished representation of Earth hewn from blue marble, which itself was perched upon a large mound of bronze cast to resemble a pile of dog poop.

This work of art has stood at the center of the park, surrounded by a gently bubbling fountain, for about three years. We've sat here many nights, pondering the meaning of this creation, intrigued and edified and challenged — but not particularly enlightened — by it.

Initially we believed that the meaning was clear. The scimitar represents war or death. The tumbling dice represent fate. The blue marble sphere, which is Earth, is a symbol of our lives. Put it all together, and you have a statement about the human condition: We live or die according to the whims of fate, our lives on this world ruled by cold chance. The bronze dog poop at the bottom is a minimalist repetition of the same theme: Life is shit.

Many learned analyses have followed the first. The scimitar, for example, might not be a scimitar at all; it might be a crescent moon. The dice-like forms might be sugar cubes. The blue sphere might not be our nurturing planet —

merely a bowling ball. What the various forms symbolize can be interpreted in a virtually infinite number of ways, although it is impossible to conceive of the bronze casting as anything but dog poop.

Seen as a moon, sugar cubes, and a bowling ball, this masterwork may be warning that our highest aspirations (reaching for the moon) cannot be achieved if we punish our bodies and agitate our minds by eating too many sweets or if we sustain lower-back injury by trying too hard to torque the ball when we're desperate to pick up a seven-ten split. The bronze dog poop, therefore, reveals to us the ultimate consequences of a bad diet combined with obsessive bowling: Life is shit.

Four benches are placed around the broad walkway that encircles the fountain in which the sculpture stands. We have viewed the piece from every perspective.

The park lamps are on a timer, and they are all extinguished at midnight to conserve city funds. The fountain stops bubbling as well. The gently splashing water is conducive to meditation, and we wish that it spritzed all night; although even if I were not an XPer, we would prefer no lamplight. Ambient light is not only sufficient but ideal for the study of this sculpture, and a good thick fog can add immeasurably to your appreciation of the artist's vision.

Prior to the erection of this monument, a simple bronze statue of Junipero Serra stood on the plinth at the center of the fountain for over a hundred years. He was a Spanish missionary to the Indians of California, two and a half centuries ago: the man who established the network of missions that are now landmark buildings, public treasures, and magnets for history-minded tourists.

Bobby's parents and a group of like-minded citizens had formed a committee to press for the banishment of the Junipero Serra statue on the grounds that a monument to a religious figure did not belong in a park created and maintained with public funds. Separation of Church and State. The United States Constitution, they said, was clear on this issue.

Wisteria Jane (Milbury) Snow — "Wissy" to her friends, "Mom" to me — in spite of being a scientist and rationalist, led the opposing committee that wished to preserve the statue of Serra. "When a society erases its past, for whatever reason," she said, "it cannot have a future."

Mom lost the debate. Bobby's folks won.

The night the decision came down, Bobby and I met in the most solemn circumstances of our long friendship, to determine if family honor and the sacred obligations of bloodline required us to conduct a vicious, unrelenting feud — in the manner of the legendary Hatfields and McCoys — until even the most distant cousins had been sent to sleep with the worms and until one or both of us was dead. After consuming enough beer to clear our heads, we decided that it was impossible to conduct a proper feud and still find the time to ride every set of glassy, pumping monoliths that the good sea sent to shore. To say nothing of all the time spent on murder and mayhem that might have been spent ogling girls in bun-floss bikinis.

Now I entered Bobby's number in the keypad on my phone and pressed *send*.

I turned the volume up a little so Orson might be able to hear both sides of the conversation. When I realized what I had done, I knew that unconsciously I had accepted the most fantastic possibility of the Wyvern project as proven fact — even though I was still pretending to have my doubts.

Bobby answered on the second ring: "Go away."

"You asleep?"

"Yeah."

"I'm sitting here in Life Is Shit Park."

"Do I care?"

"Some really bad stuff has gone down since I saw you."

"It's the salsa on those chicken tacos," he said.

"I can't talk about it on the phone."

"Good."

"I'm worried about you," I said.

"That's sweet."

"You're in real danger, Bobby."

"I swear I flossed, Mom."

Orson chuffed with amusement. The hell he didn't.

"Are you awake now?" I asked Bobby.

"No."

"I don't think you were asleep in the first place."

He was silent. Then: "Well, there's been a way spooky movie on all night since you left."

"*Planet of the Apes?*" I guessed.

"On a three-hundred-sixty-degree, wrap-around screen."

"What're they doing?"

"Oh, you know, the usual monkeyshines."

"Nothing more threatening?"

"They think they're cute. One of them's at the window right now, mooning me."

"Yeah, but did you start it?"

"I get the feeling they're trying to irritate me until I come outside again."

Alarmed, I said, "Don't go."

"I'm not a moron," he said sourly.

"Sorry."

"I'm an asshole."

"That's right."

"There's a critical difference between a moron and an asshole."

"I'm clear on that."

"I wonder."

"Do you have the shotgun with you?"

"Jesus, Snow, didn't I just say I'm not a moron?"

"If we can ride this barrel until dawn, then I think we're safe until sundown tomorrow."

"They're on the roof now."

"Doing what?"

"Don't know." He paused, listening. "At least two of them. Running back and forth. Maybe looking for a way in."

Orson jumped off the bench and stood tensely, one ear pricked toward the phone, a worried air about him. He seemed to be willing to shed some doggy pretenses if that didn't disturb me.

"*Is* there a way in from the roof?" I asked Bobby.

"The bathroom and kitchen vent ducts aren't large enough for these bastards."

Surprisingly, considering all its other amenities, the cottage had no fireplace. Corky Collins — formerly Toshiro Tagawa — had most likely decided against a fireplace because, unlike the warm waters of a spa, the stone hearth and hard bricks of a firebox didn't provide an ideal spot to get it on with a couple of naked beach girls. Thanks to his single-minded lasciviousness, there was now no convenient chimney to admit the monkeys.

I said, "I've got some more Nancy work to squeeze in before dawn."

"How's that panning out?" Bobby asked.

"I'm awesomely good at it. Come morning, I'll spend the day at Sasha's, and we'll both be at your place first thing tomorrow evening."

"You mean I've got to make dinner again?"

"We'll bring pizza. Listen, we're gonna get slammed, I think. One of us, anyway. And the only way to prevent it is hang together. Better get what sleep you can during the day. Tomorrow night might be radically hairy out there on the point."

"So you've got a handle on this?" Bobby said.

"There isn't a handle on it."

"You're not as cheerful as Nancy Drew."

I wasn't going to lie to him, not to him any more than to Orson or Sasha. "There's no solution. There's no way to zip it shut or put a button on it. Whatever's going down here —

436

we'll have to live with it the rest of our lives. But maybe we can find a way to ride the wave, even though it's a huge spooky slab."

After a silence, Bobby said, "What's wrong, bro?"

"Didn't I just say?"

"Not everything."

"I told you, some of it's not for the phone."

"I'm not talking about details. I'm talking about you."

Orson put his head in my lap, as if he thought I would take some consolation from petting him and scratching behind his ears. In fact, I did. It always works. A good dog is a medicine for melancholy and a better stress reliever than Valium.

"You're doing cool," Bobby said, "but you're not being cool."

"Bob Freud, bastard grandson of Sigmund."

"Lie down on my couch."

Smoothing Orson's coat in an attempt to smooth my nerves, I sighed and said, "Well, what it boils down to is, I think maybe my mom destroyed the world."

"Solemn."

"It is, isn't it?"

"This science thing of hers?"

"Genetics."

"Remember how I warned you against trying to leave your mark."

"I think it's worse than that. I think maybe, at the start, she was trying to find a way to help me."

"End of the world, huh?"

"End of the world as we know it," I said, remembering Roosevelt Frost's qualification.

"Beaver Cleaver's mom never did much more than bake a cake."

I laughed. "How would I make it without you, bro?"

"There's only one important thing I ever did for you."

"What's that?"

"Taught you perspective."

I nodded. "What's important and what isn't."

"Most isn't," he reminded me.

"Even this?"

"Make love to Sasha. Get some solid sleep. We'll have a bitchin' dinner tomorrow night. We'll kick some monkey ass. Ride some epic waves. A week from now, in your heart, your mom is just your mom again — if you want to let it be that way."

"Maybe," I said doubtfully.

"Attitude, bro. It's everything."

"I'll work on it."

"One thing surprises me, though."

"What?"

"Your mom must've been really *pissed* about losing the fight to keep that statue in the park."

Bobby broke the connection. I switched off my phone.

Is this really a wise strategy for living? Insisting that most of life isn't to be taken seriously. Relentlessly viewing it as a cosmic joke. Having only four guiding principles: one, do as little harm to others as possible; two, be there always for your friends; three, be responsible for yourself and ask nothing of others; four, grab all the fun you can. Put no stock in the opinions of anyone but those closest to you. Forget about leaving a mark on the world. Ignore the great issues of your time and thereby improve your digestion. Don't dwell in the past. Don't worry about the future. Live in the moment. Trust in the purpose of your existence and let meaning come to you instead of straining to discover it. When life throws a hard punch, roll with it — but roll with laughter. Catch the wave, dude.

This is how Bobby lives, and he is the happiest and most well-balanced person I have ever known.

I try to live as Bobby Halloway does, but I'm not as successful at it as he is. Sometimes I thrash when I should float. I spend too much time anticipating and too little time letting life surprise me. Maybe I don't try hard enough to live like Bobby. Or maybe I try too hard.

Orson went to the pool that surrounded the sculpture. He lapped noisily at the clear water, obviously savoring the taste and the coolness of it.

I remembered that July night in our backyard when he had stared at the stars and fallen into blackest despair. I had no accurate way to determine how much smarter Orson was than an ordinary dog. Because his intelligence had somehow been enhanced by the project at Wyvern, however, he understood vastly more than nature ever intended a dog to understand. That July night, recognizing his revolutionary potential yet — perhaps for the first time — grasping the terrible limitations placed on him by his physical nature, he'd sunk into a slough of despondency that almost claimed him permanently. To be intelligent but without the complex larynx and other physical equipment to make speech possible, to be intelligent but without the hands to write or make tools, to be intelligent but trapped in a physical package that will forever prevent the full expression of your intelligence: This would be akin to a person being born deaf, mute, and limbless.

I watched Orson now with astonishment, with a new appreciation for his courage, and with a tenderness I had never felt before for anyone on this earth.

He turned from the pool, licking at the water that dripped from his chops, grinning with pleasure. When he saw me looking at him, he wagged his tail, happy to have my attention or just happy to be with me on this strange night.

For all his limitations and in spite of all the good reasons why he should be perpetually anguished, my dog, for God's sake, was better at being Bobby Halloway than I was.

Does Bobby have a wise strategy for living? Does Orson? I hope one day to have matured enough to live as well by their philosophy as they do.

Getting up from the bench, I pointed to the sculpture. "Not a scimitar. Not a moon. It's the smile of the invisible Cheshire cat from *Alice in Wonderland.*"

Orson turned to gaze up at the masterwork.

"Not dice. Not sugar cubes," I continued. "A pair of either the grow-small or grow-big pills that Alice took in the story."

Orson considered this with interest. On video, he had seen Disney's animated version of this classic tale.

"Not a symbol of the earth. Not a blue bowling ball. A big blue eye. Put it all together and what does it mean?"

Orson looked at me for elucidation.

"The Cheshire smile is the artist laughing at the gullible people who paid him so handsomely. The pair of pills represent the drugs he was high on when he created this junk. The blue eye is his eye, and the reason you can't see his other eye is because he's winking it. The bronze pile at the bottom is, of course, dog poop, which is intended to be a pungent critical comment on the work — because, as everyone knows, dogs are the most perceptive of all critics."

If the vigor with which Orson wagged his tail was a reliable indication, he enjoyed this interpretation enormously.

He trotted around the entire fountain pool, reviewing the sculpture from all sides.

Perhaps the purpose for which I was born is *not* to write about my life in search of some universal meaning that may help others to better understand their own lives — which, in my more egomaniacal moments, is a mission I have embraced. Instead of striving to make even the tiniest mark on the world, perhaps I should consider that, possibly, the sole purpose for which I was born is to amuse Orson, to be not his master but his loving brother, to make his strange and difficult life as easy, as full of delight, and as rewarding as it can be. This would constitute a purpose as meaningful as most and more noble than some.

Pleased by Orson's wagging tail at least as much as he seemed to be pleased by my latest riff on the sculpture, I consulted my wristwatch. Less than two hours remained until dawn.

I had two places I wanted to go before the sun chased me into hiding. The first was Fort Wyvern.

From the park at Palm Street and Grace Drive in the southeast quadrant of Moonlight Bay, the trip to Fort Wyvern takes less than ten minutes by bicycle, even allowing for a pace that will not tire your canine brother. I know a shortcut through a storm culvert that runs under Highway 1. Beyond the culvert is an open, ten-foot-wide, concrete drainage channel that continues deep into the grounds of the military base after being bisected by the chain-link fence — crowned with razor wire — that defines the perimeter of the facility.

Everywhere along the fence — and throughout the grounds of Fort Wyvern — large signs in red and black warn that trespassers will be prosecuted under federal statutes and that the minimum sentence upon conviction involves a fine of no less than ten thousand dollars and a prison sentence of no less than one year. I have always ignored these threats, largely because I know that because of my condition, no judge will sentence me to prison for this minor offense. And I can afford the ten thousand bucks if it comes to that.

One night, eighteen months ago, shortly after Wyvern officially closed forever, I used a bolt cutter to breach the chain-link where it descended into the drainage channel. The opportunity to explore this vast new realm was too enticing to resist.

If my excitement seems strange to you — considering that I was not an adventuresome boy at the time but a twenty-six-year-old man — then you are probably someone who can catch a plane to London if you wish, sail off to Puerto Vallarta on a whim, or take the Orient Express from Paris to Istanbul. You probably have a driver's license and a car. You probably have not spent your entire life within the confines of a town of twelve thousand people, ceaselessly traveling it by night until you know its every byway as intimately as you know your own bedroom, and you are probably, therefore, not just a little crazy for new places, new experiences. So cut me some slack.

Fort Wyvern, named for General Harrison Blair Wyvern, a highly decorated hero of the First World War, was commissioned in 1939, as a training and support facility. It covers 134,456 acres, which makes it neither the largest nor by far not the smallest military base in the state of California.

During the Second World War, Fort Wyvern established a school for tank warfare, offering training in the operation and maintenance of every tread-driven vehicle in use in the battlefields of Europe and in the Asian theater. Other schools under the Wyvern umbrella provided first-rate education in demolitions and bomb disposal, sabotage, field artillery, field medical service, military policing, and cryptography, as well as basic training to tens of thousands of infantrymen. Within its boundaries were an artillery range, a huge network of bunkers serving as an ammunition dump, an airfield, and more buildings than exist within the city limits of Moonlight Bay.

At the height of the Cold War, active-duty personnel assigned to Fort Wyvern numbered — officially — 36,400. There were also 12,904 dependents and over four thousand civilian personnel associated with the base. The military payroll was well over seven hundred million dollars annually, and the contract expenditures exceeded one hundred and fifty million per annum.

When Wyvern was shut down at the recommendation of the Defense Base Closure and Realignment Commission, the sound of money being sucked out of the county economy was so loud that local merchants were unable to sleep because of the noise and their babies cried in the night for fear of having no college tuition when eventually they would need it. KBAY, which lost nearly a third of its potential county-wide audience and fully half of its late-night listeners, was forced to trim staff, which was why Sasha found herself serving as both the post-midnight jock and the general manager and why Doogie Sassman worked eight hours of overtime per week for regular wage and never flexed his tattooed biceps in protest.

By no means continuous but nevertheless frequent major building projects of a high-security nature were undertaken on the grounds of Fort Wyvern by military contractors whose laborers were reportedly sworn to secrecy and remained, for life, at risk of being charged with treason for a slip of the tongue. According to rumor, because of its proud history as a center of military training and education, Wyvern was chosen as the site of a major chemical-biological warfare research facility constructed as a huge self-contained, biologically secure, subterranean complex.

Given the events of the past twelve hours, I felt confident in assuming that more than a scrap of truth underlay these rumors, although I have never seen a single thread of evidence that such a stronghold exists.

The abandoned base offers sights that are, however, as likely to amaze you, give you the creeps, and make you ponder the extent of human folly as anything you will see in a cryobiological warfare laboratory. I think of Fort Wyvern, in its present state, as a macabre theme park, divided into various lands much the same as Disneyland is divided, with the difference that only one patron, along with his faithful dog, is admitted at any one time.

Dead Town is one of my favorites.

Dead Town is my name for it, not what it was called when Fort Wyvern thrived. It consists of more than three thousand single-family cottages and duplex bungalows in which married active-duty personnel and their dependents were housed if they chose to live on base. Architecturally, these humble structures have little to recommend them, and each is virtually identical to the one next door; they provided the minimum of comforts to the mostly young families who occupied them, each for only a couple of years at a time, over the war-filled decades. But in spite of their sameness, these are pleasant houses, and when you walk through their empty rooms, you can feel that life was lived well in them, with lovemaking and laughter and gatherings of friends.

These days the streets of Dead Town, laid out in a military grid, feature drifts of dust against the curbs and dry tumbleweeds waiting for wind. After the rainy season, the grass quickly turns brown and stays that shade most of the year. The shrubs are all withered, and many of the trees are dead, their leafless branches blacker than the black sky at which they seem to claw. Mice have the houses to themselves, and birds build nests on the front-door lintels, painting the stoops with their droppings.

You might expect that the structures would either be maintained against the real possibility of future need or efficiently razed, but there is no money for either solution. The materials and the fixtures of the buildings have less value than the cost of salvaging them, so no contract can be negotiated to dispose of them in that manner. For the time being, they are left to deteriorate in the elements much as the ghost towns of the gold-mining era were abandoned.

Wandering through Dead Town, you feel as

though everyone in the world has vanished or died of a plague and that you are alone on the face of the earth. Or that you have gone mad and exist now in a grim solipsist fantasy, surrounded by people you refuse to see. Or that you have died and gone to Hell, where your particular damnation consists of eternal isolation. When you see a scruffy coyote or two prowling between the houses, lean of flank, with long teeth and fiery eyes, they appear to be demons, and the Hades fantasy is the easiest one to believe. If your father was a professor of poetry, however, and if you are blessed or cursed with a three-hundred-ring circus of a mind, you can imagine countless scenarios to explain the place.

This night in March, I cycled through a couple of streets in Dead Town, but I didn't stop to visit. The fog had not reached this far inland, and the dry air was warmer than the humid murk along the coast; though the moon had set, the stars were bright, and the night was ideal for sightseeing. To thoroughly explore even this one land in the theme park that is Wyvern, however, you need to devote a week to the task.

I was not aware of being watched. After what I'd learned in the past few hours, I knew that I must have been monitored at least intermittently on my previous visits.

Beyond the borders of Dead Town lie numerous barracks and other buildings. A once-fine commissary, a barber shop, a dry cleaner, a florist, a bakery, a bank: their signs peeling and caked with dust. A day-care center. High-school-age military brats attended classes in Moonlight

Bay; but there are a kindergarten and an elementary school here. In the base library, the cobwebbed shelves are stripped of books except for one overlooked copy of *The Catcher in the Rye*. Dental and medical clinics. A movie theater with nothing on its flat marquee except a single enigmatic word: WHO. A bowling alley. An Olympic-size pool now drained and cracked and blown full of debris. A fitness center. In the rows of stables, which no longer shelter horses, the unlatched stall doors swing with an ominous chorus of rasping and creaking each time the wind stiffens. The softball field is choked with weeds, and the rotting carcass of a mountain lion that lay for more than a year in the batter's cage is at last only a skeleton.

I was not interested in any of these destinations, either. I cycled past them to the hangarlike building that stands over the warren of subterranean chambers in which I found the Mystery Train cap last autumn.

Clipped to the back rack of my bicycle is a police flashlight with a switch that allows the beam to be adjusted to three degrees of brightness. I parked at the hangar and unsnapped the flashlight from the rack.

Orson finds Fort Wyvern alternately frightening and fascinating, but regardless of his reaction on any particular night, he stays at my side, uncomplaining. This time, he was clearly spooked, but he didn't hesitate or whine.

The smaller man-size door in one of the larger hangar doors was unlocked. Switching on the flashlight, I went inside with Orson at my heels.

This hangar isn't adjacent to the airfield, and it's unlikely that aircraft were stored or serviced here. Overhead are the tracks on which a mobile crane, now gone, once moved from end to end of the structure. Judging by the sheer mass and complexity of the steel supports for these elaborate rails, the crane lifted objects of great weight. Steel bracing plates, still bolted to the concrete, once must have been surmounted by substantial machinery. Elsewhere, curiously shaped wells in the floor, now empty, appear to have housed hydraulic mechanisms of unknowable purpose.

In the passing beam of my flashlight, geometric patterns of shadow and light leaped off the crane tracks. Like the ideograms of an unknown language, they stenciled the walls and the Quonset-curve of the ceiling, revealing that half the panes in the high clerestory windows were broken.

Unnervingly, the impression wasn't of a vacated machine shop or maintenance center, but of an abandoned church. The oil and chemical stains on the floor gave forth an incenselike aroma. The penetrating cold was not solely a physical sensation but affected the spirit as well, as if this were a deconsecrated place.

A vestibule in one corner of the hangar houses a set of stairs and a large elevator shaft from which the lift mechanism and the cab have been removed. I can't be sure, but judging from the aftermath left by those who had gutted the building, access to the vestibule once must have been through another chamber; and I suspect that the existence of the stairs and elevator were kept secret from most of the personnel who had worked in the hangar or who'd had occasion to pass through it.

A formidable steel frame and threshold remain at the top of the stairwell, but the door is gone. With the flashlight beam, I chased spiders and pill bugs from the steps and led Orson downward through a film of dust that bore no footprints except those that we had left during other visits.

The steps serve three subterranean floors, each with a footprint considerably larger than the hangar above. This webwork of corridors and windowless rooms has been assiduously stripped of every item that might provide a clue to the nature of the enterprise conducted here — stripped all the way to the bare concrete. Even the smallest elements of the air-filtration and plumbing systems have been torn out.

I have a sense that this meticulous eradication is only partly explained by their desire to prevent anyone from ascertaining the purpose of the place. Although I'm operating strictly on intuition, I believe that as they scrubbed away every trace of the work done here, they were motivated in part by *shame.*

I don't believe, however, that this is the chemical-biological warfare facility that I mentioned earlier. Considering the high degree of biological isolation required, that subterranean complex is surely in a more remote corner of Fort Wyvern, dramatically larger than these three immense floors, more elaborately hidden, and buried far deeper beneath the earth.

Besides, that facility is apparently still operative.

Nevertheless, I am convinced that dangerous and extraordinary activities of one kind or another were conducted beneath this hangar. Many of the chambers, reduced only to their basic concrete forms, have features that are at once baffling and — because of their sheer strangeness — profoundly disquieting.

One of these puzzling chambers is on the deepest level, down where no dust has yet drifted, at the center of the floor plan, ringed by corridors and smaller rooms. It is an enormous ovoid, a hundred and twenty feet long, not quite sixty feet in diameter at its widest point, tapering toward the ends. The walls, ceiling, and floor are curved, so that when you stand here, you feel as if you are within the empty shell of a giant egg.

Entrance is through a small adjacent space that might have been fitted out as an airlock. Rather than a door, there must have been a hatch; the only opening in the walls of this ovoid chamber is a circle five feet in diameter.

Moving across the raised, curved threshold and passing through this aperture with Orson, I swept the light over the width of the surrounding wall, marveling at it as always: five feet of poured-in-place, steel-reinforced concrete.

Inside the giant egg, the continuous smooth curve that forms the walls, the floor, and the ceiling is sheathed in what appears to be milky, vaguely golden, translucent glass at least two or three inches thick. It's not glass, however, because it's shatterproof and because, when tapped hard, it rings like tubular bells. Furthermore, no seams are evident anywhere.

This exotic material is highly polished and appears as slick as wet porcelain. The flashlight beam penetrates this coating, quivers and flickers through it, flares off the faint golden whorls within, and shimmers across its surface. Yet the stuff was not in the least slippery as we crossed to the center of the chamber.

My rubber-soled shoes barely squeaked. Orson's claws made faint elfin music, ringing off the floor with a *tink-ting* like finger bells.

On this night of my father's death, on this night of nights, I wanted to return to this place where I'd found my Mystery Train cap the past autumn. It had been lying in the center of the egg room, the only object left behind in the entire three floors below the hangar.

I had thought that the cap had merely been forgotten by the last worker or inspector to leave. Now I suspected that on a certain October night, persons unknown had been aware of me exploring this facility, that they had been following me floor to floor without my knowledge, and that they had eventually slipped ahead of me to place the cap where I would be sure to find it.

If this was the case, it seemed to be not a mean or taunting act but more of a greeting, perhaps even a kindness. Intuition told me that the words *Mystery Train* had something to do with my mother's work. Twenty-one months after her death, someone had given me the cap because it was a link to her, and whoever had made the gift was someone who admired my mother and respected me if only because I was her son.

This is what I wanted to believe: that there were, indeed, those involved in this seemingly impenetrable conspiracy who did not see my mother as a villain and who felt friendly toward me, even if they did not revere me, as Roosevelt insisted. I wanted to believe that there were good guys in this, not merely bad, because when I learned what my mother had done to destroy the world as we know it, I preferred to receive that information from people who were convinced, at least, that her *intentions* had been good.

I didn't want to learn the truth from people who looked at me, saw my mother, and bitterly spat out that curse and accusation: *You!*

"Is anyone here?" I asked.

My question spiraled in both directions along the walls of the egg room and returned to me as two separate echoes, one to each ear.

Orson chuffed inquiringly. This soft sound lingered along the curved planes of the chamber, like a breeze whispering across water.

Neither of us received an answer.

"I'm not out for vengeance," I declared. "That's behind me."

Nothing.

"I don't even intend to go to outside authorities anymore. It's too late to undo whatever's been done. I accept that."

The echo of my voice gradually faded. As it sometimes did, the egg room filled with an uncanny silence that felt as dense as water.

I waited a minute before breaking that silence again: "I don't want Moonlight Bay wiped from the map — and me and my friends with it — for no good reason. All I want now is to understand."

No one cared to enlighten me.

Well, coming here had been a long shot anyway.

I wasn't disappointed. I have rarely allowed myself to feel disappointment about anything. The lesson of my life is patience.

Above these man-made caverns, dawn was rapidly approaching, and I couldn't spare more time for Fort Wyvern. I had one more essential stop to make before retreating to Sasha's house to wait out the reign of the murderous sun.

Orson and I crossed the dazzling floor, in which the flashlight beam was refracted along glimmering golden whorls like galaxies of stars underfoot.

Beyond the entry portal, in the drab concrete vault that might have once been an airlock, we found my father's suitcase. The one that I had put down in the hospital garage before hiding under the hearse, that had been gone when I'd come out of the cold-holding room.

It had not, of course, been here when we had passed through five minutes ago.

I stepped around the suitcase, into the room beyond the vault, and swept that space with the light. No one was there.

Orson waited diligently at the suitcase, and I returned to his side.

When I lifted the bag, it was so light that I thought it must be empty. Then I heard something tumble softly inside.

As I was releasing the latches, my heart clutched at the thought that I might find another pair of eyeballs in the bag. To counter this hideous image, I conjured Sasha's lovely face in my mind, which started my heart beating again.

When I opened the lid, the suitcase appeared to contain only air. Dad's clothes, toiletries, paperback books, and other effects were gone.

Then I saw the photograph in one corner of the bag. It was the snapshot of my mother that I had promised would be cremated with my father's body.

I held the picture under the flashlight. She was lovely. And such fierce intelligence shone from her eyes.

In her face, I saw certain aspects of my own countenance that made me understand why Sasha could, after all, look favorably on me. My mother was smiling in this picture, and her smile was so like mine.

Orson seemed to want to look at the photograph, so I turned it toward him. For long seconds his gaze traveled the image. His thin whine, when he looked away from her face, was the essence of sadness.

We *are* brothers, Orson and I. I am the fruit of Wisteria's heart and womb. Orson is the fruit of her mind. He and I share no blood, but we share things more important than blood.

When Orson whined again, I firmly said, "Dead and gone," with that ruthless focus on the future that gets me through the day.

Forgoing one more look at the photograph, I tucked it into my shirt pocket.

No grief. No despair. No self-pity.

Anyway, my mother is not entirely dead. She lives in me and in Orson and perhaps in others like Orson.

Regardless of any crimes against humanity of which my mother might stand accused by others, she is alive in us, alive in the Elephant Man and his freak dog. And with all due humility, I think the world is better for us being in it. We are not the bad guys.

As we left the vault, I said "Thank you" to whoever had left the photograph for me, though I didn't know if they could hear and though I was only assuming that their intentions had been kind.

Above ground, outside the hangar, my bicycle was where I'd left it. The stars were where I'd left them, too.

I cycled back through the edge of Dead Town and toward Moonlight Bay, where the fog — and more — waited for me.

FIVE

NEAR DAWN

30

The Nantucket-style house, with dark wood-shingle siding and deep white porches, seems to have slid three thousand miles during an unnoticed tipping of the continent, coming to rest here in the California hills above the Pacific. Looking more suitable to the landscape than logic says it should, sitting toward the front of the one-acre lot, shaded by stone pines, the residence exudes the charm, grace, and warmth of the loving family that lives within its walls.

All the windows were dark, but before long, light would appear in a few of them. Rosalina Ramirez would rise early to prepare a lavish breakfast for her son, Manuel, who would soon return from a double shift of policework — assuming he wouldn't be delayed by the extensive paperwork associated with Chief Stevenson's immolation. As he was a better cook than his mother, Manuel would prefer to make his own breakfast, but he would eat what she gave him and praise it. Rosalina was still sleeping; she had the large bedroom that had once belonged to her son, a room he'd not used since his wife died giving birth to Toby.

Beyond a deep backyard, shingled to match the house and with windows flanked by white shutters, stands a small barn with a gambrel roof. Because the property is at the extreme southern end of town, it offers access to riding trails and the open hills; the original owner had stabled horses in the barn. Now the structure is a studio, where Toby Ramirez builds his life from glass.

Approaching through the fog, I saw the windows glowing. Toby often wakes long before dawn and comes out to the studio.

I propped the bike against the barn wall and went to the nearest window. Orson put his forepaws on the windowsill and stood beside me, peering inside.

When I pay a visit to watch Toby create, I usually don't go into the studio. The fluorescent ceiling panels are far too bright. And because borosilicate glass is worked at temperatures exceeding twenty-two hundred degrees Fahrenheit, it emits significant amounts of intense light that can damage anyone's eyes, not just mine. If Toby is between tasks, he may turn the lights off, and then we talk for a while.

Now, wearing a pair of goggles with didymium lenses, Toby was in his work chair at the glass-blowing table, in front of the Fisher Multi-Flame burner. He had just finished forming a graceful pear-shaped vase with a long neck, which was still so hot that it was glowing gold and red; now he was annealing it.

When a piece of glassware is removed suddenly from a hot flame, it will usually cool too quickly, develop stresses — and crack. To preserve the item, it must be annealed — that is, cooled in careful stages.

The flame was fed by natural gas mixed with pure oxygen from a pressurized tank that was chained to the glassblowing table. During the annealing process, Toby would feather out the oxygen, gradually reducing the temperature, giving the glass molecules time to shift to more stable positions.

Because of the numerous dangers involved in glassblowing, some people in Moonlight Bay thought it was irresponsible of Manuel to allow his Down's-afflicted son to practice this technically demanding art and craft. Fiery catastrophes were envisioned, predicted, and awaited with impatience in some quarters.

Initially, no one was more opposed to Toby's dream than Manuel. For fifteen years, the barn had served as a studio for Carmelita's older brother, Salvador, a first-rank glass artist. As a child, Toby had spent uncounted hours with his uncle Salvador, wearing goggles, watching the master at work, on rare occasion donning Kevlar mittens to transfer a vase or bowl to or from the annealing oven. While he'd appeared to many to be passing those hours in stupefaction, with a dull gaze and a witless smile, he had actually been learning without being directly taught. To cope, the intellectually disadvantaged often must have superhuman patience. Toby sat day after day, year after year, in his uncle's studio, watching and slowly learning. When Salvador died two years ago, Toby — then only fourteen — asked his father if he might continue his uncle's work. Manuel had not taken the request seriously, and he'd gently discouraged his son from dwelling on this impossible dream.

One morning before dawn, he found Toby in

the studio. At the end of the worktable, standing on the fire-resistant Ceramfab top, was a family of simple blown-glass swans. Beside the swans stood a newly formed and annealed vase into which had been introduced a calculated mixture of compatible impurities that imparted to the glass mysterious midnight-blue swirls with a silvery glitter like stars. Manuel knew at once that this piece was equal to the finest vases that Salvador had ever produced; and Toby was at that very moment flame-annealing an equally striking piece of work.

The boy had absorbed the technical aspects of glass craft from his uncle, and in spite of his mild retardation, he obviously knew the proper procedures for avoiding injury. The magic of genetics was involved, too, for he possessed a striking talent that could not have been learned. He wasn't merely a craftsman but an artist, and not merely an artist but perhaps an idiot savant to whom the inspiration of the artist and the techniques of the craftsman came with the ease of waves to the shore.

Gift shops in Moonlight Bay, Cambria, and as far north as Carmel sold all the glass Toby produced. In a few years, he might become self-supporting.

Sometimes, nature throws a bone to those she maims. Witness my own ability to compose sentences and paragraphs with some skill.

Now, in the studio, orange light flared and billowed from the large, bushy annealing flame. Toby took care to turn the pear-shaped vase so that it was bathed uniformly by the fire.

With a thick neck, rounded shoulders, and proportionately short arms and stocky legs, he might have been a storybook gnome before a watch fire deep in the earth. Brow sloped and heavy. Bridge of the nose flat. Ears set too low on a head slightly too small for his body. His soft features and the inner epicanthic folds of his eyes give him a perpetual dreamy expression.

Yet on his high work chair, turning the glass in the flame, adjusting the oxygen flow with intuitive precision, face shimmering with reflected light, eyes concealed behind didymium goggles, Toby did not in any way seem below average, did not in any way impress me as being diminished by his condition. To the contrary, observed in his element, in the act of creation, he appeared exalted.

Orson snorted with alarm. He dropped his forepaws from the window, turned away from the studio, and tightened into a wary crouch.

Turning as well, I saw a shadowy figure crossing the backyard, coming toward us. In spite of the darkness and fog, I recognized him at once because of the easy way that he carried himself. It was Manuel Ramirez: Toby's dad, number two in the Moonlight Bay Police Department but now at least temporarily risen by succession to the top post, due to the fiery death of his boss.

I put both hands in my jacket pockets. I closed my right hand around the Glock.

Manuel and I were friends. I wouldn't feel comfortable pointing a gun at him, and I certainly couldn't shoot him. Unless he was not

Manuel anymore. Unless, like Stevenson, he had become someone else.

He stopped eight or ten feet from us. In the annealing flame's coruscating orange glow, which pierced the nearby window, I could see that Manuel was wearing his khaki uniform. His service pistol was holstered on his right hip. Although he stood with his thumbs hooked in his gun belt, he would be able to draw his weapon at least as quickly as I could pull the Glock from my jacket.

"Your shift over already?" I asked, although I knew it wasn't.

Instead of answering me, he said, "I hope you're not expecting beer, tamales, and Jackie Chan movies at this hour."

"I just stopped by to say hello to Toby if he happened to be between jobs."

Manuel's face, too worn with care for his forty years, had a naturally friendly aspect. Even in this Halloween light, his smile was still engaging, reassuring. As far as I could see, the only luminosity in his eyes was the reflected light from the studio window. Of course, that reflection might mask the same transient flickers of animal eyeshine that I'd seen in Lewis Stevenson.

Orson was reassured enough to ease out of his crouch. But he remained wary.

Manuel exhibited none of Stevenson's simmering rage or electric energy. As always, his voice was soft and almost musical. "You never did come around to the station after you called."

I considered my answer and decided to go

with the truth. "Yes, I did."

"So when you phoned me, you were already close," he guessed.

"Right around the corner. Who's the bald guy with the earring?"

Manuel mulled over his answer and followed my lead with some truth of his own. "His name's Carl Scorso."

"But who is he?"

"A total dirtbag. How far are you going to carry this?"

"Nowhere."

He was silent, disbelieving.

"It started out a crusade," I admitted. "But I know when I'm beaten."

"That sure would be a new Chris Snow."

"Even if I could contact an outside authority or the media, I don't understand the situation well enough to convince them of anything."

"And you have no proof."

"Nothing substantive. Anyway, I don't think I'd be allowed to make that contact. If I could get someone to come investigate, I don't think I or any of my friends would be alive to greet them when they got here."

Manuel didn't reply, but his silence was all the answer I needed.

He might still be a baseball fan. He might still like country music, Abbott and Costello. He still understood as much as I did about limitations and still felt the hand of fate as I did. He might even still like me — but he was no longer my friend. If he wouldn't be sufficiently treacherous to pull the trigger on me himself, he would watch as someone else did.

Sadness pooled in my heart, a greasy despondency that I'd never felt before, akin to nausea. "The entire police department has been co-opted, hasn't it?"

His smile had faded. He looked tired.

When I saw weariness in him rather than anger, I knew that he was going to tell me more than he should. Riven by guilt, he would not be able to keep all his secrets.

I already suspected that I knew one of the revelations he would make about my mother. I was so loath to hear it that I almost walked away. Almost.

"Yes," he said. "The entire department."

"Even you."

"Oh, *mi amigo*, especially me."

"Are you infected by whatever bug came out of Wyvern?"

" 'Infection' isn't quite the word."

"But close enough."

"Everyone else in the department has it. But not me. Not that I know. Not yet."

"So maybe they had no choice. You did."

"I decided to cooperate because there might be a lot more good that comes from this than bad."

"From the end of the world?"

"They're working to undo what's happened."

"Working out there at Wyvern, underground somewhere?"

"There and other places, yeah. And if they find a way to combat it . . . then wonderful things could come from this."

As he spoke, his gaze moved from me to the studio window.

"Toby," I said.

Manuel's eyes shifted to me again.

I said, "This thing, this plague, whatever it is — you're hoping that if they can bring it under control, they'll be able to use it to help Toby somehow."

"You have a selfish interest here, too, Chris."

From the barn roof, an owl asked its single question of identity five times in quick succession, as if suspicious of everyone in Moonlight Bay.

I took a deep breath and said, "That's the only reason my mother would work on biological research for military purposes. The only reason. Because there was a very good chance that something would come of it that might cure my XP."

"And something may still come of it."

"It was a weapons project?"

"Don't blame her, Chris. Only a weapons project would have tens of billions of dollars behind it. She'd never have had a chance to do this work for the *right* reasons. It was just too expensive."

This was no doubt true. Nothing but a weapons project would have the bottomless resources needed to fund the complex research that my mother's most profound concepts necessitated.

Wisteria Jane (Milbury) Snow was a theoretical geneticist. This means that she did the heavy thinking while other scientists did the heavy lifting. She didn't spend much of her time in laboratories or even working in the virtual lab of a computer. Her lab was her mind, and it was extravagantly equipped. She theorized, and with guidance from her, others sought to prove her theories.

I have said that she was brilliant but perhaps not that she was extraordinarily brilliant. Which she was. She could have chosen any university affiliation in the world. They all sought her.

My father loved Ashdon, but he would have followed her where she wished to go. He would have thrived in any academic environment.

She restricted herself to Ashdon because of me. Most of the truly great universities are in either major or midsize cities, where I'd be no more limited by day than I am in Moonlight Bay, but where I'd have no hope of a rich life by night. Cities are bright even after sunset. And the few dark precincts of a city are not places where a young boy on a bicycle could safely go adventuring between dusk and dawn.

She made less of her life in order to make more of mine. She confined herself to a small town, willing to leave her full potential unrealized, to give me a chance at realizing mine.

Tests to determine genetic damage in a fetus were rudimentary when I was born. If the analytic tools had been sufficiently advanced for my XP to have been detected in the weeks following my conception, perhaps she would have chosen not to bring me into the world.

How I love the world in all its beauty and strangeness.

Because of me, however, the world will grow

ever stranger in the years to come — and perhaps less beautiful.

If not for me, she would have refused to put her mind to work for the project at Wyvern, would never have led them on new roads of inquiry. And we would not have followed one of those roads to the precipice on which we now stand.

As Orson moved to make room for him, Manuel came to the window. He stared in at his son, and with his face more brightly lit, I could see not a wild light in his eyes but only overwhelming love.

"Enhancing the intelligence of animals," I said. "How would that have military applications?"

"For one thing, what better spy than a dog as smart as a human being, sent behind enemy lines? An impenetrable disguise. And they don't check dogs' passports. What better scout on a battlefield?"

Maybe you engineer an exceptionally powerful dog that's smart but also savagely vicious when it needs to be. You have a new kind of soldier: a biologically designed killing machine with the capacity for strategizing.

"I thought intelligence depended on brain size."

He shrugged. "I'm just a cop."

"Or on the number of folds in the brain surface."

"Evidently they discovered different. Anyway," Manuel said, "there was a previous success. Something called the Francis Project, several years ago. An amazingly smart golden retriever. The Wyvern operation was launched to capitalize on what they learned from that. And at Wyvern it wasn't just about animal intelligence. It was about enhancing human intelligence, about lots of things, *many* things."

In the studio, hands covered with Kevlar gloves, Toby placed the hot vase into a bucket half filled with vermiculite. This was the next stage of the annealing process.

Standing at Manuel's side, I said, "Many things? What else?"

"They wanted to enhance human agility, speed, longevity — by finding ways not just to transfer genetic material from one person to another but from species to species."

Species to species.

I heard myself say, "Oh, my God."

Toby poured more of the granular vermiculite over the vase, until it was covered. Vermiculite is a superb insulator that allows the glass to continue cooling very slowly and at a constant rate.

I remembered something Roosevelt Frost had said: that the dogs, cats, and monkeys were not the only experimental subjects in the labs at Wyvern, that there was something worse.

"People," I said numbly. "They experimented on people?"

"Soldiers court-martialed and found guilty of murder, condemned to life sentences in military prisons. They could rot there . . . or take part in the project and maybe win their freedom as a reward."

"But experimenting on people . . ."

"I doubt your mother knew anything about that. They didn't always share with her *all* the ways they applied her ideas."

Toby must have heard our voices at the window, because he took off the insulated gloves and raised the big goggles from his eyes to squint at us. He waved.

"It all went wrong," Manuel said. "I'm no scientist. Don't ask me how. But it went wrong not just in one way. Many ways. It blew up in their faces. Suddenly things happened they weren't expecting. Changes they didn't contemplate. The experimental animals and the prisoners — their genetic makeup underwent changes that weren't desired and couldn't be controlled. . . ."

I waited a moment, but he apparently wasn't prepared to tell me more. I pressed him: "A monkey escaped. A rhesus. They found it in Angela Ferryman's kitchen."

The searching look that Manuel turned on me was so penetrating that I was sure he had seen into my heart, knew the contents of my every pocket, and had an accurate count of the number of bullets left in the Glock.

"They recaptured the rhesus," he said, "but made the mistake of attributing its escape to human error. They didn't realize it had been let go, *released.* They didn't realize there were a few scientists in the project who were . . . becoming."

"Becoming what?"

"Just . . . becoming. Something new. Changing."

Toby switched off the natural gas. The Fisher burner swallowed its own flames.

"Changing how?" I asked Manuel.

"Whatever delivery system they developed to insert new genetic material in a research animal or prisoner . . . that system just took on a life of its own."

Toby turned off all but one panel of fluorescents, so I could go inside for a visit.

Manuel said, "Genetic material from other species was being carried into the bodies of the project scientists without their being aware of it. Eventually, some of them began to have a lot in common with the animals."

"Jesus."

"Too much in common maybe. There was some kind of . . . episode. I don't know the details. It was extremely violent. People died. And all the animals either escaped or were let out."

"The troop."

"About a dozen smart, vicious monkeys, yes. But also dogs and cats . . . and nine of the prisoners."

"And they're still loose?"

"Three of the prisoners were killed in the attempt to recapture them. The military police enlisted our help. That's when most of the cops in the department were contaminated. But the other six and all the animals . . . they were never found."

The man-size barn door opened, and Toby stepped into the threshold. "Daddy?" Shuffling as much as walking, he came to his father and hugged him fiercely. He grinned at me. "Hello, Christopher."

"Hi, Toby."

"Hi, Orson," the boy said, letting go of his father and dropping to his knees to greet the dog.

Orson liked Toby. He allowed himself to be petted.

"Come visit," Toby said.

To Manuel, I said, "There's a whole new troop now. Not violent like the first. Or at least . . . not violent yet. All tagged with transponders, which means they were set loose on purpose. Why?"

"To find the first troop and report their whereabouts. They're so elusive that all other attempts to locate them have failed. It's a desperation plan, an attempt to do *something* before the first troop breeds too large. But this isn't working, either. It's just creating another problem."

"And not only because of Father Eliot."

Manuel stared at me for a long moment. "You've learned a lot, haven't you?"

"Not enough. And too much."

"You're right — Father Tom isn't the problem. Some have sought him out. Others chew the transponders out of each other. This new troop . . . they're not violent but they're plenty smart and they've become disobedient. They want their freedom. At any cost."

Hugging Orson, Toby repeated his invitation to me: "Come visit, Christopher."

Before I could respond, Manuel said, "It's almost dawn, Toby. Chris has to be going home."

I looked toward the eastern horizon, but if the night sky was beginning to turn gray in that direction, the fog prevented me from seeing the change.

"We've been friends for quite a few years," Manuel said. "Seems like I owed you some pieces of the explanation. You've always been good to Toby. But you know enough now. I've done what's right for an old friend. Maybe I've done too much. You go on home now." Without my noticing, he had moved his right hand to the gun in his holster. He patted the weapon. "We won't be watching any Jackie Chan movies anymore, you and me."

He was telling me not to come back. I wouldn't have tried to maintain our friendship, but I might have returned to see Toby from time to time. Not now.

I called Orson to my side, and Toby reluctantly let him go.

"Maybe one more thing," Manuel said as I gripped the handlebars of my bike. "The benign animals who've been enhanced — the cats, the dogs, the new monkeys — they know their origins. Your mother . . . well, maybe you could say she's a legend to them . . . their maker . . . almost like their god. They know who you are, and they revere you. None of them would ever hurt you. But the original troop and most of the people who've been altered . . . even if on some level they like what they're becoming, they still hate your mother because of what they've lost. And they hate you for obvious reasons. Sooner or later, they're going to act on that. Against you. Against people close to you."

I nodded. I was already acting on that assumption. "And you can't protect me?"

He didn't reply. He put his arm around his son. In this new Moonlight Bay, family might still matter for a while, but already the concept of community was slipping away.

"Can't or won't protect me?" I wondered. Without waiting through another silence, I said, "You never told me who Carl Scorso is," referring to the bald man with the earring, who had apparently taken my father's body to an autopsy room in some secure facility still operative beneath a far corner of Fort Wyvern.

"He's one of the original prisoners who signed on for the experiments. The genetic damage related to his previous sociopathic behavior has been identified and edited out. He's not a dangerous man anymore. He's one of their few successes."

I stared at him but couldn't read his true thoughts. "He killed a transient and tore the guy's eyes out."

"No. The troop killed the transient. Scorso just found the body along the road and brought it to Sandy Kirk for disposal. It happens now and then. Hitchhikers, drifters . . . there's always been lots of them moving up and down the California coast. These days, some of them don't get farther than Moonlight Bay."

"And you live with that, too."

"I do what I'm told," he said coldly.

Toby put his arms around his father as if to

protect him, giving me a look of dismay because of the way that I'd challenged his dad.

Manuel said, "We do what we're told. That's the way it is here, these days, Chris. Decisions have been made at a very high level to let this business play out quietly. A very high level. Just suppose the President of the United States himself was something of a science buff, and suppose that he saw a chance to make history by putting huge funds behind genetic engineering the way Roosevelt and Truman funded the Manhattan Project, the way Kennedy funded the effort to put a man on the moon, and suppose he and everyone around him — and the politicians who've come after him — are now determined to cover this up."

"Is that what's happened?"

"No one at the top wants to risk the public's wrath. Maybe they're not just afraid of being booted out of office. Maybe they're afraid of being tried for crimes against humanity. Afraid of being torn apart by angry mobs. I mean . . . soldiers from Wyvern and their families, who might've been contaminated — they're all over the country now. How many have they passed it to? Could be panic in the streets. An international movement to quarantine the whole U.S. And for no good reason. Because the powers that be think the whole thing might run its course without a major effect, peak soon and then just peter out."

"Is there a chance of that?"

"Maybe."

"I don't think there's a chance of that."

He shrugged and with one hand smoothed Toby's hair, which was spiky and disarranged from the strap on the goggles that he'd been wearing. "Not all the people with symptoms of change are like Lewis Stevenson. What's happening to them has infinite variety. And some who go through a bad phase . . . they get over it. They're in flux. This isn't an event, like an earthquake or a tornado. This is a process. If it had ever gotten to be necessary, I would've dealt with Lewis myself."

Admitting nothing, I said, "Maybe it was more necessary than you realized."

"Can't have just anybody making those judgment calls. There's got to be order, stability."

"But there is none."

"There's me," he said.

"Is it possible you're infected and don't know it?"

"No. Not possible."

"Is it possible you're changing and don't realize it?"

"No."

"Becoming?"

"No."

"You scare the hell out of me, Manuel."

The owl hooted again.

A faint but welcome breeze stirred like a ladle through the soupy fog.

"Go home," Manuel said. "It'll be light soon."

"Who ordered Angela Ferryman killed?"

"Go home."

"Who?"

"No one."

"I think she was murdered because she was going to try to go public. She had nothing to lose, she told me. She was afraid of what she was . . . becoming."

"The troop killed her."

"Who controls the troop?"

"No one. We can't even *find* the fuckers."

I thought I knew one place where they hung out: the drainage culvert in the hills, where I'd found the collection of skulls. But I wasn't going to share this information with Manuel, because at this point I couldn't be sure who were my most dangerous enemies: the troop — or Manuel and the other cops.

"If no one sent them after her, why'd they do it?"

"They have their own agenda. Maybe sometimes it matches ours. They don't want the world to know about this, either. Their future isn't in undoing what's been done. Their future is the new world coming. So if somehow they learned Angela's plans, they'd deal with her. There's no mastermind behind this, Chris. There're all these factions — the benign animals, the malevolent ones, the scientists at Wyvern, people who've been changed for the worse, people who've been changed for the better. Lots of competing factions. Chaos. And the chaos will get worse before it gets better. Now go home. Drop this. Drop it before someone targets you like they targeted Angela."

"Is that a threat?"

He didn't reply.

As I started away, walking the bicycle across

the backyard, Toby said, "Christopher Snow. Snow for Christmas. Christmas and Santa. Santa and sleigh. Sleigh on snow. Snow for Christmas. Christopher Snow." He laughed with innocent delight, entertained by this awkward word game, and he was clearly pleased by my surprise.

The Toby Ramirez I had known would not have been capable of even such a simple word-association game as this one.

To Manuel, I said, "They've begun to pay for your cooperation, haven't they?"

His fierce pride in Toby's exhibition of this new verbal skill was so touching and so deeply sad that I could not look at him.

"In spite of all that he didn't have, he was always happy," I said of Toby. "He found a purpose, fulfillment. Now what if they can take him far enough that he's dissatisfied with what he is . . . but then they can't take him all the way to normal?"

"They will," Manuel said with a measure of conviction for which there could be no justification. "They will."

"The same people who've created this nightmare?"

"It's not got only a dark side."

I thought of the pitiful wails of the visitor in the rectory attic, the melancholy quality of its changeling voice, the terrible yearning in its desperate attempts to convey meaning in a caterwaul. I thought of Orson on that summer night, despairing under the stars.

"God help you, Toby," I said, because he was

my friend, too. "God bless you."

"God had His chance," Manuel said. "From now on, we'll make our own luck."

I had to get away from there, and not solely because dawn was soon to arrive. I started walking the bike across the backyard again — and didn't realize that I'd broken into a run until I was past the house and in the street.

When I glanced back at the Nantucket-style residence, it looked different from the way that it had always been before. Smaller than I remembered. Huddled. Forbidding.

In the east, a silver-gray paleness was forming high above the world, either sunrise seeping in or Judgment coming.

In twelve hours I had lost my father, the friendship of Manuel and Toby, many illusions, and much innocence. I was overcome by the terrifying feeling that more and perhaps worse losses lay ahead.

Orson and I fled to Sasha's house.

31

Sasha's house is owned by KBAY and is a perk of her position as general manager of the station. It's a small two-story Victorian with elaborate millwork enhancing the faces of the dormers, all the gableboards, the eaves, the window and door surrounds, and the porch railings.

The house would be a jewel box if it weren't painted the station colors. The walls are canary yellow. The shutters and porch railings are coral pink. All the other millwork is the precise shade of Key-lime pie. The result is as though a flock of Jimmy Buffett fans, high on Margaritas and piña coladas, painted the place during a long party weekend.

Sasha doesn't mind the flamboyant exterior. As she notes, she lives within the house, not outside where she can see it.

The deep back porch is enclosed with glass; and with the help of an electric space heater in cooler months, Sasha has transformed it into an herb greenhouse. On tables and benches and sturdy metal racks stand hundreds of terra-cotta pots and plastic trays in which she cultivates tarragon and thyme, angelica and arrowroot, chervil and cardamom and coriander and chicory, spearmint and sweet cicely, ginseng, hyssop, balm and basil, marjoram and mint and mullein, dill, fennel, rosemary, chamomile, tansy. She uses these in her cooking, to make wonderful, subtly scented potpourris, and to brew health teas that challenge the gag reflex far less than you would expect.

I don't bother to carry a key of my own. A spare is tucked into a terra-cotta pot shaped like a toad, under the yellowish leaves of a rue plant. As the deadly dawn brightened to a paler gray in the east and the world prepared to murder dreams, I let myself into the shelter of Sasha's home.

In the kitchen, I immediately switched on the radio. Sasha was winding through the last half hour of her show, giving a weather report. We were still in the wet season, and a storm was coming in from the northwest. We would have rain shortly after nightfall.

If she had predicted that we were due for a hundred-foot tidal wave and volcanic eruptions with major rivers of lava, I would have listened with pleasure. When I heard her smooth, slightly throaty radio voice, a big stupid smile came over my face, and even on this morning near the end of the world, I couldn't help but be simultaneously soothed and aroused.

As the day brightened beyond the windows, Orson padded directly to the pair of hard-plastic bowls that stood on a rubber mat in one corner. His name is painted on each: Wherever he goes, whether to Bobby's cottage or to Sasha's, he is family.

As a puppy, my dog was given a series of names, but he didn't care to respond to any of them on a regular basis. After noticing how intently the mutt focused on old Orson Welles movies when we ran them on video — and especially on the appearance of Welles himself in any scene — we jokingly renamed him after the actor-director. He has ever since answered to this moniker.

When he found both bowls empty, Orson picked up one of them in his mouth and brought it to me. I filled it with water and returned it to the rubber mat, which prevented it from sliding on the white ceramic-tile floor.

He snatched up the second bowl and looked beseechingly at me. As is true of virtually any dog, Orson's eyes and face are better designed for a beseeching look than are the expressive features of the most talented actor who ever trod the boards.

At the dining table with Roosevelt and Orson and Mungojerrie aboard the *Nostromo*, I had recalled those well-executed but jokey paintings of dogs playing poker and it had occurred to me that my subconscious had been trying to tell me something important by so vividly resurrecting this image from my memory. Now I understood. Each of the dogs in those paintings represents a familiar human type, and each is obviously as smart as any human being. On the *Nostromo*, because of the game that Orson and the cat had played with each other, "mocking their stereotypes," I had realized that some of these animals out of Wyvern might be far smarter than I had previously thought — so smart that I wasn't yet ready to face the awesome truth. If they could hold cards and talk, they might win their share of poker hands; they might even take me to the cleaners.

"It's a little early," I said, taking the food dish from Orson. "But you did have a very active night."

After shaking a serving of his favorite dry dog food from the box into his bowl, I circled the kitchen, closing the Levolor blinds against the growing threat of the day. As I was shutting the last of them, I thought I heard a door close softly elsewhere in the house.

I froze, listening.

"Something?" I whispered.

Orson looked up from his bowl, sniffed the air, cocked his head, then chuffed and once more turned his attention to his food.

The three-hundred-ring circus of my mind.

At the sink I washed my hands and splashed some cold water on my face.

Sasha keeps an immaculate kitchen, gleaming and sweet-smelling, but it's cluttered. She's a superb cook, and clusters of exotic appliances take up at least half the counter space. So many pots, pans, ladles, and utensils dangle from overhead racks that you feel as if you're spelunking through a cavern where every inch of the ceiling is hung with stalactites.

I moved through her house, closing blinds, feeling the vibrant spirit of her in every corner. She is so *alive* that she leaves an aura behind her that lingers long after she has gone.

Her home has no interior-design theme, no harmony in the flow of furniture and artwork. Rather, each room is a testament to one of her consuming passions. She is a woman of many passions.

All meals are taken at a large kitchen table, because the dining room is dedicated to her music. Along one wall is an electronic keyboard, a full-scale synthesizer with which she could compose for an orchestra if she wished, and adjacent to this is her composition table with music stand and a stack of pages with blank musical staffs awaiting her pencil. In the center of the room is a drum set. In a corner stands a high-quality cello with a low, cellist's stool. In another corner, beside a music stand, a saxophone hangs on a brass sax rack. There are two guitars as well, one acoustic and one electric.

The living room isn't about appearances but about books — another of her passions. The walls are lined with bookshelves, which overflow with hardcovers and paperbacks. The furniture is not trendy, neither stylish nor styleless: neutral-tone chairs and sofas selected for the comfort they provide, for the fact that they're perfect for sitting and talking or for spending long hours with a book.

On the second floor, the first room from the head of the stairs features an exercise bicycle, a rowing machine, a set of hand weights from two to twenty pounds, calibrated in two-pound increments, and exercise mats. This is her homeopathic-medicine room, as well, where she keeps scores of bottles of vitamins and minerals, and where she practices yoga. When she uses the Exercycle, she won't get off until she's streaming sweat and has churned up at least thirty miles on the odometer. She stays on the rowing machine until she's crossed Lake Tahoe in her mind, keeping a steady rhythm by singing tunes by Sarah McLachlan or Juliana Hatfield or Meredith Brooks or Sasha Goodall, and when she does stomach crunches and leg lifts, the padded mats under her seem as if they will start smoking before she's half done. When she's finished exercising, she's always more energetic than when she began, flushed and buoyant. And when she concludes a session of meditation in various yoga positions, the intensity of her *relaxation* seems powerful enough to blow out the walls of the room.

God, I love her.

As I stepped from the exercise room into the upstairs hall, I was stricken once more by that premonition of impending loss. I began to shake so badly that I had to lean against the wall until the episode passed.

Nothing could happen to her in daylight, not on the ten-minute drive from the broadcast studios on Signal Hill through the heart of town. The night is when the troop seems to roam. By day they go to ground somewhere, perhaps in the storm drains under the town or even in the hills where I'd found the collection of skulls. And the *people* who can no longer be trusted, the changelings like Lewis Stevenson, seem more in control of themselves under the sun than under the moon. As with the animal men in *The Island of Dr. Moreau*, the wildness in them will not be as easily suppressed at night. With the dusk, they lose a measure of self-control; a sense of adventure springs up in them, and they dare things that they never dream about by day.

Surely nothing could happen to Sasha now that dawn was upon us; for perhaps the first time in my life, I felt relief at the rising of the sun.

Finally I came to her bedroom. Here you will find no musical instruments, not a single book, no pots or trays of herbs, no bottles of vitamins, no exercise equipment. The bed is simple, with a plain headboard, no footboard, and it is covered with a thin white chenille spread. There's nothing whatsoever remarkable about the dresser, the nightstands, or the lamps. The walls are pale yellow, the very shade of morning sunlight in a cloud; no artwork interrupts their smooth planes. The room might seem stark to some, but when Sasha's present, this space is as elaborately decorated as any baroque drawing room in a French castle, as nurturingly serene as any meditation point in a Zen garden. She never sleeps fitfully but always as deep and still as a stone at the bottom of the sea, so you find yourself reaching out to touch her, to feel the warmth of her skin or the throb of her pulse, to quiet the sudden fear for her that grips you from time to time. As with so many things, she has a passion for sleep. She has a passion for passion, too, and when she makes love to you, the room ceases to exist, and you're in a timeless time and a placeless place, where there's only Sasha, only the light and the heat of her, the glorious light of her that blazes but doesn't burn.

As I passed the foot of the bed, heading toward the first of three windows to close the blinds, I saw an object on the chenille spread. It was small, irregular, and highly polished: a fragment of hand-painted, glazed china. Half a smiling mouth, a curve of cheek, one blue eye. A shard from the face of the Christopher Snow doll that had shattered against the wall in Angela Ferryman's house just before the lights had gone out and the smoke had poured into the stairwell from above and below.

At least one of the troop had been here during the night.

Shaking again but with fury rather than fear this time, I ripped the pistol out of my jacket and set out to search the house, from the attic down, every room, every closet, every cupboard, every smallest space in which one of these hateful creatures might be able to conceal itself. I wasn't stealthy or cautious. Cursing, making threats that I had every intention of fulfilling, I tore open doors, slammed drawers shut, poked under furniture with a broom handle. In general I created such a racket that Orson sprinted to my side with the expectation of finding me in a battle for my life — then followed me at a cautious distance, as if he feared that, in my current state of agitation, I might shoot myself in the foot and him in the paw if he stayed too close.

None of the troop was in the house.

When I concluded the search, I had the urge to fill a pail with strong ammonia water and sponge off every surface that the intruder — or intruders — might have touched: walls, floor, stair treads and railings, furniture. Not because I believed that they'd left behind any microorganisms that could infect us. Rather, because I found them to be unclean in a profoundly spiritual sense, as though they had come not out of laboratories at Wyvern but out of a vent in the earth from which also rose sulfur fumes, a terrible light, and the distant cries of the damned.

Instead of going for the ammonia, I used the kitchen phone to call the direct booth line at KBAY. Before I entered the last number, I realized that Sasha was off the air and already on her way home. I hung up and keyed in her mobile number.

"Hey, Snowman," she said.

"Where are you?"

"Five minutes away."

"Are your doors locked?"

"What?"

"For Christ's sake, are your doors locked?"

She hesitated. Then: "They are now."

"Don't stop for anyone. Not anyone. Not for a friend, not even for a cop. Especially not for a cop."

"What if I accidentally run down a little old lady?"

"She won't be a little old lady. She'll only look like one."

"You've suddenly gotten spooky, Snowman."

"Not me. The rest of the world. Listen, I want you to stay on the phone until you're in the driveway."

"Explorer to control tower: The fog's pulling back already. You don't need to talk me in."

"I'm not talking you in. You're talking me *down*. I'm in a state here."

"I sorta noticed."

"I need to hear your voice. All the way. All

the way home, your voice."

"Smooth as the bay," she said, trying to get me to lighten up.

I kept her on the phone until she drove her truck into the carport and switched off the engine.

Sun or no sun, I wanted to go outside and meet her as she opened the driver's door. I wanted to be at her side with the Glock in my hand as she walked across the house to the rear porch, which was the entrance that she always used.

An hour seemed to pass before I heard her footsteps on the back porch, as she walked between the tables of potted herbs.

When she swung open the door, I was standing in the wide blade of morning light that slashed into the kitchen. I pulled her into my arms, slammed the door behind her, and held her so tightly that for a moment neither of us could breathe. I kissed her then, and she was warm and real, real and glorious, glorious and alive.

No matter how tightly I held her, however, no matter how sweet her kisses, I was still haunted by that presentiment of worse losses to come.

SIX

THE DAY
AND THE NIGHT

32

With all that had happened during the previous night and with all that loomed in the night to come, I didn't imagine that we would make love. Sasha couldn't imagine *not* making love. Even though she didn't know the reason for my terror, the sight of me so fearful and so shaken by the thought of losing her was an aphrodisiac that put her in a mood not to be refused.

Orson, ever a gentleman, remained downstairs in the kitchen. We went upstairs to the bedroom and from there into the timeless time and placeless place where Sasha is the only energy, the only form of matter, the only force in the universe. So bright.

Afterward, in a mood that made even the most apocalyptic news seem tolerable, I told her about my night from sundown until dawn, about the millennium monkeys and Stevenson, about how Moonlight Bay was now a Pandora's box swarming with myriad evils.

If she thought I was insane, she hid her judgment well. When I told her of the taunting by the troop, which Orson and I had endured after leaving Bobby's house, she broke out in gooseflesh and had to pull on a robe. As she gradually realized fully how dire our situation was, that we had no one to whom we could turn and nowhere to run even if we were allowed to leave town, that we might already be tainted by this

Wyvern plague, with effects to come that we could not even imagine, she pulled the collar of the robe tighter around her neck.

If she was repulsed by what I'd done to Stevenson, she managed to suppress her emotions with remarkable success, because when I was finished, when I had told her about even the fragment of the doll's face that I'd found on her bed, she slipped out of her robe and, although still stippled with gooseflesh, brought me into her light again.

This time, when we made love, we were quieter than before, moved more slowly, more gently than we had the first time. Although tender before, the motion and the act were more tender now. We clung to each other with love and need but also with desperation, because a new and poignant appreciation of our isolation was upon us. Strangely, though we shared a sense of being two condemned people with an executioner's clock ticking relentlessly, our fusion was sweeter than it had been previously.

Or maybe that isn't strange at all. Perhaps extreme danger strips us of all pretenses, all ambitions, all confusions, focusing us more intensely than we are otherwise ever focused, so that we remember what we otherwise spend most of our lives forgetting: that our nature and purpose is, more than anything else, to love and to make love, to take joy from the beauty of the world, to live with an awareness that the future is not as real a place for any one of us as are the present and the past.

If the world as we knew it was this minute

being flushed away, then my writing and Sasha's songwriting didn't matter. To paraphrase Bogart to Bergman: In this crazy future tumbling like an avalanche straight at us, the ambitions of two people didn't amount to a hill of beans. All that mattered was friendship, love, and surf. The wizards of Wyvern had given me and Sasha an existence as reduced to the essentials as was Bobby Halloway's.

Friendship, love, and surf. Get them while they're hot. Get them before they're gone. Get them while you're still human enough to know how precious they are.

For a while we lay in silence, holding each other, waiting for time to start flowing again. Or maybe hoping that it never would.

Then Sasha said, "Let's cook."

"I think we just did."

"I mean omelets."

"Mmmmmm. All those delicious egg whites," I said, ridiculing her tendency to carry the concept of a healthy diet to extremes.

"I'll use the whole eggs today."

"Now I *know* it's the end of the world."

"Cooked in butter."

"With cheese?"

"Somebody's got to keep the cows in business."

"Butter, cheese, egg yolks. So you've decided on suicide."

We were doing cool, but we weren't *being* cool.

We both knew it, too.

We kept at it anyway, because to do otherwise

would be to admit how scared we were.

The omelets were exceptionally good. So were the fried potatoes and the heavily buttered English muffins.

As Sasha and I ate by candlelight, Orson circled the kitchen table, mewling plaintively and making starving-child-of-the-ghetto eyes at us when we looked down at him.

"You already ate everything I put in your bowl," I told him.

He chuffed as if astonished that I would make such a claim, and he resumed mewling pitiably at Sasha as though trying to assure her that I was lying, that no food whatsoever had yet been provided him. He rolled onto his back, wriggled, and pawed at the air in an all-out assault of merciless cuteness, trying to earn a nibble. He stood on his hind feet and turned in a circle. He was shameless.

With one foot, I pushed a third chair away from the table and said, "Okay, sit up here."

Immediately he leaped onto the chair and sat at eager attention, regarding me intently.

I said, "Ms. Goodall here has bought a fully radical, way insane story from me, without any proof except a few months of diary entries by an obviously disturbed priest. She probably did this because she is critically sex crazy and needs a man, and I'm the only one that'll have her."

Sasha threw a corner of buttered toast at me. It landed on the table in front of Orson.

He darted for it.

"No way, bro!" I said.

He stopped with his mouth open and his teeth bared, an inch from the scrap of toast. Instead of eating the morsel, he sniffed it with obvious pleasure.

"If you help me prove to Ms. Goodall that what I've told her about the Wyvern project is true, I'll share some of my omelet and potatoes with you."

"Chris, his heart," Sasha worried, backsliding into her Grace Granola persona.

"He doesn't have a heart," I said. "He's all stomach."

Orson looked at me reproachfully, as if to say that it wasn't fair to engage in put-down humor when he was unable to participate.

To the dog I said, "When someone nods his head, that means *yes*. When he shakes his head side to side, that means *no*. You understand that, don't you?"

Orson stared at me, panting and grinning stupidly.

"Maybe you don't trust Roosevelt Frost," I said, "but you have to trust this lady here. You don't have a choice, because she and I are going to be together from now on, under the same roof, for the rest of our lives."

Orson turned his attention to Sasha.

"Aren't we?" I asked her. "The rest of our lives?"

She smiled. "I love you, Snowman."

"I love you, Ms. Goodall."

Looking at Orson, she said, "From now on, pooch, it's not the two of you anymore. It's the three of us."

Orson blinked at me, blinked at Sasha, stared with unblinking desire at the bite of toast on the table in front of him.

"Now," I said, "do you understand about nods and shakes?"

After a hesitation, Orson nodded.

Sasha gasped.

"Do you think she's nice?" I asked.

Orson nodded.

"Do you like her?"

Another nod.

A giddy delight swept through me. Sasha's face was shining with the same elation.

My mother, who destroyed the world, had also helped to bring marvels and wonders into it.

I had wanted Orson's cooperation not only to confirm my story but to lift our spirits and give us reason to hope that there might be life after Wyvern. Even if humanity was now faced with dangerous new adversaries like the members of the original troop that escaped the labs, even if we were swept by a mysterious plague of gene-jumping from species to species, even if few of us survived the coming years without fundamental changes of an intellectual, emotional, and even physical nature — perhaps there was nevertheless some chance that when we, the current champions of the evolutionary game, stumbled and fell out of the race and passed away, there would be worthy heirs who might do better with the world than we did.

Cold comfort is better than none.

"Do you think Sasha's pretty?" I asked the dog.

Orson studied her thoughtfully for long seconds. Then he turned to me and nodded.

"That could have been a little quicker," Sasha complained.

"Because he took his time, checked you out good, you know he's being sincere," I assured her.

"I think you're pretty, too," Sasha told him.

Orson wagged his tail across the back of his chair.

"I'm a lucky guy, aren't I, bro?" I asked him. He nodded vigorously.

"And I'm a lucky girl," she said.

Orson turned to her and shook his head: *No.*

"Hey," I said.

The dog actually winked at me, grinning and making that soft wheezing sound that I swear is laughter.

"He can't even talk," I said, "but he can do put-down humor."

We weren't just doing cool now. We were being cool.

If you're genuinely cool, you'll get through anything. That's one of the primary tenets of Bobby Halloway's philosophy, and from my current vantage point, post-Wyvern, I have to say that Philosopher Bob offers a more effective guide to a happy life than all of his big-browed competitors from Aristotle to Kierkegaard to Thomas More to Schelling — to Jacopo Zabarella, who believed in the primacy of logic, order, method. Logic, order, method. All important, sure. But can all of life be analyzed and understood with only those tools? Not that I'm about to claim to have met Bigfoot or to be able to channel dead spirits or to be the reincarnation of Kahuna, but when I see where diligent attention to logic, order, and method have at last brought us, to this genetic storm . . . well, I think I'd be happier catching some epic waves.

For Sasha, apocalypse was no cause for insomnia. As always, she slept deeply.

Although exhausted, I dozed fitfully. The bedroom door was locked, and a chair was wedged under the knob. Orson was sleeping on the floor, but he would be a good early-warning system if anyone entered the house. The Glock was on my nightstand, and Sasha's Smith & Wesson .38 Chiefs Special was on her nightstand. Yet I repeatedly woke with a start, sure that someone had crashed into the bedroom, and I didn't feel safe.

My dreams didn't soothe me. In one of them, I was a drifter, walking alongside a desert highway under a full moon, thumbing a ride without success. In my right hand was a suitcase exactly like my father's. It couldn't have been heavier if it had been filled with bricks. Finally, I put it down, opened it, and recoiled as Lewis Stevenson rose out of it like a cobra from a basket, golden light shimmering in his eyes, and I knew that if something as strange as the dead chief could be in my suitcase, something even stranger could be in me, whereupon I felt the top of my head unzipping — and woke up.

An hour before sundown, I telephoned Bobby

from Sasha's kitchen.

"How's the weather out there at monkey central?" I asked.

"Storm coming in later. Big thunderheads far out to sea."

"Did you get some sleep?"

"After the jokesters left."

"When was that?"

"After I turned the tables and started mooning *them.*"

"They were intimidated," I said.

"Damn right. I've got the bigger ass, and they know it."

"You have a lot of ammunition for that shotgun?"

"A few boxes."

"We'll bring more."

"Sasha's not on the air tonight?"

"Not Saturdays," I said. "Maybe not weeknights anymore, either."

"Sounds like news."

"We're an item. Listen, do you have a fire extinguisher out there?"

"Now you're bragging, bro. The two of you aren't *that* hot together."

"We'll bring a couple of extinguishers. These dudes have a thing for fire."

"You really think it'll get that real?"

"Totally."

Immediately after sunset, while I waited in the Explorer, Sasha went into Thor's Gun Shop to buy ammunition for the shotgun, the Glock, and her Chiefs Special. The order was so large and heavy that Thor Heissen himself carried it out to the truck for her and loaded it in back.

He came to the passenger window to say hello. He is a tall, fat man with a face pitted by acne scars, and his left eye is glass. He's not one of the world's best-looking guys, but he's a former L.A. cop who quit on principle, not because of scandal, an active deacon at his church and founder of — and largest contributor to — the orphanage associated with it.

"Heard about your dad, Chris."

"At least he's not suffering anymore," I said — and wondered just what had been different about his cancer that made the people at Wyvern want to do an autopsy on him.

"Sometimes, it's a blessing," Thor said. "Just being allowed to slip away when it's your time. Lots of folks will miss him, though. He was a fine man."

"Thanks, Mr. Heissen."

"What're you kids up to, anyway? Gonna start a war?"

"Exactly," I said as Sasha twisted her key in the ignition and raced the engine.

"Sasha says you're gonna go shoot clams."

"That's not environmentally correct, is it?"

He laughed as we pulled away.

In the backyard of my house, Sasha swept a flashlight beam across the craters that had been clawed out of the grass by Orson the previous night, before I'd taken him with me to Angela Ferryman's.

"What's he have buried here?" she asked.

"The whole skeleton of a T-Rex?"

"Last night," I said, "I thought all the digging was just a grief reaction to Dad's death, a way for Orson to work off negative energy."

"Grief reaction?" she said, frowning.

She'd seen how smart Orson was, but she still didn't have a full grasp on the complexity of his inner life or on its similarity to our own. Whatever techniques were used to enhance the intelligence of these animals, it had involved the insertion of some human genetic material into their DNA. When Sasha finally got a handle on that, she would have to sit down for a while; maybe for a week.

"Since then," I said, "it's occurred to me that he was searching for something that he knew I needed to have."

I knelt on the grass beside Orson. "Now, bro, I know you were in a lot of distress last night, grieving over Dad. You were rattled, couldn't quite remember where to dig. He's been gone a day now, and it's a little easier to accept, isn't it?"

Orson whined thinly.

"So give it another try," I said.

He didn't hesitate, didn't debate where to start, but went to one hole and worked to enlarge it. In five minutes, his claws clinked against something.

Sasha directed the flashlight on a dirt-caked Mason jar, and I worked it the rest of the way out of the ground.

Inside was a roll of yellow pages from a legal tablet, held together by a rubber band.

I unrolled them, held the first page to the light, and at once recognized my father's handwriting. I read only the first paragraph:

If you're reading this, Chris, I am dead and Orson has led you to the jar in the yard, because only he knows of its existence. And that's where we should begin. Let me tell you about your dog. . . .

"Bingo," I said.

Rolling up the papers and returning them to the jar, I glanced at the sky. No moon. No stars. The scudding clouds were low and black, touched here and there by a sour-yellow glow from the rising lights of Moonlight Bay.

"We can read these later," I said. "Let's move. Bobby's alone out there."

33

As Sasha opened the tailgate of the Explorer, shrieking gulls wheeled low overhead, tumbling inland toward safer roosts, frightened by a wind that shattered the sea and flung the wet fragments across the point of the horn.

With the box from Thor's Gun Shop in my arms, I watched the white wings dwindle across the turbulent black sky.

The fog was long gone. Under the lowering clouds, the night was crystalline.

Around us on the peninsula, the sparse shore grass thrashed. Tall sand devils whirled off the tops of the dunes, like pale spirits spun up from graves.

I wondered if more than the wind had harried the seagulls from their shelter.

"They're not here yet," Bobby assured me as he took the two pizza-shop boxes from the back of the Explorer. "It's early for them."

"Monkeys are usually eating at this hour," I said. "Then a little dancing."

"Maybe they won't even come at all tonight," Sasha hoped.

"They'll come," I said.

"Yeah. They'll come," Bobby agreed.

Bobby went inside with our dinner. Orson stayed close by his side, not out of fear that the murderous troop might be among the dunes even now but, in his role as food cop, to guard against the unfair distribution of the pizza.

Sasha removed two plastic shopping bags from the Explorer. They contained the fire extinguishers that she'd purchased at Crown Hardware.

She closed the tailgate and used the remote on her key chain to lock the doors. Since Bobby's Jeep occupied his one-car garage, we were leaving the Explorer in front of the cottage.

When Sasha turned to me, the wind made a glorious banner of her lustrous mahogany hair, and her skin glowed softly, as if the moon had managed to press one exquisite beam through the clotted clouds to caress her face. She seemed larger than life, an elemental spirit.

"What?" she said, unable to interpret my stare.

"You're so beautiful. Like a wind goddess drawing the storm to you."

"You're so full of shit," she said, but she smiled.

"It's one of my most charming qualities."

A sand devil did a dervish dance around us, spitting grit in our faces, and we hurried into the house.

Bobby was waiting inside, where the lights were dialed down to a comfortable murk. He locked the front door behind us.

Looking around at the large panes of glass, Sasha said, "I sure wish we could nail some plywood over these."

"This is my house," Bobby said. "I'm not going to board up the windows, hunker down, and live like a prisoner just because of some damn monkeys."

To Sasha, I said, "As long as I've known him,

this amazing dude hasn't been intimidated by monkeys."

"Never," Bobby agreed. "And I'm not starting now."

"Let's at least draw the blinds," Sasha said.

I shook my head. "Bad idea. That'll just make them suspicious. If they can watch us, and if we don't appear to be lying in wait for them, they'll be less cautious."

Sasha took the two fire extinguishers from their boxes and clipped the plastic presale guards from the triggers. They were ten-pound, marine-type models, easy to handle. She put one in a corner of the kitchen where it couldn't be seen from the windows, and tucked the second beside one of the sofas in the living room.

While Sasha dealt with the extinguishers, Bobby and I sat in the candlelit kitchen, boxes of ammunition in our laps, working below table level in case the monkey mafia showed up while we were at work. Sasha had purchased three extra magazines for the Glock and three speed-loaders for her revolver, and we snapped cartridges into them.

"After I left here last night," I said, "I visited Roosevelt Frost."

Bobby looked at me from under his eyebrows. "He and Orson have a broly chat?"

"Roosevelt tried. Orson wasn't having any of it. But there was this cat named Mungojerrie."

"Of course," he said drily.

"The cat said the people at Wyvern wanted me to walk away from this, just move on."

"You talk to the cat personally?"

"No. Roosevelt passed the message to me."

"Of course."

"According to the cat, I was going to get a warning. If I didn't stop Nancying this, they'd kill my friends one by one until I did."

"They'll blow *me* away to warn you off?"

"Their idea, not mine."

"They can't just kill you? They think they need kryptonite?"

"They revere me, Roosevelt says."

"Well, who doesn't?" Even after the monkeys, he remained dubious about this issue of anthropomorphizing animal behavior. But he sure had cranked down the volume of his sarcasm.

"Right after I left the *Nostromo*," I said, "I was warned, just like the cat said I would be."

I told Bobby about Lewis Stevenson, and he said, "He was going to kill Orson?"

From his guard post where he stared up at the pizza boxes on the counter, Orson whined as if to confirm my account.

"So," Bobby said, "you shot the sheriff."

"He was the chief of police."

"You shot the sheriff," Bobby insisted.

A lot of years ago, he had been a radical Eric Clapton junkie, so I knew why he liked it better this way. "All right. I shot the sheriff — but I did not shoot the deputy."

"I can't let you out of my sight."

He finished with the speedloaders and tucked them into the dump pouch that Sasha had also purchased.

"Bitchin' shirt," I said.

Bobby was wearing a rare long-sleeve Hawaiian shirt featuring a spectacular, colorful mural of a tropical festival: oranges, reds, and greens.

He said, "Kamehameha Garment Company, from about 1950."

Having dealt with the fire extinguishers, Sasha came into the kitchen and switched on one of the two ovens to warm up the pizza.

To Bobby, I said, "Then I set the patrol car on fire to destroy the evidence."

"What's on the pizza?" he asked Sasha.

"Pepperoni on one, sausage and onions on the other."

"Bobby's wearing a used shirt," I told her.

"Antique," Bobby amended.

"Anyway, after I blew up the patrol car, I went over to St. Bernadette's and let myself in."

"Breaking and entering?"

"Unlocked window."

"So it's just criminal trespass," he said.

As I finished loading the spare magazines for the Glock, I said, "Used shirt, antique shirt — seems like the same thing to me."

"One's cheap," Sasha explained, "and the other isn't."

"One's art," Bobby said. He held out the leather holder with the speedloaders. "Here's your dump pouch."

Sasha took it from him and snapped it onto her belt.

I said, "Father Tom's sister was an associate of my mother's."

Bobby said, "Mad-scientist-blow-up-the-world type?"

"No explosives are involved. But, yeah, and now she's infected."

"Infected." He grimaced. "Do we really have to get into this?"

"Yeah. But it's way complex. Genetics."

"Big-brain stuff. Boring."

"Not this time."

Far out to sea, bright arteries of lightning pulsed in the sky and a low throb of thunder followed.

Sasha had also purchased a cartridge belt designed for duck hunters and skeet shooters, and Bobby began to stuff shotgun shells into the leather loops.

"Father Tom's infected, too," I said, putting one of the spare 9-millimeter magazines in my shirt pocket.

"Are you infected?" Bobby asked.

"Maybe. My mom had to be. And Dad was."

"How's it passed?"

"Bodily fluids," I said, standing the other two magazines behind a fat red candle on the table, where they could not be seen from the windows. "And maybe other ways."

Bobby looked at Sasha, who was transferring the pizzas to baking sheets.

She shrugged and said, "If Chris is, then I am."

"We've been holding hands for over a year," I told Bobby.

"You want to heat your own pizza?" Sasha asked him.

"Nah. Too much trouble. Go ahead and infect me."

I closed the box of ammo and put it on the floor. My pistol was still in my jacket, which hung on the back of my chair.

As Sasha continued preparing the pizzas, I said, "Orson might not be infected, exactly. I mean, he might be more like a carrier or something."

Passing a shotgun shell between his fingers and across his knuckles, like a magician rolling a coin, Bobby said, "So when does the pus and puking start?"

"It's not a disease in that sense. It's more a process."

Lightning flared again. Beautiful. And too brief to do any damage to me.

"Process," Bobby mused.

"You're not actually sick. Just . . . changed."

Sliding the pizzas into the oven to reheat them, Sasha said, "So who owned the shirt before you did?"

Bobby said, "Back in the fifties? Who knows?"

"Were dinosaurs alive then?" I wondered.

"Not many," Bobby said.

Sasha said, "What's it made of?"

"Rayon."

"Looks in perfect condition."

"You don't abuse a shirt like this," Bobby said solemnly, "you treasure it."

At the refrigerator, I plucked out bottles of Corona for everyone but Orson. Because of his body weight, the mutt can usually handle one beer without getting sloppy, but this night he needed to keep a totally clear head. The rest of us actually needed the brew; calming our nerves a little would increase our effectiveness.

As I stood beside the sink, popping the caps off the beers, lightning tore at the sky again, unsuccessfully trying to rip rain out of the clouds, and in the flash I saw three hunched figures racing from one dune to another.

"They're here," I said, bringing the beers to the table.

"They always need a while to get up their nerve," Bobby said.

"I hope they give us time for dinner."

"I'm starved," Sasha agreed.

"Okay, so what're the basic symptoms of this not-disease, this process?" Bobby asked. "Do we end up looking like we have gnarly oak fungus?"

"Some may degenerate psychologically like Stevenson," I said. "Some may change physically, too, in minor ways. Maybe in major ways, for all I know. But it sounds as if each case is different. Maybe some people aren't affected, or not so you'd notice, and then others really *change*."

As Sasha fingered the sleeve of Bobby's shirt, admiring it, he said, "The pattern's a Eugene Savage mural called *Island Feast.*"

"The buttons are fully stylin'," she said, in the mood now.

"Totally stylin'," Bobby agreed, rubbing his thumb over one of the yellow-brown, striated buttons, smiling with the pride of a passionate collector and with pleasure at the sensuous texture. "Polished coconut shell."

Sasha got a stack of paper napkins from a

drawer and brought them to the table.

The air was thick and damp. You could feel the skin of the storm swelling like a balloon. It would burst soon.

After taking a swallow of the icy Corona, I said to Bobby, "Okay, bro, before I tell you the rest of it, Orson has a little demonstration for you."

"I've got all the Tupperware I need."

I called Orson to my side. "There are some throw pillows on the living-room sofas. One was a gift from me to Bobby. Would you go get it for him, please?"

Orson padded out of the room.

"What's going on?" Bobby wondered.

Sitting down with her beer, Sasha grinned and said, "Just wait." Her .38 Chiefs Special was on the table. She unfolded a paper napkin and covered the weapon with it. "Just wait."

Every year, Bobby and I exchange gifts at Christmas. One gift each. Because we both have everything we need, value and usefulness are not criteria when we shop. The idea is to give the tackiest items that can be found for sale. This has been a hallowed tradition since we were twelve. In Bobby's bedroom are shelves on which he keeps the collection of tasteless gifts that I've given to him; the only one he finds insufficiently tacky to warrant space on those shelves is the pillow.

Orson returned to the kitchen with this inadequately tacky item in his mouth, and Bobby accepted it, trying to look unimpressed with the dog's feat.

The twelve-by-eight-inch pillow featured a needlepoint sampler on the front. It was among items that had been manufactured by — and sold to raise funds for — a popular television evangelist. Inside an elaborate border were eight words in scrollwork stitching: JESUS EATS SINNERS AND SPITS OUT SAVED SOULS.

"You didn't find this tacky?" Sasha asked disbelievingly.

"Tacky, yes," Bobby said, strapping the loaded ammo belt around his waist without getting up from his chair. "But not tacky enough."

"We have awesomely high standards," I said.

The year after I gave Bobby the pillow, I presented him with a ceramic sculpture of Elvis Presley. Elvis is depicted in one of his glitziest white-silk-and-sequins Vegas stage outfits while sitting on the toilet where he died; his hands are clasped in prayer, his eyes are raised to Heaven, and there's a halo around his head.

In this yuletide competition, Bobby is at a disadvantage because he insists on actually going into gift shops in search of the perfect trash. Because of my XP, I am restricted to mail order, where one can find enough catalogs of exquisitely tacky merchandise to fill all the shelves in the Library of Congress.

Turning the pillow over in his hands, frowning at Orson, Bobby said, "Neat trick."

"No trick," I said. "There were evidently a lot of different experiments going on at Wyvern. One of them dealt with enhancing the intelligence of both humans and animals."

"Bogus."

"Truth."

"Insane."

"Entirely."

I instructed Orson to take the pillow back where he'd found it, then to go to the bedroom, nudge open the sliding door, and return with one of the black dress loafers that Bobby had bought when he'd discovered that he had only thongs, sandals, and athletic shoes to wear to my mother's memorial service.

The kitchen was redolent with the aroma of pizza, and the dog gazed longingly at the oven.

"You'll get your share," I assured him. "Now scoot."

As Orson started out of the kitchen, Bobby said, "Wait."

Orson regarded him expectantly.

"Not just a shoe. And not just a loafer. The loafer for my left foot."

Chuffing as if to say that this complication was insignificant, Orson proceeded on his errand.

Out over the Pacific, a blazing staircase of lightning connected the heavens to the sea, as if signaling the descent of archangels. The subsequent crash of thunder rattled the windows and reverberated in the cottage walls.

Along this temperate coast, our storms are rarely accompanied by pyrotechnics of this kind. Apparently we were scheduled for a major hammering.

I put a can of red-pepper flakes on the table, then paper plates and the insulated serving pads on which Sasha placed the pizzas.

"Mungojerrie," said Bobby.

"It's a name from a book of poems about cats."

"Seems pretentious."

"It's cute," Sasha disagreed.

"Fluffy," Bobby said. "Now that's a name for a cat."

The wind rose, rattling a vent cap on the roof and whistling in the eaves. I couldn't be sure, but I thought that I heard, in the distance, the loonlike cries of the troop.

Bobby reached down with one hand to reposition the shotgun, which was on the floor beside his chair.

"Fluffy or Boots," he said. "Those are solid cat names."

With a knife and fork, Sasha cut a slice of pepperoni pizza into bite-size pieces and set it aside to cool for Orson.

The dog returned from the bedroom with one loafer in his mouth. He presented it to Bobby. It was for the left foot.

Bobby carried the shoe to the flip-top trash can and disposed of it. "It's not the tooth marks or the dog drool," he assured Orson. "I don't plan ever to wear dress shoes again, anyway."

I remembered the envelope from Thor's Gun Shop that had been on my bed when I'd found the Glock there the night before. It had been slightly damp and stippled with curious indentations. Saliva. Tooth marks. Orson was the person who had put my father's pistol where I would be sure to find it.

Bobby returned to the table and sat staring at the dog.

"So?" I asked.

"What?"

"You know what."

"I need to say it?"

"Yeah."

Bobby sighed. "I feel as if one honking huge mondo crashed through my head and just about sucked my brain out in the backwash."

"You're a hit," I told Orson.

Sasha had been fanning one hand over the dog's share of pizza to ensure that the cheese wouldn't be hot enough to stick to the roof of his mouth and burn him. Now she put the plate on the floor.

Orson banged his tail against table and chair legs as he set about proving that high intelligence does not necessarily correlate with good table manners.

"Silky," Bobby said. "Simple name. A cat name. Silky."

As we ate pizza and drank beer, the three flickering candles provided barely enough light for me to scan the pages of yellow lined tablet paper on which my father had written a concise account of the activities at Wyvern, the unanticipated developments that had spiraled into catastrophe, and the extent of my mother's involvement. Although Dad wasn't a scientist and could only recount — largely in layman's terms — what my mother had told him, there was a wealth of information in the document he had left for me.

" 'A little delivery boy,' " I said. "That's what Lewis Stevenson said to me last night when I asked what had changed him from the man he'd once been. 'A little delivery boy that wouldn't die.' He was talking about a retrovirus. Apparently, my mother theorized a new kind of retrovirus . . . with the selectivity of a retrotransposon."

When I looked up from Dad's pages, Sasha and Bobby were staring at me blank-eyed.

He said, "Orson probably knows what you're talking about, bro, but I dropped out of college."

"I'm a deejay," Sasha said.

"And a good one," Bobby said.

"Thank you."

"Though you play too much Chris Isaak," he added.

This time lightning didn't step down the sky but dropped straight and fast, like a blazing express elevator carrying a load of high explosives, which detonated when it slammed into the earth. The entire peninsula seemed to leap, and the house shook, and rain like a shower of blast debris rattled across the roof.

Glancing at the windows, Sasha said, "Maybe they won't like the rain. Maybe they'll stay away."

I reached into the pocket of the jacket hanging on my chair and drew the Glock. I placed it on the table where I could get at it more quickly, and I used Sasha's trick with the paper napkin to conceal it.

"Mostly in clinical trials, scientists have been treating lots of illnesses — AIDS, cancer, inherited diseases — with various gene therapies. The idea is, if the patient has certain defective genes or maybe lacks certain genes altogether, you replace the bad genes with working copies or add the missing genes that will make his cells better at fighting disease. There've been encouraging results. A growing number of modest successes. And failures, too, unpleasant surprises."

Bobby said, "There's always a Godzilla. Tokyo's humming along, all happy and prosperous one minute — and the next minute, you've got giant lizard feet stamping everything flat."

"The problem is getting the healthy genes into the patient. Mostly they use crippled viruses to carry the genes into the cells. Most of these are retroviruses."

"Crippled?" Bobby asked.

"It means they can't reproduce. That way they're no threat to the body. Once they carry the human gene into the cell, they have the ability to neatly splice it into the cell's chromosomes."

"Delivery boys," Bobby said.

"And once they do their job," Sasha said, "they're supposed to die?"

"Sometimes they don't go easily," I said. "They can cause inflammation or serious immune responses that destroy the viruses *and* the cells into which they delivered genes. So some researchers have been studying ways to modify retroviruses by making them more like retrotransposons, which are bits of the body's own DNA that can already copy and slot themselves into chromosomes."

"Here comes Godzilla," Bobby told Sasha.

She said, "Snowman, how do you know all this crap? You didn't get it by looking at those pages for two minutes."

"You tend to find the driest research papers interesting when you know they could save your life," I said. "If anyone can find a way to replace my defective genes with working copies, my body will be able to produce the enzymes that repair the ultraviolet damage to my DNA."

Bobby said, "Then you wouldn't be the Nightcrawler anymore."

"Goodbye freakhood," I agreed.

Above the noisy drumming of the rain on the roof came the patter of something running across the back porch.

We looked toward the sound in time to see a large rhesus leap up from the porch floor onto the windowsill over the kitchen sink. Its fur was wet and matted, which made it look scrawnier than it would have appeared when dry. It balanced adroitly on that narrow ledge and pinched a vertical mullion in one small hand. Peering in at us with what appeared to be only ordinary monkey curiosity, the creature looked quite benign — except for its baleful eyes.

"They'll probably get annoyed quicker if we pretty much ignore them," Bobby said.

"The more annoyed they are," Sasha added, "the more careless they might get."

Biting into another slice of the sausage-and-onion pizza, tapping one finger against the stack of yellow pages on the table, I said, "Just scanning, I see this paragraph where my dad explains as much as he understood about this new theory of my mother's. For the project at Wyvern, she developed this revolutionary new approach to engineering retroviruses so they could more safely be used to ferry genes into the patient's cells."

"I definitely hear giant lizard feet," Bobby said. "Boom, boom, boom, boom."

At the window, the monkey shrieked at us.

I glanced at the nearer window, beside the table, but nothing was peering in there.

Orson stood on his hind legs with his forepaws on the table and theatrically expressed an interest in more pizza, lavishing all his charm on Sasha.

"You know how kids try to play one parent against the other," I warned her.

"I'm more like his sister-in-law," she said. "Anyway, this could be his last meal. Ours, too."

I sighed. "All right. But if we aren't killed, then we're setting a lousy precedent."

A second monkey leaped onto the windowsill. They were both shrieking and baring their teeth at us.

Sasha selected the narrowest of the remaining slices of pizza, cut it into pieces, and placed it on the dog's plate on the floor.

Orson glanced worriedly at the goblins at the window, but even the primates of doom couldn't spoil his appetite. He turned his attention to his dinner.

One of the monkeys began to slap a hand rhythmically against the windowpane, shrieking louder than ever.

Its teeth looked larger and sharper than those of a rhesus ought to have been, plenty large enough and sharp enough to help it fulfill the demanding role of a predator. Maybe this was a physical trait engineered into it by the playful weapons-research boys at Wyvern. In my mind's eye, I saw Angela's torn throat.

"This might be meant to distract us," Sasha suggested.

"They can't get into the house anywhere else without breaking glass," Bobby said. "We'll hear them."

"Over this racket and the rain?" she wondered.

"We'll hear them."

"I don't think we should split up in different rooms unless we're absolutely driven to it," I said. "They're smart enough to know about dividing to conquer."

Again, I squinted through the window near which the table was placed, but no monkeys were on that section of porch, and nothing but the rain and the wind moved through the dark dunes beyond the railing.

Over the sink, one of the monkeys had managed to turn its back and still cling to the window. It was squealing as if with laughter as it mooned us, pressing its bare, furless, ugly butt to the glass.

"So," Bobby asked me, "what happened after you let yourself into the rectory?"

Sensing time running out, I swiftly summarized the events in the attic, at Wyvern, and at the Ramirez house.

"Manuel, a pod person," Bobby said, shaking his head sadly.

"Ugh," Sasha said, but she wasn't commenting on Manuel.

At the window, the male monkey facing us was urinating copiously on the glass.

"Well, this is new," Bobby observed.

On the porch beyond the sink windows, more monkeys started popping into the air like kernels of corn bursting off a hot oiled pan, tumbling up into sight and then dropping away. They were all squealing and shrieking, and there seemed to be scores of them, though it was surely the same half dozen springing-spinning-popping repeatedly into view.

I finished the last of my beer.

Being cool was getting harder minute by minute. Perhaps even *doing* cool required energy and more concentration than I possessed.

"Orson," I said, "it wouldn't be a bad idea if you sauntered around the house."

He understood and set out immediately to police the perimeter.

Before he was out of the kitchen, I said, "No heroics. If you see anything wrong, bark your head off and come running straight back here."

He padded out of sight.

Immediately, I regretted having sent him, even though I knew it was the right thing to do.

The first monkey had emptied its bladder, and now the second one had turned to face the kitchen and had begun to loose his own stream. Others were scampering along the handrail outside and swinging from the porch-roof rafters.

Bobby was sitting directly opposite the window that was adjacent to the table. He searched that comparatively calm part of the night with suspicion equal to mine.

The lightning seemed to have passed, but volleys of thunder still boomed across the sea. This cannonade excited the troop.

"I hear the new Brad Pitt movie is really hot," Bobby said.

Sasha said, "Haven't seen it."

"I always wait for video," I reminded him.

Something tried the door to the back porch. The knob rattled and squeaked, but the lock was securely engaged.

The two monkeys at the sink windows dropped away. Two more sprang up from the porch to take their places, and both began to urinate on the glass.

Bobby said, "I'm not cleaning this up."

"Well, *I'm* not cleaning it up," Sasha declared.

"Maybe they'll get their aggression and anger out this way and then just leave," I said.

Bobby and Sasha appeared to have studied withering sarcastic expressions at the same school.

"Or maybe not," I reconsidered.

From out of the night, a stone about the size of a cherry pit struck one of the windows, and the peeing monkeys dropped away to escape from the line of fire. More small stones quickly followed the first, rattling like hail.

No stones were flung at the nearest window.

Bobby plucked the shotgun from the floor and placed it across his lap.

When the barrage was at its peak, it abruptly ended.

The frenzied monkeys were screaming more fiercely now. Their escalating cries were shrill, eerie, and seemed to have supernatural effect, feeding back into the night with such demonic energy that rain pounded the cottage harder than ever. Merciless hammers of thunder cracked the shell of the night, and once again bright tines of lightning dug at the meat of the sky.

A stone, larger than any in the previous assault, rebounded off one of the sink windows: *snap*. A second of approximately the same size immediately followed, thrown with greater force than the first.

Fortunately their hands were too small to allow them to hold and properly operate pistols or revolvers; and with their relatively low body weight, they would be kicked head over heels by the recoil. These creatures were surely smart enough to understand the purpose and operation of handguns, but at least the horde of geniuses in the Wyvern labs hadn't chosen to work with gorillas. Although, if the idea occurred to them, they would no doubt immediately seek funding for that enterprise and would not only provide the gorillas with firearms training but instruct them, as well, in the fine points of nuclear-weapons design.

Two more stones snapped against the targeted window glass.

I touched the cell phone clipped to my belt.

There ought to be someone we could call for help. Not the police, not the FBI. If the former responded, the friendly officers on the Moonlight Bay force would probably provide cover fire for the monkeys. Even if we could get through to the nearest office of the FBI and could sound more credible than all the callers reporting abduction by flying saucers, we would be talking to the enemy; Manuel Ramirez said the decision to let this nightmare play itself out had been made at "very high levels," and I believed him.

With a concession of responsibility unmatched by generations before ours, we have entrusted our lives and futures to professionals and experts who convince us that we have too little knowledge or wit to make any decisions of importance about the management of society. This is the consequence of our gullibility and laziness. Apocalypse with primates.

A still larger stone struck the window. The pane cracked but didn't shatter.

I picked up the two spare 9-millimeter magazines on the table and tucked one into each of my jean pockets.

Sasha slipped one hand under the rumpled napkin that concealed the Chiefs Special.

I followed her lead and got a grip on the hidden Glock.

We looked at each other. A tide of fear washed through her eyes, and I was sure that she saw the same dark currents in mine.

I tried to smile reassuringly, but my face felt as though it would crack like hard plaster. "Gonna be fine. A deejay, a surf rebel, and the

Elephant Man — the perfect team to save the world."

"If possible," Bobby said, "don't immediately waste the first one or two that come in. Let a few inside. Delay as long as you can. Let them feel confident. Sucker the little geeks. Then let me open on them first, teach them respect. With the shotgun, I don't even have to aim."

"Yes, sir, General Bob," I said.

Two, three, four stones — about as hefty as peach pits — struck the windows. The second large pane cracked, and a subsidiary fissure opened off that line, like lightning branching.

I was experiencing a physiological rearrangement that would have fascinated any physician. My stomach had squeezed up through my chest and was pressing insistently at the base of my throat, while my pounding heart had dropped down into the space formerly occupied by my stomach.

Half a dozen more substantial stones, whaled harder than before, battered the two large windows, and both panes shattered inward. With a burst of brittle music, glass rained into the stainless-steel sink, across the granite counters, onto the floor. A few shards sprayed as far as the dinette, and I shut my eyes briefly as sharp fragments clinked onto the tabletop and plopped into the remaining slices of cold pizza.

When I opened my eyes an instant later, two shrieking monkeys, each as large as the one that Angela had described, were already at the window again. Wary of the broken glass and of us, the pair swung inside, onto the granite counter.

Wind churned in around them, plucking at their rain-matted fur.

One of them looked toward the broom closet, where the shotgun was usually locked away. Since their arrival, they hadn't seen any of us approach that cupboard, and they couldn't possibly spot the 12-gauge balanced on Bobby's knees, under the table.

Bobby glanced at them but was more interested in the window opposite him, across the table.

Hunched and agile, the two creatures already in the room moved along the counter in opposite directions from the sink. In the dimly lighted kitchen, their malevolent yellow eyes were as bright as the flames leaping on the points of the candle wicks.

The intruder to the left encountered a toaster and angrily swept it to the floor. Sparks spurted from the wall receptacle when the plug tore out of the socket.

I remembered Angela's account of the rhesus bombarding her with apples hard enough to split her lip. Bobby maintained an uncluttered kitchen, but if these beasts opened cabinet doors and started firing glasses and dishes at us, they could do serious damage even if we did enjoy an advantage in firepower. A dinner plate, spinning like a Frisbee, catching you across the bridge of the nose, might be nearly as effective as a bullet.

Two more dire-eyed creatures sprang up from the porch floor into the frame of the shattered window. They bared their teeth at us and hissed.

The paper napkin over Sasha's gun hand trembled visibly — and not because it was caught by a draft from the window.

In spite of the shrieking-chattering-hissing of the intruders, in spite of the bluster of the March wind at the broken windows and the rolling thunder and the drumming rain, I thought I heard Bobby singing under his breath. He was largely ignoring the monkeys on the far side of the kitchen, focusing intently on the window that remained intact, across the table from him — and his lips were moving.

Perhaps emboldened by our lack of response, perhaps believing us to be immobilized by fear, the two increasingly agitated creatures in the broken-out windows now swung inside and moved in opposite directions along the counter, forming pairs with each of the first two intruders.

Either Bobby began to sing louder or stark terror sharpened my hearing, because suddenly I could recognize the song that he was singing. "Daydream Believer." It was golden-oldie teen pop, first recorded by the Monkees.

Sasha must have heard it, too, because she said, "A blast from the past."

Two *more* members of the troop climbed into the windows above the sink, clinging to the frames, hellfire in their eyes, squealing monkey-hate at us.

The four already in the room were shrieking louder than ever, bouncing up and down on the counters, shaking their fists in the air, baring their teeth and spitting at us.

They were smart but not smart enough. Their rage was rapidly clouding their judgment.

"Wipeout," Bobby said.

Here we go.

Instead of scooting backward in his chair to clear the table, he swung sideways in it, rose fluidly to his feet, and brought up the shotgun as if he'd had both military training and ballet lessons. Flame spouted from the muzzle, and the first deafening blast caught the two latest arrivals at the windows, blowing them backward onto the porch, as though they were only a child's stuffed toys, and the second round chopped down the pair on the counter to the left of the sink.

My ears were ringing as though I were inside a tolling cathedral bell, and although the roar of the gunfire in this confined space was loud enough to be disorienting, I was on my feet before the 12-gauge boomed the second time, as was Sasha, who turned away from the table and squeezed off a round toward the remaining pair of intruders just as Bobby dealt with numbers three and four.

As they fired and the kitchen shook with the blasts, the nearest window exploded at me. Air-surfing on a cascade of glass, a screaming rhesus landed on the table in our midst, knocking over two of the three candles and extinguishing one of them, spraying rain off its coat, sending a pan of pizza spinning to the floor.

I brought up the Glock, but the latest arrival flung itself onto Sasha's back. If I shot it, the slug would pass straight through the damn thing and probably kill her, too.

By the time I kicked a chair out of the way and got around the table, Sasha was screaming, and the squealing monkey on her back was trying to tear out handfuls of her hair. Reflexively, she'd dropped her .38 to reach blindly behind herself for the rhesus. It snapped at her hands, teeth audibly cracking together on empty air. Her body was bent backward over the table, and her assailant was trying to pull her head back farther still, to expose her throat.

I dropped the Glock on the table and seized the creature from behind, getting my right hand around its neck, using my left to clutch the fur and skin between its shoulder blades. I twisted that handful of fur and skin so fiercely that the beast screamed in pain. It wouldn't let go of Sasha, however, and as I struggled to tear it away from her, it tried to pull her hair out by the roots.

Bobby pumped another round into the chamber and squeezed off a third shot, the cottage walls seemed to shake as if an earthquake had rumbled under us, and I figured that was the end of the final pair of intruders, but I heard Bobby cursing and knew more trouble had come our way.

Revealed more by their blazing yellow eyes than by the guttering flames of the remaining two candles, another pair of monkeys, total kamikazes, had sprung into the windows above the sink.

And Bobby was reloading.

In another part of the cottage, Orson barked

loudly. I didn't know if he was racing toward us to join the fray or whether he was calling for help.

I heard myself cursing with uncharacteristic vividness and snarling with animal ferocity as I shifted my grip on the rhesus, getting both hands around its neck. I choked it, choked it until finally it had no choice but to let go of Sasha.

The monkey weighed only about twenty-five pounds, less than one-sixth of my weight, but it was all bone and muscle and seething hatred. Screaming thinly and spitting even as it struggled for breath, the thing tried to tuck its head down to bite at the hands encircling its throat. It wrenched, wriggled, kicked, flailed, and I can't imagine that an eel could have been harder to hold on to, but my fury at what the little fucker had tried to do to Sasha was so great that my hands were like iron, and at last I felt its neck snap. Then it was just a limp, dead thing, and I dropped it on the floor.

Gagging with disgust, gasping for breath, I picked up my Glock as Sasha, having recovered her Chiefs Special, stepped to the broken window near the table and opened fire at the night beyond.

While reloading, apparently having lost track of the last two monkeys in spite of their glowing eyes, Bobby had gone to the light switch by the door. Now he cranked up the rheostat far enough to make me squint.

One of the little bastards was standing on a counter beside the cooktop. It had extracted the smallest of the knives from the wall rack, and before any of us could open fire, it threw the blade at Bobby.

I don't know whether the troop had been busy learning simple military arts or whether the monkey was lucky. The knife tumbled through the air and sank into Bobby's right shoulder.

He dropped the shotgun.

I fired two rounds at the knife thrower, and it pitched backward onto the cooktop burners, dead.

The remaining monkey might have once heard that old saw about discretion being the better part of valor, because he curled his tail up against his back and fled over the sink and out the window. I got two shots off, but both missed.

At the other window, with surprisingly steady nerves and nimble fingers, Sasha fumbled a speedloader from the dump pouch on her belt and slipped it into the .38. She twisted the speedloader, neatly filling all chambers at once, dropped it on the floor, and snapped the cylinder shut.

I wondered what school of broadcasting offered would-be disc jockeys courses on weaponry and grace under fire. Of all the people in Moonlight Bay, Sasha had been the sole one remaining who seemed genuinely to be only what she *appeared* to be. Now I suspected that she had a secret or two of her own.

She began squeezing off shots into the night once more. I don't know if she had any targets in view or whether she was just laying down a suppressing fire to discourage whatever remained of the troop.

Ejecting the half-empty magazine from the Glock, slamming in a full one, I went to Bobby as he pulled the knife out of his shoulder. The blade appeared to have penetrated only an inch or two, but there was a spreading bloodstain on his shirt.

"How bad?" I asked.

"Damn!"

"Can you hold on?"

"This was my best shirt!"

Maybe he would be all right.

Toward the front of the house, Orson's barking continued — but it was punctuated now with squeals of terror.

I tucked the Glock under my belt, against the small of my back, picked up Bobby's shotgun, which was fully loaded, and ran toward the barking.

The lights were on but dimmed down in the living room, as we had left them. I dialed them up a little.

One of the big windows had been shattered. Hooting wind drove rain under the porch roof and into the living room.

Four screaming monkeys were perched on the backs of chairs and on the arms of sofas. When the lights brightened, they turned their heads toward me and hissed as one.

Bobby had estimated that the troop was composed of eight or ten individuals, but it was obviously a lot larger than that. I'd already seen twelve or fourteen, and in spite of the fact that they were more than half crazed with rage and hatred, I didn't think they were so reckless —

or stupid — that they would sacrifice most of their community in a single assault like this.

They'd been loose for two to three years. Plenty of time to breed.

Orson was on the floor, surrounded by this quartet of goblins, which now began to shriek at him again. He was turning worriedly in a circle, trying to watch all of them at once.

One of the troop was at such a distance and angle that I didn't have to worry that any stray buckshot would catch the dog. Without hesitation, I blew away the creature on which I had a clear line of fire, and the resulting spray of buckshot and monkey guts would cost Bobby maybe five thousand bucks in redecorating costs.

Squealing, the remaining three intruders bounded from one piece of furniture to another, heading toward the windows. I brought down another one, but the third round in the shotgun only peppered a teak-paneled wall and cost Bobby another five or ten grand.

I pitched the shotgun aside, reached to the small of my back, drew the Glock from under my belt, started after the two monkeys that were fleeing through the broken window onto the front porch — and was nearly lifted off my feet when someone grabbed me from behind. A beefy arm swung around my throat, instantly choking off my air supply, and a hand seized the Glock, tearing it away from me.

The next thing I knew, I *was* off my feet, lifted and tossed as though I were a child. I crashed into a coffee table, which collapsed under me.

Flat on my back in the ruins of the furniture,

I looked up and saw Carl Scorso looming over me, even more gigantic from this angle than he actually was. The bald head. The earring. Though I'd dialed up the lights, the room was still sufficiently shadowy that I could see the animal shine in his eyes.

He was the troop leader. I had no doubt about that. He was wearing athletic shoes and jeans and a flannel shirt, and there was a watch on his wrist, and if he were put in a police lineup with four gorillas, no one would have the least difficulty identifying him as the sole human being. Yet in spite of the clothes and the human form, he radiated the savage aura of something subhuman, not merely because of the eyeshine but because his features were twisted into an expression that mirrored no human emotion I could identify. Though clothed, he might as well have been naked; though clean-shaven from his neck to the crown of his head, he might as well have been as hairy as an ape. If he lived two lives, it was clear that he was more attuned to the one that he lived at night, with the troop, than to the one that he lived by day, among those who were not changelings like him.

He held the Glock at arm's length, executioner style, aiming it at my face.

Orson flew at him, snarling, but Scorso was the quicker of the two. He landed a solid kick against the dog's head, and Orson went down and stayed down, without even a yelp or a twitch of his legs.

My heart dropped like a stone in a well.

Scorso swung the Glock toward me again and

fired a round into my face. Or that was how it seemed for an instant. But a split second before he pulled the trigger, Sasha shot him in the back from the far end of the room, and the *crack* I heard was the report of her Chiefs Special.

Scorso jerked from the impact of the slug, pulling the Glock off-target. The teak floor beside my head splintered as the bullet tore through it.

Wounded but less fazed than most of us would have been once shot in the back, Scorso swung around, pumping out rounds from the Glock as he turned.

Sasha dropped and rolled backward out of the room, and Scorso emptied the pistol at the place where she had stood. He kept trying to pull the trigger even after the magazine was empty.

I could see rich, dark blood spreading across the back of his flannel shirt.

Finally he threw down the Glock, turned toward me, and appeared to contemplate whether to stomp my face or to tear my eyes from my head, leaving me blinded and dying. Opting for neither pleasure, he headed toward the broken-out window through which the last two monkeys had escaped.

He was just stepping out of the house onto the porch when Sasha reappeared and, incredibly, pursued him.

I shouted at her to stop, but she looked so wild that I wouldn't have been surprised to see that dreadful light in her eyes, too. She was across the living room and onto the front porch while I was still getting up from the splintered remains of the coffee table.

Outside, the Chiefs Special cracked, cracked again, and then a third time.

Although it seemed clear now that Sasha could take care of herself, I wanted to go after her and drag her back. Even if she finished Scorso, the night was probably home to more monkeys than even a first-rate disc jockey could handle — and the night was their domain, not hers.

A fourth shot boomed. A fifth.

I hesitated because Orson lay limp, so still that I couldn't see his black flank rising and falling with his breathing. He was either dead or unconscious. If unconscious, he might need help quickly. He had been kicked in the head. Even if he was alive, there was the danger of brain damage.

I realized I was crying. I bit back my grief, blinked back my tears. As I always do.

Bobby was crossing the living room toward me, one hand clamped to the stab wound in his shoulder.

"Help Orson," I said.

I refused to believe that nothing could help him now, because even to think such a terrible thing might ensure that it be true.

Pia Klick would understand that concept.

Maybe Bobby would understand it now, too.

Dodging furniture and dead monkeys, crunching glass underfoot, I ran to the window. Silvery whips of cold, windblown rain lashed past the jagged fragments of glass still prickling from the frame. I crossed the porch, leaped down the steps, and raced into the heart of the downpour, toward Sasha, where she stood thirty feet away in the dunes.

Carl Scorso lay facedown in the sand.

Soaked and shivering, she stood over him, twisting her third and last speedloader into the revolver. I suspected that she had hit him with most if not all the rounds that I'd heard, but she seemed to feel she might need a few more.

Indeed, Scorso twitched and worked both out-flung hands in the sand, as if he were burrowing into cover, like a crab.

With a shudder of horror, she leaned down and fired one last round, this time into the back of his skull.

When she turned to me, she was crying. Making no attempt to repress her tears.

I was tearless now. I told myself that one of us had to hold it together.

"Hey," I said gently.

She came into my arms.

"Hey," she whispered against my throat.

I held her.

The rain was coming down in such torrents that I couldn't see the lights of town, three-quarters of a mile to the east. Moonlight Bay might have been dissolved by this flood out of Heaven, washed away as if it had been only an elaborate sand sculpture of a town.

But it was back there, all right. Waiting for this storm to pass, and for another storm after this one, and others until the end of all days. There was no escaping Moonlight Bay. Not for us. Not ever. It was, quite literally, in our blood.

"What happens to us now?" she asked, still

holding fast to me.

"Life."

"It's all screwed up."

"It always was."

"They're still out there."

"Maybe they'll leave us alone — for a while."

"Where do we go from here, Snowman?"

"Back to the house. Get a beer."

She was still shivering, and not because of the rain. "And after that? We can't drink beer forever."

"Big surf coming in tomorrow."

"It's going to be that easy?"

"Got to catch those epic waves while you can get them."

We walked back to the cottage, where we found Orson and Bobby sitting on the wide front-porch steps. There was just enough room for us to sit down beside them.

Neither of my brothers was in the best mood of his life.

Bobby felt that he needed only Neosporin and a bandage. "It's a shallow wound, thin as a paper cut, and hardly more than half an inch from top to bottom."

"Sorry about the shirt," Sasha said.

"Thanks."

Whimpering, Orson got up, wobbled down the steps into the rain, and puked in the sand. It was a night for regurgitation.

I couldn't take my eyes off him. I was trembling with dread.

"Maybe we should take him to a vet," Sasha said.

I shook my head. No vet.

I would not cry. I do not cry. How bitter do you risk becoming by swallowing too many tears?

When I could speak, I said, "I wouldn't trust any vet in town. They're probably part of it, co-opted. If they realize what he is, that he's one of the animals from Wyvern, they might take him away from me, back to the labs."

Orson stood with his face turned up to the rain, as if he found it refreshing.

"They'll be back," Bobby said, meaning the troop.

"Not tonight," I said. "And maybe not for a way long time."

"But sooner or later."

"Yeah."

"And who else?" Sasha wondered. "What else?"

"It's chaos out there," I said, remembering what Manuel had told me. "A radical new world. Who the hell knows what's in it — or what's being born right now?"

In spite of all that we had seen and all that we had learned about the Wyvern project, perhaps it was not until this moment on the porch steps that we believed in our bones that we were living near the end of civilization, on the brink of Armageddon. Like the drums of Judgment, the hard and ceaseless rain beat on the world. This night was like no other night on earth, and it couldn't have felt more alien if the clouds had parted to reveal three moons instead of one and a sky full of unfamiliar stars.

Orson lapped puddled rainwater off the lowest porch step. Then he climbed to my side with more confidence than he had shown when he had descended.

Hesitantly, using the nod-for-*yes*-shake-for-*no* code, I tested him for concussion or worse. He was okay.

"Jesus," Bobby said with relief. I'd never heard him as shaken as this.

I went inside and got four beers and the bowl on which Bobby had painted the word *Rosebud.* I returned to the porch.

"A couple of Pia's paintings took some buckshot," I said.

"We'll blame it on Orson," Bobby said.

"Nothing," Sasha said, "is more dangerous than a dog with a shotgun."

We sat in silence awhile, listening to the rain and breathing the delicious, fresh-scrubbed air.

I could see Scorso's body out there in the sand. Now Sasha was a killer just like me.

Bobby said, "This sure is live."

"Totally," I said.

"Way radical."

"Insanely," Sasha said.

Orson chuffed.

34

That night we wrapped the dead monkeys in sheets. We wrapped Scorso's body in a sheet, too. I kept expecting him to sit up and reach out for me, trailing his cotton windings, as though he were a mummy from one of those long-ago movies filmed in an era when people were more spooked by the supernatural than the real world allows them to be these days. Then we loaded them into the back of the Explorer.

Bobby had a stack of plastic drop cloths in the garage, left over from the most recent visit by the painters, who periodically hand-oiled the teak paneling. We used them and a staple gun to seal the broken windows as best we could.

At two o'clock in the morning, Sasha drove all four of us to the northeast end of town and up the long driveway, past the graceful California pepper trees that waited like a line of mourners weeping in the storm, past the concrete *Pietà*. We stopped under the portico, before the massive Georgian house.

No lights were on. I don't know if Sandy Kirk was sleeping or not home.

We unloaded the sheet-wrapped corpses and piled them at his front door.

As we drove away, Bobby said, "Remember when we came up here as kids — to watch Sandy's dad at work?"

"Yeah."

"Imagine if one night we'd found something like that on his doorstep."

"Cool."

There were days of cleanup and repairs to be undertaken at Bobby's place, but we weren't ready to bend to that task. We went to Sasha's house and passed the rest of the night in her kitchen, clearing our heads with more beer and going through my father's account of the origins of our new world, our new life.

My mother had dreamed up a revolutionary new approach to the engineering of retroviruses for the purpose of ferrying genes into the cells of patients — or experimental subjects. In the secret facility at Wyvern, a world-class team of big brows had realized her vision. These new microbe delivery boys were more spectacularly successful and selective than anyone had hoped.

"Then comes Godzilla," as Bobby said.

The new retroviruses, though crippled, proved to be so clever that they were able not merely to deliver their package of genetic material but to select a package from the patient's — or lab animal's — DNA to replace what they had delivered. Thus they became a two-way messenger, carrying genetic material in *and* out of the body.

They also proved capable of capturing other viruses naturally present in a subject's body, selecting from those organisms' traits, and remaking themselves. They mutated more radically and faster than any microbe had ever mutated before. Wildly they mutated, becoming something new within hours. They had also become able to reproduce in spite of having been crippled.

Before anyone at Wyvern grasped what was happening, Mom's new bugs were ferrying as much genetic material out of the experimental animals as into them — and transferring that material not only among the different animals but among the scientists and other workers in the labs. Contamination is not solely by contact with bodily fluids. Skin contact alone is sufficient to effect the transfer of these bugs if you have even the tiniest wound or sore: a paper cut, a nick from shaving.

In the years ahead, as each of us is contaminated, he or she will take on a load of new DNA different from the one that anybody else receives. The effect will be singular in every case. Some of us will not change appreciably at all, because we will receive so many bits and pieces from so many sources that there will be no *focused* cumulative effect. As our cells die, the inserted material might or might not appear in the new cells that replace them. But some of us may become psychological or even physical monsters.

To paraphrase James Joyce: It will darkle, tinct-tint, all this our fun animal world. Darkle with strange variety.

We know not if the change will accelerate, the effects become more widely visible, the secret be exposed by the sheer momentum of the retrovirus's work — or whether it will be a process that remains subtle for decades or centuries. We can only wait. And see.

Dad seemed to think the problem didn't arise entirely because of a flaw in the theory. He believed the people at Wyvern — who tested my mother's theories and developed them until actual organisms could be produced — were more at fault than she, because they deviated from her vision in ways that may have seemed subtle at the time but proved calamitous in the end.

However you look at it, my mom destroyed the world as we know it — but, for all that, she's still my mom. On one level, she did what she did for love, out of the hope that my life could be saved. I love her as much as ever — and marvel that she was able to hide her terror and anguish from me during the last years of her life, after she realized what kind of new world was coming.

My father was less than half-convinced that she killed herself, but in his notes, he admits the possibility. He felt that murder was more likely. Although the plague had spread too far — too fast — to be contained, Mom finally had wanted to go public with the story. Maybe she was silenced. Whether she killed herself or tried to stand up to the military and government doesn't matter; she's gone in either case.

Now that I understand my mother better, I know where I get the strength — or the obsessive will — to repress my own emotions when I find them too hard to deal with. I'm going to try to change that about myself. I don't see why I shouldn't be able to do it. After all, that's what the world is now about: change. Relentless change.

Although some hate me for being my mother's son, I'm permitted to live. Even my father wasn't sure why I should be granted this dispensation, considering the savage nature of some of my enemies. He suspected, however, that my mother used fragments of my genetic material to engineer this apocalyptic retrovirus; perhaps, therefore, the key to undoing or at least limiting the scope of the calamity will eventually be found in my genes. My blood is drawn each month not, as I've been told, for reasons related to my XP but for study at Wyvern. Perhaps I am a walking laboratory: containing the potential for immunity to this plague — or containing a clue as to the ultimate destruction and terror it will cause. As long as I keep the secret of Moonlight Bay and live by the rules of the infected, I will most likely remain alive and free. On the other hand, if I attempt to tell the world, I will no doubt live out my days in a dark room in some subterranean chamber under the fields and hills of Fort Wyvern.

Indeed, Dad was afraid that they would take me anyway, sooner or later, to imprison me and thus ensure a continuing supply of blood samples. I'll have to deal with that threat if and when it comes.

Sunday morning and early afternoon, as the storm passed over Moonlight Bay, we slept — and of the four of us, only Sasha didn't wake from a nightmare.

After four hours in the sack, I went down to

Sasha's kitchen and sat with the blinds drawn. For a while, in the dim light, I studied the words *Mystery Train* on my cap, wondering how they related to my mother's work. Although I couldn't guess their significance, I felt that Moonlight Bay isn't merely on a roller-coaster ride to Hell, as Stevenson had claimed. We're on a journey to a mysterious destination that we can't entirely envision: maybe something wondrous — or maybe something far worse than the tortures of Hell.

Later, using a pen and tablet, I wrote by candlelight. I intend to record all that happens in the days that remain to me.

I don't expect ever to see this work published. Those who wish the truth of Wyvern to remain unrevealed will never permit me to spread the word. Anyway, Stevenson was right: It's too late to save the world. In fact, that's the same message Bobby's been giving me throughout most of our long friendship.

Although I don't write for publication anymore, it's important to have a record of this catastrophe. The world as we know it should not pass away without the explanation of its passing preserved for the future. We are an arrogant species, full of terrible potential, but we also have a great capacity for love, friendship, generosity, kindness, faith, hope, and joy. How we perished by our own hand may be more important than how we came into existence in the first place — which is a mystery that we will now never solve.

I might diligently record all that happens in Moonlight Bay and, by extension, in the rest of the world as the contamination spreads — but record it to no avail, because there might one day be no one left to read my words or no one capable of reading them. I'll take my chances. If I were a betting man, I'd bet that some species will arise from the chaos to replace us, to be masters of the earth as we were. Indeed, if I were a betting man, I'd put my money on the dogs.

Sunday night, the sky was as deep as the face of God, and the stars were as pure as tears. The four of us went to the beach. Fourteen-foot, fully macking, glassy monoliths pumped ceaselessly out of far Tahiti. It was epic. It was so *live*.

AUTHOR'S NOTE

Moonlight Bay's radio station, KBAY, is entirely a fictional enterprise. The real KBAY is located in Santa Cruz, California, and none of the employees of the Moonlight Bay station is based on any past or present employee of the Santa Cruz station. These call letters were borrowed here for one reason: They're cool.

In chapter seventeen, Christopher Snow quotes a line from a poem by Louise Glück. The title of the poem is "Lullaby," and it appears in Ms. Glück's wonderful and moving *Ararat*.

Christopher Snow, Bobby Halloway, Sasha Goodall, and Orson are real. I have spent many months with them. I like their company, and I intend to spend a lot more time with them in the years to come.

— DK

Recent Results
in Cancer Research

180

Rüdiger Liersch · Wolfgang E. Berdel
Torsten Kessler (Eds.)

Angiogenesis Inhibition

 Springer

Editors
Dr. Rüdiger Liersch
Department of Medicine
Hematology/Oncology
University Hospital Münster
Albert-Schweitzer-Str. 33
48129 Münster
Germany
rliersch@uni-muenster.de

Prof. Dr. Wolfgang E. Berdel
Department of Medicine
Hematology/Oncology
University Hospital Münster
Albert-Schweitzer-Str. 33
48129 Münster
Germany
berdel@uni-muenster.de

Dr. Torsten Kessler
Department of Medicine
Hematology/Oncology
University Hospital Münster
Albert-Schweitzer-Str. 33
48129 Münster
Germany
torstenkessler@uni-muenster.de

ISBN: 978-3-540-78280-3   e-ISBN: 978-3-540-78281-0

DOI: 10.1007/978-3-540-78281-0

Springer Heidelberg Dordrecht London New York

Library of Congress Control Number: 2009933610

© Springer-Verlag Berlin Heidelberg 2010

Cover design: eStudioCalamar Figueres/Berlin

Printed on acid-free paper

Springer is part of Springer Science+Business Media (www.springer.com)

Contents

1   Introduction   1
Judah Folkman   1

2   Angiopoietins   3
Yvonne Reiss

2.1   Introduction   3
2.2   Importance of the Angiopoietin/Tie System During
        Developmental Angiogenesis   4
2.3   Angiopoietins and Tumor-Associated Angiogenesis   6
2.4   Therapeutic Implications   9
2.5   Conclusions   9
        References   10

3   HIF-1α and Cancer Therapy   15
Mei Yee Koh, Taly R. Spivak-Kroizman, and Garth Powis

3.1   Background   15
3.2   Molecular and Cellular Biology of HIF-1   16
3.3   HIF-1 Regulation   16
3.3.1 Regulation of HIF-1α Translation   16
3.3.2 Regulation of HIF-1α Degradation   20
3.3.3 Regulation of HIF-1 Transactivation   21
3.4   Relationship Between HIF-1 and Other Key Oncogenic Pathways . . .   22
3.4.1 HIF-1 Activation by Growth Factors   22
3.4.2 Interplay Between HIF-1 and the p53 Tumor Suppressor   22
3.4.3 Interplay Between HIF-1 and Myc   22
3.5   Hypoxia and HIF-1 Effects on Cancer Stem Cells   23
3.6   HIF-1 as a Cancer Drug Target   23
3.7   HIF-1 Inhibitors   24
3.8   Conclusions   27
        References   28

4   Chemokines 35
Andreas Hippe, Bernhard Homey, and Anja Mueller-Homey

4.1   Angiogenesis 35
4.2   Chemokines in Angiogenesis 37
4.2.1   CXC Chemokine Subfamily 37
4.2.2   CC Chemokine Subfamily 38
4.2.3   CX3C Chemokine Subfamily 39
4.3   Chemokine Receptor Repertoire of Endothelial Cells 39
4.4   Angiogenesis, Chemokines, and Cancer 40
4.4.1   Breast Cancer 41
4.4.2   Malignant Melanoma 41
4.4.3   Lung Cancer 42
4.5   Inhibition of Chemokine-Induced Angiogenesis
         as a Therapeutic Strategy 43
         References 45

5   Angiogenesis Inhibition in Cancer Therapy 51
Iris Appelmann, Rüdiger Liersch, Torsten Kessler, Rolf M. Mesters,
and Wolfgang E. Berdel

5.1   Introduction 51
5.2   VEGF 52
5.2.1   VEGF Isoforms and Their Expression 52
5.2.2   VEGF Receptors 53
5.2.3   Structure of VEGFR1 and VEGFR2 54
5.2.4   Signaling and Biological Functions of VEGFR1 55
5.2.5   Expression and Signaling of VEGFR2 56
5.2.6   VEGF and Malignancy 57
5.3   PDGF 59
5.3.1   Platelet-Derived Growth Factor and Its Isoforms 59
5.3.2   PDGF Receptors 61
5.3.3   PDGF Ligand and Receptor Expression Patterns 61
5.3.4   PDGF Biosynthesis, Secretion, and Distribution 62
5.3.5   PDGFR Signal Transduction 64
5.3.6   Cellular Responses to PDGFR Signaling 65
5.3.7   PDGF and PDGFR in Malignancy 67
         References 69

**6   Vascular Integrins: Therapeutic and Imaging Targets
of Tumor Angiogenesis** 83
Curzio Rüegg and Gian Carlo Alghisi

6.1   Integrin Structure 83
6.2   Integrin Functions 84
6.2.1   Cell Adhesion 84
6.2.2   Cell Signaling 84

6.3   Integrins in Tumor Angiogenesis   86
6.4   Integrin Antagonists with Antiangiogenic Activities   87
6.4.1   Antibodies.   87
6.4.2   Endogenous Antagonists   89
6.4.3   Peptides.   90
6.4.4   Non-peptidic Inhibitors.   90
6.5   Open Questions and Current Developments.   91
6.5.1   Most Relevant Targets   91
6.5.2   Combination Therapies.   91
6.5.3   Drug Targeting   92
6.5.4   Tumor Imaging.   93
6.6   Future Directions   93
6.6.1   New Generation of Extracellular Antagonists   93
6.6.2   Targeting the Integrin Intracellular Domains   94
6.6.3   Targeting Angiogenic Precursor Cells
           and Inflammatory Cells.   94
6.7   Conclusions.   94
           References.   95

7   **PDGF and Vessel Maturation**   103
           Carina Hellberg, Arne Östman, and C.-H. Heldin

7.1   Introduction.   103
7.2   The PDGF Family.   103
7.3   Pericytes   104
7.3.1   Role of Pericytes.   104
7.3.2   Identification of Pericytes.   104
7.3.3   The Origin of Pericytes.   105
7.4   Vessel Maturation   106
7.4.1   Normal Vessels   106
7.4.2   Tumor Vessels.   108
7.5   Tumor Therapy Targeting PDGF Receptors on the Vasculature . .   109
7.5.1   Antiangiogenic Therapy Targeting Pericytes   110
7.5.2   Improving the Efficacy of Conventional Therapies   110
7.6   Future Perspectives.   111
           References.   112

8   **Lymphangiogenesis in Cancer: Current Perspectives**.   115
           Rüdiger Liersch, Christoph Biermann, Rolf M. Mesters,
           and Wolfgang E. Berdel

8.1   Introduction.   115
8.2   Embryonic Lymphatic Development   116
8.3   The Lymphatic Function.   117
8.3.1   Molecular Players in the Regulation
           of Lymphangiogenesis   118

8.4   Pathology of the Lymphatic Vasculature   122
8.4.1   Secondary Lymphedema.   122
8.4.2   Primary Lymphedema.   123
8.5   Role of Lymphangiogenesis in Cancer.   124
8.5.1   Lymphvascular Invasion.   124
8.5.2   Tumor-Lymphangiogenesis   124
8.5.3   Lymphatic Endothelial Cell Activation   125
8.5.4   Lymph Node Lymphangiogenesis   125
8.6   Targeting Lymphangiogenesis   126
8.6.1   Antibodies.   127
8.6.2   Soluble Receptors   127
8.6.3   Small Molecule Inhibitor   127
8.7   Conclusions.   127
           References.   127

9   Compounds in Clinical Phase III and beyond   137
      Torsten Kessler, Michael Bayer, Christian Schwöppe, Rüdiger Liersch,
      Rolf M. Mesters, and Wolfgang E. Berdel

9.1   Introduction.   137
9.1.1   Anti-VEGF Antibody (Bevacizumab, Avastin)   138
9.1.2   Aflibercept (VEGF – Trap).   140
9.1.2.1   Sorafenib (Nexavar)   140
9.1.3   Sunitinib Malate (SU11248; Sutent).   144
9.1.4   Axitinib (AG-013736)   146
9.1.5   Cediranib (AZD2171; Recentin)   147
9.1.6   Vandetanib (ZD6474; Zactima)   148
9.1.7   Vatalanib (PTK787/ZK222584)   149
9.1.8   Endostatin (rh-Endostatin, YH-16, Endostar)   150
9.1.9   Thalidomide   151
9.1.10   Vascular Disrupting Agents   152
9.1.11   Accidental Antiangiogenesis Agents   154
9.1.12   Conclusions and Future Perspectives   155
           References.   156

10   Metronomic Chemotherapy: Principles and Lessons Learned
      from Applications in the Treatment of Metastatic Prostate Cancer   165
      Urban Emmenegger, Giulio Francia, Yuval Shaked,
      and Robert S. Kerbel

10.1   Introduction.   165
10.2   Mechanisms of Action of Metronomic Chemotherapy   166
10.2.1   Preferential Antiproliferative Effects of Metronomic
           Chemotherapy Toward Endothelial Cells.   167
10.2.2   Circulating Bone Marrow-Derived Endothelial
           Precursor Cells as Targets of Metronomic Chemotherapy   167

10.2.2.1	Benefit of Combined Bolus and Metronomic Chemotherapy Administration	168
10.2.2.2	CEPs and Optimal Biological Dose of Antiangiogenic Agents ...	169
10.2.3	Mechanisms of Action Summarized........................	170
10.3	Metronomic Chemotherapy for the Treatment of Metastatic Castration-Resistant Prostate Cancer	170
10.3.1	From Bench to Bedside	172
10.3.2	Key Findings of Metronomic Trials in Castration-Resistant Prostate Cancer and Emerging Questions....................	174
10.3.2.1	Choice of Cytotoxic Drugs Used in Metronomic Regimens	176
10.3.2.2	Optimal Biological Dose	176
10.3.2.3	Combination Therapies.................................	177
10.3.3	Integration of Metronomic Chemotherapy into Current Standards of Practice for Prostate Cancer.............	178
10.4	Conclusions and Perspectives...........................	178
	References...	179

11   Targeting Inflammatory Cells to Improve Anti-VEGF Therapies in Oncology 185
Hans-Peter Gerber, Ezogelin Olazoglu, and Iqbal S. Grewal

11.1	Role of Bone Marrow-Derived Tumor Infiltrating Cells in Tumor Angiogenesis	185
11.2	Endothelial Progenitor Cells (EPCs) and Circulatory Endothelial Progenitor Cells (CEPs)	186
11.3	Tumor-Associated Macrophages	189
11.4	CD11b+ Gr1+ Myeloid-Derived Suppressor Cells	191
11.5	Lymphocytes and Mast Cells (MCs)	191
11.6	Neutrophils...	192
11.7	Therapeutic Targets to Overcome Anti-VEGF Refractoriness....	193
11.7.1	Bv8	193
11.8	VEGF-B, -C, -D, and PlGF	193
11.9	Targeting MDSCs and TAMs............................	194
11.10	Targeting EPCs......................................	195
11.11	Conclusions...	195
	References...	195

12   Antibody-Based Vascular Tumor Targeting...................... 201
Christoph Schliemann and Dario Neri

12.1	Concept and Definitions	201
12.2	Discovery of Novel Vascular Targets	203
12.3	Validated Markers of the Tumor Vasculature.................	204
12.3.1	Extra Domains of Fibronectin	205
12.3.2	Large Isoforms of Tenascin C...........................	206
12.3.3	Phosphatidylserine	206

12.3.4	Annexin A1	206
12.3.5	Prostate-Specific Membrane Antigen (PSMA)	207
12.3.6	Endoglin	207
12.3.7	Integrins	207
12.3.8	Vascular Endothelial Growth Factors (VEGFs) and Receptors	208
12.3.9	Nucleolin	208
12.4	Vascular Tumor Targeting: Imaging Applications	208
12.5	Vascular Tumor Targeting: Therapeutic Applications	209
	References	212

13 Caveolae and Cancer 217

Kerri A. Massey and Jan E. Schnitzer

13.1	Vascular Endothelium	217
13.2	Caveolae Structure	218
13.3	Isolation of Caveolae	218
13.4	Caveolae in Signal Transduction	219
13.5	Caveolae as Active Transport Vesicles	220
13.6	Vascular Targeting	221
13.7	Phage Display Libraries	222
13.8	Large-Scale Approaches	223
13.9	Reducing Complexity	223
13.10	Tissue-Specific Targets	224
13.11	Tumor-Specific Targets	225
13.12	Clinical Implications	226
	References	227

Contributors

Gian Carlo Alghisi
Division of Experimental Oncology
Centre Pluridisciplinaire d'Oncologie
Lausanne Cancer Center
University of Lausanne
Lausanne
Switzerland

Iris Appelmann
Department of Medicine
Hematology and Oncology
University of Münster
Albert-Schweitzer-Strasse 33
48129 Münster
Germany
Iris.Appelmann@ukmuenster.de

Michael Bayer
Department of Medicine
Hematology and Oncology
University of Münster
Albert-Schweitzer-Strasse 33
48129 Münster
Germany

Wolfgang E. Berdel
Department of Medicine
Hematology/Oncology
University of Münster
Albert-Schweitzer-Strasse 33
48129 Münster, Germany
berdel@uni-muenster.de

Christoph Biermann
Department of Medicine
Hematology and Oncology
University Hospital Münster
Albert-Schweitzerstrasse 33
48129 Münster
Germany

Urban Emmenegger
Department of Medicine
Division of Medical Oncology, and
Department of Medical Biophysics
Division of Molecular and Cellular Biology
Sunnybrook Health Sciences Centre
University of Toronto
2075 Bayview Avenue Toronto ON
Canada M4N3M5
urban.emmenegger@sri.utoronto.ca

Giulio Francia
Department of Medical Biophysics
Division of Molecular and Cellular Biology
Sunnybrook Health Sciences Centre
University of Toronto
2075 Bayview Avenue
Toronto, ON
Canada M4N3M5

Hans-Peter Gerber
Sr Dir Discovery Tumor Prog
Pharma, Research & Development
Pearl River, NY
gerberh@wyeth.com

Iqbal S. Grewal
Department of Preclinical Therapeutics
Seattle Genetics Inc.
Bothell
Washington 98021
USA

C.-H. Heldin
Ludwig Institute for Cancer Research
Uppsala University
S-751 24 Uppsala
Sweden
C-H.Heldin@LICR.uu.e

Carina Hellberg
Ludwig Institute for Cancer Research
Uppsala University
S-751 24 Uppsala
Sweden
Carina.Hellberg@LICR.uu.se

Andreas Hippe
Department of Dermatology
Heinrich-Heine-University
Moorenstrasse 5
40225 Düsseldorf
Germany
ahippe@gmail.com

Bernhard Homey
Department of Dermatology
Heinrich-Heine-University
Moorenstrasse 5
40225 Düsseldorf
Germany
Bernhard.Homey@uni-duesseldorf.de

Robert S. Kerbel
Department of Medical Biophysics
Division of Molecular and Cellular Biology
Sunnybrook Health Sciences Centre
University of Toronto
2075 Bayview Avenue
Toronto, ON,
Canada M4N3M5

Torsten Kessler
Department of Medicine
Hematology/Oncology
University Hospital Münster
Albert-Schweitzer-Str. 33
48129 Münster
Germany
torstenkessler@uni-muenster.de

Mei Yee Koh
Department of Experimental Therapeutics
M.D. Anderson Cancer Center
Houston, TX 77030
USA

Rüdiger Liersch
Department of Medicine
Hematology/Oncology
University Hospital Münster
Albert-Schweitzer-Str. 33
48129 Münster
Germany
rliersch@uni-muenster.de

Kerri A. Massey
Sidney Kimmel Cancer Center
10905 Road to the Cure
San Diego, CA 92121
USA

Rolf M. Mesters
Department of Medicine
Hematology and Oncology
University of Münster
Albert-Schweitzer-Strasse 33
48129 Münster
Germany

Anja Mueller-Homey
Department of Radiation Therapy
and Radiation Oncology
Heinrich-Heine-University
Moorenstrasse 4
40225 Düsseldorf
Germany
A.Mueller@uni-duesseldorf.de

Dario Neri
Institute of Pharmaceutical Sciences
Department of Chemistry and
Applied Biosciences
Swiss Federal Institute of Technology Zürich
Wolfgang-Pauli-Strasse 10
CH-8093 Zürich
Switzerland
dario.neri@pharma.ethz.ch

Ezogelin Olazoglu
Department of Preclinical Therapeutics
Seattle Genetics Inc.
Bothell
Washington, DC 98021
USA

Arne Östman
Department of Pathology-Oncology
Cancer Center Karolinska
Karolinska Institute
171 76, Stockholm
Sweden
Arne.Ostman@cck.ki.se

Garth Powis
MD Anderson Cancer Center
1400 Holcombe Blvd.
FC6.3044
Unit 422
Houston, TX 77030
USA
gpowis@mdanderson.org

Yvonne Reiss
Institute of Neurology/Edinger Institute
Frankfurt University Medical School
Heinrich-Hoffmann-Strasse
760528 Frankfurt
Germany
Yvonne.Reiss@kgu.de

Curzio Rüegg
Division of Experimental Oncology
Centre Pluridisciplinaire d'Oncologie
155 Chemin des Boveresses
CH1066 Epalinges
Switzerland
curzio.ruegg@unil.ch

Christoph Schliemann
Institute of Pharmaceutical Sciences,
Department of Chemistry and Applied
Biosciences
Swiss Federal Institute of Technology Zürich
Wolfgang-Pauli-Strasse 10
CH-8093 Zürich
Switzerland
Christoph.schliemann@pharma.ethz.ch

Jan E. Schnitzer
Proteogenomics Research Institute
for Systems Medicine,
11107 Roselle St,
San Diego, CA 92121
USA
jschnitzer@prism-sd.org

Christian Schwöppe
Department of Medicine
Hematology and Oncology
University of Münster
Albert-Schweitzer-Strasse 33
48129 Münster
Germany

Yuval Shaked
Department of Medical Biophysics
Division of Molecular and Cellular Biology
Sunnybrook Health Sciences Centre
University of Toronto
2075 Bayview Avenue
Toronto
ON, Canada M4N3M5

Taly R. Spivak-Kroizman
Department of Experimental Therapeutics
M.D. Anderson Cancer Center
Houston, TX 77030
USA

Introduction

Judah Folkman

Judah Folkman agreed to write an introductory overview on the field of angiogenesis and cancer for this book. The topic was his field of research, indeed his passion, and he put it into the center of interest for a whole generation of researchers and clinicians working to combat and treat cancer. Judah Folkman died suddenly on January 14, 2008 at age 74, on the way to a scientific conference on angiogenesis. He could not finish his chapter. This day witnessed the loss of a scientific pioneer and humanitarian.

Born in 1933, Dr. Folkman was trained at Ohio State University and Harvard Medical School. During his time of serving in the U.S. Navy, he began studying tumors and soon concentrated on the dependence of tumor growth and spread from the formation of new blood vessels. In 1971 the *New England Journal of Medicine* published his ground-breaking hypothesis on angiogenesis and antiangiogenic therapy. Initially met with skepticism, this paper opened the field of neoangiogenesis and cancer for a growing community of scientists and physician–scientists working on biological mechanisms of the connections between the vascular systems and cancer and on the development of antiangiogenic therapy against cancer. Judah Folkman and his team of scientists were always on the forefront of this research. He and his team isolated the first proangiogenic factor bFGF, identified multiple angiogenic inhibitors such as endostatin, angiostatin, and fumagillin, and made numerous other discoveries that moved the field forward. His laboratory also studied molecular pathways of angiogenesis and helped to develop numerous antiangiogenic drugs.

Today antiangiogenic therapy, as envisaged by Judah Folkman, has made a difference for many patients with cancer. This book will provide the reader with an overview of the field of antiangiogenic therapy for cancer, but because of the large scope of the field, it concentrates on certain aspects as well. The editors hope that it contains interesting and stimulating information for scientists and physicians alike working on aspects of the vascular systems and cancer. In a very real sense, we hope this book will commemorate the tremendous influence Judah Folkman's farsighted thinking and pioneering work has had on all of us.

Germany   Wolfgang E. Berdel

R. Liersch et al. (eds.), *Angiogenesis Inhibition,* Recent Results in Cancer Research,
DOI: 10.1007/978-3-540-78281-0_1, © Springer Verlag Berlin Heidelberg 2010

Angiopoietins

2

Yvonne Reiss

Abstract The formation of new blood vessels plays an important role during the development and progression of a disease. In recent years, there has been a tremendous effort to uncover the molecular mechanisms that drive blood vessel growth in adult tissues. Angiopoietins belong to a family of growth factors that are critically involved in blood vessel formation during developmental and pathological angiogenesis. The importance of Angiopoietin signaling has been recognized in transgenic mouse models as the genetic ablation of Ang-1, and its primary receptor Tie2 has led to early embryonic lethality. Interesting and unusual for a family of ligands, Ang-2 has been identified as an antagonist of Ang-1 in endothelial cells as evidenced by a similar embryonic phenotype when Ang-2 was overexpressed in transgenic mice. In this review, we focus on the functional consequences of autocrine Angiopoietin signaling in endothelial cells.

Y. Reiss
Institute of Neurology/Edinger Institute,
Frankfurt University Medical School,
Heinrich-Hoffmann-Strasse,
760528, Frankfurt,
Germany
e-mail: Yvonne.Reiss@kgu.de

2.1
Introduction

Angiogenesis involves the complex signaling between multiple angiogenic growth factors, and requires the coordinated interaction between endothelial and adjacent cells. Vascular endothelial growth factor (VEGF) possesses a dominant role in mediating endothelial cell sprouting, migration, and network formation as indicated by the early lethality of VEGF-deficient mice (Carmeliet et al. 1996; Ferrara et al. 1996; for review see Ferrara et al. 2003; Conway et al. 2001; Risau 1997). The Angiopoietin (Ang) family has primary roles in the latter stages of vascular development and in the adult vasculature, where it controls vessel remodeling and stabilization. Ang-1 has the capability to stimulate Tie2 receptor activation while Ang-2 has been identified as an antagonizing ligand (Suri et al. 1998; Maisonpierre et al. 1997). Ang-2 overexpression in transgenic mice led to embryonic death with a phenotype similar to Ang-1 or Tie2 deletion (Maisonpierre et al. 1997). Thus, genetic evidence suggests that signaling through Tie2 appears to depend on the balance between Ang1 and Ang2. In the quiescent vasculature in adults, Ang1 provides a basal signal to maintain the integrity of the endothelial cells (Brindle et al. 2006). In contrast, Ang-2 induced by VEGF or hypoxia suppresses these effects

R. Liersch et al. (eds.), *Angiogenesis Inhibition,* Recent Results in Cancer Research,
DOI: 10.1007/978-3-540-78281-0_2, © Springer Verlag Berlin Heidelberg 2010

and leads to vessel destabilization. Consequently, effects mediated by Ang-2 allow vessel growth or regression, depending on the presence of additional growth factors (Hanahan 1997).

2.2
Importance of the Angiopoietin/Tie System During Developmental Angiogenesis

Ang-1 and Ang-2 (Davis et al. 1996; Maisonpierre et al. 1997) are best characterized among the Angiopoietin family. Additional members are designated as Ang-3 and Ang-4, and represent diverging counterparts in mice and humans (Valenzuela et al. 1999). Ang-1 and Ang-2 are ligands for the receptor tyrosine kinase with immunoglobulin and epidermal growth factor homology domains 2 (Tie2; Maisonpierre et al. 1997; Davis et al. 1996; Sato et al. 1995; Dumont et al. 1995) with predominant expression in endothelial cells. They share approximately 60% of aminoacid identity (Maisonpierre et al. 1997). Ang-1 has initially been discovered as the primary Tie2 ligand (Davis et al. 1996). Although Ang-1 and Ang-2 act as antagonizing molecules, they bind to Tie2 with similar affinities. They share the same binding domains of the Tie2 receptor, including the first Ig-like loop and the epidermal growth factor-like repeats (Barton et al. 2006; Fiedler et al. 2003). The two highly related members of the Tie receptor tyrosine kinase family, Tie1 and Tie2, display unique extracellular domains: epidermal growth factor repeats, immunoglobulin-like domains, fibronectin-type III repeats, and a separated tyrosine kinase domain in the cytoplasmic region (Dumont et al. 1993; Sato et al. 1993; Schnurch and Risau 1993; Partanen et al. 1992). Although Tie2 is the best established receptor for Ang-1, there are emerging data showing that the ligand may also signal through the related tyrosine kinase Tie1 (Saharinen et al. 2005).

Engagement of Tie2 by Ang-1 is responsible for receptor phosphorylation and the induction of survival signals in endothelial cells (Jones et al. 1999; Papapetropoulos et al. 2000). There is additional evidence that Ang-1 plays an active role in vessels sprouting as Ang-1 overexpression in mice increased vessel density and branching (Suri et al. 1998). Ang-1-mediated endothelial cell sprouting and migration has also been proven in in vitro models (Audero et al. 2004; Hayes et al. 1999; Koblizek et al. 1998). Consistent with these findings, interactions between endothelial and pericytes/smooth muscle cells are stabilized only in the presence of Ang-1, and decreased association of endothelial cells with support cells is evident in Ang-1 mutant mice (Suri et al. 1996). In the adult vasculature, Ang-1 binding to Tie2 is constitutive and essential to maintain endothelium in the quiescent state (Wong et al. 1997; Saharinen et al. 2008; Fukuhara et al. 2008). By contrast, opposing functions have been described for Ang-2. Binding of Tie2 by Ang-2 antagonizes receptor phosphorylation in transgenic animals (Maisonpierre et al. 1997; Reiss et al. 2007), thereby disrupting contacts between endothelial- and periendothelial support cells. Ang-2 also disrupts endothelial monolayer interaction with smooth muscle cells in culture (Scharpfenecker et al. 2005). This process is fundamental for the initiation of vessel sprouting or regression.

Evidence for the importance of the Angiopoietin/Tie2 system for the vascular development is derived from genetic experiments following the ablation of Ang-1 or Tie2 in transgenic mice (Suri et al. 1996; Sato et al. 1995; Dumont et al. 1995). A summary of genetic mouse models available of Angiopoietins and Tie receptors are displayed in Table 2.1. Embryos lacking Tie2 receptor tyrosine kinase or Ang-1 ligand display aberrant vascular development and die around embryonic day E11 as a consequence of insufficient remodeling of the primary capillary plexus. Analysis of the vasculature of mice deficient for Tie2 or Ang-1 has indicated abnormal interactions between endothelial cells and peri-endothelial support cells (Suri et al. 1996; Sato et al. 1995; Dumont et al. 1995). Contrary to these findings, mice with targeted expression of Ang-1 in the skin exhibit larger and

Table 2.1 Transgenic mice resulting from Angiopoietin/Tie deletion and overexpression

Ang-1

Ang-1$^{-/-}$

Lethal at E11–12.5, defective vessel remodeling, enlarged vessels, and poor endothelial cell interaction with perivascular cells, complementary to Tie2$^{-/-}$ phenotype (Suri et al. 1996)

Ang-1 overexpression

Overexpression in skin increases number, size and branching of vessels (hypervascularization), vessel sealing, anti-inflammatory (Suri et al. 1998; Thurston et al. 1999)

Ang-2

Ang-2$^{-/-}$

Lethal at postnatal day 14 (depending on genetic background), normal embryonic vascular development, defects in postnatal angiogenic remodeling (disturbed hyaloid vessel regression), and defects in the lymphatic vasculature (disorganization/hypoplasia in dermal and intestinal lymphatics) (Gale et al. 2002)

Ang-2 overexpression

Ang-2 overexpression in the vasculature, lethal at E9.5–10.5. complementary to Ang-1 and Tie2 mutant phenotypes but more severe, rounded endothelial cells, poor interaction with matrix, endocardial defects (Maisonpierre et al. 1997)

Inducible Ang-2 overexpression in endothelial cells

Tie1 promoter driven, Tet-inducible expression of Ang-2 in endothelial cells, embryonic lethality during gestation, defective collateral artery growth, and smooth muscle cell coverage during pathological angiogenesis (limb ischemia) (Reiss et al. 2007)

Tie receptors

Tie1$^{-/-}$

Die embryonic day >13.5 (E13.5), vessel hemorrhage, edema, rupture, endocardial defects (Sato et al. 1995; Puri et al. 1995; Puri et al. 1999)

Tie2$^{-/-}$

Lethal E9.5–10.5, complementary phenotype to Ang-1$^{-/-}$, defective vessel remodeling, dilated vessels, decreased branching, rounded endothelial cells lacking pericytes, hemorrhage, vessel rupture (Dumont et al. 1994; Sato et al. 1995)

Tie1 and Tie2$^{-/-}$

Similar to Tie2$^{-/-}$ but more severe. Tie1$^{-/-}$embryos sensitive to Tie2 gene dosage, Tie1$^{-/-}$/Tie2$^{-/-}$endothelial cells absent from capillaries of adult chimeric wildtype/double knockout mice (Puri et al. 1999)

Tie1$^{-/-}$/Tie2$^{-/-}$cells have reduced capacity to contribute to hematopoiesis in the adult, but not in the fetus (Puri and Bernstein 2003)

more numerous branched vessels that are resistant to vascular leakage induced by permeability factors, such as VEGF (Suri et al. 1998). These findings support the present concept that the Angiopoietin/Tie2 system plays an important role in the interaction between endothelial and mural cells. Angiogenic remodeling of the mature vasculature requires a progressive disengagement of endothelial cells from the surrounding support cells, and this destabilization can result in vessels sprouting or regression. The distinct expression pattern of Ang-2 at sites of active vascular remodeling (Maisonpierre et al. 1997) and in highly vascularized tumors (Holash et al. 1999; Stratmann et al. 1998) has implicated Ang-2 in the blockade of the Ang-1 stabilizing function to facilitate angiogenesis. In addition, transgenic overexpression in embryonic endothelial cells resulted in a similar phenotype as the deletion of the Tie2 gene, supporting the view that Ang-2 is an antagonistic ligand (Maisonpierre et al. 1997). However, genetic ablation of Ang-2 in mice resulted in a less severe phenotype, which is compatible with life, as such providing evidence that Ang-2 is not redundant with Ang-1 (Gale et al. 2002). Ang-2 is selectively upregulated in tumor vessels before the onset of VEGF in adjacent tumor cells, and can synergize with VEGF to enhance neovascularization. This indicated that Ang-2 might be antagonist in particular environments, such as in postnatal remodeling or pathological angiogenesis (Gale et al. 2002; Holash et al. 1999).

2.3
Angiopoietins and Tumor-Associated Angiogenesis

The essential role of angiogenesis for the expansion of solid tumors is demonstrated by the observation that avascular tumors are not able to grow beyond a certain size unless they acquire new blood vessels for the supply of nutrients and oxygen (Folkman 1971; Hanahan and Folkman 1996; Yancopoulos et al. 2000). Co-option of existing vessels from the neighboring tissue thereby displays one possible mechanism to promote tumor growth (Holash et al. 1999). In addition, tumor cells provide endothelium-specific growth factors such as VEGF and Angiopoietins for the recruitment of new blood vessel.

During development, Tie2 expression is present on virtually all endothelial cells (Dumont et al. 1995; Sato et al. 1995). In addition, Tie2 expression is increased during physiological and pathological angiogenesis in the adult. However, endothelial cells of the vasculature remain quiescent during adult life. Numerous studies have demonstrated altered expression patterns for Angiopoietin ligands and corresponding Tie receptors in a variety of tumors. This clearly

indicated important roles for Angiopoietin/Tie signaling beyond development in experimental models of tumor growth (Reiss et al. 2005; Tait and Jones 2004). Tumor vessels are known to have abnormal phenotypes that include changes in the architecture and assembly of the vessel wall (Morikawa et al. 2002; Ward and Dumont 2002). These vessel abnormalities are likely the cause for increased vascular permeability within the tumor. With respect to potential targeted interventions of angiogenesis in tumors, it is required to decipher the mechanisms that promote or inhibit the vessel growth. Regarding the current knowledge of Angiopoietin biology during tumor angiogenesis, results are controversial and include pro- and antiangiogenic functions for both, Ang-1 and Ang-2. In detail, overexpression of Ang-1 in experimental tumors induced stabilization by the recruitment of pericytes and smooth muscle cells to recently formed vessels (for review see (Reiss et al. 2005; Tait and Jones 2004)). Consequently, reduced tumor growth or tumor stasis has been reported by a number of research laboratories in experimental tumors, such as colon-, lung-, mammary- and squamous cell carcinoma (Stoeltzing et al. 2003; Hawighorst et al. 2002; Tian et al. 2002; Stoeltzing et al. 2002; Ahmad et al. 2001; Yu and Stamenkovic 2001; Hayes et al. 2000). However, findings derived from certain tumor types, including our own results, indicate proangiogenic functions when overexpressing Ang-1 (Shim et al. 2002; Machein et al. 2004). These controversial findings may be related to differences in the presence of growth factors within the tumor types investigated. Although effector functions of Ang-1 on the outcome of tumor growth are not completely resolved, an improved vessel architecture in the presence of Ang-1 is typically observed. This is mainly exerted by a higher degree of pericyte coverage. Ang-2 in contrast, is necessary to initiate vessel sprouting and is associated with pericyte loss of the host tumor vasculature (Reiss et al. 2009; Cao et al. 2007; Machein et al. 2004; Zhang et al. 2003; Hu et al. 2003; Ahmad et al. 2001; Yu and

Stamenkovic 2001; Etoh et al. 2001; Tanaka et al. 1999). This is achieved through the destabilizing actions on the previously quiescent vasculature. At present, findings that have been reported for the role of Ang-2 during tumor progression are not well understood. However, what can be concluded from the literature with regard to Ang-2 functions in tumors is a shift in the balance of Ang-1 and Ang-2 in favor of Ang-2. Consequently, instability of the host vasculature and aberrant, nonfunctional vessels were often observed (Reiss et al. 2009; Reiss et al. 2005). Furthermore, Lewis lung carcinoma, mammary carcinoma, gastric

and brain tumors overexpressing Ang-2 display increased frequencies of metastatic dissemination and are highly invasive (Hu et al. 2003; Yu and Stamenkovic 2001; Etoh et al. 2001). In summary, evidence from the literature implies that vessel destabilizing defects of Ang-2 might be caused by the disengagement of pericytes from the tumor vessels, and the defective cellular linings caused by openings between endothelial cells might to some extent explain increased permeabilities within tumor vessels (Hashizume et al. 2000). Ang-2-mediated functions during tumor angiogenesis are illustrated in Fig. 2.1.

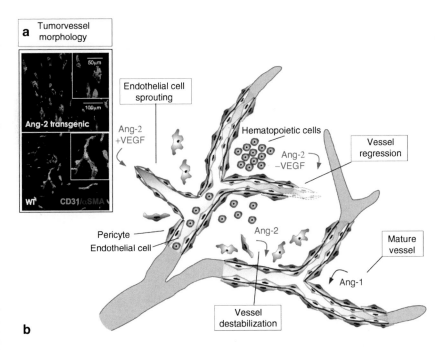

Fig. 2.1 Influence of the Angiopoietin/Tie system on the formation of new blood vessels in tumors. Inducible Ang-2 expression in the vasculature of transgenic animals (adapted from Reiss et al. 2007) leads to increased vascular densities (*green*: αCD31 immunohistochemistry) in subcutaneous Lewis lung tumors, indicative for excessive vessel sprouting (**a**). Furthermore, reduced in red pericyte coverage (**a**, indicated by αSMA labeling) in red is prominent within the tumor vasculature (insets: higher magnification). A schematic drawing of Angiopoietin/Tie mediated functions in tumors is illustrated in (**b**). Ang-1 contributes to the stabilization and maturation of new blood vessels in tumors. In concert with VEGF, Ang-2 destabilizes the vasculature and leads to vessel sprouting or regression (modified after (Reiss et al. 2005)) Ang-2 additionally might be able to promote the recruitment of hematopoietic cells during tumor progression or other pathological conditions as Ang-2 deficient mice display delayed inflammatory cell recruitment (Fiedler et al., 2006)

Ang-2 is highly regulated at the transcriptional level (Hegen et al. 2004) and induced in endothelial cells in areas of active angiogenesis (Holash et al. 1999; Stratmann et al. 1998) such as in tumors, making it an attractive target for therapeutic intervention. Moreover, Ang-2 has been associated with poor prognosis and lymph-node metastasis in human tumors pointing towards a need for therapeutic intervention (Ochiumi et al. 2004; Hu et al. 2003; Sfiligoi et al. 2003; Etoh et al. 2001). Pharmacological inhibition of Angiopoietin functions by sequestration with soluble Tie2 (Siemeister et al. 1999; Lin et al. 1998; Lin et al. 1997) or by the usage of dominant-negative Tie2 mutants has earlier been shown to have a negative impact on tumor growth and progression. Furthermore, neutralization of Ang-2-Tie2 interactions (Oliner et al. 2004) or overexpression of Ang-2 (Cao et al. 2007) inhibited tumor angiogenesis and tumor growth in mice. Whether targeted intervention of Ang-2 will be applicable in human tumors as well remains to be elucidated in the future.

In spite of the intense research on Angiopoietin functions during physiological angiogenesis (Suri et al. 1998; Maisonpierre et al. 1997) and tumor angiogenesis (Holash et al. 1999; Stratmann et al. 1998), the biological actions of Angiopoietins during tumor progression have not been fully ascertained. Clearly, molecular mechanisms for a more precise understanding of Angiopoietin/Tie-mediated effector functions that may lead to increased vessel integrity or drive vascular remodeling/regression are largely missing. In detail, it is well established that tumor vessels display highly permeable vessels, but only few studies focused on the cellular basis of tumor vessel permeability (McDonald et al. 1999; Morikawa et al. 2002; Hashizume et al. 2000). For instance, it is largely unknown how Ang-1 prevents and Ang-2 increases vessel permeability, although they both seem to interfere with cell–cell interactions and junctional proteins (e.g., stabilize or destabilize EC junctions in vitro) (Gamble et al. 2000; Scharpfenecker et al. 2005). Recently, two reports provided some insight in the molecular mechanism of Ang-1-induced Tie2 signaling in regulating endothelial cell quiescence vs. angiogenic activation (Saharinen et al. 2008; Fukuhara et al. 2008). Using an in vitro system, the authors elegantly showed that Ang1-activated Tie2 assembles novel signaling complexes leading to preferential activation of different downstream signal transduction proteins in the presence vs. absence of cell–cell contacts.

In our own studies, we analyzed the cellular consequences of Angiopoietin expression on tumor vessel morphology in two mouse mammary carcinoma models which naturally displayed distinct Ang/Tie2 expression profiles and generated mammary carcinomas to express Ang-1 and Ang-2 (Reiss et al. 2009). Analysis of Angiopoietin-overexpressing mammary xenografts at the ultrastructural level strongly supported the hypothesis that Ang-1/Tie2 signaling is essential for proper vessel organization, and suggested that Ang-2 is mainly responsible for the induction of disrupted endothelial cells (Reiss et al. 2009). Furthermore, our findings supported the hypothesis that Ang-2 can trigger important signals that are decisive for a switch of vascular phenotypes within tumors. Current results also imply that disruption of cell–cell contacts between endothelial cells might be inversely regulated by Ang-1 and Ang-2. For instance, it has been shown that VEGF-mediated disruption of cell–cell interactions is attributed to the dissociation of β-catenin from VE-cadherin (Wang et al. 2004). Interestingly, this effect can be opposed by Ang-1 as it specifically counteracts the ability of VEGF to induce the phosphorylation-dependent redistribution of VE-cadherin, thereby rescueing the endothelial barrier function (Gavard et al. 2008). Our own observations in tumors of Ang-2 transgenic animals (unpublished data);

(Reiss et al. 2007) suggest that high serum levels of Ang-2 are mainly responsible for improper vessel function. Future studies will help to unravel participating cellular elements during pathological angiogenesis more precisely.

2.4
Therapeutic Implications

Clearly, the effects of Angiopoietins in vivo suggest that manipulation of this ligand could have therapeutical potential. Pharmacological inhibition of Angiopoietin functions by sequestration with soluble Tie2 (Siemeister et al. 1999; Lin et al. 1998; Lin et al. 1997), or by the usage of dominant-negative Tie2 mutants has previously been shown to have a negative impact on tumor growth and progression. Until now, novel inhibition strategies for cancer treatment are at the preclinical level in murine angiogenesis models. Possible manipulation includes neutralization of Ang-2-Tie2 interactions (Oliner et al. 2004) or overexpression of Ang-2 (Cao et al. 2007), which inhibited tumor angiogenesis and tumor growth in mice. Whether targeted intervention of Ang-2 will be favorable in human tumors needs to be determined in the future. However, interfering with Ang-2 will shift the relative level of Ang1 and Ang-2. In case of Ang-2 inhibition, increased levels of Ang-1 will be beneficial for vessel perfusion and permeability and might lead to increased angiogenesis. Thus, Angiopoietin dosage is critical for the net outcome on angiogenesis inhibition and has to be taken into account for possible therapeutic interventions. Interestingly, VEGFR2 blockage can temporarily normalize tumor vessel structure (increased pericyte coverage) and lead to vascular normalization via expression of Ang-1 (Winkler et al. 2004). As a consequence, transient stabilization of vessels and improved oxygen delivery to hypoxic zones is achieved following VEGF neutralization which may facilitate drug delivery into tumors. The delivery of drugs utilizing the Angiopoietin/Tie system as a vehicle has recently been reported by De Palma et al. (De Palma et al. 2008). In this study, the authors exploited the tumor-homing ability of proangiogenic Tie2-expressing monocytes to deliver IFN-α to tumors which inhibited tumor growth and metastasis.

The complex interplay between complementary and yet conflicting roles of both Angiopoietins during tumor angiogenesis has impeded the development of drugs interfering with this angiogenic pathway. Collectively, a better understanding of the molecular mechanisms of Ang-1 and Ang-2 signaling during pathological angiogenesis may set the stage for novel therapies targeting this pathway.

2.5
Conclusions

Angiopoietins (Ang-1 and Ang-2) and their Tie receptors have wide-ranging effects on tumor malignancy that includes angiogenesis, vascular stabilization and permeability, and the recruitment of inflammatory cells. These multifaceted pathways present a valuable opportunity in developing novel inhibition strategies for cancer treatment. Ang-1 is not significantly upregulated in the majority of tumors. In contrast, Ang-2 is highly induced in the tumor vasculature, even prior to the induction of VEGF. As such, a shift in the Ang-1:Ang-2 balance in advantage of Ang-2 is the consequence. Therefore, it is evident that Ang-2 dosage is critical in shaping the outcome of angiogenesis. However, the regulatory role of Ang-1 and Ang-2 in tumor angiogenesis remains controversial, and the complex interplay between complementary yet conflicting

2

roles of both the Angiopoietins during adult angiogenesis need to be addressed more precisely, for example, by using Ang-2 transgenic animals. Further studies are needed to discern how Angiopoietins cooperate with other molecules and to develop new strategies for therapy targeting the Ang/Tie pathway.

Acknowledgment I gratefully acknowledge Jutta Reiss for helping with the illustrations and cartoons, and Andrea Tal for confocal images. This work is supported by the SFB/TR23 – C1 and the Excellence Cluster Cardio-Pulmonary System (ECCPS).

References

Carmeliet P, Ferreira V, Breier G et al (1996) Abnormal blood vessel development and lethality in embryos lacking a single VEGF allele. Nature 380:435–439

Ferrara N, Carver-Moore K, Chen H et al (1996) Heterozygous embryonic lethality induced by targeted inactivation of the VEGF gene. Nature 380:439–442

Ferrara N, Gerber HP, LeCouter J (2003) The biology of VEGF and its receptors. Nat Med 9:669–676

Conway EM, Collen D, Carmeliet P (2001) Molecular mechanisms of blood vessel growth. Cardiovasc Res 49:507–521

Risau W (1997) Mechanisms of angiogenesis. Nature 386:671–674

Suri C, McClain J, Thurston G et al (1998) Increased vascularization in mice overexpressing angiopoietin-1. Science 282:468–471

Maisonpierre PC, Suri C, Jones PF et al (1997) Angiopoietin-2, a natural antagonist for Tie2 that disrupts in vivo angiogenesis. Science 277:55–60

Brindle NP, Saharinen P, Alitalo K (2006) Signaling and functions of angiopoietin-1 in vascular protection. Circ Res 98:1014–1023

Hanahan D (1997) Signaling vascular morphogenesis and maintenance. Science 277:48–50

Davis S, Aldrich TH, Jones PF et al (1996) Isolation of angiopoietin-1, a ligand for the TIE2 receptor, by secretion-trap expression cloning. Cell 87:1161–1169

Valenzuela DM, Griffiths JA, Rojas J et al (1999) Angiopoietins 3 and 4: diverging gene counterparts in mice and humans. Proc Natl Acad Sci U S A 96:1904–1909

Sato TN, Tozawa Y, Deutsch U et al (1995) Distinct roles of the receptor tyrosine kinases Tie-1 and Tie-2 in blood vessel formation. Nature 376:70–74

Dumont DJ, Fong GH, Puri MC, Gradwohl G, Alitalo K, Breitman ML (1995) Vascularization of the mouse embryo: a study of flk-1, tek, tie, and vascular endothelial growth factor expression during development. Dev Dyn 203:80–92

Barton WA, Tzvetkova-Robev D, Miranda EP et al (2006) Crystal structures of the Tie2 receptor ectodomain and the angiopoietin-2-Tie2 complex. Nat Struct Mol Biol 13:524–532

Fiedler U, Krissl T, Koidl S et al (2003) Angiopoietin-1 and angiopoietin-2 share the same binding domains in the Tie-2 receptor involving the first Ig-like loop and the epidermal growth factor-like repeats. J Biol Chem 278:1721–1727

Dumont DJ, Gradwohl GJ, Fong GH, Auerbach R, Breitman ML (1993) The endothelial-specific receptor tyrosine kinase, tek, is a member of a new subfamily of receptors. Oncogene 8:1293–1301

Sato TN, Qin Y, Kozak CA, Audus KL (1993) Tie-1 and tie-2 define another class of putative receptor tyrosine kinase genes expressed in early embryonic vascular system. Proc Natl Acad Sci U S A 90:9355–9358

Schnurch H, Risau W (1993) Expression of tie-2, a member of a novel family of receptor tyrosine kinases, in the endothelial cell lineage. Development 119:957–968

Partanen J, Armstrong E, Makela TP et al (1992) A novel endothelial cell surface receptor tyrosine kinase with extracellular epidermal growth factor homology domains. Mol Cell Biol 12:1698–1707

Saharinen P, Kerkela K, Ekman N et al (2005) Multiple angiopoietin recombinant proteins activate the Tie1 receptor tyrosine kinase and promote its interaction with Tie2. J Cell Biol 169:239–243

Jones N, Master Z, Jones J et al (1999) Identification of Tek/Tie2 binding partners. Binding to a multifunctional docking site mediates cell survival and migration. J Biol Chem 274:30896–30905

Papapetropoulos A, Fulton D, Mahboubi K et al (2000) Angiopoietin-1 inhibits endothelial cell apoptosis via the Akt/survivin pathway. J Biol Chem 275:9102–9105

Audero E, Cascone I, Maniero F et al (2004) Adaptor ShcA protein binds tyrosine kinase Tie2 receptor and regulates migration and sprouting but not survival of endothelial cells. J Biol Chem 279: 13224–13233

Hayes AJ, Huang WQ, Mallah J, Yang D, Lippman ME, Li LY (1999) Angiopoietin-1 and its receptor Tie-2 participate in the regulation of capillary-like tubule formation and survival of endothelial cells. Microvasc Res 58:224–237

Koblizek TI, Weiss C, Yancopoulos GD, Deutsch U, Risau W (1998) Angiopoietin-1 induces sprouting angiogenesis in vitro. Curr Biol 8:529–532

Suri C, Jones PF, Patan S et al (1996) Requisite role of angiopoietin-1, a ligand for the TIE2 receptor, during embryonic angiogenesis. Cell 87: 1171–1180

Wong AL, Haroon ZA, Werner S, Dewhirst MW, Greenberg CS, Peters KG (1997) Tie2 expression and phosphorylation in angiogenic and quiescent adult tissues. Circ Res 81:567–574

Saharinen P, Eklund L, Miettinen J et al (2008) Angiopoietins assemble distinct Tie2 signalling complexes in endothelial cell-cell and cell-matrix contacts. Nat Cell Biol 10:527–537

Fukuhara S, Sako K, Minami T et al (2008) Differential function of Tie2 at cell-cell contacts and cell-substratum contacts regulated by angiopoietin-1. Nat Cell Biol 10:513–526

Reiss Y, Droste J, Heil M et al (2007) Angiopoietin-2 impairs revascularization after limb ischemia. Circ Res 101(1):88–96

Scharpfenecker M, Fiedler U, Reiss Y, Augustin HG (2005) The Tie-2 ligand angiopoietin-2 destabilizes quiescent endothelium through an internal autocrine loop mechanism. J Cell Sci 118:771–780

Holash J, Maisonpierre PC, Compton D et al (1999) Vessel cooption, regression, and growth in tumors mediated by angiopoietins and VEGF. Science 284:1994–1998

Stratmann A, Risau W, Plate KH (1998) Cell type-specific expression of angiopoietin-1 and angiopoietin-2 suggests a role in glioblastoma angiogenesis. Am J Pathol 153:1459–1466

Gale NW, Thurston G, Hackett SF et al (2002) Angiopoietin-2 is required for postnatal angiogenesis and lymphatic patterning, and only the latter role is rescued by Angiopoietin-1. Dev Cell 3:411–423

Folkman J (1971) Tumor angiogenesis: therapeutic implications. N Engl J Med 285:1182–1186

Hanahan D, Folkman J (1996) Patterns and emerging mechanisms of the angiogenic switch during tumorigenesis. Cell 86:353–364

Yancopoulos GD, Davis S, Gale NW, Rudge JS, Wiegand SJ, Holash J (2000) Vascular-specific growth factors and blood vessel formation. Nature 407:242–248

Reiss Y, Machein MR, Plate KH (2005) The role of angiopoietins during angiogenesis in gliomas. Brain Pathol 15:311–317

Tait CR, Jones PF (2004) Angiopoietins in tumours: the angiogenic switch. J Pathol 204:1–10

Morikawa S, Baluk P, Kaidoh T, Haskell A, Jain RK, McDonald DM (2002) Abnormalities in pericytes on blood vessels and endothelial sprouts in tumors. Am J Pathol 160:985–1000

Ward NL, Dumont DJ (2002) The angiopoietins and Tie2/Tek: adding to the complexity of cardiovascular development. Semin Cell Dev Biol 13:19–27

Stoeltzing O, Ahmad SA, Liu W et al (2003) Angiopoietin-1 inhibits vascular permeability, angiogenesis, and growth of hepatic colon cancer tumors. Cancer Res 63:3370–3377

Hawighorst T, Skobe M, Streit M et al (2002) Activation of the tie2 receptor by angiopoietin-1 enhances tumor vessel maturation and impairs squamous cell carcinoma growth. Am J Pathol 160:1381–1392

Tian S, Hayes AJ, Metheny-Barlow LJ, Li LY (2002) Stabilization of breast cancer xenograft tumour neovasculature by angiopoietin-1. Br J Cancer 86:645–651

Stoeltzing O, Ahmad SA, Liu W et al (2002) Angiopoietin-1 inhibits tumour growth and ascites formation in a murine model of peritoneal carcinomatosis. Br J Cancer 87:1182–1187

Ahmad SA, Liu W, Jung YD et al (2001) The effects of angiopoietin-1 and -2 on tumor growth and angiogenesis in human colon cancer. Cancer Res 61:1255–1259

Yu Q, Stamenkovic I (2001) Angiopoietin-2 is implicated in the regulation of tumor angiogenesis. Am J Pathol 158:563–570

Hayes AJ, Huang WQ, Yu J et al (2000) Expression and function of angiopoietin-1 in breast cancer. Br J Cancer 83:1154–1160

Shim WS, Teh M, Bapna A et al (2002) Angiopoietin 1 promotes tumor angiogenesis and tumor vessel plasticity of human cervical cancer in mice. Exp Cell Res 279:299–309

Machein MR, Knedla A, Knoth R, Wagner S, Neuschl E, Plate KH (2004) Angiopoietin-1 promotes tumor angiogenesis in a rat glioma model. Am J Pathol 165:1557–1570

Cao Y, Sonveaux P, Liu S et al (2007) Systemic

overexpression of angiopoietin-2 promotes tumor microvessel regression and inhibits angiogenesis and tumor growth. Cancer Res 67:3835–3844

Zhang L, Yang N, Park JW et al (2003) Tumor-derived vascular endothelial growth factor up-regulates angiopoietin-2 in host endothelium and destabilizes host vasculature, supporting angiogenesis in ovarian cancer. Cancer Res 63:3403–3412

Hu B, Guo P, Fang Q et al (2003) Angiopoietin-2 induces human glioma invasion through the activation of matrix metalloprotease-2. Proc Natl Acad Sci U S A 100:8904–8909

Etoh T, Inoue H, Tanaka S, Barnard GF, Kitano S, Mori M (2001) Angiopoietin-2 is related to tumor angiogenesis in gastric carcinoma: possible in vivo regulation via induction of proteases. Cancer Res 61:2145–2153

Tanaka S, Mori M, Sakamoto Y, Makuuchi M, Sugimachi K, Wands JR (1999) Biologic significance of angiopoietin-2 expression in human hepatocellular carcinoma. J Clin Invest 103:341–345

Hashizume H, Baluk P, Morikawa S et al (2000) Openings between defective endothelial cells explain tumor vessel leakiness. Am J Pathol 156:1363–1380

Hegen A, Koidl S, Weindel K, Marme D, Augustin HG, Fiedler U (2004) Expression of angiopoietin-2 in endothelial cells is controlled by positive and negative regulatory promoter elements. Arterioscler Thromb Vasc Biol 24:1803–1809

Ochiumi T, Tanaka S, Oka S et al (2004) Clinical significance of angiopoietin-2 expression in the deepest invasive tumor site of advanced colorectal carcinoma. Int J Oncol 24:539–547

Sfiligoi C, de Luca A, Cascone I et al (2003) Angiopoietin-2 expression in breast cancer correlates with lymph node invasion and short survival. Int J Cancer 103:466–474

Siemeister G, Schirner M, Weindel K et al (1999) Two independent mechanisms essential for tumor angiogenesis: inhibition of human melanoma xenograft growth by interfering with either the vascular endothelial growth factor receptor pathway or the Tie-2 pathway. Cancer Res 59:3185–3191

Lin P, Buxton JA, Acheson A et al (1998) Antiangiogenic gene therapy targeting the endothelium-specific receptor tyrosine kinase Tie2. Proc Natl Acad Sci U S A 95:8829–8834

Lin P, Polverini P, Dewhirst M, Shan S, Rao PS, Peters K (1997) Inhibition of tumor angiogenesis using a soluble receptor establishes a role for Tie2 in pathologic vascular growth. J Clin Invest 100:2072–2078

Oliner J, Min H, Leal J et al (2004) Suppression of angiogenesis and tumor growth by selective inhibition of angiopoietin-2. Cancer Cell 6:507–516

McDonald DM, Thurston G, Baluk P (1999) Endothelial gaps as sites for plasma leakage in inflammation. Microcirculation 6:7–22

Gamble JR, Drew J, Trezise L et al (2000) Angiopoietin-1 is an antipermeability and anti-inflammatory agent in vitro and targets cell junctions. Circ Res 87:603–607

Wang Y, Pampou S, Fujikawa K, Varticovski L (2004) Opposing effect of angiopoietin-1 on VEGF-mediated disruption of endothelial cell-cell interactions requires activation of PKC beta. J Cell Physiol 198:53–61

Gavard J, Patel V, Gutkind JS (2008) Angiopoietin-1 prevents VEGF-induced endothelial permeability by sequestering Src through mDia. Dev Cell 14:25–36

Murdoch C, Muthana M, Coffelt SB, Lewis CE (2008) The role of myeloid cells in the promotion of tumour angiogenesis. Nat Rev Cancer 8:618–631

Grunewald M, Avraham I, Dor Y et al (2006) VEGF-induced adult neovascularization: recruitment, retention, and role of accessory cells. Cell 124:175–189

De Palma M, Murdoch C, Venneri MA, Naldini L, Lewis CE (2007) Tie2-expressing monocytes: regulation of tumor angiogenesis and therapeutic implications. Trends Immunol 28:519–524

De Palma M, Venneri MA, Roca C, Naldini L (2003) Targeting exogenous genes to tumor angiogenesis by transplantation of genetically modified hematopoietic stem cells. Nat Med 9: 789–795

De Palma M, Venneri MA, Galli R et al (2005) Tie2 identifies a hematopoietic lineage of proangiogenic monocytes required for tumor vessel formation and a mesenchymal population of pericyte progenitors. Cancer Cell 8: 211–226

Machein MR, Renninger S, de Lima-Hahn E, Plate KH (2003) Minor contribution of bone marrow-derived endothelial progenitors to the vascularization of murine gliomas. Brain Pathol 13:582–597

Fiedler U, Reiss Y, Scharpfenecker M et al (2006) Angiopoietin-2 sensitizes endothelial cells to TNF-alpha and has a crucial role in the induction of inflammation. Nat Med 12:235–239

Winkler F, Kozin SV, Tong RT et al (2004) Kinetics of vascular normalization by VEGFR2 blockade governs brain tumor response to radiation: role of oxygenation, angiopoietin-1, and matrix metalloproteinases. Cancer Cell 6:553–563

De Palma M, Mazzieri R, Politi LS et al (2008) Tumor-targeted interferon-alpha delivery by Tie2-expressing monocytes inhibits tumor growth and metastasis. Cancer Cell 14:299–311

Thurston G, Suri C, Smith K et al (1999) Leakage-resistant blood vessels in mice transgenically overexpressing angiopoietin-1. Science 286: 2511–2514

Puri MC, Rossant J, Alitalo K, Bernstein A, Partanen J (1995) The receptor tyrosine kinase TIE is required for integrity and survival of vascular endothelial cells. EMBO J 14:5884–5891

Puri MC, Partanen J, Rossant J, Bernstein A (1999) Interaction of the TEK and TIE receptor tyrosine kinases during cardiovascular development. Development 126:4569–4580

Dumont DJ, Gradwohl G, Fong GH et al (1994) Dominant-negative and targeted null mutations in the endothelial receptor tyrosine kinase, tek, reveal a critical role in vasculogenesis of the embryo. Genes Dev 8:1897–1909

Puri MC, Bernstein A (2003) Requirement for the TIE family of receptor tyrosine kinases in adult but not fetal hematopoiesis. Proc Natl Acad Sci U S A 100:12753–12758

Reiss Y, Knedla A, Tal AO et al (2009) Switching of vascular phenotypes within a murine breast cancer model induced by Angiopoietin-2. J Path 217 (4):571–580

HIF-1α and Cancer Therapy

3

Mei Yee Koh, Taly R. Spivak-Kroizman, and Garth Powis

Abstract Most solid tumors develop regions of hypoxia as they grow and outstrip their blood supply. In order to survive in the stressful hypoxic environment, tumor cells have developed a coordinated set of responses orchestrating their adaptation to hypoxia. The outcomes of the cellular responses to hypoxia are aggressive disease, resistance to therapy, and decreased patient survival. A critical mediator of the hypoxic response is the transcription factor hypoxia-inducible factor 1 (HIF-1) that upregulates expression of proteins that promote angiogenesis, anaerobic metabolism, and many other survival pathways. Regulation of HIF-1α, a component of the HIF-1 heterodimer, occurs at multiple levels including translation, degradation, and transcriptional activation, and serves as a testimony to the central role of HIF-1. Studies demonstrating the importance of HIF-1α expression for tumor survival have made HIF-1α an attractive target for cancer therapy. The growing l.ist of pharmacological inhibitors of HIF-1 and their varied targets mirrors the complex molecular mechanisms controlling HIF-1. In this chapter, we summarize recent findings regarding the regulation of HIF-1α and the progress made in identifying new therapeutic agents that inhibit HIF-1α.

3.1
Background

More than 50% of locally advanced solid tumors exhibit hypoxic tissue areas (i.e., areas with oxygen tensions of <2.5 mmHg) heterogeneously distributed within the tumor mass (Vaupel and Mayer 2007). Tumor hypoxia occurs due to the inability of the local vasculature to supply sufficient oxygen to the rapidly growing tumor. In an attempt to alleviate hypoxia, tumor cells release factors that generate new vasculature, which is itself highly irregular, tortuous, and leaky with arterio-venous shunts and blind ends (Brown and Giaccia 1998). The insufficient/intermittent oxygen supply, both from the existing vasculature and from the irregular tumor neovasculature, gives rise to a highly dynamic tumor microenvironment containing hypoxic/reoxygenation gradients (Bristow and Hill 2008). Tumor hypoxia is of major significance since it can promote both tumor progression and resistance to radiation and chemotherapy.

The tumor response to hypoxia includes the induction of angiogenesis, a switch from aerobic metabolism to anaerobic glycolysis, and the

G. Powis (✉)
MD Anderson Cancer Center, 1400 Holcombe Blvd., FC6.3044, Unit 422, Houston, TX 77030, USA
e-mail: gpowis@mdanderson.org

R. Liersch et al. (eds.), *Angiogenesis Inhibition,* Recent Results in Cancer Research,
DOI: 10.1007/978-3-540-78281-0_3, © Springer Verlag Berlin Heidelberg 2010

expression of a variety of stress proteins regulating cell death or survival (Table 3.1).The hypoxia-inducible factor-1 (HIF-1 or HIF) transcription factor is the master regulator of the hypoxic response, inducing the expression of a large number of genes critical for adaptation to hypoxia (Semenza and Wang 1992). Indeed, hypoxia has been recognized as a primary physiological regulator of the angiogenic switch in which HIF-1 acts as a focal point, tipping the balance of anti- and proangiogenic factors toward hypoxia-induced angiogenesis (Bergers and Benjamin 2003; Giordano and Johnson 2001). Hypoxic cells are also more genetically unstable, more resistant to treatment by ionizing radiation and chemotherapy, and generally more invasive and metastatic (Vaupel and Mayer 2007). Hence, HIF-1 is a positive factor in tumor growth and its increased expression has been correlated with poor patient prognosis, making targeting tumor hypoxia/HIF-1 an attractive approach for the development of novel anticancer therapies (Semenza 2004; Welsh et al. 2006).

3.2
Molecular and Cellular Biology of HIF-1

The HIF-1 transcription factor is a heterodimer of the oxygen-regulated HIF-α subunit, and the constitutively expressed HIF-1β subunit (also known as the aryl hydrocarbon receptor nuclear translocator (ARNT)) (Wang et al. 1995). When HIF-α is stabilized (such as during hypoxia), it enters the nucleus and heterodimerizes with HIF-1β and binds to a conserved DNA sequence known as the hypoxia responsive element (HRE) to transactivate a variety of hypoxia-responsive genes (Maxwell et al. 2001). Both subunits are basic helix-loop-helix-Per-ARNT-Sim (bHLH-PAS) domain proteins in which DNA binding and dimerization is mediated by the basic HLH domains, whilst the PAS domain is involved in dimer formation (Jiang et al. 1996) (Fig. 3.1). The HIF-α subunit also

contains an oxygen-dependent degradation (ODD) domain that regulates its ODD and two transactivation domains (N-TAD and C-TAD). To date, three HIF-α isoforms (HIF-1/2/3α) have been described, of which HIF-1α and HIF-2α are the best characterized. HIF-1α is expressed ubiquitously, whereas HIF-2α displays more tissue-specific expression (Wiesener et al. 2003). Both have been shown to regulate common and unique target genes (Hu et al. 2003), and may be differentially regulated depending on the duration and severity of hypoxia exposure (Holmquist-Mengelbier et al. 2006). The least studied HIF-α isoform, HIF-3α, is regulated in a similar manner to HIF-1α and HIF-2α and can also dimerize with HIF-1β (Gu et al. 1998). HIF-3α has high similarity with HIF-1α and HIF-2α in the bHLH and PAS domains, but lacks the C-TAD found in HIF-1α and HIF-2α. HIF-3α has multiple splice variants, including the best-known, inhibitory PAS domain protein (IPAS), which is a truncated protein that acts as a dominant negative inhibitor of HIF-1 (Makino et al. 2002).

The HIF-1 heterodimer binds a conserved HIF binding sequence (HBS) within the HRE in the promoter or enhancer regions of target genes, thereby eliciting their transactivation and an adaptive hypoxic response (Semenza 2003). To date, more than 70 genes have been confirmed as HIF-1 target genes (Table 3.1). These genes regulate a diverse set of cellular processes critical for the physiological response to hypoxia important both for normal development and for the hypoxic adaptation of tumor cells.

3.3
HIF-1 Regulation

3.3.1
Regulation of HIF-1α Translation

Numerous studies support the idea that in addition to inhibition of ODD, continued translation also contributes to the accumulation of HIF-1α

Table 3.1 Role of HIF-1 in the response to hypoxia

Hypoxic response	HIF-1 target genes
Angiogenesis: HIF-1 directly activates the expression of a number of proangiogenic factors, the best characterized of which is the vascular endothelial growth factor (VEGF). This event promotes the formation of new blood vessels, thus restoring the supply of oxygen and nutrients. Increased angiogenesis is one of the key HIF-1-dependent protumorigenic events that enable continued tumor growth	Vascular endothelial growth factor (VEGF), VEGF receptor 1 (Flt-1), erythropoietin (EPO), plasminogen activator inhibitor 1 (PAI-1), adrenomedullin (ADM), endothelin-1 (EDN1), nitric oxide synthase-2 (NOS2A). leptin (LEP)
Anaerobic metabolism: HIF-1 promotes both the uptake and metabolism of glucose through anaerobic glycolysis by upregulating the expression of glucose transporters (GLUT1, GLUT3) and of glycolytic enzymes (PFKFB3). To maintain the metabolic flux through glycolysis, HIF-1 activation also leads to the inhibition of the Kreb's cycle by upregulating PDK1 and LDHA. This shift from aerobic to anaerobic metabolism is frequently observed in cancer cells, even in normoxia, and is known as the Warburg effect	Glucose transporter 1 and 3 (GLUT1, GLUT3), 6-phosphofructo-2-kinase/fructose-2,6-bisphosphatase (PFKFB3), pyruvate dehydrogenase kinase 1 (PDK1), lactate dehydrogenase A (LDHA), hexokinase 1 and 2 (HK1, HK2), glucose phosphate isomerase (AMF/GP1), enolase 1 (ENO1), glyceraldehyde-3-phosphate dehydrogenase (GAPDH), phosphofructokinase L (PFKL), phosphoglycerate kinase 1 (PGK1), pyruvate kinase M (PKM)
pH regulation: To counter the potentially toxic intracellular acidosis owing to increased production of lactic acid and CO by anaerobic glycolysis, HIF-1 also upregulates MCT4, which mediates lactic acid efflux, and CA IX, which catalyzes the conversion of extracellular CO_2 to carbonic acid (H_2CO_3)	Carbonic anhydrase 9 and 12 (CAIX, CAXII), monocarboxylic acid transporter 4 (MCT4)
Apoptosis, survival and proliferation: HIF-1 regulates a complex array of pro- and antiapoptotic genes as well as genes regulating cell cycle and proliferation. The final outcome of HIF-1 activation on cell growth and survival may be dictated by the severity and duration of hypoxia as well as the presence of other regulatory cofactors	BCL2/adenovirus E1B 19 kDa interacting protein 3 (BNIP3), BNIP3-like (BNIP3L/NIX), DNA-damage-inducible transcript 4 (DDIT4), ADM, Insulin-likegrowth factor 2 (IGF2), Insulin-like growth factor binding protein 1, 2, and 3 (IGF-BP1, IGF-BP2, IGF-BP3), NOS2, transforming growth factor α (TGF-α), cyclin G2
Invasion, metastasis, differentiation: HIF-1 promotes tumor cell invasion and metastasis and particularly when composed of the HIF-2α isoform, has been implicated in the inhibition of differentiation and maintenance of the stem cell phenotype	AMF/GP1, hepatocyte growth factor receptor (c-MET), low density lipoprotein-related protein 1 (LRP1), lysyl oxidase (LOX), TWIST1, POU class 5 homeobox 1(POU5F1/OCT4)

Poorly vascularized regions are associated with hypoxia and nutrient deprivation, thereby limiting ATP production, a requirement for cell proliferation. Hypoxia induces HIF-1, which activates a variety of genes that regulate the cellular response to hypoxia. These are summarized below. This list is by no means exhaustive and has been described in greater detail previously (Semenza 2002; Semenza 1999)

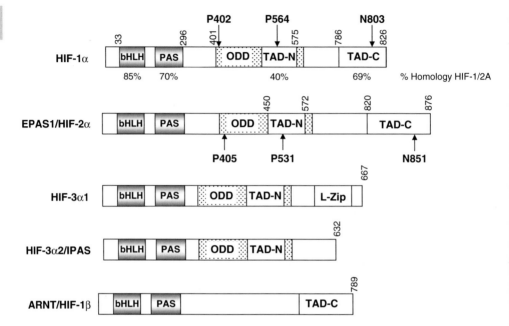

Fig. 3.1 Domain structures of HIF-1α, HIF-2α, HIF-3α and HIF-1β/ARNT. The HIF-α and HIF-β subunits are basic helix-loop-helix/Per-ARNT-Sim homology (bHLH/PAS) transcription factors. HIF-1α and HIF-2α contain two transactivation (TAD) domains, one at the amino terminal and the other at the carboxy terminal. Six splice versions of HIF-3α have been identified (only two are depicted here) and those that have been mapped contain only an N-TAD. HIF-1β/ARNT, the constitutive member of the HIF-1 heterodimer contains a C-TAD which is not required for HIF-1 transcriptional activity

protein in hypoxia (Koh et al. 2008c). However, it is well-known that hypoxia inhibits global protein translation by 20–70%, and the precise mechanism which allows sustained translation of HIF-1α as well as other stress proteins during hypoxia is unclear. Hypoxia-mediated inhibition of overall protein translation is controlled mainly by two distinct pathways that are regulated in a biphasic manner. The first pathway, the unfolded protein response (UPR) is activated rapidly by hypoxia, leading to phosphorylation of the eukaryotic initiation factor 2 (eIF2α) by PERK. This prevents the assembly of the 40S ribosome-binding eIF2-GTP-met-tRNA ternary complex required for initiation of translation. The second pathway, activated by prolonged hypoxia, inhibits the activity of the mammalian target of rapamycin (mTOR) that promotes protein synthesis by phosphorylating

the inhibitory eukaryotic initiation factor 4E (eIF4E)-binding proteins (4E-BPs). Active mTOR phosphorylates 4E-BPs on multiple sites thus releasing eIF4E allowing it thus, to mediate the binding of the eIF4F complex to the 5' cap of the mRNA and engage in translation (Fig. 3.2).

Initially it was suggested that HIF-1α translation occurs through internal ribosome-entry-site (IRES) elements, which are RNA sequences that form secondary or tertiary structures and direct ribosome binding without the need for the eIF4F cap-binding complex. Several studies have reported that the 5'UTR of HIF-1α contains an IRES capable of promoting translation of a downstream reporter in bicistronic reporter assay (Lang et al. 2002; Zhou et al. 2004; Schepens et al. 2005). However, recent work convincingly disputes the role of IRES in HIF1-α translation, and suggests that the measured activity is due to cryptic

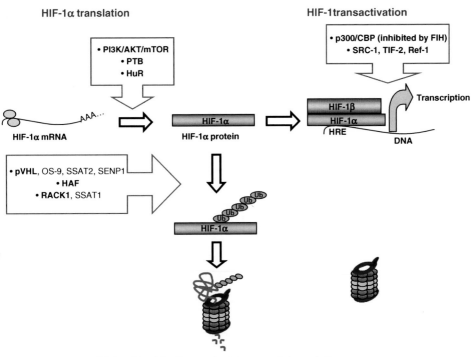

Fig. 3.2 Focal points of HIF-1 regulation. HIF-1α translation is regulated by the PI3K-AKT/mTOR pathway and the RNA binding proteins PTB and HuR. HIF-1α protein is degraded by the ubiquitin-proteasome system through either oxygen-dependent or oxygen-independent mechanisms. The mediators of HIF-1α degradation are pVHL (oxygen-dependent), HAF and RACK1 (oxygen-independent) which are themselves regulated by OS-9, SSAT2, SENP1, and SSAT1 as indicated. Stabilized HIF-1α enters the nucleus where it heterodimerizes with HIF-1β forming the HIF-1 transcription factor and initiating transcription of targets genes containing the HRE sequence. HIF-1 transactivating activity requires the cofactors p300/CBP through an interaction inhibiting by FIH. Other transcriptional cofactors recruited by HIF-1 are SRC-1, TIF-2, and Ref-1

promoter activity rather than IRES-mediated translation (Young et al. 2008; Bert et al. 2006).

The RNA-binding proteins polypyrimidine tract-binding protein (PTB) and HuR bind the HIF-1α 3'UTR and 5'UTR, respectively, and have also been proposed to enhance HIF-1α translation (Galban et al. 2008; Schepens et al. 2005). A role for calcium in the regulation of HIF-1α translation during hypoxia is receiving increased attention. Most cells respond to hypoxia with a sustained increase in cytoplasmic free calcium that results from the combined influx of extracellular calcium and the release of calcium present in the ER lumen (Seta et al. 2004). Studies addressing the role of calcium in the regulation of HIF-1α levels have been inconsistent with regard to the effect or the mechanism (Berchner-Pfannschmidt et al. 2004; Liu et al. 2007b; Hui et al. 2006; Liu et al. 2004; Metzen et al. 1999; Mottet et al. 2002; Salnikow et al. 2002; Werno et al. 2008; Zhou et al. 2006). This reflects the complexity of calcium-dependent signaling which is involved in pathways regulating degradation, translation, and transcription of HIF-1α. Further studies are needed to define the role of calcium in HIF-1α regulation.

A recent study provides a new molecular mechanism for maintaining translation of HIF-2α in hypoxia (Zimmer et al. 2008). The authors showed that in normoxia, the iron-regulatory protein 1 (IRP1) binds to an iron-responsive element (IRE) within the 5'UTR of HIF2α mRNA and represses HIF-2α translation. Hypoxia induces posttranslational changes in IRP1 that impair its ability to bind IRE, allowing translation of HIF-2α. The authors also identified small-molecule inhibitors that selectively decrease HIF-2α translation by enhancing the binding of IRP1 to IRE. Interestingly, the IRP1 mechanism does not appear to contribute to translation of HIF-1α in hypoxia despite the presence of a putative IRE sequence within the 5'UTR of HIF-1α (Zimmer et al. 2008).

Phosphorylation of eIF2α may allow preferential translation of stress proteins such as HIF-1α by creating a shift in translation, referred to as "translational reprogramming" (Ron and Walter 2007). This mechanism proposes that eIF2α phosphorylation allows resetting of the translational machinery by liberating ribosomes and translation factors from their binding to preexisting mRNA (Harding et al. 2000). Thus, HIF-1α mRNA is able to compete more effectively for the limited number of translation factors present in hypoxia, possibly through its binding to PTB and HuR (Galban et al. 2008; Schepens et al. 2005).

mTOR has been implicated as contributing to HIF-1α accumulation in both normoxia and hypoxia (Bernardi et al. 2006; Brugarolas et al. 2004; Hudson et al. 2002; Majumder et al. 2004). The mechanism that may allow translation of HIF-1α in cancer cells is through accumulation of mutations in pathways regulating mTOR activity that bypass the hypoxia-mediated mTOR inhibition. For example, loss of the tumor suppressor PTEN leads to activation of the PI3K/AKT pathway, and is associated with the induction of mTOR-dependent HIF-1α translation (Zundel et al. 2000). Another study has shown that growth of AKT-dependent prostate intraepithelial neoplasia requires mTOR-dependent activation

of HIF-1α, and that clinical resistance to mTOR inhibitors may emerge through upregulation of HIF-1α activity (Majumder et al. 2004). Also, loss of the VHL gene has been found to sensitize kidney cancer cells to the mTOR inhibitor CCI-779 and correlated with inhibition of HIF-1α translation (Thomas et al. 2006). Another example of mutation that promotes HIF-1α translation was demonstrated in breast cancer where overexpressed 4E-BP1 and eIF4G function as a hypoxia-activated switch that facilitate cap-independent translation over cap-dependent translation of HIF-1α and other key proangiogenic and prosurvival mRNAs (Braunstein et al. 2007).

In addition, the antitumor activity of several mTOR inhibitors has been shown to be related to their ability to inhibit HIF-1α and its targets, again supporting the involvement of mTOR in HIF-1α translation in tumors. The antitumor activity of CCI-779 (temsirolimus, Wyeth) was attributed to its ability to inhibit HIF-1α and VEGF in both normoxia and hypoxia in the Her-2 amplified breast cancer cells, BT-747 (Del Bufalo et al. 2006), and to inhibition of mTOR/HIF-1α/VEGF pathway in human rhabdomyosarcoma xenografts (Wan et al. 2006). Similarly, the activity of another mTOR inhibitors RAD001 (everolimus, Novartis) was also shown to be dependent on HIF-1α (Majumder et al. 2004). Taken together, this information suggests that the continued translation of HIF-1α in hypoxia promotes tumorigenesis, and hence translation may be a promising therapeutic target.

3.3.2
Regulation of HIF-1α Degradation

Under aerobic conditions, HIF-1α is hydroxylated by specific prolyl hydroxylases (PHD1, PHD2, and PHD3) at two conserved proline residues (402 and 564) situated within its ODD domain in a reaction requiring oxygen, 2-oxoglutarate, and ascorbate (Jaakkola et al. 2001). A fourth PHD containing a transmembrane domain,

P4H-TM has recently been described (Koivunen et al. 2007). Under hypoxic conditions, PHD activity is inhibited, resulting in HIF-1α stabilization. In addition to the enzymatic inhibition of the PHDs, hypoxia causes perturbations in the mitochondrial electron transport chain, thus increasing the levels of cytoplasmic reactive oxygen species (ROS) which alters the oxidation state of Fe^{2+}, a cofactor for PHD activity, to Fe^{3+}, which cannot be utilized. This alteration inhibits PHD activity and promotes HIF-1α stabilization. Thus the disruption of mitochondrial function using either pharmacological or genetic inhibition/knockout of the mitochondrial electron transport chain prevents HIF-1α stabilization during hypoxia (Hagen et al. 2003; Simon 2006). In addition to mitochondrial-dependent mechanisms, the PHDs are subject to regulation by other factors including intracellular calcium concentration (Berchner-Pfannschmidt et al. 2004) and the Siah1 and Siah2 E3 ubiquitin ligases (Nakayama and Ronai 2004).

HIF-1α hydroxylation facilitates binding of pVHL to the HIF-1α ODD (Ohh et al. 2000). pVHL forms the substrate recognition module of an E3 ubiquitin ligase complex comprising elongin C, elongin B, cullin-2, and ring-box 1 (Rbx1), which directs HIF-1α poly-ubiquitylation and proteasomal degradation. The central role of pVHL in HIF-1α regulation is manifested in VHL disease where the inactivation of the *VHL* gene results in the development of highly vascularized tumors of the kidney, retina, and central nervous system (Kaelin 2007).

Although pVHL has been well established as the key player in the regulation of the ODD of HIF-1α, a number of alternative pathways have recently been described (Koh et al. 2008c). HIF-1α can be ubiquitylated and degraded in a manner mechanistically similar to the pVHL pathway through the binding of receptor of activated protein kinase C (RACK1) to HIF-1α. As RACK1 competes with Hsp90 for binding to HIF-1α, Hsp90 inhibitors such as 17-(Allylamino)-17-demethoxygeldanamycin (17-AAG) cause the oxygen-independent degradation of HIF-1α through RACK1 (Liu et al. 2007a). The hypoxia-associated factor (HAF) is a new E3 ligase specific for HIF-1α that causes HIF-1α ubiquitination and proteasomal degradation in an oxygen- and pVHL-independent manner (Koh et al. 2008a). HAF is the first HIF-1α specific E3 ligase to be identified, and may provide a mechanism for HIF-1α/HIF-2α isoform selectivity. The characterization of these novel modulators of HIF-1α degradation may provide novel approaches for HIF-1 inhibition.

3.3.3
Regulation of HIF-1 Transactivation

The transactivation activity of the HIF-1 heterodimer is mediated by the N-TAD and the C-TAD on the HIF-α subunit. Both the N-TAD and the C-TAD recruit the coactivators p300/CBP, SRC-1, and TIF-2 (Arany et al. 1996; Carrero et al. 2000). p300 and CBP are homologous transcriptional coactivators and are essential for linking HIF-1 and other transcription factors with coactivator complexes and the basal transcriptional machinery. p300/CBP, SRC-1, and TIF-2 have histone acetyltransferase activity allowing chromatin remodeling prior to transcription (Carrero et al. 2000; Lando et al. 2002). Although HIF-1β also contains a C-TAD, it appears to be dispensable for HIF-1 transcription activity. A key difference between the N-TAD and C-TAD is the oxygen-dependent regulation of the C-TAD. Under normoxic conditions, the ability of HIF-1α to activate transcription is prevented by another oxygen-regulated enzyme, factor inhibiting HIF-1 (FIH-1). FIH-1 hydroxylates asparagine 803 within the C-TAD of HIF-1α, disrupting its interaction with the transcription coactivators p300/CBP (Mahon et al. 2001). As with the PHDs, asparagine hydroxylation is inhibited under hypoxic conditions allowing the p300/CBP complex to bind to HIF-1α allowing HIF-1 transactivation.

3.4
Relationship Between HIF-1 and Other Key Oncogenic Pathways

3.4.1
HIF-1 Activation by Growth Factors

In addition to hypoxia-dependent regulation, HIF-1 may be activated by a wide range of growth-promoting stimuli and oncogenic pathways such as insulin, insulin-like growth factor-1, epidermal growth factor and mutant Ras, Src and/or PI-3K pathways (Brugarolas et al. 2004; Gray et al. 2005; Hudson et al. 2002; Zundel et al. 2000). Dysregulation of growth factors and/or their cognate receptors due to loss-of-function of tumor suppressor genes or activation of oncogenes may result in constitutive activation of HIF-1, such as through the PI3K/mTOR pathway (Zhong et al. 2000), or in increased HIF-1α activity through p42/p44 MAPK phosphorylation (Berra et al. 2000; Richard et al. 1999). Activation of these oncogenic pathways is associated with increased angiogenesis through HIF-1 activation (Jiang and Liu 2008).

3.4.2
Interplay Between HIF-1 and the p53 Tumor Suppressor

The p53 tumor suppressor is a transcription factor with an important role in the regulation of the cellular response to environmental stress and DNA damage (Giaccia and Kastan 1998). The p53 gene is one of the most frequently mutated genes in human cancer (Levine 1997). In normal, unstressed cells, p53 is present at low levels due to its association with MDM2, an E3-ubiquitin ligase that targets p53 for proteasomal degradation. Chronic hypoxia or anoxia may cause the upregulation of p53 through posttranslational modifications (including N-terminal phosphorylation) that disrupt the p53-MDM2 interaction, leading to p53 nuclear translocation and transactivation (An et al. 1998; Giaccia and Kastan 1998; Graeber et al. 1994). Hypoxia alone may be insufficient to induce p53 (Wenger et al. 1998) but may induce p53 accumulation when accompanied by acidosis and nutrient deprivation (Pan et al. 2004). Hypoxia-induced p53 protein is stabilized by a direct interaction with the ODD of HIF-1α, whereby one p53 dimer interacts with a single HIF-1α ODD domain. However, by binding to HIF-1α, p53 may also promote the ubiquitin-mediated degradation of HIF-1α via recruitment of MDM2 (Ravi et al. 2000). Consequently, loss of p53 in tumor cells results in an increase in hypoxia-induced HIF-1α and augments HIF-1-dependent transactivation. p53 may also attenuate HIF-1α signaling by competing for binding to p300/CBP. Both HIF-1α and p53 bind to p300/CBP, which is required for full activity of both transactivators (Gu et al. 1997). The repression of HIF-1α transactivation or protein levels by p53 is supported by a significant correlation between HIF-1α levels and the presence of mutant p53, suggesting that increased HIF-1α in cancer may be due at least partly, to a loss of p53 function (Zhong et al. 1999). A further link between p53 and HIF-1α is mediated by pVHL. pVHL ubiquitinates and degrades HIF-1α under normoxic conditions. Under DNA-damaging conditions, pVHL has been shown to physically associate with p53, thus stabilizing and transactivating p53, ATM, and p300 (Roe et al. 2006). Hence pVHL-deficient renal carcinoma cells (RCC), in addition to increased HIF-1 activity, also exhibit attenuated p53 activation in response to DNA damage.

3.4.3
Interplay Between HIF-1 and Myc

Myc is a transcription factor that heterodimerizes with Myc-associated protein (Max) to regulate a large number of processes important for normal biology and tumorigenesis such as growth, differentiation, apoptosis, and metabolism

(Adhikary and Eilers 2005). The Myc transcription factors contribute to almost every aspect of tumor cell biology and aberrantly high and/or deregulated Myc activity has been implicated causally in the majority of cancers (Adhikary and Eilers 2005; Shchors and Evan 2007). Myc regulates its many target genes by either promoting or inhibiting transcription. In certain scenarios, HIF-1α can act by displacing Myc from binding to its promoter. For example, hypoxia-induced HIF-1α increases the expression of the cyclin-dependent kinase inhibitors (CKIs) p21^{cip1} and p27^{kip1} by displacing the inhibitory Myc from their promoters (Koshiji et al. 2004). Myc displacement by HIF-1α has also been shown to account for repression of Myc activated genes including genes *hTERT* and *BRCA1*, the DNA repair genes *MSH2*, *MSH6*, and *NBS1* and the cell-cycle gene *CDC25A* (Huang 2008; Koshiji et al. 2004). Intriguingly, in contrast to the Myc-antagonizing properties of HIF-1α, HIF-2α, can enhance Myc activity by stimulating its interaction with Max (Gordan et al. 2007). Hence, HIF-2α overexpression promotes tumorigenesis in pVHL-deficient RCC, while HIF-1α inhibits RCC growth. However, both HIF-α isoforms can also act in concert to inhibit the Myc-activated gene *PPARGC1B* (encoding PGC-1β) important in mitochondria biogenesis by transcriptionally activating Mxi1, a protein that competes with Myc for binding to Max (Corn et al. 2005). Additionally severe or prolonged hypoxia results in Myc degradation via the ubiquitin-proteasome pathway in a HIF-α dependent but Mxi1-independent manner (Zhang et al. 2007). To add to the complexity, HIF-1α can also cooperate with Myc in cancer settings to enhance the expression of shared target genes such as those involved in glycolysis (*HK2*, *PDK1*) and angiogenesis (*VEGFA*) (Kim et al. 2007). Hence, although Myc may function as a critical hub for the control of normal cellular growth and proliferation, it appears that under hypoxic conditions, its activities can be usurped by HIF-α for tumor-cell adaptation and survival (Dang et al. 2008).

3.5
Hypoxia and HIF-1 Effects on Cancer Stem Cells

A new concept of "cancer stem cells" has emerged over the past 10 years (Pardal et al. 2003) defined as a subset population of cancer cells endowed with extensive potential for cell division. Experimentally, it has been shown that cancer stem cells have an increased potential to form tumors and only relatively few cells are required to initiate tumors in mice. How cells acquire properties such as self-renewal potential that turn them into cancer stem cells can in some cases be explained by mutational transformation of either normal stem cells or differentiated cells (Takahashi and Yamanaka 2006). Another theory suggests that hypoxia, through activation of HIF-1α and HIF-2α, contributes by activating pathways that induce dedifferentiation of cancer cells, maintenance of stem cell identity, and increased metastatic potential (Barnhart and Simon 2007). For example, HIF-1α stabilizes Notch1, which maintains the undifferentiated state, and induces lysyl oxidase (LOX) and matrix metalloproteases (MMP) that are important for invasive and metastatic phenotypes. HIF-2α, on the other hand, induces the expression of OCT-4, one of the most important stem cell maintenance factors, and enhances the activity of c-Myc which increases proliferation. Thus, despite being mostly speculative at this stage, the idea that hypoxia, through HIF-1/2α, may impact specific pathways supporting stem cell maintenance is highly intriguing and holds promise for future novel therapies.

3.6
HIF-1 as a Cancer Drug Target

HIF-1 provides a major defense against hypoxic stress in the growing tumor by increasing the expression of survival genes. However, the fact that HIF-1 also increases the expression of proapoptotic genes such as BNIP3, BNIP3L (NIX) (Bruick 2000; Sowter et al. 2001), RTP801(DDIT4) (Shoshani et al. 2002) and Noxa (Kim et al. 2004) has raised the question of whether HIF-1α is a good target for chemotherapy because inhibition of the proapoptotic effects of hypoxia could conceivably lead to increased tumor growth (Patiar and Harris 2006). It is well known that anoxia or severe and prolonged hypoxia induces apoptotic death in cells (Brown and Giaccia 1998). This is likely to occur in areas of the tumor where blood vessels are compressed or obstructed by tumor cells. However, the type of hypoxia that has been observed within tumors appears to be less severe due to the abnormal architecture and blood-flow dynamics of tumor vasculature that leads to cycles of vasoconstriction and dilation, and periods of poor perfusion (Nordsmark et al. 1996; Thomlinson and Gray 1955). Thus, under the levels of hypoxia found within tumors, HIF-1-induced proapoptotic genes may play little role in inducing apoptotic cell death. Indeed, the overwhelming evidence is that the antiapototic effects of HIF-1 outweigh any proapoptotic effects and that HIF-1 expression increases tumor growth. Studies with HIF-1α null knockout immortalized murine embryonic fibroblasts (MEFs) (Ryan et al. 2000; Unruh et al. 2003), CHO cells with mutagen-induced loss of HIF-1α (Williams et al. 2002) and human colon tumor cells with deleted HIF-1α (Dang et al. 2006) have all shown decreased tumor growth with increased apoptosis when injected into mice. The ability of antisense RNA (Chang et al. 2006; Sun et al. 2001; Sun et al. 2003), RNAi (Li et al. 2005), and dominant negative HIF-1α (Chen et al. 2003) to inhibit tumor growth in animal models also suggest that the cell survival effects of HIF-1 outweigh its apoptotic effects. There are, however, a few reports that HIF-1α inhibition may stimulate tumor growth. Murine embryonic stem (ES) cells with deleted HIF-1α injected into mice were reported to form tumors and after several weeks delay, shown to grow faster and show decreased apoptosis compared

to tumors from wild type cells (Carmeliet et al. 1998). However, this could not be confirmed in another study where ES HIF-1α null cells formed tumors that grew more slowly and had increased apoptosis (Ryan et al. 1998). Human HIF-1α deficient transformed astrocytes injected subcutaneously into mice have been reported to form tumors with poor vascularization and slower growth than wild type astrocytomas. However, when the same cells were injected intracranially, the HIF-1α deficient astrocytomas were highly vascularized and grew faster than wild type astrocytomas (Blouw et al. 2003), although apoptosis was similar in both HIF-1α and wild type tumors. A study with A549 human non small cell lung cancer cells overexpressing HIF-1α also reported slower growth together with increased apoptosis compared to empty vector transfected control tumors, although this occurred despite increased angiogenesis in the HIF-1α transfected tumors (Savai et al. 2005). It is noteworthy that A549 tumors have only low levels of HIF-1α and VEGF, and their growth does not respond to HIF-1α inhibition, suggesting that A-549 is a tumor where HIF-1α is not critical for angiogenesis and tumor growth (Jordan et al. 2005). Thus, except for the limited examples given here, there is overwhelming evidence that HIF-1α is a rational and an exciting target for anticancer drug discovery.

3.7
HIF-1 Inhibitors

The relative ease of cell-based screening for inhibitors of HIF-1 transcriptional activity typically using an HRE-fluorescent or chemiluminescent reporter under conditions where HIF-1α is elevated, such as by hypoxia or artificially with a chemical inhibitor of HIF-1α degradation such as cobalt chloride or desferrioxamine, has led to the identification of a number of HIF-1 inhibitors (reviewed in (Melillo 2007; Patiar and Harris 2006; Powis and Kirkpatrick

2004; Semenza 2007)). Although such screens provide little information on the mechanism of HIF-1 inhibition, follow-up studies have identified potential mechanisms for the inhibition of transcription by the CDK inhibitor flavopiridol (Newcomb et al. 2005), inhibition of translation by temsirolimus, an inhibitor of mTOR (Del Bufalo et al. 2006), increased HIF-1α degradation by Hsp90 inhibitors (Hur et al. 2002; Isaacs et al. 2002; Kurebayashi et al. 2001), and by SCH6636, a farnesyl transferase inhibitor (Han et al. 2005), inhibition of growth factor-induced HIF-1 signaling by imatinib, a BCR-ABL, c-Kit inhibitor (Mayerhofer et al. 2002), by the EGF receptor small molecule inhibitors imatinib and erlotinib (Pore et al. 2006) and the EGF receptor monoclonal antibody cetuximab (Luwor et al. 2005). Specific screens have also identified agents that inhibit the interaction of HIF-1α with p300 (Kung et al. 2004). However, for most of the agents, the ability to inhibit tumor HIF-1 transcriptional activity in an in vivo setting has not been demonstrated. Agents that have been shown to inhibit tumor HIF-1α are listed in Table 3.2, and those that have antitumor activity in animal models are described below.

YC-1 [3-(5′-hydroxymethyl-2-furyl)-1-benzyl indazole] was developed as an activator of soluble guanyl cyclase for treating circulatory disorders caused by platelet aggregation and vascular contraction. It was also found to decrease HIF-1α levels in vitro (Chun et al. 2001) and in tumors (Yeo et al. 2003). YC-1 has been reported to accelerate HIF-1α degradation (Kim et al. 2006), to inhibit PI-3K/AKT/mTor mediated HIF-1α synthesis (Sun et al. 2007) and most recently, to stimulate the FIH-dependent dissociation of p300 from HIF-1α (Li et al. 2008). Although used experimentally, a clinical application for YC-1 as an antitumor agent remains in doubt because of its potential for increasing bleeding time, to cause hypotension and to act as an erectogenic (Chun et al. 2004).

Topotecan, a cytotoxic agent that causes DNA replication-mediated DNA damage through its action as a topoisomerase poison and approved for clinical use in lung and ovarian cancer, was identified as an inhibitor of HIF-1 activity in a cell-based screen (Rapisarda et al. 2002). It was subsequently shown to be an inhibitor of HIF-1α translation through a topoisomerase dependent mechanism (Rapisarda et al. 2004a). When administered on a daily schedule to mice with human glioma tumor xenografts, topotecan inhibited tumor growth, accompanied by decreased tumor HIF-1α expression and angiogenesis (Rapisarda et al. 2004b). Based on these results, topotecan is being tested in a pilot study in patients with advanced malignancies to determine if it inhibits HIF-1α in patients with tumor over-expressing HIF-1α (Melillo et al. 2007). If HIF-1α inhibition can be confirmed, it will still have to be demonstrated that this contributes to the antitumor activity of topotecan.

It is worth noting that a number of histone deacetylase (HDAC) inhibitors, particularly those targeting Class I and II HDACs, decrease HIF-1α levels in cells (Liang et al. 2006). It is generally accepted that a major function of HDAC inhibitors is to decrease tumor angiogenesis by inhibiting the formation of proangiogenic factors such as VEGF (Kim et al. 2001; Mie Lee et al. 2003). This has led to the assumption that it is inhibition of HIF-1 that is responsible for this effect (Liang et al. 2006). The mechanism responsible for this activity is a subject of debate, but may involve pVHL and p53 independent HIF-1α destabilization and proteasomal degradation. This could be due to either direct HIF-1α acetylation (Kim et al. 2001) or a mechanism involving Hsp90 acetylation (Liang et al. 2006). HDAC inhibitors could also repress HIF-1 transactivating activity by targeting the HIF-1α/p300 complex (Fath et al. 2006). However, what is lacking is the clear demonstration that HDAC inhibitors at doses that inhibit tumor growth also lower tumor HIF-1α levels or decrease HIF-1 transactivating activity. In two early studies of the HDAC inhibitors trichostatin A (Kim et al. 2001) and FK228 (Mie Lee et al. 2003), HIF-1α levels appear to be increased or unchanged in tumors on drug treatment.

Table 3.2 Compounds reported to inhibit HIF-1α

Compound	Mechanism of HIF inhibition	Reference
Hsp90 inhibitors		
17AAG	Degradation	(Isaacs et al. 2002)
Radicicol	DNA binding	(Hur et al. 2002)
KF58333 (radicicol analog)	Degradation	(Kurebayashi et al. 2001)
Topoisomerase inhibitors		
Topotecan (topoisomerase 1)	Translation	(Rapisarda et al. 2002; Rapisarda et al. 2004a)
GL331 (toposiomerase 2)	Transcription	(Chang et al. 2003)
Antimicrotubule		
Taxol	Translation	(Mabjeesh et al. 2003)
Vincristine	Translation	(Mabjeesh et al. 2003)
2ME2	Translation	(Mabjeesh et al. 2003)
HDAC inhibitors		
Trichostatin A	Degradation/transactivation	(Fath et al. 2006; Kong et al. 2006)
FK228	Transcription	(Mie Lee et al. 2003)
mTOR inhibitors		
Temsirolimus (CCI779)	Translation	(Del Bufalo et al. 2006; Wan et al. 2006)
Everolimus (RAD001)	Translation	(Majumder et al. 2004)
Thioredoxin inhibitors		
PX-12	Unknown	(Welsh and Powis 2003)
Pleurotin	Unknown	(Welsh and Powis 2003)
PX-916 (TXN reductase I)	Unknown	(Powis et al. 2006)
Soluble guanyl cyclase stimulator		
YC-1	Degradation/transactivation	(Yeo et al. 2003)
Farnesyl transferase inhibitor		
SCH66336	Degradation	(Han et al. 2005)
Growth factor signaling inhibitors		
Imatinib (BCR-ABL, c-Kit)	Translation/ Other	(Litz and Krystal 2006)
Erlotinib, gefitinib (EGFR)	Translation	(Pore et al. 2006)
Cetuximab (EGFR)	Translation	(Luwor et al. 2005)
Other		
Chetomin	Transactivation	(Kung et al. 2004)
PX-478	Translation/other	(Koh et al. 2008b; Welsh et al. 2004)

A more exhaustive list of compounds has been provided elsewhere (Melillo 2007; Powis and Kirkpatrick 2004)

2-Methoxyestradiol (2ME2) is an antiproliferative and antiangiogenic estrogen metabolite with weak estrogen receptor-binding activity (Sutherland et al. 2007). 2ME2 has been reported to have a number of effects which could account for its biological activity, including oxidative stress associated with inhibition of superoxide dismutase and increased production of nitric

oxide and binding to tubulin to cause microtubule disruption and mitotic arrest (reviewed in
(Sutherland et al. 2007)). 2ME2 has also been
identified as an inhibitor of HIF-1α translation
and nuclear translocation (Mabjeesh et al. 2003).
It is noteworthy that other microtubule agents
destabilizing agents such as *Vinca* alkaloids and
colchicine-like compounds, as well as microtubule stabilizing agents such as taxanes and
epothilones, have also been reported to inhibit
HIF-1α expression (Escuin et al. 2005). 2ME2
has been reported to lower HIF-1α protein in an
animal human orthotopic human glioblastoma
model (Kang et al. 2006) and is currently in
Phase II clinical trials. It may be difficult to separate HIF-1α inhibitory activity from 2ME2's
other effects in relation to its antitumor activity.

Chetomin, a dithiodiketopiperazine fungal
metabolite, was identified in a high-throughput
screen of over half a million natural and synthetic compounds for inhibitors of the interaction of HIF-1α with p300 that regulates HIF-1
transcriptional activity (Kung et al. 2004).
Chetomin also disrupts the binding of other proteins to p300, including HIF-2α and STAT2,
indicating that it is a nonspecific inhibitor of
transcription. When administered intravenously
to mice with tumor xenografts, chetomin was
shown to inhibit the interaction of HIF-1α and
p300, and to block HIF-1 transcriptional activity and downstream gene expression. Significant
antitumor activity was also seen against HCT-
116 colon and PC-3 prostate tumor xenografts.
Unfortunately, local toxicity at the site of intravenous injection limited the amount of chetomin
that could be administered and whether it will
be pursued as an antitumor agent is in doubt.

The small redox protein thioredoxin, which
is found in high levels in many human tumors,
has been reported to increase HIF-1α protein
levels in hypoxic cells by an unknown mechanism (Welsh et al. 2002). The thioredioxin
inhibitor PX-12 (1-methylpropyl-2-imidazoly
disulfide) has been found to decrease HIF-1α
protein levels, HIF-1 transactivating activity and
downstream gene expression, including *VEGF*

in cells and in tumor xenografts in mice (Jordan
et al. 2005; Welsh et al. 2004). PX-12 is currently in Phase I/II clinical trial as an antitumor
agent, but whether HIF-1α inhibition contributes to its activity remains to be determined. An
inhibitor of thioredoxin reductase, PX-916, a
water-soluble prodrug of the naphthoquinone
spiroketal fungal metabolite palmarumycin CP1,
has also shown the ability to decrease HIF-1α
and VEGF protein levels,in tumor xenografts in
mice, and to cause growth inhibition in a number of tumor xenografts (Powis et al. 2006).

PX-478   (S-2-amino-3-[4'-*N*,*N*,-bis(chloro-
ethyl)amino]-phenyl propionic acid *N*-oxide dihy-
drochloride) was identified through a screen for
compounds that lowered cellular HIF-1α levels,
HIF-1 transactivating activity and downstream
gene expression through a process that is independent of oxygen, pVHL, or p53. The primary mechanism for lowering of HIF-1α protein by PX-478
appears to be inhibition of HIF-1α translation
since HIF-1α translation is maintained in hypoxia,
whereas translation of most proteins is inhibited.
However, PX478 also decreases levels of HIF-1α
mRNA and causes inhibition of HIF-1α deubiq-
uitination (Koh et al. 2008b). PX-478 administered intravenously or per orem to mice lowered
HIF-1α levels in tumor xenografts and inhibited
the expression of HIF-1 target genes *VEGF* and
GLUT-1. PX-478 showed antitumor activity
against a variety of established tumors with marked
tumor regression accompanied by massive apoptosis, and in some cases cures (Jordan et al. 2005;
Welsh et al. 2004). The antitumor response to
PX-478 positively correlated with tumor HIF-1α
levels. PX-478 is currently in Phase I clinical trial
as an antitumor agent and HIF-1 inhibitor.

3.8
Conclusions

While a number of agents have been found to
inhibit HIF-1α levels in cells, only a few agents
have been demonstrated to inhibit HIF-1α or

HIF-1 activity in tumors in vivo. This has, however, been accompanied by antitumor activity that in some cases, is quite marked. In most cases the exact molecular target of the agent is not known. Some agents have properties or biological activities that preclude their use in humans. Of agents that are currently being tested in humans, some have other mechanisms of action that could more rationally account for their activity. For these agents it will be difficult, if not impossible, to determine whether HIF-1 inhibition contributes in any way to antitumor activity. In this regard, PX-478 is one agent that appears to show selective inhibition of HIF-1α. Thus, HIF-1 presents a novel target for cancer drug discovery and development and, while it is still early days, agents are being tested in the clinic that will show whether its preclinical potential as a target will be realized.

Aknowledgments   Supported by NIH grants CA-0179094, CA095060, CA0179094 and CA109552.

References

Adhikary S, Eilers M (2005) Transcriptional regulation and transformation by Myc proteins. Nat Rev Mol Cell Biol 6:635–645

An WG, Kanekal M, Simon MC, Maltepe E, Blagosklonny MV, Neckers LM (1998) Stabilization of wild-type p53 by hypoxia-inducible factor 1alpha. Nature 392:405–408

Arany Z, Huang LE, Eckner R, Bhattacharya S, Jiang C, Goldberg MA, Bunn HF, Livingston DM (1996) An essential role for p300/CBP in the cellular response to hypoxia. Proc Natl Acad Sci U S A 93:12969–12973

Barnhart BC, Simon MC (2007) Metastasis and stem cell pathways. Cancer Metastasis Rev 26:261–271

Berchner-Pfannschmidt U, Petrat F, Doege K, Trinidad B, Freitag P, Metzen E, de Groot H, Fandrey J (2004) Chelation of cellular calcium modulates hypoxia-inducible gene expression through activation of hypoxia-inducible factor-1alpha. J Biol Chem 279:44976–44986

Bergers G, Benjamin LE (2003) Tumorigenesis and the angiogenic switch. Nat Rev Cancer 3:401–410

Bernardi R, Guernah I, Jin D, Grisendi S, Alimonti A, Teruya-Feldstein J, Cordon-Cardo C, Simon MC, Rafii S, Pandolfi PP (2006) PML inhibits HIF-1alpha translation and neoangiogenesis through repression of mTOR. Nature 442:779–785

Berra E, Milanini J, Richard DE, Le Gall M, Vinals F, Gothie E, Roux D, Pages G, Pouyssegur J (2000) Signaling angiogenesis via p42/p44 MAP kinase and hypoxia. Biochem Pharmacol 60:1171–1178

Bert AG, Grepin R, Vadas MA, Goodall GJ (2006) Assessing IRES activity in the HIF-1alpha and other cellular 5' UTRs. Rna 12:1074–1083

Blouw B, Song H, Tihan T, Bosze J, Ferrara N, Gerber HP, Johnson RS, Bergers G (2003) The hypoxic response of tumors is dependent on their microenvironment. Cancer Cell 4:133–146

Braunstein S, Karpisheva K, Pola C, Goldberg J, Hochman T, Yee H, Cangiarella J, Arju R, Formenti SC, Schneider RJ (2007) A hypoxia-controlled cap-dependent to cap-independent translation switch in breast cancer. Mol Cell 28:501–512

Bristow RG, Hill RP (2008) Hypoxia and metabolism. Hypoxia, DNA repair and genetic instability. Nat Rev Cancer 8:180–192

Brown JM, Giaccia AJ (1998) The unique physiology of solid tumors: opportunities (and problems) for cancer therapy. Cancer Res 58:1408–1416

Brugarolas J, Lei K, Hurley RL, Manning BD, Reiling JH, Hafen E, Witters LA, Ellisen LW, Kaelin WG Jr (2004) Regulation of mTOR function in response to hypoxia by REDD1 and the TSC1/TSC2 tumor suppressor complex. Genes Dev 18:2893–2904

Bruick RK (2000) Expression of the gene encoding the proapoptotic Nip3 protein is induced by hypoxia. Proc Natl Acad Sci U S A 97:9082–9087

Carmeliet P, Dor Y, Herbert JM, Fukumura D, Brusselmans K, Dewerchin M, Neeman M, Bono F, Abramovitch R, Maxwell P, Koch CJ, Ratcliffe P, Moons L, Jain RK, Collen D, Keshert E, Keshet E (1998) Role of HIF-1alpha in hypoxia-mediated apoptosis, cell proliferation and tumour angiogenesis. Nature 394:485–490

Carrero P, Okamoto K, Coumailleau P, O'Brien S, Tanaka H, Poellinger L (2000) Redox-regulated recruitment of the transcriptional coactivators CREB-binding protein and SRC-1 to hypoxia-inducible factor 1alpha. Mol Cell Biol 20:402–415

Chang H, Shyu KG, Lee CC, Tsai SC, Wang BW, Hsien Lee Y, Lin S (2003) GL331 inhibits

HIF-1alpha expression in a lung cancer model. Biochem Biophys Res Commun 302:95–100

Chang Q, Qin R, Huang T, Gao J, Feng Y (2006) Effect of antisense hypoxia-inducible factor 1alpha on progression, metastasis, and chemosensitivity of pancreatic cancer. Pancreas 32:297–305

Chen J, Zhao S, Nakada K, Kuge Y, Tamaki N, Okada F, Wang J, Shindo M, Higashino F, Takeda K, Asaka M, Katoh H, Sugiyama T, Hosokawa M, Kobayashi M (2003) Dominant-negative hypoxia-inducible factor-1 alpha reduces tumorigenicity of pancreatic cancer cells through the suppression of glucose metabolism. Am J Pathol 162:1283–1291

Chun YS, Yeo EJ, Choi E, Teng CM, Bae JM, Kim MS, Park JW (2001) Inhibitory effect of YC-1 on the hypoxic induction of erythropoietin and vascular endothelial growth factor in Hep3B cells. Biochem Pharmacol 61:947–954

Chun YS, Yeo EJ, Park JW (2004) Versatile pharmacological actions of YC-1: anti-platelet to anticancer. Cancer Lett 207:1–7

Corn PG, Ricci MS, Scata KA, Arsham AM, Simon MC, Dicker DT, El-Deiry WS (2005) Mxi1 is induced by hypoxia in a HIF-1-dependent manner and protects cells from c-Myc-induced apoptosis. Cancer Biol Ther 4:1285–1294

Dang CV, Kim JW, Gao P, Yustein J (2008) The interplay between MYC and HIF in cancer. Nat Rev Cancer 8:51–56

Dang DT, Chen F, Gardner LB, Cummins JM, Rago C, Bunz F, Kantsevoy SV, Dang LH (2006) Hypoxia-inducible factor-1alpha promotes non-hypoxia-mediated proliferation in colon cancer cells and xenografts. Cancer Res 66:1684–1936

Del Bufalo D, Ciuffreda L, Trisciuoglio D, Desideri M, Cognetti F, Zupi G, Milella M (2006) Antiangiogenic potential of the Mammalian target of rapamycin inhibitor temsirolimus. Cancer Res 66:5549–5554

Escuin D, Kline ER, Giannakakou P (2005) Both microtubule-stabilizing and microtubule-destabilizing drugs inhibit hypoxia-inducible factor-1alpha accumulation and activity by disrupting microtubule function. Cancer Res 65: 9021–9028

Fath DM, Kong X, Liang D, Lin Z, Chou A, Jiang Y, Fang J, Caro J, Sang N (2006) Histone deacetylase inhibitors repress the transactivation potential of hypoxia-inducible factors independently of direct acetylation of HIF-alpha. J Biol Chem 281:13612–13619

Galban S, Kuwano Y, Pullmann R Jr, Martindale JL, Kim HH, Lal A, Abdelmohsen K, Yang X, Dang Y, Liu JO, Lewis SM, Holcik M, Gorospe M (2008) RNA-binding proteins HuR and PTB promote the translation of hypoxia-inducible factor 1alpha. Mol Cell Biol 28:93–107

Giaccia AJ, Kastan MB (1998) The complexity of p53 modulation: emerging patterns from divergent signals. Genes Dev 12:2973–2983

Giordano FJ, Johnson RS (2001) Angiogenesis: the role of the microenvironment in flipping the switch. Curr Opin Genet Dev 11:35–40

Gordan JD, Bertout JA, Hu CJ, Diehl JA, Simon MC (2007) HIF-2alpha promotes hypoxic cell proliferation by enhancing c-myc transcriptional activity. Cancer Cell 11:335–347

Graeber TG, Peterson JF, Tsai M, Monica K, Fornace AJ Jr, Giaccia AJ (1994) Hypoxia induces accumulation of p53 protein, but activation of a G1-phase checkpoint by low-oxygen conditions is independent of p53 status. Mol Cell Biol 14:6264–6277

Gray MJ, Zhang J, Ellis LM, Semenza GL, Evans DB, Watowich SS, Gallick GE (2005) HIF-1alpha, STAT3, CBP/p300 and Ref-1/APE are components of a transcriptional complex that regulates Src-dependent hypoxia-induced expression of VEGF in pancreatic and prostate carcinomas. Oncogene 24:3110–3120

Gu W, Shi XL, Roeder RG (1997) Synergistic activation of transcription by CBP and p53. Nature 387:819–823

Gu YZ, Moran SM, Hogenesch JB, Wartman L, Bradfield CA (1998) Molecular characterization and chromosomal localization of a third alpha-class hypoxia inducible factor subunit, HIF3alpha. Gene Expr 7:205–213

Hagen T, Taylor CT, Lam F, Moncada S (2003) Redistribution of intracellular oxygen in hypoxia by nitric oxide: effect on HIF1alpha. Science 302:1975–1978

Han JY, Oh SH, Morgillo F, Myers JN, Kim E, Hong WK, Lee HY (2005) Hypoxia-inducible factor 1alpha and antiangiogenic activity of farnesyltransferase inhibitor SCH66336 in human aerodigestive tract cancer. J Natl Cancer Inst 97:1272–1286

Harding HP, Novoa I, Zhang Y, Zeng H, Wek R, Schapira M, Ron D (2000) Regulated translation initiation controls stress-induced gene expression in mammalian cells. Mol Cell 6:1099–1108

Holmquist-Mengelbier L, Fredlund E, Lofstedt T, Noguera R, Navarro S, Nilsson H, Pietras A,

Vallon-Christersson J, Borg A, Gradin K, Poellinger L, Pahlman S (2006) Recruitment of HIF-1alpha and HIF-2alpha to common target genes is differentially regulated in neuroblastoma: HIF-2alpha promotes an aggressive phenotype. Cancer Cell 10:413–423

Hu CJ, Wang LY, Chodosh LA, Keith B, Simon MC (2003) Differential roles of hypoxia-inducible factor 1alpha (HIF-1alpha) and HIF-2alpha in hypoxic gene regulation. Mol Cell Biol 23:9361–9374

Huang LE (2008) Carrot and stick: HIF-alpha engages c-Myc in hypoxic adaptation. Cell Death Differ 15:672–677

Hudson CC, Liu M, Chiang GG, Otterness DM, Loomis DC, Kaper F, Giaccia AJ, Abraham RT (2002) Regulation of hypoxia-inducible factor 1alpha expression and function by the mammalian target of rapamycin. Mol Cell Biol 22:7004–7014

Hui AS, Bauer AL, Striet JB, Schnell PO, Czyzyk-Krzeska MF (2006) Calcium signaling stimulates translation of HIF-alpha during hypoxia. Faseb J 20:466–475

Hur E, Kim HH, Choi SM, Kim JH, Yim S, Kwon HJ, Choi Y, Kim DK, Lee MO, Park H (2002) Reduction of hypoxia-induced transcription through the repression of hypoxia-inducible factor-1alpha/aryl hydrocarbon receptor nuclear translocator DNA binding by the 90-kDa heat-shock protein inhibitor radicicol. Mol Pharmacol 62:975–982

Isaacs JS, Jung YJ, Mimnaugh EG, Martinez A, Cuttitta F, Neckers LM (2002) Hsp90 regulates a von Hippel Lindau-independent hypoxia-inducible factor-1 alpha-degradative pathway. J Biol Chem 277:29936–29944

Jaakkola P, Mole DR, Tian YM, Wilson MI, Gielbert J, Gaskell SJ, Kriegsheim A, Hebestreit HF, Mukherji M, Schofield CJ, Maxwell PH, Pugh CW, Ratcliffe PJ (2001) Targeting of HIF-alpha to the von Hippel-Lindau ubiquitylation complex by O2-regulated prolyl hydroxylation. Science 292:468–472

Jiang BH, Liu LZ (2008) PI3K/PTEN signaling in tumorigenesis and angiogenesis. Biochim Biophys Acta 1784:150–158

Jiang BH, Rue E, Wang GL, Roe R, Semenza GL (1996) Dimerization, DNA binding, and transactivation properties of hypoxia-inducible factor 1. J Biol Chem 271:17771–17778

Jordan BF, Runquist M, Raghunand N, Baker A, Williams R, Kirkpatrick L, Powis G, Gillies RJ (2005) Dynamic contrast-enhanced and diffusion MRI show rapid and dramatic changes in tumor microenvironment in response to inhibition of HIF-1alpha using PX-478. Neoplasia 7:475–485

Kaelin WG (2007) Von hippel-lindau disease. Annu Rev Pathol 2:145–173

Kang SH, Cho HT, Devi S, Zhang Z, Escuin D, Liang Z, Mao H, Brat DJ, Olson JJ, Simons JW, Lavallee TM, Giannakakou P, Van Meir EG, Shim H (2006) Antitumor effect of 2-methoxyestradiol in a rat orthotopic brain tumor model. Cancer Res 66:11991–11997

Kim HL, Yeo EJ, Chun YS, Park JW (2006) A domain responsible for HIF-1alpha degradation by YC-1, a novel anticancer agent. Int J Oncol 29:255–260

Kim JW, Gao P, Liu YC, Semenza GL, Dang CV (2007) Hypoxia-inducible factor 1 and dysregulated c-Myc cooperatively induce vascular endothelial growth factor and metabolic switches hexokinase 2 and pyruvate dehydrogenase kinase 1. Mol Cell Biol 27:7381–7393

Kim JY, Ahn HJ, Ryu JH, Suk K, Park JH (2004) BH3-only protein Noxa is a mediator of hypoxic cell death induced by hypoxia-inducible factor 1alpha. J Exp Med 199:113–124

Kim MS, Kwon HJ, Lee YM, Baek JH, Jang JE, Lee SW, Moon EJ, Kim HS, Lee SK, Chung HY, Kim CW, Kim KW (2001) Histone deacetylases induce angiogenesis by negative regulation of tumor suppressor genes. Nat Med 7:437–443

Koh MY, Darnay BG, Powis G (2008a) Hypoxia-associated factor, a novel E3-ubiquitin ligase, binds and ubiquitinates hypoxia-inducible factor 1alpha, leading to its oxygen-independent degradation. Mol Cell Biol 28:7081–7095

Koh MY, Spivak-Kroizman T, Venturini S, Welsh S, Williams RR, Kirkpatrick DL, Powis G (2008b) Molecular mechanisms for the activity of PX-478, an antitumor inhibitor of the hypoxia-inducible factor-1alpha. Mol Cancer Ther 7:90–100

Koh MY, Spivak-Kroizman TR, Powis G (2008c) HIF-1 regulation: not so easy come, easy go. Trends Biochem Sci 33(11):526–534

Koivunen P, Tiainen P, Hyvarinen J, Williams KE, Sormunen R, Klaus SJ, Kivirikko KI, Myllyharju J (2007) An endoplasmic reticulum transmembrane prolyl 4-hydroxylase is induced by hypoxia and acts on hypoxia-inducible factor alpha. J Biol Chem 282:30544–30552

Kong X, Lin Z, Liang D, Fath D, Sang N, Caro J (2006) Histone deacetylase inhibitors induce VHL and ubiquitin-independent proteasomal degradation of hypoxia-inducible factor 1alpha. Mol Cell Biol 26:2019–2028

Koshiji M, Kageyama Y, Pete EA, Horikawa I, Barrett JC, Huang LE (2004) HIF-1alpha induces cell cycle arrest by functionally counteracting Myc. Embo J 23:1949–1956

Kung AL, Zabludoff SD, France DS, Freedman SJ, Tanner EA, Vieira A, Cornell-Kennon S, Lee J, Wang B, Wang J, Memmert K, Naegeli HU, Petersen F, Eck MJ, Bair KW, Wood AW, Livingston DM (2004) Small molecule blockade of transcriptional coactivation of the hypoxia-inducible factor pathway. Cancer Cell 6:33–43

Kurebayashi J, Otsuki T, Kurosumi M, Soga S, Akinaga S, Sonoo H (2001) A radicicol derivative, KF58333, inhibits expression of hypoxia-inducible factor-1alpha and vascular endothelial growth factor, angiogenesis and growth of human breast cancer xenografts. Jpn J Cancer Res 92:1342–1351

Lando D, Peet DJ, Whelan DA, Gorman JJ, Whitelaw ML (2002) Asparagine hydroxylation of the HIF transactivation domain a hypoxic switch. Science 295:858–861

Lang KJD, Kappel A, Goodall GJ (2002) Hypoxia-inducible factor-1 contains an interna ribosome entry site that allows efficient translation during normoxia and hypoxia. Mol Biol Cell 13:1792–1801

Levine AJ (1997) p53, the cellular gatekeeper for growth and division. Cell 88:323–331

Li L, Lin X, Staver M, Shoemaker A, Semizarov D, Fesik SW, Shen Y (2005) Evaluating hypoxia-inducible factor-1alpha as a cancer therapeutic target via inducible RNA interference in vivo. Cancer Res 65:7249–7258

Li SH, Shin DH, Chun YS, Lee MK, Kim MS, Park JW (2008) A novel mode of action of YC-1 in HIF inhibition: stimulation of FIH-dependent p300 dissociation from HIF-1{alpha}. Mol Cancer Ther 7:3729–3738

Liang D, Kong X, Sang N (2006) Effects of histone deacetylase inhibitors on HIF-1. Cell Cycle 5:2430–2435

Litz J, Krystal GW (2006) Imatinib inhibits c-Kit-induced hypoxia-inducible factor-1alpha activity and vascular endothelial growth factor expression in small cell lung cancer cells. Mol Cancer Ther 5:1415–1422

Liu Q, Moller U, Flugel D, Kietzmann T (2004) Induction of plasminogen activator inhibitor I gene expression by intracellular calcium via hypoxia-inducible factor-1. Blood 104:3993–4001

Liu YV, Baek JH, Zhang H, Diez R, Cole RN, Semenza GL (2007a) RACK1 competes with HSP90 for binding to HIF-1alpha and is required for O(2)-independent and HSP90 inhibitor-induced degradation of HIF-1alpha. Mol Cell 25:207–217

Liu YV, Hubbi ME, Pan F, McDonald KR, Mansharamani M, Cole RN, Liu JO, Semenza GL (2007b) Calcineurin promotes hypoxia-inducible factor 1alpha expression by dephosphorylating RACK1 and blocking RACK1 dimerization. J Biol Chem 282:37064–37073

Luwor RB, Lu Y, Li X, Mendelsohn J, Fan Z (2005) The antiepidermal growth factor receptor monoclonal antibody cetuximab/C225 reduces hypoxia-inducible factor-1 alpha, leading to transcriptional inhibition of vascular endothelial growth factor expression. Oncogene 24:4433–4441

Mabjeesh NJ, Escuin D, LaVallee TM, Pribluda VS, Swartz GM, Johnson MS, Willard MT, Zhong H, Simons JW, Giannakakou P (2003) 2ME2 inhibits tumor growth and angiogenesis by disrupting microtubules and dysregulating HIF. Cancer Cell 3:363–375

Mahon PC, Hirota K, Semenza GL (2001) FIH-1: a novel protein that interacts with HIF-1alpha and VHL to mediate repression of HIF-1 transcriptional activity. Genes Dev 15:2675–2686

Majumder PK, Febbo PG, Bikoff R, Berger R, Xue Q, McMahon LM, Manola J, Brugarolas J, McDonnell TJ, Golub TR, Loda M, Lane HA, Sellers WR (2004) mTOR inhibition reverses Akt-dependent prostate intraepithelial neoplasia through regulation of apoptotic and HIF-1-dependent pathways. Nat Med 10:594–601

Makino Y, Kanopka A, Wilson WJ, Tanaka H, Poellinger L (2002) Inhibitory PAS domain protein (IPAS) is a hypoxia-inducible splicing variant of the hypoxia-inducible factor-3alpha locus. J Biol Chem 277:32405–32408

Maxwell PH, Pugh CW, Ratcliffe PJ (2001) Activation of the HIF pathway in cancer. Curr Opin Genet Dev 11:293–299

Mayerhofer M, Valent P, Sperr WR, Griffin JD, Sillaber C (2002) BCR/ABL induces expression of vascular endothelial growth factor and its transcriptional activator, hypoxia inducible factor-1alpha, through a pathway involving phosphoinositide 3-kinase and the mammalian target of rapamycin. Blood 100:3767–3775

Melillo G (2007) Targeting hypoxia cell signaling for cancer therapy. Cancer Metastasis Rev 26:341–352

Melillo G, Gutierrez M, Holkova B, Rapisarda A, Raffeld M, Horneffer Y, Chang R, Murgo AJ, Doroshow JH, Kummar S (2007) A pilot trial of topotecan administered orally in patients with advanced solid tumors expressing hypoxia inducible factor (HIF)- 1alpha. J Clin Oncol 25:14103

Metzen E, Fandrey J, Jelkmann W (1999) Evidence against a major role for Ca2+ in hypoxia-induced gene expression in human hepatoma cells (Hep3B). J Physiol 517(Pt 3):651–657

Mie Lee Y, Kim SH, Kim HS, Jin Son M, Nakajima H, Jeong Kwon H, Kim KW (2003) Inhibition of hypoxia-induced angiogenesis by FK228, a specific histone deacetylase inhibitor, via suppression of HIF-1alpha activity. Biochem Biophys Res Commun 300:241–246

Mottet D, Michel G, Renard P, Ninane N, Raes M, Michiels C (2002) ERK and calcium in activation of HIF-1. Ann N Y Acad Sci 973:448–453

Nakayama K, Ronai Z (2004) Siah: new players in the cellular response to hypoxia. Cell Cycle 3:1345–1347

Newcomb EW, Ali MA, Schnee T, Lan L, Lukyanov Y, Fowkes M, Miller DC, Zagzag D (2005) Flavopiridol downregulates hypoxia-mediated hypoxia-inducible factor-1alpha expression in human glioma cells by a proteasome-independent pathway: implications for in vivo therapy. Neuro Oncol 7:225–235

Nordsmark M, Hoyer M, Keller J, Nielsen OS, Jensen OM, Overgaard J (1996) The relationship between tumor oxygenation and cell proliferation in human soft tissue sarcomas. Int J Radiat Oncol Biol Phys 35:701–708

Ohh M, Park CW, Ivan M, Hoffman MA, Kim TY, Huang LE, Pavletich N, Chau V, Kaelin WG (2000) Ubiquitination of hypoxia-inducible factor requires direct binding to the beta-domain of the von Hippel-Lindau protein. Nat Cell Biol 2:423–427

Pan Y, Oprysko PR, Asham AM, Koch CJ, Simon MC (2004) p53 cannot be induced by hypoxia alone but responds to the hypoxic microenvironment. Oncogene 23:4975–4983

Pardal R, Clarke MF, Morrison SJ (2003) Applying the principles of stem-cell biology to cancer. Nat Rev Cancer 3:895–902

Patiar S, Harris AL (2006) Role of hypoxia-inducible factor-1alpha as a cancer therapy target. Endocr Relat Cancer 13(Suppl 1):S61–S75

Pore N, Jiang Z, Gupta A, Cerniglia G, Kao GD, Maity A (2006) EGFR tyrosine kinase inhibitors decrease VEGF expression by both hypoxia-inducible factor (HIF)-1-independent and HIF-1-dependent mechanisms. Cancer Res 66:3197–3204

Powis G, Kirkpatrick L (2004) Hypoxia inducible factor-1alpha as a cancer drug target. Mol Cancer Ther 3:647–654

Powis G, Wipf P, Lynch SM, Birmingham A, Kirkpatrick DL (2006) Molecular pharmacology and antitumor activity of palmarumycin-based inhibitors of thioredoxin reductase. Mol Cancer Ther 5:630–636

Rapisarda A, Uranchimeg B, Scudiero DA, Selby M, Sausville EA, Shoemaker RH, Melillo G (2002) Identification of small molecule inhibitors of hypoxia-inducible factor 1 transcriptional activation pathway. Cancer Res 62:4316–4324

Rapisarda A, Uranchimeg B, Sordet O, Pommier Y, Shoemaker RH, Melillo G (2004a) Topoisomerase I-mediated inhibition of hypoxia-inducible factor 1: mechanism and therapeutic implications. Cancer Res 64:1475–1482

Rapisarda A, Zalek J, Hollingshead M, Braunschweig T, Uranchimeg B, Bonomi CA, Borgel SD, Carter JP, Hewitt SM, Shoemaker RH, Melillo G (2004b) Schedule-dependent inhibition of hypoxia-inducible factor-1alpha protein accumulation, angiogenesis, and tumor growth by topotecan in U251-HRE glioblastoma xenografts. Cancer Res 64:6845–6848

Ravi R, Mookerjee B, Bhujwalla ZM, Sutter CH, Artemov D, Zeng Q, Dillehay LE, Madan A, Semenza GL, Bedi A (2000) Regulation of tumor angiogenesis by p53-induced degradation of hypoxia-inducible factor 1alpha. Genes Dev 14:34–44

Richard DE, Berra E, Gothie E, Roux D, Pouyssegur J (1999) p42/p44 mitogen-activated protein kinases phosphorylate hypoxia-inducible factor 1alpha (HIF-1alpha) and enhance the transcriptional activity of HIF-1. J Biol Chem 274:32631–32637

Roe JS, Kim H, Lee SM, Kim ST, Cho EJ, Youn HD (2006) p53 stabilization and transactivation by a von Hippel-Lindau protein. Mol Cell 22:395–405

Ron D, Walter P (2007) Signal integration in the endoplasmic reticulum unfolded protein response. Nat Rev Mol Cell Biol 8:519–529

Ryan HE, Lo J, Johnson RS (1998) HIF-1 alpha is required for solid tumor formation and embryonic vascularization. Embo J 17:3005–3015

Ryan HE, Poloni M, McNulty W, Elson D, Gassmann M, Arbeit JM, Johnson RS (2000) Hypoxia-inducible factor-1alpha is a positive factor in solid tumor growth. Cancer Res 60:4010–4015

Salnikow K, Kluz T, Costa M, Piquemal D, Demidenko ZN, Xie K, Blagosklonny MV (2002) The regulation of hypoxic genes by calcium involves c-Jun/AP-1, which cooperates with hypoxia-inducible factor 1 in response to hypoxia. Mol Cell Biol 22:1734–1741

Savai R, Schermuly RT, Voswinckel R, Renigunta A, Reichmann B, Eul B, Grimminger F, Seeger W, Rose F, Hanze J (2005) HIF-1alpha attenuates tumor growth in spite of augmented vascularization in an A549 adenocarcinoma mouse model. Int J Oncol 27:393–400

Schepens B, Tinton SA, Bruynooghe Y, Beyaert R, Cornelis S (2005) The polypyrimidine tract-binding protein stimulates HIF-1alpha IRES-mediated translation during hypoxia. Nucleic Acids Res 33:6884–6894

Semenza G (2002) Signal transduction to hypoxia-inducible factor 1. Biochem Pharmacol 64: 993–998

Semenza GL (2007) Evaluation of HIF-1 inhibitors as anticancer agents. Drug Discov Today 12: 853–859

Semenza GL (2004) Intratumoral hypoxia, radiation resistance, and HIF-1. Cancer Cell 5:405–406

Semenza GL (1999) Regulation of mammalian O_2 homeostasis by hypoxia-inducible factor 1. Annu Rev Cell Dev Biol 15:551–578

Semenza GL (2003) Targeting HIF-1 for cancer therapy. Nat Rev Cancer 3:721–732

Semenza GL, Wang GL (1992) A nuclear factor induced by hypoxia via de novo protein synthesis binds to the human erythropoietin gene enhancer at a site required for transcriptional activation. Mol Cell Biol 12:5447–5454

Seta KA, Yuan Y, Spicer Z, Lu G, Bedard J, Ferguson TK, Pathrose P, Cole-Strauss A, Kaufhold A, Millhorn DE (2004) The role of calcium in hypoxia-induced signal transduction and gene expression. Cell Calcium 36:331–340

Shchors K, Evan G (2007) Tumor angiogenesis: cause or consequence of cancer? Cancer Res 67:7059–7061

Shoshani T, Faerman A, Mett I, Zelin E, Tenne T, Gorodin S, Moshel Y, Elbaz S, Budanov A, Chajut A, Kalinski H, Kamer I, Rozen A, Mor O, Keshet E, Leshkowitz D, Einat P, Skaliter R, Feinstein E (2002) Identification of a novel hypoxia-inducible factor 1-responsive gene, RTP801, involved in apoptosis. Mol Cell Biol 22:2283–2293

Simon MC (2006) Mitochondrial reactive oxygen species are required for hypoxic HIF alpha stabilization. Adv Exp Med Biol 588:165–170

Sowter HM, Ratcliffe PJ, Watson P, Greenberg AH, Harris AL (2001) HIF-1-dependent regulation of hypoxic induction of the cell death factors BNIP3 and NIX in human tumors. Cancer Res 61:6669–6673

Sun HC, Qiu ZJ, Liu J, Sun J, Jiang T, Huang KJ, Yao M, Huang C (2007) Expression of hypoxia-inducible factor-1 alpha and associated proteins in pancreatic ductal adenocarcinoma and their impact on prognosis. Int J Oncol 30:1359–1367

Sun X, Kanwar JR, Leung E, Lehnert K, Wang D, Krissansen GW (2001) Gene transfer of antisense hypoxia inducible factor-1 alpha enhances the therapeutic efficacy of cancer immunotherapy. Gene Ther 8:638–645

Sun X, Kanwar JR, Leung E, Vale M, Krissansen GW (2003) Regression of solid tumors by engineered overexpression of von Hippel-Lindau tumor suppressor protein and antisense hypoxia-inducible factor-1alpha. Gene Ther 10:2081–2089

Sutherland TE, Anderson RL, Hughes RA, Altmann E, Schuliga M, Ziogas J, Stewart AG (2007) 2-Methoxyestradiol–a unique blend of activities generating a new class of anti-tumour/anti-inflammatory agents. Drug Discov Today 12:577–584

Takahashi K, Yamanaka S (2006) Induction of pluripotent stem cells from mouse embryonic and adult fibroblast cultures by defined factors. Cell 126:663–676

Thomas GV, Tran C, Mellinghoff IK, Welsbie DS, Chan E, Fueger B, Czernin J, Sawyers CL (2006) Hypoxia-inducible factor determines sensitivity to inhibitors of mTOR in kidney cancer. Nat Med 12:122–127

Thomlinson RH, Gray LH (1955) The histological structure of some human lung cancers and the possible implications for radiotherapy. Br J Cancer 9:539–549

Unruh A, Ressel A, Mohamed HG, Johnson RS, Nadrowitz R, Richter E, Katschinski DM, Wenger RH (2003) The hypoxia-inducible factor-1 alpha is a negative factor for tumor therapy. Oncogene 22:3213–3220

Vaupel P, Mayer A (2007) Hypoxia in cancer: significance and impact on clinical outcome. Cancer Metastasis Rev 26:225–239

Wan X, Shen N, Mendoza A, Khanna C, Helman LJ (2006) CCI-779 inhibits rhabdomyosarcoma xenograft growth by an antiangiogenic mechanism linked to the targeting of mTOR/Hif-1alpha/VEGF signaling. Neoplasia 8:394–401

Wang GL, Jiang BH, Rue EA, Semenza GL (1995) Hypoxia-inducible factor 1 is a basic-helix-loop-helix-PAS heterodimer regulated by cellular O2 tension. Proc Natl Acad Sci U S A 92:5510–5514

Welsh S, Williams R, Kirkpatrick L, Paine-Murrieta G, Powis G (2004) Antitumor activity and pharmacodynamic properties of PX-478, an inhibitor of hypoxia-inducible factor-1alpha. Mol Cancer Ther 3:233–244

Welsh SJ, Bellamy WT, Briehl MM, Powis G (2002) The redox protein thioredoxin-1 (Trx-1) increases hypoxia-inducible factor 1alpha protein expression: Trx-1 overexpression results in increased vascular endothelial growth factor production and enhanced tumor angiogenesis. Cancer Res 62:5089–5095

Welsh SJ, Koh MY, Powis G (2006) The hypoxic inducible stress response as a target for cancer drug discovery. Semin Oncol 33:486–497

Welsh SJ, Powis G (2003) Hypoxia inducible factor as a cancer drug target. Curr Cancer Drug Targets 3:391–405

Wenger RH, Camenisch G, Desbaillets I, Chilov D, Gassmann M (1998) Up-regulation of hypoxia-inducible factor-1alpha is not sufficient for hypoxic/anoxic p53 induction. Cancer Res 58:5678–5680

Werno C, Zhou J, Brune B (2008) A23187, ionomycin and thapsigargin upregulate mRNA of HIF-1alpha via endoplasmic reticulum stress rather than a rise in intracellular calcium. J Cell Physiol 215:708–714

Wiesener MS, Jurgensen JS, Rosenberger C, Scholze CK, Horstrup JH, Warnecke C, Mandriota S, Bechmann I, Frei UA, Pugh CW, Ratcliffe PJ, Bachmann S, Maxwell PH, Eckardt KU (2003) Widespread hypoxia-inducible expression of HIF-2alpha in distinct cell populations of different organs. Faseb J 17:271–273

Williams KJ, Telfer BA, Airley RE, Peters HP, Sheridan MR, van der Kogel AJ, Harris AL, Stratford IJ (2002) A protective role for HIF-1 in response to redox manipulation and glucose deprivation: implications for tumorigenesis. Oncogene 21:282–290

Yeo EJ, Chun YS, Cho YS, Kim J, Lee JC, Kim MS, Park JW (2003) YC-1: a potential anticancer drug targeting hypoxia-inducible factor 1. J Natl Cancer Inst 95:516–525

Young RM, Wang SJ, Gordan JD, Ji X, Liebhaber SA, Simon MC (2008) Hypoxia-mediated selective mRNA translation by an internal ribosome entry site-independent mechanism. J Biol Chem 283: 16309–16319

Zhang H, Gao P, Fukuda R, Kumar G, Krishnamachary B, Zeller KI, Dang CV, Semenza GL (2007) HIF-1 inhibits mitochondrial biogenesis and cellular respiration in VHL-deficient renal cell carcinoma by repression of C-MYC activity. Cancer Cell 11:407–420

Zhong H, Chiles K, Feldser D, Laughner E, Hanrahan C, Georgescu MM, Simons JW, Semenza GL (2000) Modulation of hypoxia-inducible factor 1alpha expression by the epidermal growth factor/phosphatidylinositol 3-kinase/ PTEN/AKT/FRAP pathway in human prostate cancer cells: implications for tumor angiogenesis and therapeutics. Cancer Res 60:1541–1545

Zhong H, De Marzo AM, Laughner E, Lim M, Hilton DA, Zagzag D, Buechler P, Isaacs WB, Semenza GL, Simons JW (1999) Overexpression of hypoxia-inducible factor 1alpha in common human cancers and their metastases. Cancer Res 59:5830–5835

Zhou J, Callapina M, Goodall GJ, Brune B (2004) Functional integrity of nuclear factor kappaB, phosphatidylinositol 3'-kinase, and mitogen-activated protein kinase signaling allows tumor necrosis factor alpha-evoked Bcl-2 expression to provoke internal ribosome entry site-dependent translation of hypoxia-inducible factor 1alpha. Cancer Res 64:9041–9048

Zhou J, Kohl R, Herr B, Frank R, Brune B (2006) Calpain mediates a von Hippel-Lindau protein-independent destruction of hypoxia-inducible factor-1alpha. Mol Biol Cell 17:1549–1558

Zimmer M, Ebert BL, Neil C, Brenner K, Papaioannou I, Melas A, Tolliday N, Lamb J, Pantopoulos K, Golub T, Iliopoulos O (2008) Small-molecule inhibitors of HIF-2a translation link its 5'UTR iron-responsive element to oxygen sensing. Mol Cell 32:838–848

Zundel W, Schindler C, Haas-Kogan D, Koong A, Kaper F, Chen E, Gottschalk AR, Ryan HE, Johnson RS, Jefferson AB, Stokoe D, Giaccia AJ (2000) Loss of PTEN facilitates HIF-1-mediated gene expression. Genes Dev 14:391–396

Chemokines

4

Andreas Hippe, Bernhard Homey, and Anja Mueller-Homey

Abstract Tumor growth is restricted to approximately 2 μm diameters by simple dissociation of nutrients and oxygen. Hence, tumors require the formation of new blood vessels for further growth progression. This process is referred to as tumor neo-angiogenesis. The process of tumor neo-angiogenesis is directed by complex bidirectional interactions between the tumor and the vessels, and creates a favorable microenvironment for angiogenesis. The tumor vessel system not only facilitates tumor growth by providing nutrients and oxygen but also functions as a convenient route for metastasis.

A group of small cytokine-like molecules called chemokines have been shown to participate in angiogenesis under homeostatic and neoplastic conditions. This review summarizes their role in tumor-associated angiogenesis.

B. Homey (✉)
Department of Dermatology,
Heinrich-Heine-University, Moorenstrasse 5,
40225, Düsseldorf, Germany
e-mail: Bernhard.Homey@uni-duesseldorf.de

4.1
Angiogenesis

The physiological process of blood vessel formation from preexisting microvasculature is referred to as angiogenesis. The process of angiogenesis has been reported to play an important role in both health and disease (Auerbach et al. 1976; Folkman 1995; Folkman and Shing 1992; Polverini 1995). The regulation of angiogenesis is dependent on the balance of angiogenic and angiostatic factors present in the microenvironment. Under homeostatic conditions, turnover of endothelial cells forming the vasculature is measured in months or years (Engerman et al. 1967; Tannock and Hayashi 1972). However, under conditions requiring rapid neo-vascularization such as wound healing, the balance between angiogenic and angiostatic factors in the microenvironment is rapidly shifted in favor of angiogenic factors, enabling the development of new vessels efficiently within days (Leibovich and Wiseman 1988). Such a predominance of angiogenic factors is transient and is followed by an equally rapid decline of these factors to achieve a steady state. Thus, under healthy conditions, the process of angiogenesis is controlled, fast, and transient, regressing back to a steady-state level (Strieter et al. 1995a). The termination of angiogenesis after wound healing is accomplished at

R. Liersch et al. (eds.), *Angiogenesis Inhibition,* Recent Results in Cancer Research,
DOI: 10.1007/978-3-540-78281-0_4, © Springer Verlag Berlin Heidelberg 2010

Table 4.1 Known chemokines, their synonyms, as well as their corresponding receptors are shown on the table

Name	Synonyms	Chemokine receptor	ELR-motif	Role in angiogenesis
CXC family				
CXCL1	Groα	CXCR2>CXCR1	+	Angiogenic
CXCL2	Groβ	CXCR2	+	Angiogenic
CXCL3	Groγ	CXCR2	+	Angiogenic
CXCL4	PF4	CXCR3B	−	Angiostatic
CXCL5	ENA-78	CXCR2	+	Angiogenic
CXCL6	GCP-2	CXCR1, CXCR2	+	Angiogenic
CXCL7	NAP-2	Unknown	+	Angiogenic
CXCL8	IL-8	CXCR1, CXCR2	+	Angiogenic
CXCL9	MIG	CXCR3, CXCR3B	−	Angiostatic
CXCL10	IP-10	CXCR3, CXCR3B	−	Angiostatic
CXCL11	I-TAC	CXCR3, CXCR3B	−	Angiostatic
CXCL12	SDF-1α/β	CXCR4, CXCR7	−	Angiogenic
CXCL13	BLC, BCA-1	Unknown	−	Angiostatic
CXCL14	BRAK, Bolekine	Unknown	−	
CXCL15	Unknown	Unknown	+	
CXCL16		CXCR6	−	
CXCL17	DMC	Unknown	−	
CC family				
CCL1	I-309	CCR8	−	Angiogenic
CCL2	MCP-1	CCR2	−	Angiogenic
CCL3	Mip-1α, LD78α	CCR1, CCR5	−	
CCL3L1	LD78β		−	
CCL3L3	LD78β		−	
CCL4	MIP-1β	CCR5	−	
CCL4L1	AT744.2		−	
CCL4L2			−	
CCL5	RANTES	CCR1, CCR3, CCR5	−	Angiogenic
CCL7	MCP-3	CCR1, CCR2, CCR3	−	
CCL8	MCP-2	CCR1, CCR2, CCR3, CCR5	−	
CCL11	Eotaxin	CCR3	−	Angiogenic
CCL13	MCP-4	CCR1, CCR2, CCR3	−	
CCL14	HCC-1	CCR1	−	
CCL15	HCC-2	CCR1, CCR3	−	Angiogenic
CCL16	HCC-4	CCR1, CCR2, CCR5	−	Angiogenic
CCL17	TARC	CCR4	−	
CCL18	DC-CK1, PARC	Unknown	−	
CCL19	MIP-3β, ELC	CCR7	−	
CCL20	MIP-3α, LARC	CCR6	−	
CCL21	SLC, 6Ckine	CCR7	−	Angiostatic
CCL22	MDC, STCP-1	CCR4	−	

Table 4.1 (continued)

Name	Synonyms	Chemokine receptor	ELR-motif	Role in angiogenesis
CCL23	MPIF-1	CCR1	–	Angiogenic
CCL24	Eotaxin-2	CCR3	–	
CCL25	TECK	CCR9	–	
CCL26	Eotaxin-3	CCR3	–	
CCL27	CTACK/ILC	CCR10	–	
CCL28	MEC	CCR10S	–	
C family			–	
XCL1	Lymphotactin, SCM-1α	XCR1	–	
XCL2	SCM-1β		–	
CX3C family			–	
CX3CL1	Fractalkine	CX3CR1	–	Angiogenic

The occurrence of the ELR-motif in CXC chemokines is listed, as well as any known angiogenic or angiostatic properties. If the entry under role in angiogenesis is left blank, the chemokine in question either has no or no known role in angiogenesis

two levels: (a) a reduction of angiogenic factors, and (b) an increase in expression of angiostatic molecules (Bouck 1990).

If this tightly controlled mechanism is defective, pathological conditions occur, as exemplified by aberrant angiogenesis during tumor progression or rheumatoid arthritis (Harris 1976).

4.2
Chemokines in Angiogenesis

Chemokines are a family of small (8–14 kDa) cytokine-like, mostly basic, structurally related molecules that are known to regulate leukocyte trafficking through interactions with G-protein-coupled receptors with seven transmembrane-spanning domains (Zlotnik and Yoshie 2000). Chemokines can be subdivided into four classes based on the alignment of the first two cysteine residues in their amino acid sequence. If the cysteines follow each other, the respective chemokine is part of the CC subgroup, whereas if the two cysteines are separated by one amino acid in between, then the respective chemokine

is part of the CXC subgroup. In addition, there are two subgroups consisting of chemokines with only one residue (XC) or with three residues between the cysteines (CX3C) (Zlotnik and Yoshie 2000). A comprehensive listing of known chemokines, their receptors, and known roles in angiogenesis is summarized in Table 4.1.

4.2.1
CXC Chemokine Subfamily

First, the angiogenic potential of members of the CXC subfamily was identified. The CXC chemokines can be further subdivided based on the presence or absence of a three-amino-acid motif (Glu-Leu-Arg) present at the NH_2-terminus, namely the ELR-motif (Strieter et al. 1995b). Initially, CXC chemokines lacking an ELR-motif such as CXCL4 (PF4), CXCL9 (MIG), and CXCL10 (IP-10) were considered as angiostatic chemokines, whereas those CXC chemokines endowed with the ELR-motif such as CXC-L1-3 (GRO-α-γ), CXCL5 (ENA-78), CXCL6 (GCP-2), CXCL7 (NAP-2), and CXCL8 (IL-8) were considered as angiogenic chemokines

(Belperio et al. 2000). The role of the motif as a structural domain for angiogenic activity was first demonstrated by a site-directed mutagenesis substitution of the motif. A switch of the ELR motif from CXCL8 to CXCL9 caused a shift in the angiogenic properties of these molecules both *in vitro* and *in vivo* (Strieter et al. 1995b). In addition, angiostatic interferons upregulated ELR-motif lacking angiostatic chemokines (Cole et al. 1998; Miller and Krangel 1992) and downregulated the expression of ELR-motif containing angiogenic chemokines (Strieter et al. 1995a). Analysis of chemokine–chemokine receptor interactions demonstrated that angiogenic ELR-motif containing chemokines bound to CXCR2. The angiostatic non-ELR-motif chemokines bound to CXCR3 instead, suggesting receptor-specificity to be responsible for effects on angiogenesis. Indeed, Martins-Green and Hanafusa demonstrated that CXCL12 (SDF-1), a chemokine lacking the motif, had angiogenic properties (Martins-Green and Hanafusa 1997). CXCL12 binds to CXCR4; therefore the more important factor contributing to the angiogenic property of a chemokine is receptor specificity. A typical example is the non-ELR-motif angiostatic chemokine CXCL4. Recently, Lasagni et al. demonstrated that CXCL4 along with CXCL9, 10, 11 bound to CXCR3-B (a splice variant of CXCR3) where as CXCL 9, 10, 11 bound to an another variant (CXCR3-A) (Lasagni et al. 2003). CXCR3-B and not CXCR3-A was specifically expressed by primary cultures of human microvascular endothelial cells (HMEC) and a treatment with CXCL4, 9, 10, 11 resulted in inhibition of growth, thus implicating not only CXCR3-B to be the angiostatic receptor but consequently CXCL4 to be an angiostatic chemokine by virtue of its receptor specificity (Lasagni et al. 2003).

The chemokine CXCL14 (BRAK) was first reported in 1999 by Hromas et al. It is a non-ELR-motif chemokine (Hromas et al. 1999) reported to induce chemotaxis in prostaglandin E_2-treated monocytes (Kurth et al. 2001), neutrophils, and dendritic cells (Cao et al. 2000), as well as cell lines from B-cell and monocytic cell lineages (Sleeman et al. 2000). In one report by Shellenberger et al., CXCL14 potently inhibited angiogenesis in vivo in a rat corneal micropocket assay (Shellenberger et al. 2004). The corresponding receptor for CXCL14 is still unknown and might present itself as another putative angiostatic CXC receptor.

4.2.2
CC Chemokine Subfamily

Recent findings indicate that CC chemokines, in addition to the CXC chemokine sub-family members, also modulate angiogenesis. (Yan et al. 2006). Out of the CC chemokine subfamily CCL1, 2, 11, 15, 16, 21, and 23 are involved under homeostatic, inflammatory, and neoplastic conditions (Bernardini et al. 2000; Goede et al. 1999; Hwang et al. 2004; Salcedo et al. 2001; Soto et al. 1998; Strasly et al. 2004). CCL2 induced migration of human endothelial cells (Salcedo et al. 2000) and exhibited an angiogenic potency similar to vascular endothelial growth factor (VEGF)-A (Goede et al. 1999). However, unlike angiogenesis induced by angiogenic factors such as VEGF, CCL2-mediated angiogenesis was also accompanied by macrophage recruitment (Goede et al. 1999). Hence, indirect effects might be involved as well.

CCL11, a ligand for the receptor CCR3, has been demonstrated to induce angiogenesis in vivo. In a study by Salcedo et al. HMEC migrated toward CCL11 (Salcedo et al. 2001). In rat aortic assays, matrigel plug assays, as well as chicken chorian allantois membrane (CAM) assays, CCL11 was able to induce vascularization (Salcedo et al. 2001). Additionally, CCL15, which also binds to CCR3, induced angiogenic effects (Hwang et al. 2004). This effect was stronger when using a truncated form of CCL15, which consisted of the amino acids 25–92 of full-length CCL15 (Hwang et al. 2004). It promoted sprouting from rat aortic rings, as well as induced neovascularization in a chicken CAM assay (Hwang et al. 2004). Therefore, CCR3 is considered to be an angiogenic receptor.

An interesting case is presented by the CC chemokine CCL21. CCL21 differs from other CC chemokines, having six cysteines in its amino acid sequence rather than the four cysteines characterizing most of the CC chemokine family members (Hedrick and Zlotnik 1997). It is known for the recruitment of activated, matured dendritic cells and naive T cells to T cell zones of lymph nodes (Arenberg et al. 2001). Interestingly, it has been demonstrated that murine CCL21 is able to bind to CCR7 and CXCR3 (Soto et al. 1998), whereas human CCL21 can only bind to CCR7 (Jenh et al. 1999). Hence, murine CCL21 is able to act as an angiostatic chemokine, as demonstrated in a rat corneal micropocket assay in vivo (Soto et al. 1998). Contrary to mCCL21, human CCL21 was not able to bind to either human CXCR3 or murine CXCR3, as well as showing no effect on tumor growth, demonstrating that the angiostatic effect of CCL21 is caused by CXCR3 binding and is specific to the mouse model (Arenberg et al. 2001).

4.2.3
CX3C Chemokine Subfamily

CX3CL1 (Fractalkine) presents itself as a unique chemokine not only by being the sole member of the CX3C chemokine family, but also by its presence as a membrane-bound form as well as a cleaved soluble one (Fong et al. 2000). Inflammatory cytokines induce CX3CL1 expression on endothelial cells, and in the membrane-bound form, it is able to promote a robust adhesion of CX3CR1-expressing monocytes and T-lymphocytes (Imaizumi et al. 2004). By proteolytic cleavage, CX3CL1 enters a soluble state, acting as a chemotatic agent for monocytes and lymphocytes (Imaizumi et al. 2004). Recently, CX3CL1 has also been implicated to play a role in angiogenesis. It was found to be an angiogenic mediator in rheumatoid arthritis (Volin et al. 2001), as well as in ocular angiogenesis (You et al.

2007). CX3CL1/CX3CR1 interaction on endothelial cells activates the Raf-1/MEK/ERK- and PI3K/Akt/eNOS-dependent signal pathways (Lee et al. 2006). This induces hypoxia inducible factor 1α (HIF-1α), which in turn induces VEGF-A production, inducing angiogenesis via VEGF receptor 2 (Ryu et al. 2007).

4.3
Chemokine Receptor Repertoire of Endothelial Cells

For modulation of angiogenesis by chemokines, chemokine–chemokine receptor interaction is necessary. This necessity implicates the study of receptor repertoires of cells involved in angiogenesis. The typical vessel is comprised of an inner lining of endothelial cells and an outer layer of mural cells, which can be smooth muscle cells in larger vessels and pericytes in the microvasculature, divided by a basal membrane (Alberts et al. 2007). Both cell types play a role in angiogenesis. Since the mid-1990s, several studies were published investigating the presence of chemokine receptors on endothelial cells. These studies were reviewed in Bernardini et al. 2003, and demonstrated that HMEC expressed CXCR2, CXCR3, CXCR4, and CX3CR1 (Bernardini et al. 2003). HMECs of a dermal lineage were reported to additionally express CCR2 (Salcedo et al. 2000). There are two isoforms of CCR2, namely CCR2A and B, encoded in a single gene, created by alternative splicing (Charo et al. 1994). De Paepe and De Bleecker studied the expression of these two isoforms, demonstrating CCR2A as the most prominent endothelial CCR2 variant (De Paepe and De Bleecker 2005). Human umbilical vein endothelial cells (HUVEC) expressed only low levels of CXCR2 and CXCR3, while abundantly expressing CXCR4. Additionally, HUVECs expressed CXCR5, CCR2, CCR3, CCR4, and CCR8, which were not expressed on HMEC, but they lacked the HMEC receptor CX3CR1

(Bernardini 2003). Aortic endothelial cells were shown to express CXCR4, CCR2, CCR4, and CCR5 (Bernardini 2003).

Knockout of CXCR4 in mice demonstrated a prenatal lethal phenotype due to defects in development of arteries of the gastrointestinal tract as well as defects in vascular development and cardiogenesis (Tachibana et al. 1998). Similarly, CXCR2-deficient mice demonstrated impaired angiogenesis in the cornea in response to CXCR2-ligand-induced angiogenic activity (Addison et al. 2000). These observations emphasize the importance of both CXCR2 and CXCR4 in angiogenesis and organogenesis in vivo.

Despite this progress, there are several challenges and limitations in the identification of endothelial cell receptor repertoires. Three major concerns being, (a) differential expression of the aforesaid receptors in different endothelial cells of different origin in vitro, (b) faithfulness of model systems, and (c) expression in vivo. For instance, HUVEC (derived from umbilical vessels) are part of the macrocirculation, as described by Garlanda and Dejana (Garlanda and Dejana 1997), and hence may not be an ideal representative for cells involved in angiogenic processes. Similarly, most microvascular endothelial cells in culture are derived from both blood and lymphatic vessels, raising the issue of differences between these lineages of endothelial cells. These differences were observed by Kriehuber et al. after separation of podoplanin-positive lymphatic endothelial cells and podoplanin-negative blood endothelial cells from dermal cell suspensions. Besides podoplanin, LYVE-1 and VEGF-C receptor, among others, were found to be differentially expressed (Kriehuber et al. 2001). Currently, no data for the differential expression of chemokine receptors between lymphatic and blood endothelial cells have been reported. The expression data acquired to date mostly concentrates on cell line receptor expression. The few data on in vivo tissue expression showed that CXCR3 was on middle and large endothelial cells in vivo (Garcia-Lopez et al.

2001), while CXCR4 was expressed on aortic endothelium as well as on coronary vessels of the heart (Berger et al. 1999; Volin et al. 1998). Of the CC chemokine receptors, high CCR2a expression could be demonstrated on coronary vessels, while only low expression of CCR3 and 5 could be demonstrated on these cells (Berger et al. 1999).

Mural cells associated with the endothelial cell, for example, pericytes, have not yet been extensively studied for their chemokine receptor repertoire. Some studies reported chemokine receptor expression of pericytes, for example, CXCR3 was demonstrated to be functionally expressed (Bonacchi et al. 2001). Additionally, CXCR4 (Pablos et al. 1999) and CCR2 (Carulli et al. 2005) expression on pericytes was demonstrated.

4.4
Angiogenesis, Chemokines, and Cancer

Tumor-associated angiogenesis is dependent on several key factors to accomplish neo-vascularization. Microvascular endothelial and mural cells need to proliferate and sprout from preexisting microvasculature in a directional migration toward the tumor. Tumors therefore need to establish a favorable microenvironment (consisting of extracellular matrix and stromal cells, e.g., fibroblasts, endothelial cells, and leukocytes), which in turn influences the preexisting nearby microvasculature to change from a homeostatic condition to a migratory one. Tumor-associated chemokine production is an important event in forming the tumor microenvironment as it plays a key role in facilitating angiogenesis and attracting endothelial cells and leukocytes to the tumor (Belperio et al. 2000; Ben-Baruch 2003; Bernardini et al. 2003). The neo-vasculature of the tumor then (a) feeds the tumor mass and allows tumor growth and (b) presents an accessible route for metastasizing cells from the primary site to distant locations. Here we focus on three cancer types, namely breast cancer, malignant melanoma, and lung cancer, and summarize the current knowledge on chemokine-associated angiogenesis in these malignancies.

4.4.1
Breast Cancer

Breast cancer represents the leading cause of cancer-related deaths among women in developed countries (Parkin et al. 2005). Lack of estrogen receptor (ER) has been associated with a poor prognosis of the disease (Skoog et al. 1987). Interestingly, ER-negative breast cancer cells express CCL2 abundantly (Chavey et al. 2007). In xenomodels, immunodeficient mice infected with human MDA-MB 231 tumor cells show significantly inhibited formation of lung metastases following neutralization of CCL2. This decrease of metastatic dissemination was associated with decreased tumor angiogenesis in vivo (Salcedo et al. 2000). Interestingly, CCL2 expression of breast cancer cells was accompanied by the recruitment of tumor-associated macrophages (Chavey et al. 2007). These macrophages secreted TNF-α and in turn were able to stimulate breast cancer cells to express more CCL2 and 5, forming a vicious circle (Yaal-Hahoshen et al. 2006). Tumor-secreted CCL2 is therefore able to both stimulate angiogenesis and draw macrophages into the tumor. These tumor-associated macrophages are then able to modulate the microenvironment via their cytokine and growth factor expression to a tumor-favorable state. Similarly, CXCL8 expression was inversely correlated with the expression of ER in breast cancers (Freund et al. 2003). The CXCL8-expressing tumor cells not only demonstrated increased invasiveness into matrigel, but also when media-conditioned by CXCL8-expressing tumor cells matrigel was able to facilitate angiogenesis when injected subcutaneously into nude mice (Lin et al. 2004). Therefore, apart from CCL2, CXCL8 might also increase angiogenesis in breast tumors. Interestingly, CCL2 and CXCL8 expression was inversely correlated to ER expression (Chavey et al. 2007; Lin et al. 2004). Loss of ER in breast cancer cells is accompanied by poor prognosis and high risk of locoregional recurrence and distant metastases (Kyndi et al. 2008), giving evidence that an increase in angiogenic chemokine expression might increase the probability of metastasis formation.

4.4.2
Malignant Melanoma

Melanoma, a malignant tumor of melanocytes, is the main cause for skin-cancer-related deaths. The large variety of different chemokines expressed by melanoma cells is evidence for tumor-associated angiogenesis in this malignancy. Hs294T melanoma cell culture supernatants contained CXCL1, which induced autocrine growth stimulatory activity (Balentien et al. 1991; Richmond and Thomas 1986). CXCL1 mRNA was also reported to be constitutively expressed in cultured nevocytes and melanoma cells, but was undetectable in primary melanocytes (Bordoni et al. 1990). This change in expression from melanocytes to premalignant and malignant forms was identified to be dependent on NF-κB activation (Shattuck-Brandt and Richmond 1997). CXCL8 has been demonstrated to be constitutively expressed by melanoma cell lines in vitro, too. CXCL8 exhibited an autocrine effect on melanoma cells as inferred from the decrease of melanoma cell proliferation either by neutralizing CXCL8 by antibodies or by decreasing CXCL8 expression in melanoma cells by transfection of antisense oligonucleotides (Schadendorf et al. 1993). As expected, CXCR1 and CXCR2 expression (the chemokine receptors of CXCL8) could be identified on melanoma cells in tissue sections by immunohistochemistry

(Varney et al. 2006). Interestingly, CXCR2 expression was more abundant in Clark level III to V specimens, than in Clark level I–II specimens. In contrast, CXCR1 expression was ubiquitously detected in the majority of analyzed specimens (Varney et al. 2006). Therefore, autocrine stimulation of melanoma cells by CXCL8, which enhances proliferation, might be dependent on CXCR2 signaling, as more advanced stages of melanoma express more CXCR2. In addition, CXCL8 expression by melanoma cells enhanced angiogenesis. Increased proliferation of endothelial cells was observed during both in vitro and in vivo vessel formation assays using matrigel plugs containing conditioned media of M14 melanoma cells, which was enriched with CXCL8 (Giorgini et al. 2007). Furthermore, the importance of the tumor microenvironment for tumor progression and angiogenesis could be observed in melanoma. Metastatic human melanoma cells harvested from subcuteanous areas expressed CXCL8 much more abundantly than metastases from liver. Subcutaneous metastases lost their abundant CXCL8 expression when reinjected and reharvested from liver lesions. This could be reproduced in coculture experiments of melanoma cells with either keratinocytes or hepatocytes. Paracrine induction of CXCL8 in melanoma cells by keratinocyte-derived IL-1 was observed to be the reason for high levels of CXCL8, while hepatocyte-derived TGF-β was responsible for a negative regulation of CXCL8 in melanoma, demonstrating the vital importance of the microenvironment for tumors (Gutman et al. 1995). Furthermore, CCL2 is expressed in melanoma and blocking of CCL2 function was able to prevent tumor angiogenesis and tumor growth (Koga et al. 2008). The role of CCL2 might therefore be similar to its role in breast cancers. Additionally, a more aggressive behaviour of melanoma in nude mice was observed after CCL5 induction in melanoma cells by TNF-α (Mrowietz et al.

1999). This is compelling evidence that tumor infiltrating macrophages might, through enhancement of CCL2 and CCL5 production, transform the microenvironment to one favorable for angiogenesis and tumor progression, which in turn leads to a tumor in a more aggressive stage.

4.4.3
Lung Cancer

The role of chemokines in lung cancer angiogenesis has been well established by Strieter et al. CXCL8 expression was elevated in non-small cell lung cancer (NSCLC) and significantly contributed to tumor-derived angiogenesis (Smith et al. 1994). Neutralizing antibodies to CXCL8 were able to significantly reduce endothelial cell chemotactic activity in response to NSCLC tissue (Smith et al. 1994). Furthermore, in a human NSCLC/SCID mouse chimera model, the cell line A549 (adenocarcinoma) and the cell line Calu 1 (squamous cell carcinoma) were studied. In A549-bearing animals, a progressive increase of tumor size was observed, while Calu 1-bearing mice demonstrated little tumor growth (Arenberg et al. 1996a). Correspondingly, A549 tumors produced greater levels of CXCL8 than Calu 1 tumors and were up to 50-fold larger in size than Calu 1 tumors (Arenberg et al. 1996a). When A549 tumors were treated with neutralizing antibodies to CXCL8, a marked reduction of tumor growth compared to control tumors followed (Arenberg et al. 1996a). Furthermore, in corneal micropocket assays and assessments of vessel density in tumors, inhibition of CXCL8 by antibody treatment resulted in lower vessel density as well as reduced angiogenesis, demonstrating that tumor-associated CXCL8 mediated tumor angiogenesis in A549 (Arenberg et al. 1996a). It is important to note that, although CXCL8 is unknown in mice (Zlotnik and Yoshie 2000), both corresponding receptors,

CXCR1 and CXCR2, have been identified in mice and being responsive to human CXCL8 (Fan et al. 2007). Interestingly, an inversely correlated phenomenon was observed after assessing expression of CXCL10 in adenocarcinomas compared to squamous cell carcinomas. In squamous cell carcinomas elevated levels of CXCL10 were observed (Arenberg et al. 1996b). Corresponding to the CXCL8 experiments, CXCL10 expression was studied in the same NSCLC/SCID mouse chimera model. Not surprisingly, CXCL10 expression was inversely correlated to tumor growth showing high levels in Calu 1 tumors and low levels in A549 tumors, and the antibody neutralization of CXCL10 caused an increase in growth of Calu 1 tumors (Arenberg et al. 1996b). Furthermore, neutralization of CXCL10 by antibodies increased neovascularization of squamous cell carcinomas in the cornea as well as showing an increased endothelial cell chemotactic activity (Arenberg et al. 1996b). The balance of CXCL8 vs. CXCL10 expression of adenocarcinomas and squamous cell carcinomas of the lung corresponded to the prognosis of patients. Patient survival is poorer and metastatic potential is greater in patients with adenocarcinomas when compared to patients with squamous cell carcinomas (Carney 1988; Minna 1991). Therefore, the difference of behavior observed in these two tumor entities might be dependent on the balance of angiogenic CXCL8 and angiostatic CXCL10, demonstrating an opposing system of angiogenic and angiostatic factors in the microenvironment controlling tumorangiogenesis. Furthermore, tumor-infiltrating macrophages were able to induce CXCL8 expression in lung cancer cells, as demonstrated by a significant increase in CXCL8 mRNA in lung cancer cells cocultured with phorbol myristate acetate-treated THP-1 cells and human primary lung macrophages (Yao et al. 2005), demonstrating the vital importance of crosstalk between tumor-associated macrophages and tumor cells in modulating the microenvironment.

In contrast, abundant CXCL8 expression could not be observed in small cell lung cancer (SCLC) (Zhu et al. 2004). Instead, SCLC cell lines H711, H69, H345, Lu165, and GLC19 expressed CXCL6 abundantly, where as in tested NSCLC cell lines CXCL6 expression could not be observed (Zhu et al. 2006). Additionally, IL-1β as well as hypoxic conditions induced the production of CXCL6 in SCLC cell lines. Furthermore, CXCL6 is able to promote cell proliferation by autocrine stimulation, as evidenced by inhibition of proliferation when SCLC cells were treated with neutralizing anti-CXCL6 antibodies (Zhu et al. 2006). Interestingly, the receptor for CXCL6 is the same as for CXCL8, namely CXCR2 (Zlotnik and Yoshie 2000). It might be possible that CXCL6 is the agent modulating angiogenesis in a SCLC scenario, instead of CXCL8, although this still needs to be further elucidated.

4.5
Inhibition of Chemokine-Induced Angiogenesis as a Therapeutic Strategy

Today, cancer therapeutic strategies targeting angiogenesis are in clinical use. The most prominent of antiangiogenic drugs for cancer therapy is bevacizumab, an antibody targeting VEGF (John et al. 2008). Use of bevacizumab in addition to standard chemotherapy shows some promising results in prolonging the survival of treated patients (John et al. 2008). There are several other drugs in preclinical and clinical evaluation which target the receptors of VEGF, matrix-metallo proteinases, and cyclooxygenase-2 (COX-2) (John et al. 2008). COX-2 is an inducible enzyme, which catalyzes the conversion of arachidonic acid to prostaglandin H_2 (PGH_2) (Williams et al. 1999). PGH_2 serves as a subtrate for a number of prostaglandin synthetases (Williams et al. 1999). One prostaglandin endproduct, prostaglandin E_2 (PGE_2), has been implicated in acting as an inducer of angiogenesis regulators like VEGF, endothelin-1 and others (Chiarugi et al. 1998). Not surprisingly, COX-2 is upregulated in many cancer types and represents a valuable target for antitumor therapy (Harris 2007).

The role of chemokines in angiogenesis presents an opportunity for novel approaches in cancer therapy. It might be worthwhile to pursue a therapeutic role for angiostatic chemokines like CXCL4, CXCL9, CXCL10, and CXCL11. These chemokines could be introduced into a tumor either by direct application or by gene therapy approaches to shift the balance of the tumor microenvironment towards angiostasis, thereby inhibiting tumor growth. One prominent example of a tumor therapy strategy utilizing an inhibiting drug is exemplified by Interferon-α (INFα). A tumor-limiting effect of INFα was demonstrated more than 25 years ago in B16 melanoma (Bart et al. 1980). Today, it has found clinical application as a treatment of several malignancies, including non-Hodgkin's lymphoma, Kaposi sarcoma, melanoma, and renal cell carcinoma (Parmar and Platanias 2003). INFα not only acts through activation of immune cells, but it was demonstrated to also directly act on tumor cells by induction of apoptosis (Parmar and Platanias 2003).

One risk involved in such an approach could be that the loss of vasculature inside the tumor could result in hypoxic conditions. Hypoxia in the tumor might drive the tumor cells toward different ways to escape hypoxic-related cell death. In fact, antiangiogenic therapies might select resistant subclones and boost tumor progression and growth, giving rise to the paradox, that in antiangiogenic therapy, the induced hypoxic condition of the tumor needs to be fought, too (Abbadessa et al. 2007). For example, hypoxia induced CXCR4 expression in mononuclear phagocytes, HUVEC, and the ovarian cancer cell line CAOV3 (Schioppa et al. 2003). Furthermore, in mouse embryonic fibroblasts hypoxia-induced CXCR4 induction was alleviated in HIF-1α-deficient cells, implicating that CXCR4 is under regulation by HIF-1α (Schioppa et al. 2003). CXCR4 expression on cancer cells plays a role in invasion and targeted metastasis to distant sites (Muller et al. 2001). Therefore, chemokine receptor expression induced by hypoxia might represent the danger involved in therapy targeting angiogensis.

Another approach might be the inhibition of angiogenic chemokines present in the tumor microenvironment. Drugs which inhibit the corresponding chemokine receptor or using chemokine-specific antibodies to neutralize the angiogenic effect would realize this approach. This strategy is already in use with VEGF or VEGFR-targeting drugs mentioned at the beginning of this chapter. The goal of both general strategies (a) supplementing the tumor microenvironment with agents inhibiting angiogenesis directly or (b) agents targeting angiogenic modulators, thereby inhibiting angiogenesis indirectly, are to shift the microenvironment from an angiogenesis favoring to an angiogenesis limiting state.

The research for chemokine-based cancer therapy has mostly been directed toward stimulating immune response (immunotherapy) to tumors or to inhibit metastasis. One prominent example is the use of antagonists against CXCR4. The focus on research of CXCR4 antagonists is founded on its role as a coreceptor for viral infection in HIV (Feng et al. 1996), as well as its role in cancer metastasis (Geminder et al. 2001; Muller et al. 2001; Payne and Cornelius 2002; Taichman et al. 2002; Zeelenberg et al. 2001). Several small molecule antagonists to CXCR4 are in development, among them BKT140 and its analogs (Takenaga et al. 2004; Tamamura et al. 2003), CTCE-9908 by Chemokine Therapeutics (Vancouver, Canada) (Kim et al. 2005), as well as AMD3100 by AnorMED Inc. (Langley, Canada) (De Clercq 2003). AMD3100, now renamed Mozobil™, completed Phase II studies (Devine et al. 2004) for stem cell transplantaion treatment of multiple myeloma and non-Hodgkin's lymphoma patients in 2004. Recently, GenzymeCorporation (Cambridge, MA, USA), developing Mozobil(TM) after its acquisition of AnorMED Inc., announced after successful Phase III trials the FDA approval for Mozobil(TM) at the end of 2008 for the mobilization of stem cells from the bone marrow for collection and autologous transplantation. Incidentally, CXCR4 antagonists might not only present a way to inhibit metastasis, but also due to its role in angiogenesis (see Chap. 2), be a viable antiangiogenesis therapeutic.

The research focusing on finding chemokine-derived agents which inhibit angiogenesis is much smaller. Abgenix (Thousand Oaks, CA, USA) has developed an anti-CXCL8 antibody, ABX-IL8 (Yang et al. 1999). ABX-IL8 inhibited angiogenesis, tumor growth, and metastasis in human melanoma both in vitro and in vivo (Huang et al. 2002) in preclinical trials and inhibited tumor growth and matrix metalloproteinase activity in orthotopic bladder cancer xenografts as well (Mian et al. 2003). A Phase II study of ABX-IL8 in patients with malignant melanoma was planned in 2002, but this study never commenced due to failure to meet its endpoint in a seperate psoriasis trial (Yan et al. 2006).

About 25% of human malignancies contain activated forms of the *Ras* protooncogene (Bos 1989). Interestingly, CXCL8, a chemokine with a prominent role in angiogenesis, is induced by activation of the epidermal growth factor receptor (EGFR)/Ras signal transduction pathway (Sparmann and Bar-Sagi 2004). Moreover, activation of EGFR/Ras signal transduction in skin malignancies facilitates escape of immune surveillance via downregulation of homeostatic CCL27 by the tumor (Pivarcsi et al. 2007). Targeting the EGFR/Ras signal transduction pathway therefore might not only inhibit angiogenesis but also establish an immune response to the tumor. EGFR inhibitors like erlotinib, geftinib, and cetuximab (John et al. 2008) are either already in clinical use or in clinical study phases and present a promising antiproliferative, immunomodulating, apoptosis-enhancing, and antiangiogenetic therapeutic approach in cancer therapy.

The possibility of inhibiting tumor angiogenesis by (a) antibodies to angiogenic chemokines or anatgonists against angiogenic receptors, (b) raising the angiostatic chemokine level in the tumor microenvironment or (c) targeting signal transduction pathways modulating chemokine expression, presents a promising strategy for novel anticancer therapeutics. Further investigations and screening for new antagonists to chemokine receptors or chemokines might provide physicians with further tools to inhibit tumor growth and to combat progression of tumors.

References

Abbadessa G, Vogiatzi P, Rimassa L, Claudio PP (2007) Antiangiogenic drugs currently used for colorectal cancer: what other pathways can we target to prolong responses? Drug News Perspect 20:307–313

Addison CL, Daniel TO, Burdick MD, Liu H, Ehlert JE, Xue YY, Buechi L, Walz A, Richmond A, Strieter RM (2000) The CXC chemokine receptor 2, CXCR2, is the putative receptor for ELR+ CXC chemokine-induced angiogenic activity. J Immunol 165:5269–5277

Arenberg DA, Kunkel SL, Polverini PJ, Glass M, Burdick MD, Strieter RM (1996a) Inhibition of interleukin-8 reduces tumorigenesis of human non-small cell lung cancer in SCID mice. J Clin Invest 97:2792–2802

Arenberg DA, Kunkel SL, Polverini PJ, Morris SB, Burdick MD, Glass MC, Taub DT, Iannettoni MD, Whyte RI, Strieter RM (1996b) Interferon-gamma-inducible protein 10 (IP-10) is an angiostatic factor that inhibits human non-small cell lung cancer (NSCLC) tumorigenesis and spontaneous metastases. J Exp Med 184:981–992

Arenberg DA, Zlotnick A, Strom SR, Burdick MD, Strieter RM (2001) The murine CC chemokine, 6C-kine, inhibits tumor growth and angiogenesis in a human lung cancer SCID mouse model. Cancer Immunol Immunother 49:587–592

Auerbach R, Kubai L, Sidky Y (1976) Angiogenesis induction by tumors, embryonic tissues, and lymphocytes. Cancer Res 36:3435–3440

Alberts B, Johnson A, Lewis J, Raff M, Roberts K, Walter P (2007) Molecular biology of the cell. Garland Science, London

Balentien E, Mufson BE, Shattuck RL, Derynck R, Richmond A (1991) Effects of MGSA/GRO alpha on melanocyte transformation. Oncogene 6:1115–1124

Bart RS, Porzio NR, Kopf AW, Vilcek JT, Cheng EH, Farcet Y (1980) Inhibition of growth of B16 murine malignant melanoma by exogenous interferon. Cancer Res 40:614–619

Belperio JA, Keane MP, Arenberg DA, Addison CL, Ehlert JE, Burdick MD, Strieter RM (2000) CXC chemokines in angiogenesis. J Leukoc Biol 68:1–8

Ben-Baruch A (2003) Host microenvironment in breast cancer development: inflammatory cells, cytokines and chemokines in breast cancer progression: reciprocal tumor-microenvironment interactions. Breast Cancer Res 5:31–36

Berger O, Gan X, Gujuluva C, Burns AR, Sulur G, Stins M, Way D, Witte M, Weinand M, Said J, Kim KS, Taub D, Graves MC, Fiala M (1999) CXC and CC chemokine receptors on coronary and brain endothelia. Mol Med 5:795–805

Bernardini G, Ribatti D, Spinetti G, Morbidelli L, Ziche M, Santoni A, Capogrossi MC, Napolitano M (2003) Analysis of the role of chemokines in angiogenesis. J Immunol Methods 273: 83–101

Bernardini G, Spinetti G, Ribatti D, Camarda G, Morbidelli L, Ziche M, Santoni A, Capogrossi MC, Napolitano M (2000) I-309 binds to and activates endothelial cell functions and acts as an angiogenic molecule in vivo. Blood 96: 4039–4045

Bonacchi A, Romagnani P, Romanelli RG, Efsen E, Annunziato F, Lasagni L, Francalanci M, Serio M, Laffi G, Pinzani M, Gentilini P, Marra F (2001) Signal transduction by the chemokine receptor CXCR3: activation of Ras/ERK, Src, and phosphatidylinositol 3-kinase/Akt controls cell migration and proliferation in human vascular pericytes. J Biol Chem 276:9945–9954

Bordoni R, Fine R, Murray D, Richmond A (1990) Characterization of the role of melanoma growth stimulatory activity (MGSA) in the growth of normal melanocytes, nevocytes, and malignant melanocytes. J Cell Biochem 44:207–219

Bos JL (1989) ras oncogenes in human cancer: a review. Cancer Res 49:4682–4689

Bouck N (1990) Tumor angiogenesis: the role of oncogenes and tumor suppressor genes. Cancer Cells 2:179–185

Cao X, Zhang W, Wan T, He L, Chen T, Yuan Z, Ma S, Yu Y, Chen G (2000) Molecular cloning and characterization of a novel CXC chemokine macrophage inflammatory protein-2 gamma chemoattractant for human neutrophils and dendritic cells. J Immunol 165:2588–2595

Carney DN (1988) Cancers of the lungs. In: Fishman AP (ed) Pulmonary diseases and disorders. McGraw-Hill, New York, pp 1885–2068

Carulli MT, Ong VH, Ponticos M, Shiwen X, Abraham DJ, Black CM, Denton CP (2005) Chemokine receptor CCR2 expression by systemic sclerosis fibroblasts: evidence for autocrine regulation of myofibroblast differentiation. Arthritis Rheum 52:3772–3782

Charo IF, Myers SJ, Herman A, Franci C, Connolly AJ, Coughlin SR (1994) Molecular cloning and functional expression of two monocyte chemoattractant protein 1 receptors reveals alternative splicing of the carboxyl-terminal tails. Proc Natl Acad Sci U S A 91:2752–2756

Chavey C, Bibeau F, Gourgou-Bourgade S, Burlinchon S, Boissiere F, Laune D, Roques S, Lazennec G (2007) Oestrogen receptor negative breast cancers exhibit high cytokine content. Breast Cancer Res 9:R15

Chiarugi V, Magnelli L, Gallo O (1998) Cox-2, iNOS and p53 as play-makers of tumor angiogenesis (review). Int J Mol Med 2:715–719

Cole KE, Strick CA, Paradis TJ, Ogborne KT, Loetscher M, Gladue RP, Lin W, Boyd JG, Moser B, Wood DE, Sahagan BG, Neote K (1998) Interferon-inducible T cell alpha chemoattractant (I-TAC): a novel non-ELR CXC chemokine with potent activity on activated T cells through selective high affinity binding to CXCR3. J Exp Med 187:2009–2021

De Clercq E (2003) The bicyclam AMD3100 story. Nat Rev Drug Discov 2:581–587

De Paepe B, De Bleecker JL (2005) Beta-chemokine receptor expression in idiopathic inflammatory myopathies. Muscle Nerve 31:621–627

Devine SM, Flomenberg N, Vesole DH, Liesveld J, Weisdorf D, Badel K, Calandra G, DiPersio JF (2004) Rapid mobilization of CD34+ cells following administration of the CXCR4 antagonist AMD3100 to patients with multiple myeloma and non-Hodgkin's lymphoma. J Clin Oncol 22:1095–1102

Engerman RL, Pfaffenbach D, Davis MD (1967) Cell turnover of capillaries. Lab Invest 17:738–743

Fan X, Patera AC, Pong-Kennedy A, Deno G, Gonsiorek W, Manfra DJ, Vassileva G, Zeng M, Jackson C, Sullivan L, Sharif-Rodriguez W,

Opdenakker G, Van Damme J, Hedrick JA, Lundell D, Lira SA, Hipkin RW (2007) Murine CXCR1 is a functional receptor for GCP-2/CXCL6 and interleukin-8/CXCL8. J Biol Chem 282:11658–11666

Feng Y, Broder CC, Kennedy PE, Berger EA (1996) HIV-1 entry cofactor: functional cDNA cloning of a seven-transmembrane, G protein-coupled receptor. Science 272:872–877

Folkman J (1995) Angiogenesis in cancer, vascular, rheumatoid and other disease. Nat Med 1:27–31

Folkman J, Shing Y (1992) Angiogenesis. J Biol Chem 267:10931–10934

Fong AM, Erickson HP, Zachariah JP, Poon S, Schamberg NJ, Imai T, Patel DD (2000) Ultrastructure and function of the fractalkine mucin domain in CX(3)C chemokine domain presentation. J Biol Chem 275:3781–3786

Freund A, Chauveau C, Brouillet JP, Lucas A, Lacroix M, Licznar A, Vignon F, Lazennec G (2003) IL-8 expression and its possible relationship with estrogen-receptor-negative status of breast cancer cells. Oncogene 22:256–265

Garcia-Lopez MA, Sanchez-Madrid F, Rodriguez-Frade JM, Mellado M, Acevedo A, Garcia MI, Albar JP, Martinez C, Marazuela M (2001) CXCR3 chemokine receptor distribution in normal and inflamed tissues: expression on activated lymphocytes, endothelial cells, and dendritic cells. Lab Invest 81:409–418

Garlanda C, Dejana E (1997) Heterogeneity of endothelial cells. Specific markers. Arterioscler Thromb Vasc Biol 17:1193–1202

Geminder H, Sagi-Assif O, Goldberg L, Meshel T, Rechavi G, Witz IP, Ben-Baruch A (2001) A possible role for CXCR4 and its ligand, the CXC chemokine stromal cell-derived factor-1, in the development of bone marrow metastases in neuroblastoma. J Immunol 167:4747–4757

Giorgini S, Trisciuoglio D, Gabellini C, Desideri M, Castellini L, Colarossi C, Zangemeister-Wittke U, Zupi G, Del Bufalo D (2007) Modulation of bcl-xL in tumor cells regulates angiogenesis through CXCL8 expression. Mol Cancer Res 5:761–771

Goede V, Brogelli L, Ziche M, Augustin HG (1999) Induction of inflammatory angiogenesis by monocyte chemoattractant protein-1. Int J Cancer 82:765–770

Gutman M, Singh RK, Xie K, Bucana CD, Fidler IJ (1995) Regulation of interleukin-8 expression in human melanoma cells by the organ environment. Cancer Res 55:2470–2475

Harris ED Jr (1976) Recent insights into the pathogenesis of the proliferative lesion in rheumatoid arthritis. Arthritis Rheum 19:68–72

Harris RE (2007) Cyclooxygenase-2 (cox-2) and the inflammogenesis of cancer. Subcell Biochem 42:93–126

Hedrick JA, Zlotnik A (1997) Identification and characterization of a novel beta chemokine containing six conserved cysteines. J Immunol 159:1589–1593

Hromas R, Broxmeyer HE, Kim C, Nakshatri H, Christopherson K 2nd, Azam M, Hou YH (1999) Cloning of BRAK, a novel divergent CXC chemokine preferentially expressed in normal versus malignant cells. Biochem Biophys Res Commun 255:703–706

Huang S, Mills L, Mian B, Tellez C, McCarty M, Yang XD, Gudas JM, Bar-Eli M (2002) Fully humanized neutralizing antibodies to interleukin-8 (ABX-IL8) inhibit angiogenesis, tumor growth, and metastasis of human melanoma. Am J Pathol 161:125–134

Hwang J, Kim CW, Son KN, Han KY, Lee KH, Kleinman HK, Ko J, Na DS, Kwon BS, Gho YS, Kim J (2004) Angiogenic activity of human CC chemokine CCL15 in vitro and in vivo. FEBS Lett 570:47–51

Imaizumi T, Yoshida H, Satoh K (2004) Regulation of CX3CL1/fractalkine expression in endothelial cells. J Atheroscler Thromb 11:15–21

Jenh CH, Cox MA, Kaminski H, Zhang M, Byrnes H, Fine J, Lundell D, Chou CC, Narula SK, Zavodny PJ (1999) Cutting edge: species specificity of the CC chemokine 6Ckine signaling through the CXC chemokine receptor CXCR3: human 6Ckine is not a ligand for the human or mouse CXCR3 receptors. J Immunol 162:3765–3769

John AR, Bramhall SR, Eggo MC (2008) Antiangiogenic therapy and surgical practice. Br J Surg 95:281–293

Kim S, Mendoza A, Midura B et al (2005) Inhibition of murine osteosarcoma lung metastases using the CXCR4 antagonist, CTCE-9908. In Proceedings of the 96th AACR annual meeting. Anaheim, CA.

Koga M, Kai H, Egami K, Murohara T, Ikeda A, Yasuoka S, Egashira K, Matsuishi T, Kai M, Kataoka Y, Kuwano M, Imaizumi T (2008) Mutant MCP-1 therapy inhibits tumor angiogenesis and growth of malignant melanoma in mice. Biochem Biophys Res Commun 365:279–284

4

Kriehuber E, Breiteneder-Geleff S, Groeger M, Soleiman A, Schoppmann SF, Stingl G, Kerjaschki D, Maurer D (2001) Isolation and characterization of dermal lymphatic and blood endothelial cells reveal stable and functionally specialized cell lineages. J Exp Med 194: 797–808

Kurth I, Willimann K, Schaerli P, Hunziker T, Clark-Lewis I, Moser B (2001) Monocyte selectivity and tissue localization suggests a role for breast and kidney-expressed chemokine (BRAK) in macrophage development. J Exp Med 194:855–861

Kyndi M, Sorensen FB, Knudsen H, Overgaard M, Nielsen HM, Overgaard J (2008) Estrogen receptor, progesterone receptor, HER-2, and response to postmastectomy radiotherapy in high-risk breast cancer: the Danish Breast Cancer Cooperative Group. J Clin Oncol 26(9):1419–1426

Lasagni L, Francalanci M, Annunziato F, Lazzeri E, Giannini S, Cosmi L, Sagrinati C, Mazzinghi B, Orlando C, Maggi E, Marra F, Romagnani S, Serio M, Romagnani P (2003) An alternatively spliced variant of CXCR3 mediates the inhibition of endothelial cell growth induced by IP-10, Mig, and I-TAC, and acts as functional receptor for platelet factor 4. J Exp Med 197:1537–1549

Lee SJ, Namkoong S, Kim YM, Kim CK, Lee H, Ha KS, Chung HT, Kwon YG (2006) Fractalkine stimulates angiogenesis by activating the Raf-1/MEK/ERK- and PI3K/Akt/eNOS-dependent signal pathways. Am J Physiol Heart Circ Physiol 291:H2836–H2846

Leibovich SJ, Wiseman DM (1988) Macrophages, wound repair and angiogenesis. Prog Clin Biol Res 266:131–145

Lin Y, Huang R, Chen L, Li S, Shi Q, Jordan C, Huang RP (2004) Identification of interleukin-8 as estrogen receptor-regulated factor involved in breast cancer invasion and angiogenesis by protein arrays. Int J Cancer 109:507–515

Martins-Green M, Hanafusa H (1997) The 9E3/CEF4 gene and its product the chicken chemotactic and angiogenic factor (cCAF): potential roles in wound healing and tumor development. Cytokine Growth Factor Rev 8:221–232

Mian BM, Dinney CP, Bermejo CE, Sweeney P, Tellez C, Yang XD, Gudas JM, McConkey DJ, Bar-Eli M (2003) Fully human anti-interleukin 8 antibody inhibits tumor growth in orthotopic bladder cancer xenografts via down-regulation of matrix metalloproteases and nuclear factor-kappaB. Clin Cancer Res 9:3167–3175

Miller MD, Krangel MS (1992) Biology and biochemistry of the chemokines: a family of chemotactic and inflammatory cytokines. Crit Rev Immunol 12:17–46

Minna JD (1991) Neoplasms of the lung. In: Isselbacher KJ (ed) Principles of internal medicine. McGraw-Hill, New York, pp 1102–1110

Mrowietz U, Schwenk U, Maune S, Bartels J, Kupper M, Fichtner I, Schroder JM, Schadendorf D (1999) The chemokine RANTES is secreted by human melanoma cells and is associated with enhanced tumour formation in nude mice. Br J Cancer 79:1025–1031

Muller A, Homey B, Soto H, Ge N, Catron D, Buchanan ME, McClanahan T, Murphy E, Yuan W, Wagner SN, Barrera JL, Mohar A, Verastegui E, Zlotnik A (2001) Involvement of chemokine receptors in breast cancer metastasis. Nature 410:50–56

Pablos JL, Amara A, Bouloc A, Santiago B, Caruz A, Galindo M, Delaunay T, Virelizier JL, Arenzana-Seisdedos F (1999) Stromal-cell derived factor is expressed by dendritic cells and endothelium in human skin. Am J Pathol 155:1577–1586

Parkin DM, Bray F, Ferlay J, Pisani P (2005) Global cancer statistics, 2002. CA Cancer J Clin 55:74–108

Parmar S, Platanias LC (2003) Interferons: mechanisms of action and clinical applications. Curr Opin Oncol 15:431–439

Payne AS, Cornelius LA (2002) The role of chemokines in melanoma tumor growth and metastasis. J Invest Dermatol 118:915–922

Pivarcsi A, Muller A, Hippe A, Rieker J, van Lierop A, Steinhoff M, Seeliger S, Kubitza R, Pippirs U, Meller S, Gerber PA, Liersch R, Buenemann E, Sonkoly E, Wiesner U, Hoffmann TK, Schneider L, Piekorz R, Enderlein E, Reifenberger J, Rohr UP, Haas R, Boukamp P, Haase I, Nurnberg B, Ruzicka T, Zlotnik A, Homey B (2007) Tumor immune escape by the loss of homeostatic chemokine expression. Proc Natl Acad Sci U S A 104:19055–19060

Polverini PJ (1995) The pathophysiology of angiogenesis. Crit Rev Oral Biol Med 6:230–247

Richmond A, Thomas HG (1986) Purification of melanoma growth stimulatory activity. J Cell Physiol 129:375–384

Ryu J, Lee CW, Hong KH, Shin JA, Lim SH, Park CS, Shim J, Nam KB, Choi KJ, Kim YH, Han KH (2007) Activation of Fractalkine/CX3CR1 by

Vascular Endothelial Cells Induces Angiogenesis through VEGF-A/KDR and Reverses Hindlimb Ischemia. Cardiovasc Res 78(2):333–340

Salcedo R, Ponce ML, Young HA, Wasserman K, Ward JM, Kleinman HK, Oppenheim JJ, Murphy WJ (2000) Human endothelial cells express CCR2 and respond to MCP-1: direct role of MCP-1 in angiogenesis and tumor progression. Blood 96:34–40

Salcedo R, Young HA, Ponce ML, Ward JM, Kleinman HK, Murphy WJ, Oppenheim JJ (2001) Eotaxin (CCL11) induces in vivo angiogenic responses by human CCR3+ endothelial cells. J Immunol 166:7571–7578

Schadendorf D, Moller A, Algermissen B, Worm M, Sticherling M, Czarnetzki BM (1993) IL-8 produced by human malignant melanoma cells in vitro is an essential autocrine growth factor. J Immunol 151:2667–2675

Schioppa T, Uranchimeg B, Saccani A, Biswas SK, Doni A, Rapisarda A, Bernasconi S, Saccani S, Nebuloni M, Vago L, Mantovani A, Melillo G, Sica A (2003) Regulation of the chemokine receptor CXCR4 by hypoxia. J Exp Med 198: 1391–1402

Shattuck-Brandt RL, Richmond A (1997) Enhanced degradation of I-kappaB alpha contributes to endogenous activation of NF-kappaB in Hs294T melanoma cells. Cancer Res 57:3032–3039

Shellenberger TD, Wang M, Gujrati M, Jayakumar A, Strieter RM, Burdick MD, Ioannides CG, Efferson CL, El-Naggar AK, Roberts D, Clayman GL, Frederick MJ (2004) BRAK/CXCL14 is a potent inhibitor of angiogenesis and a chemotactic factor for immature dendritic cells. Cancer Res 64:8262–8270

Skoog L, Humla S, Axelsson M, Frost M, Norman A, Nordenskjold B, Wallgren A (1987) Estrogen receptor levels and survival of breast cancer patients. A study on patients participating in randomized trials of adjuvant therapy. Acta Oncol 26:95–100

Sleeman MA, Fraser JK, Murison JG, Kelly SL, Prestidge RL, Palmer DJ, Watson JD, Kumble KD (2000) B cell- and monocyte-activating chemokine (BMAC), a novel non-ELR alpha-chemokine. Int Immunol 12:677–689

Smith DR, Polverini PJ, Kunkel SL, Orringer MB, Whyte RI, Burdick MD, Wilke CA, Strieter RM (1994) Inhibition of interleukin 8 attenuates angiogenesis in bronchogenic carcinoma. J Exp Med 179:1409–1415

Soto H, Wang W, Strieter RM, Copeland NG, Gilbert DJ, Jenkins NA, Hedrick J, Zlotnik A (1998) The CC chemokine 6Ckine binds the CXC chemokine receptor CXCR3. Proc Natl Acad Sci U S A 95:8205–8210

Sparmann A, Bar-Sagi D (2004) Ras-induced interleukin-8 expression plays a critical role in tumor growth and angiogenesis. Cancer Cell 6:447–458

Strasly M, Doronzo G, Capello P, Valdembri D, Arese M, Mitola S, Moore P, Alessandri G, Giovarelli M, Bussolino F (2004) CCL16 activates an angiogenic program in vascular endothelial cells. Blood 103:40–49

Strieter RM, Polverini PJ, Arenberg DA, Kunkel SL (1995a) The role of CXC chemokines as regulators of angiogenesis. Shock 4:155–160

Strieter RM, Polverini PJ, Kunkel SL, Arenberg DA, Burdick MD, Kasper J, Dzuiba J, Van Damme J, Walz A, Marriott D et al (1995b) The functional role of the ELR motif in CXC chemokine-mediated angiogenesis. J Biol Chem 270:27348–27357

Tachibana K, Hirota S, Iizasa H, Yoshida H, Kawabata K, Kataoka Y, Kitamura Y, Matsushima K, Yoshida N, Nishikawa S, Kishimoto T, Nagasawa T (1998) The chemokine receptor CXCR4 is essential for vascularization of the gastrointestinal tract. Nature 393:591–594

Taichman RS, Cooper C, Keller ET, Pienta KJ, Taichman NS, McCauley LK (2002) Use of the stromal cell-derived factor-1/CXCR4 pathway in prostate cancer metastasis to bone. Cancer Res 62:1832–1837

Takenaga M, Tamamura H, Hiramatsu K, Nakamura N, Yamaguchi Y, Kitagawa A, Kawai S, Nakashima H, Fujii N, Igarashi R (2004) A single treatment with microcapsules containing a CXCR4 antagonist suppresses pulmonary metastasis of murine melanoma. Biochem Biophys Res Commun 320:226–232

Tamamura H, Hori A, Kanzaki N, Hiramatsu K, Mizumoto M, Nakashima H, Yamamoto N, Otaka A, Fujii N (2003) T140 analogs as CXCR4 antagonists identified as anti-metastatic agents in the treatment of breast cancer. FEBS Lett 550:79–83

Tannock IF, Hayashi S (1972) The proliferation of capillary endothelial cells. Cancer Res 32:77–82

Varney ML, Johansson SL, Singh RK (2006) Distinct expression of CXCL8 and its receptors CXCR1 and CXCR2 and their association with vessel density and aggressiveness in malignant melanoma. Am J Clin Pathol 125:209–216

Volin MV, Joseph L, Shockley MS, Davies PF (1998) Chemokine receptor CXCR4 expression in endothelium. Biochem Biophys Res Commun 242:46–53

Volin MV, Woods JM, Amin MA, Connors MA, Harlow LA, Koch AE (2001) Fractalkine: a novel angiogenic chemokine in rheumatoid arthritis. Am J Pathol 159:1521–1530

Williams CS, Mann M, DuBois RN (1999) The role of cyclooxygenases in inflammation, cancer, and development. Oncogene 18:7908–7916

Yaal-Hahoshen N, Shina S, Leider-Trejo L, Barnea I, Shabtai EL, Azenshtein E, Greenberg I, Keydar I, Ben-Baruch A (2006) The chemokine CCL5 as a potential prognostic factor predicting disease progression in stage II breast cancer patients. Clin Cancer Res 12:4474–4480

Yan L, Anderson GM, DeWitte M, Nakada MT (2006) Therapeutic potential of cytokine and chemokine antagonists in cancer therapy. Eur J Cancer 42:793–802

Yang XD, Corvalan JR, Wang P, Roy CM, Davis CG (1999) Fully human anti-interleukin-8 monoclonal antibodies: potential therapeutics for the treatment of inflammatory disease states. J Leukoc Biol 66:401–410

Yao PL, Lin YC, Wang CH, Huang YC, Liao WY, Wang SS, Chen JJ, Yang PC (2005) Autocrine and paracrine regulation of interleukin-8 expression in lung cancer cells. Am J Respir Cell Mol Biol 32:540–547

You JJ, Yang CH, Huang JS, Chen MS, Yang CM (2007) Fractalkine, a CX3C chemokine, as a mediator of ocular angiogenesis. Invest Ophthalmol Vis Sci 48:5290–5298

Zeelenberg IS, Ruuls-Van Stalle L, Roos E (2001) Retention of CXCR4 in the endoplasmic reticulum blocks dissemination of a T cell hybridoma. J Clin Invest 108:269–277

Zhu YM, Bagstaff SM, Woll PJ (2006) Production and upregulation of granulocyte chemotactic protein-2/CXCL6 by IL-1beta and hypoxia in small cell lung cancer. Br J Cancer 94: 1936–1941

Zhu YM, Webster SJ, Flower D, Woll PJ (2004) Interleukin-8/CXCL8 is a growth factor for human lung cancer cells. Br J Cancer 91: 1970–1976

Zlotnik A, Yoshie O (2000) Chemokines: a new classification system and their role in immunity. Immunity 12:121–127

Angiogenesis Inhibition in Cancer Therapy

5

Platelet-Derived Growth Factor (PDGF) and Vascular Endothelial Growth Factor (VEGF) and their Receptors: Biological Functions and Role in Malignancy

Iris Appelmann, Rüdiger Liersch, Torsten Kessler,
Rolf M. Mesters, and Wolfgang E. Berdel

Abstract Vascular endothelial growth factor (VEGF) is an endothelial cell-specific mitogen in vitro and an angiogenic inducer in a variety of in vivo models. VEGF gene transcription is induced in particular in hypoxic cells. In developmental angiogenesis, the role of VEGF is demonstrated by the finding that the loss of a single VEGF allele results in defective vascularization and early embryonic lethality. Substantial evidence also implicates VEGF as a mediator of pathological angiogenesis. In situ hybridization studies demonstrate expression of VEGF mRNA in the majority of human tumors. Platelet-derived growth factor (PDGF) is mainly believed to be an important mitogen for connective tissue, and also has important roles during embryonal development. Its overexpression has been linked to different types of malignancies. Thus, it is important to understand the physiology of VEGF and PDGF and their receptors as well as their roles in malignances in order to develop antiangiogenic strategies for the treatment of malignant disease.

I. Appelmann (✉)
Department of Medicine/Hematology and Oncology,
University of Münster, Albert-Schweitzer-Strasse 33,
48129 Münster, Germany
e-mail: Iris.Appelmann@ukmuenster.de

5.1 Introduction

In vertebrates, virtually all tissues depend on oxygen and nutrition supply provided by the blood-vessel system (Risau 1997). The diffusion limit for oxygen is between 100 and 200 μm; thus nearly all cells need to reside in proximity of a capillary (Carmeliet 2003). In addition, the progression of major diseases and of malignancies in particular is related to an abnormally increased formation of vascular networks (Hanahan and Folkman 1996), whereas other important diseases such as cardiac or brain infarction are caused by poor blood supply. Thus, in order to overcome diseases related to the vascular system, an understanding of the molecular basis of angiogenesis is of major importance. Several factors have been identified to play relevant roles in angiogenesis, for example, VEGF, PDGF, and angiopoietin. Among them, VEGF and its receptors are involved in mammalian blood and lymph vessel formation from earliest stages in embryogenesis (Alitalo and Carmeliet 2002; Ferrara and Davis-Smyth 1997), and also play pivotal roles in pathologic angiogenesis (Cornali et al. 1996; Ferrara et al. 1998; Ferrara and Gerber 2001; Plate et al. 1992; Shweiki et al. 1992). PDGF is mainly believed to be an important mitogen for connective

R. Liersch et al. (eds.), *Angiogenesis Inhibition*, Recent Results in Cancer Research,
DOI: 10.1007/978-3-540-78281-0_5, © Springer Verlag Berlin Heidelberg 2010

5

tissue, especially for fibroblasts that serve in wound healing. However, PDGF also has important roles during embryonal development, and its overexpression has been linked to different types of fibrotic disorders and malignancies. Thus, it is important to understand the physiology of VEGF and PDGF and their receptors as well as their roles in malignancies. This chapter summarizes the biosynthesis and physiologic activity of VEGF and PDGF, and the role of VEGF and PDGF expression in malignant disease. For detailed information on particular aspects of VEGF and PDGF biology (e.g., signal transduction) the reader is kindly referred to other reviews and original literature, some of which are cited later in the chapter.

5.2
VEGF

5.2.1
VEGF Isoforms and Their Expression

In 1983, VEGF was first described as having an important impact on vessel formation (Senger et al. 1983). It was observed that this factor induced vascular leakage, and thus it was first called vascular permeability factor (VPF). Sequencing and purification of VPF took place in

1990 (Connolly et al. 1989a). Independently, the term "vascular endothelial growth factor" was used by Ferrara and Henzel for a specific endothelial mitogen isolated from conditioned medium. Finally, Connolly was able to prove in 1989 that VPF and VEGF were the same molecule (Connolly et al. 1989a, b).

VEGF is now recognized to play an essential role in physiological as well as pathological angiogenesis (Cornali et al. 1996; Ferrara et al. 1998; Ferrara and Gerber 2001; Plate et al. 1992; Shweiki et al. 1992). Different structurally related dimeric glycoproteins which are highly homologous to PDGF have been identified (Keck et al. 1989; Leung et al. 1989), and constitute the VEGF family. This VEGF family includes VEGF-A, VEGF-B (Olofsson et al. 1996), VEGF-C (Joukov et al. 1996), VEGF-D (Achen et al. 1998), VEGF-E, and placenta-derived growth factor (PlGF) (Maglione et al. 1991; Maglione et al. 1993). Homodimers or heterodimers of the VEGF family form the active VEGF molecule. VEGF-A as the predominant form is a heparin-binding homodimeric glycoprotein of 45 kDa and is generated by alternative exon splicing in four different isoforms (VEGF121, VEGF165, VEGF189, VEGF205) (Houck et al. 1992; Keyt et al. 1996; Tischer et al. 1991) which are generated concomitantly (Fig. 5.1). In humans, the VEGF gene consists of eight exons with seven introns

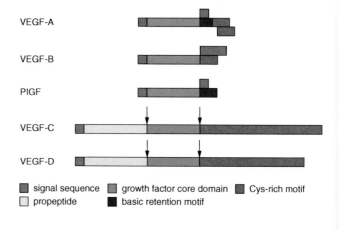

Fig. 5.1 Mammalian VEGFs. *Arrows* indicates proteolytic cleavage sites

■ signal sequence   ■ growth factor core domain   ■ Cys-rich motif
□ propeptide   ■ basic retention motif

and is localized on chromosome 6p21.3 (Vincenti et al. 1996). The two shorter isoforms show mitogenic activity as well as permeability-inducing activity. The longer isoforms are only capable of inducing vascular permeability (Keyt et al. 1996). VEGF 121 lacks the parts encoded by Exon 6 and 7 so that it loses its heparin-binding capability. This lack of heparin-binding capacity causes a significant reduction of the mitogenic potential of VEGF (Keyt et al. 1996). A complete recovery of a tumorigenic pheno-type in VEGF −/− mice is only caused by the murine isoform VEGF164 (which is shorter by one amino acid compared to the human isoform) (Grunstein et al. 2000). Furthermore, mice which exclusively express VEGF120 die as newborns or within the first two weeks (Carmeliet et al. 1999). Thus, for the initiation of vascular branch formation, the heparin-binding capacity seems to play a pivotal role (Carmeliet 1999). An increase in VEGF levels has been observed in several different human malignan-cies, for example, breast, lung, pancreatic, ovar-ian, kidney, and bladder carcinomas (Boocock et al. 1995; Brown et al. 1993a; Ellis et al. 1998; Hatva et al. 1995; Volm et al. 1997a; Yoshiji et al. 1996). Since low oxygen tension serves as major stimulus for VEGF expression, the high-est expression is found in proximity to necrotic areas (Ferrara et al. 1998; Shweiki et al. 1992). There is a close relationship between the hypoxic mechanism leading to VEGF expression and the regulative mechanism of erythropoietin (Epo) expression (Goldberg and Schneider 1994). The VEGF gene, as well as the Epo gene, contains a highly homologous promoter region with simi-lar affinity to hypoxia-inducible factor 1 (HIF-1) (Levy et al. 1995; Liu et al. 1995), which is one of the essential mediators for a response to low oxygen tension (Madan and Curtin 1993). Other important mediators linked to the HIF-1 path-way include products of tumor suppressor genes like the von-Hippel-Lindau (VHL) protein (Iliopoulos et al. 1996) and the tumor suppressor gene PTEN. PTEN is a negative regulator to the

PI3-kinase pathway and is constitutively mutated in glioblastomas (Li et al. 1997; Zundel et al. 2000). Furthermore, a stimulus for increased VEGF expression is the amplification of the oncogene ras (Grugel et al. 1995; Rak et al. 1995), which directly links an upregulation of VEGF to oncogenic transformation in malig-nant cells. This strongly suggests a role for VEGF as autocrine growth factor not only for endothelial cells. In addition, the expression of VEGF is upregulated by other growth fac-tors, cytokines, and hormones such as PDGF, fibroblast growth factor (FGF), insulin-like growth factor 1 (IGF-1), tumor necrosis factor α (TNF-α), and estradiol (Cohen et al. 1996; Frank et al. 1995; Mueller et al. 2000; Mueller et al. 2003; Pertovaara et al. 1994; Warren et al. 1996).

5.2.2
VEGF Receptors

There is evidence that mammalian VEGF recep-tors (VEGFRs) are derived from the tyrosine kinase receptor D-VEGFR/PVR found in Droso-phila, where it is mainly needed to mediate cell migration (e.g., migration of border cells, hema-topoietic cells, and epithelial cells for thorax closure) (Cho et al. 2002; Duchek et al. 2001; Ishimaru et al. 2004). Only one VEGFR-related gene has been identified in nonvertebrates like Drosophila; thus it is believed that the variety of VEGFR family genes and structurally similar PDGFR genes in vertebrates have been gener-ated by gene duplication or triplication during early stages of evolution of vertebrates. The phylogenetical developments of VEGFRs and PDGFRs in vertebrates seem to have occured in a step-wise manner due to which a gain of func-tion has developed. It explains that vertebrate VEGFRs do not only transduce signals for cell migration, but also generate mitotic signals for vascular/lymphatic endothelial cells. In close relationship, PDGFRs even generate signals

5

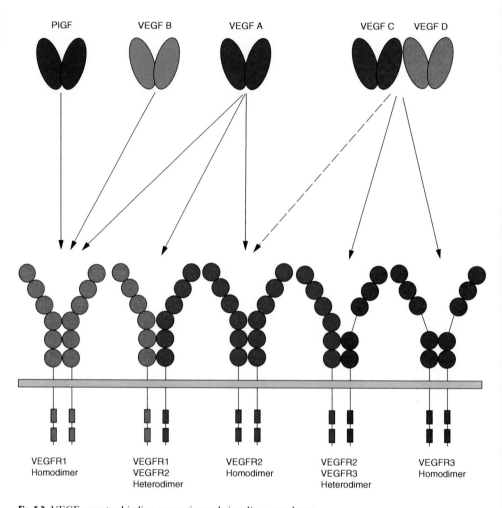

Fig. 5.2 VEGF receptor-binding properties and signaling complexes

for the activation of the PI3-kinase and ras pathways for cell growth and transformation (Shibuya 2002; Shibuya and Claesson-Welsh 2006) (Fig 5.2).

5.2.3
Structure of VEGFR1 and VEGFR2

In humans the VEGFR1 consists of 1338 amino acids and VEGFR2 contains 1356 amino acids. Both receptors can be separated into four regions:

an extracellular ligand-binding domain, a transmembrane domain, a tyrosine kinase domain, and a downstream carboxy terminal region (Matthews et al. 1991; Millauer et al. 1993; Shibuya et al. 1990; Terman et al. 1991). There is a homology in the overall structure of VEGFR1 (Flt1), VEGFR2 (KDR/Flk-1), and VEGFR3 (Flt-4) (Alitalo and Carmeliet 2002; Shibuya et al. 1990). The VEGF receptors are closely related to the PDGF receptor family, for example, PDGFR, CSF-1 receptor (c-Fms), SCF receptor (c-Kit), and Flt-3. There is, however, a difference between the two receptor families in the number of Ig-like domains: the VEGFRs contain 7 Ig-like domains, whereas the PDGFRs contain only 5 Ig-like domains.

The binding sites for VEGF-A are located on the second Ig-like domain in the VEGFR1 and on the second/third Ig-like domain in VEGFR2. Several authors observed that the downstream structure of the fourth to seventh Ig-like domains plays an important role for receptor dimerization and thus activation (Fuh et al. 1998; Keyt et al. 1996; Shinkai et al. 1998; Tanaka et al. 1997). In both VEGFR and PDGFR, a tyronsine residue can be found in position 801, which in PDGFR is phosphorylated and binds to c-Src, thereby provoking a negative signaling (Heldin and Westermark 1999). In contrast to PDGFR, this tyrosine residue is not well autophosphorylated in VEGFR2. Even an exchange of this tyrosine residue in a phenylalanine mutant did not elicit a significant difference in MAP-kinase activation and DNA synthesis (Takahashi et al. 2001).

In the tyrosine kinase domain of VEGFR1 and R2 and PDGFR, similarities can again be found: the length of the kinase insert shows a high grade of homology (two inserts of 70 amino acids), whereas the structure differs between VEGFRs and PDGFRs. (Shibuya 1995; Terman et al. 1991). Two Tyr-x-x-Met motifs for auto-phosphorylation can be found in the PDGFR insert sequence. These are critical activating sites for the PI3-kinase/Akt pathway to activate Ras as survival signal. In the entire sequence of VEGFR1 and R2, these motifs are not present. The lack of these critical motifs suggests only a weak cross-talk between VEGFR1/R2 and the PI3K/Akt pathway (Gerber et al. 1998).

The neuropilins (NRP-1 and NRP-2) act as coreceptors for the VEGFs and increase the binding affinity of VEGF to VEGFRs. There is evidence that NRP-1 and NRP-2 can also induce signal transduction independent from their coreceptor function. The effects of NRP-mediated VEGF activation have not yet been completely understood. However, recent studies have shown that dual targeting of the vasculature with antibodies to VEGF and NRP is more effective than single-agent therapy (Pan et al. 2007).

5.2.4
Signaling and Biological Functions of VEGFR1

On the one hand, different authors observed that the affinity of VEGF-A to VEGFR1 is very high with a kDa of 2–10 pM (de Vries et al. 1992; Sawano et al. 1997). On the other hand, the tyrosine kinase activity of VEGFR1 is relatively weak and it does not stimulate the proliferation of NIH3T3 cells overexpressing VEGFR1. Furthermore, the proliferation of VEGFR1 and R2-expressing endothelial cells is not stimulated by VEGFR1-specific ligands (PlGF, VEGF-B) (Waltenberger et al. 1994).

The VEGFR1 gene encodes not only the mRNA for a full-length receptor, but also a short mRNA for a soluble form of the VEGFR1 protein, which carries only the extracellular ligand-binding domain (Kendall and Thomas 1993; Shibuya et al. 1990). The soluble ligand-binding domain could serve as a natural inhibitor of VEGF-A. Thus, VEGFR1 seems to function as a positive regulator via its tyrosine kinase domain and also as a negative regulator via its ligand-binding domain.

The relatively weak biological activity of VEGFR1 makes it difficult to assess the downstream signaling of VEGFR1. It is autophosphorylated in five positions: Tyr-1169, 1213, 1242, 1327, and 1333 (Cunningham et al. 1995; Ito et al. 2001; Sawano et al. 1997). The major binding site for the MAP-kinase pathway leading toward angiogenesis in VEGFR2 is Tyr-1175. In VEGFR1, Tyr-1169 corresponds to this binding site, but the phosphorylation here is again relatively weak, and in conclusion the aforementioned pathway is only mildly activated (Sawano et al. 1997). 1213-Tyr is highly autophosphorylated on VEGFR1 but its downstream pathway remains unclear.

It was observed by Fong et al. that VEGFR1-null mutant mice die at embryonic stage E-8.5–9.0 due to the overgrowth and disorganization of blood vessels (Fong et al. 1995). This strongly suggests a negative role for VEGFR1 by suppressing proangiogenic signals in the early embryo in order to establish a balance essential for physiological angiogenesis. Hiratsuka et al. tested if the negative role of VEGFR1 involves the ligand-binding domain or not. Knock-out mice lacking the tyrosine kinase domain of VEGFR1 were basically healthy with nearly normal blood vessels but showed a defect in the migration of macrophages toward VEGF-A (Hiratsuka et al. 2001; Hiratsuka et al. 1998). These results indicate that ligand-binding domain and transmembrane domain of VEGFR1 together are sufficient for a suppressive effect on angiogenesis in embryogenesis.

In contrast to the negative role in embryogenesis, a positive role of VEGFR1 has been described concerning tumor growth, metastasis, and inflammation. The rate of tumor growth in VEGFR1 TK $(-/-)$ mice is slower than in wild-type mice. In particular, the tumor cells grow faster in VEGFR1 TK $(-/-)$ mice if PlGF. a VEGFR1-specific ligand, is overexpressed at the same time (Hiratsuka et al. 2001). The mechanisms underlying this phenomenon remain unclear.

In lung carcinomas, the rate of growth in VEGFR TK $(-/-)$ mice was similar to the rate of growth in wildtype mice, but the VEGFR TK $(-/-)$ mice showed a significant reduction in the rate of lung-orientated metastasis (Hiratsuka et al. 2002). Hiratsuka et al. reported furthermore that there was a significant infiltration of monocytes/macrophages in the pulmonary tissue before the occurrence of metastasis in tumor-bearing wildtype mice. This infiltration also occurs in VEGFR TK $(-/-)$ mice, but to a considerably lower degree. It was also observed that the expression of matrix metalloproteinase 9 (MMP9) was induced in both tumor-bearing wildtype mice and VEGFR TK $(-/-)$ mice, but the extent was again different: the expression of MMP9 was threefold higher in VEGFR TK $(-/-)$ mice than in tumor-bearing wildtype mice. In tumor-bearing MMP9-knockout mice, macrophage-lineage cells also infiltrate the lung but metastasis is significantly decreased. These results support the theory that signaling of VEGFR1 tyrosine kinase promotes lung metastasis by premetastatic induction of MMP9 expression. Similar results have been reported by Kaplan et al. in 2005 when bone-marrow derived cells (e.g., macrophage lineage cells) infiltrate the lung before the occurrence of metastasis and thus provide a pre-metastatic niche for the original tumor (Kaplan et al. 2005). This implies the importance of VEGFR signaling as target for the suppression of tumor metastasis.

5.2.5
Expression and Signaling of VEGFR2

The expression of VEGFR2 is first perceived at E7.5 in murine development in mesodermal cells of the tail (Kaipainen et al. 1993; Shalaby et al. 1995). Differentiation into primitive endothelial cells then takes place in E 7.5–8.0 when VEGFR2-positive cells migrate into the head region and yolk sac (Hiratsuka et al. 2005; Shalaby et al. 1995). In the yolk sac, these cells begin to form blood islands and initiate hematopoiesis (Eichmann et al. 1997; Shalaby et al. 1995). Postnatally, there is still an expression of VEGFR2 on hematopoietic cells found, but to a much lower extent compared to its expression on vascular endothelial cells. The role of these relatively low expression levels of VEGFR2 on hematopoietic cells remains to be determined as well as its role in nonendothelial cells (lower levels are also described on neuronal cells, osteoblasts, pancreatic duct cells, retinal progenitor cells, and megakaryocytes) (Matsumoto and Claesson-Welsh 2001).

Plate et al. reported a 3–5-fold higher expression of VEGFR2 on tumor vessels compared to normal vasculature, and VEGF-A is a stimulus for VEGFR2 expression via a positive feedback loop (Ferrara and Davis-Smyth 1997; Plate et al. 1992). Within the tumor tissue, in contrast to tumor vasculature, only little VEGFR2 is expressed, whereas expression levels of VEGF-A are high. Hence this implies a paracrine regulation loop of VEGF-A and VEGFR2 between tumor cells and vascular endothelial cells to stimulate pathological angiogenesis (Alitalo and Carmeliet 2002; Ferrara and Davis-Smyth 1997; Shibuya 1995).

VEGFR2 has a pivotal role for signal transduction in both physiological and pathological angiogenesis: VEGFR2 knockout mice die at E 8.0–8.5 with a lack of vasculogenesis. This shows the importance of VEGFR2 signaling for the differentiation of VEGFR2-positive endothelial precursor cells into vascular endothelial cells and for their proliferation (Shalaby et al. 1995). Carmeliet et al. and other groups reported a lethal effect of reduced VEGFR2 signaling due to VEGF-A (+/−) heterozygosity and neuropilin 1 (−/−) gene homozygosity. Death in this case was caused by a critical abnormality of the vascular system, in particular by an impaired aortic heart connection and vascular remodeling in the yolk sac, although the blood vessel formation itself was carried out normally (Carmeliet et al. 1996; Ferrara et al. 1996; Kawasaki et al. 1999; Maes et al. 2002). These results signify that vasculogenesis may sufficiently be promoted with reduced VEGFR2 TK activation, but in this condition, however, critical steps such as morphogenesis of the aorta and the heart are carried out insufficiently.

Several tyrosine inserts are phosphorylated in the carboxy tail and kinase insert region when stimulation of VEGFR2 by VEGF-A takes place, whereas only one of them, Tyr-1175, is the only binding site for the SH2 domain of phospholipase Cγ (PLCγ). The PKC-c-Raf-MEK-MAP pathway is activated by tyrosine phosphorylation of PLCγ (Takahashi et al. 2001). Despite this, DURING VEGFR2 pathway activation the

active Ras (GTP-form of Ras) is only rarely found. Furthermore, dominant negative Ras mutants were not able to inhibit PKC-dependent MAP-kinase activation via VEGFR2 (Takahashi et al. 1999). This is unique since other growth-promoting receptor tyrosine kinases such as EGFR utilize the activation of Ras for various downstream signaling events. In addition, Sakurai et al. detected a death at embryonic stage 9.0 which was again due to a lack of vasculogenesis in knock-in mutant carrying a Tyr-to-Ph substitution at position 1173 (in analogy to human 1175-Tyr) (Sakurai et al. 2005). These results suggest that the VEGFR2-1175PY-PLCγ-PKC pathway has an important role in vivo, although its exact biological meaning remains unclear. There is evidence that signaling via VEGFR2 might be critical for the maintenance of the tubular structure of blood vessels during angiogenesis as well as vascular remodeling. Interactions of VEGFR2 and VE-cadherin and integrins have been observed (Shay-Salit et al. 2002; Stupack and Cheresh 2004). The exact mechanism and the interacting residues involved have not yet been detected. VEGFR2 is also expressed on lymph vessels, and thus might be involved in lymphangiogenesis (Hirakawa et al. 2005; Veikkola et al. 2001).

5.2.6
VEGF and Malignancy

Neovascularization in the proximity of tumors was first described a century ago, (Goldmann 1907; Ide et al. 1939) and was named angiogenesis in contrast to the term vasculogenesis referring to the development of the vascular system in embryogenesis. In 1971, the paradigm-shifting work of Folkman (Folkman 1971; Folkman et al. 1971) proposed a new strategy against malignant tumor: blocking angiogenesis. In the concerted play of growth factors (e.g., FGF, PDGF, VEGF, angiopoietins), which at least partly causes the angiogenic switch in malignant tumors, VEGF is believed to be one of the key molecules as it stimulates permeability, endothelial cell activation, survival and proliferation, proliferation of tumor cells, and facilitates invasion and migration. In situ hybridization studies have demonstrated the expression of VEGF mRNA in the majority of human tumors, including carcinoma of the lung (Volm et al. 1997a, b), breast (Brown et al. 1995; Yoshiji et al. 1996), gastrointestinal tract (Brown et al. 1993b; Ellis et al. 1998; Suzuki et al. 1996; Uchida et al. 1998), kidney (Nicol et al. 1997; Tomisawa et al. 1999), bladder (Brown et al. 1993a), ovary (Olson et al. 1994; Sowter et al. 1997; Yamamoto et al. 1997), endometrium (Guidi et al. 1996), and several intracranial tumors, for example, glioblastoma multiforme (Plate et al. 1992; Shweiki et al. 1992). Sporadic expression has also been observed in capillary hemangioblastoma (Wizigmann-Voos et al. 1995). In a variety of pituitary tumors, VEGF expression has also been described (Lloyd et al. 1999). VEGF is expressed in various cell lines derived from different hematological malignancies, including T-cell lymphoma, acute lymphoblastic leukemia, Burkitt's lymphoma, acute lymphocytic leukemia, histiocytic lymphoma, promyelocytic leukemia, etc. (for review see (Gerber and Ferrara 2003)). Expression of both VEGFRs has been detected in some, but not all, leukemia cell lines, and VEGFR-1 was found to be more frequently expressed than VEGFR-2. These observations suggest that the production of VEGF by malignant myeloid precursors might serve both as an autocrine growth stimulus and a diffusible, paracrine, signal-mediating angiogenesis within the bone marrow.

Although tumor cells usually represent the major source of VEGF, tumor-associated stroma is also an important site of VEGF production (Fukumura et al. 1998; Gerber et al. 2000). Chemotactic signals from tumor cells cause recruitment of stromal cells, which also produce VEGF and other angiogenic factors. The growth of several human tumor cell lines transplanted in nude mice is substantially reduced, but not completely suppressed, by antihuman VEGF monoclonal antibodies (Kim et al. 1993). Administration of mFlt (1–3)-IgG, a chimeric receptor containing the first three Ig-like domains of VEGFR-1, that binds both human and mouse VEGF, results in a nearly complete suppression of tumor growth and tumor cells necrosis in a nude mouse model of human rhabdomyosarcoma (Gerber et al. 2000). Similar observations were made using a chimeric soluble receptor consisting of domain 2 of VEGFR-1 fused with domain 3 of VEGFR-2, referred to as "VEGF-trap" (Holash et al. 2002). Thus, the use of VEGF inhibitors that only target human VEGF in human xenograft models might result in an underestimation of the role of VEGF in the process of tumor angiogenesis.

The overexpression of VEGF has been observed to be a bad prognostic parameter in carcinomas of the lung (Imoto et al. 1998; O'Byrne et al. 2000; Volm et al. 1997a), breast (Gasparini et al. 1997; Toi et al. 1995), gastrointestinal tract (Amaya et al. 1997; Ishigami et al. 1998; Maeda et al. 2000; Ogata et al. 2003; Shih et al. 2000), kidney (Jacobsen et al. 2004), and ovary (Paley et al. 1997; Yamamoto et al. 1997). Klein et al. (2001) have shown that VEGF expression detected by immunohistochemistry is a negative prognostic marker in papillary thyroid carcinoma. In prostate carcinoma, VEGF expression is regulated by androgens, and recent studies suggest a correlation between angiogenesis and biological aggressiveness of the disease. In hematologic malignancies, the overexpression of VEGF also led to an unfavorable outcome (Aguayo et al. 2002).

A potent inhibitory effect on the growth of several tumor cell lines in nude mice is exerted by anti-VEGF monoclonal antibodies (Kim et al. 1993), but this antibody had no effect on the tumor cells in vitro. As a consequence, various other tumor cell lines were found to be inhibited in vivo by anti-VEGF monoclonal antibodies (Asano et al. 1995; Borgstrom et al. 1996, 1998,

1999; Melnyk et al. 1996; Mesiano et al. 1998; Warren et al. 1995). Tumor growth inhibition was demonstrated also with other anti-VEGF treatments, including a retrovirus-delivered dominant negative Flk-1 mutant (Millauer et al. 1994), small molecule inhibitors of VEGFR-2 signaling (Fiedler et al. 2003; Strawn et al. 1996; Wedge et al. 2000; Wood et al. 2000), antisense oligonucleotides (Oku et al. 1998; Saleh et al. 1996), anti-VEGFR-2 antibodies (334), and soluble VEGF receptors (Gerber et al. 2000; Goldman et al. 1998; Kong et al. 1998; Prewett et al. 1999). The inhibitory effects of small molecule inhibitors targeting VEGFR-1 and VEGFR-2 on the growth of human myeloid leukemia cell lines have been documented (Smolich et al. 2001). Further evidence for a functional role of VEGFR-2 in leukemic cell growth was provided by experiments showing that an anti-VEGFR-2 antibody inhibits proliferation of xenotransplanted human leukemia cells and significantly increased survival of nude mice (Dias et al. 2000). Clinical results with anti-VEGF strategies are detailed in Chap. 9 in this volume.

5.3
PDGF

PDGFs and their receptors are known to play important roles in animal development, for example, in gastrulation, the development of cranial and cardiac neural crest, gonads, lung, intestine, skin, CNS, and skeleton, and thus have been intensively studied over the past two decades. Similarly, models for PDGFR-β signaling have been developed in angiogenesis and early hematopoiesis and are widely accepted. Furthermore, PDGF signaling is observed in various pathological conditions and diseases. Autocrine activation of PDGF signaling pathways is observed in gliomas, sarcomas, and leukemias, whereas paracrine PDGF signaling pathways are important for the development of

epithelial cancers. Here PDGF triggers the recruitment of stromal cells and seems to be involved in epithelial–mesenchymal transition. This has an influence on tumor growth by affecting angiogenesis, invasion, and metastasis. Besides, PDGF is not only important in malignancy, but also drives the development of various other pathological conditions such as vascular disorders (e.g., atherosclerosis, pulmonary hypertension, retinopathies) and fibrotic diseases (e.g., pulmonary or hepatic fibrosis, scleroderma, and glomerulosclerosis). In the following paragraphs, current knowledge on PDGF functions in health and disease are summarized and a background to PDGF biochemistry and cell biology is discussed. The regulation of bioavailability and tissue distribution of the PDGFs by certain different mechanisms are shown.

5.3.1
Platelet-Derived Growth Factor and Its Isoforms

PDGF was identified more than three decades ago for the first time as a serum growth factor for fibroblasts, smooth muscle cells (SMCs), and glia cells (Kohler and Lipton 1974; Ross et al. 1974; Wasteson et al. 1976), and was shown to be a cationic disulfide-linked homo- or heterodimer of two different polypeptide chains, A and B, separable by using reversed phase chromatography (Johnsson et al. 1982).

For almost two decades, the theory existed that the PDGF family consists of three proteins—PDGF-AA, PDGF-AB, and PDGF-BB—encoded by two genes, PDGF-A and PDGF-B.

Between the B-chain of PDGF (PDGF-B) and the product of the retroviral oncogene v-sis of simian sarcoma virus (SSV) (Doolittle et al. 1983; Waterfield et al. 1983) some homology was characterized by amino acid sequencing. Subsequently, it was confirmed by different studies that the human cellular counterpart to v-sis was identical to PDGF-B, and that autocrine PDGF activity was sufficient for SSV transformation in vitro. For the relationship between neoplastic cell transformation and normal growth control, this was a staggering discovery because the importance of autocrine growth stimulation in neoplastic transformation was demonstrated for the first time. It is now a well-established model that autocrine PDGF stimulation is also of significance in some human cancers.

PDGF-A was characterized by cDNA cloning (Betsholtz et al. 1986) and most cell lines express PDGF-A and secrete PDGF-AA homodimers (Heldin et al. 1986), whereas PDGF-BB homodimers are produced by SSV-transformed or PDGF-B-expressing cells. The view of two encoding genes for PDGF dimers was corrected 20 years after the first description of PDGF when two additional PDGF genes were identified by Li et al. and Bergsten et al. (PDGF-C and PDGF-D) (Bergsten et al. 2001; Li et al. 2000). To current knowledge, the PDGF genes and polypeptides belong to a family of growth factors that also includes the VEGFs (see earlier) (Fredriksson et al. 2004).

Although the PDGFs play crucial roles during development, there is only limited evidence for, and knowledge about, their physiological functions in the adult. However, increased PDGF activity is important in several diseases and pathological conditions, and even causal pathogenic roles of the PDGFs have been established for some diseases. This might provide prospects for therapy, using PDGF antagonists. Intensive testing of PDGF receptor-inhibiting substances on the one hand and recombinant human PDGF-BB on the other hand is now taking place in preclinical models as well as in human clinical trials.

Nine different genes encode four different PDGF chains (PDGF-A, PDGF-B, PDGF-C, and PDGF-D) and five different VEGF chains (VEGF-A, VEGF-B, VEGF-C, VEGF-D, and placenta growth factor, PlGF) in mammals (Ferrara et al. 2003; Fredriksson et al. 2004) (Fig. 5.3). All PDGFs and VEGFs are dimers of disulfide-linked polypeptide chains (Heldin and Westermark 1999).

One heterodimer (PDGF-AB) has been demonstrated specifically in human platelets whose physiological importance remains unclear although its signaling properties have been shown to be different from those of the homodimers (Ekman et al. 1999; Stroobant and Waterfield 1984).

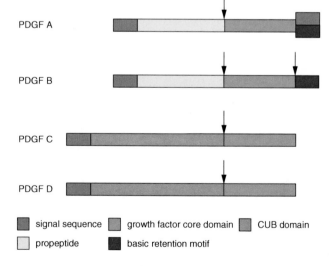

Fig. 5.3 Mammalian PDGFs. *Arrows* indicate proteolytic cleavage sites

■ signal sequence   ■ growth factor core domain   ■ CUB domain
□ propeptide   ■ basic retention motif

The nonoverlapping endogenous expression patterns of PDGF-A and PDGF-B (Hoch and Soriano 2003) suggest that heterodimers are infrequent in vivo. Also, there is no evidence for genetic interactions between PDGF-A and PDGF-B (Li et al. 2000). Thus, homodimers appear to dominate, at least during development. Mammalian PDGFs and VEGFs separate into four distinguishable classes of proteins (VEGF structure and isoforms shown earlier). All members have a growth factor core domain containing a set of cysteine residues. The core domain is necessary and sufficient for receptor binding and activation. The classification into PDGFs or VEGFs is based on receptor binding. The model that PDGFs and VEGFs are selective for their own receptors had been generally accepted until recently this was challenged by the demonstration that VEGF-A may bind to and activate PDGF receptors in bone-marrow-derived mesenchymal stem cells (Ball et al. 2007). The view that VEGFs target mainly endothelial cells, whereas mesenchymal cells are targeted by PDGFs is also called into question by the study mentioned earlier and by findings that VEGF-C and PDGF-A both regulate oligodendrocyte development, however, through distinct receptors. Both VEGFs and PDGFs also appear to be of importance in hematopoietic development, neurogenesis, and neuroprotection (Andrae et al. 2008).

5.3.2
PDGF Receptors

PDGFs act via two RTKs that share structures with c-Kit, c-Fms, and Flt3. The domain structures include five extracellular immunoglobulin loops and an intracellular tyrosine kinase (TK) domain (Fig. 5.4).

Receptor dimerization is promoted by ligand binding. The dimerization then initiates signaling. Depending on ligand configuration and the pattern of receptor expression, different receptor dimers may form (Heldin and Westermark 1999). Only a few interactions between PDGF and the PDGF receptors have been shown in vivo, whereas in cell culture experiments, the interactions seem to be multiple and complex. An overview of PDGF receptor signal transduction mechanisms is provided in further reviews on this topic (Heldin and Westermark 1999; Ronnstrand and Heldin 2001; Tallquist and Kazlauskas 2004).

5.3.3
PDGF Ligand and Receptor Expression Patterns

Although there is evidence for paracrine as well as autocrine functions of PDGF, autocrine roles, similar to those recently described for VEGF-A in endothelial cells (Lee et al. 2007), have not been demonstrated for the PDGFs. Their function as paracrine growth factors seems to be of greater importance; they act locally to drive different cellular responses (Betsholtz 2004; Hoch and Soriano 2003). The expression patterns of PDGF and PDGFR are spatio-temporally regulated in vivo during development and in some physiological hypertrophic responses. Expression of PDGF in cultured cells is dynamic and responds to certain stimuli, for example, low oxygen tension, thrombin, cytokines, and growth factors including PDGF itself (Heldin and Westermark 1999). Expression of PDGF-A also increases in human uterine SMCs during pregnancy (physiological hypertrophy). Similarly, the expression of PDGFR is dynamic. In physiological conditions, the expression of PDGFR on mesenchymal cells is low in vivo but increases in conditions of inflammation. Several factors induce PDGFR expression, including TGF-β, estrogen, interleukin-1 (IL-1), fibroblast growth factor-2 (FGF-2), tumor necrosis factor-α, and lipopolysaccharide (Heldin and Westermark 1999). Although the detailed expression patterns of the individual PDGF ligands and receptors are complex and have been reviewed elsewhere

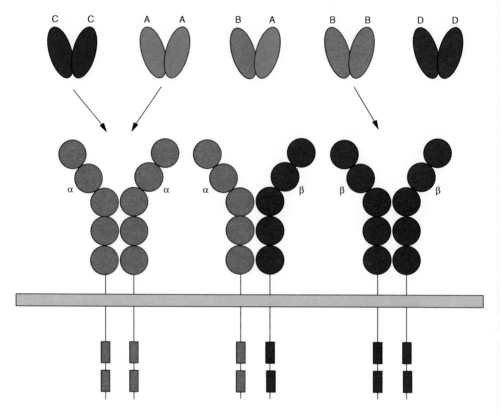

Fig. 5.4 PDGF and PDGF receptor interactions. Each part of the PDGF dimer interacts with the PDGFR and thus influences receptor configuration and activity. *Arrows* show interactions which have been observed to be of importance in mammalian development

(Heldin and Westermark 1999; Hoch and Soriano 2003), there are some general patterns of expression: PDGF-B is mainly expressed in vascular endothelial cells, megakaryocytes, and neurons. PDGF-A and PDGF-C are expressed in epithelial cells, muscle, and neuronal progenitors. PDGF-D expression has been described in fibroblasts and SMCs at certain locations but is less well-characterized. PDGFR-α is expressed in mesenchymal cells as well as in subtypes of mesenchymal progenitors in lung, skin, and intestine and in pericytes of the vessel wall. In mesenchymal progenitors, a particularly strong expression of PDGFR-α has been described. The PDGF and PDGFR genes are located on different chromosomes. Their transcriptional

regulation seems mostly independent. The transcriptional regulation of the PDGF-A and PDGF-B genes has been extensively studied and is reviewed elsewhere (Heldin and Westermark 1999; Kaetzel 2003). The transcriptional regulation of PDGF-C and PDGF-D and the PDGFRs has not been widely studied to date.

5.3.4
PDGF Biosynthesis, Secretion, and Distribution

There are control mechanisms of PDGF biosynthesis and processing at multiple levels. Biosynthesis and processing vary for the different PDGFs. There is currently no evidence for regulated secretion of the PDGFs. PDGFs instead appear to be constitutively released (Fruttiger et al. 2000). PDGF-A and PDGF-B become disulfide-linked into dimers already as propeptides. PDGF-C and PDGF-D have been less studied in this regard. Intracellularly, the N-terminal prodomains of PDGF-A and PDGF-B are removed by furin or related pro-protein convertases (for review, see (Fredriksson et al. 2004)). N-terminal processing is necessary for PDGF-A to acquire receptor-binding ability (for review, see (Fredriksson et al. 2004; Heldin and Westermark 1999)). Likewise, PDGF-B also requires N-terminal propeptide removal to become active. PDGF-C and PDGF-D are not processed intracellularly but are instead secreted as conditionally inactive ligands (Fredriksson et al. 2004; Reigstad et al. 2005). Dissociation of the growth factor domain from the CUB domain leads to activation in the extra-cellular space. Plasmin and tissue plasminogen activator (tPA) have been shown to remove the CUB domain in PDGF-C proteolytically, leading to biological activity (Fredriksson et al. 2004). Although the endogenous protease responsible for PDGF-C activation in vivo remains to be identified, tPA endogenously expressed in cultured fibroblasts activates PDGF-CC expressed by the same cells. Activation of PDGF-D can also take place by plasmin cleavage, but not tPA cleavage (Fredriksson et al. 2004). The tPA needs to interact with both the CUB domain and the core domain in order to cleave and activate PDGF-C, which likely explains its specificity. Biological activity and action range of growth factors, cytokines, and morphogens is explained by their uneven distribution with gradients and depots. Binding to extracellular matrix components plays an important role for the diffusion of PDGF in the tissue interstitium. The binding is attained partly by the positively charged C-terminal motifs (referred to as retention motifs) for PDGF-A and PDGF-B. The C-terminal motifs contain a high proportion of basic amino acid residues. PDGF-C and

PDGF-D lack basic retention motifs. Still, the existence of CUB domains results in protein–protein and protein–carbohydrate interactions in other contexts. This may be a regulatory factor for extracellular distribution of constitutively inactive PDGF-C and PDGF-D. Proteolytic processing determines the retention motifs in PDGF-B, whereas alternative splicing is the major determinant for the retention motif in PDGF-A. Alternative splicing of the PDGF-A transcript is specific for different cell types and also differs among tumor cell lines (Afrakhte et al. 1996) and in different organs during development. The C-terminal proteolytic processing of PDGF-B may take place intracellularly or extracellularly. There are hints that thrombin is the endogenous protease for extracellular proteolysis, and thus might release endogenously expressed PDGF-B adherent to the cell surface and the extracellular matrix (Kelly et al. 1993; Soyombo and DiCorleto 1994).

PDGF interacts with heparin and heparan sulfate proteoglycans (HSPGs) like many other growth factor and morphogens as well, and the roles of these interactions remained unclear until phenotypic analysis of PDGF-B retention motif knockout mice were carried out by different groups (Abramsson et al. 2007; Feyzi et al. 1997; Hacker et al. 2005; Lin et al. 2004; Lustig et al. 1999). Targeted deletion of the retention motif led to detachment of pericytes from the microvessel wall (Abramsson et al. 2003; Lindblom et al. 2003). Reduced heparan sulfate (HS) N-sulfation (caused by lack of the responsible enzyme N-deacetylase/N- sulfotransferase-1) similarly led to pericyte detachment and delayed pericyte migration in vivo (Abramsson et al. 2007). This might be caused by reduced PDGF-BB binding to HS. PDGF-BB/HS interaction appears to depend on overall N- and O-sulfation of HS. Considering these observations, a model in which PDGF-BB secreted from endothelial cells interacts with HS at the endothelial surface or in the periendothelial matrix can be developed. Consecutively, this would lead to local deposits of PDGF-BB that are critical for the correct investment of pericytes in the vessel wall. HS binding is also necessary for proper localization and function of VEGF-A (Ruhrberg et al. 2002).

PDGF also binds to certain non-HSPG extracellular proteins. The physiological significance of these interactions remains unclear. Binding of PDGF-B to α-2-macroglobulin (Bonner et al. 1995; Bonner and Osornio-Vargas 1995) has been observed. In this context, α-2-macroglobulin is potentially acting as a scavenger for PDGF-B through low-density lipoprotein (LDL) receptor-related protein (LRP) receptors on macrophages and other cells (Bonner et al. 1995). PDGF-B also binds to SPARC and adiponectin, which may keep the growth factor in the extracellular space (Arita et al. 2002; Raines et al. 1992; Raines and Ross 1992).

5.3.5
PDGFR Signal Transduction

Dimerization is crucial in PDGF receptor activation as it causes receptor autophosphorylation on tyrosine residues in the intracellular domain (Kelly et al. 1991). By autophosphorylation the receptor kinase is activated and docking sites for downstream signaling molecules are allocated (Kazlauskas and Cooper 1989). Docking of receptor substrates and further signal transmission involves protein–protein interactions. For these interactions specific domains are essential; for example, Src homology 2 (SH2) and phosphotyrosine-binding (PTB) domains recognizing phosphorylated tyrosines, SH3 domains recognizing proline-rich regions, pleckstrin homology (PH) domains recognizing membrane phospholipids, and PDZ domains recognizing C-terminal-specific sequences (for review, see (Heldin et al. 1998)). Binding to specific sites on the phosphorylated receptors is mostly affected by the SH2 domains of the PDGFR effectors. PDGFR-α and PDGFR-β signaling involves several well-described signaling pathways, for example, Ras-MAPK, PI3K, and PLC. These signaling pathways are involved in various cellular and developmental responses (Fig. 5.5).

PDGFRs connect to Ras-MAPK through the adaptor proteins Grb2 and Shc. Grb2 binds the activated PDGFR through its SH2 domain and complexes Sos1 through its SH3 domains. Sos1 then activates Ras, followed by downstream activation of Raf-1 and the MAPK cascade. Gene transcription is activated by MAPK signaling, leading to stimulation of cell growth, differentiation, and migration (Bar-Sagi and Feramisco 1986; Campbell et al. 1995). PI3K is a family of enzymes phosphorylating phosphoinositides, and effectors of PI3K signaling include serine/threonine kinases such as Akt/PKB (Burgering and Coffer 1995; Franke et al. 1995), some members of the PKC family including atypical isoforms (Akimoto et al. 1996; Nakanishi et al. 1993), p70 S6 kinase (Chung et al. 1994), JNK (Lopez-Ilasaca et al. 1997), and small GTPases of the Rho family (Nobes et al. 1995). Activation of the PI3K pathway by PDGFRs stimulates actin reorganization, directed cell movements, cell growth, and inhibition of apoptosis (Hu et al. 1995). PLC-γ binds PDGFRs, which results in its phosphorylation and thereby activation (for review, see (Tallquist and Kazlauskas 2004)). PLC-γ activation leads to mobilization of intracellular calcium ions and the activation of PKC (Berridge 1993a, b). The effects of PDGFR-β-mediated PLC-γ activation include promotion of cell growth and motility (Kundra et al. 1994). Several additional signaling molecules are engaged by PDGFRs, including enzymes, adaptors, and transcription factors. Activation of the Src TK promotes Myc transcription and mitogenic responses (for review, see (Erpel and Courtneidge 1995)). PKC-δ is phosphorylated by PDGFR-β, leading to its activation and translocation to the cell membrane. This in turn promotes cell differentiation (Li and Pierce 1996). STAT transcription factors may bind to

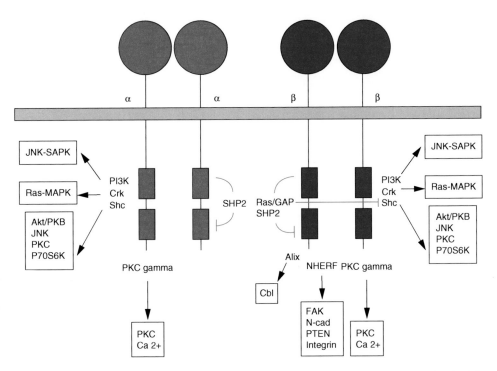

Fig. 5.5 PDGFR signal transduction: PDGFR α and β with intracellular domains. Negative feedback is illustrated in red. *Arrows* show linkage to important signaling pathways and effectors

PDGF receptors, causing their phosphorylation and activation (Darnell 1997). Interactions between PDGF receptors and integrins have been reported, and these interactions enhance cell proliferation, migration, and survival (Assoian 1997; Frisch and Ruoslahti 1997). PDGFR interaction with integrins helps localizing PDGFRs and interacting molecules at focal adhesions, which are sites where several signaling pathways initiate and cross-talk (Clark and Brugge 1995). Recently, Na$^+$/H$^+$ exchanger regulatory factors (NHERFs) were observed to bind PDGFR-β and thereby cause a linkage with focal adherence kinase and the cortical actin cytoskeleton (James et al. 2004), as well as to N-cadherin (Theisen et al. 2007) and the phosphatase PTEN (Takahashi et al. 2006).

Feedback control mechanisms accurately regulate PDGF signaling. Stimulatory and inhibitory signals arise in a parallel way. The final response depends on the balance between these signals (Heldin et al. 1998). The SHP-2 tyrosine phosphatase binds PDGFR through its SH2 domain and dephosphorylates the receptor and its substrates (Lechleider et al. 1993). The negative regulator of Ras, Ras-GAP, also binds PDGFR-β through its SH2 domain (Fantl et al. 1992).

5.3.6
Cellular Responses to PDGFR Signaling

There are certain rapid cellular responses to PDGFs that proceed within seconds to minutes after PDGFR activation. These reactions are not dependent on gene expression and protein synthesis. There are similarities between responses caused by PDGFR-α and PDGFR-β, nevertheless the responses are not identical. Both receptors are able to promote the rearrangement of actin filaments, but only PDGFR-β causes the formation of circular ruffles. PDGFR-β also mobilizes calcium ions more efficiently than PDGFR-α does(Diliberto et al. 1992; Fatatis and Miller 1997). Inhibition of cell communication by phosphorylated gap junctions is observed to be caused by PDGFR-β (Hossain et al. 1998). It is unclear whether this ability is shared with PDGFR-α.

Like other RTKs, PDGFRs initiate fast transcriptional changes involving so-called immediate early genes (IEGs) (Cochran et al. 1983). IEGs are direct targets of the transcription factors, which get activated through various signaling pathways by posttranslational modification. The IEG responses seem to be necessary for many of the long-term effects of PDGFs in vitro and in vivo. The extent of specificity contributed to PDGFR signaling by IEG responses remains unclear. Different RTKs induce similar or even identical sets of IEGs (Fambrough et al. 1999). Furthermore, different signaling pathways activated by the same receptor (PDGFR-β) induce largely overlapping sets of IEGs in vitro (Fambrough et al. 1999). These studies implicate that quantitative rather than qualitative differences in the IEG responses are regulators for the specific responses to different RTKs and signaling pathways. In vivo analysis of an allelic series of pdgfrb tyrosine-to-phenylalanine mutations supports this view: it leads to disrupting connection to different substrates and signaling pathways. Mutations in single or multiple tyrosine residues caused quantitatively different but qualitatively similar developmental effects (Tallquist et al. 2003; Tallquist and Soriano 2003). In contrast, similar analyzes of PDGFR-α revealed a remarkable difference in the roles of the downstream signaling pathways. For PDGFR-β, there is no or only limited consequence from the disruption of signaling through PI3K alone (Heuchel et al. 1999; Tallquist et al. 2000). Quite contrary to this observation, PI3K is essential for PDGFR-α function during development (Klinghoffer et al.

2002). Deficient coupling to Src from PDGFR-α resulted in specific problems with the oligodendrocyte lineage. In contrast, other processes, such as skeletal development, remained normal.

There appears to be cooperation between different IEGs in their regulation of downstream cellular and developmental events. Analysis of gene trap mutants for >20 IEGs downstream from PDGFR signaling showed a striking degree of phenotypic overlap and genetic interaction. Different mutated IEGs produced qualitatively similar responses. Furthermore, the combination of mutations in several genes strengthened specific phenotypic outcomes known to depend on PDGFR signaling, such as craniofacial, cardiovascular, or kidney developmental processes (Schmahl et al. 2007).

The overlap and coincidence between signaling pathways, IEGs, and biological processes leads to a model in which specifity is determined by quantitative and spatial differences in dimension and duration of responses in the signaling cascade. Meanwhile, cell type- and context-specific PDGFR expression is the major reason for PDGFR specificity in developmental functions, and correlations between the expression patterns of the PDGFRs and their major sites of functions have been described (e.g., PDGFR-β is strongly expressed in pericyte progenitors). Lack of redundancy therefore depends in part on the different transcriptional regulation of the two pdgfr genes. If a PDGFR-β intracellular domain is knocked into the pdgfra gene, phenotypically normal animals are obtained, showing that PDGFR-β signaling might be a full substitute for PDGFR-α signaling if it is expressed in a spatially and temporally correct manner (Klinghoffer et al. 2001). In contrast, PDGFR-α signaling can only compensate for the loss of PDGFR-β signaling to some extent and targeted substitution in PDGFR-α with other RTK signaling domains also showed only partial rescue (Klinghoffer et al. 2001). Thus, specificity of PDGFR signaling might be obtained by a combination of cell type-specific expression and variable engagement of downstream signaling pathways.

Ligand occupancy of PDGFRs drives endocytotic receptor internalization, which is followed by lysosomal degradation, and according to this PDGFR signaling is temporally limited (Heldin et al. 1998; Sorkin et al. 1991). A lack of phosphatase TC-PTP, a negative regulator for PDGFR-β phosphorylation (Persson et al. 2004), signs for a recycling of PDGFR-β can be observed. PDGFR-α does not undergo such a recycling process (Karlsson et al. 2006). Trafficking toward lysosomal degradation of PDGFR-β depends on interactions with c-Cbl and receptor ubiquitination. Alix, an adapter protein which interacts with the C-terminal domain of PDGFR-β, facilitates ubiquitination and degradation of c-Cbl, and thus inhibits PDGFR-β-downregulation (Lennartsson et al. 2006).

5.3.7
PDGF and PDGFR in Malignancy

PDGF not only has an important role in many disease processes, but its role might even be causative, that is, in some malignancies, when genetic abnormalities cause uncontrolled PDGFR signaling in tumor cells. A functional role of PDGFR signaling has also been shown in various animal models by genetic or pharmacological loss-of-function-approaches, which implicates the reversibility of the disease process by PDGF pathway inhibitors. However, the limitation of this approach originates in the lack of specificity of all inhibitors currently available. Furthermore, it often remains unclear as to what degree the animal models are relevant for the corresponding human disease process. Considering these limitations, there is still a growing evidence for the involvement of PDGF signaling in several disease processes. Potent and nontoxic PDGFR inhibitors such as imatinib give augmenting possibilities to test theories about causative roles of

PDGF signaling in malignancy in humans too.

In general, two types of cells have been described to respond in a pathological way to PDGFs – SMCs and fibroblasts – leading to vessel wall pathologies and tissue fibrosis. PDGFR-β appears to be the dominant PDGFR involved in vascular pathology, whereas growing evidence in contrast suggests a crucial role for PDGFR-α signaling in various types of mesenchymal cell/fibroblast-driven pathologies. Thus, there is a certain homology between the pathological roles of PDGFRs and their developmental roles in which PDGFR-β signaling has a key role in vascular mural cell formation, whereas PDGFR-α has both general and specific roles in the development of various mesenchymal and fibroblastic cell compartments.

Six acquired capabilities of cancer cells are described in the review on hallmarks of cancer by Hanahan and Weinberg – self-sufficiency in growth signals, insensitivity to antigrowth signals, escape from apoptosis, sustained angiogenesis, tissue invasion and metastasis, and limitless replicative potential (Hanahan and Weinberg 2000).

Several studies have recently shown that self-sufficiency in growth signals may be established for certain cell types via autocrine growth stimulatory loops involving PDGF-B/PDGFR-β signaling (Andrae et al. 2008; Heldin and Westermark 1999).

Autocrine PDGF signaling drives proliferative expansion of clones of genetically unstable or preneoplasitc cells, which then become malignant by further genetic alteration and thus contributes to tumorigenesis. Johnsson et al. demonstrated no difference between autocrine PDGF stimulation compared to exogenous PDGF stimulation (Johnsson et al. 1985). In addition, Uhrbom et al. showed that PDGF stimulation by injection of PDGF-B producing retroviruses into the mouse brain results in a malignant phenotype only by the additive induction of genetic changes by the retrovirus

(Uhrbom et al. 1998). PDGF expression and autocrine signaling has been described particularly in human gliomas (Hermansson et al. 1988; Lokker et al. 2002; Nister et al. 1988), and an overexpression is likely to cause the formation of glioma-like tumors (Newton 2003; Uhrbom et al. 1998). Subsequently, inhibition of PDGF signaling (e.g., by administration of imatinib which has also been tested in clinical trials (Newton 2003)) slows down the growth of glioma-like tumors (Lokker et al. 2002; Uhrbom et al. 2000). The mechanism by which PDGF signaling induces the formation of gliomas is not well understood yet, but there is evidence for a link between PDGF signaling and TGFβ signaling via Smad2/3/4. Futhermore, genetic alterations also lead to overexpression and/or altered gene products. Several different mechanisms cause genetic changes, for example, amplification, translocations, and activating mutation, which have all been described in human tumors with high PDGF expression. Upregulation of PDGFR-α is observed again in human gliomas of all malignant grades; the higher the expression, the more malignant is the tumor (Hermanson et al. 1996; Smith and Jenkins 2000; Smith et al. 2000). Gene amplifications have also been described in other tumor entities such as oesophageal squamous cell carcinoma (Arai et al. 2003), sarcomas (Zhao et al. 2002), and epithelial carcinomas (see later). Gastrointestinal stroma tumors (GISTs) carry activating mutations in the Kit receptor tyrosine kinase. In a subset of GISTs with wild-type Kit, gain-of-function mutations in PDGFR-A have been observed (Heinrich et al. 2003; Hirota et al. 2003). Kit and PDGFR-α mutations are mutually exclusive, but around 90% of all GISTs carry one of the two mutations. Constitutive activation of the receptor is a consequence of PDGFR-α mutation found either in the juxtamembrane region or in any of the two TK domains. Signaling via PI3K and STAT3 seems to be crucial for this activation (for review, see (Ali et al. 2007).

In leukemias and myeloid disorders, several different translocations of the PDGFR-B gene have been described by Sirvent et al. (2003), but since most of these translocations are very rare, their exact role in leukemogenesis remains to be elucidated. In epithelial carcinomas, PDGF signaling is mostly described as acting in a paracrine fashion (Heldin and Westermark 1999). There is evidence, however, that autocrine PDGF signaling is also important for tumorigenesis in carcinomas with ectopic onset of PDGFR expression (Heldin et al. 1988).

Beyond the consequences of autocrine PDGF signaling as a proliferative stimulus, it also seems to be of importance in invasion and metastasis of epithelial malignancies.

Paracrine PDGF signaling is necessary to recruit different stromal cells (e.g., vascular and fibroblastic stromal cells) and to regulate their functions (Abramsson et al. 2003; Forsberg et al. 1993; Furuhashi et al. 2004; Pietras et al. 2001; Skobe and Fusenig 1998). This seems to be an explanation for the frequently compromised drug delivery to tumors (e.g., due to high interstitial pressure caused by PDGF signaling). Tumor stroma is composed of nonneoplastic cells and extracellular matrix recruited from the circulation or from neighboring cells and makes up a variable proportion of the total tumor mass. The stroma composition itself is varied as well. In stromal cells of carcinomas, PDGFR expression is frequent and is found in lung, colorectal, breast, skin, and different other carcinomas (see (Andrae et al. 2008; Heldin and Westermark 1999; Ostman 2004) for further review).

In conclusion, PDGF signaling contributes to the causes for three of the six cancer cell traits summarized by Hanahan and Weinberg: self-sufficient growth, angiogenesis, and metastasis, and moreover is partly responsible for resistance to cytotoxic therapy.

Thus, VEGF and PDGF both play important roles in neovascularization, in particular in several human malignancies. Oxygen and nutrient support must be provided by vasculature to enable a tumor to grow beyond 1–2 mm diameter. VEGF and PDGF are causally involved in an angiogenic switch, which then provides vasculature for the tumor. Different factors precede and cause the upregulation of PDGF and VEGF in malignancy, for example, oncogene activation, inhibition of tumor supressors, release of growth factors and tumor hxpoxia, and necrosis, and furthermore, a certain protection against apoptotic signals is provided for tumor vasculature. The characteristics of both VEGF and PDGF make them a putative therapeutic target for anticancer strategies.

References

Abramsson A, Kurup S, Busse M, Yamada S, Lindblom P, Schallmeiner E, Stenzel D, Sauvaget D, Ledin J, Ringvall M, Landegren U, Kjellen L, Bondjers G, Li JP, Lindahl U, Spillmann D, Betsholtz C, Gerhardt H (2007) Defective N-sulfation of heparan sulfate proteoglycans limits PDGF-BB binding and pericyte recruitment in vascular development. Genes Dev 21:316–331

Abramsson A, Lindblom P, Betsholtz C (2003) Endothelial and nonendothelial sources of PDGF-B regulate pericyte recruitment and influence vascular pattern formation in tumors. J Clin Invest 112:1142–1151

Achen MG, Jeltsch M, Kukk E, Makinen T, Vitali A, Wilks AF, Alitalo K, Stacker SA (1998) Vascular endothelial growth factor D (VEGF-D) is a ligand for the tyrosine kinases VEGF receptor 2 (Flk1) and VEGF receptor 3 (Flt4). Proc Natl Acad Sci U S A 95:548–553

Afrakhte M, Nister M, Ostman A, Westermark B, Paulsson Y (1996) Production of cell-associated PDGF-AA by a human sarcoma cell line: evidence for a latent autocrine effect. Int J Cancer 68:802–809

Aguayo A, Kantarjian HM, Estey EH, Giles FJ, Verstovsek S, Manshouri T, Gidel C, O'Brien S, Keating MJ, Albitar M (2002) Plasma vascular endothelial growth factor levels have prognostic significance in patients with acute myeloid leukemia but not in patients with myelodysplastic syndromes. Cancer 95:1923–1930

Akimoto K, Takahashi R, Moriya S, Nishioka N, Takayanagi J, Kimura K, Fukui Y, Osada S,

Mizuno K, Hirai S, Kazlauskas A, Ohno S (1996) EGF or PDGF receptors activate atypical PKClambda through phosphatidylinositol 3-kinase. EMBO J 15:788–798

Ali Y, Lin Y, Gharibo MM, Gounder MK, Stein MN, Lagattuta TF, Egorin MJ, Rubin EH, Poplin EA (2007) Phase I and pharmacokinetic study of imatinib mesylate (Gleevec) and gemcitabine in patients with refractory solid tumors. Clin Cancer Res 13:5876–5882

Alitalo K, Carmeliet P (2002) Molecular mechanisms of lymphangiogenesis in health and disease. Cancer Cell 1:219–227

Amaya H, Tanigawa N, Lu C, Matsumura M, Shimomatsuya T, Horiuchi T, Muraoka R (1997) Association of vascular endothelial growth factor expression with tumor angiogenesis, survival and thymidine phosphorylase/platelet-derived endothelial cell growth factor expression in human colorectal cancer. Cancer Lett 119:227–235

Andrae J, Gallini R, Betsholtz C (2008) Role of platelet-derived growth factors in physiology and medicine. Genes Dev 22:1276–1312

Arai H, Ueno T, Tangoku A, Yoshino S, Abe T, Kawauchi S, Oga A, Furuya T, Oka M, Sasaki K (2003) Detection of amplified oncogenes by genome DNA microarrays in human primary esophageal squamous cell carcinoma: comparison with conventional comparative genomic hybridization analysis. Cancer Genet Cytogenet 146:16–21

Arita Y, Kihara S, Ouchi N, Maeda K, Kuriyama H, Okamoto Y, Kumada M, Hotta K, Nishida M, Takahashi M, Nakamura T, Shimomura I, Muraguchi M, Ohmoto Y, Funahashi T, Matsuzawa Y (2002) Adipocyte-derived plasma protein adiponectin acts as a platelet-derived growth factor-BB-binding protein and regulates growth factor-induced common postreceptor signal in vascular smooth muscle cell. Circulation 105:2893–2898

Asano M, Yukita A, Matsumoto T, Kondo S, Suzuki H (1995) Inhibition of tumor growth and metastasis by an immunoneutralizing monoclonal antibody to human vascular endothelial growth factor/vascular permeability factor121. Cancer Res 55:5296–5301

Assoian RK (1997) Anchorage-dependent cell cycle progression. J Cell Biol 136:1–4

Ball SG, Shuttle CA, Kielty CM (2007) Mesenchymal stem cells and neovascularization: role of platelet-derived growth factor receptors. J Cell Mol Med 11:1012–1030

Bar-Sagi D, Feramisco JR (1986) Induction of membrane ruffling and fluid-phase pinocytosis in quiescent fibroblasts by ras proteins. Science 233:1061–1068

Bergsten E, Uutela M, Li X, Pietras K, Ostman A, Heldin CH, Alitalo K, Eriksson U (2001) PDGF-D is a specific, protease-activated ligand for the PDGF beta-receptor. Nat Cell Biol 3: 512–516

Berridge MJ (1993a) Cell signalling. A tale of two messengers. Nature 365:388–389

Berridge MJ (1993b) Inositol trisphosphate and calcium signalling. Nature 361:315–325

Betsholtz C (2004) Insight into the physiological functions of PDGF through genetic studies in mice. Cytokine Growth Factor Rev 15:215–228

Betsholtz C, Johnsson A, Heldin CH, Westermark B, Lind P, Urdea MS, Eddy R, Shows TB, Philpott K, Mellor AL et al (1986) cDNA sequence and chromosomal localization of human platelet-derived growth factor A-chain and its expression in tumour cell lines. Nature 320:695–699

Bonner JC, Badgett A, Hoffman M, Lindroos PM (1995) Inhibition of platelet-derived growth factor-BB-induced fibroblast proliferation by plasmin-activated alpha 2-macroglobulin is mediated via an alpha 2-macroglobulin receptor/low density lipoprotein receptor-related protein-dependent mechani. J Biol Chem 270:6389–6395

Bonner JC, Osornio-Vargas AR (1995) Differential binding and regulation of platelet-derived growth factor A and B chain isoforms by alpha 2-macroglobulin. J Biol Chem 270:16236–16242

Boocock CA, Charnock-Jones DS, Sharkey AM, McLaren J, Barker PJ, Wright KA, Twentyman PR, Smith SK (1995) Expression of vascular endothelial growth factor and its receptors flt and KDR in ovarian carcinoma. J Natl Cancer Inst 87:506–516

Borgstrom P, Bourdon MA, Hillan KJ, Sriramarao P, Ferrara N (1998) Neutralizing anti-vascular endothelial growth factor antibody completely inhibits angiogenesis and growth of human prostate carcinoma micro tumors in vivo. Prostate 35:1–10

Borgstrom P, Gold DP, Hillan KJ, Ferrara N (1999) Importance of VEGF for breast cancer angiogenesis in vivo: implications from intravital microscopy of combination treatments with an anti-VEGF neutralizing monoclonal antibody and doxorubicin. Anticancer Res 19:4203–4214

Borgstrom P, Hillan KJ, Sriramarao P, Ferrara N (1996) Complete inhibition of angiogenesis and growth of microtumors by anti-vascular endothelial growth factor neutralizing antibody: novel concepts of angiostatic therapy from intravital videomicroscopy. Cancer Res 56:4032–4039

Brown LF, Berse B, Jackman RW, Tognazzi K, Guidi AJ, Dvorak HF, Senger DR, Connolly JL, Schnitt SJ (1995) Expression of vascular permeability factor (vascular endothelial growth factor) and its receptors in breast cancer. Hum Pathol 26:86–91

Brown LF, Berse B, Jackman RW, Tognazzi K, Manseau EJ, Dvorak HF, Senger DR (1993a) Increased expression of vascular permeability factor (vascular endothelial growth factor) and its receptors in kidney and bladder carcinomas. Am J Pathol 143:1255–1262

Brown LF, Berse B, Jackman RW, Tognazzi K, Manseau EJ, Senger DR, Dvorak HF (1993b) Expression of vascular permeability factor (vascular endothelial growth factor) and its receptors in adenocarcinomas of the gastrointestinal tract. Cancer Res 53:4727–4735

Burgering BM, Coffer PJ (1995) Protein kinase B (c-Akt) in phosphatidylinositol-3-OH kinase signal transduction. Nature 376:599–602

Campbell JS, Seger R, Graves JD, Graves LM, Jensen AM, Krebs EG (1995) The MAP kinase cascade. Recent Prog Horm Res 50:131–159

Carmeliet P (1999) Developmental biology. Controlling the cellular brakes. Nature 401:657–658

Carmeliet P (2003) Blood vessels and nerves: common signals, pathways and diseases. Nat Rev Genet 4:710–720

Carmeliet P, Ferreira V, Breier G, Pollefeyt S, Kieckens L, Gertsenstein M, Fahrig M, Vandenhoeck A, Harpal K, Eberhardt C, Declercq C, Pawling J, Moons L, Collen D, Risau W, Nagy A (1996) Abnormal blood vessel development and lethality in embryos lacking a single VEGF allele. Nature 380:435–439

Carmeliet P, Ng YS, Nuyens D, Theilmeier G, Brusselmans K, Cornelissen I, Ehler E, Kakkar VV, Stalmans I, Mattot V, Perriard JC, Dewerchin M, Flameng W, Nagy A, Lupu F, Moons L, Collen D, D'Amore PA, Shima DT (1999) Impaired myocardial angiogenesis and ischemic cardiomyopathy in mice lacking the vascular endothelial growth factor isoforms VEGF164 and VEGF188. Nat Med 5:495–502

Cho NK, Keyes L, Johnson E, Heller J, Ryner L, Karim F, Krasnow MA (2002) Developmental control of blood cell migration by the Drosophila VEGF pathway. Cell 108:865–876

Chung J, Grammer TC, Lemon KP, Kazlauskas A, Blenis J (1994) PDGF- and insulin-dependent pp 70S6k activation mediated by phosphatidylinositol-3-OH kinase. Nature 370:71–75

Clark EA, Brugge JS (1995) Integrins and signal transduction pathways: the road taken. Science 268:233–239

Cochran BH, Reffel AC, Stiles CD (1983) Molecular cloning of gene sequences regulated by platelet-derived growth factor. Cell 33:939–947

Cohen T, Nahari D, Cerem LW, Neufeld G, Levi BZ (1996) Interleukin 6 induces the expression of vascular endothelial growth factor. J Biol Chem 271:736–741

Connolly DT, Heuvelman DM, Nelson R, Olander JV, Eppley BL, Delfino JJ, Siegel NR, Leimgruber RM, Feder J (1989a) Tumor vascular permeability factor stimulates endothelial cell growth and angiogenesis. J Clin Invest 84:1470–1478

Connolly DT, Olander JV, Heuvelman D, Nelson R, Monsell R, Siegel N, Haymore BL, Leimgruber R, Feder J (1989b) Human vascular permeability factor. Isolation from U937 cells. J Biol Chem 264:20017–20024

Cornali E, Zietz C, Benelli R, Weninger W, Masiello L, Breier G, Tschachler E, Albini A, Sturzl M (1996) Vascular endothelial growth factor regulates angiogenesis and vascular permeability in Kaposi's sarcoma. Am J Pathol 149: 1851–1869

Cunningham SA, Waxham MN, Arrate PM, Brock TA (1995) Interaction of the Flt-1 tyrosine kinase receptor with the p85 subunit of phosphatidylinositol 3-kinase. Mapping of a novel site involved in binding. J Biol Chem 270:20254–20257

Darnell JE Jr (1997) STATs and gene regulation. Science 277:1630–1635

de Vries C, Escobedo JA, Ueno H, Houck K, Ferrara N, Williams LT (1992) The fms-like tyrosine kinase, a receptor for vascular endothelial growth factor. Science 255:989–991

Dias S, Hattori K, Zhu Z, Heissig B, Choy M, Lane W, Wu Y, Chadburn A, Hyjek E, Gill M, Hicklin DJ, Witte L, Moore MA, Rafii S (2000) Autocrine stimulation of VEGFR-2 activates human leukemic cell growth and migration. J Clin Invest 106:511–521

Diliberto PA, Gordon GW, Yu CL, Earp HS, Herman B (1992) Platelet-derived growth factor (PDGF) alpha receptor activation modulates the calcium mobilizing activity of the PDGF beta receptor in Balb/c3T3 fibroblasts. J Biol Chem 267:11888–11897

Doolittle RF, Hunkapiller MW, Hood LE, Devare SG, Robbins KC, Aaronson SA, Antoniades HN (1983) Simian sarcoma virus onc gene, v-sis, is derived from the gene (or genes) encoding a platelet-derived growth factor. Science 221:275–277

Duchek P, Somogyi K, Jekely G, Beccari S, Rorth P (2001) Guidance of cell migration by the Drosophila PDGF/VEGF receptor. Cell 107:17–26

Eichmann A, Corbel C, Nataf V, Vaigot P, Breant C, Le Douarin NM (1997) Ligand-dependent development of the endothelial and hemopoietic lineages from embryonic mesodermal cells expressing vascular endothelial growth factor receptor 2. Proc Natl Acad Sci U S A 94:5141–5146

Ekman S, Thuresson ER, Heldin CH, Ronnstrand L (1999) Increased mitogenicity of an alphabeta heterodimeric PDGF receptor complex correlates with lack of RasGAP binding. Oncogene 18:2481–2488

Ellis LM, Takahashi Y, Fenoglio CJ, Cleary KR, Bucana CD, Evans DB (1998) Vessel counts and vascular endothelial growth factor expression in pancreatic adenocarcinoma. Eur J Cancer 34: 337–340

Erpel T, Courtneidge SA (1995) Src family protein tyrosine kinases and cellular signal transduction pathways. Curr Opin Cell Biol 7:176–182

Fambrough D, McClure K, Kazlauskas A, Lander ES (1999) Diverse signaling pathways activated by growth factor receptors induce broadly overlapping, rather than independent, sets of genes. Cell 97:727–741

Fantl WJ, Escobedo JA, Martin GA, Turck CW, del Rosario M, McCormick F, Williams LT (1992) Distinct phosphotyrosines on a growth factor receptor bind to specific molecules that mediate different signaling pathways. Cell 69:413–423

Fatatis A, Miller RJ (1997) Platelet-derived growth factor (PDGF)-induced Ca2+ signaling in the CG4 oligodendroglial cell line and in transformed oligodendrocytes expressing the beta-PDGF receptor. J Biol Chem 272:4351–4358

Ferrara N, Carver-Moore K, Chen H, Dowd M, Lu L, O'Shea KS, Powell-Braxton L, Hillan KJ, Moore MW (1996) Heterozygous embryonic lethality induced by targeted inactivation of the VEGF gene. Nature 380:439–442

Ferrara N, Chen H, Davis-Smyth T, Gerber HP, Nguyen TN, Peers D, Chisholm V, Hillan KJ, Schwall RH (1998) Vascular endothelial growth factor is essential for corpus luteum angiogenesis. Nat Med 4:336–340

Ferrara N, Davis-Smyth T (1997) The biology of vascular endothelial growth factor. Endocr Rev 18:4–25

Ferrara N, Gerber HP (2001) The role of vascular endothelial growth factor in angiogenesis. Acta Haematol 106:148–156

Ferrara N, Gerber HP, LeCouter J (2003) The biology of VEGF and its receptors. Nat Med 9:669–676

Feyzi E, Lustig F, Fager G, Spillmann D, Lindahl U, Salmivirta M (1997) Characterization of heparin and heparan sulfate domains binding to the long splice variant of platelet-derived growth factor A chain. J Biol Chem 272:5518–5524

Fiedler W, Mesters R, Tinnefeld H, Loges S, Staib P, Duhrsen U, Flasshove M, Ottmann OG, Jung W, Cavalli F, Kuse R, Thomalla J, Serve H, O'Farrell AM, Jacobs M, Brega NM, Scigalla P, Hossfeld DK, Berdel WE (2003) A phase 2 clinical study of SU5416 in patients with refractory acute myeloid leukemia. Blood 102:2763–2767

Folkman J (1971) Tumor angiogenesis: therapeutic implications. N Engl J Med 285:1182–1186

Folkman J, Merler E, Abernathy C, Williams G (1971) Isolation of a tumor factor responsible for angiogenesis. J Exp Med 133:275–288

Fong GH, Rossant J, Gertsenstein M, Breitman ML (1995) Role of the Flt-1 receptor tyrosine kinase in regulating the assembly of vascular endothelium. Nature 376:66–70

Forsberg K, Valyi-Nagy I, Heldin CH, Herlyn M, Westermark B (1993) Platelet-derived growth factor (PDGF) in oncogenesis: development of a vascular connective tissue stroma in xenotransplanted human melanoma producing PDGF-BB. Proc Natl Acad Sci U S A 90:393–397

Frank S, Hubner G, Breier G, Longaker MT, Greenhalgh DG, Werner S (1995) Regulation of vascular endothelial growth factor expression in cultured keratinocytes. Implications for normal and impaired wound healing. J Biol Chem 270:12607–12613

Franke TF, Yang SI, Chan TO, Datta K, Kazlauskas A, Morrison DK, Kaplan DR, Tsichlis PN (1995) The protein kinase encoded by the Akt proto-oncogene is a target of the PDGF-activated phosphatidylinositol 3-kinase. Cell 81:727–736

Fredriksson L, Li H, Eriksson U (2004) The PDGF family: four gene products form five dimeric isoforms. Cytokine Growth Factor Rev 15:197–204

Frisch SM, Ruoslahti E (1997) Integrins and anoikis. Curr Opin Cell Biol 9:701–706

Fruttiger M, Calver AR, Richardson WD (2000) Platelet-derived growth factor is constitutively secreted from neuronal cell bodies but not from axons. Curr Biol 10:1283–1286

Fuh G, Li B, Crowley C, Cunningham B, Wells JA (1998) Requirements for binding and signaling of the kinase domain receptor for vascular endothelial growth factor. J Biol Chem 273:11197–11204

Fukumura D, Xavier R, Sugiura T, Chen Y, Park EC, Lu N, Selig M, Nielsen G, Taksir T, Jain RK, Seed B (1998) Tumor induction of VEGF promoter activity in stromal cells. Cell 94:715–725

Furuhashi M, Sjoblom T, Abramsson A, Ellingsen J, Micke P, Li H, Bergsten-Folestad E, Eriksson U, Heuchel R, Betsholtz C, Heldin CH, Ostman A (2004) Platelet-derived growth factor production by B16 melanoma cells leads to increased pericyte abundance in tumors and an associated increase in tumor growth rate. Cancer Res 64:2725–2733

Gasparini G, Toi M, Gion M, Verderio P, Dittadi R, Hanatani M, Matsubara I, Vinante O, Bonoldi E, Boracchi P, Gatti C, Suzuki H, Tominaga T (1997) Prognostic significance of vascular endothelial growth factor protein in node-negative breast carcinoma. J Natl Cancer Inst 89:139–147

Gerber HP, Ferrara N (2003) The role of VEGF in normal and neoplastic hematopoiesis. J Mol Med 81:20–31

Gerber HP, Kowalski J, Sherman D, Eberhard DA, Ferrara N (2000) Complete inhibition of rhabdomyosarcoma xenograft growth and neovascularization requires blockade of both tumor and host vascular endothelial growth factor. Cancer Res 60:6253–6258

Gerber HP, McMurtrey A, Kowalski J, Yan M, Keyt BA, Dixit V, Ferrara N (1998) Vascular endothelial growth factor regulates endothelial cell survival through the phosphatidylinositol 3'-kinase/Akt signal transduction pathway. Requirement for Flk-1/KDR activation. J Biol Chem 273:30336–30343

Goldberg MA, Schneider TJ (1994) Similarities between the oxygen-sensing mechanisms regulating the expression of vascular endothelial growth factor and erythropoietin. J Biol Chem 269:4355–4359

Goldman CK, Kendall RL, Cabrera G, Soroceanu L, Heike Y, Gillespie GY, Siegal GP, Mao X, Bett AJ, Huckle WR, Thomas KA, Curiel DT (1998) Paracrine expression of a native soluble vascular endothelial growth factor receptor inhibits tumor growth, metastasis, and mortality rate. Proc Natl Acad Sci U S A 95:8795–8800

Goldmann E (1907) Growth of the malignant disease in man and the lower animals with special reference to vascular system. Lancet 170:1236–1240

Grugel S, Finkenzeller G, Weindel K, Barleon B, Marme D (1995) Both v-Ha-Ras and v-Raf stimulate expression of the vascular endothelial growth factor in NIH 3T3 cells. J Biol Chem 270:25915–25919

Grunstein J, Masbad JJ, Hickey R, Giordano F, Johnson RS (2000) Isoforms of vascular endothelial growth factor act in a coordinate fashion to recruit and expand tumor vasculature. Mol Cell Biol 20:7282–7291

Guidi AJ, Abu-Jawdeh G, Tognazzi K, Dvorak HF, Brown LF (1996) Expression of vascular permeability factor (vascular endothelial growth factor) and its receptors in endometrial carcinoma. Cancer 78:454–460

Hacker U, Nybakken K, Perrimon N (2005) Heparan sulphate proteoglycans: the sweet side of development. Nat Rev Mol Cell Biol 6:530–541

Hanahan D, Folkman J (1996) Patterns and emerging mechanisms of the angiogenic switch during tumorigenesis. Cell 86:353–364

Hanahan D, Weinberg RA (2000) The hallmarks of cancer. Cell 100:57–70

Hatva E, Kaipainen A, Mentula P, Jaaskelainen J, Paetau A, Haltia M, Alitalo K (1995) Expression of endothelial cell-specific receptor tyrosine kinases and growth factors in human brain tumors. Am J Pathol 146:368–378

Heinrich MC, Corless CL, Duensing A, McGreevey L, Chen CJ, Joseph N, Singer S, Griffith DJ, Haley A, Town A, Demetri GD, Fletcher CD, Fletcher JA (2003) PDGFRA activating mutations in gastrointestinal stromal tumors. Science 299:708–710

Heldin CH, Johnsson A, Wennergren S, Wernstedt C, Betsholtz C, Westermark B (1986) A human osteosarcoma cell line secretes a growth factor structurally related to a homodimer of PDGF A-chains. Nature 319:511–514

Heldin CH, Ostman A, Ronnstrand L (1998) Signal transduction via platelet-derived growth factor receptors. Biochim Biophys Acta 1378:F79–F113

Heldin CH, Westermark B (1999) Mechanism of action and in vivo role of platelet-derived growth factor. Physiol Rev 79:1283–1316

Heldin NE, Gustavsson B, Claesson-Welsh L, Hammacher A, Mark J, Heldin CH, Westermark B (1988) Aberrant expression of receptors for platelet-derived growth factor in an anaplastic thyroid carcinoma cell line. Proc Natl Acad Sci U S A 85:9302–9306

Hermanson M, Funa K, Koopmann J, Maintz D, Waha A, Westermark B, Heldin CH, Wiestler OD, Louis DN, von Deimling A, Nister M (1996) Association of loss of heterozygosity on chromosome 17p with high platelet-derived growth factor alpha receptor expression in human malignant gliomas. Cancer Res 56:164–171

Hermansson M, Nister M, Betsholtz C, Heldin CH, Westermark B, Funa K (1988) Endothelial cell hyperplasia in human glioblastoma: coexpression of mRNA for platelet-derived growth factor (PDGF) B chain and PDGF receptor suggests autocrine growth stimulation. Proc Natl Acad Sci U S A 85:7748–7752

Heuchel R, Berg A, Tallquist M, Ahlen K, Reed RK, Rubin K, Claesson-Welsh L, Heldin CH, Soriano P (1999) Platelet-derived growth factor beta receptor regulates interstitial fluid homeostasis through phosphatidylinositol-3' kinase signaling. Proc Natl Acad Sci U S A 96:11410–11415

Hirakawa S, Kodama S, Kunstfeld R, Kajiya K, Brown LF, Detmar M (2005) VEGF-A induces tumor and sentinel lymph node lymphangiogenesis and promotes lymphatic metastasis. J Exp Med 201:1089–1099

Hiratsuka S, Kataoka Y, Nakao K, Nakamura K, Morikawa S, Tanaka S, Katsuki M, Maru Y, Shibuya M (2005) Vascular endothelial growth factor A (VEGF-A) is involved in guidance of VEGF receptor-positive cells to the anterior portion of early embryos. Mol Cell Biol 25:355–363

Hiratsuka S, Maru Y, Okada A, Seiki M, Noda T, Shibuya M (2001) Involvement of Flt-1 tyrosine kinase (vascular endothelial growth factor receptor-1) in pathological angiogenesis. Cancer Res 61:1207–1213

Hiratsuka S, Minowa O, Kuno J, Noda T, Shibuya M (1998) Flt-1 lacking the tyrosine kinase domain is sufficient for normal development and angiogenesis in mice. Proc Natl Acad Sci U S A 95: 9349–9354

Hiratsuka S, Nakamura K, Iwai S, Murakami M, Itoh T, Kijima H, Shipley JM, Senior RM,

Shibuya M (2002) MMP9 induction by vascular endothelial growth factor receptor-1 is involved in lung-specific metastasis. Cancer Cell 2:289–300

Hirota S, Ohashi A, Nishida T, Isozaki K, Kinoshita K, Shinomura Y, Kitamura Y (2003) Gain-of-function mutations of platelet-derived growth factor receptor alpha gene in gastrointestinal stromal tumors. Gastroenterology 125:660–667

Hoch RV, Soriano P (2003) Roles of PDGF in animal development. Development 130:4769–4784

Holash J, Davis S, Papadopoulos N, Croll SD, Ho L, Russell M, Boland P, Leidich R, Hylton D, Burova E, Ioffe E, Huang T, Radziejewski C, Bailey K, Fandl JP, Daly T, Wiegand SJ, Yancopoulos GD, Rudge JS (2002) VEGF-Trap: a VEGF blocker with potent antitumor effects. Proc Natl Acad Sci U S A 99:11393–11398

Hossain MZ, Ao P, Boynton AL (1998) Platelet-derived growth factor-induced disruption of gap junctional communication and phosphorylation of connexin43 involves protein kinase C and mitogen-activated protein kinase. J Cell Physiol 176:332–341

Houck KA, Leung DW, Rowland AM, Winer J, Ferrara N (1992) Dual regulation of vascular endothelial growth factor bioavailability by genetic and proteolytic mechanisms. J Biol Chem 267:26031–26037

Hu Q, Klippel A, Muslin AJ, Fantl WJ, Williams LT (1995) Ras-dependent induction of cellular responses by constitutively active phosphatidylinositol-3 kinase. Science 268:100–102

Ide AG, Baker NH, Warren SL (1939) Vascularization of the Brown-Pearce rabbi epithelioma transplant as seen in the transparent ear chamber. Am J Radiol 42:891–899

Iliopoulos O, Levy AP, Jiang C, Kaelin WG Jr, Goldberg MA (1996) Negative regulation of hypoxia-inducible genes by the von Hippel-Lindau protein. Proc Natl Acad Sci U S A 93:10595–10599

Imoto H, Osaki T, Taga S, Ohgami A, Ichiyoshi Y, Yasumoto K (1998) Vascular endothelial growth factor expression in non-small-cell lung cancer: prognostic significance in squamous cell carcinoma. J Thorac Cardiovasc Surg 115:1007–1014

Ishigami SI, Arii S, Furutani M, Niwano M, Harada T, Mizumoto M, Mori A, Onodera H, Imamura M (1998) Predictive value of vascular endothelial growth factor (VEGF) in metastasis and prognosis of human colorectal cancer. Br J Cancer 78:1379–1384

Ishimaru S, Ueda R, Hinohara Y, Ohtani M, Hanafusa H (2004) PVR plays a critical role via JNK activation in thorax closure during Drosophila metamorphosis. EMBO J 23:3984–3994

Ito N, Huang K, Claesson-Welsh L (2001) Signal transduction by VEGF receptor-1 wild type and mutant proteins. Cell Signal 13:849–854

Jacobsen J, Grankvist K, Rasmuson T, Bergh A, Landberg G, Ljungberg B (2004) Expression of vascular endothelial growth factor protein in human renal cell carcinoma. BJU Int 93: 297–302

James MF, Beauchamp RL, Manchanda N, Kazlauskas A, Ramesh V (2004) A NHERF binding site links the betaPDGFR to the cytoskeleton and regulates cell spreading and migration. J Cell Sci 117:2951–2961

Johnsson A, Betsholtz C, von der Helm K, Heldin CH, Westermark B (1985) Platelet-derived growth factor agonist activity of a secreted form of the v-sis oncogene product. Proc Natl Acad Sci U S A 82:1721–1725

Johnsson A, Heldin CH, Westermark B, Wasteson A (1982) Platelet-derived growth factor: identification of constituent polypeptide chains. Biochem Biophys Res Commun 104:66–74

Joukov V, Pajusola K, Kaipainen A, Chilov D, Lahtinen I, Kukk E, Saksela O, Kalkkinen N, Alitalo K (1996) A novel vascular endothelial growth factor, VEGF-C, is a ligand for the Flt4 (VEGFR-3) and KDR (VEGFR-2) receptor tyrosine kinases. EMBO J 15:290–298

Kaetzel DM (2003) Transcription of the platelet-derived growth factor A-chain gene. Cytokine Growth Factor Rev 14:427–446

Kaipainen A, Korhonen J, Pajusola K, Aprelikova O, Persico MG, Terman BI, Alitalo K (1993) The related FLT4, FLT1, and KDR receptor tyrosine kinases show distinct expression patterns in human fetal endothelial cells. J Exp Med 178: 2077–2088

Kaplan RN, Riba RD, Zacharoulis S, Bramley AH, Vincent L, Costa C, MacDonald DD, Jin DK, Shido K, Kerns SA, Zhu Z, Hicklin D, Wu Y, Port JL, Altorki N, Port ER, Ruggero D, Shmelkov SV, Jensen KK, Rafii S, Lyden D (2005) VEGFR1-positive haematopoietic bone marrow progenitors initiate the pre-metastatic niche. Nature 438:820–827

Karlsson S, Kowanetz K, Sandin A, Persson C, Ostman A, Heldin CH, Hellberg C (2006) Loss of T-cell protein tyrosine phosphatase induces recycling of the platelet-derived growth factor (PDGF) beta-receptor but not the PDGF alpha-receptor. Mol Biol Cell 17:4846–4855

Kawasaki T, Kitsukawa T, Bekku Y, Matsuda Y, Sanbo M, Yagi T, Fujisawa H (1999) A requirement for neuropilin-1 in embryonic vessel formation. Development 126:4895–4902

Kazlauskas A, Cooper JA (1989) Autophosphorylation of the PDGF receptor in the kinase insert region regulates interactions with cell proteins. Cell 58:1121–1133

Keck PJ, Hauser SD, Krivi G, Sanzo K, Warren T, Feder J, Connolly DT (1989) Vascular permeability factor, an endothelial cell mitogen related to PDGF. Science 246:1309–1312

Kelly JD, Haldeman BA, Grant FJ, Murray MJ, Seifert RA, Bowen-Pope DF, Cooper JA, Kazlauskas A (1991) Platelet-derived growth factor (PDGF) stimulates PDGF receptor subunit dimerization and intersubunit trans-phosphorylation. J Biol Chem 266:8987–8992

Kelly JL, Sanchez A, Brown GS, Chesterman CN, Sleigh MJ (1993) Accumulation of PDGF B and cell-binding forms of PDGF A in the extracellular matrix. J Cell Biol 121:1153–1163

Kendall RL, Thomas KA (1993) Inhibition of vascular endothelial cell growth factor activity by an endogenously encoded soluble receptor. Proc Natl Acad Sci U S A 90:10705–10709

Keyt BA, Nguyen HV, Berleau LT, Duarte CM, Park J, Chen H, Ferrara N (1996) Identification of vascular endothelial growth factor determinants for binding KDR and FLT-1 receptors. Generation of receptor-selective VEGF variants by site-directed mutagenesis. J Biol Chem 271: 5638–5646

Kim KJ, Li B, Winer J, Armanini M, Gillett N, Phillips HS, Ferrara N (1993) Inhibition of vascular endothelial growth factor-induced angiogenesis suppresses tumour growth in vivo. Nature 362:841–844

Klein M, Vignaud JM, Hennequin V, Toussaint B, Bresler L, Plenat F, Leclere J, Duprez A, Weryha G (2001) Increased expression of the vascular endothelial growth factor is a pejorative prognosis marker in papillary thyroid carcinoma. J Clin Endocrinol Metab 86:656–658

Klinghoffer RA, Hamilton TG, Hoch R, Soriano P (2002) An allelic series at the PDGFalphaR locus indicates unequal contributions of distinct signaling pathways during development. Dev Cell 2:103–113

Klinghoffer RA, Mueting-Nelsen PF, Faerman A, Shani M, Soriano P (2001) The two PDGF receptors maintain conserved signaling in vivo despite divergent embryological functions. Mol Cell 7:343–354

Kohler N, Lipton A (1974) Platelets as a source of fibroblast growth-promoting activity. Exp Cell Res 87:297–301

Kong HL, Hecht D, Song W, Kovesdi I, Hackett NR, Yayon A, Crystal RG (1998) Regional suppression of tumor growth by in vivo transfer of a cDNA encoding a secreted form of the extracellular domain of the flt-1 vascular endothelial growth factor receptor. Hum Gene Ther 9:823–833

Kundra V, Soker S, Zetter BR (1994) Excess early signaling activity inhibits cellular chemotaxis toward PDGF-BB. Oncogene 9:1429–1435

Lechleider RJ, Sugimoto S, Bennett AM, Kashishian AS, Cooper JA, Shoelson SE, Walsh CT, Neel BG (1993) Activation of the SH2-containing phosphotyrosine phosphatase SH-PTP2 by its binding site, phosphotyrosine 1009, on the human platelet-derived growth factor receptor. J Biol Chem 268:21478–21481

Lee S, Chen TT, Barber CL, Jordan MC, Murdock J, Desai S, Ferrara N, Nagy A, Roos KP, Iruela-Arispe ML (2007) Autocrine VEGF signaling is required for vascular homeostasis. Cell 130: 691–703

Lennartsson J, Wardega P, Engstrom U, Hellman U, Heldin CH (2006) Alix facilitates the interaction between c-Cbl and platelet-derived growth factor beta-receptor and thereby modulates receptor down-regulation. J Biol Chem 281: 39152–39158

Leung DW, Cachianes G, Kuang WJ, Goeddel DV, Ferrara N (1989) Vascular endothelial growth factor is a secreted angiogenic mitogen. Science 246:1306–1309

Levy AP, Levy NS, Wegner S, Goldberg MA (1995) Transcriptional regulation of the rat vascular endothelial growth factor gene by hypoxia. J Biol Chem 270:13333–13340

Li J, Yen C, Liaw D, Podsypanina K, Bose S, Wang SI, Puc J, Miliaresis C, Rodgers L, McCombie R, Bigner SH, Giovanella BC, Ittmann M, Tycko B, Hibshoosh H, Wigler MH, Parsons R (1997) PTEN, a putative protein tyrosine phosphatase gene mutated in human brain, breast, and prostate cancer. Science 275:1943–1947

Li W, Pierce JH (1996) Protein kinase C-delta, an important signaling molecule in the platelet-derived growth factor beta receptor pathway. Curr Top Microbiol Immunol 211:55–65

Li X, Ponten A, Aase K, Karlsson L, Abramsson A, Uutela M, Backstrom G, Hellstrom M, Bostrom H, Li H, Soriano P, Betsholtz C, Heldin CH, Alitalo K, Ostman A, Eriksson U (2000) PDGF-C is a new protease-activated ligand for the PDGF alpha-receptor. Nat Cell Biol 2:302–309

Lin ZH, Fukuda N, Suzuki R, Takagi H, Ikeda Y, Saito S, Matsumoto K, Kanmatsuse K, Mugishima H (2004) Adenovirus-encoded hammerhead ribozyme to PDGF A-chain mRNA inhibits neointima formation after arterial injury. J Vasc Res 41:305–313

Lindblom P, Gerhardt H, Liebner S, Abramsson A, Enge M, Hellstrom M, Backstrom G, Fredriksson S, Landegren U, Nystrom HC, Bergstrom G, Dejana E, Ostman A, Lindahl P, Betsholtz C (2003) Endothelial PDGF-B retention is required for proper investment of pericytes in the microvessel wall. Genes Dev 17:1835–1840

Liu Y, Cox SR, Morita T, Kourembanas S (1995) Hypoxia regulates vascular endothelial growth factor gene expression in endothelial cells. Identification of a 5' enhancer. Circ Res 77: 638–643

Lloyd RV, Scheithauer BW, Kuroki T, Vidal S, Kovacs K, Stefaneanu L (1999) Vascular endothelial growth factor (VEGF) expression in human pituitary adenomas and carcinomas. Endocr Pathol 10:229–235

Lokker NA, Sullivan CM, Hollenbach SJ, Israel MA, Giese NA (2002) Platelet-derived growth factor (PDGF) autocrine signaling regulates survival and mitogenic pathways in glioblastoma cells: evidence that the novel PDGF-C and PDGF-D ligands may play a role in the development of brain tumors. Cancer Res 62:3729–3735

Lopez-Ilasaca M, Li W, Uren A, Yu JC, Kazlauskas A, Gutkind JS, Heidaran MA (1997) Requirement of phosphatidylinositol-3 kinase for activation of JNK/SAPKs by PDGF. Biochem Biophys Res Commun 232:273–277

Lustig F, Hoebeke J, Simonson C, Ostergren-Lunden G, Bondjers G, Ruetchi U, Fager G (1999) Processing of PDGF gene products determines interactions with glycosaminoglycans. J Mol Recognit 12:112–120

Madan A, Curtin PT (1993) A 24-base-pair sequence 3' to the human erythropoietin gene contains a hypoxia-responsive transcriptional enhancer. Proc Natl Acad Sci U S A 90:3928–3932

Maeda K, Nishiguchi Y, Yashiro M, Yamada S, Onoda N, Sawada T, Kang SM, Hirakawa K (2000) Expression of vascular endothelial growth factor and thrombospondin-1 in colorectal carcinoma. Int J Mol Med 5:373–378

Maes C, Carmeliet P, Moermans K, Stockmans I, Smets N, Collen D, Bouillon R, Carmeliet G (2002) Impaired angiogenesis and endochondral bone formation in mice lacking the vascular endothelial growth factor isoforms VEGF164 and VEGF188. Mech Dev 111:61–73

Maglione D, Guerriero V, Viglietto G, Delli-Bovi P, Persico MG (1991) Isolation of a human placenta cDNA coding for a protein related to the vascular permeability factor. Proc Natl Acad Sci U S A 88:9267–9271

Maglione D, Guerriero V, Viglietto G, Ferraro MG, Aprelikova O, Alitalo K, Del Vecchio S, Lei KJ, Chou JY, Persico MG (1993) Two alternative mRNAs coding for the angiogenic factor, placenta growth factor (PlGF), are transcribed from a single gene of chromosome 14. Oncogene 8: 925–931

Matsumoto T, Claesson-Welsh L (2001) VEGF receptor signal transduction. Sci STKE 2001:RE21

Matthews W, Jordan CT, Gavin M, Jenkins NA, Copeland NG, Lemischka IR (1991) A receptor tyrosine kinase cDNA isolated from a population of enriched primitive hematopoietic cells and exhibiting close genetic linkage to c-kit. Proc Natl Acad Sci U S A 88:9026–9030

Melnyk O, Shuman MA, Kim KJ (1996) Vascular endothelial growth factor promotes tumor dissemination by a mechanism distinct from its effect on primary tumor growth. Cancer Res 56: 921–924

Mesiano S, Ferrara N, Jaffe RB (1998) Role of vascular endothelial growth factor in ovarian cancer: inhibition of ascites formation by immunoneutralization. Am J Pathol 153:1249–1256

Millauer B, Shawver LK, Plate KH, Risau W, Ullrich A (1994) Glioblastoma growth inhibited in vivo by a dominant-negative Flk-1 mutant. Nature 367:576–579

Millauer B, Wizigmann-Voos S, Schnurch H, Martinez R, Moller NP, Risau W, Ullrich A (1993) High affinity VEGF binding and developmental expression suggest Flk-1 as a major regulator of vasculogenesis and angiogenesis. Cell 72:835–846

Mueller MD, Vigne JL, Minchenko A, Lebovic DI, Leitman DC, Taylor RN (2000) Regulation of vascular endothelial growth factor (VEGF) gene transcription by estrogen receptors alpha and beta. Proc Natl Acad Sci U S A 97:10972–10977

Mueller MD, Vigne JL, Pritts EA, Chao V, Dreher E, Taylor RN (2003) Progestins activate vascular endothelial growth factor gene transcription in endometrial adenocarcinoma cells. Fertil Steril 79:386–392

Nakanishi S, Nakajima Y, Yokota Y (1993) Signal transduction and ligand-binding domains of the tachykinin receptors. Regul Pept 46:37–42

Newton HB (2003) Molecular neuro-oncology and development of targeted therapeutic strategies for brain tumors. Part 1: growth factor and Ras signaling pathways. Expert Rev Anticancer Ther 3:595–614

Nicol D, Hii SI, Walsh M, Teh B, Thompson L, Kennett C, Gotley D (1997) Vascular endothelial growth factor expression is increased in renal cell carcinoma. J Urol 157:1482–1486

Nister M, Hammacher A, Mellstrom K, Siegbahn A, Ronnstrand L, Westermark B, Heldin CH (1988) A glioma-derived PDGF A chain homodimer has different functional activities from a PDGF AB heterodimer purified from human platelets. Cell 52:791–799

Nobes CD, Hawkins P, Stephens L, Hall A (1995) Activation of the small GTP-binding proteins rho and rac by growth factor receptors. J Cell Sci 108(Pt 1):225–233

O'Byrne KJ, Koukourakis MI, Giatromanolaki A, Cox G, Turley H, Steward WP, Gatter K, Harris AL (2000) Vascular endothelial growth factor, platelet-derived endothelial cell growth factor and angiogenesis in non-small-cell lung cancer. Br J Cancer 82:1427–1432

Ogata Y, Fujita H, Yamana H, Sueyoshi S, Shirouzu K (2003) Expression of vascular endothelial growth factor as a prognostic factor in node-positive squamous cell carcinoma in the thoracic esophagus: long-term follow-up study. World J Surg 27: 584–589

Oku T, Tjuvajev JG, Miyagawa T, Sasajima T, Joshi A, Joshi R, Finn R, Claffey KP, Blasberg RG (1998) Tumor growth modulation by sense and antisense vascular endothelial growth factor gene expression: effects on angiogenesis, vascular permeability, blood volume, blood flow, fluorodeoxyglucose uptake, and proliferation of human melanoma intracerebral xenografts. Cancer Res 58:4185–4192

Olofsson B, Pajusola K, Kaipainen A, von Euler G, Joukov V, Saksela O, Orpana A, Pettersson RF,

Alitalo K, Eriksson U (1996) Vascular endothelial growth factor B, a novel growth factor for endothelial cells. Proc Natl Acad Sci U S A 93:2576–2581

Olson TA, Mohanraj D, Carson LF, Ramakrishnan S (1994) Vascular permeability factor gene expression in normal and neoplastic human ovaries. Cancer Res 54:276–280

Ostman A (2004) PDGF receptors-mediators of autocrine tumor growth and regulators of tumor vasculature and stroma. Cytokine Growth Factor Rev 15:275–286

Paley PJ, Staskus KA, Gebhard K, Mohanraj D, Twiggs LB, Carson LF, Ramakrishnan S (1997) Vascular endothelial growth factor expression in early stage ovarian carcinoma. Cancer 80:98–106

Pan Q, Chantery Y, Liang WC, Stawicki S, Mak J, Rathore N, Tong RK, Kowalski J, Yee SF, Pacheco G, Ross S, Cheng Z, Le Couter J, Plowman G, Peale F, Koch AW, Wu Y, Bagri A, Tessier-Lavigne M, Watts RJ (2007) Blocking neuropilin-1 function has an additive effect with anti-VEGF to inhibit tumor growth. Cancer Cell 11:53–67

Persson C, Savenhed C, Bourdeau A, Tremblay ML, Markova B, Bohmer FD, Haj FG, Neel BG, Elson A, Heldin CH, Ronnstrand L, Ostman A, Hellberg C (2004) Site-selective regulation of platelet-derived growth factor beta receptor tyrosine phosphorylation by T-cell protein tyrosine phosphatase. Mol Cell Biol 24:2190–2201

Pertovaara L, Kaipainen A, Mustonen T, Orpana A, Ferrara N, Saksela O, Alitalo K (1994) Vascular endothelial growth factor is induced in response to transforming growth factor-beta in fibroblastic and epithelial cells. J Biol Chem 269:6271–6274

Pietras K, Ostman A, Sjoquist M, Buchdunger E, Reed RK, Heldin CH, Rubin K (2001) Inhibition of platelet-derived growth factor receptors reduces interstitial hypertension and increases transcapillary transport in tumors. Cancer Res 61:2929–2934

Plate KH, Breier G, Weich HA, Risau W (1992) Vascular endothelial growth factor is a potential tumour angiogenesis factor in human gliomas in vivo. Nature 359:845–848

Prewett M, Huber J, Li Y, Santiago A, O'Connor W, King K, Overholser J, Hooper A, Pytowski B, Witte L, Bohlen P, Hicklin DJ (1999) Antivascular endothelial growth factor receptor (fetal liver kinase 1) monoclonal antibody inhibits tumor angiogenesis and growth of several mouse and human tumors. Cancer Res 59:5209–5218

Raines EW, Lane TF, Iruela-Arispe ML, Ross R, Sage EH (1992) The extracellular glycoprotein SPARC interacts with platelet-derived growth factor (PDGF)-AB and -BB and inhibits the binding of PDGF to its receptors. Proc Natl Acad Sci U S A 89:1281–1285

Raines EW, Ross R (1992) Compartmentalization of PDGF on extracellular binding sites dependent on exon-6-encoded sequences. J Cell Biol 116:533–543

Rak J, Mitsuhashi Y, Bayko L, Filmus J, Shirasawa S, Sasazuki T, Kerbel RS (1995) Mutant ras oncogenes upregulate VEGF/VPF expression: implications for induction and inhibition of tumor angiogenesis. Cancer Res 55:4575–4580

Reigstad LJ, Varhaug JE, Lillehaug JR (2005) Structural and functional specificities of PDGF-C and PDGF-D, the novel members of the platelet-derived growth factors family. FEBS J 272: 5723–5741

Risau W (1997) Mechanisms of angiogenesis. Nature 386:671–674

Ronnstrand L, Heldin CH (2001) Mechanisms of platelet-derived growth factor-induced chemotaxis. Int J Cancer 91:757–762

Ross R, Glomset J, Kariya B, Harker L (1974) A platelet-dependent serum factor that stimulates the proliferation of arterial smooth muscle cells in vitro. Proc Natl Acad Sci U S A 71:1207–1210

Ruhrberg C, Gerhardt H, Golding M, Watson R, Ioannidou S, Fujisawa H, Betsholtz C, Shima DT (2002) Spatially restricted patterning cues provided by heparin-binding VEGF-A control blood vessel branching morphogenesis. Genes Dev 16: 2684–2698

Sakurai Y, Ohgimoto K, Kataoka Y, Yoshida N, Shibuya M (2005) Essential role of Flk-1 (VEGF receptor 2) tyrosine residue 1173 in vasculogenesis in mice. Proc Natl Acad Sci U S A 102:1076–1081

Saleh M, Stacker SA, Wilks AF (1996) Inhibition of growth of C6 glioma cells in vivo by expression of antisense vascular endothelial growth factor sequence. Cancer Res 56:393–401

Sawano A, Takahashi T, Yamaguchi S, Shibuya M (1997) The phosphorylated 1169-tyrosine containing region of flt-1 kinase (VEGFR-1) is a major binding site for PLCgamma. Biochem Biophys Res Commun 238:487–491

Schmahl J, Raymond CS, Soriano P (2007) PDGF signaling specificity is mediated through multiple immediate early genes. Nat Genet 39:52–60

Senger DR, Asch BB, Smith BD, Perruzzi CA, Dvorak HF (1983) A secreted phosphoprotein marker for neoplastic transformation of both epithelial and fibroblastic cells. Nature 302:714–715

Shalaby F, Rossant J, Yamaguchi TP, Gertsenstein M, Wu XF, Breitman ML, Schuh AC (1995) Failure of blood-island formation and vasculogenesis in Flk-1-deficient mice. Nature 376:62–66

Shay-Salit A, Shushy M, Wolfovitz E, Yahav H, Breviario F, Dejana E, Resnick N (2002) VEGF receptor 2 and the adherens junction as a mechanical transducer in vascular endothelial cells. Proc Natl Acad Sci U S A 99:9462–9467

Shibuya M (1995) Role of VEGF-flt receptor system in normal and tumor angiogenesis. Adv Cancer Res 67:281–316

Shibuya M (2002) Vascular endothelial growth factor receptor family genes: when did the three genes phylogenetically segregate? Biol Chem 383:1573–1579

Shibuya M, Claesson-Welsh L (2006) Signal transduction by VEGF receptors in regulation of angiogenesis and lymphangiogenesis. Exp Cell Res 312:549–560

Shibuya M, Yamaguchi S, Yamane A, Ikeda T, Tojo A, Matsushime H, Sato M (1990) Nucleotide sequence and expression of a novel human receptor-type tyrosine kinase gene (flt) closely related to the fms family. Oncogene 5:519–524

Shih CH, Ozawa S, Ando N, Ueda M, Kitajima M (2000) Vascular endothelial growth factor expression predicts outcome and lymph node metastasis in squamous cell carcinoma of the esophagus. Clin Cancer Res 6:1161–1168

Shinkai A, Ito M, Anazawa H, Yamaguchi S, Shitara K, Shibuya M (1998) Mapping of the sites involved in ligand association and dissociation at the extracellular domain of the kinase insert domain-containing receptor for vascular endothelial growth factor. J Biol Chem 273:31283–31288

Shweiki D, Itin A, Soffer D, Keshet E (1992) Vascular endothelial growth factor induced by hypoxia may mediate hypoxia-initiated angiogenesis. Nature 359:843–845

Sirvent N, Maire G, Pedeutour F (2003) Genetics of dermatofibrosarcoma protuberans family of tumors: from ring chromosomes to tyrosine kinase inhibitor treatment. Genes Chromosomes Cancer 37:1–19

Skobe M, Fusenig NE (1998) Tumorigenic conversion of immortal human keratinocytes through stromal cell activation. Proc Natl Acad Sci U S A 95:1050–1055

Smith JS, Jenkins RB (2000) Genetic alterations in adult diffuse glioma: occurrence, significance, and prognostic implications. Front Biosci 5:D213–D231

Smith JS, Wang XY, Qian J, Hosek SM, Scheithauer BW, Jenkins RB, James CD (2000) Amplification of the platelet-derived growth factor receptor-A (PDGFRA) gene occurs in oligodendrogliomas with grade IV anaplastic features. J Neuropathol Exp Neurol 59:495–503

Smolich BD, Yuen HA, West KA, Giles FJ, Albitar M, Cherrington JM (2001) The antiangiogenic protein kinase inhibitors SU5416 and SU6668 inhibit the SCF receptor (c-kit) in a human myeloid leukemia cell line and in acute myeloid leukemia blasts. Blood 97:1413–1421

Sorkin A, Westermark B, Heldin CH, Claesson-Welsh L (1991) Effect of receptor kinase inactivation on the rate of internalization and degradation of PDGF and the PDGF beta-receptor. J Cell Biol 112:469–478

Sowter HM, Corps AN, Evans AL, Clark DE, Charnock-Jones DS, Smith SK (1997) Expression and localization of the vascular endothelial growth factor family in ovarian epithelial tumors. Lab Invest 77:607–614

Soyombo AA, DiCorleto PE (1994) Stable expression of human platelet-derived growth factor B chain by bovine aortic endothelial cells. Matrix association and selective proteolytic cleavage by thrombin. J Biol Chem 269:17734–17740

Strawn LM, McMahon G, App H, Schreck R, Kuchler WR, Longhi MP, Hui TH, Tang C, Levitzki A, Gazit A, Chen I, Keri G, Orfi L, Risau W, Flamme I, Ullrich A, Hirth KP, Shawver LK (1996) Flk-1 as a target for tumor growth inhibition. Cancer Res 56:3540–3545

Stroobant P, Waterfield MD (1984) Purification and properties of porcine platelet-derived growth factor. EMBO J 3:2963–2967

Stupack DG, Cheresh DA (2004) Integrins and angiogenesis. Curr Top Dev Biol 64:207–238

Suzuki K, Hayashi N, Miyamoto Y, Yamamoto M, Ohkawa K, Ito Y, Sasaki Y, Yamaguchi Y, Nakase H, Noda K, Enomoto N, Arai K, Yamada Y, Yoshihara H, Tujimura T, Kawano K, Yoshikawa K, Kamada T (1996) Expression of vascular permeability factor/vascular endothelial growth factor in human hepatocellular carcinoma. Cancer Res 56:3004–3009

Takahashi T, Ueno H, Shibuya M (1999) VEGF activates protein kinase C-dependent, but Ras-independent Raf-MEK-MAP kinase pathway for DNA synthesis in primary endothelial cells. Oncogene 18:2221–2230

Takahashi T, Yamaguchi S, Chida K, Shibuya M (2001) A single autophosphorylation site on KDR/Flk-1 is essential for VEGF-A-dependent activation of PLC-gamma and DNA synthesis in vascular endothelial cells. EMBO J 20:2768–2778

Takahashi Y, Morales FC, Kreimann EL, Georgescu MM (2006) PTEN tumor suppressor associates with NHERF proteins to attenuate PDGF receptor signaling. EMBO J 25:910–920

Tallquist M, Kazlauskas A (2004) PDGF signaling in cells and mice. Cytokine Growth Factor Rev 15:205–213

Tallquist MD, French WJ, Soriano P (2003) Additive effects of PDGF receptor beta signaling pathways in vascular smooth muscle cell development. PLoS Biol 1:E52

Tallquist MD, Klinghoffer RA, Heuchel R, Mueting-Nelsen PF, Corrin PD, Heldin CH, Johnson RJ, Soriano P (2000) Retention of PDGFR-beta function in mice in the absence of phosphatidylinositol 3′-kinase and phospholipase C gamma signaling pathways. Genes Dev 14:3179–3190

Tallquist MD, Soriano P (2003) Cell autonomous requirement for PDGFRalpha in populations of cranial and cardiac neural crest cells. Development 130:507–518

Tanaka K, Yamaguchi S, Sawano A, Shibuya M (1997) Characterization of the extracellular domain in vascular endothelial growth factor receptor-1 (Flt-1 tyrosine kinase). Jpn J Cancer Res 88:867–876

Terman BI, Carrion ME, Kovacs E, Rasmussen BA, Eddy RL, Shows TB (1991) Identification of a new endothelial cell growth factor receptor tyrosine kinase. Oncogene 6:1677–1683

Theisen CS, Wahl JK 3rd, Johnson KR, Wheelock MJ (2007) NHERF links the N-cadherin/catenin complex to the platelet-derived growth factor receptor to modulate the actin cytoskeleton and regulate cell motility. Mol Biol Cell 18:1220–1232

Tischer E, Mitchell R, Hartman T, Silva M, Gospodarowicz D, Fiddes JC, Abraham JA (1991) The human gene for vascular endothelial growth factor. Multiple protein forms are encoded through alternative exon splicing. J Biol Chem 266:11947–11954

Toi M, Inada K, Suzuki H, Tominaga T (1995) Tumor angiogenesis in breast cancer: its importance as a prognostic indicator and the association with vascular endothelial growth factor expression. Breast Cancer Res Treat 36: 193–204

Tomisawa M, Tokunaga T, Oshika Y, Tsuchida T, Fukushima Y, Sato H, Kijima H, Yamazaki H, Ueyama Y, Tamaoki N, Nakamura M (1999) Expression pattern of vascular endothelial growth factor isoform is closely correlated with tumour stage and vascularisation in renal cell carcinoma. Eur J Cancer 35:133–137

Uchida S, Shimada Y, Watanabe G, Tanaka H, Shibagaki I, Miyahara T, Ishigami S, Imamura M (1998) In oesophageal squamous cell carcinoma vascular endothelial growth factor is associated with p53 mutation, advanced stage and poor prognosis. Br J Cancer 77:1704–1709

Uhrbom L, Hesselager G, Nister M, Westermark B (1998) Induction of brain tumors in mice using a recombinant platelet-derived growth factor B-chain retrovirus. Cancer Res 58:5275–5279

Uhrbom L, Hesselager G, Ostman A, Nister M, Westermark B (2000) Dependence of autocrine growth factor stimulation in platelet-derived growth factor-B-induced mouse brain tumor cells. Int J Cancer 85:398–406

Veikkola T, Jussila L, Makinen T, Karpanen T, Jeltsch M, Petrova TV, Kubo H, Thurston G, McDonald DM, Achen MG, Stacker SA, Alitalo K (2001) Signalling via vascular endothelial growth factor receptor-3 is sufficient for lymphangiogenesis in transgenic mice. EMBO J 20:1223–1231

Vincenti V, Cassano C, Rocchi M, Persico G (1996) Assignment of the vascular endothelial growth factor gene to human chromosome 6p21.3. Circulation 93:1493–1495

Volm M, Koomagi R, Mattern J (1997a) Prognostic value of vascular endothelial growth factor and its receptor Flt-1 in squamous cell lung cancer. Int J Cancer 74:64–68

Volm M, Koomagi R, Mattern J, Stammler G (1997b) Angiogenic growth factors and their receptors in non-small cell lung carcinomas and their relationships to drug response in vitro. Anticancer Res 17:99–103

Waltenberger J, Claesson-Welsh L, Siegbahn A, Shibuya M, Heldin CH (1994) Different signal transduction properties of KDR and Flt1, two receptors for vascular endothelial growth factor. J Biol Chem 269:26988–26995

Warren RS, Yuan H, Matli MR, Ferrara N, Donner DB (1996) Induction of vascular endothelial growth factor by insulin-like growth factor 1 in colorectal carcinoma. J Biol Chem 271:29483–29488

Warren RS, Yuan H, Matli MR, Gillett NA, Ferrara N (1995) Regulation by vascular endothelial growth factor of human colon cancer tumorigenesis in a mouse model of experimental liver metastasis. J Clin Invest 95:1789–1797

Wasteson A, Hook M, Westermark B (1976) Demonstration of a platelet enzyme, degrading heparan sulphate. FEBS Lett 64:218–221

Waterfield MD, Scrace GT, Whittle N, Stroobant P, Johnsson A, Wasteson A, Westermark B, Heldin CH, Huang JS, Deuel TF (1983) Platelet-derived growth factor is structurally related to the putative transforming protein p28sis of simian sarcoma virus. Nature 304:35–39

Wedge SR, Ogilvie DJ, Dukes M, Kendrew J, Curwen JO, Hennequin LF, Thomas AP, Stokes ES, Curry B, Richmond GH, Wadsworth PF (2000) ZD4190: an orally active inhibitor of vascular endothelial growth factor signaling with broad-spectrum antitumor efficacy. Cancer Res 60:970–975

Wizigmann-Voos S, Breier G, Risau W, Plate KH (1995) Up-regulation of vascular endothelial growth factor and its receptors in von Hippel-Lindau disease-associated and sporadic hemangioblastomas. Cancer Res 55:1358–1364

Wood JM, Bold G, Buchdunger E, Cozens R, Ferrari S, Frei J, Hofmann F, Mestan J, Mett H, O'Reilly T, Persohn E, Rosel J, Schnell C, Stover D, Theuer A, Towbin H, Wenger F, Woods-Cook K, Menrad A, Siemeister G, Schirner M, Thierauch KH, Schneider MR, Drevs J, Martiny-Baron G, Totzke F (2000) PTK787/ZK 222584, a novel and potent inhibitor of vascular endothelial growth factor receptor tyrosine kinases, impairs vascular endothelial growth factor-induced responses and tumor growth after oral administration. Cancer Res 60:2178–2189

Yamamoto S, Konishi I, Mandai M, Kuroda H, Komatsu T, Nanbu K, Sakahara H, Mori T (1997) Expression of vascular endothelial growth factor (VEGF) in epithelial ovarian neoplasms: correlation with clinicopathology and patient survival, and analysis of serum VEGF levels. Br J Cancer 76:1221–1227

Yoshiji H, Gomez DE, Shibuya M, Thorgeirsson UP (1996) Expression of vascular endothelial growth factor, its receptor, and other angiogenic factors in human breast cancer. Cancer Res 56:2013–2016

Zhao J, Roth J, Bode-Lesniewska B, Pfaltz M, Heitz PU, Komminoth P (2002) Combined comparative genomic hybridization and genomic microarray for detection of gene amplifications in pulmonary artery intimal sarcomas and adrenocortical tumors. Genes Chromosomes Cancer 34:48–57

Zundel W, Schindler C, Haas-Kogan D, Koong A, Kaper F, Chen E, Gottschalk AR, Ryan HE, Johnson RS, Jefferson AB, Stokoe D, Giaccia AJ (2000) Loss of PTEN facilitates HIF-1-mediated gene expression. Genes Dev 14:391–396

Vascular Integrins: Therapeutic and Imaging Targets of Tumor Angiogenesis

6

Curzio Rüegg and Gian Carlo Alghisi

Abstract Cells, including endothelial cells, continuously sense their surrounding environment and rapidly adapt to changes in order to assure tissues and organs homeostasis. The extracellular matrix (ECM) provides a physical scaffold for cell positioning and represents an instructive interface allowing cells to communicate over short distances. Cell surface receptors of the integrin family emerged through evolution as essential mediators and integrators of ECM-dependent communication. In preclinical studies, pharmacological inhibition of vascular integrins suppressed angiogenesis and inhibited tumor progression. $\alpha_v\beta_3$ and $\alpha_v\beta_5$ were the first integrins targeted to suppress tumor angiogenesis. Subsequently, additional integrins, in particular $\alpha_1\beta_1$, $\alpha_2\beta_1$, $\alpha_5\beta_1$, and $\alpha_6\beta_4$, emerged as potential therapeutic targets. Integrin inhibitors are currently tested in clinical trials for their safety and antiangiogenic/antitumor activity. In this chapter, we review the role of integrins in angiogenesis and present recent advances in the use of integrin antagonists as potential therapeutics in cancer and discuss future perspectives.

C. Rüegg (✉)
Division of Experimental Oncology,
Centre Pluridisciplinaire d'Oncologie,
155, Chemin des Boveresses,
CH1066 Epalinges, Switzerland
e-mail: curzio.ruegg@unil.ch

6.1
Integrin Structure

Integrins comprise a family of cell surface heterodimeric complexes formed by the noncovalent association of two subunits, α and β (Takada et al. 2007). There are 18 α and 8 β subunits capable of forming 24 different functional heterodimers. The $\alpha\beta$ composition of the heterodimer largely determines the ligand specificity, although some ligands can bind directly to individual subunits, such as collagens, to the I-domain on the α subunit. Each individual subunit consists of a large extracellular domain (about 750 amino acids for the β subunits and around to 1000 amino acids for the α subunits), a single transmembrane domain (22–24 amino acids), and a short cytoplasmic tail (15–58 amino acids, except for the β_4 subunit, which contains over 1000 intracellular residues). The cytoplasmic domain is essential for the regulation of integrin activity and function: on the one side it controls extracellular ligand-binding activity of the complex ("inside-out" signaling), while on the other, it initiates cellular responses upon ligand binding ("outside-in" signaling) (Ginsberg et al. 2005). In resting, nonligated integrins, the β subunit cytoplasmic domain interacts with the α subunit cytoplasmic domain, thereby maintaining the receptor in its inactive state

R. Liersch et al. (eds.), *Angiogenesis Inhibition,* Recent Results in Cancer Research,
DOI: 10.1007/978-3-540-78281-0_6, © Springer Verlag Berlin Heidelberg 2010

6

(Luo et al. 2007). Binding of the cytoplasmic protein talin to the β subunit cytoplasmic domain disrupts this interaction, resulting in a conformational change of the extracellular domain leading to a high affinity ligand-binding state (affinity maturation). The "released" β cytoplasmic tail interacts with additional intracellular structural (e.g., paxillin, vinculin), adaptor (e.g., Shc, Cas), and signaling (e.g., FAK, ILK) proteins, thereby initiating cytoskeletal rearrangement and cell signaling events. Ligated integrins can cluster to form small focal contacts at the cell periphery, large focal adhesions retracted from the cell border, or fibrillar adhesions located underneath the cell body along actin stress fibers (Romer et al. 2006).

6.2
Integrin Functions

6.2.1
Cell Adhesion

Integrins are the main cell adhesion receptors for ECM proteins for virtually every cell, including endothelial cells (Hynes 2007). A particular feature of integrins is their ability to recognize short amino acid sequences on exposed loops of their cognate ligands, the tripeptide RGD being the best known and studied. In addition, integrins also bind matricellular proteins, such as thrombospondins, and cell surface molecules, such as ICAMs (for a comprehensive detailed list of ligands, see (Takada et al. 2007)). Ligand binding specificity is promiscuous and redundant: that is, one integrin can bind several different ligands, and many different integrins can bind to the same ligand. Redundancy may be an advantage when the cellular response needed in a particular context (e.g., survival or migration during matrix remodeling) is more important than the nature of the ECM protein eliciting. For example integrin $\alpha_v\beta_3$ binds to many ECM proteins present at sites of inflammation, coagulation, and tissue remodeling. Promiscuity may reflect the need to initiate different signaling events and cellular responses from the same ECM. For example, integrin $\alpha_5\beta_1$ and $\alpha_v\beta_6$ bind to fibronectin, but $\alpha_5\beta_1$ suppresses cell migration, while $\alpha_v\beta_6$ stimulates it (Coutifaris et al. 2005; Scott et al. 2004). More recently, integrins have been reported to bind to a multitude of noncanonical ligands, which themselves are known modulators of vascular functions, including VEGF (Vlahakis et al. 2007), FGF (Murakami et al. 2008), angiopoietins (Camenisch et al. 2002), or matrix-bound VEGFR-1 (Orecchia et al. 2003). These observations open the intriguing possibility that angiogenic growth factors, when associated to the ECM, may modulate endothelial cell functions by signaling through integrins in complement to their activities mediated by their canonical receptors.

6.2.2
Cell Signaling

Integrin ligation also initiates signaling cascades, modulating complex cell functions like spreading, migration, survival, proliferation, or differentiation (Alghisi and Ruegg 2006; Stupack 2007) (Fig. 6.1). As integrins do not have intrinsic enzymatic activity, they need to recruit cytoplasmic structural (e.g., α-actinin, talin, vinculin) and signaling (e.g., FAK, paxillin, and Src family kinases) proteins at adhesion complexes to initiate signal transduction (Luo et al. 2007; Romer et al. 2006). Many signaling pathways activated by integrins are also activated by growth factor receptors, and maximal signal transduction is achieved when integrins and growth factor receptors are concomitantly engaged. Signaling pathways activated by integrins, including in angiogenesis, comprise: MAPK, Akt/PKB, Rho family GTPases, and NF-κB (Mahabeleshwar et al. 2006).

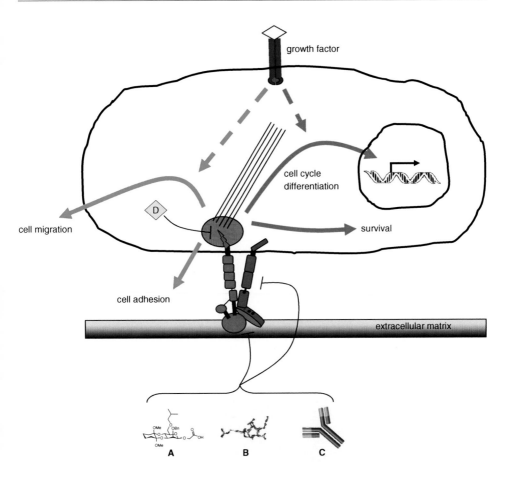

growth factor

cell cycle
differentiation

D

cell migration

survival

cell adhesion

extracellular matrix

A   B   C

Fig. 6.1 Integrin functions and how to inhibit them. Integrins act as cell adhesion and motility mediators (*green arrows*) or as signal transducers (*red arrows*). These functions can be modulated by growth factors and their receptors (*green and red dashed arrows*). On one hand, the inhibition or integrin function can be achieved extracellularly by the action of peptidomimetics (**a**), peptides, most frequently RGD-based, but also as noncanonical peptides (**b**) or antibodies (**c**). These three classes of inhibitors could also be used as imaging tools if they are labeled with a detectable tracers. On the other hand, peptides disrupting or blocking the interaction between the β integrin cytoplasmic tail with cytoplasmic adaptor or signaling proteins inhibit integrin function and may be developed in the future as therapeutic tools (**d**)

A pathway activated by integrin, particularly relevant to vascular biology and angiogenesis, is the COX-2/prostaglandin pathway. Integrin-mediated adhesion and binding of soluble ligands induce COX-2 mRNA expression and stabilize COX-2 protein in endothelial cells resulting in enhanced prostaglandin production (Zaric and Ruegg 2005). In turn, prostaglandins activate the adenylcyclase via prostane receptor signaling, resulting in PKA activation, accelerated $\alpha_v\beta_3$-dependent cell adhesion, spreading, and migration in a Rac1-dependent manner (Dormond and Ruegg 2003). Consistent with these findings, COX-2 inhibitors inhibit $\alpha_v\beta_3$-dependent endothelial cell spreading and migration in vitro and angiogenesis in vivo.

6.3
Integrins in Tumor Angiogenesis

- Integrin $\alpha_V\beta_3$ was the first integrin associated with angiogenesis (Brooks et al. 1994). $\alpha_V\beta_3$ is highly expressed in angiogenic endothelial cells in granulation tissue and in malignant tumors, but is virtually absent from quiescent endothelial cells (Hynes 2007). Inhibition of $\alpha_V\beta_3$ with a function-blocking monoclonal antibody, or RGD-based peptides, or peptidomimetics suppressed corneal neovascularization (Klotz et al. 2000), hypoxia-induced retinal neovascularization (Hammes et al. 1996), tumor angiogenesis, and tumor progression in various in vivo models (MacDonald et al. 2001; Reinmuth et al. 2003), and endothelial cell sprouting and angiogenesis in an in vitro 3D model of angiogenesis (Nisato et al. 2004). Importantly, quiescent and pre-existing vessels were not perturbed by these treatments. The results obtained with pharmacological antagonists of integrins $\alpha_V\beta_3/\alpha_V\beta_5$ contrast with results obtained through genetic approaches. Mice deficient in α_V integrins and lacking $\alpha_V\beta_1$, $\alpha_V\beta_3$, $\alpha_V\beta_5$, $\alpha_V\beta_6$, and $\alpha_V\beta_8$ expression, were still able to undergo extensive developmental vasculogenesis and angiogenesis, although they died in utero or shortly after birth (Bader et al. 1998). Analysis of the phenotype of individual β integrin knock-out mice showed that the β_8 knock-out was the only one to reproduce the α_V knock-out phenotype (Zhu et al. 2002), thereby revealing a role for $\alpha_V\beta_8$ in the association between cerebral microvessels and brain parenchymal cells. Deletion of the β_3 subunit did not significantly disrupt vascular development, although some embryos died in utero due to placenta defects, while others died postnatally due to bleeding and anemia (Hodivala-Dilke et al. 1999). β_3-deficiency reproduce the inherited human bleeding disorder known as Glanzmann thrombasthenia due to the concomitant lack of $\alpha_{IIb}\beta_3$ (Tomiyama 2000). Paradoxically, mice lacking $\alpha_V\beta_3$ integrins had enhanced pathological angiogenesis, including tumor angiogenesis (Reynolds et al. 2002), associated with enhanced VEGFR-2 signaling (Reynolds et al. 2004). The reason for the divergence of the results obtained with pharmacological inhibition vs. genetic deletion of $\alpha_V\beta_3$ are not yet fully clear (Hynes 2002).

- More recently, β_1 integrins (i.e., $\alpha_1\beta_1$, $\alpha_2\beta_1$, $\alpha_3\beta_1$, $\alpha_4\beta_1$, $\alpha_5\beta_1$, $\alpha_V\beta_1$), $\alpha_V\beta_8$, and $\alpha_6\beta_4$ have also been shown to promote angiogenesis (Alghisi and Ruegg 2006; Serini et al. 2006). β_1 integrin expression on vascular endothelial cells is dispensable for vasculogenesis, but crucial for embryonic angiogenesis (Tanjore et al. 2007). Deletion of the α_5 gene is embryonically lethal and is associated with vascular and cardiac defects (Francis et al. 2002). $\alpha_5\beta_1$ is up regulated in angiogenesis and blocking anti-α_5 antibodies suppressed VEGF-induced tumor angiogenesis in both chick embryo and murine models (Collo and Pepper 1999; Kim et al. 2000). An $\alpha_5\beta_1$ antagonist in combination with chemotherapy reduced metastasis and suppressed angiogenesis at metastatic lesions (Stoeltzing et al. 2003).

- Integrins $\alpha_1\beta_1$ and $\alpha_2\beta_1$ are highly upregulated by VEGF in cultured endothelial cells, resulting in enhanced cell spreading on collagen I, while anti-$\alpha_1\beta_1$ and anti-$\alpha_2\beta_1$ antibodies inhibited VEGF-driven angiogenesis in vivo. Combined administration of anti-$\alpha_1\beta_1$ and anti-$\alpha_2\beta_1$ antibodies to mice bearing squamous cell carcinoma xenografts, resulted in reduced tumor angiogenesis and tumor growth (Hong et al. 2004; Perruzzi et al. 2003; Senger et al. 2002). The role of $\alpha_2\beta_1$ for the regulation of murine wound angiogenesis was confirmed in a genetic approach (Zweers et al. 2007).

- $\alpha_6\beta_4$ promotes an invasive endothelial cell phenotype at the early phase of angiogenesis in response to growth factors (FGF-2, VEGF)

(Nikolopoulos et al. 2004). Genetic studies have revealed that $\alpha_6\beta_4$ signaling promotes both angiogenesis and tumorigenesis. Importantly, $\alpha_6\beta_4$ combines with multiple receptor tyrosine kinases, including ErbB2, EGF-R and c-Met, and enhances their signaling function (Giancotti 2007).

6.4
Integrin Antagonists with Antiangiogenic Activities

Four different types of integrin antagonists have been developed: antibodies, endogenous inhibitors, peptides, and nonpeptidic antagonists. We describe here the main representative drugs within each class that have shown antiangiogenic activity in preclinical models, with particular emphasis on drugs that entered clinical testing. These and additional inhibitors are summarized in Table 6.1.

6.4.1
Antibodies

- *LM609/MEDI-522/Vitaxin.* The anti-$\alpha_v\beta_3$ monoclonal antibody LM609 blocked endothelial cell adhesion, migration, and sprouting in vitro and angiogenesis in vivo in the CAM assay (Brooks et al. 1994). Subsequently, LM609 was humanized and affinity matured allowing the isolation of an antibody with a 90-fold improved affinity (MEDI-522 or Vitaxin) (Wu et al. 1998). Phase I studies demonstrated that treatment was well tolerated with little or no toxicity. The most common side effect was infusion-related fevers. Doses of 1 mg/kg/week or more produced plasma concentrations sufficient to saturate $\alpha_v\beta_3$ in vitro. Vitaxin demonstrated a half-life longer than five days with no tendency to accumulation. One partial response and several stable diseases were observed (Posey et al. 2001). Combination of Vitaxin with chemotherapy was well tolerated. There was possible effect on tumor perfusion detected by dynamic computed tomography imaging, but no objective antitumor responses (McNeel et al. 2005). In treated patients, there was evidence of reduced FAK phosphorylation in skin wound vessels, consistent with inhibition of $\alpha_v\beta_3$ signaling (Zhang et al. 2007). Vitaxin has entered Phase II trials mostly on hormone-refractory prostate cancers or metastatic melanoma (www.clinicaltrials.gov).

- *CNTO 95.* CNTO 95 is a pan anti-α_v fully humanized antibody. In a human melanoma xenograft model, wherein CNTO 95 recognized $\alpha_v\beta_3$ and $\alpha_v\beta_5$ on human tumor cells but not mouse cells, CNTO 95 treatment inhibited tumor growth by 80%. In a nude rat, human skin xenograft tumor model where CNTO 95 blocks $\alpha_v\beta_3$ and $\alpha_v\beta_5$ on both human tumor cells and human skin endothelial cells, treatment reduced final tumor weight by >99% (Trikha et al. 2004). The antibody did not show any adverse effects in monkeys (Martin et al. 2005) and entered Phase I clinical trials in various solid tumors, including ovarian, colorectal, melanoma, and renal cell carcinoma. Results on these patients showed that CNTO 95 was well tolerated up to weekly doses of 10 mg/kg (www.asco.org). CNTO 95 is now in Phase I/II in combination with other chemotherapeutic drugs in Stage IV melanoma or metastatic HRPC.

- *M200/Volociximab.* M200 is an affinity matured humanized chimeric monoclonal antibody blocking $\alpha_5\beta_1$ integrin. It inhibited tumor angiogenesis and tumor growth in a rabbit syngenic tumor model (M200 does not bind to rodent $\alpha_5\beta_1$) despite a 20-fold lower affinity for rabbit integrin, relative to human (Bhaskar et al. 2007a). A function blocking rat-anti-mouse $\alpha_5\beta_1$ antibody with features similar to M200 was shown to inhibit angiogenesis and suppress tumor growth and metastasis in mice (Bhaskar et al. 2007b;

Table 6.1 Integrin antagonists in clinical trials

	Inhibitor	Targeted integrins	Clinical development	References
Antibodies	LM609, MEDI-522, vitaxin®	$\alpha_V\beta_3$	Passed phase I In phase II	(Gutheil et al. 2000; McNeel et al. 2005; Posey et al. 2001)
	Volociximab, M200	$\alpha_5\beta_1$	Passed phase I, currently in phase II	(Kuwada 2007; Ramakrishnan et al. 2006) www.pdl.com
	CNTO 95	α_V family, strong affinity for $\alpha_V\beta_3$ and $\alpha_V\beta_5$	Phase I or phaseI/II	(Mullamitha et al. 2007; Trikha et al. 2004) www.clinicaltrials.gov
	17E6	α_V family, strong affinity for $\alpha_V\beta_3$, $\alpha_V\beta_5$ and $\alpha_V\beta_1$		(Mitjans et al. 1995, 2000)
	7E3, abciximab, ReoPro	$\alpha_{IIb}\beta_3$ primarily but also $\alpha_V\beta_3$ and $\alpha_M\beta_2$ (Mac-1)	Passed phase I and II. Currently in phase III for the prevention of restenosis	(Nakada et al. 2006; Varner et al. 1999)
	Ha 31/8	$\alpha_1\beta_1$		(Senger et al. 1997, 2002)
	Ha 1/29	$\alpha_2\beta_1$		(Senger et al. 1997, 2002)
	NKI-SAM-1, JBS5 or IIA1	$\alpha_5\beta_1$		(Francis et al. 2002; Kim et al. 2000)
Endogenous inhibitors	Endostatin (C-terminal fragment of collagen XVIII)	$\alpha_5\beta_1$	Phase I	(Herbst et al. 2002), www.clinicaltrials.gov
	Tumstatin (C-terminal fragment of collagen IV)	$\alpha_V\beta_3$		(Hamano and Kalluri 2005; Maeshima et al. 2002)
	Endorepellin (C-terminal module of perlecan)	$\alpha_2\beta_1$		(Woodall et al., 2008)
	Angiocidin	$\alpha_2\beta_1$		(Sabherwal et al. 2006)
	PEX (MMP-2 proteolytic fragment)	$\alpha_V\beta_3$		(Bello et al. 2001; Pfeifer et al. 2000)
	Fastatin (FAS1 domain of βig-h3	$\alpha_V\beta_3$		(Nam et al. 2005)

Table 6.1 (continued)

	Inhibitor	Targeted integrins	Clinical development	References
Synthetic peptides	EMD121974, cilengitide	$\alpha_v\beta_3$	Passed phase I Phase II	(Eskens et al. 2003; Nabors et al. 2007) www.clinicaltrials.gov
	TP508 (thrombospondin derived peptide)	$\alpha_v\beta_3$		(Tsopanoglou et al. 2004)
	S247	$\alpha_v\beta_3$		(Abdollahi et al. 2005)
	ATN-161	$\alpha_5\beta_1$	Phase I Phase II	(Cianfrocca et al. 2006) www.clinicaltrials.gov
	CRRETAWAC (fibronectin peptide)	$\alpha_5\beta_1$		(Koivunen et al. 1994; Mould et al. 1998)
Peptidomimetics	SCH221153	$\alpha_v\beta_3$ and $\alpha_v\beta_5$		(Kumar et al. 2001)
	BCH-14661 BCH-15056	$\alpha_v\beta_3$ and $\alpha_v\beta_5$		(Meerovitch et al. 2003)
	ST1646	$\alpha_v\beta_3$ and $\alpha_v\beta_5$		(Belvisi et al. 2005)
	Thiolutin	$\alpha_v\beta_3$ (indirect), decreases paxillin levels		(Minamiguchi et al. 2001)
	SJ749	$\alpha_5\beta_1$		(Kim et al. 2000; Marinelli et al. 2005)
	JSM6427	$\alpha_5\beta_1$		(Umeda et al. 2006)

A nonexhaustive list of available antibody, peptide and peptidomimetic antagonists of integrins with anti-angiogenic activities developed so far is presented (some compounds are further described in the text)

Ramakrishnan et al. 2006). Based on this activity profile, Volociximab was tested in Phase I trials in various refractory solid tumors including renal cell carcinoma and metastatic melanoma. The study data showed that adverse events were generally mild to moderate in intensity and there were no dose limiting toxicities. Volociximab is currently evaluated in Phase II trials as a single agent (Kuwada 2007). Combination trials with chemotherapy are planned.

- *c7E3/Abciximab/ReoPro*. c7E3 is a humanized monoclonal antibody Fab fragment approved for use as adjunct therapy to prevent cardiac ischemic complications in patients undergoing coronary angioplasty (Cohen et al. 2000). c7E3 also interacts with integrins $\alpha_v\beta_3$ and Mac-1 ($\alpha_M\beta_2$). In animal models, c7E3 inhibited tumor growth and angiogenesis (Nakada et al. 2006).

6.4.2
Endogenous Antagonists

- *Endostatin* is a carboxyl-terminal fragment of Collagen XVIII inhibiting endothelial cell proliferation in vitro and angiogenesis and

6

tumor growth in vivo (O'Reilly et al. 1997). The generation of endostatin from Collagen XII is mediated by various proteases (e.g., cathepsin L and MMPs). The antiangiogenic activity of endostatin is due, at least in part, to binding to integrin $\alpha_5\beta_1$ and caveolin-1 on endothelial cells, causing downregulation of RhoA activity and Src family kinase-dependent disassembly of focal adhesions and actin stress fibers, resulting in decreased matrix deposition and migration (Wickstrom et al. 2005). Recombinant human endostatin entered clinical testing and was found to be safe and well tolerated (Hansma et al. 2005; Herbst et al. 2002).

- *Tumstatin* consists of the carboxyl-terminal noncollagenous 1 (NC1) domain of the α3 chain of Collagen IV. It inhibited in vivo neovascularization in Matrigel plug assays, suppressed tumor growth in xenograft models, and induced endothelial cell apoptosis (Hamano and Kalluri 2005). Tumstatin binds to $\alpha_V\beta_3$ integrin in endothelial cells, and selectively inhibits protein synthesis by suppressing mTOR (Maeshima et al. 2002).

6.4.3
Peptides

- *EMD121974/Cilengitide.* The discovery that many integrins recognize their ligands through short amino acid sequences, most notably RGD, led to the development of small peptides that competitively blocked ligand–receptor interaction. Cyclized peptides were up to 100-fold more selective than linear counterparts, and cyclic pentapeptides that possessed two hydrophobic amino acids next to the recognition sequence proved to be highly active and selective for $\alpha_V\beta_3/\alpha_V\beta_5$. The cyclic pentapeptide cyclo(-Arg-Gly-Asp-D-Phe-Val-) (EMD66203 Merck KGaA) showed nanomolar inhibition of vitronectin binding to the $\alpha_V\beta_3$ integrin without

interfering with $\alpha_{IIb}\beta_3$ integrin (Haubner et al. 1996). Modification of the amino acids flanking the RGD sequence led to the synthesis of EMD121974 (Cilengitide) inhibiting $\alpha_V\beta_3$ integrin binding to vitronectin with an IC_{50} of 0.6 nM versus 900 nM for the $\alpha_{IIb}\beta_3$ integrin (Smith 2003). Cilengitide showed antitumor effects in brain, melanoma, head and neck, and brain tumors (MacDonald et al. 2001; Mitjans et al. 2000; Raguse et al. 2004; Taga et al. 2002). In Phase I, studies of cilengitide were well tolerated with no dose-limiting toxicities, and showed evidence of activity in recurrent malignant gliomas (Nabors et al. 2007). Cilengitide is now in Phase II clinical trials, alone and in combination with radio and chemotherapies, in solid tumors, leukemia, and lymphoma (Stupp and Ruegg 2007).

- *ATN-161* is a peptide derived from the $\alpha_5\beta_1$-binding sequence PHSRN present in fibronectin (Livant et al. 2000). Chemical modifications of this sequence led to the synthesis of ATN-161 (Ac-PHSCN-NH$_2$) that, in contrast to other integrin antagonist peptides, is not a RGD-based peptide. ATN-161 possesses antitumorigenic antiangiogenic activities in mice in the absence of toxicities (Livant et al. 2000). ATN-161 was tested in a Phase I study in patients with advanced solid tumors for up to 14 cycles of 4 weeks and was well tolerated at all dose levels. Approximately, one-third of the treated patients manifested prolonged stable disease (Cianfrocca et al. 2006).

6.4.4
Non-peptidic Inhibitors

Peptidomimetics are compounds containing non-peptidic structural elements mimicking the action(s) of a natural parent peptide. Peptidomimetics can be administered orally, are insensitive to protease-mediated degradation, and have longer stability (Cacciari and Spalluto 2005).

- *SCH221153* was obtained by screening and further modifying an RGD-based peptidomimetic library. It targets $\alpha_v\beta_3$ and $\alpha_v\beta_5$ integrins with IC_{50} of 3.2 and 1.7 nM, respectively. SCH221153 inhibited endothelial cell adhesion to vitronectin and suppressed angiogenesis in a CAM assay (Kumar et al. 2001).
- *BCH-14661* and *BCH-15046* are integrin antagonists that induce cell detachment and apoptosis of angiogenic endothelial grown on RGD-based matrices (i.e., vitronectin and fibronectin). BCH-14661 is specific for $\alpha_v\beta_3$, while BCH-15046 antagonizes $\alpha_v\beta_3$, $\alpha_v\beta_5$ and $\alpha_5\beta_1$ (Meerovitch et al. 2003). BCH-15046 was also capable to induce endothelial cell apoptosis independently of cell detachment.
- *Thiolutin* is a non-peptidic antagonist of cell adhesion interfering with integrin-post-receptor events (Minamiguchi et al. 2001). The antiadhesive effect of thiolutin is due to decreased paxillin protein expression, disruption of focal adhesions, and cell detachment.
- *SJ749*, which structure mimics RGD-based sequences, is a potent inhibitor of $\alpha_5\beta_1$ integrin (IC_{50} around 0.8 nM), and it inhibited angiogenesis in the CAM assay (Kim et al. 2000). The structure of this non-peptidic compound bound to the head of the $\alpha_5\beta_1$ integrin has been resolved, thereby opening new perspectives in rational design to improve its specificity and binding constant (Marinelli et al. 2005).
- *JSM6427* is another $\alpha_5\beta_1$-specific peptidomimetic inhibitor with antiangiogenic activities (Umeda et al. 2006). Interestingly, JSM6427 inhibited inflammatory lymphangiogenesis (Dietrich et al. 2007) suggesting the possibility of combined targeting angiogenesis and lymphangiogenesis by targeting one integrin.

6.5
Open Questions and Current Developments

Preclinical studies suggest that vascular integrins are valuable targets for antiangiogenic treatments. Results obtained in Phase I clinical trials have shown that the integrin antagonists tested so far are well tolerated and hint some antitumor activity. Phase II trials aimed at demonstrating antiangiogenic/antitumor activities are ongoing (Stupp and Ruegg 2007). Important basic questions on the role of integrins in angiogenesis and their therapeutic targeting, however, have remained unanswered and new ones have emerged. In this section we review some of the open outstanding questions.

6.5.1
Most Relevant Targets

Endothelial cells can express up to 12 integrins ($\alpha_v\beta_3$, $\alpha_v\beta_5$, $\alpha_5\beta_1$, $\alpha_1\beta_1$, $\alpha_2\beta_1$, $\alpha_6\beta_4$, $\alpha_3\beta_1$, $\alpha_4\beta_1$, $\alpha_6\beta_1$, $\alpha_8\beta_1$, $\alpha_v\beta_1$, and $\alpha_v\beta_8$) (Alghisi and Ruegg 2006). At this point, we do not know which one of these integrins is the best therapeutic target for antiangiogenic treatments, and if angiogenic vessels in different tumors or at different stages of development may use different integrins. More preclinical work is needed to test and compare the suitability of individual integrins as therapeutic target and to evaluate the possibility of combined targeting.

6.5.2
Combination Therapies

Combined treatment with integrin antagonists and chemotherapy or radiotherapy has shown enhanced therapeutic efficacy in preclinical models (Ruegg and Mutter 2007). Since combination therapy appears to be a general rule for

6

antiangiogenic treatments in humans, the critical issue is to define the best combination in term of drug association, timing, and schedule.

- *Radiotherapy.* Integrin antagonists enhance efficacy of radiotherapy. Radiation was found to upregulate $\alpha_v\beta_3$ expression in endothelial cells and to induce activation of Akt/PKB, possibly as a mechanism for the tumor vasculature to escape or recover from radiation-induced injury. Inhibitors of $\alpha_v\beta_3$ integrin suppressed radiation-induced Akt/PKB phosphorylation, increased cell death and enhanced antiangiogenic and antitumor effects in xenograft models (Abdollahi et al. 2005; Ning et al. 2007). Using a different model, cilengitide sensitized tumors to radioimmunotherapy (Burke et al. 2002). These results reinforce the rationale of combining vascular integrin antagonists with radiotherapy.
- *Chemotherapy.* Combination of ATN-161 ($\alpha_5\beta_1$ antagonist) with 5-fluoroacil synergized the reduction of the number of liver metastases and tumor burden of CT26 colon cancer cells in mice (Stoeltzing et al. 2003). Liver tumors in the ATN-161 and ATN-161/5-FU groups had significantly fewer microvessels than tumors in the control or 5-FU-treated groups.
- *Tumor Necrosis Factor (TNF).* TNF is used in combination with high dose chemotherapy in an isolation limb perfusion setting to treat advanced cancers of the limbs (Lejeune et al. 2006). The mechanism by which TNF exerts its antitumor activity involves detachment and death of angiogenic endothelial cells expressing $\alpha_v\beta_3$ (Ruegg et al. 1998). Integrin-mediated adhesion is required for TNF-induced Akt/PKB activation, an event essential for the survival of TNF-stimulated endothelial cells (Bieler et al. 2007). Consistent with these results, cilengitide sensitizes endothelial cells to TNF-induced death in vitro. Thus, combined administration of cilengitide may open new perspectives to the therapeutic use of TNF as anticancer agent.

- Tyrosine Kinase Inhibitors (TKI). Since integrins facilitate signaling from several receptor tyrosine kinases, including ErbB2, VEGFR-2, EGF-R, and Met, it is reasonable to hypothesize that integrin inhibition may sensitize endothelial cells to currently available TKI antiangiogenic drugs (e.g., bevacizumab, sorafenib, sunitinib, temsirolimus) or to other TKI with antiangiogenic activities, such as EGFR antagonists (e.g., cetuximab or gefitinib), or PDGFRs inhibitors (e.g., Imatinib). Indeed, combined administration of cilengitide and SU5416, a VEGR-2 TKI reduced tumoral vessel density and intratumoral blood flow compared to single drug treatments (Strieth et al. 2006). $\alpha_6\beta_4$ might be an interesting integrin to target in combination with ErbB2, EGFR, and Met inhibitors, since, in addition to antiangiogenic effects, it may also have direct antitumor activity, as $\alpha_6\beta_4$ and ErbB2, EGF-R and Met are expressed on many carcinoma cells (Giancotti 2007). The endogenous antiangiogenic peptide tumstatin was shown to exert direct antitumoral effects in $\alpha_v\beta_3$ expressing glioma cells in vitro and in vivo by suppressing $\alpha_v\beta_3$-dependent Akt and mTOR signaling (Kawaguchi et al. 2006), suggesting the possibility that a combination strategy may be chosen in a way to target angiogenic endothelial cells and tumor cells.

6.5.3
Drug Targeting

Vascular integrins expressed on tumoral vessels, such as $\alpha_v\beta_3$ have been used to target drugs to tumors. Cationic nanoparticles coupled with an integrin $\alpha_v\beta_3$-targeting ligand were used to deliver a dominant-negative mutant Raf gene to angiogenic blood vessels in tumor-bearing mice, resulting in apoptosis of the tumor vessels and regression of established primary and metastatic tumors (Hood et al. 2002). Paclitaxel

(Taxol), an antitumor drug commonly used for the treatment of advanced metastatic breast cancer, conjugated with an RGD-based peptide had a better uptake kinetic in vivo compared to free paclitaxel (i.e., 4 h for free PTX vs. 2 h for the PTX-RGD conjugate), although it did not show enhanced potency at the cellular level(Chen et al. 2005). These experiments demonstrate the feasibility of integrin-based targeted drug delivery to tumors. More recently, several studies reported that conjugation of $\alpha_V\beta_3$-targeting RGD peptides or peptidomimetics to carrier proteins (e.g., antibody), synthetic scaffold structures, or micelles (e.g., PEG-polyLys-associated with plasmid DNA) resulted in improved pharmacokinetics, retention in the tumor tissue, and cellular uptake (Mitra et al. 2006; Oba et al. 2007; Shin et al. 2007). $\alpha_V\beta_3$-integrin-targeted nanoparticles rapidly taken up by $\alpha_V\beta_3$-positive angiogenic vessels and tumors were developed for delivery and imaging purposes (Xie et al. 2007).

6.5.4
Tumor Imaging

Vascular integrins upregulated in angiogenic vessels have also been explored for noninvasive tumor imaging purposes. Most approaches have targeted $\alpha_V\beta_3$ in combination with positron emission tomography (PET) and Magnetic Resonance Imaging (MRI) imaging techniques (Choe and Lee 2007). The proof of concept experiment was reported already in 1998, where gadolinium-labeled LM609 was used to detect angiogenesis in a rabbit tumor model.

Before this approach be successfully translated into the clinic, however, substantial gains in sensitivity brought about by improved coils, pulse sequences, and contrast agents were needed (Barrett et al. 2007). Thanks to its high sensitivity, PET technology has been preferred and used in animal models and in humans to detect $\alpha_V\beta_3$ using ^{18}F-labeled monomeric or multimeric RGD peptides. The level of expression $\alpha_V\beta_3$ detected by PET, correlated with the level of $\alpha_V\beta_3$ determined by immunohistochemistry, suggesting that this approach may be used for the noninvasive measurement of $\alpha_V\beta_3$ and monitoring antiangiogenic therapy in patients (Beer et al. 2006). ^{64}Cu-DOTA-labeled Vitaxin (Abegrin) were used in animal models and showed high levels of late tumor activity accumulation (i.e., 71 h) post injection (Cai et al. 2006). Similarly, ^{99m}Tc-labeled RGD peptides were used to image tumors and angiogenic vascular beds by gamma camera (Decristoforo et al. 2006) or single photon emission computed tomography (SPECT) in experimental models (Liu et al. 2007). Recently, near-infrared fluorescence imaging coupled with 3D optical imaging systems have been used to image $\alpha_V\beta_3$-positive tumor vessels and tumor cells in mice using Cy5.5-RGD peptides (Hsu et al. 2006). Taken together, these results illustrate the potential of employing integrin-targeted molecular probes to image tumor vasculature and monitoring response to therapy.

6.6
Future Directions

6.6.1
New Generation of Extracellular Antagonists

While most efforts have been focused on the generation of small molecular inhibitors based on the RGD sequence or the ligand-binding pocket, recent studies have reported inhibitors acting in a RGD-independent manner, such as tumstatin (Maeshima et al. 2000) or ATN-161 (Livant et al. 2000). The resolution of the 3D structure of cilengitide-$\alpha_V\beta_3$ complex (Xiong et al. 2002) and of SJ749-$\alpha_5\beta_1$ complex (Marinelli et al. 2005), allows for the exploration of additional regions of the receptor for binding of novel inhibitory molecules, "*in silico*" design and virtual screenings of improved or fully novel antagonists (Zhou et al. 2006). Furthermore, "broad spectrum" inhibitors blocking several angiogenic integrins (e.g., β_1 and β_3) may be developed, as suggested by the recent report of BCH-15046, a $\alpha_v\beta_3$, $\alpha_v\beta_5$ and $\alpha_5\beta_1$ antagonist (Meerovitch et al. 2003).

6.6.2
Targeting the Integrin Intracellular Domains

Interaction of the cytoplasmic tail of the β subunit is essential for integrin function (Travis et al. 2003). Expression of isolated β integrin subunit cytoplasmic and transmembrane domains in adherent endothelial cells caused cell detachment and death in vitro and in vivo (Hasmim et al. 2005; Oguey et al. 2000), consistent with the notion that overexpression of isolated β-cytoplasmic domain competes for binding of essential cytoplasmic adaptor proteins (e.g., talin), resulting in "mechanical uncoupling"of the integrins from focal adhesions and cytoskeletal structures. These results also suggest the possibility of targeting the cytoplasmic domain for therapeutic purposes. Two main problems need to be addressed: the first one concerns integrin specificity (current constructs that do not differentiate between β_1 and β_3 integrins). The second problem concerns intracellular delivery: to allow penetration into the cell, an inhibitory peptide has to be fused to cytoplasmic transduction peptides (Kim et al. 2006). Alternatively, non-peptidic drugs may be developed to disrupt β_3-tail interaction with structural or signaling cytoplasmic proteins.

6.6.3
Targeting Angiogenic Precursor Cells and Inflammatory Cells

Bone marrow cells are mobilized during tumor growth and recruited at tumor sites to promote tumor angiogenesis. While some of the cells include true endothelial precursors giving rise to mature endothelial cells, most of them are of monocyte/macrophage lineage (De Palma and Naldini 2006). Monocyte/macrophage is very sensitive to hypoxia and produces angiogenic factors and chemokines that stimulate tumor angiogenesis, progression, and metastasis (Condeelis and Pollard 2006). Since leukocytes and inflammatory cells use integrins to extravasate and migrate through the stroma, such as $\alpha_L\beta_2$, $\alpha_4\beta_1$, $\alpha_M\beta_2$, $\alpha_v\beta_3$, or $\alpha_5\beta_1$, it may be reasonable to inhibit their recruitment to tumor sites by targeting their integrins (Ulbrich et al. 2003). For example, antagonists of integrin $\alpha_4\beta_1$ blocked extravasation of monocytes into tumor tissue and prevented monocyte macrophage colonization of tumors and tumor angiogenesis (Jin et al. 2006). Since it is also possible that some of the antiangiogenic effects observed with $\alpha_v\beta_3$ or $\alpha_5\beta_1$ antagonists may be due to the inhibition of leukocyte recruitment, in future experimental and clinical studies it will be important to monitor the effect of integrin inhibitors on the recruitment of inflammatory cells to tumor sites. Of note is the observation that Cilengitide inhibited proliferation and differentiation of human endothelial progenitor cells in vitro (Loges et al. 2007).

6.7
Conclusions

Preclinical evidence indicates that integrins expressed in angiogenic endothelial cells are potentially relevant targets for antiangiogenic therapies in cancer. Early clinical trials have provided initial evidence of activity in human cancers, and ongoing clinical trials tell us whether they may bring benefits to human cancer treatment. If this is the case, besides further clinical trials, there will be a race to generate novel, more potent, and orally bioavailable "second generation" antagonists as well as to define the best combination strategy. The possibility of coupling the use of integrin antagonists for therapeutic purposes with non-invasive imaging of vascular integrins would open the possibility to select patients expressing high levels of the target, and therefore those who are most likely to benefit from the treatment.

Acknowledgments   Work in our laboratory was supported by funds from the Molecular Oncology Program of the National Center for Competence in Research (NCCR), a research instrument of the Swiss National Science Foundation, the Swiss Cancer League/Oncosuisse, the Swiss National Science Foundation, and the Medic Foundation. We apologize to those colleagues whose work could not be cited due to space limitations.

References

Abdollahi A, Griggs DW, Zieher H, Roth A, Lipson KE, Saffrich R, Grone H-J, Hallahan DE, Reisfeld RA, Debus J, Niethammer AG, Huber PE (2005) Inhibition of alpha(v)beta3 integrin survival signaling enhances antiangiogenic and antitumor effects of radiotherapy. Clin Cancer Res 11: 6270–6279

Alghisi GC, Ruegg C (2006) Vascular integrins in tumor angiogenesis: mediators and therapeutic targets. Endothelium 13:113–135

Bader B, Rayburn H, Crowley D, Hynes R (1998) Extensive vasculogenesis, angiogenesis, and organogenesis precede lethality in mice lacking all alpha v integrins. Cell 95:507–519

Barrett T, Brechbiel M, Bernardo M, Choyke PL (2007) MRI of tumor angiogenesis. J Magn Reson Imaging 26:235–249

Beer AJ, Haubner R, Sarbia M, Goebel M, Luderschmidt S, Grosu AL, Schnell O, Niemeyer M, Kessler H, Wester HJ, Weber WA, Schwaiger M (2006) Positron emission tomography using [18F]Galacto-RGD identifies the level of integrin alpha(v)beta3 expression in man. Clin Cancer Res 12:3942–3949

Bello L, Lucini V, Carrabba G, Giussani C, Machluf M, Pluderi M, Nikas D, Zhang J, Tomei G, Villani RM, Carroll RS, Bikfalvi A, Black PM (2001) Simultaneous inhibition of glioma angiogenesis, cell proliferation, and invasion by a naturally occurring fragment of human metalloproteinase-2. Cancer Res 61: 8730–8736

Belvisi L, Riccioni T, Marcellini M, Vesci L, Chiarucci I, Efrati D, Potenza D, Scolastico C, Manzoni L, Lombardo K, Stasi MA, Orlandi A, Ciucci A, Nico B, Ribatti D, Giannini G, Presta M, Carminati P, Pisano C (2005) Biological and molecular properties of a new alpha(v)beta3/alpha(v)beta5 integrin antagonist. Mol Cancer Ther 4:1670–1680

Bhaskar V, Fox M, Breinberg D, Wong MH, Wales PE, Rhodes S, Dubridge RB, Ramakrishnan V (2007a) Volociximab, a chimeric integrin alpha5beta1 antibody, inhibits growth of VX2 tumors in rabbits. Invest New Drugs 26(1):7–12

Bhaskar V, Zhang D, Fox M, Seto P, Wong MH, Wales PE, Powers D, Chao DT, Dubridge RB, Ramakrishnan V (2007b) A function blocking anti-mouse integrin alpha5beta1 antibody inhibits angiogenesis and impedes tumor growth in vivo. J Transl Med 5:61

Bieler G, Hasmim M, Monnier Y, Imaizumi N, Ameyar M, Bamat J, Ponsonnet L, Chouaib S, Grell M, Goodman SL, Lejeune F, Ruegg C (2007) Distinctive role of integrin-mediated adhesion in TNF-induced PKB/Akt and NF-kappaB activation and endothelial cell survival. Oncogene 26: 5722–5732

Brooks PC, Clark RA, Cheresh DA (1994) Requirement of vascular integrin alpha v beta 3 for angiogenesis. Science 264:569–571

Burke PA, DeNardo SJ, Miers LA, Lamborn KR, Matzku S, DeNardo GL (2002) Cilengitide targeting of alpha(v)beta3 integrin receptor synergizes with radioimmunotherapy to increase efficacy and apoptosis in breast cancer xenografts. Cancer Res 62:4263–4272

Cacciari B, Spalluto G (2005) Non peptidic alphav-beta3 antagonists: recent developments. Curr Med Chem 12:51–70

Cai W, Wu Y, Chen K, Cao Q, Tice DA, Chen X (2006) In vitro and in vivo characterization of 64Cu-labeled Abegrin, a humanized monoclonal antibody against integrin alpha v beta 3. Cancer Res 66:9673–9681

Camenisch G, Pisabarro MT, Sherman D, Kowalski J, Nagel M, Hass P, Xie MH, Gurney A, Bodary S, Liang XH, Clark K, Beresini M, Ferrara N, Gerber HP (2002) ANGPTL3 stimulates endothelial cell adhesion and migration via integrin alpha vbeta 3 and induces blood vessel formation in vivo. J Biol Chem 277: 17281–17290

Chen X, Plasencia C, Hou Y, Neamati N (2005) Synthesis and biological evaluation of dimeric RGD peptide-paclitaxel conjugate as a model for integrin-targeted drug delivery. J Med Chem 48:1098–1106

Choe YS, Lee KH (2007) Targeted in vivo imaging of angiogenesis: present status and perspectives. Curr Pharm Des 13:17–31

Cianfrocca ME, Kimmel KA, Gallo J, Cardoso T, Brown MM, Hudes G, Lewis N, Weiner L, Lam GN, Brown SC, Shaw DE, Mazar AP, Cohen RB (2006) Phase 1 trial of the antiangiogenic peptide ATN-161 (Ac-PHSCN-NH(2)), a beta integrin antagonist, in patients with solid tumours. Br J Cancer 94:1621–1626

Cohen S, Trikha M, Mascelli M (2000) Potential future clinical applications for the GPIIb/IIIa antagonist, abciximab in thrombosis, vascular and oncological indications. Pathol Oncol Res 6: 163–174

Collo G, Pepper MS (1999) Endothelial cell integrin alpha5beta1 expression is modulated by cytokines and during migration in vitro. J Cell Sci 112: 569–578

Condeelis J, Pollard JW (2006) Macrophages: obligate partners for tumor cell migration, invasion, and metastasis. Cell 124:263–266

Coutifaris C, Omigbodun A, Coukos G (2005) The fibronectin receptor alpha5 integrin subunit is upregulated by cell-cell adhesion via a cyclic AMP-dependent mechanism: implications for human trophoblast migration. Am J Obstet Gynecol 192:1240–1253; discussion 1253–1255

De Palma M, Naldini L (2006) Role of haematopoietic cells and endothelial progenitors in tumour angiogenesis. Biochim Biophys Acta 1766: 159–166

Decristoforo C, Faintuch-Linkowski B, Rey A, von Guggenberg E, Rupprich M, Hernandez-Gonzales I, Rodrigo T, Haubner R (2006) [99mTc]HYNIC-RGD for imaging integrin alphavbeta3 expression. Nucl Med Biol 33:945–952

Dietrich T, Onderka J, Bock F, Kruse FE, Vossmeyer D, Stragies R, Zahn G, Cursiefen C (2007) Inhibition of inflammatory lymphangiogenesis by integrin alpha5 blockade. Am J Pathol 171: 361–372

Dormond O, Ruegg C (2003) Regulation of endothelial cell integrin function and angiogenesis by COX-2, cAMP and protein kinase A. Thromb Haemost 90:577–585

Eskens FALM, Dumez H, Hoekstra R, Perschl A, Brindley C, Bottcher S, Wynendaele W, Drevs J, Verweij J, van Oosterom AT (2003) Phase I and pharmacokinetic study of continuous twice weekly intravenous administration of Cilengitide (EMD 121974), a novel inhibitor of the integrins [alpha]v[beta]3 and [alpha]v[beta]5 in patients with advanced solid tumours. Eur J Cancer 39: 917–926

Francis SE, Goh KL, Hodivala-Dilke K, Bader BL, Stark M, Davidson D, Hynes RO (2002) Central roles of alpha5beta1 integrin and fibronectin in vascular development in mouse embryos and embryoid bodies. Arterioscler Thromb Vasc Biol 22:927–933

Giancotti FG (2007) Targeting integrin beta4 for cancer and anti-angiogenic therapy. Trends Pharmacol Sci 28:506–511

Ginsberg MH, Partridge A, Shattil SJ (2005) Integrin regulation. Curr Opin Cell Biol 17:509–516

Gutheil JC, Campbell TN, Pierce PR, Watkins JD, Huse WD, Bodkin DJ, Cheresh DA (2000) Targeted antiangiogenic therapy for cancer using vitaxin: a humanized monoclonal antibody to the integrin aVb3. Clin Cancer Res 6:3056–3061

Hamano Y, Kalluri R (2005) Tumstatin, the NC1 domain of alpha3 chain of type IV collagen, is an endogenous inhibitor of pathological angiogenesis and suppresses tumor growth. Biochem Biophys Res Commun 333:292–298

Hammes H, Brownlee M, Jonczyk A, Sutter A, Preissner K (1996) Subcutaneous injection of a cyclic peptide antagonist of vitronectin receptor-type integrins inhibits retinal neovascularization. Nat Med 2:529–533

Hansma AHG, Broxterman HJ, van der Horst I, Yuana Y, Boven E, Giaccone G, Pinedo HM, Hoekman K (2005) Recombinant human endostatin administered as a 28-day continuous intravenous infusion, followed by daily subcutaneous injections: a phase I and pharmacokinetic study in patients with advanced cancer. Ann Oncol 16: 1695–1701

Hasmim M, Vassalli G, Alghisi G, Bamat J, Ponsonnet L, Bieler G, Bonnard C, Paroz C, Oguey D, Rüegg C (2005) Expressed isolated integrin b1 subunit cytodomain induces endothelial cell death secondary to detachment. Thromb Haemost 94: 1060–1070

Haubner R, Gratias R, Diefenbach B, Goodman SL, Jonczyk A, Kessler H (1996) Structural and functional aspects of rgd-containing cyclic penta-peptides as highly potent and selective integrin $\alpha v \beta 3$ antagonists. J. Am. Chem. Soc. 118:7461–7472

Herbst RS, Hess KR, Tran HT, Tseng JE, Mullani NA, Charnsangavej C, Madden T, Davis DW, McConkey DJ, O'Reilly MS, Ellis LM, Pluda J, Hong WK, Abbruzzese JL (2002) Phase I study of recombinant human endostatin in patients with advanced solid tumors. J Clin Oncol 20: 3792–3803

Hodivala-Dilke KM, McHugh KP, Tsakiris DA, Rayburn H, Crowley D, Ullman-Cullere M, Ross FP, Coller BS, Teitelbaum S, Hynes RO (1999) $\beta 3$-integrin–deficient mice are a model for Glanzmann thrombasthenia showing placental defects and reduced survival. J Clin Invest 103:229–238

Hong YK, Lange-Asschenfeldt B, Velasco P, Hirakawa S, Kunstfeld R, Brown LF, Bohlen P, Senger DR, Detmar M (2004) VEGF-A promotes tissue repair-associated lymphatic vessel formation via VEGFR-2 and the alpha1beta1 and alpha2beta1 integrins. Faseb J 18: 1111–1113

Hood JD, Bednarski M, Frausto R, Guccione S, Reisfeld RA, Xiang R, Cheresh DA (2002) Tumor regression by targeted gene delivery to the neovasculature. Science 296:2404–2407

Hsu AR, Hou LC, Veeravagu A, Greve JM, Vogel H, Tse V, Chen X (2006) In vivo near-infrared fluorescence imaging of integrin alphavbeta3 in an orthotopic glioblastoma model. Mol Imaging Biol 8:315–323

Hynes RO (2002) A reevaluation of integrins as regulators of angiogenesis. Nat Med 8:918–921

Hynes RO (2007) Cell-matrix adhesion in vascular development. J Thromb Haemost 5(Suppl 1): 32–40

Jin H, Su J, Garmy-Susini B, Kleeman J, Varner J (2006) Integrin alpha4beta1 promotes monocyte trafficking and angiogenesis in tumors. Cancer Res 66:2146–2152

Kawaguchi T, Yamashita Y, Kanamori M, Endersby R, Bankiewicz KS, Baker SJ, Bergers G, Pieper RO (2006) The PTEN/Akt pathway dictates the direct alphaVbeta3-dependent growth-inhibitory action of an active fragment of tumstatin in glioma cells in vitro and in vivo. Cancer Res 66:11331–11340

Kim D, Jeon C, Kim JH, Kim MS, Yoon CH, Choi IS, Kim SH, Bae YS (2006) Cytoplasmic transduction peptide (CTP): new approach for the delivery of biomolecules into cytoplasm in vitro and in vivo. Exp Cell Res 312:1277–1288

Kim S, Bell K, Mousa SA, Varner JA (2000) Regulation of angiogenesis in vivo by ligation of integrin a5b1 with the central cell-binding domain of fibronectin. Am J Pathol 156: 1345–1362

Klotz O, Park JK, Pleyer U, Hartmann C, Baatz H (2000) Inhibition of corneal neovascularization by alpha(v)-integrin antagonists in the rat. Graefes Arch Clin Exp Ophthalmol 238:88–93

Koivunen E, Wang B, Ruoslahti E (1994) Isolation of a highly specific ligand for the alpha 5 beta 1 integrin from a phage display library. J Cell Biol 124:373–380

Kumar CC, Malkowski M, Yin Z, Tanghetti E, Yaremko B, Nechuta T, Varner J, Liu M, Smith EM, Neustadt B, Presta M, Armstrong L (2001) Inhibition of angiogenesis and tumor growth by SCH221153, a dual avb3 and avb5 integrin receptor antagonist. Cancer Res 61:2232–2238

Kuwada SK (2007) Drug evaluation: volociximab, an angiogenesis-inhibiting chimeric monoclonal antibody. Curr Opin Mol Ther 9:92–98

Lejeune FJ, Lienard D, Matter M, Ruegg C (2006) Efficiency of recombinant human TNF in human cancer therapy. Cancer Immun 6:6

Liu S, Hsieh WY, Jiang Y, Kim YS, Sreerama SG, Chen X, Jia B, Wang F (2007) Evaluation of a (99m)Tc-labeled cyclic RGD tetramer for noninvasive imaging integrin alpha(v)beta3-positive breast cancer. Bioconjug Chem 18:438–446

Livant DL, Brabec RK, Pienta KJ, Allen DL, Kurachi K, Markwart S, Upadhyaya A (2000) Anti-invasive, antitumorigenic, and antimetastatic activities of the PHSCN sequence in prostate carcinoma. Cancer Res 60:309–320

Loges S, Butzal M, Otten J, Schweizer M, Fischer U, Bokemeyer C, Hossfeld DK, Schuch G, Fiedler W (2007) Cilengitide inhibits proliferation and differentiation of human endothelial progenitor cells in vitro. Biochem Biophys Res Commun 357:1016–1020

Luo BH, Carman CV, Springer TA (2007) Structural basis of integrin regulation and signaling. Annu Rev Immunol 25:619–647

MacDonald T, Taga T, Shimada H, Tabrizi P, Zlokovic B, Cheresh D, Laug W (2001) Preferential susceptibility of brain tumors to the antiangiogenic effects of an alpha(v) integrin antagonist. Neurosurgery 48:151–157

Maeshima Y, Colorado PC, Torre A, Holthaus KA, Grunkemeyer JA, Ericksen MB, Hopfer H, Xiao Y, Stillman IE, Kalluri R (2000) Distinct antitumor properties of a Type IV collagen domain derived from basement membrane. J Biol Chem 275:21340–21348

Maeshima Y, Sudhakar A, Lively JC, Ueki K, Kharbanda S, Kahn CR, Sonenberg N, Hynes RO, Kalluri R (2002) Tumstatin, an endothelial cell-specific inhibitor of protein synthesis. Science 295:140–143

Mahabeleshwar GH, Feng W, Phillips DR, Byzova TV (2006) Integrin signaling is critical for pathological angiogenesis. J Exp Med 203: 2495–2507

Marinelli L, Meyer A, Heckmann D, Lavecchia A, Novellino E, Kessler H (2005) Ligand binding analysis for human alpha5beta1 integrin: strategies for designing new alpha5beta1 integrin antagonists. J Med Chem 48:4204–4207

Martin PL, Jiao Q, Cornacoff J, Hall W, Saville B, Nemeth JA, Schantz A, Mata M, Jang H, Fasanmade AA, Anderson L, Graham MA, Davis HM, Treacy G (2005) Absence of adverse effects in cynomolgus macaques treated with CNTO 95, a fully human anti-av integrin monoclonal antibody, despite widespread tissue binding. Clin Cancer Res 11:6959–6965

McNeel DG, Eickhoff J, Lee FT, King DM, Alberti D, Thomas JP, Friedl A, Kolesar J, Marnocha R, Volkman J, Zhang J, Hammershaimb L, Zwiebel JA, Wilding G (2005) Phase I trial of a monoclonal antibody specific for avb3 integrin (MEDI-522) in patients with advanced malignancies, including an assessment of effect on tumor perfusion. Clin Cancer Res 11:7851–7860

Meerovitch K, Bergeron F, Leblond L, Grouix B, Poirier C, Bubenik M, Chan L, Gourdeau H, Bowlin T, Attardo G (2003) A novel RGD antagonist that targets both alphavbeta3 and alpha5beta1 induces apoptosis of angiogenic endothelial cells on type I collagen. Vascul Pharmacol 40:77–89

Minamiguchi K, Kumagai H, Masuda T, Kawada M, Ishizuka M, Takeuchi T (2001) Thiolutin, an inhibitor of HUVEC adhesion to vitronectin, reduces paxillin in HUVECs and suppresses tumor cell-induced angiogenesis. Int J Cancer 93:307–316

Mitjans F, Sander D, Adan J, Sutter A, Martinez JM, Jaggle CS, Moyano JM, Kreysch HG, Piulats J, Goodman SL (1995) An anti-alpha v-integrin antibody that blocks integrin function inhibits the development of a human melanoma in nude mice. J Cell Sci 108:2825–2838

Mitjans F, Meyer T, Fittschen C, Goodman S, Jonczyk A, Marshall J, Reyes G, Piulats J (2000) In vivo therapy of malignant melanoma by means of antagonists of alphav integrins. Int J Cancer 87: 716–723

Mitra A, Coleman T, Borgman M, Nan A, Ghandehari H, Line BR (2006) Polymeric conjugates of mono- and bi-cyclic alphaVbeta3 binding peptides for tumor targeting. J Control Release 114:175–183

Mould AP, Burrows L, Humphries MJ (1998) Identification of amino acid residues that form part of the ligand-binding pocket of integrin alpha 5beta 1. J. Biol. Chem. 273:25664–25672

Mullamitha SA, Ton NC, Parker GJ, Jackson A, Julyan PJ, Roberts C, Buonaccorsi GA, Watson Y, Davies K, Cheung S, Hope L, Valle JW, Radford JA, Lawrence J, Saunders MP, Munteanu MC, Nakada MT, Nemeth JA, Davis HM, Jiao Q, Prabhakar U, Lang Z, Corringham RE, Beckman RA, Jayson GC (2007) Phase I evaluation of a fully human anti-alphav integrin monoclonal antibody (CNTO 95) in patients with advanced solid tumors. Clin Cancer Res 13:2128–2135

Murakami M, Elfenbein A, Simons M (2008) Non-canonical fibroblast growth factor signaling in angiogenesis. Cardiovasc Res 78(2):223–231

Nabors LB, Mikkelsen T, Rosenfeld SS, Hochberg F, Akella NS, Fisher JD, Cloud GA, Zhang Y, Carson K, Wittemer SM, Colevas AD, Grossman SA (2007) Phase I and correlative biology study of cilengitide in patients with recurrent malignant glioma. J Clin Oncol 25:1651–1657

Nakada MT, Cao G, Sassoli PM, DeLisser HM (2006) c7E3 Fab inhibits human tumor angiogenesis in a SCID mouse human skin xenograft model. Angiogenesis 9:171–176

Nam JO, Jeong HW, Lee BH, Park RW, Kim IS (2005) Regulation of tumor angiogenesis by fastatin, the fourth FAS1 domain of betaig-h3, via alphavbeta3 integrin. Cancer Res 65:4153–4161

Nikolopoulos SN, Blaikie P, Yoshioka T, Guo W, Giancotti FG (2004) Integrin [beta]4 signaling promotes tumor angiogenesis. Cancer Cell 6:471–483

Ning S, Chen Z, Dirks A, Husbeck B, Hsu M, Bedogni B, O'Neill M, Powell MB, Knox SJ (2007) Targeting integrins and PI3K/Akt-mediated signal transduction pathways enhances radiation-induced anti-angiogenesis. Radiat Res 168: 125–133

Nisato RE, Tille J-C, Jonczyk A, Goodman SL, Pepper MS (2004) alphav beta3 and alphav beta5 integrin antagonists inhibit angiogenesis in vitro. Angiogenesis 6:105–119

O'Reilly MS, Boehm T, Shing Y, Fukai N, Vasios G, Lane WS, Flynn E, Birkhead JR, Olsen BR, Folkman J (1997) Endostatin: an endogenous inhibitor of angiogenesis and tumor growth. Cell 88:277–285

Oba M, Fukushima S, Kanayama N, Aoyagi K, Nishiyama N, Koyama H, Kataoka K (2007) Cyclic RGD peptide-conjugated polyplex micelles as a targetable gene delivery system directed to cells possessing alphavbeta3 and alphavbeta5 integrins. Bioconjug Chem 18:1415–1423

Oguey D, George P, Ruegg C (2000) Disruption of integrin-dependent adhesion and survival of endothelial cells by recombinant adenovirus expressing isolated beta integrin cytoplasmic domains. Gene Ther 7:1292–1303

Orecchia A, Lacal PM, Schietroma C, Morea V, Zambruno G, Failla CM (2003) Vascular endothelial growth factor receptor-1 is deposited in the extracellular matrix by endothelial cells and is a ligand for the alpha 5 beta 1 integrin. J Cell Sci 116:3479–3489

Perruzzi CA, de Fougerolles AR, Koteliansky VE, Whelan MC, Westlin WF, Senger DR (2003) Functional overlap and cooperativity among alphav and beta1 integrin subfamilies during skin angiogenesis. J Invest Dermatol 120: 1100–1109

Pfeifer A, Kessler T, Silletti S, Cheresh DA, Verma IM (2000) Suppression of angiogenesis by lentiviral delivery of PEX, a noncatalytic fragment of matrix metalloproteinase 2. PNAS 97:12227–12232

Posey J, Khazaeli M, DelGrosso A, Saleh M, Lin C, Huse W, LoBuglio A (2001) A pilot trial of Vitaxin, a humanized anti-vitronectin receptor (anti alpha v beta 3) antibody in patients with metastatic cancer. Cancer Biother Radiopharm 16:125–132

Raguse J-D, Gath HJ, Bier J, Riess H, Oettle H (2004) Cilengitide (EMD 121974) arrests the growth of a heavily pretreated highly vascularised head and neck tumour. Oral Oncol 40:228–230

Ramakrishnan V, Bhaskar V, Law DA, Wong MH, DuBridge RB, Breinberg D, O'Hara C, Powers DB, Liu G, Grove J, Hevezi P, Cass KM, Watson S, Evangelista F, Powers RA, Finck B, Wills M, Caras I, Fang Y, McDonald D, Johnson D, Murray R, Jeffry U (2006) Preclinical evaluation of an anti-alpha5beta1 integrin antibody as a novel anti-angiogenic agent. J Exp Ther Oncol 5: 273–286

Reinmuth N, Liu W, Ahmad SA, Fan F, Stoeltzing O, Parikh AA, Bucana CD, Gallick GE, Nickols MA, Westlin WF, Ellis LM (2003) Alphavbeta3 integrin antagonist S247 decreases colon cancer metastasis and angiogenesis and improves survival in mice. Cancer Res 63:2079–2087

Reynolds AR, Reynolds LE, Nagel TE, Lively JC, Robinson SD, Hicklin DJ, Bodary SC, Hodivala-Dilke KM (2004) Elevated Flk1 (vascular endothelial growth factor receptor 2) signaling mediates enhanced angiogenesis in b3-integrin-deficient mice. Cancer Res 64:8643–8650

Reynolds L, Wyder L, Lively J, Taverna D, Robinson S, Huang X, Sheppard D, Hynes R, Hodivala-Dilke K (2002) Enhanced pathological angiogenesis in mice lacking beta3 integrin or beta3 and beta5 integrins. Nat Med 8:27–34

Romer LH, Birukov KG, Garcia JG (2006) Focal adhesions: paradigm for a signaling nexus. Circ Res 98:606–616

Ruegg C, Yilmaz A, Bieler G, Bamat J, Chaubert P, Lejeune FJ (1998) Evidence for the involvement of endothelial cell integrin alphaVbeta3 in the disruption of the tumor vasculature induced by TNF and IFN-gamma. Nat Med 4:408–414

Ruegg C, Mutter N (2007) Anti-angiogenic therapies in cancer: achievements and open questions. Bull Cancer 94:753–762

Sabherwal Y, Rothman VL, Dimitrov S, L'Heureux DZ, Marcinkiewicz C, Sharma M, Tuszynski GP (2006) Integrin alpha2beta1 mediates the anti-angiogenic and anti-tumor activities of angiocidin, a novel tumor-associated protein. Exp Cell Res 312: 2443–2453

Scott KA, Arnott CH, Robinson SC, Moore RJ, Thompson RG, Marshall JF, Balkwill FR (2004) TNF-alpha regulates epithelial expression of MMP-9 and integrin alphavbeta6 during tumour promotion. A role for TNF-alpha in keratinocyte migration? Oncogene 23:6954–6966

Senger DR, Claffey KP, Benes JE, Perruzzi CA, Sergiou AP, Detmar M (1997) Angiogenesis promoted by vascular endothelial growth factor: regulation through alpha 1beta 1 and alpha 2beta 1 integrins. Proc Natl Acad Sci 94: 13612–13617

Senger DR, Perruzzi CA, Streit M, Koteliansky VE, de Fougerolles AR, Detmar M (2002) The a1b1 and a2b1 integrins provide critical support for vascular endothelial growth factor signaling, endothelial cell migration, and tumor angiogenesis. Am J Pathol 160:195–204

6

Serini G, Valdembri D, Bussolino F (2006) Integrins and angiogenesis: a sticky business. Exp Cell Res 312(5):651–658

Shin IS, Jang BS, Danthi SN, Xie J, Yu S, Le N, Maeng JS, Hwang IS, Li KC, Carrasquillo JA, Paik CH (2007) Use of antibody as carrier of oligomers of peptidomimetic alphavbeta3 antagonist to target tumor-induced neovasculature. Bioconjug Chem 18:821–828

Smith JW (2003) Cilengitide Merck. Curr Opin Investig Drugs 4:741–745

Stoeltzing O, Liu W, Reinmuth N, Fan F, Parry G, Parikh A, McCarty M, Bucana C, Mazar A, Ellis L (2003) Inhibition of integrin alpha5beta1 function with a small peptide (ATN-161) plus continuous 5-FU infusion reduces colorectal liver metastases and improves survival in mice. Int J Cancer 104:496–503

Strieth S, Eichhorn ME, Sutter A, Jonczyk A, Berghaus A, Dellian M (2006) Antiangiogenic combination tumor therapy blocking alpha(v)-integrins and VEGF-receptor-2 increases therapeutic effects in vivo. Int J Cancer 119:423–431

Stupack DG (2007) The biology of integrins. Oncology (Williston Park) 21:6–12

Stupp R, Ruegg C (2007) Integrin inhibitors reaching the clinic. J Clin Oncol 25:1637–1638

Taga T, Suzuki A, Gonzalez-Gomez I, Gilles FH, Stins M, Shimada H, Barsky L, Weinberg KI, Laug WE (2002) Alphav-Integrin antagonist EMD 121974 induces apoptosis in brain tumor cells growing on vitronectin and tenascin. Int J Cancer 98:690–697

Takada Y, Xiaojing X, Scott S (2007) The integrins. Genome Biol 8:215

Tanjore H, Zeisberg EM, Gerami-Naini B, Kalluri R (2007) Beta1 integrin expression on endothelial cells is required for angiogenesis but not for vasculogenesis. Dev Dyn 237:75–82

Tomiyama Y (2000) Glanzmann thrombasthenia: integrin alpha IIb beta 3 deficiency. Int J Hematol 72:448–454

Travis MA, Humphries JD, Humphries MJ (2003) An unraveling tale of how integrins are activated from within. Trends Pharmacol Sci 24:192–197

Trikha M, Zhou Z, Nemeth J, Chen Q, Sharp C, Emmell E, Giles-Komar J, Nakada M (2004) CNTO 95, a fully human monoclonal antibody that inhibits av integrins, has antitumor and antiangiogenic activity in vivo. Int J Cancer 110:326–335

Tsopanoglou NE, Papaconstantinou ME, Flordellis CS, Maragoudakis ME (2004) On the mode of action of thrombin-induced angiogenesis: thrombin peptide, TP508, mediates effects in endothelial cells via alphavbeta3 integrin. Thromb Haemost 92:846–857

Ulbrich H, Eriksson EE, Lindbom L (2003) Leukocyte and endothelial cell adhesion molecules as targets for therapeutic interventions in inflammatory disease. Trends Pharmacol Sci 24:640–647

Umeda N, Kachi S, Akiyama H, Zahn G, Vossmeyer D, Stragies R, Campochiaro PA (2006) Suppression and regression of choroidal neovascularization by systemic administration of an alpha5beta1 integrin antagonist. Mol Pharmacol 69:1820–1828

Varner JA, Nakada MT, Jordan RE, Coller BS (1999) Inhibition of angiogenesis and tumor growth by murine 7E3, the parent antibodyof c7E3 Fab (abciximab; ReoProTM). Angiogenesis 3:53–60

Vlahakis NE, Young BA, Atakilit A, Hawkridge AE, Issaka RB, Boudreau N, Sheppard D (2007) Integrin alpha9beta1 directly binds to vascular endothelial growth factor (VEGF)-A and contributes to VEGF-A-induced angiogenesis. J Biol Chem 282:15187–15196

Wickstrom SA, Alitalo K, KeskiOja J (2005) Endostatin signaling and regulation of endothelial cell-matrix interactions. Adv Cancer Res 94:197–229

Woodall BP, Nystrom A, Iozzo RA, Eble JA, Niland S, Krieg T, Eckes B, Pozzi A, Iozzo RV (2008) Integrin alpha 2beta 1 is the required receptor for endorepellin angiostatic activity. J Biol Chem 283(4):2335–2343

Wu H, Beuerlein G, Nie Y, Smith H, Lee BA, Hensler M, Huse WD, Watkins JD (1998) Stepwise in vitro affinity maturation of Vitaxin, an alpha vbeta 3-specific humanized mAb. Proc Natl Acad Sci 95:6037–6042

Xie J, Shen Z, Li KC, Danthi N (2007) Tumor angiogenic endothelial cell targeting by a novel integrin-targeted nanoparticle. Int J Nanomed 2:479–485

Xiong JP, Stehle T, Zhang R, Joachimiak A, Frech M, Goodman SL, Arnaout MA (2002) Crystal structure of the extracellular segment of integrin alpha

Vbeta3 in complex with an Arg-Gly-Asp ligand. Science 296:151–155

Zaric J, Ruegg C (2005) Integrin-mediated adhesion and soluble ligand binding stabilize COX-2 protein levels in endothelial cells by inducing expression and preventing degradation. J Biol Chem 280:1077–1085

Zhang D, Pier T, McNeel DG, Wilding G, Friedl A (2007) Effects of a monoclonal anti-alphavbeta3 integrin antibody on blood vessels – a pharmacodynamic study. Invest New Drugs 25:49–55

Zhou Y, Peng H, Ji Q, Qi J, Zhu Z, Yang C (2006) Discovery of small molecule inhibitors of integrin alphavbeta3 through structure-based virtual screening. Bioorg Med Chem Lett 16: 5878–5882

Zhu J, Motejlek K, Wang D, Zang K, Schmidt A, Reichardt LF (2002) β8 integrins are required for vascular morphogenesis in mouse embryos. Development 129:2891–2903

Zweers MC, Davidson JM, Pozzi A, Hallinger R, Janz K, Quondamatteo F, Leutgeb B, Krieg T, Eckes B (2007) Integrin alpha2beta1 is required for regulation of murine wound angiogenesis but is dispensable for reepithelialization. J Invest Dermatol 127:467–478

PDGF and Vessel Maturation

Carina Hellberg, Arne Östman, and C.-H. Heldin

Abstract Pericytes are smooth muscle-like cells found in close contact with the endothelium in capillaries, where they regulate the morphology and function of the vessels. During vessel formation, platelet-derived growth factor-BB (PDGF-BB) is required for the recruitment and differentiation of pericytes. Tumor vessels display abnormal morphology and increased endothelial proliferation, resulting in leaky, tortuous vessels that are often poorly perfused. These vessels typically display decreased pericyte density, and the tumor-associated pericytes often express abnormal markers and show abnormal morphology. Anti-angiogenic therapy targeting pro-angiogenic growth factor pathways has been applied to a broad range of solid tumors with varying results. Studies utilizing mouse models indicate that the presence of pericytes protect endothelial cells against inhibition of vascular endothelial growth factor (VEGF) signaling. Simultaneous inhibition of PDGF receptors on pericytes therefore improves the effect of VEGF inhibitors on endothelial cells and enhances anti-angiogenic therapy.

C.-H. Heldin (✉)
Ludwig Institute for Cancer Research,
Uppsala University, S-751 24, Uppsala, Sweden
e-mail: C-H.Heldin@LICR.uu.e

7.1
Introduction

Newly formed capillaries are stabilized through the recruitment of a specialized form of mural cells termed pericytes. In addition to providing physical stabilization, the presence of pericytes reduces endothelial cell proliferation and promotes differentiation, a process termed vascular maturation. During this process, activation of the platelet-derived growth factor (PDGF) β-receptor plays a crucial role in the recruitment of pericytes to the newly formed vessels. In the present communication, we review the role of PDGF in vessel maturation.

7.2
The PDGF Family

The PDGF family of growth factors is composed of disulfide-bonded homodimers of four polypeptide chains, the classical PDGF-A and -B chains and the more recently described PDGF-C and -D chains (Fredriksson et al. 2004). In addition, the A and B chains heterodimerize to form PDGF-AB. PDGF isoforms exert their biological effects through the

R. Liersch et al. (eds.), *Angiogenesis Inhibition,* Recent Results in Cancer Research,
DOI: 10.1007/978-3-540-78281-0_7, © Springer Verlag Berlin Heidelberg 2010

activation of two tyrosine kinase receptors, PDGF α- and β-receptors (Heldin et al. 1998).

PDGF family are major mitogens for a number of cell types, including mesenchymal cells such as fibroblasts and smooth muscle cells. During the embryonal development, PDGF isoforms are important for the development of mesenchymal cells of different organs, such as mesangial cells of the kidney, alveolar smooth muscle cells of the lung, smooth muscle cells and pericytes of blood vessels, and glial cells of the central nervous system. Overactivity of PDGF has been linked to atherosclerosis, fibrotic diseases, and malignancies. In certain types of rather rare solid tumors, PDGF is involved in autocrine stimulation of tumor cell growth. In addition, PDGF is commonly involved in paracrine recruitment of tumor stroma fibroblasts and stimulation of angiogenesis (Ostman and Heldin 2007).

(Betsholtz 2004). Moreover, a basic retention motif in the common C-terminus of PDGF-BB is crucial for this process, since it makes contact with sulfated heparan proteoglycans and ensures that PDGF-BB remains in the close environment of the producing endothelial cells (Lindblom et al. 2003; Abramsson et al. 2007). Since pericytes are contractile cells they presumably exert parts of their morphogenic control of capillary diameter through PDGF-BB-induced pericyte contractility. In addition, pericytes also regulate capillary diameter by regulating endothelial proliferation and differentiation. Absence of pericytes in PDGF-B/PDGF β-receptor null mice coincides with endothelial hyperplasia, suggesting that pericytes negatively control endothelial proliferation (Hellstrom et al. 2001). Absence of pericytes also leads to defects in endothelial junction formation, suggesting that pericytes control endothelial differentiation in vivo.

7.3
Pericytes

7.3.1
Role of Pericytes

Mature blood vessels are composed of endothelial cells and mural cells, including pericytes and smooth muscle cells. Arteries and veins are surrounded by vascular smooth muscle cells, whereas pericytes are present on capillaries, postcapillary venules, and collecting venules throughout the body. Pericytes are smooth muscle-like single cells found in close contact with endothelial cells within the basement membrane, where they are wrapped around the vessel sending out long protrusions that make contact with a number of endothelial cells and other pericytes (Fig. 7.1) (Bergers and Song 2005). The presence of pericytes on these vessel types is plastic, and varies between tissues.

PDGF made by endothelial cells has a crucial role in the recruitment of pericytes to vessels

7.3.2
Identification of Pericytes

Despite their physiological importance, pericytes still remain an understudied cell type. Part of the problem when studying pericytes is the difficulty in identifying them, since there is no convenient pan-pericyte marker. Pericytes reside within the basement membrane; thus morphological identification by electron microscopy remains the most reliable means of identifying a pericyte in mature tissues (Baluk et al. 2005). However, during angiogenic sprouting and vascular remodeling, the basement membrane is not fully developed, making this method of identification more difficult to apply (Baluk et al. 2003). Therefore, several marker proteins are used for studying pericytes during angiogenesis (Bergers and Song 2005).

As expected from its importance for the recruitment of pericytes, the PDGF β-receptor is one of the most widely used markers for pericytes. However, this receptor is also expressed

a   b

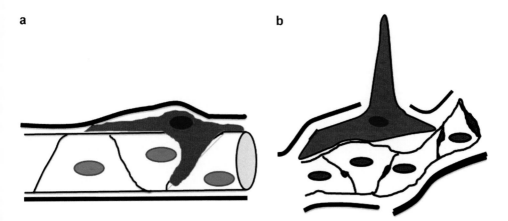

Fig. 7.1 (**a**) Morphology of capillaries of normal tissues. The pericytes reside between the basement membrane and the endothelial cells. Each pericyte makes contact with several endothelial cells and wraps itself around the vessel. (**b**) Morphology of capillaries of tumors. The tumor vessels are contorted and often flattened. Pericytes make contact with the endothelium, but are often partly dethatched and often extend protrusions away from the vessel. The basement membrane varies in thickness and has gaps in it.

on other stromal cells such as smooth muscle cells, fibroblasts and myofibroblasts. Another commonly used marker is α-smooth muscle actin (ASMA) that is expressed by pericytes, smooth muscle cells, and myofibroblasts. The expression of ASMA by pericytes is primarily restricted to sites of vascular remodeling. Desmin is a component of intermediate filaments, and is found in mature skeletal, cardiac, and smooth muscle cells. On pericytes, its expression appears to be restricted to differentiated cells in close physical contact with the endothelium. The expression of ASMA and desmin is likely to reflect the role of pericytes as contractile cells that participate in the regulation of capillary blood flow. The NG2 chondroitin sulfate proteoglycan (also known as high-molecular-weight melanoma-associated antigen, or sometimes AN2 in mice) is expressed on the surface of activated pericytes during vasculogenesis and angiogenesis. The regulator of G-protein signaling-5 (RGS-5), a regulator of signaling pathways downstream of heterotrimeric G-protein coupled receptors, was recently described as a marker for developing pericytes.

Its expression overlaps with the expression of NG2 and the PDGF β-receptor.

Not much is known about the regulation of the expression of these markers, and they may represent either distinct or overlapping populations of pericytes. The expressions of pericyte markers are dynamic, and their expression varies, depending on the species and tissue studied. When addressing the involvement of pericytes in vessel maturation, the difficulty to identify pericytes still present a problem, and most studies therefore contain the analysis of several marker proteins.

7.3.3
The Origin of Pericytes

During embryonic development, pericytes and smooth muscle cells, as well as endothelial cells, are believed to be derived from mesenchymal precursors (Bergers and Song 2005). During this process, PDGF-BB/PDGF β-receptor signaling is essential for the recruitment and differentiation of pericytes. Postnatally, pericytes are presumed to either migrate with the endothelial sprouts during the initiation of angiogenesis, or to differentiate from a local source of mesenchymal cells in response to PDGF and/or transforming growth factor β (TGF-β). However, recent studies have also described the existence of bone marrow-derived pericyte progenitor cells (Lamagna and Bergers 2006) and tissue-specific pericyte progenitors (Howson et al. 2005; Dore-Duffy et al. 2006; Tamaki et al. 2007).

The adult bone marrow contains both hematopoietic and mesenchymal stem and progenitor cells. Therefore, the recruitment of bone marrow-derived progenitors into tumors supports the initiation of tumor angiogenesis by incorporating endothelial and pericyte progenitor cells into the newly formed vessels. It has been proposed that the release of cytokines from tumors induces the mobilization of hematopoietic bone marrow stem cells (Petit et al. 2007). The recruitment of endothelial progenitor cells and their incorporation into tumor vessels have been demonstrated in a number of studies (Lyden et al. 2001; Shirakawa et al. 2002), and was recently shown to have an important role in the vascularization of at least two types of lung metastases. Circulating progenitor cells positive for PDGF β-receptor, the stem cell antigen-1 (Sca-1) and CD11b have been demonstrated to incorporate into blood vessels and to mature into NG2-, ASMA- and desmin-positive pericytes (Song et al. 2005). Circulating cells positive for CD11b and CD45 have also been shown to incorporate into vessels as pericyte-like cells, although these cells only expressed NG2 (Rajantie et al. 2004).

Several studies have also demonstrated the presence of pericyte progenitor cells in various other tissues, which appear to contribute to postnatal vasculogenesis and angiogenesis. Since these progenitor cells give rise to cell populations expressing different pericyte markers (see later in the text), it is unclear as to what extent the presence of these cells on vessels stabilizes

the vascular function. Thus, the neonatal rat aorta contains cells positive for the PDGF β-receptor, Tie2 and CD34, but negative for endothelial markers (Howson et al. 2005). These cells differentiates into pericytes when cocultured with endothelial cells or aorta ring explants in vitro. In the microvasculature of the adult rat CNS, cells positive for nestin and NG2 that has the capacity to differentiate into pericyte-like cells in vitro were identified (Dore-Duffy et al. 2006). In mice, skeletal muscle-derived stem cells negative for CD31 and CD45 were reported to differentiate into pericytes, endothelial cells, and smooth muscle in vivo (Tamaki et al. 2007). Although these studies indicate the presence of cells with the capability to differentiate into pericytes in adult tissues, most of the studies were performed in vitro. Information is still scarce about differentiation of tissue pericytes in vivo during vascular remodeling, or during tumor angiogenesis. Further studies addressing the physiological function of vessels that contain pericytes recruited from different sources are required.

7.4
Vessel Maturation

7.4.1
Normal Vessels

During embryonic development, the nascent vascular network is formed through de novo vessel formation from angioblasts or stem cells, a process termed vasculogenesis. From these vessels, new vessels sprout and form bridges by angiogenesis. The vessels are then stabilized through the recruitment of mural cells, and through generation of the basal membrane. The final patterning of the vascular network is determined by signals provided by soluble angiogenesis factors as well as components of the basement membrane and ECM, which stimulates proliferation, survival, migration, and differentiation of endothelial and mural cells. As already described, PDGF-BB is secreted by the endothelial cells during angiogenesis, presumably in response to vascular endothelial growth factor (VEGF), which facilitates the recruitment of mural cells. The endothelial differentiation sphingolipid G-protein coupled receptor 1 (EDG1 or S1P$_1$) (Allende and Proia 2002), which is activated by sphingosine 1-phosphate, appears to be important for mural-cell migration, and its genetic ablation in mouse led to a similar phenotype as that of PDGF ko mice. It remains to be investigated whether these signals are unrelated or if the EDG1 receptor signals downstream of the PDGF β-receptor.

Angiopoietin (Ang) 1 and 2 both act through the Tie2 receptor, but with different outcomes (Morisada et al. 2006). Ang1 stabilizes the physical contacts between endothelial cells and pericytes, thereby making the vessels less leaky. The role of Ang2 appears to be contextual. When VEGF is absent, Ang2 destabilizes vessels by inhibiting Ang1 signaling, but in the presence of VEGF Ang2 facilitates vascular sprouting. TGF-β is expressed by both endothelial and mural cells. It promotes vessel maturation not only by inducing differentiation of mesenchymal cells to mural cells, but also by stimulating ECM production. As with Ang2, TGF-β can be either pro- or antiangiogenic, depending on the context (Bertolino et al. 2005).

The presence of pericytes on the capillary bed is necessary for normal vessel function. Genetic studies in mice showed that loss of PDGF-BB or the PDGF β-receptor leads to a severe deficiency in pericyte recruitment, causing microvascular leakage and hemorrhage (Lindahl et al. 1997; Hellstrom et al. 1999). When investigating animals chimaeric for the PDGF β-receptor, it was evident that only PDGF β-receptor positive cells populated the vascular smooth muscle and pericyte compartment, directly demonstrating a need for PDGF signaling for the development of these cells (Crosby et al. 1998).

During angiogenic sprouting, PDGF-B is expressed by the endothelial tip cell (Gerhardt et al. 2003). Tissue-specific knockout of PDGF-BB in endothelial cells resulted in a similar phenotype as that of PDGF β-receptor ko, indicating that paracrine signaling between the endothelium and pericytes is required in the process of pericyte recruitment (Bjarnegard et al. 2004). When examining animals chimaeric for endothelial PDGF-BB, they displayed a variation in pericyte coverage and morphology of individual brain capillaries indicative of segments of PDGF-BB, expressing endothelium with normal recruitment of pericytes (Bjarnegard et al. 2004). The PDGF-BB molecule contains a short, basic sequence that functions as a retention motif allowing the secreted growth factor to remain on the tip cell. Mutational loss of the retention sequence resulted in partial detachment of the pericytes from the angiogenic sprout, presumably due to diffusion of PDGF-BB into the surrounding tissue (Lindblom et al. 2003). These findings highlight the need for a paracrine PDGF signal and a physical contact with endothelial cells for pericyte recruitment and differentiation.

Although PDGF β-receptor ko mice die from bleedings due to microanuerysms and a lack of mural cells, loss of pericytes in all tissues is not complete (Hellstrom et al. 1999). It thus appears as if PDGF is critical for the proliferation and migration of both pericytes and vascular smooth muscle cells, but that the initial formation of these cell types can also be induced by other factors. It is presently unclear where these cells originate from and what are the factors that induce their differentiation. It has been proposed that endothelial cells only express PDGF-BB at the sites of the vessels where pericyte recruitment occurs (Lindahl et al. 1997; Hellstrom et al. 1999). This is supported by the finding that in the developing CNS, PDGF-BB is mainly expressed by the endothelial cells situated at the tip of the sprouting vessels (Gerhardt et al. 2003).

7.4.2
Tumor Vessels

The growth of large, solid tumors is directly dependent on the presence of a tumor vasculature (Folkman 1971). As the tumor grows, hypoxia induces the expression of VEGF by tumor cells. This induces angiogenesis by activating the endothelial cells on surrounding vessels, thereby stimulating the branching and growth of new blood vessels into the tumor (Bergers and Benjamin 2003) (Fig. 7.2). During this process, the connections between the endothelial cells are loosened. Matrix metalloproteases are activated, leading to the degradation of the basement membrane. This serves two purposes. First, it allows the detachment of both endothelial cells and pericytes from the basement membrane, facilitating their migration into the tumor. Second, it may also activate proangiogenic factors within the basement membrane. Endothelial cells and pericytes migrate into the tumor tissue, where they proliferate and reconnect to form new vessels. Although most studies suggest that the endothelial cells lead the formation of new vessels, there are also studies suggesting that the pericytes migrate into the tissue first.

Tumor blood vessels have a number of structural and functional abnormalities (Jain 2003). They are dynamic, and vessels are continuously being initiated, remodeled, and regressed. The vessels are irregular in size and shape, tortuous and lack the normal hierarchical arrangement of arterioles, capillaries, and venules. The structure of the vessel wall is also abnormal. The tumor vessel diameter varies greatly, and the endothelial cells form an imperfect lining and contain a large number of fenestrations (Baluk et al. 2005). Although the presence of a basement membrane surrounding tumor vessels have been reported, it appears to be morphologically and functionally altered due to the vessel remodeling (Baluk et al. 2003). As a result of the

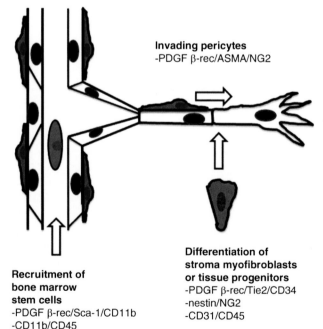

Fig. 7.2 Angiogenic sprouting. A new capillary is formed as a tip cell leads the sprouting capillary into the tissue. Pericytes may be recruited through the invasion and proliferation of pericytes from the mother vessel, by differentiation of stromal precursors, or through the recruitment of bone marrow precursor cells. Different molecular markers described for pericytes derived from mother vessels (Gerhardt et al., 2003), bone marrow-derived progenitors (Song et al., 2005; Rajantie et al., 2004, respectively) and tissue progenitors (Dore-Duffy et al., 2006; Howson et al., 2005; Tamaki et al., 2007, respectively) are given.

Invading pericytes
-PDGF β-rec/ASMA/NG2

Recruitment of bone marrow stem cells
-PDGF β-rec/Sca-1/CD11b
-CD11b/CD45

Differentiation of stroma myofibroblasts or tissue progenitors
-PDGF β-rec/Tie2/CD34
-nestin/NG2
-CD31/CD45

abnormal organization and ultrastructure of the vessels, the blood flow in the tumor vessels is chaotic and the vessels are leaky (Hashizume et al. 2000), resulting in an increase the interstitial fluid pressure (IFP) in the tumor. Furthermore, because of continuous remodeling of the vasculature, the blood flow and permeability varies not only between tumors, but also between regions of the same tumor, between the same region over time, and between the tumor and metastases. This is at least partly due to an imbalance between various pro- and antiangiogenic factors such as VEGF and Ang1/2. Taken together, the vessel abnormalities render the tumor vasculature inefficient at delivering not only oxygen and nutrients, but also drugs.

The density of pericytes covering normal capillaries varies between tissues, which is the case also for the pericyte coverage of tumor vessels (Baluk et al. 2005). In some studies no pericytes were found around the tumor capillaries, whereas other studies found the vessels covered to varying extents. It is unclear as to what extent these variations are due to differences between the tissues or the tumor types studied. Since PDGF-BB expression by endothelial cells is heterogeneous (Hellstrom et al. 1999), this may explain the uneven pericyte coverage of tumor vessels. Also, as discussed earlier, there may also be differences in the expression of the various molecular markers between tumor types, making an accurate pericyte count difficult. It is not just the pericyte density that is abnormal. Tumor-associated pericytes often display both an abnormal expression of markers, as well as abnormal morphology (Baluk et al. 2005). In tumors, pericytes are often found to express both ASMA and NG2, which are known to be expressed during vascular remodeling. Where normal pericytes are in close contact with the endothelium and reside within the basement membrane, tumor pericytes are often loosely associated with the endothelium, and may extend long protrusions into the surrounding tissue. At present, it is not clear whether the cells displaying the abnormal morphology are truly pericytes, if they are in the process of differentiation from myofibroblasts, or if they represent pericytes that are partially detaching from the endothelium to divide. Furthermore, it is unclear as to what extent these pericytes are able to participate in vessel function.

There are several sources described for pericyte progenitors during normal vascular remodeling, but it is currently unclear where tumor pericytes originate from. In angiogenesis in the retina, pericytes have been shown to migrate along the angiogenic sprout in response to the PDGF-BB expressed by the endothelial cells (Gerhardt et al. 2003). In tumors, it is also possible that components of the tumor microenvironment induce the differentiation of fibroblasts into myofibroblasts. Such cues may be TGF-β or PDGF expressed by tumor cells or the surrounding stroma. The incorporation of bone marrow-derived circulating pericyte progenitors into tumors have also been described (Song et al. 2005). The relative importance of these sources of pericytes is yet to be determined.

7.5
Tumor Therapy Targeting PDGF Receptors on the Vasculature

The genetic instability of tumor cells poses a serious problem when developing specific drugs targeting mutated proteins in tumors. Tumors that initially respond well to targeted therapies often develop resistance to the therapy, partly because of the enrichment of cells with new mutations. It has been proposed that targeting of tumor stroma, tumor vessels, and fibroblasts could be a means to avoid drug resistance since these tissues are more genetically stable (Hofmeister et al. 2008). Given the importance of PDGF in tumor stroma formation, the PDGF receptors are interesting targets in antistromal therapy.

7.5.1
Antiangiogenic Therapy Targeting Pericytes

Targeting of tumor angiogenesis has long been an attractive idea for the treatment of solid tumors (Folkman 1971; Cao 2004). Although therapies targeting the VEGF pathway are efficient in mouse tumor models, the results of several clinical trials suggests that therapies targeting VEGF alone may not be enough for efficient antiangiogenic therapy (Cobleigh et al. 2003; Yang et al. 2003).

When revisiting the mouse models, studies indicated that the response to VEGF-targeting therapy may be dependent on the maturity of the tumor vessels. Established, mature tumor vessels with richer pericyte coverage appear to be less sensitive to the antiangiogenic therapy than vessels with fewer pericytes. The notion that PDGF-BB may protect endothelial cells from antiangiogenic therapy was further supported by a study by Huang et al. (Huang et al. 2004), where an increased expression of PDGF-BB was detected around vessels that became resistant to anti-VEGF therapy. These observations initiated the idea that antiangiogenic therapy may be more efficient if both endothelial cells and pericytes are targeted using both VEGF receptor and PDGF receptor kinase inhibitors. This notion has recently been corroborated in a study of vessels in a nonmalignant tissue, chicken chorioallantoic membranes, displaying different stages of vascular maturity during development (Hlushchuk et al. 2007). In tumors, this type of combination therapy have been shown to give synergistic antiangiogenic and antitumor effects (Bergers et al. 2003; Erber et al. 2004; Hasumi et al. 2007), although the magnitude of the effect of PDGF inhibitors on the vasculature may be contextual (Sennino et al. 2007). It is currently not known why tumor pericytes are targeted during this treatment, while the vast majority of mural cells in the body are unaffected. It is possible that only a subset of abnormal, activated pericytes that are in the process of being remodeled, are targeted while more mature subsets are unaffected (Hasumi et al. 2007).

7.5.2
Improving the Efficacy of Conventional Therapies

As a consequence of the poor perfusion and abnormal functions of tumor vessels, the delivery of nutrients and oxygen into the tumor is poor (Jain 2005). This also affects the therapeutic outcome of both chemotherapy and radiotherapy. In the clinic, hypoxia strongly correlates with tumor radioresistance (Moeller et al. 2007), and preclinical data showed that increased tumor oxygenation improved the response to radiation therapy. Different approaches to modify the tumor vasculature have been taken to correct for this problem.

The abnormal tumor vasculature and stroma results in an elevated IFP in tumors compared to normal tissues. In addition to forming a barrier to transcapillary transport of nutrients and oxygen, the elevated IFP also results in inefficient uptake of therapeutic agents, especially macromolecules such as liposomes and antibodies (Heldin et al. 2004). Thus, lowering of IFP could be used to improve the therapeutic efficiency of both chemotherapy and radiation therapy. There are several factors affecting the IFP in tumors. The excess VEGF produced by hypoxic tumor cells induce capillary leakiness, resulting in an increased outflow of plasma proteins into the interstitium. Tumors are typically void of functional lymph vessels, which impair the fluid drainage from the tumor. Also, fibrosis and contraction of interstitial matrix mediated by stroma fibroblasts participates in the elevation of tumor IFP. PDGF contributes to the regulation of IFP through the phosphatidylinositol-3' kinase (PI3K) signaling pathway (Heuchel et al. 1999). Activation of PDGF β-receptors on stromal fibroblasts induce αvβ3 intergrin-mediated contraction of the extracellular matrix thereby controlling the dermal IFP (Liden et al. 2006). The PDGF β-receptor may also participate in the regulation of vessel leakiness by recruiting pericytes that stabilizes the capillaries (Lindahl et al. 1997). Lowering of IFP by VEGF inhibitors (Lee et al. 2000; Tong et al. 2004) as well as PDGF inhibitors (Pietras et al. 2001) have been demonstrated. At present, it is not clear if the PDGF inhibitors reduce IFP by acting on pericytes or fibroblasts, or on both cell types. The reduction in IFP has been correlated to increased drug uptake (Pietras et al. 2001; Willett et al. 2004) and increased effect of chemotherapy (Pietras et al. 2002).

It has been proposed that restoring the balance between pro-and antiangiogenic factors could temporary normalize the vasculature, allowing for drug delivery (Jain 2005). According to this notion, removal of VEGF signaling would target the immature vasculature, pruning the less functional vessels and promoting the blood flow through the remaining vessels. Part of the normalization of vessel function seen after anti-VEGF therapy can be explained by decreased vessel leakiness, which reduces the osmotic pressure of the interstitium and consequently reduces the tumor IFP. The reported effects of anti-VEGF therapy have been transient, which would be expected if prolonged treatment disrupt also mature vessel function. Studies have demonstrated that targeting VEGF receptors alters vessel morphology (Miller et al. 2005; Taguchi et al. 2008), with temporary improvements in tumor oxygenation and response to radiotherapy (Dings et al. 2007). Another study demonstrated decreased effects of chemotherapy on glioblastomas, presumably due to restoration of the blood–brain barrier (Claes et al. 2008).

7.6
Future Perspectives

It is increasingly clear that the properties of the tumor vasculature are important for the outcome of both antiangiogenic targeted therapies and conventional cancer therapies. The presence of pericytes on the vessels gives structural stability to capillaries, resulting in improved perfusion, and provides endothelial cells with protection to anti-angiogenic therapy targeting the VEGF pathway. Understanding the precise mechanisms underlying vascular maturation should provide cues for refining therapies targeting the vasculature, whether to inhibit tumor angiogenesis or to normalize the vascular function for more efficient drug delivery. To achieve this, further studies evaluating the effects of antiangiogenic inhibitors on vessel function, both in animal models and in patients, are needed. The approval of several PDGF receptor inhibitors for use in the clinic (Ostman and Heldin 2007) will be important for further validation of the concept of vascular normalization after antiangiogenic therapy and the concomitant increase in drug uptake in patients. Such studies should reveal the extent to which different tumor types vary regarding their response to the combined targeting of VEGF- and PDGF receptor signaling, and may provide markers for the prediction of the therapeutic outcome in subsets of tumors.

The pericytes on tumor vessels are abnormal, both in the expression of molecular markers and in morphology. Nevertheless, B16 mouse melanoma tumors expressing PDGF-BB display increased pericyte coverage of the vessels, and an increased growth rate (Furuhashi et al. 2004), which correlates to an increased perfusion of small vessels and increased blood-flow rate (Robinson et al. 2008), indicating that the presence of abnormal pericytes exert effects on tumor vessel function. So how do these pericytes differ from the function of a fully differentiated pericyte? Further studies are required to understand the molecular mechanisms underlying pericyte differentiation and their interactions with endothelial cells. It will also be important to determine the source of tumor pericytes and the signaling pathways involved in their recruitment into the tumor vasculature. These studies require further development of more refined methods for studying vessel function in vivo.

References

Abramsson A, Kurup S, Busse M, Yamada S, Lindblom P, Schallmeiner E, Stenzel D, Sauvaget D, Ledin J, Ringvall M, Landegren U, Kjellen L, Bondjers G, Li JP, Lindahl U, Spillmann D, Betsholtz C, Gerhardt H (2007) Defective N-sulfation of heparan sulfate proteoglycans limits PDGF-BB binding and pericyte recruitment in vascular development. Genes Dev 21:316–331

Allende ML, Proia RL (2002) Sphingosine-1-phosphate receptors and the development of the vascular system. Biochim Biophys Acta 1582: 222–227

Baluk P, Hashizume H, McDonald DM (2005) Cellular abnormalities of blood vessels as targets in cancer. Curr Opin Genet Dev 15:102–111

Baluk P, Morikawa S, Haskell A, Mancuso M, McDonald DM (2003) Abnormalities of basement membrane on blood vessels and endothelial sprouts in tumors. Am J Pathol 163: 1801–1815

Bergers G, Benjamin LE (2003) Tumorigenesis and the angiogenic switch. Nat Rev Cancer 3: 401–410

Bergers G, Song S (2005) The role of pericytes in blood-vessel formation and maintenance. Neuro-Oncol 7:452–464

Bergers G, Song S, Meyer-Morse N, Bergsland E, Hanahan D (2003) Benefits of targeting both pericytes and endothelial cells in the tumor vasculature with kinase inhibitors. J Clin Invest 111:1287–1295

Bertolino P, Deckers M, Lebrin F, ten Dijke P (2005) Transforming growth factor-beta signal transduction in angiogenesis and vascular disorders. Chest 128:585S–590S

Betsholtz C (2004) Insight into the physiological functions of PDGF through genetic studies in mice. Cytokine Growth Factor Rev 15:215–228

Bjarnegard M, Enge M, Norlin J, Gustafsdottir S, Fredriksson S, Abramsson A, Takemoto M, Gustafsson E, Fässler R, Betsholtz C (2004) Endothelium-specific ablation of PDGFB leads to pericyte loss and glomerular, cardiac and placental abnormalities. Development 131:1847–1857

Cao Y (2004) Antiangiogenic cancer therapy. Semin Cancer Biol 14:139–145

Claes A, Wesseling P, Jeuken J, Maass C, Heerschap A, Leenders WP (2008) Antiangiogenic compounds interfere with chemotherapy of brain tumors due to vessel normalization. Mol Cancer Ther 7:71–78

Cobleigh MA, Langmuir VK, Sledge GW, Miller KD, Haney L, Novotny WF, Reimann JD, Vassel A (2003) A phase I/II dose-escalation trial of bevacizumab in previously treated metastatic breast cancer. Semin Oncol 30:117–124

Crosby JR, Seifert RA, Soriano P, Bowen-Pope DF (1998) Chimaeric analysis reveals role of Pdgf receptors in all muscle lineages. Nat Genet 18:385–388

Dings RP, Loren M, Heun H, McNiel E, Griffioen AW, Mayo KH, Griffin RJ (2007) Scheduling of radiation with angiogenesis inhibitors anginex and Avastin improves therapeutic outcome via vessel normalization. Clin Cancer Res 13:3395–3402

Dore-Duffy P, Katychev A, Wang X, Van Buren E (2006) CNS microvascular pericytes exhibit multipotential stem cell activity. J Cereb Blood Flow Metab 26:613–624

Erber R, Thurnher A, Katsen AD, Groth G, Kerger H, Hammes HP, Menger MD, Ullrich A, Vajkoczy P (2004) Combined inhibition of VEGF and PDGF signaling enforces tumor vessel regression by interfering with pericyte-mediated endothelial cell survival mechanisms. FASEB J 18:338–340

Folkman J (1971) Tumor angiogenesis: therapeutic implications. N Engl J Med 285:1182–1186

Fredriksson L, Li H, Eriksson U (2004) The PDGF family: four gene products form five dimeric isoforms. Cytokine Growth Factor Rev 15:197–204

Furuhashi M, Sjöblom T, Abramsson A, Ellingsen J, Micke P, Li H, Bergsten-Folestad E, Eriksson U, Heuchel R, Betsholtz C, Heldin CH, Östman A (2004) Platelet-derived growth factor production by B16 melanoma cells leads to increased pericyte abundance in tumors and an associated increase in tumor growth rate. Cancer Res 64: 2725–2733

Gerhardt H, Golding M, Fruttiger M, Ruhrberg C, Lundkvist A, Abramsson A, Jeltsch M, Mitchell C, Alitalo K, Shima D, Betsholtz C (2003) VEGF guides angiogenic sprouting utilizing endothelial tip cell filopodia. J Cell Biol 161:1163–1177

Hashizume H, Baluk P, Morikawa S, McLean JW, Thurston G, Roberge S, Jain RK, McDonald DM (2000) Openings between defective endothelial cells explain tumor vessel leakiness. Am J Pathol 156:1363–1380

Hasumi Y, Klosowska-Wardega A, Furuhashi M, Östman A, Heldin CH, Hellberg C (2007) Identification of a subset of pericytes that respond to combination therapy targeting PDGF and VEGF signaling. Int J Cancer 121:2606–2614

Heldin CH, Rubin K, Pietras K, Östman A (2004) High interstitial fluid pressure – an obstacle in cancer therapy. Nat Rev Cancer 4:806–813

Heldin CH, Östman A, Rönnstrand L (1998) Signal transduction via platelet-derived growth factor receptors. Biochim Biophys Acta 1378:F79–F113

Hellström M, Gerhardt H, Kalen M, Li X, Eriksson U, Wolburg H, Betsholtz C (2001) Lack of pericytes leads to endothelial hyperplasia and abnormal vascular morphogenesis. J Cell Biol 153:543–553

Hellström M, Kalén M, Lindahl P, Abramsson A, Betsholtz C (1999) Role of PDGF-B and PDGFR-beta in recruitment of vascular smooth muscle cells and pericytes during embryonic blood vessel formation in the mouse. Development 126: 3047–3055

Heuchel R, Berg A, Tallquist M, Åhlen K, Reed RK, Rubin K, Claesson-Welsh L, Heldin CH, Soriano P (1999) Platelet-derived growth factor beta receptor regulates interstitial fluid homeostasis through phosphatidylinositol-3' kinase signaling. Proc Natl Acad Sci U S A 96:11410–11415

Hlushchuk R, Baum O, Gruber G, Wood J, Djonov V (2007) The synergistic action of a VEGF-receptor tyrosine-kinase inhibitor and a sensitizing PDGF-receptor blocker depends upon the stage of vascular maturation. Microcirculation 14:813–825

Hofmeister V, Schrama D, Becker JC (2008) Anti-cancer therapies targeting the tumor stroma. Cancer Immunol Immunother 57:1–17

Howson KM, Aplin AC, Gelati M, Alessandri G, Parati EA, Nicosia RF (2005) The postnatal rat aorta contains pericyte progenitor cells that form spheroidal colonies in suspension culture. Am J Physiol Cell Physiol 289:C1396–C1407

Huang J, Soffer SZ, Kim ES, McCrudden KW, New T, Manley CA, Middlesworth W, O'Toole K, Yamashiro DJ, Kandel JJ (2004) Vascular remodeling marks tumors that recur during chronic suppression of angiogenesis. Mol Cancer Res 2:36–42

Jain RK (2003) Molecular regulation of vessel maturation. Nat Med 9:685–693

Jain RK (2005) Normalization of tumor vasculature: an emerging concept in antiangiogenic therapy. Science 307:58–62

Lamagna C, Bergers G (2006) The bone marrow constitutes a reservoir of pericyte progenitors. J Leukoc Biol 80:677–681

Lee CG, Heijn M, di Tomaso E, Griffon-Etienne G, Ancukiewicz M, Koike C, Park KR, Ferrara N, Jain RK, Suit HD, Boucher Y (2000) Anti-vascular endothelial growth factor treatment augments tumor radiation response under normoxic or hypoxic conditions. Cancer Res 60:5565–5570

Liden A, Berg A, Nedrebo T, Reed RK, Rubin K (2006) Platelet-derived growth factor BB-mediated normalization of dermal interstitial fluid pressure after mast cell degranulation depends on beta3 but not beta1 integrins. Circ Res 98:635–641

Lindahl P, Johansson BR, Leveen P, Betsholtz C (1997) Pericyte loss and microaneurysm formation in PDGF-B-deficient mice. Science 277: 242–245

Lindblom P, Gerhardt H, Liebner S, Abramsson A, Enge M, Hellström M, Bäckstrom G, Fredriksson S, Landegren U, Nystrom HC, Bergström G, Dejana E, Ostman A, Lindahl P, Betsholtz C (2003) Endothelial PDGF-B retention is required for proper investment of pericytes in the microvessel wall. Genes Dev 17:1835–1840

Lyden D, Hattori K, Dias S, Costa C, Blaikie P, Butros L, Chadburn A, Heissig B, Marks W, Witte L, Wu Y, Hicklin D, Zhu Z, Hackett NR, Crystal RG, Moore MA, Hajjar KA, Manova K, Benezra R, Rafii S (2001) Impaired recruitment of bone-marrow-derived endothelial and hematopoietic precursor cells blocks tumor angiogenesis and growth. Nat Med 7: 1194–1201

Miller DW, Vosseler S, Mirancea N, Hicklin DJ, Bohlen P, Volcker HE, Holz FG, Fusenig NE (2005) Rapid vessel regression, protease inhibition, and stromal normalization upon short-term vascular endothelial growth factor receptor 2 inhibition in skin carcinoma heterotransplants. Am J Pathol 167:1389–1403

Moeller BJ, Richardson RA, Dewhirst MW (2007) Hypoxia and radiotherapy: opportunities for improved outcomes in cancer treatment. Cancer Metastasis Rev 26:241–248

Morisada T, Kubota Y, Urano T, Suda T, Oike Y (2006) Angiopoietins and angiopoietin-like proteins in angiogenesis. Endothelium 13:71–79

Östman A, Heldin CH (2007) PDGF receptors as targets in tumor treatment. Adv Cancer Res 97: 247–274

Petit I, Jin D, Rafii S (2007) The SDF-1-CXCR4 signaling pathway: a molecular hub modulating neo-angiogenesis. Trends Immunol 28:299–307

Pietras K, Östman A, Sjöquist M, Buchdunger E, Reed RK, Heldin CH, Rubin K (2001) Inhibition of platelet-derived growth factor receptors reduces interstitial hypertension and increases transcapillary transport in tumors. Cancer Res 61:2929–2934

Pietras K, Rubin K, Sjöblom T, Buchdunger E, Sjöquist M, Heldin CH, Östman A (2002)

Inhibition of PDGF receptor signaling in tumor stroma enhances antitumor effect of chemotherapy. Cancer Res 62:5476–5484

Rajantie I, Ilmonen M, Alminaite A, Ozerdem U, Alitalo K, Salven P (2004) Adult bone marrow-derived cells recruited during angiogenesis comprise precursors for periendothelial vascular mural cells. Blood 104:2084–2086

Robinson SP, Ludwig C, Paulsson J, Östman A (2008) The effects of tumor-derived platelet-derived growth factor on vascular morphology and function in vivo revealed by susceptibility MRI. Int J Cancer 122:1548–1556

Sennino B, Falcon BL, McCauley D, Le T, McCauley T, Kurz JC, Haskell A, Epstein DM, McDonald DM (2007) Sequential loss of tumor vessel pericytes and endothelial cells after inhibition of platelet-derived growth factor B by selective aptamer AX102. Cancer Res 67: 7358–7367

Shirakawa K, Shibuya M, Heike Y, Takashima S, Watanabe I, Konishi F, Kasumi F, Goldman CK, Thomas KA, Bett A, Terada M, Wakasugi H (2002) Tumor-infiltrating endothelial cells and endothelial precursor cells in inflammatory breast cancer. Int J Cancer 99:344–351

Song S, Ewald AJ, Stallcup W, Werb Z, Bergers G (2005) PDGFRbeta+ perivascular progenitor cells in tumours regulate pericyte differentiation and vascular survival. Nat Cell Biol 7:870–879

Taguchi E, Nakamura K, Miura T, Shibuya M, Isoe T (2008) Anti-tumor activity and tumor vessel normalization by the vascular endothelial growth factor receptor tyrosine kinase inhibitor KRN951 in a rat peritoneal disseminated tumor model. Cancer Sci 99(3):623–630

Tamaki T, Okada Y, Uchiyama Y, Tono K, Masuda M, Wada M, Hoshi A, Akatsuka A (2007) Synchronized reconstitution of muscle fibers, peripheral nerves and blood vessels by murine skeletal muscle-derived CD34(-)/45 (-) cells. Histochem Cell Biol 128:349–360

Tong RT, Boucher Y, Kozin SV, Winkler F, Hicklin DJ, Jain RK (2004) Vascular normalization by vascular endothelial growth factor receptor 2 blockade induces a pressure gradient across the vasculature and improves drug penetration in tumors. Cancer Res 64:3731–3736

Willett CG, Boucher Y, di Tomaso E, Duda DG, Munn LL, Tong RT, Chung DC, Sahani DV, Kalva SP, Kozin SV, Mino M, Cohen KS, Scadden DT, Hartford AC, Fischman AJ, Clark JW, Ryan DP, Zhu AX, Blaszkowsky LS, Chen HX, Shellito PC, Lauwers GY, Jain RK (2004) Direct evidence that the VEGF-specific antibody bevacizumab has antivascular effects in human rectal cancer. Nat Med 10:145–147

Yang JC, Haworth L, Sherry RM, Hwu P, Schwartzentruber DJ, Topalian SL, Steinberg SM, Chen HX, Rosenberg SA (2003) A randomized trial of bevacizumab, an anti-vascular endothelial growth factor antibody, for metastatic renal cancer. N Engl J Med 349:427–434

Lymphangiogenesis in Cancer: Current Perspectives

8

Rüediger Liersch, Christoph Biermann, Rolf M. Mesters, and Wolfgang E. Berdel

Abstract Although the lymphatic system has been initially described in the sixteenth century, basic research has been limited. Despite its importance for the maintenance of tissue fluid homeostasis and for the afferent immune response, research of the molecular mechanisms of lymphatic vessel formation and function has for a long time been hampered. One reason could be because of the difficulties of visibility due to the lack of lymphatic markers. But since the discovery of several molecules specifically expressed in lymphatic endothelial cells, a rediscovery of the lymphatic vasculature has taken place. New scientific insights has facilitated detailed analysis of the nature and organization of the lymphatic system in physiological and pathophysiological conditions, such as in chronic inflammation and metastatic cancer spread. Knowledge about the molecules that control lymphangiogenesis and tumor-associated lymphangiogenesis is now expanding, allowing better opportunities for the development of drugs interfering with the relevant signaling pathways. Advances in our understanding of the mechanisms have translated into a number of novel therapeutic studies.

8.1 Introduction

The lymphatic vasculature develops separately, but is functionally related to the blood vascular system. While the blood vascular system is a closed circulatory system, the lymphatic system is open-ended. It collects the interstitial fluid in the periphery and drains the absorbed lymph in the nuchal region into the subclavian veins. This loop controls the balance of various factors and 10% of the body fluid volume. Next to the transport of interstitial fluid, the lymphatic system plays an essential role in the circulation of macromolecules, dietary fats, lymphocytes, and antigen-presenting cells. In the immune-regulatory network, the lymphatic system directs the trafficking of cytokines and immune cells. However, the lymphatic system is also a common pathway for lymphatic metastasis, and therefore plays an essential role for overall survival of cancer patients.

R. Liersch (✉)
Department of Medicine, Hematology/Oncology,
University Hospital Münster,
Albert-Schweitzer-Str. 33, 48129,
Münster, Germany
e-mail: rliersch@uni-muenster.de

R. Liersch et al. (eds.), *Angiogenesis Inhibition,* Recent Results in Cancer Research,
DOI: 10.1007/978-3-540-78281-0_8, © Springer Verlag Berlin Heidelberg 2010

8.2
Embryonic Lymphatic Development

The lymphatic system develops in parallel with the blood vascular system, but although major progress has been made, it remains controversial as to whether the lymphatic vasculature is developing from embryonic veins, from lymphangioblasts, or from both (Wilting et al. 1999). In 1902, Florence Sabin proposed the most widely accepted theory that the lymphatic vasculature develops from embryonic veins (Sabin 1902; Sabin 1904) and that the peripheral lymphatic system expands from the primary lymph sacs, originates from vascular endothelial cells, and then spreads by endothelial sprouting, forming capillaries. Upon the formation of the vascular system, Lyve-1 (lymphatic vessel endothelial hyaluron receptor) starts to be expressed in venous endothelial cells of the cardinal vein, and endothelial cells become competent to respond to lymphatic signals (lymphatic competence). Induced by a so far unknown signal almost at the same time, Prox-1 expression occurs in restricted areas of the cardinal vein, determining the lymphatic fate (lymphatic bias) of budding endothelial cells. Homebox gene Prox-1 is a transcription factor related to the Drosophila gene prospero, and expressing endothelial cells are detected in a polarized manner in a subset of cells of the cardinal vein, leading to budding of endothelial cells, initially in the jugular and mesonephric regions (Wigle and Oliver 1999). The analysis of Prox-1 null mice revealed that Prox-1 is required to promote lymphangiogenesis in a specific subpopulation in the embryonic vein. The importance becomes evident by the fact that in Prox-1 null mice the lymphatics do not develop, whereas the blood vessels seem to be unaffected (Wigle and Oliver 1999). Prox-1 promotes the lymphatic differentiation and leads to the downregulation of blood vessel markers (Wigle et al. 2002).

The vascular endothelial growth factor (VEGF)-C plays another essential role during lymphatic development. Binding of its receptor, the VEGF-Receptor-3 (VEGFR-3), expressed on early blood vessels and on lymphatic endothelium is required for migration and budding. In VEGF-C knockout mice, endothelial cells commit to the lymphatic lineage but do not sprout to form lymph vessels (Karkkainen et al. 2004). Xenopus tadpoles with VEGF-C knockdown had lymphatic commitment but impaired the directional migration and budding (Ny et al. 2005). Taken together, these results suggest that Prox-1 activity is required for the commitment of the venous endothelial cells to lymphatic differentiation, whereas VEGF-C/VEGFR-3 signaling provides essential signals for sprouting (Karkkainen et al. 2004; Wigle and Oliver 1999). The development of the lymphatic vasculature during embryogenesis lags behind that of the blood vessels, and these vessels at a later point in time develop Prox-1, Lyve-1, and CD31 positive vessel structures. Vascular endothelial growth factor–A and –C, but not basic FGF-2 (basic FGF), hepatocyte growth factor (HGF), and hypoxia, stimulate the development of early lymphatics (Kreuger et al. 2006; Liersch et al. 2006). Additional molecules, including the mucin-type glycoprotein podoplanin, Neuropilin-2 (Nrp-2), and angiopoietin-2 (Ang2) play major roles in the further maturation of the developing lymphatic system. Integrin $\alpha9\beta1$ is required for the development of the fully functional lymphatic system and is involved in mediating the effects of VEGF-C and VEGF-D via VEGFR-3. Mice deficient in the integrin $\alpha9$-subunit show edema and chylothorax, and die shortly after birth.

An alternative model suggested that the primary lymphatics develop in the mesenchyme from precursor cells, so-called lymphangioblasts, independent from veins, and only later establish connections with the venous system (Huntington and McClure 1910). This was supported by the findings obtained in birds, where the lymph sacs develop by sprouting and form the embryonic mesenchyme (Schneider et al. 1999). Recently it has been shown in the tadpole model that both mechanisms can also contribute to lymph vessel development (Ny et al. 2005). Evidence for both models has been recently found in murine embroid bodies. In these

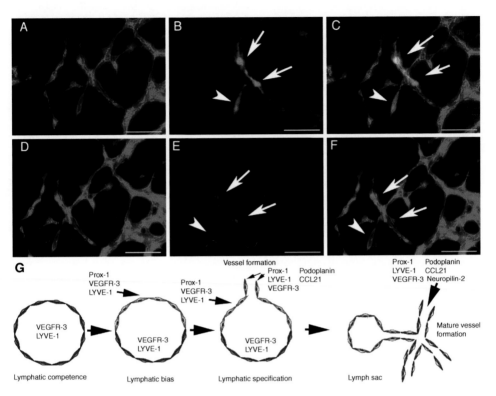

Fig. 8.1 Embryonic development of the lymph system. Lymphatic competence of vascular structures in embryoid bodies (EB) show differential expression of Lyve-1 and Prox-1. Double immunofluorescence stains of 21 days old EBs for CD31 (*red*; **a, d**) and Prox-1 (*green*, **e**) revealed CD31-positive blood vessels and CD31+/Prox-1+ (**e**; *arrow*) positive lymphatic vessels (f; merged image). Differential immunofluorescence stains for CD31 (**a, d**; *red*) and LYVE-1 (**b**; *green*) revealed that vascular structures are CD31+/Lyve-1 positive (b; *arrow/arrowhead*) with no expression of Prox-1 (e; *arrowhead*). (**c, f**) Merged images. Scale bars: 100 μm. (**g**) At early embryonic development endothelial cells of the cardinal vein express LYVE-1 and VEGFR-3 (lymphatic competence). Upon stimulation a subset of endothelial cells express the transcription factor Prox-1, a master regulator of lymphatic differentiation (lymphatic bias). These Prox-1 cells bud off and migrate out to form the primitive lymph sacs and then the mature lymphatic network. During this process, they upregulate the expression of additional lymphatic lineage markers

three-dimensional structures lymphatic endothelial cells (LEC) seem to develop not only from blood vessels. In agreement with earlier observation, LYVE-1/CD31 positive vessels develop much earlier than Prox-1 expression occurs. But Prox-1 was partially expressed not only in a subpopulation of LYVE-1/CD31 positive blood endothelial vessels (Fig. 8.1), but also in additional areas of newly formed lymphatic vessels not associated to any blood vessel.

In summary, until now published data suggest that the lymphatic vasculature is budding of from pre-existing veins, with a contribution from mesenchymal progenitors.

8.3
The Lymphatic Function

The lymphatic system consists of capillaries, collecting vessels, lymph nodes, trunks, and ducts. In the periphery, the blind-ended, finger shaped capillaries consist of a single layer of overlapping cells, connected to the surrounding tissue by fibrillin-containing anchoring filaments (Gerli et al. 2000). Due to an absent basal membrane, no smooth muscle cells, and lack of tight cell–cell junctions (Barsky et al. 1983; Leak and Burke 1968; Sauter et al. 1998), only these filaments stabilize the lymphatic capillaries and facilitate lymphatic flow and drainage (Leak and Burke 1966). Under physiological conditions, lymphatic capillaries remain collapsed, but especially in the case of increased interstitial pressure the anchoring filaments provide a better drainage by increasing their luminal volume. After the capillaries merge into collecting vessels, they consist of valves and are surrounded by smooth muscle cells. Intrinsic pump activity, nitric oxide–responsiveness (Shirasawa et al. 2000; von der Weid 2001), skeletal muscle action and valves regulate the unidirectional lymph flow (von der Weid 2001). Collecting vessels become the afferent lymphatics of lymph nodes, emptying into the subcapsular sinus. Lymph nodes are discrete structures surrounded by a capsule composed of connective tissue. Lymph nodes function as filters and reservoirs and exist for the activation of T-lymphocytes and B-lymphocytes. The capsule is perforated at various points by afferent lymphatics. Lymph fluid, macromolecules, and cells travel through the subcapsular, the trabecular, and marginal sinuses to reach the efferent lymphatic. The lining endothelium of the sinuses is lymphatic endothelium, expressing the typical lymphatic markers. Lymph node sinuses have an irregular surface with many reticular cells and fibers protruding into or crossing the lumen and, equivalent to the anchoring filaments of the peripheral capillaries, these fibers support the intranodal vessel lumen (Okada et al. 2002). Casts of these sinuses are connected with the surrounded nodal parenchyma and blood vessels by lymphaticovenous shunts (Okada et al. 2002). All collecting lymphatic vessels pass through lymph nodes, which are organized in clusters through the lymphatic systems. After leaving the lymph node,

the efferent lymphatic vessels merge to thoracic ducts and drain the collected fluids, proteins, and cells back into the blood vascular circulation. Reflecting this specialized function in drainage, transport, and dissemination the lymphatic vasculature is crucially involved in the pathogenesis of various diseases or inflammatory conditions.

8.3.1
Molecular Players in the Regulation of Lymphangiogenesis

The lymphatic endothelium expresses most of the common endothelial cell markers and shares various biological similarities with the blood endothelium (Sauter et al. 1998; Wissmann and Detmar 2006). The main regulator of lymphatic differentiation is the homebox transcription factor *Prox-1* (Drosophila prospero related homeobox gene) (Alitalo and Carmeliet 2002; Wigle et al. 2002). Essential for lymph vessel growth are growth factors like *VEGF-C* and *VEGF-D* (Jeltsch et al. 1997; Oh et al. 1997; Veikkola et al. 2001). These were the first described stimulators of lymphangiogenesis (Fig. 8.2). Both are members of the VEGF-family, and they bind and activate the vascular endothelial growth factor receptor (VEGFR)-3 (Achen et al. 1998; Cao et al. 2004; Joukov et al. 1996; Lee et al. 1996; Makinen et al. 2001a; Veikkola et al. 2001), but after stepwise proteolytic processing by enzymes such as plasmin and proprotein convertases, they also bind VEGFR-2 (Joukov et al. 1997; Stacker et al. 1999) influencing angiogenesis as well (Cao et al. 1998; Marconcini et al. 1999; Witzenbichler et al. 1998). VEGFR-3, also known as FLT-4, was the first lymphangiogenic specific growth factor receptor (Kaipainen et al. 1995). It is expressed in early embryonic development in venous and lymphatic endothelium (Kaipainen et al. 1995) and synthesis is in parts controlled via activation of the p42/p44 MAPK signaling cascade, in protein C kinase dependent fashion, and via AKT phosphorylation (Makinen

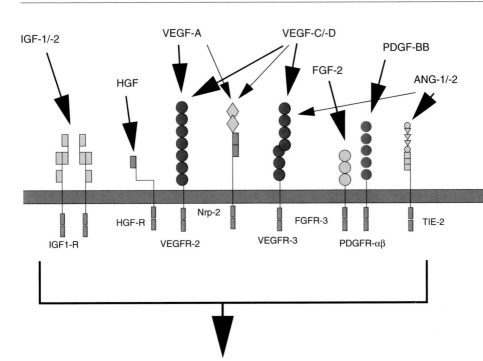

Fig. 8.2 Lymphangiogenic growth factors and their receptors. *VEGFR* vascular endothelial growth factor receptor; *HGFR* hepatocyte growth factor receptor; *IGFR* insulin-like growth factor receptor; *PDGFR* platelet derived growth factor receptor, *FGF* fibroblast growth factor, *TIE* Tyrosine kinase with immunoglobulin-like and EGF-like domains

et al. 2001b). However, in adults the expression of VEGFR-3 becomes confined to the lymphatic endothelium (Kaipainen et al. 1995), but in addition also monocytes, macrophages, dendritic cells, and fenestrated capillaries and veins express VEGFR-3 (Hamrah et al. 2003; Partanen et al. 2000; Schoppmann et al. 2002). Interestingly, VEGFR-3 is reexpressed on capillary endothelium in tumor tissue and is even involved in tumor-angiogenesis and tumor growth (Laakkonen et al. 2007). Signaling via VEGFR-3 is also important for the remodeling of primary vascular networks into larger blood vessels, a function essential for the development of the cardiovascular system in embryos (Dumont et al. 1998). Targeted inactivation of VEGFR-3 results in embryonic lethality as a result of failure to remodel the capillary network before the emergence of lymphatic vessels (Dumont et al. 1998). VEGF-C induces lymphangiogenesis both in embryos and tumors mainly by its interaction with VEGFR-3 (Jeltsch et al. 2003). VEGF-C knockouts fail to form initial lymphatic vessels indicating the pivotal role in embryogenesis (Karkkainen et al. 2004). In contrast, VEGF-D is not required for embryogenesis (Baldwin et al. 2005), but is the strongest inducer of lymphangiogenesis in the adult when given via adenoviral delivery (Rissanen et al. 2003). Exogenous VEGF-D can rescue the phenotype of VEGF-C deficient mice (Karkkainen et al. 2004). Recent studies revealed that VEGF-A also supports lymphangiogenesis through interaction with VEGFR-2, expressed on LEC (Fig. 8.2). VEGF-A induces proliferation of LEC

8

and overexpression in vivo induces lymphangiogenesis in tissue repair and inflammation (Hong et al. 2004; Kunstfeld et al. 2004; Nagy et al. 2002). Even neutralizing anti-VEGF-A antibodies reduce both lymphatic vessel density (LVD) and lymph node metastasis in xenograft models (Whitehurst et al. 2007). Recently, it has been suggested that VEGF-A predominantly promotes lymphatic enlargement, but not the formation of lymphatic vessels (Wirzenius et al. 2007). However, whether the effect is mainly direct or indirect is still not well understood, because VEGF-A also might stimulate lymphangiogenesis indirectly by recruitment of VEGF-C/-D secreting mononuclear cells (Cursiefen et al. 2004b).

Podoplanin is a transmembrane sialomucoprotein expressed at high levels on lymphatic vessel endothelium (Breiteneder-Geleff et al. 1999). It appears to be important for their correct function and formation. In humans, podoplanin is also expressed in osteoblastic cells, kidney podocytes, and lung alveolar Type-I cells (Wetterwald et al. 1996). The precise function of podoplanin is unclear; however, mice with a targeted gene deletion were shown to have impaired lymphatic function and lymphedema (Schacht et al. 2003). Podoplanin knockout mice having defects in lymphatic, but not blood vessel patterning, show symptoms of lymphedema and die at birth due to respiratory failure (Schacht et al. 2003). Podoplanin is also able to aggregate platelets by interaction with the -C-type lectin-like receptor2 (CLEC-2), preventing leaks between the both vasculatures (Kato et al. 2003; Suzuki-Inoue et al. 2007). Interestingly, Wicki et al. (2006) recently published that podoplanin is upregulated in the invasive front of a number of human carcinomas and promotes tumor-cell invasion.

LYVE-1, the primary lymphatic endothelial receptor for hyaluronan has been shown to be a highly specific marker for lymphatic endothelium in a wide variety of different tissues, and to distinguish lymphatic from blood vascular endothelium in numerous human tumors

(Banerji et al. 1999). The considerable structural similarity between LYVE-1 and the leukocyte inflammatory homing receptor CD44 suggests a potential role for LYVE-1 in lymphatic trafficking (Banerji et al. 1999). However, the precise function of LYVE-1 remains unknown, and LYVE-1 $^{-/-}$ mice display no obvious phenotype (Gale et al. 2007). Recently, Lyve-1 expression has also been reported to be absent in some tumor- and inflammation-associated lymphatic vessels (Rubbia-Brandt et al. 2004). It could be downregulated upon incubation of cultured LEC with tumor necrosis factor-alpha (Johnson et al. 2007).

Evidence is mounting concerning the role of *integrins* in lymphangiogenesis. Especially α9β1 seems to have a crucial role in lymphangiogenesis. Mice deficient in the integrin α9 subunit show edema, extra vascular lymphocytes surrounding lymphatic vessels, and die shortly after birth (Huang et al. 2000). Because integrin β1 can stimulate to some degree VEGFR-3, and VEGF-C and VEGF-D can bind α9β1, the integrin-complex might be involved in lymphatic vessel formation and stabilization (Wang et al. 2001). Integrin α9β1 has a role in growth factor induced lymphangiogenesis as Prox-1 upregulates the integrin and VEGFR-3 (Mishima et al. 2007). Antagonism of α9β1 suppressed VEGF-C induced motility. Additional studies revealed that α1β1 and α2β1 are expressed on LEC in healing wounds, and antagonists could block lymphangiogenesis (Hong et al. 2004). Antagonists of α4β1, which is expressed on tumor lymphatic endothelium, has been shown to block tumor metastasis as well as lymphangiogenesis (Garmy-Susini et al. 2007).

While Neuropilin-1 is mainly expressed on arterial endothelial cells, Neuropilin-2 is restricted to veins and lymphatics and is known to mediate axonal guidance during neuronal development. Neuropilin-2 is expressed by LEC and deficient mice develop a reduced small lymphatic endothelium (Yuan et al. 2002). It is also a receptor for VEGF-C and VEGF-D, raising the possibility that VEGF-C signaling is enhanced by Neuropilin, similar to Neuropilin-1 promotion of VEGF-A binding to VEGFR-2 (Karkkainen et al. 2001).

Subsequent studies have also identified *additional lymphangiogenic factors*, including fibroblast growth factor-2 (bFGF), platelet derived growth factor (PDGF-BB), HGF, insulin-like growth factor (IGF), and angiopoietins (Ang-1/-2). bFGF promotes lymphangiogensis in a mouse cornea assay, but it is more likely that this is due to an indirect effect by inducing VEGF-C production (Chang et al. 2004; Kubo et al. 2002). Recently, HGF was described as a novel lymphangiogenic growth factor. HGF promoted lymphangiogenesis and promoted peritumoral lymphangiogenesis (Kajiya et al. 2005). Of interest, HGF-receptor, also known as MET/c-met has been reported to correlate with metastatic spread of cancer (Danilkovitch-Miagkova and Zbar 2002). Studies also revealed that the insulin-like growth factor 1 and 2 (IGF-1/-2) induce lymphangiogenesis, but the effect could not be blocked by antagonist of VEGFR-3 (Bjorndahl et al. 2005), although IGF-receptors promoted expression of VEGF-C and lymph node metastasis in a Lewis lung carcinoma model (Tang et al. 2003). Whether IGF-1/-2 has a direct or indirect effect has to be further analyzed. In addition to Prox-1, VEGF-C, VEGF-D, and VEGFR-3, several molecules are known to be especially important for *later stages of lymphatic development.*

While *angiopoietin-2 (Ang-2)* is not required for the formation of lymphatics, it plays a key role in their subsequent remodeling and maturation. Mice lacking Ang-2 develop subcutaneous oedema and chylous ascites and die shortly after birth, due to impaired lymphatic vessel formation (Gale et al. 2002). Ang-1 can rescue these effects, although the abnormal angiogenesis also observed in Ang-2 $^{-/-}$ mice is not corrected (Gale et al. 2002). Interestingly, VEGF-C induces Ang-2 expression in cultured LEC through VEGFR-2, indicating a possible connection between the VEGF and angiopoietin families during lymphangiogenesis (Veikkola et al. 2003). However, so far there are no data published about the angiopoietins enhancing tumor-lymphangiogenesis and lymphatic metastasis, although a majority of tumors show an increased expression (for review (Tait and Jones 2004).

The *PDGF*-family (Platelet derived growth factor) includes at least four structurally related members, PDGF-AA, PDGF-BB, PDGF-CC, and PDGF-DD, that can form both homodimers and hetereodimers (Heldin and Westermark 1999). PDGF signaling is critical for proper embryonic development, whereas in the adult it plays a role in wound healing and in the control of interstitial fluid pressure. Besides stimulation of stromal cell recruitment, PDGF seems to be an important factor in regulating angiogenesis, pericyte recruitment, and tumor growth (Heldin and Westermark 1999; Ostman and Heldin 2007; Reinmuth et al. 2009). PDGF-BB plays a direct role in promoting lymphangiogenesis and metastasis. Expression of PDGF-BB in murine fibrosarcoma cells induce tumor lymphangiogenesis, leading to enhanced metastasis in lymph nodes (Cao et al. 2004). Cao et al. suggest that PDGF-BB acts as a survival factor for newly formed lymphatics through interaction with receptors PDGFR-alpha and -beta, both detected on isolated primary lymphatic endothelia cells. PDGFs may modulate the postnatal remodeling of lymphatic vessels, but not the development of rudimentary lymphatic vessels. This has to be validated in future.

Several other molecules were additionally found to be required for the development. The tyrosine kinase Syk and the adaptor protein SLP-76 were found to be involved in the separation of blood and lymph vessels (Abtahian et al. 2003). Deficiency resulted in arteriovenous shunting and connections between blood vessels and blood-filled lymph vessels. A similar role has been reported for Spred-1/Spred-2. In knockout mice, blood-filled lymphatic vessels have been reported indicating a possible role in vascular separation (Taniguchi et al. 2007) and angiopoietin-like protein-4 might be required for sustained separation of the two vasculatures (Backhed et al. 2007). Recently, two membrane proteins have been described specifically expressed in activated tumor-associated LEC. Applying double-staining techniques with established LEC markers, Fiedler et al. (2006) have screened endothelial cell differentiation antigens for their expression in LECs. Their experiments identified the sialomucin CD34 as being exclusively expressed by LECs in human tumors but not in corresponding normal tissues. LyP-1, a molecular marker of tumor lymphatics in the MDA-MB-435 breast carcinoma cell line, which was grown in nude mice, was identified by combining ex vivo screening of phage-displayed peptides and in vivo screening for tumor homing. LyP-1 does not appear in normal lymphatics, and it remains to be determined whether it is expressed in other tumor types (Laakkonen et al. 2002). Since LEC's can be successfully isolated by tissue micropreparation from lymphatic channels, embryonic stem cells, even when established in primary culture, provide a valuable opportunity to further explore molecular mechanisms of lymphangiogenesis and the biology of lymphatic metastasis (Hirakawa et al. 2003; Kono et al. 2006; Petrova et al. 2002; Podgrabinska et al. 2002; Wick et al. 2007). This may lead to the identification of endothelial lineage specific signatures.

8.4
Pathology of the Lymphatic Vasculature

Lymphatic vessels have multiple functions and play an important role in various diseases. Impaired function of lymphatic vessels results in lymphedema. Based on the cause, lymphedema occurs as a hereditary (primary) edema or acquired (secondary) edema, but share common features—the dysfunctional lymphatic vessel showing fibrosis and susceptibility to inflammation and infection. The secondary lymphedema is a frequent clinical finding in industrialized countries due to cancer treatment including surgery, radiotherapy, and chemotherapy.

8.4.1
Secondary Lymphedema

In the setting of *inflammation*, lymphatic vessels have multiple functions. In acute inflammation, edema is one typical sign and a significant feature. It results when the amount of inflamed tissue fluid exceeds the capacity of lymphatic vessel for drainage. Lymphatic vessels have the passive role to transport the interstitial fluid and cytokines to the sentinel lymph nodes. In addition, the lymphatic vessels actively participate in the inflammatory process and are responsible for the afferent immune response by enhancing the migration of dendritic cells, which could be induced in two different ways. One is the increasing level of markers such as the secondary lymphoid chemokine (CCL21) or by increased lymphangiogenesis, triggered by infiltrating immune cells. In the case of an inflammatory response, the infiltrating immune cells are a major source of growth factors and even stromal fibroblasts secrete chemokines and other cytokines such as VEGF-A, VEGF-C, and monocyte-colony stimulating factor (M-CSF). They are chemotactic for further monocytes and macrophages (Barleon et al. 1996; Melder et al. 1996). Macrophages, in particular, secrete many angiogenic and lymphangiogenic factors, including VEGF-C and VEGF-D (Schoppmann et al. 2002), and therefore trigger lymphangiogenesis. It has even been reported that macrophages contribute to lymphangiogenesis by incorporation into newly formed lymphatic vessels in the inflamed cornea (Kerjaschki et al. 2006). Thus, VEGFR-3 might have crucial roles in amplification of pathological lymphangiogenesis. Cornea inflammation increased the expression of VEGFR-3 and induced VEGF-C in dendritic cells, possibly by the secretion of proinflammatory cytokines (Hamrah et al. 2003).

It further induces pronounced recruitment of dendritic cells to lymph nodes and triggers graft-rejection. VEGF-C producing macrophages were also found to participate in lymphangiogenesis in human renal transplant rejection (Kerjaschki et al. 2004). Therefore, antilymphangiogenic strategies may improve transplant survival in the setting of transplantation (Cursiefen et al. 2004a, 2003).

In one setting of *lymphatic dysfunction*, the clinical finding of lymphedema is associated with a blockade of the lymphatic fluid uptake. Filiariasis, a parasitic worm infection (*Brugia malayi* or *Wuchereria bancrofti*), often causes massive fibrosis of the lymph nodes and lymph channels in the inguinal region. The resulting edema of the external genitalia and the lower limbs is so extreme that it is called elephantiasis. In Europe, one often finds edema resulting from trauma, surgery, tissue grafting, and congenital edema (Daroczy 1995; Gerber 1998; Mortimer 1998; Witte et al. 1998). Treatment of cancer by removal or irradiation of lymph nodes induces posttreatment lymphedema. Impaired lymphatic drainage produces swelling, scarring, and immundysregulatory disorders. Lymphedema can be a result of an induced imbalance between lymph formation and absorption. The induced fluid accumulation causes pain, chronic and disabling swelling, tissue fibrosis, adipose degeneration, poor immune function, and susceptibility to infections, as well as impaired wound healing (Rockson 2001). Recent studies of experimental lymphedema revealed that VEGF-C protein injection into the wounded area and virus-mediated VEGF-C gene therapy induce the growth of functional lymphatics (Karkkainen et al. 2001; Szuba et al. 2002). Furthermore, it has been shown that adenoviral delivery regenerated lymphatic vessels in mice (Tammela et al. 2007). Postsurgical lymphedemas might be a future indication for VEGF-C-based therapies; however, in the case of cancer treatment related lymphedema, future studies are warranted. VEGF-C might increase the risk of distant organ metastasis if not all tumor cells have been removed.

8.4.2
Primary Lymphedema

Primary lymphedemas are rare genetic developmental disorders which can manifest at birth (Milroy's disease) or at the onset of puberty (Meige's disease) (Witte et al. 1998). Milroy's disease is a congenital form of disease. It has been mapped to the telomeric part of chromosome 5q, in the region 5q34-q35 and Irrthum et al. (2000) have shown that this region includes a VEGFR-3 intragenic polymorphism. Several heterozygous VEGFR-3 missense mutations have been found in Milroy's disease, resulting in the expression of an inactive tyrosine kinase (Irrthum et al. 2003; Karkkainen et al. 2000). The effect of these mutations was the inhibition of autophosphorylation of the receptor causing this congenital hereditary lymphedema (Irrthum et al. 2000). In Milroy's disease, the superficial or subcutaneous lymphatic vessels are usually aplastic or hypoplastic, whereas in other lymphedema syndromes, such as in lymphedema distichiasis (LD), the microlymphatic network is normal or larger than in healthy controls (Bollinger et al. 1983). The inactivating mutation of the forkhead transcription factor FOXC2 in autosomal dominant LD syndrome relates to pubertal onset of lymphedema and double row of eyelashes (distichiasis) (Fang et al. 2000). FOXC2 is a member of the forkhead/winged helix family of transcription factors involved in developmental pathways. FOXC2 knockout mice display aortic arch and ventricular septal defects and also defective lymphatic valve formation and abnormal pericyte recruitment (Petrova et al. 2004). FOXC2 is necessary in lymphatic maturation and is expressed in the developing lymphatic vessels and lymphatic valves of adults (Dagenais et al. 2004; Petrova et al. 2004). Dysfunction of SOX18, a transcription factor of the SOX family, has been identified as a cause for hypotrichosis ly mphedema-teleangiectasia syndrome in humans (Irrthum et al. 2003), and is interestingly regulated by VEGFR-3 activation (Cermenati et al. 2008).

8

However, the detailed function is unclear. Reelin mutations, a gene coding for a protein guiding neuronal-cell migration, is accompanied with congenital lymphedema and chylous ascites (Hong et al. 2000).

In many lymphedema patients none of the aforementioned genetic defects are visible, indicating more relevant genes in human lymphatic development. Different familial lymphedema syndromes emphasize even bigger phenotypic and genotypic heterogeneity in inherited lymphedema angiodysplasia syndromes, where the mutated genes have not been characterized yet (Northup et al. 2003).

cells protrude and migrate between LEC, known as lymphovascular invasion (LVI), an important parameter in the prognosis of cancer patients associated with relapse-free and overall survival in various cancers (Lee et al. 2006, 2007; Lotan et al. 2005; May et al. 2007). Once tumor cells gain access to lymphatic vessels, they embolize as single cells or in clusters to the sentinel lymph node (SLN) (Yancopoulos et al. 2000). When tumor cells infiltrate, the SLN further metastasis to distant lymph nodes or distant organs occurs. Through lymphaticovenous connections cancer cells metastasize via blood vessels, although hematogenous metastasis could also occur without SLN metastasis (Fisher and Fisher 1966).

8.5
Role of Lymphangiogenesis in Cancer

The metastatic spread of tumor cells is responsible for the majority of cancer deaths, and with few exceptions, all cancers can metastasize. The lymphatic system is the primary pathway of metastasis for most human cancers. For migrating tumor cells, the lymphatic system has many advantages over the blood circulation. Even the smallest lymphatic vessels are larger than blood capillaries; flow velocities are lower and there is less interference with serum factors. High shear stress and mechanic deformation in the blood vascular system often kills metastatic cells (Liotta et al. 1991; Weiss 1992). Lymphatic vessels have no or a discontinuous basal membrane, intercellular gaps, and lymphatic capillaries are not surrounded by pericytes.

8.5.1
Lymphvascular Invasion

Lymphatic vessels in comparison to blood vessels are easier to invade and provide ideal conduits. In addition, LEC's secret chemotactic agents attract malignant tumor cells toward areas of high LVD (Shields et al. 2007). Tumor

8.5.2
Tumor-Lymphangiogenesis

Lymphangiogenesis has been found in the tissue of many malignancies. Studies revealed that tumors can actively induce the formation of tumor lymphangiogenesis and promote metastasis (Mandriota et al. 2001; Skobe et al. 2001; Stacker et al. 2001). VEGF-C and VEGF-D induced lymphatic vessel proliferation intratumorally and peritumorally. Size of the peritumoral lymphatic vessel was observed to be a most reliable and significant predictor for cutaneous melanoma metastasis and survival (Dadras et al. 2003). There is still an ongoing controversy regarding the significance and functionality of intratumoral lymphatics or intratumoral lymphangiogenesis. Although there have been studies demonstrating that intratumoral lymphatics are nonfunctional for fluid drainage (Padera et al. 2002), others could describe the prognostic influence of intratumoral lymphatics in immunhistochemical analysis (Dadras et al. 2003). Tumor lymphangiogenesis predicts the presence of melanoma metastasis in sentinel lymph nodes at time of surgery (Dadras et al. 2003). In addition, several clinical studies have correlated intratumoral LVD with metastasis (reviewed by (Achen et al. 2005; Stacker et al. 2002), but nevertheless the importance of intratumoral lymphangiogenesis in regard to metastasis is debatable and may depend on the organ and/or experimental model used. This leads to the general problem that current methodology of lymphangiogenesis quantification is still characterized by high intra- and inter-observer variability. For using the amount of lymphatic vessels in a tumor as a clinically useful parameter, a reliable quantification technique needs to be developed.

8.5.3
Lymphatic Endothelial Cell Activation

Aside from peritumoral lymphangiogenesis, activation of lymphatic vessels has also been proposed as a way to enhance tumor cell infiltration and sentinel lymph node metastasis. He et al. (2005) recently noted that peritumoral LEC proximal to subcutaneous LNM35 lung tumors often displayed an activated phenotype – characterized by increased vessel sprouting, dilation, and permeability. VEGF-C may also activate lymphatics to promote tumor cell chemotaxis, lymphatic intravasation, blood vessel leakage with enhanced lymphatic vessel dilatation and hence tumor cell dissemination (Hoshida et al. 2006). Others have speculated that activated lymphatics might upregulate secretion of chemokines that could attract tumor cells (Alitalo et al. 2004). This activated phenotype can apparently be reversed by adenoviral delivery of soluble Flt-4 (He et al. 2005). Experimental evidence has been obtained suggesting that LEC's could attract tumor cells by secreting chemokines, and therefore actively promote lymphatic metastasis. One of the chemokines, named secondary lymphoid chemokine (SLC/CCL21), is highly expressed in lymph nodes, specifically in endothelial cells of high endothelial venules and T cell-rich areas, and also in the lymphatic endothelium of multiple organs (Gunn et al. 1998). CCL19 and CCL21, chemokines produced by LEC (Saeki et al. 1999), induce a biochemical change

when bound to CCR7. Inactivation of CCR7 or CCL21 blocked dendritic cells to migrate from peripheral tissues to draining lymph nodes (Gunn et al. 1999). Recent reports have also shown that human (Takeuchi et al. 2004) and murine (Wiley et al. 2001) melanomas express CCR7, the receptor for CCL21 and CCL19 and that in gastric carcinoma, head/neck squamous cell carcinoma, nonsmall cell lung cancer, and breast cancer, these two factors are associated with lymph node metastasis (Mashino et al. 2002; Muller et al. 2001; Takanami 2003; Wang et al. 2004; Yan et al. 2004). It has been reported earlier that CCR7 and CXCR4, receptors for SLC/CCL21 and CXCL12, respectively, are significantly expressed in human breast cancer cells. Their ligands exhibit high levels of expression in regional lymph nodes, bone marrow, lung, and liver, which represent the first destinations of breast cancer metastasis (Muller et al. 2001). Inhibiting the interaction between this receptor–ligand pair in vivo reduced the ability of MDA-MB-231 breast cancer cells to metastasize to both lung and lymph nodes. These data suggest active interactions between tumor cells and endothelial cells. Furthermore, overexpression of CCR7 by B16 murine melanoma cells enhanced the incidence of lymph node but not lung metastasis when the tumor cells were implanted into the footpads of mice (Wiley et al. 2001). CCR7-mediated enhancement of lymphatic metastasis could be completely suppressed by treatment with neutralizing anti-SLC antibodies (Wiley et al. 2001). These data indicate that chemokines and their receptors play a critical role in determining the metastatic destination of tumor cells.

8.5.4
Lymph Node Lymphangiogenesis

Paget (1889) concluded that metastasis occurred only when certain favored tumor cells (the seed) had a special affinity for the growth milieu provided by certain specific organs (the soil). The

8

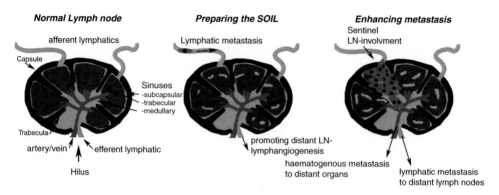

Fig. 8.3 Lymph node lymphangiogenesis. Cancer promotes tumor-associated lymphangiogenesis leading to enhanced metastasis to sentinel lymph nodes (SLN). Lymphangiogenic factors (VEGF-C or VEGF-A) are drained to the SLN where they induce expansion of the lymphatic network (lymph node lymphangiogenesis) preparing the lymph node for the later arrival of the metastatic cells. Metastatic cells then further stimulate sentinel lymph node lymphangiogenesis and distant lymph node lymphangiogenesis, enhancing cancer spread to distant lymph nodes and organs

concept of the *"Seed and soil hypothesis"* (Fig. 8.3) for tumor lymphangiogenesis has been recently described by Hirakawa et al. (2007, 2005). They describe an increased lymphangiogenesis in the sentinel lymph node, even prior to, and after metastatic colonization (Hirakawa et al. 2007, 2005) (Fig. 8.3). Similar observations have been also made in malignant melanoma experiments (Harrell et al. 2007) and in hematological malignancies such as lymphomas (Ruddell et al. 2003). Interestingly, these investigators also observed a 20-30-fold increase in lymph flow. Equivalent changes of lymph node lymphangiogenesis have been recently described in uninvolved axillary lymph nodes of human breast cancer patients (Qian et al. 2006), and lymph node lymphangiogenesis was even associated with nonsentinel lymph node metastasis (Van den Eynden et al. 2006, 2007). That lymph nodes respond to inflammation or neoplasia is a long-known fact. Activated lymph nodes can increase many-fold in size and weight (Cahill et al. 1976; Hall and Morris 1965; Hay and Hobbs 1977). This can be a morphological change known as reactive lymphadenopathy also observed during inflammatory processes. Although the exact mechanism underlying cancer-associated lymph node lymphangiogenesis remains unclear, it could be proposed as a possible way for tumors to disseminate faster throughout the lymphatic system and, subsequently, to distant sites.

8.6
Targeting Lymphangiogenesis

Dissemination of tumor cells is an early and common event and is associated with poorer prognosis for human cancer patients. Targeting lymphangiogenesis could prevent lymphatic metastasis and further dissemination to distant lymph nodes or even distant organs. In the setting of adjuvant tumor therapy, antilymphangiogenic treatment may be an interesting approach after the primary tumor has been surgically removed. Preventing the dissemination of micrometastasis and keeping the metastasis in a localized stage might increase the therapeutic opportunities and improve prognosis. Thus far, therapeutic agents include antibodies, soluble receptors, and tyrosine kinase inhibitors.

8.6.1
Antibodies

The most extensively targeted molecular system is the VEGFR-3/VEGF-C and VEGFR-3/VEGF-D system. Inhibition by neutralizing antibodies reduced lymphangiogenesis and prevented lymphatic metastasis in various animal models (He et al. 2002, 2005; Hoshida et al. 2006; Roberts et al. 2006; Stacker et al. 2001). Interestingly, neutralizing VEGFR-3 antibody blocked the formation of new lymphatics, while the preexisting lymphatics have not been affected (Pytowski et al. 2005). Of further importance is the expression of VEGFR-2 and the stimulation of LEC by VEGF-A and by proteolytically processed VEGF-C. Clinical studies inhibiting the activation of VEGFR-2 by the neutralizing VEGF-A antibody (bevacizumab) showed to be beneficial in human tumors (for review (Ferrara et al. 2004). An antilymphangiogenic effect of this antibody has never been evaluated systematically so far. Treatment of breast carcinoma in animal models with an anti-VEGF-A antibody revealed a reduced LVD and lymph node metastasis (Whitehurst et al. 2007). The effect might be more pronounced by a combined blockade of both VEGF-C and VEGF-A, leading to dual blocking of angiogenesis and lymphangiogenesis. Double blockade by an anti-receptor targeting may lead to enhanced antiangiogenic and antitumor effect (Tammela et al. 2008).

8.6.2
Soluble Receptors

Soluble receptors compete with membrane-bound receptors. They comprise their extracellular portions and retain the ability to bind their ligand. Even due to the binding of multiple soluble factors they might be very effective. Inhibition of VEGFR-3 signaling with a soluble receptor, VEGFR-3-Ig, suppressed tumor lymphangiogenesis and lymphatic metastasis in a breast and lung carcinoma model (He et al. 2002; Karpanen et al. 2001).

8.6.3
Small Molecule Inhibitor

A similar approach, but interacting intracellularly with the signal transduction are the receptor tyrosine kinase inhibitors such as sorafenib and sunitinib. Both interact with the VEGFR-2 and VEGFR-3 phosphorylation pockets and inhibit consecutive signaling pathways, but no studies have been published so far on their specific anti-lymphangiogenic effect. Cedarinib and vandetanib, which block VEGFR-2 and VEGFR-3 signaling, yielded no inhibition of lymphatic metastasis in animal models, suggesting that kinase inhibition of both receptors may not be enough (Padera et al. 2008). But further studies are warranted to determine the role of tyrosine kinase inhibitors in antilymphangiogenic treatment.

8.7
Conclusions

Lymphangiogenesis is currently receiving increasing scientific and clinical interest. The identification of novel mediators of lymphangiogenesis will likely lead to new advances in our understanding of the mechanisms underlying tumor metastasis. Comprehensive research strategies have revealed a number of novel targets supporting biologically based therapeutic studies. Novel lymphangiogenic targets for the treatment of cancers and inflammation support the future development of individualized therapies, possibly avoiding adverse side effects.

References

Abtahian F, Guerriero A, Sebzda E, Lu MM, Zhou R, Mocsai A, Myers EE, Huang B, Jackson DG, Ferrari VA, Tybulewicz V, Lowell CA, Lepore JJ,

8

Koretzky GA, Kahn ML (2003) Regulation of blood and lymphatic vascular separation by signaling proteins SLP-76 and Syk. Science 299: 247–251

Achen MG, Jeltsch M, Kukk E, Makinen T, Vitali A, Wilks AF, Alitalo K, Stacker SA (1998) Vascular endothelial growth factor D (VEGF-D) is a ligand for the tyrosine kinases VEGF receptor 2 (Flk1) and VEGF receptor 3 (Flt4). Proc Natl Acad Sci U S A 95:548–553

Achen MG, McColl BK, Stacker SA (2005) Focus on lymphangiogenesis in tumor metastasis. Cancer Cell 7:121–127

Alitalo K, Carmeliet P (2002) Molecular mechanisms of lymphangiogenesis in health and disease. Cancer Cell 1:219–227

Alitalo K, Mohla S, Ruoslahti E (2004) Lymphangiogenesis and cancer: meeting report. Cancer Res 64:9225–9229

Backhed F, Crawford PA, O'Donnell D, Gordon JI (2007) Postnatal lymphatic partitioning from the blood vasculature in the small intestine requires fasting-induced adipose factor. Proc Natl Acad Sci U S A 104:606–611

Baldwin ME, Halford MM, Roufail S, Williams RA, Hibbs ML, Grail D, Kubo H, Stacker SA, Achen MG (2005) Vascular endothelial growth factor D is dispensable for development of the lymphatic system. Mol Cell Biol 25:2441–2449

Banerji S, Ni J, Wang SX, Clasper S, Su J, Tammi R, Jones M, Jackson DG (1999) LYVE-1, a new homologue of the CD44 glycoprotein, is a lymph-specific receptor for hyaluronan. J Cell Biol 144:789–801

Barleon B, Sozzani S, Zhou D, Weich HA, Mantovani A, Marme D (1996) Migration of human monocytes in response to vascular endothelial growth factor (VEGF) is mediated via the VEGF receptor flt-1. Blood 87:3336–3343

Barsky SH, Baker A, Siegal GP, Togo S, Liotta LA (1983) Use of anti-basement membrane antibodies to distinguish blood vessel capillaries from lymphatic capillaries. Am J Surg Pathol 7: 667–677

Bjorndahl M, Cao R, Nissen LJ, Clasper S, Johnson LA, Xue Y, Zhou Z, Jackson D, Hansen AJ, Cao Y (2005) Insulin-like growth factors 1 and 2 induce lymphangiogenesis in vivo. Proc Natl Acad Sci U S A 102:15593–15598

Bollinger A, Isenring G, Franzeck UK, Brunner U (1983) Aplasia of superficial lymphatic capillaries in hereditary and connatal lymphedema (Milroy's disease). Lymphology 16:27–30

Breiteneder-Geleff S, Soleiman A, Horvat R, Amann G, Kowalski H, Kerjaschki D (1999) Podoplanin–a specific marker for lymphatic endothelium expressed in angiosarcoma. Verh Dtsch Ges Pathol 83:270–275

Cahill RN, Frost H, Trnka Z (1976) The effects of antigen on the migration of recirculating lymphocytes through single lymph nodes. J Exp Med 143:870–888

Cao Y, Linden P, Farnebo J, Cao R, Eriksson A, Kumar V, Qi JH, Claesson-Welsh L, Alitalo K (1998) Vascular endothelial growth factor C induces angiogenesis in vivo. Proc Natl Acad Sci U S A 95:14389–14394

Cao R, Bjorndahl MA, Religa P, Clasper S, Garvin S, Galter D, Meister B, Ikomi F, Tritsaris K, Dissing S, Ohhashi T, Jackson DG, Cao Y (2004) PDGF-BB induces intratumoral lymphangiogenesis and promotes lymphatic metastasis. Cancer Cell 6:333–345

Cermenati S, Moleri S, Cimbro S, Corti P, Del Giacco L, Amodeo R, Dejana E, Koopman P, Cotelli F, Beltrame M (2008) Sox18 and Sox7 play redundant roles in vascular development. Blood 111:2657–2666

Chang LK, Garcia-Cardena G, Farnebo F, Fannon M, Chen EJ, Butterfield C, Moses MA, Mulligan RC, Folkman J, Kaipainen A (2004) Dose-dependent response of FGF-2 for lymphangiogenesis. Proc Natl Acad Sci U S A 101:11658–11663

Cursiefen C, Chen L, Dana MR, Streilein JW (2003) Corneal lymphangiogenesis: evidence, mechanisms, and implications for corneal transplant immunology. Cornea 22:273–281

Cursiefen C, Cao J, Chen L, Liu Y, Maruyama K, Jackson D, Kruse FE, Wiegand SJ, Dana MR, Streilein JW (2004a) Inhibition of hemangiogenesis and lymphangiogenesis after normal-risk corneal transplantation by neutralizing VEGF promotes graft survival. Invest Ophthalmol Vis Sci 45:2666–2673

Cursiefen C, Chen L, Borges LP, Jackson D, Cao J, Radziejewski C, D'Amore PA, Dana MR, Wiegand SJ, Streilein JW (2004b) VEGF-A stimulates lymphangiogenesis and hemangiogenesis in inflammatory neovascularization via macrophage recruitment. J Clin Invest 113:1040–1050

Dadras SS, Paul T, Bertoncini J, Brown LF, Muzikansky A, Jackson DG, Ellwanger U, Garbe C, Mihm MC, Detmar M (2003) Tumor lymphangiogenesis: a novel prognostic indicator for cutaneous melanoma metastasis and survival. Am J Pathol 162:1951–1960

Dagenais SL, Hartsough RL, Erickson RP, Witte MH, Butler MG, Glover TW (2004) Foxc2 is expressed in developing lymphatic vessels and other tissues associated with lymphedema-distichiasis syndrome. Gene Expr Patterns 4:611–619

Danilkovitch-Miagkova A, Zbar B (2002) Dysregulation of Met receptor tyrosine kinase activity in invasive tumors. J Clin Invest 109:863–867

Daroczy J (1995) Pathology of lymphedema. Clin Dermatol 13:433–444

Dumont DJ, Jussila L, Taipale J, Lymboussaki A, Mustonen T, Pajusola K, Breitman M, Alitalo K (1998) Cardiovascular failure in mouse embryos deficient in VEGF receptor-3. Science 282: 946–949

Fang J, Dagenais SL, Erickson RP, Arlt MF, Glynn MW, Gorski JL, Seaver LH, Glover TW (2000) Mutations in FOXC2 (MFH-1), a forkhead family transcription factor, are responsible for the hereditary lymphedema-distichiasis syndrome. Am J Hum Genet 67:1382–1388

Ferrara N, Hillan KJ, Gerber HP, Novotny W (2004) Discovery and development of bevacizumab, an anti-VEGF antibody for treating cancer. Nat Rev Drug Discov 3:391–400

Fisher B, Fisher ER (1966) The interrelationship of hematogenous and lymphatic tumor cell dissemination. Surg Gynecol Obstet 122:791–798

Gale NW, Thurston G, Hackett SF, Renard R, Wang Q, McClain J, Martin C, Witte C, Witte MH, Jackson D, Suri C, Campochiaro PA, Wiegand SJ, Yancopoulos GD (2002) Angiopoietin-2 is required for postnatal angiogenesis and lymphatic patterning, and only the latter role is rescued by Angiopoietin-1. Dev Cell 3: 411–423

Gale NW, Prevo R, Espinosa J, Ferguson DJ, Dominguez MG, Yancopoulos GD, Thurston G, Jackson DG (2007) Normal lymphatic development and function in mice deficient for the lymphatic hyaluronan receptor LYVE-1. Mol Cell Biol 27:595–604

Garmy-Susini B, Makale M, Fuster M, Varner JA (2007) Methods to study lymphatic vessel integrins. Methods Enzymol 426:415–438

Gerber LH (1998) A review of measures of lymphedema. Cancer 83:2803–2804

Gerli R, Solito R, Weber E, Agliano M (2000) Specific adhesion molecules bind anchoring filaments and endothelial cells in human skin initial lymphatics. Lymphology 33:148–157

Gunn MD, Tangemann K, Tam C, Cyster JG, Rosen SD, Williams LT (1998) A chemokine

expressed in lymphoid high endothelial venules promotes the adhesion and chemotaxis of naive T lymphocytes. Proc Natl Acad Sci U S A 95: 258–263

Gunn MD, Kyuwa S, Tam C, Kakiuchi T, Matsuzawa A, Williams LT, Nakano H (1999) Mice lacking expression of secondary lymphoid organ chemokine have defects in lymphocyte homing and dendritic cell localization. J Exp Med 189:451–460

Hall JG, Morris B (1965) The immediate effect of antigens on the cell output of a lymph node. Br J Exp Pathol 46:450–454

Hamrah P, Chen L, Zhang Q, Dana MR (2003) Novel expression of vascular endothelial growth factor receptor (VEGFR)-3 and VEGF-C on corneal dendritic cells. Am J Pathol 163:57–68

Harrell MI, Iritani BM, Ruddell A (2007) Tumor-induced sentinel lymph node lymphangiogenesis and increased lymph flow precede melanoma metastasis. Am J Pathol 170:774–786

Hay JB, Hobbs BB (1977) The flow of blood to lymph nodes and its relation to lymphocyte traffic and the immune response. J Exp Med 145:31–44

He Y, Kozaki K, Karpanen T, Koshikawa K, Yla-Herttuala S, Takahashi T, Alitalo K (2002) Suppression of tumor lymphangiogenesis and lymph node metastasis by blocking vascular endothelial growth factor receptor 3 signaling. J Natl Cancer Inst 94:819–825

He Y, Rajantie I, Pajusola K, Jeltsch M, Holopainen T, Yla-Herttuala S, Harding T, Jooss K, Takahashi T, Alitalo K (2005) Vascular endothelial cell growth factor receptor 3-mediated activation of lymphatic endothelium is crucial for tumor cell entry and spread via lymphatic vessels. Cancer Res 65:4739–4746

Heldin CH, Westermark B (1999) Mechanism of action and in vivo role of platelet-derived growth factor. Physiol Rev 79:1283–1316

Hirakawa S, Hong YK, Harvey N, Schacht V, Matsuda K, Libermann T, Detmar M (2003) Identification of vascular lineage-specific genes by transcriptional profiling of isolated blood vascular and lymphatic endothelial cells. Am J Pathol 162:575–586

Hirakawa S, Kodama S, Kunstfeld R, Kajiya K, Brown LF, Detmar M (2005) VEGF-A induces tumor and sentinel lymph node lymphangiogenesis and promotes lymphatic metastasis. J Exp Med 201:1089–1099

Hirakawa S, Brown LF, Kodama S, Paavonen K, Alitalo K, Detmar M (2007) VEGF-C-induced lymphangiogenesis in sentinel lymph nodes promotes tumor metastasis to distant sites. Blood 109: 1010–1017

Hong SE, Shugart YY, Huang DT, Shahwan SA, Grant PE, Hourihane JO, Martin ND, Walsh CA (2000) Autosomal recessive lissencephaly with cerebellar hypoplasia is associated with human RELN mutations. Nat Genet 26:93–96

Hong YK, Lange-Asschenfeldt B, Velasco P, Hirakawa S, Kunstfeld R, Brown LF, Bohlen P, Senger DR, Detmar M (2004) VEGF-A promotes tissue repair-associated lymphatic vessel formation via VEGFR-2 and the alpha1beta1 and alpha2beta1 integrins. FASEB J 18: 1111–1113

Hoshida T, Isaka N, Hagendoorn J, di Tomaso E, Chen YL, Pytowski B, Fukumura D, Padera TP, Jain RK (2006) Imaging steps of lymphatic metastasis reveals that vascular endothelial growth factor-C increases metastasis by increasing delivery of cancer cells to lymph nodes: therapeutic implications. Cancer Res 66:8065–8075

Huang XZ, Wu JF, Ferrando R, Lee JH, Wang YL, Farese RV Jr, Sheppard D (2000) Fatal bilateral chylothorax in mice lacking the integrin alpha-9beta1. Mol Cell Biol 20:5208–5215

Huntington G, McClure C (1910) The anatomy and development of the jugular lymph sac in the domestic cat (Felis domestica). Am J Anat 10: 177–311

Irrthum A, Karkkainen MJ, Devriendt K, Alitalo K, Vikkula M (2000) Congenital hereditary lymphedema caused by a mutation that inactivates VEGFR3 tyrosine kinase. Am J Hum Genet 67: 295–301

Irrthum A, Devriendt K, Chitayat D, Matthijs G, Glade C, Steijlen PM, Fryns JP, Van Steensel MA, Vikkula M (2003) Mutations in the transcription factor gene SOX18 underlie recessive and dominant forms of hypotrichosis-lymphedema-telangiectasia. Am J Hum Genet 72:1470–1478

Jeltsch M, Kaipainen A, Joukov V, Meng X, Lakso M, Rauvala H, Swartz M, Fukumura D, Jain RK, Alitalo K (1997) Hyperplasia of lymphatic vessels in VEGF-C transgenic mice. Science 276:1423–1425

Jeltsch M, Tammela T, Alitalo K, Wilting J (2003) Genesis and pathogenesis of lymphatic vessels. Cell Tissue Res 314:69–84

Johnson LA, Prevo R, Clasper S, Jackson DG (2007) Inflammation-induced uptake and degradation of the lymphatic endothelial hyaluronan receptor LYVE-1. J Biol Chem 282:33671–33680

Joukov V, Pajusola K, Kaipainen A, Chilov D, Lahtinen I, Kukk E, Saksela O, Kalkkinen N, Alitalo K (1996) A novel vascular endothelial growth factor, VEGF-C, is a ligand for the Flt4 (VEGFR-3) and KDR (VEGFR-2) receptor tyrosine kinases. EMBO J 15:1751

Joukov V, Sorsa T, Kumar V, Jeltsch M, Claesson-Welsh L, Cao Y, Saksela O, Kalkkinen N, Alitalo K (1997) Proteolytic processing regulates receptor specificity and activity of VEGF-C. EMBO J 16:3898–3911

Kaipainen A, Korhonen J, Mustonen T, van Hinsbergh VW, Fang GH, Dumont D, Breitman M, Alitalo K (1995) Expression of the fms-like tyrosine kinase 4 gene becomes restricted to lymphatic endothelium during development. Proc Natl Acad Sci U S A 92:3566–3570

Kajiya K, Hirakawa S, Ma B, Drinnenberg I, Detmar M (2005) Hepatocyte growth factor promotes lymphatic vessel formation and function. EMBO J 24:2885–2895

Karkkainen MJ, Ferrell RE, Lawrence EC, Kimak MA, Levinson KL, McTigue MA, Alitalo K, Finegold DN (2000) Missense mutations interfere with VEGFR-3 signalling in primary lymphoedema. Nat Genet 25:153–159

Karkkainen MJ, Saaristo A, Jussila L, Karila KA, Lawrence EC, Pajusola K, Bueler H, Eichmann A, Kauppinen R, Kettunen MI, Yla-Herttuala S, Finegold DN, Ferrell RE, Alitalo K (2001) A model for gene therapy of human hereditary lymphedema. Proc Natl Acad Sci U S A 98: 12677–12682

Karkkainen MJ, Haiko P, Sainio K, Partanen J, Taipale J, Petrova TV, Jeltsch M, Jackson DG, Talikka M, Rauvala H, Betsholtz C, Alitalo K (2004) Vascular endothelial growth factor C is required for sprouting of the first lymphatic vessels from embryonic veins. Nat Immunol 5:74–80

Karpanen T, Egeblad M, Karkkainen MJ, Kubo H, Yla-Herttuala S, Jaattela M, Alitalo K (2001) Vascular endothelial growth factor C promotes tumor lymphangiogenesis and intralymphatic tumor growth. Cancer Res 61:1786–1790

Kato Y, Fujita N, Kunita A, Sato S, Kaneko M, Osawa M, Tsuruo T (2003) Molecular identification of Aggrus/T1alpha as a platelet aggregation-inducing factor expressed in colorectal tumors. J Biol Chem 278:51599–51605

Kerjaschki D, Regele HM, Moosberger I, Nagy-Bojarski K, Watschinger B, Soleiman A, Birner P, Krieger S, Hovorka A, Silberhumer G,

Laakkonen P, Petrova T, Langer B, Raab I (2004) Lymphatic neoangiogenesis in human kidney transplants is associated with immunologically active lymphocytic infiltrates. J Am Soc Nephrol 15:603–612

Kerjaschki D, Huttary N, Raab I, Regele H, Bojarski-Nagy K, Bartel G, Krober SM, Greinix H, Rosenmaier A, Karlhofer F, Wick N, Mazal PR (2006) Lymphatic endothelial progenitor cells contribute to de novo lymphangiogenesis in human renal transplants. Nat Med 12: 230–234

Kono T, Kubo H, Shimazu C, Ueda Y, Takahashi M, Yanagi K, Fujita N, Tsuruo T, Wada H, Yamashita JK (2006) Differentiation of lymphatic endothelial cells from embryonic stem cells on OP9 stromal cells. Arterioscler Thromb Vasc Biol 26:2070–2076

Kreuger J, Nilsson I, Kerjaschki D, Petrova T, Alitalo K, Claesson-Welsh L (2006) Early lymph vessel development from embryonic stem cells. Arterioscler Thromb Vasc Biol 26:1073–1078

Kubo H, Cao R, Brakenhielm E, Makinen T, Cao Y, Alitalo K (2002) Blockade of vascular endothelial growth factor receptor-3 signaling inhibits fibroblast growth factor-2-induced lymphangiogenesis in mouse cornea. Proc Natl Acad Sci U S A 99:8868–8873

Kunstfeld R, Hirakawa S, Hong YK, Schacht V, Lange-Asschenfeldt B, Velasco P, Lin C, Fiebiger E, Wei X, Wu Y, Hicklin D, Bohlen P, Detmar M (2004) Induction of cutaneous delayed-type hypersensitivity reactions in VEGF-A transgenic mice results in chronic skin inflammation associated with persistent lymphatic hyperplasia. Blood 104:1048–1057

Laakkonen P, Porkka K, Hoffman JA, Ruoslahti E (2002) A tumor-homing peptide with a targeting specificity related to lymphatic vessels. Nat Med 8:751–755

Laakkonen P, Waltari M, Holopainen T, Takahashi T, Pytowski B, Steiner P, Hicklin D, Persaud K, Tonra JR, Witte L, Alitalo K (2007) Vascular endothelial growth factor receptor 3 is involved in tumor angiogenesis and growth. Cancer Res 67:593–599

Leak LV, Burke JF (1966) Fine structure of the lymphatic capillary and the adjoining connective tissue area. Am J Anat 118:785–809

Leak LV, Burke JF (1968) Electron microscopic study of lymphatic capillaries in the removal of connective tissue fluids and particulate substances. Lymphology 1:39–52

Lee J, Gray A, Yuan J, Luoh SM, Avraham H, Wood WI (1996) Vascular endothelial growth factor-related protein: a ligand and specific activator of the tyrosine kinase receptor Flt4. Proc Natl Acad Sci U S A 93:1988–1992

Lee AH, Pinder SE, Macmillan RD, Mitchell M, Ellis IO, Elston CW, Blamey RW (2006) Prognostic value of lymphovascular invasion in women with lymph node negative invasive breast carcinoma. Eur J Cancer 42:357–362

Lee CC, Wu CW, Lo SS, Chen JH, Li AF, Hsieh MC, Shen KH, Lui WY (2007) Survival predictors in patients with node-negative gastric carcinoma. J Gastroenterol Hepatol 22:1014–1018

Liersch R, Nay F, Lu L, Detmar M (2006) Induction of lymphatic endothelial cell differentiation in embryoid bodies. Blood 107:1214–1216

Liotta LA, Stetler-Stevenson WG, Steeg PS (1991) Cancer invasion and metastasis: positive and negative regulatory elements. Cancer Invest 9: 543–551

Lotan Y, Gupta A, Shariat SF, Palapattu GS, Vazina A, Karakiewicz PI, Bastian PJ, Rogers CG, Amiel G, Perotte P, Schoenberg MP, Lerner SP, Sagalowsky AI (2005) Lymphovascular invasion is independently associated with overall survival, cause-specific survival, and local and distant recurrence in patients with negative lymph nodes at radical cystectomy. J Clin Oncol 23:6533–6539

Makinen T, Jussila L, Veikkola T, Karpanen T, Kettunen MI, Pulkkanen KJ, Kauppinen R, Jackson DG, Kubo H, Nishikawa S, Yla-Herttuala S, Alitalo K (2001a) Inhibition of lymphangiogenesis with resulting lymphedema in transgenic mice expressing soluble VEGF receptor-3. Nat Med 7:199–205

Makinen T, Veikkola T, Mustjoki S, Karpanen T, Catimel B, Nice EC, Wise L, Mercer A, Kowalski H, Kerjaschki D, Stacker SA, Achen MG, Alitalo K (2001b) Isolated lymphatic endothelial cells transduce growth, survival and migratory signals via the VEGF-C/D receptor VEGFR-3. EMBO J 20:4762–4773

Mandriota SJ, Jussila L, Jeltsch M, Compagni A, Baetens D, Prevo R, Banerji S, Huarte J, Montesano R, Jackson DG, Orci L, Alitalo K, Christofori G, Pepper MS (2001) Vascular endothelial growth factor-C-mediated lymphangiogenesis promotes tumour metastasis. EMBO J 20:672–682

Marconcini L, Marchio S, Morbidelli L, Cartocci E, Albini A, Ziche M, Bussolino F, Oliviero S (1999) c-fos-induced growth factor/vascular

8

endothelial growth factor D induces angiogenesis in vivo and in vitro. Proc Natl Acad Sci U S A 96:9671–9676

Mashino K, Sadanaga N, Yamaguchi H, Tanaka F, Ohta M, Shibuta K, Inoue H, Mori M (2002) Expression of chemokine receptor CCR7 is associated with lymph node metastasis of gastric carcinoma. Cancer Res 62:2937–2941

May M, Kaufmann O, Hammermann F, Loy V, Siegsmund M (2007) Prognostic impact of lymphovascular invasion in radical prostatectomy specimens. BJU Int 99:539–544

Melder RJ, Koenig GC, Witwer BP, Safabakhsh N, Munn LL, Jain RK (1996) During angiogenesis, vascular endothelial growth factor and basic fibroblast growth factor regulate natural killer cell adhesion to tumor endothelium. Nat Med 2:992–997

Mishima K, Watabe T, Saito A, Yoshimatsu Y, Imaizumi N, Masui S, Hirashima M, Morisada T, Oike Y, Araie M, Niwa H, Kubo H, Suda T, Miyazono K (2007) Prox1 induces lymphatic endothelial differentiation via integrin alpha9 and other signaling cascades. Mol Biol Cell 18: 1421–1429

Mortimer PS (1998) The pathophysiology of lymphedema. Cancer 83:2798–2802

Muller A, Homey B, Soto H, Ge N, Catron D, Buchanan ME, McClanahan T, Murphy E, Yuan W, Wagner SN, Barrera JL, Mohar A, Verastegui E, Zlotnik A (2001) Involvement of chemokine receptors in breast cancer metastasis. Nature 410:50–56

Nagy JA, Vasile E, Feng D, Sundberg C, Brown LF, Detmar MJ, Lawitts JA, Benjamin L, Tan X, Manseau EJ, Dvorak AM, Dvorak HF (2002) Vascular permeability factor/vascular endothelial growth factor induces lymphangiogenesis as well as angiogenesis. J Exp Med 196:1497–1506

Northup KA, Witte MH, Witte CL (2003) Syndromic classification of hereditary lymphedema. Lymphology 36:162–189

Ny A, Koch M, Schneider M, Neven E, Tong RT, Maity S, Fischer C, Plaisance S, Lambrechts D, Heligon C, Terclavers S, Ciesiolka M, Kalin R, Man WY, Senn I, Wyns S, Lupu F, Brandli A, Vleminckx K, Collen D, Dewerchin M, Conway EM, Moons L, Jain RK, Carmeliet P (2005) A genetic *Xenopus laevis* tadpole model to study lymphangiogenesis. Nat Med 11:998–1004

Oh SJ, Jeltsch MM, Birkenhager R, McCarthy JE, Weich HA, Christ B, Alitalo K, Wilting J (1997) VEGF and VEGF-C: specific induction of angiogenesis and lymphangiogenesis in the differentiated avian chorioallantoic membrane. Dev Biol 188:96–109

Okada S, Albrecht RM, Aharinejad S, Schraufnagel DE (2002) Structural aspects of the lymphocyte traffic in rat submandibular lymph node. Microsc Microanal 8:116–133

Ostman A, Heldin CH (2007) PDGF receptors as targets in tumor treatment. Adv Cancer Res 97:247–274

Padera TP, Kadambi A, di Tomaso E, Carreira CM, Brown EB, Boucher Y, Choi NC, Mathisen D, Wain J, Mark EJ, Munn LL, Jain RK (2002) Lymphatic metastasis in the absence of functional intratumor lymphatics. Science 296:1883–1886

Padera TP, Kuo AH, Hoshida T, Liao S, Lobo J, Kozak KR, Fukumura D, Jain RK (2008) Differential response of primary tumor versus lymphatic metastasis to VEGFR-2 and VEGFR-3 kinase inhibitors cediranib and vandetanib. Mol Cancer Ther 7:2272–2279

Paget S. The distribution of secondary growths in cancer of the breast. *Lancet*. 1889;1:571–573.

Partanen TA, Arola J, Saaristo A, Jussila L, Ora A, Miettinen M, Stacker SA, Achen MG, Alitalo K (2000) VEGF-C and VEGF-D expression in neuroendocrine cells and their receptor, VEGFR-3, in fenestrated blood vessels in human tissues. FASEB J 14:2087–2096

Petrova TV, Makinen T, Makela TP, Saarela J, Virtanen I, Ferrell RE, Finegold DN, Kerjaschki D, Yla-Herttuala S, Alitalo K (2002) Lymphatic endothelial reprogramming of vascular endothelial cells by the Prox-1 homeobox transcription factor. EMBO J 21:4593–4599

Petrova TV, Karpanen T, Norrmen C, Mellor R, Tamakoshi T, Finegold D, Ferrell R, Kerjaschki D, Mortimer P, Yla-Herttuala S, Miura N, Alitalo K (2004) Defective valves and abnormal mural cell recruitment underlie lymphatic vascular failure in lymphedema distichiasis. Nat Med 10:974–981

Podgrabinska S, Braun P, Velasco P, Kloos B, Pepper MS, Skobe M (2002) Molecular characterization of lymphatic endothelial cells. Proc Natl Acad Sci U S A 99:16069–16074

Pytowski B, Goldman J, Persaud K, Wu Y, Witte L, Hicklin DJ, Skobe M, Boardman KC, Swartz MA (2005) Complete and specific inhibition of adult lymphatic regeneration by a novel VEGFR-3 neutralizing antibody. J Natl Cancer Inst 97:14–21

Qian CN, Berghuis B, Tsarfaty G, Bruch M, Kort EJ, Ditlev J, Tsarfaty I, Hudson E, Jackson DG, Petillo D, Chen J, Resau JH, Teh BT (2006) Preparing the "soil": the primary tumor induces vasculature reorganization in the sentinel lymph node before the arrival of metastatic cancer cells. Cancer Res 66:10365–10376

Reinmuth N, Liersch R, Raedel M, Fehrmann F, Fehrmann N, Bayer M, Schwoeppe C, Kessler T, Berdel W, Thomas M, Mesters RM (2009) Combined anti-PDGFRalpha and PDGFRbeta targeting in non-small cell lung cancer. Int J Cancer 124(7):1535–1544

Rissanen TT, Markkanen JE, Gruchala M, Heikura T, Puranen A, Kettunen MI, Kholova I, Kauppinen RA, Achen MG, Stacker SA, Alitalo K, Yla-Herttuala S (2003) VEGF-D is the strongest angiogenic and lymphangiogenic effector among VEGFs delivered into skeletal muscle via adenoviruses. Circ Res 92:1098–1106

Roberts N, Kloos B, Cassella M, Podgrabinska S, Persaud K, Wu Y, Pytowski B, Skobe M (2006) Inhibition of VEGFR-3 activation with the antagonistic antibody more potently suppresses lymph node and distant metastases than inactivation of VEGFR-2. Cancer Res 66:2650–2657

Rockson SG (2001) Lymphedema. Am J Med 110: 288–295

Rubbia-Brandt L, Terris B, Giostra E, Dousset B, Morel P, Pepper MS (2004) Lymphatic vessel density and vascular endothelial growth factor-C expression correlate with malignant behavior in human pancreatic endocrine tumors. Clin Cancer Res 10:6919–6928

Ruddell A, Mezquita P, Brandvold KA, Farr A, Iritani BM (2003) B lymphocyte-specific c-Myc expression stimulates early and functional expansion of the vasculature and lymphatics during lymphomagenesis. Am J Pathol 163:2233–2245

Sabin F (1902) On the origin of the lymphatics system from the veins and the development of the lymph hearts and thorarcic duct in the pig. Am J Anat 1:367–391

Sabin F (1904) On the development of the superficial lymphatics in the skin of the pig. Am J Anat 3:183–195

Saeki H, Moore AM, Brown MJ, Hwang ST (1999) Cutting edge: secondary lymphoid-tissue chemokine (SLC) and CC chemokine receptor 7 (CCR7) participate in the emigration pathway of mature dendritic cells from the skin to regional lymph nodes. J Immunol 162:2472–2475

Sauter B, Foedinger D, Sterniczky B, Wolff K, Rappersberger K (1998) Immunoelectron microscopic characterization of human dermal lymphatic microvascular endothelial cells. Differential expression of CD31, CD34, and type IV collagen with lymphatic endothelial cells vs blood capillary endothelial cells in normal human skin, lymphangioma, and hemangioma in situ. J Histochem Cytochem 46: 165–176

Schacht V, Ramirez MI, Hong YK, Hirakawa S, Feng D, Harvey N, Williams M, Dvorak AM, Dvorak HF, Oliver G, Detmar M (2003) T1alpha/podoplanin deficiency disrupts normal lymphatic vasculature formation and causes lymphedema. EMBO J 22:3546–3556

Schneider M, Othman-Hassan K, Christ B, Wilting J (1999) Lymphangioblasts in the avian wing bud. Dev Dyn 216:311–319

Schoppmann SF, Birner P, Stockl J, Kalt R, Ullrich R, Caucig C, Kriehuber E, Nagy K, Alitalo K, Kerjaschki D (2002) Tumor-associated macrophages express lymphatic endothelial growth factors and are related to peritumoral lymphangiogenesis. Am J Pathol 161:947–956

Shields JD, Emmett MS, Dunn DB, Joory KD, Sage LM, Rigby H, Mortimer PS, Orlando A, Levick JR, Bates DO (2007) Chemokine-mediated migration of melanoma cells towards lymphatics–a mechanism contributing to metastasis. Oncogene 26:2997–3005

Shirasawa Y, Ikomi F, Ohhashi T (2000) Physiological roles of endogenous nitric oxide in lymphatic pump activity of rat mesentery in vivo. Am J Physiol Gastrointest Liver Physiol 278:G551–G556

Skobe M, Hawighorst T, Jackson DG, Prevo R, Janes L, Velasco P, Riccardi L, Alitalo K, Claffey K, Detmar M (2001) Induction of tumor lymphangiogenesis by VEGF-C promotes breast cancer metastasis. Nat Med 7:192–198

Stacker SA, Stenvers K, Caesar C, Vitali A, Domagala T, Nice E, Roufail S, Simpson RJ, Moritz R, Karpanen T, Alitalo K, Achen MG (1999) Biosynthesis of vascular endothelial growth factor-D involves proteolytic processing which generates non-covalent homodimers. J Biol Chem 274:32127–32136

Stacker SA, Caesar C, Baldwin ME, Thornton GE, Williams RA, Prevo R, Jackson DG, Nishikawa S,

8

Kubo H, Achen MG (2001) VEGF-D promotes the metastatic spread of tumor cells via the lymphatics. Nat Med 7:186–191

Stacker SA, Achen MG, Jussila L, Baldwin ME, Alitalo K (2002) Lymphangiogenesis and cancer metastasis. Nat Rev Cancer 2:573–583

Suzuki-Inoue K, Kato Y, Inoue O, Kaneko MK, Mishima K, Yatomi Y, Yamazaki Y, Narimatsu H, Ozaki Y (2007) Involvement of the snake toxin receptor CLEC-2, in podoplanin-mediated platelet activation, by cancer cells. J Biol Chem 282:25993–26001

Szuba A, Skobe M, Karkkainen MJ, Shin WS, Beynet DP, Rockson NB, Dakhil N, Spilman S, Goris ML, Strauss HW, Quertermous T, Alitalo K, Rockson SG (2002) Therapeutic lymphangiogenesis with human recombinant VEGF-C. FASEB J 16:1985–1987

Tait CR, Jones PF (2004) Angiopoietins in tumours: the angiogenic switch. J Pathol 204:1–10

Takanami I (2003) Overexpression of CCR7 mRNA in nonsmall cell lung cancer: correlation with lymph node metastasis. Int J Cancer 105:186–189

Takeuchi H, Fujimoto A, Tanaka M, Yamano T, Hsueh E, Hoon DS (2004) CCL21 chemokine regulates chemokine receptor CCR7 bearing malignant melanoma cells. Clin Cancer Res 10:2351–2358

Tammela T, Saaristo A, Holopainen T, Lyytikka J, Kotronen A, Pitkonen M, Abo-Ramadan U, Yla-Herttuala S, Petrova TV, Alitalo K (2007) Therapeutic differentiation and maturation of lymphatic vessels after lymph node dissection and transplantation. Nat Med 13:1458–1466

Tammela T, Zarkada G, Wallgard E, Murtomaki A, Suchting S, Wirzenius M, Waltari M, Hellstrom M, Schomber T, Peltonen R, Freitas C, Duarte A, Isoniemi H, Laakkonen P, Christofori G, Yla-Herttuala S, Shibuya M, Pytowski B, Eichmann A, Betsholtz C, Alitalo K (2008) Blocking VEGFR-3 suppresses angiogenic sprouting and vascular network formation. Nature 454:656–660

Tang Y, Zhang D, Fallavollita L, Brodt P (2003) Vascular endothelial growth factor C expression and lymph node metastasis are regulated by the type I insulin-like growth factor receptor. Cancer Res 63:1166–1171

Taniguchi K, Kohno R, Ayada T, Kato R, Ichiyama K, Morisada T, Oike Y, Yonemitsu Y, Maehara Y, Yoshimura A (2007) Spreds are essential for embryonic lymphangiogenesis by regulating vascular endothelial growth factor receptor 3 signaling. Mol Cell Biol 27:4541–4550

Van den Eynden GG, Van der Auwera I, Van Laere SJ, Huygelen V, Colpaert CG, van Dam P, Dirix LY, Vermeulen PB, Van Marck EA (2006) Induction of lymphangiogenesis in and around axillary lymph node metastases of patients with breast cancer. Br J Cancer 95:1362–1366

Van den Eynden GG, Vandenberghe MK, van Dam PJ, Colpaert CG, van Dam P, Dirix LY, Vermeulen PB, Van Marck EA (2007) Increased sentinel lymph node lymphangiogenesis is associated with nonsentinel axillary lymph node involvement in breast cancer patients with a positive sentinel node. Clin Cancer Res 13:5391–5397

Veikkola T, Jussila L, Makinen T, Karpanen T, Jeltsch M, Petrova TV, Kubo H, Thurston G, McDonald DM, Achen MG, Stacker SA, Alitalo K (2001) Signalling via vascular endothelial growth factor receptor-3 is sufficient for lymphangiogenesis in transgenic mice. EMBO J 20:1223–1231

Veikkola T, Lohela M, Ikenberg K, Makinen T, Korff T, Saaristo A, Petrova T, Jeltsch M, Augustin HG, Alitalo K (2003) Intrinsic versus microenvironmental regulation of lymphatic endothelial cell phenotype and function. FASEB J 17:2006–2013

von der Weid PY (2001) Lymphatic vessel pumping and inflammation–the role of spontaneous constrictions and underlying electrical pacemaker potentials. Aliment Pharmacol Ther 15:1115–1129

Wang JF, Zhang XF, Groopman JE (2001) Stimulation of beta 1 integrin induces tyrosine phosphorylation of vascular endothelial growth factor receptor-3 and modulates cell migration. J Biol Chem 276:41950–41957

Wang J, Xi L, Hunt JL, Gooding W, Whiteside TL, Chen Z, Godfrey TE, Ferris RL (2004) Expression pattern of chemokine receptor 6 (CCR6) and CCR7 in squamous cell carcinoma of the head and neck identifies a novel metastatic phenotype. Cancer Res 64:1861–1866

Weiss L (1992) Biomechanical interactions of cancer cells with the microvasculature during hematogenous metastasis. Cancer Metastasis Rev 11:227–235

Wetterwald A, Hoffstetter W, Cecchini MG, Lanske B, Wagner C, Fleisch H, Atkinson M (1996) Characterization and cloning of the E11 antigen, a marker expressed by rat osteoblasts and osteocytes. Bone 18:125–132

Whitehurst B, Flister MJ, Bagaitkar J, Volk L, Bivens CM, Pickett B, Castro-Rivera E, Brekken RA, Gerard RD, Ran S (2007) Anti-VEGF-A therapy reduces lymphatic vessel density and expression of VEGFR-3 in an orthotopic breast tumor model. Int J Cancer 121:2181–2191

Wick N, Saharinen P, Saharinen J, Gurnhofer E, Steiner CW, Raab I, Stokic D, Giovanoli P, Buchsbaum S, Burchard A, Thurner S, Alitalo K, Kerjaschki D (2007) Transcriptomal comparison of human dermal lymphatic endothelial cells ex vivo and in vitro. Physiol Genomics 28:179–192

Wicki A, Lehembre F, Wick N, Hantusch B, Kerjaschki D, Christofori G (2006) Tumor invasion in the absence of epithelial-mesenchymal transition: podoplanin-mediated remodeling of the actin cytoskeleton. Cancer Cell 9:261–272

Wigle JT, Oliver G (1999) Prox1 function is required for the development of the murine lymphatic system. Cell 98:769–778

Wigle JT, Harvey N, Detmar M, Lagutina I, Grosveld G, Gunn MD, Jackson DG, Oliver G (2002) An essential role for Prox1 in the induction of the lymphatic endothelial cell phenotype. EMBO J 21:1505–1513

Wiley HE, Gonzalez EB, Maki W, Wu MT, Hwang ST (2001) Expression of CC chemokine receptor-7 and regional lymph node metastasis of B16 murine melanoma. J Natl Cancer Inst 93:1638–1643

Wilting J, Neeff H, Christ B (1999) Embryonic lymphangiogenesis. Cell Tissue Res 297:1–11

Wirzenius M, Tammela T, Uutela M, He Y, Odorisio T, Zambruno G, Nagy JA, Dvorak HF, Yla-Herttuala S, Shibuya M, Alitalo K (2007)

Distinct vascular endothelial growth factor signals for lymphatic vessel enlargement and sprouting. J Exp Med 204:1431–1440

Wissmann C, Detmar M (2006) Pathways targeting tumor lymphangiogenesis. Clin Cancer Res 12:6865–6868

Witte MH, Erickson R, Bernas M, Andrade M, Reiser F, Conlon W, Hoyme HE, Witte CL (1998) Phenotypic and genotypic heterogeneity in familial Milroy lymphedema. Lymphology 31:145–155

Witzenbichler B, Asahara T, Murohara T, Silver M, Spyridopoulos I, Magner M, Principe N, Kearney M, Hu JS, Isner JM (1998) Vascular endothelial growth factor-C (VEGF-C/VEGF-2) promotes angiogenesis in the setting of tissue ischemia. Am J Pathol 153:381–394

Yan C, Zhu ZG, Yu YY, Ji J, Zhang Y, Ji YB, Yan M, Chen J, Liu BY, Yin HR, Lin YZ (2004) Expression of vascular endothelial growth factor C and chemokine receptor CCR7 in gastric carcinoma and their values in predicting lymph node metastasis. World J Gastroenterol 10: 783–790

Yancopoulos GD, Davis S, Gale NW, Rudge JS, Wiegand SJ, Holash J (2000) Vascular-specific growth factors and blood vessel formation. Nature 407:242–248

Yuan L, Moyon D, Pardanaud L, Breant C, Karkkainen MJ, Alitalo K, Eichmann A (2002) Abnormal lymphatic vessel development in Neuropilin-2 mutant mice. Development 129: 4797–4806

Compounds in Clinical Phase III and Beyond

9

Torsten Kessler, Michael Bayer, Christian Schwöppe,
Rüdiger Liersch, Rolf M. Mesters, and Wolfgang E. Berdel

Abstract Targeted therapies against cancer have become more and more important. In particular, the inhibition of tumor angiogenesis and vascular targeting have been the focus of new treatment strategies. Numerous new substances were developed as angiogenesis inhibitors and evaluated in clinical trials for safety, tolerance, and efficacy. With positive study results, some of these molecules have already been approved for clinical use. For example, this is true for the vascular endothelial growth factor neutralizing antibody bevacizumab (BEV) in metastatic colorectal cancer, nonsmall cell lung cancer, renal cancer, and breast cancer. The tyrosine kinase (TK) inhibitors sorafenib and sunitinib have been approved for metastatic renal cancer as well as for hepatocellular carcinoma, and sunitinib has also been approved for gastrointestinal stroma tumors. In this chapter we try to give an overview of the substances currently investigated in Phase III studies and beyond with regard to antiangiogenesis in cancer therapy.

T. Kessler (✉)
Department of Medicine,
Hematology and Oncology, University of Münster,
Albert-Schweitzer-Strasse, 33, 48129,
Münster, Germany
e-mail: torstenkessler@uni-muenster.de

9.1
Introduction

Besides surgery and radiation, chemotherapy has been the cornerstone of cancer treatment for decades. Over the past ten years, a new generation of substances has come into focus targeting molecular pathways in the malignant cell itself or in cells supporting tumor growth, more specifically. For example, strategies aiming at tumor angiogenesis have been extensively studied, following observations that the growth and metastasis of tumors depend on the development of vascular supply. This research led to the isolation of an array of mediators that are capable of inhibiting tumor angiogenesis. Possibly the most pivotal positive regulator of angiogenesis is vascular endothelial growth factor (VEGF). Strategies to either block binding of VEGF to its receptors or to block intracellular signaling events in the downstream cascade represent the basis of many new developments in antiangiogenic cancer therapy (Ferrara et al. 2003).

During the 1990s, the first angiogenesis inhibitors entered clinical trials for cancer therapy. The first drug in this class that was granted approval by the Food and Drug Administration (FDA) in the United States was the anti-VEGF antibody BEV in 2004 (Ferrara et al. 2004). Soon, broad-spectrum receptor tyrosine kinase

R. Liersch et al. (eds.), *Angiogenesis Inhibition,* Recent Results in Cancer Research,
DOI: 10.1007/978-3-540-78281-0_9, © Springer Verlag Berlin Heidelberg 2010

(TK) inhibitors (RTKI) targeting the VEGF/ VEGFR pathway followed in clinical development. The idea behind the development of these compounds was partly based on the rather modest activity of the BEV when used as monotherapy, giving a rationale for higher efficacy when aiming at more than one target. In fact, most agents currently investigated in clinical studies work by mechanisms illustrated in Fig. 9.1. By now at least the RTKIs sorafenib and sunitinib are also approved for treatment of certain cancers, and more than 40 other drugs that were preclinically screened and selected for their antiangiogenic activity are listed in clinical trials of the National Cancer Institute's (NCI) database.

This chapter summarizes some of the substances currently approved or investigated as antiangiogenic cancer drugs in Phase III studies and beyond.

9.1.1
Anti-VEGF Antibody (Bevacizumab, Avastin™)

The humanized monoclonal anti-VEGF antibody BEV is the first VEGF targeting drug which has been officially approved for cancer therapy (Ferrara et al. 2004). In particular, BEV is approved, in combination with intravenous 5-fluorouracil-based (5-FU) chemotherapy, for

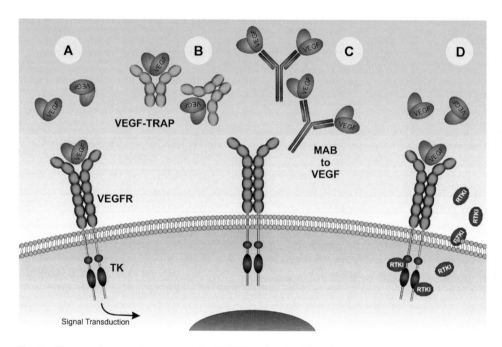

Fig. 9.1 *Therapeutic strategies to target the VEGF/ VEGF receptor (VEGFR) system.* (**a**) Tumors secrete VEGF in response to hypoxia, VEGF binds to VEGFR-2 on endothelial cells, thereby switching on the intracellular tyrosine kinase (TK) activity. Subsequent signal transduction steps promote proliferation, migration, invasion and tumor angiogenesis. Downregulation of VEGF secretion on the tumor side can be achieved by antagonists of the Epidermal Growth Factor Receptor (EGFR) and

other "accidental" antiangiogenic drugs. (**b**) VEGF-TRAP (Aflibercept), fusion protein of the second IgG domain of VEGFR-1, the third IgG domain of VEGFR-2 and the Fc region of human IgG functions as decoy receptor. (**c**) Mab against VEGF (bevacizumab; Avastin™) prevents binding to VEGFR. (**d**) Small molecule Receptor tyrosine kinase inhibitors (RTKI) suppress kinase activity of VEGFR after VEGF binding; e.g., sorafenib, sunitinib, axitinib, vatalanib, vandetanib, cediranib first- or second-line treatment of patients with metastatic carcinoma of the colon or rectum and in combination with carboplatin and paclitaxel for the first-line treatment of patients with unresectable, locally advanced, recurrent, or metastatic nonsquamous nonsmall cell lung cancer (NSCLC). Furthermore, it has been approved in combination with paclitaxel for first-line treatment of patients with metastatic breast cancer and in combination with interferon α-2a for first-line treatment of patients with advanced and/or metastatic renal cell cancer (RCC). The original FDA approval for BEV in 2004 was based on data from a large, placebo-controlled, randomized study demonstrating prolongation in the median survival of patients with metastatic colorectal cancer (CRC) treated with BEV in addition to a combination chemotherapy regimen containing 5-FU, Leucovorin, and Irinotecan (IFL) by approximately five months, compared to patients treated with the IFL chemotherapy regimen alone (20.3 vs. 15.6 months). At that time, this study represented one of the largest improvements in survival ever reported in a randomized, Phase III study of patients with metastatic CRC (Hurwitz et al. 2004). The following approval for second-line therapy was based on results of a randomized, controlled, multicenter Phase III trial (E3200) of 829 patients with advanced or metastatic CRC who had received previous treatment with irinotecan and 5-FU as initial therapy for metastatic disease or as adjuvant therapy (Giantonio et al. 2007). In detail, it could be shown that patients who received BEV plus the 5-FU-based chemotherapy regimen known as FOLFOX4 (oxaliplatin/5-FU/leucovorin) had a 33% improvement in overall survival (OS), compared to patients who received FOLFOX4 alone (hazard ratio (HR) 0.75). Median OS for patients receiving BEV plus FOLFOX4 was 13.0 months, compared to 10.8 months for those receiving FOLFOX4 alone. The third approval and first in another cancer type was based on results from E4599, a randomized, controlled, multicenter trial that enrolled 878 patients with unresectable, locally

advanced, recurrent, or metastatic nonsquamous NSCLC (Sandler et al. 2006). Results showed that patients receiving BEV plus paclitaxel and carboplatin chemotherapies had a 25% improvement in OS, the trial's primary end point, compared to patients who received chemotherapy alone (hazard ratio (HR) 0.80). One-year survival was 51% in the BEV arm vs. 44% in the chemotherapy-alone arm. Median OS of patients treated with BEV plus chemotherapy was 12.5 months, compared to 10.2 months for patients treated with chemotherapy alone. Notably, a pilot study including NSCLC patients with squamous histology prior to E4599 showed an increased death rate in the BEV arm due to fatal pulmonal hemorrhages, leading to exclusion of this subtype for further studies (Johnson et al. 2004). Subsequently, BEV has been approved in first-line therapy of metastatic breast cancer, which was based on an improvement in progression-free survival (PFS) only. In this study 722 patients who had not received chemotherapy for locally recurrent or metastatic breast cancer were randomized to receive either paclitaxel alone or in combination with BEV (Miller et al. 2007). The addition of BEV to paclitaxel resulted in an improvement in PFS (11.3 vs. 5.8 months; $p<0.0001$) with no significant improvement in OS (26.5 vs. 24.8 months; $p=0.14$). Partial response (PR) rates in patients with measurable disease were higher with BEV plus paclitaxel, but no complete responses (CR) were observed. This has led to a limited approval of BEV not including patients with breast cancer that has progressed following anthracycline and taxane chemotherapy administered for metastatic disease. The most recent approval for BEV has been granted for the combination with interferon-α (IFN-α) as first-line treatment of patients with advanced and/or metastatic clear RCC. This was based on a multicentre, randomized, Phase III study, randomizing 649 patients with previously untreated metastatic RCC to receive IFN-α plus BEV or placebo (Escudier et al. 2007a). Median duration of PFS was significantly longer in the BEV plus IFN-α group than it was in the control group (10.2 vs. 5.4 months; $p<0.0001$). With regard to OS, only a trend in favor of the BEV group could be observed.

Currently, BEV is listed in 47 clinical phase III trials, mostly evaluating new combinations for approved indications such as breast cancer, CRC, and NSCLC, but also for other entities such as lymphoma or osteosarcoma (see Table 9.1).

9.1.2
Aflibercept (VEGF – Trap)

Another approach to target the VEGF/VEGF receptor system is to deliver a soluble decoy for VEGF. To this end, a recombinant fusion protein was constructed from the second Ig domain of VEGFR-1 and the third Ig domain of VEGFR-2, fused to the Fc region of human IgG (Aflibercept; VEGF – trap, Regeneron in cooperation with Sanofi-Aventis). The resulting decoy receptor possesses an affinity for all VEGF isoforms that is significantly higher than that of the monoclonal antibody. In addition, aflibercept binds Placental Growth Factor (PLGF), which has also been implicated in tumor angiogenesis. Numerous preclinical models demonstrated significant inhibition of angiogenesis and tumor growth (Holash et al. 2002; Kim et al. 2002a). The first clinical Phase II study published is an open-label, multicenter, two-stage trial in patients with metastatic CRC with at least one prior systemic therapy and good performance status (Tang et al. 2008). Prior treatment with a VEGF or VEGFR inhibitor other than BEV was not allowed. Aflibercept (4 mg/kg) was administered every 2 weeks intravenously. In total, 51 patients were included (BEV naive=24 patients; prior BEV=27; median age=59). During 287 therapy cycles, most common adverse events (AE) of any grade were fatigue ($n=40$), hypertension ($n=28$), proteinuria ($n=25$), headache ($n=22$), voice alteration ($n=16$), anorexia ($n=12$), and joint pain ($n=9$). Serious AE (Grade 3/4) consisted of hypertension ($n=4$), proteinuria ($n=4$), fatigue ($n=3$),

headache ($n=3$). One patient died during treatment due to progressive disease (PD). In the BEV naïve group ($n=24$), disease control rate defined as either PR or stable disease (SD) for at least 16 weeks was 29% (95% Confidence Interval (CI) 13–51%), and median PFS was 2.0 months (95% CI 1.7 – not reached). In the group with prior BEV treatment ($n=27$), disease control rate was 30% (95% CI 14–50%) and median PFS was 3.4 months (95% CI 1.9 – not reached). The authors concluded that aflibercept is well tolerated in pretreated patients with CRC and shows single agent activity (Tang et al. 2008). Based on the study results, aflibercept is now tested in a randomized Phase III study in combination with irinotecan based second-line chemotherapy for patients with CRC. Other currently listed Phase III studies for aflibercept evaluate its efficacy in prostate cancer, NSCLC, advanced ovarian and pancreatic cancer (see Table 9.1).

9.1.2.1
Sorafenib (Nexavar™)

Sorafenib (Nexavar™; Bayer Pharmaceuticals) represents the class of small-molecule compounds with activity against a broad spectrum of receptor tyrosine kinases. Originally developed as RAF-1 inhibitor in a high-throughput screening program, sorafenib later was found to be active against VEGFR-1/-2/-3; platelet derived growth factor (PDGF) -β receptor; Fms-like tyrosine kinase-3 (FLT-3); c-Kit protein and RET receptor tyrosine kinases (Adnane et al. 2006). Thereby, sorafenib inhibits tumor growth by targeting the endothelial cell as well as the tumor cell and was shown to inhibit proliferation, promote apoptosis, and disrupt angiogenesis. In preclinical mechanism of action studies, sorafenib demonstrated a potent antiangiogenic effect in nearly all models tested, resulting in significant reduction of micro-vessel density (Strumberg 2005; Wilhelm et al. 2006). It also showed promising activity in tumor xenograft models in nude mice in combination with

Table 9.1 Inhibitors of angiogenesis currently approved and investigated in clinical phase III studies (Numbers in brackets according to the U.S. National Cancer Institute Clinical Trial Identifier Code)

Drug	Approved	Phase III
Bevacizumab (Avastin™) Monoclonal antibody that binds and inactivates VEGF	First approval 2004: in combination with chemotherapy for metastatic CRC (first and second line), unresectable NSCLC (2006), metastatic breast cancer (2007), in combination with IFN-α for RCC	Forty-seven active phase III trials: evaluating further combinations for approved entities but also new indications such as mesothelioma (NCT00651456), ovarian cancer (NCT00262847), GIST (NCT00324987), lymphoma (NCT00486759), gastric cancer (NCT00548548), carcinoid (NCT00569127), head-and-neck cancer (NCT00588770), osteosarcoma (NCT00667342), and cervix carcinoma (NCT00803062)
Aflibercept (VEGF-trap) binds and neutralizes VEGF as decoy receptor		Four active phase III trials: with docetaxel in metastatic HRPC (NCT00519285), with docetaxel as second-line therapy in metastatic NSCLC (NCT00532155), with irinotecan and 5-FU for metastatic CRC as second line after oxaliplation failure (NCT00561470), with gemcitabine for first-line therapy of metastatic pancreatic cancer (NCT00574275)
Sorafenib (Nexavar™) RTKI active against VEGFRs, PDGFR, c-Kit, FLT-3, RET, RAF-1	First approval 2005: advanced RCC after failure of cytokine therapy or patients unsuitable for such therapy. Advanced HCC as first-line therapy (2008)	Ten active phase III trials: further combinations for approved entities, new indications include unresectable stage III and IV melanoma (NCT00111007) and in combination with gemcitabine for advanced pancreatic cancer (NCT00541021)
Sunitinib (Sutent™) RTKI active against VEGFRs, PDGFR, c-Kit, FLT-3	First approval 2006: advanced RCC as first-line therapy. Advanced GIST after imatinib failure	Twenty active phase III trials: further combinations for approved entities, new indications include the combination with paclitaxel in breast cancer (NCT00373256), with capecitabine in breast cancer (NCT00373113), for pancreatic islet tumors (NCT00428597), with erlotinib in NSCLC (NCT00457392), with FOLFIRI in mCRC (NCT00457691), after failure of docetaxel in HRPC (NCT00676650). Head-to-head study against sorafenib for advanced HCC first line therapy (NCT00699374)
Axitinib (AG-013736) RTKI active against VEGFRs, PDGFR, c-Kit		Two active phase III trials: in combination with gemcitabine for advanced pancreatic cancer (NCT00471146), as second-line therapy for metastatic RCC (NCT00678392)

(*continued*)

9

Table 9.1 (continued)

Drug	Approved	Phase III
Cediranib (AZD2171; Recentin™) RTKI active against VEGFRs, PDGFR, c-Kit, EGFR		Five active phase III trials: in combination with FOLFOX or XELOX for first-line therapy of mCRC (NCT00384176, NCT00399035), with platinum based chemotherapy for ovarian epithelial, fallopian tube or primary peritoneal carcinoma (NCT00544973), with lomustin in recurrent glioblastoma (NCT00777153), with carboplatin/paclitaxel in stage IIIb/IV NSCLC (NCT00795340)
Vandetanib (ZD6474; Zactima™) RTKI active against VEGFR-2 and -3, RET and EGFR		Four recently completed phase III trials: vs. erlotinib in second line therapy of NSCLC (NCT00364351), after EGFR-antagonist failure as monotherapy (NCT00404924), in combination with pemetrexed in second-line therapy of NSCLC (NCT00418886), combined with docetaxel in second-line therapy of NSCLC (NCT00312377). Significant improvement in PFS for vandetanib (press release)
Vatalanib (PTK787/ ZK222584) RTKI active against VEGFRs, c-KIT and PDGFR		Two completed phase III trials: in combination with FOLFOX in first-line (NCT00056459) and second-line therapy of mCRC (NCT00068679). Clinical benefits in LDH high patients
rh-Endostatin (YH-16, Endostar™) endogenous angiogenesis inhibitor	First approval in 2005 (China): in combination with chemotherapy as first-line therapy of NSCLC	Two active phase III trials (China): in combination with Cisplatin and Vinorelbine as adjuvant therapy in stage IB-IIIA NSCLC after complete resection (NCT00576914). Combined with chemotherapy in metastatic NSCLC (biomarker analysis; NCT00657423)
Thalidomide not fully clarified mechanism: postulated direct apoptotic effect on endothelial cells via downregulation of angiogenic growth factors	First approval 1998: treatment of erythema nodosum leprosum (ENL). in combination with Dexamethason as first-line therapy of multiple myeloma (MM) (2003)	Twenty active phase III trials: new indications in MM, e.g., maintenance therapy after autologous stem cell transplantation (NCT00049673), in advanced HCC with poor liver reserve (NCT00225290), with transarterial chemoembolization in advanced HCC (NCT00522405)
Combretastatin-A4 (Zybrestat™) VDA with direct disrupting effect on the endothelial cytoskeleton	"Fast-track" status for anaplastic thyroid cancer	One active phase III trial: in combination with paclitaxel/carboplatin in the treatment of anaplastic thyroid cancer (NCT00507429)
DMXAA (ASA404) VDA with direct disrupting effect on the endothelial cytoskeleton and cytokine induction		Two active phase III trials: in combination with paclitaxel/carboplatin as first line therapy of stage IIIB/IV NSCLC (NCT00662597). In combination with docetaxel in second-line therapy of stage IIIB/IV NSCLC (NCT00738387)

chemotherapy. The first clinical entity in which sorafenib was tested again was clear-cell RCC (Kane et al. 2006). This cancer is special due to its loss of the von Hippel-Lindau tumor suppressor gene, which results in overexpression of hypoxia inducible factors (HIF) – 1 and – 2, subsequently upregulating pro-angiogenic factors (e.g., VEGF). The tumors are usually hypervascularized and increased RAF-1 activity also is found. All these pathways are within the target range for sorafenib providing a strong rationale for testing it in RCC.

In a number of Phase I/II trials, the optimal dose was determined to be 400 mg twice daily (b.i.d.) with dose-limiting toxicities (DLT) such as fatigue, skin rash, hand-foot syndrome, and diarrhea (Richly et al. 2006; Siu et al. 2006; Strumberg et al. 2006). Also, the postulated antiangiogenic effect was confirmed by diminished blood flow in dynamic contrast-enhanced magnetic resonance imaging (Flaherty et al. 2008). The most promising result was the significant increase in PFS in RCC patients treated with sorafenib (24 weeks) vs. placebo (6 weeks; $p = 0.0087$) (Ratain et al. 2006).

This prompted the Phase III treatment approach in RCC global evaluation trial (TARGET), which represents the biggest randomized treatment trial for this disease so far (Escudier et al. 2007b). From November 2003 to March 2005, the participating 117 centers in 19 countries randomized 903 patients with advanced or metastatic RCC who failed standard therapy to receive either continuous treatment with oral sorafenib (at a dose of 400 mg b.i.d.) or placebo; resulting in 451 patients who received sorafenib and 452 who received placebo. A single planned analysis of PFS in January 2005 already demonstrated a statistically significant benefit of sorafenib over placebo. Regarding this result, patients who were on placebo were allowed to crossover to the sorafenib arm later that year. In detail, the PFS was 5.5 months in the sorafenib group and 2.8 months in the placebo group (HR for disease progression in the sorafenib group=0.44; 95% CI 0.35–0.55;

$p < 0.01$). The first interim analysis of the primary end point OS in May 2005 indicated that sorafenib reduced the risk of death, as compared with placebo (HR=0.72; 95% CI 0.54–0.94; $p = 0.02$). However, this survival benefit did not meet the previously specified criteria for statistical significance. Only in a preplanned placebo-censored analysis, excluding patients who crossed over to sorafenib, results showed a significant survival advantage (17.8 months median OS vs. 14.3 months; HR=0.78; 95% CI 0.62–0.97; $p = 0.0287$) (Bukowski et al. 2007). Partial responses were reported as the best response in 10% of patients receiving sorafenib and in 2% of those receiving placebo ($p < 0.001$). Again, diarrhea, rash, fatigue, and hand-foot skin reactions were the most common AE associated with sorafenib. Hypertension and cardiac ischemia were more common in patients receiving sorafenib than in those receiving placebo. At the time of publication, the authors concluded that sorafenib prolongs PFS as compared with placebo in patients with advanced clear-cell RCC in whom previous therapy has failed. However, sorafenib therapy was associated with increased toxicities (Escudier et al. 2007b). In a concomitant quality of life (QOL) analysis it was shown that sorafenib had a positive effect on cancer-related symptoms and did not negatively impact QOL (Cella et al. 2006).

This result led to the approval of sorafenib for the treatment of patients with advanced RCC who have failed prior IFN-α or interleukin-2-based therapy, or are considered unsuitable for such therapy.

Apart from RCC, hepatocellular carcinoma (HCC) also represents a rather chemoresistant, but highly vascularized tumor with vast expression of VEGF. Furthermore, Raf-1 is constitutely overexpressed in HCC offering a rationale for treatment with sorafenib. A number of Phase I and II trials showed promising results for sorafenib either as monotherapy or in combination with doxorubicin (Abou-Alfa et al. 2006; Furuse et al. 2008; Gollob et al. 2007;

Richly et al. 2008). This prompted a randomized Phase III trial for patients with advanced or metastatic HCC in which sorafenib was compared with placebo (SHARP-trial). Patients with advanced measurable HCC in good performance status and Child-Pugh status A were treated with either sorafenib 400 mg b.i.d. or placebo. Overall, 602 patients were randomized leaving 299 in the sorafenib arm and 303 in the placebo arm. Baseline characteristics were similar for both arms. Based on 321 deaths (Sorafenib $n=143$; Placebo $n=178$), the HR for OS was 0.69 (95% CI 0.55–0.87; $p=0.0006$), representing a 44% improvement. This met early stopping criteria and median OS was 10.7 months for sorafenib vs. 7.9 for placebo. There was no accumulation of serious AE in the sorafenib arm. The most frequent grade 3/4 AE for sorafenib vs. placebo were diarrhea (11 vs. 2%), hand-foot skin reaction (8 vs. 1%), fatigue (10 vs. 15%), and bleeding (6 vs. 9%). At the time of presentation at the annual meeting of the American Society of Clinical Oncology (ASCO) in 2007, the authors concluded that sorafenib is the first drug to demonstrate a statistically significant improvement in OS for patients with advanced HCC (Llovet et al. 2007). Again, these findings led to the approval of sorafenib for this indication.

Currently, sorafenib is listed in ten active Phase III studies for treatment of RCC, HCC, NSCLC, unresectable melanoma and adenocarcinoma of the pancreas (see Table 9.1).

9.1.3
Sunitinib Malate (SU11248; Sutent™)

Sunitinib (SU11248; Sutent™; Pfizer Oncology) is a broad-spectrum orally available TK inhibitor of VEGFR, PDGFR, c-kit, and Flt-3 kinase activity. Just like sorafenib, it emerged from a drug-discovery program that was initiated to identify compounds with activity against selected receptor tyrosine kinases involved in tumor angiogenesis (Atkins et al. 2006; Roskoski 2007). Again, the highly vascularized clear cell RCC was one of the first diseases in which sunitinib was tested. After the promising Phase I and II results, a large multicentered, international randomized Phase III trial was started (Motzer et al. 2007). Single-agent sunitinib was compared with IFN-α in patients with treatment-naive advanced or metastatic RCC. Altogether, 750 patients were randomized (1:1) to receive either 50 mg sunitinib once daily in 6-week cycles (4 weeks on treatment, 2 weeks off) or to receive IFN-α administered subcutaneously at nine million units 3 times a week until disease progression or withdrawal from the trial.

Median duration of treatment was 11 months for sunitinib vs. 4 months for IFN-α. The 2008-updated response rate was 47% (95% CI 42–52%) for sunitinib vs. 12% (95% CI 9–16%) for IFN-α ($p<0.000001$), including 11 CR for sunitinib and four for IFN-α (Figlin et al. 2008). Median PFS was significantly higher in the sunitinib arm (11 months vs. 5 months; $p<0.000001$). Also the median OS was significantly longer for sunitinib (26.4 months; 95% CI 23.0–32.9) vs. IFN-α (21.8 months; 95% CI 17.9–26.9), which results in a HR of 0.821 (95% CI 0.673–1.001; $p=0.051$). The most common grade 3/4 treatment-related AEs for the sunitinib group were hypertension (12%), fatigue (11%), diarrhea and hand-foot syndrome (both 8%), and for IFN-α fatigue (13%) and anorexia (2%).

These results led to the approval of sunitinib in patients with advanced or metastatic RCC as first-line therapy and based on two other Phase II studies also as second-line therapy after cytokine or interferon failure (Motzer et al. 2006a, b).

Another malignant disease for which sunitinib has been approved is the gastrointestinal stroma tumor (GIST). Based on its strong activity against the GIST driving c-kit receptor, there was an imminent rationale for the therapy with sunitinib. Also, in cases of advanced, unresectable, or metastatic disease, the other TK inhibitor imatinib was already established as standard first-line therapy for this indication. However, after failure of imatinib, there was no accepted standard therapy available in unresectable GIST tumors (Faivre et al. 2007; Heinrich et al. 2008; Liegl et al. 2008).

Sunitinib was first tested in a population of GIST patients in two multicenter randomized studies. The first one represented a two-sided, randomized, double-blind, placebo-controlled trial of sunitinib in patients with GIST who had disease progression during prior imatinib treatment or who were intolerant of imatinib. Altogether, 312 patients were randomized (2:1) to receive either 50 mg sunitinib ($n=207$) or placebo orally ($n=105$), once daily, on the same 4 weeks on and 2 weeks off schedule until disease progression or withdrawal from the study for another reason. Patients randomized to placebo were then offered to crossover to open-label sunitinib (Demetri et al. 2006).

Demographics were comparable between the sunitinib and placebo groups with regard to age (69 vs. 72% younger than 65 years for sunitinib vs. placebo, respectively), gender (male: 64 vs. 61%), performance status (ECOG 0: 44 vs. 46%, ECOG 1: 55 vs. 52% and ECOG 2: 1 vs. 2%). Prior treatment included surgery (94 vs. 93%) and radiotherapy (8 vs. 15%). Reasons for imatinib failure were also comparably balanced between both arms; being intolerance (4 vs. 4%), progression within 6 months of starting treatment (17 vs. 16%), or progression beyond 6 months (78 vs. 80%).

The trial was unblinded early after the preplanned interim analysis including the first 149 cases of disease progression or death revealed significantly longer time to tumor progression (TTP) in patients initially treated with sunitinib than in those who started with placebo. In detail, the primary study endpoint, median TTP, was more than 4 times as long with sunitinib (27.3 weeks; 95% CI 16.0–32.1) as with placebo treatment (6.4 weeks; 95% CI 4.4–10.0; HR 0.33, 95% CI 0.23–0.47; $p<0.0001$). All other efficacy analyzes were uniformly statistically and clinically significant and confirmed the findings of the primary endpoint data. The median PFS was similar to TPP (24.1 weeks; 95% CI 11.1–28.3 for sunitinib; 6.0 weeks for placebo, respectively; HR 0.33; 95% CI 0.24–0.47; $p<0.0001$). Moreover, 16% (33) of patients in the sunitinib group were progression-free for at least 26 weeks, compared with 1% (one) in the placebo group. As more than half the patients in the initial sunitinib group were still alive at the time of the interim analysis, OS data were not mature at the time of publication and a median OS was not calculated. However, there was a gain in OS in patients treated initially with sunitinib compared to those who started on placebo despite the availability of the crossover option (HR 0.49, 95% CI 0.29–0.83; $p=0.007$). Later on, an update presented at the ASCO 2008 conventional analysis showed that OS converged in the two treatment groups (Sunitinib median 74.7 weeks; 95% CI 61.4–85.7; placebo 64.9 weeks, 45.7–98.4; HR 0.82, $p=0.128$) as expected for the crossover design (Demetri et al. 2008). However, rank-preserving structural failure time analysis yielded an estimated median OS for placebo of 36.0 weeks (95% CI 25.9–51.0), revealing a significant sunitinib treatment effect (HR 0.46, $p<0.0001$) comparable to that of the blinded phase. The most common treatment-related AEs throughout the entire study were fatigue, diarrhea, nausea, and skin discoloration, mainly grade 1/2; incidences increased slightly with extended duration of sunitinib treatment. In terms of best overall objective tumor response, 7% (14) of patients in the sunitinib group showed PR as the best response, 58% (120) had SD, and 19% (39) had PD, compared with rates of 0 48 (50), and 37% (39), respectively, for placebo. Six of fifty-nine patients who crossed over to sunitinib from the placebo group also had confirmed PR (10.2%, 95% CI 3.8–20.8). Four patients (7% overall) who crossed over to sunitinib from placebo had SD for at least 26 weeks after crossover. Based on these results, sunitinib is now approved for the therapy of GIST patients with advanced or unresectable disease after imatinib failure or intolerance (Goodman et al. 2007).

Currently, sunitinib is listed for 20 Phase III studies involving the approved indications RCC and GIST, as well as NSCLC, breast cancer, CRC, and pancreatic islet cell tumors (see Table 9.1).

9.1.4
Axitinib (AG-013736)

Axitinib (AG-013736; Pfizer Oncology) represents a potent small molecule TK inhibitor of all known VEGFRs at subnanomolar concentrations and PDGFR-ß and c-Kit in low nanomolar concentrations. Structurally, it is a substituted indazole derivative discovered by using a structure-based drug design. In vitro, axitinib selectively blocks VEGF stimulated receptor auto-phosphorylation leading to inhibition of endothelial cell proliferation and survival. In numerous preclinical models, axitinib inhibited tumor angiogenesis and the growth of human colorectal and murine lung tumors. In a transgenic mouse model of spontaneous islet cell tumors, axitinib eliminated suppressed vascular sprouting within 24 h. At 7 days, vascular density decreased more than 70%, and significant tumor shrinkage was seen at 21 days (Inai et al. 2004).

The first-in-human Phase I trial was conducted to test axitinib in patients with advanced solid malignancies in order to determine DLTs and the maximum-tolerated dose (MTD). Altogether, 36 patients received axtinib at doses ranging from 5 to 30 mg orally b.i.d. (Rugo et al. 2005). Similar to other TK inhibitors, observed DLTs included hypertension, hemoptysis, and stomatitis primarily seen at higher dose levels. All toxicities were manageable with medication or drug holidays. The MTD and recommended Phase II dose of AG-013736 was specified for 5 mg b.i.d. The trial demonstrated three confirmed partial responses and other evidence of clinical activity (Rugo et al. 2005). Subsequently, axitinib was tested in advanced or metastatic RCC in a multicenter, open-label, Phase II study (Dutcher et al. 2008). Altogether, 58 patients with sorafenib or sunitinib-refractory (progression or unacceptable toxicity) metastatic RCC, and measurable disease, regardless of additional prior therapies, were enrolled. All patients received a starting dose of axitinib 5 mg orally b.i.d., which was titrated to 7 mg b.i.d. and then to 10 mg b.i.d. according to tolerance. Stratification was performed by prior therapy into three groups: 14 patients were refractory to sunitinib and sorafenib (Group 1), 29 patients were refractory to cytokines and sorafenib (Group 2), and 15 patients were refractory to sorafenib alone (Group 3). With a median follow-up of 10.3 months, the overall response rate (ORR) was 7, 28, and 27% and the median PFS was 7.1, 9.0, and 7.7 months for groups 1, 2, and 3, respectively. Overall, grade 3/4 treatment-related AEs included fatigue (13%), hypertension (11%), hand-foot syndrome (11%), diarrhea (5%), and dyspnea (5%). The authors concluded, that axitinib appears to have antitumor activity in metastatic RCC refractory to sunitinib and sorafenib (Dutcher et al. 2008). To this end, a randomized Phase III trial is currently recruiting patients. The Axis-trial is a head-to-head comparison of axitinib (5 mg b.i.d.) and sorafenib (400 mg b.i.d.) for second-line therapy of metastatic RCC and is designed to enroll 540 patients until 2010 (NCT00678392).

The other malignant disease in which axitinib is currently evaluated in a Phase III trial is pancreatic cancer (see Table 9.1). So far, standard of care for patients with advanced pancreatic cancer is gemcitabine-based chemotherapy. Therefore, axitinib was tested in a Phase I/II trial in combination with gemcitabine in patients with pancreatic cancer (Spano et al. 2008). In detail, eight patients were treated on the Phase I part and 103 for the Phase II part of the trial. Prior gemcitabine or VEGF/VEGFR inhibitors were not allowed. The randomization took place between standard dose gemcitabine (1,000 mg/m^2 over 30 min on days 1, 8, 15) plus axitinib (5 mg b.i.d.) or placebo. The median number of days on axitinib was 158 days (range: 57–330 days). The most commonly reported AEs were anemia (48%), alkaline phosphatase elevations (48%), leukopenia (45%), and thrombocytopenia (27%). The most common nonhematologic AEs were nausea (24%), vomiting (20%), fatigue (19%), diarrhea (18%), anorexia (18%), constipation (13%), dyspnea (12%), and fever (12%). In the axitinib group 66% of patients ($n=45$) reached at least disease stabilization, including 7% PRs compared to 59% SD ($n=20$) and no PR for gemcitabine plus placebo. This yielded a median OS of 210 days in the axitinib group in comparison to 169 days for gemcitabine plus placebo (HR 0.74; 95% CI 0.427–1.284) for the whole study group. For the subpopulation in very good performance status (ECOG PS 0/1), the calculated death risk reduction for axitinib was even bigger with 33% (HR 0.67; 95% CI 0.372–1.196). These results prompted the currently recruiting randomized, double-blind Phase III study of gemcitabine plus axitinib vs. gemcitabine plus placebo for the first-line treatment of patients in good performance status with locally advanced, unresectable, or metastatic pancreatic cancer. The trial is estimated to enroll more than 500 patients until planned completion date in September 2009 (NCT00471146).

9.1.5
Cediranib (AZD2171; Recentin™)

Another broad-spectrum kinase inhibitor is cediranib (AZD2171; Recentin™; AstraZeneca). Its predominant effect is directed against VEGFR-2 with additional potent inhibition of VEGFR-1 and -3, c-Kit, Flt-3 and to a lesser extent against epidermal growth factor receptor (EGFR). This broad activity range was deter-mined in a wide range of cell lines (Wedge et al. 2005). Cediranib significantly inhibits VEGF driven vascular sprouting and demonstrated potent antitumor effects in a number of preclinical studies. It is orally bioavailable and was preclinically tested at a dose range of 1.5–6 mg/kg bodyweight per day. Based on these observations, a range of clinical Phase I studies were performed, the first being a dose-finding trial with 83 patients suffering of different solid tumors. In this study, cediranib was generally well tolerated at doses not higher than 45 mg/day and gave encouraging antitumor activity. Pharmacokinetic data revealed a half-life of approximately 20 h and the optimal dosing was determined to be 20–30 mg once daily (Drevs et al. 2007).

The next step was the initiation of Phase I/II study in conjunction with standard doses of carboplatin (AUC 6) and paclitaxel (200 mg/m^2) in order to assess the tolerability, safety, and antitumor activity of this combination in patients with stage IIIB / IV NSCLC of any histology in first-line therapy (Laurie et al. 2006; Laurie et al. 2008). Cediranib was started on Day 2 of the first cycle at a dose of 30 mg p.o. daily. Of the 20 enrolled patients, nine received cediranib at 30 mg/day, 11 at 45 mg/day. Again, most common grade 3/4 toxicity was hypertension, other common toxicities were: fatigue, anorexia, mucositis, and diarrhea. Hematologic toxicity was not greater than that expected with chemotherapy alone. At time of presentation, 15 patients were evaluable for response, with 6 PR, 8 SD, and 1 PD. The authors concluded that, full single-agent dose of cediranib may be administered with standard chemotherapy. However, the subsequent started randomized Phase II/III trial CTG BR.24 comparing carboplatin/paclitaxel plus cediranib (30 mg/day) vs. this chemotherapy combination plus placebo did not reach Phase III. The National Cancer Institute of Canada Clinical Trials Group (NCIC-CTG) decided in 2008 that the BR.24 study should not continue into Phase III following the planned end of

Phase II efficacy and tolerability analysis by the study's data safety monitoring committee, mostly because of an imbalance in toxicity. Although cediranib gave evidence of clinical activity, the study did not meet the predefined criteria for automatic continuation into Phase III (Laurie et al. 2008). Instead, NCIC-CTG agreed to start a new randomized Phase III study evaluating this combination in advanced or metastatic NSCLC with a lower dose of cediranib (20 mg/day); this BR.29 trial is expected to enroll the first patients in 2009.

Another step in the clinical development of cediranib was the initiation of a two-stage, multicenter Phase II clinical trial in patients with recurrent ovarian, peritoneal, or fallopian tube cancer (Hirte et al. 2008). Of the 60 patients who were enrolled; 49 had ovarian, 8 peritoneal, and 3 fallopian tube cancer; follow up was available for 154 cycles of treatment given to 46 patients. As in other Phase I studies with cediranib, the most frequent AEs were fatigue (85%), diarrhea (80%), hypertension (72%), anorexia (57%). Hypertension (33%) and fatigue (20%) were the most frequent grade 3/4 AEs. The median TTP and median OS for all patients was 4.1 months (95% CI 3.4–7.6) and 11.9 months (95% CI 9.9-not reached). This prompted a randomized Phase III study evaluating the combination of carboplatin/paclitaxel with or without cediranib in treating women with relapsed ovarian epithelial cancer, fallopian tube cancer, or primary peritoneal cancer.

Altogether, cediranib is currently listed in five active Phase III studies, such as the HORIZON II Phase II/III study of chemotherapy with cediranib vs. placebo in first-line metastatic CRC and HORIZON III, which represents a head-to-head comparison with bevacizumab (Avastin™) for this indication. Both studies completed recruitment by the end of 2008 and results are eagerly awaited. Also, the Phase III REGAL trial, in recurrent glioblastoma comparing cediranib monotherapy vs. lomustine±cediranib began enrolling patients in late 2008 (see Table 9.1).

9.1.6
Vandetanib (ZD6474; Zactima®)

Vandetanib (ZD6474; Zactima™; AstraZeneca), an orally bioavailable 4-anilinoquinazoline derivate, acts as selective and reversible inhibitor of ATP binding to TK receptors VEGFR-2, -3, RET, and EGFR. In comparison to other kinase inhibitors, vandetanib is somehow more selective, which is demonstrated by a lack of effect against structurally related receptors such as PDGFR or c-Kit. Its antiangiogenic and antitumor activity has been shown in a wide range of preclinical animal models (Herbst et al. 2007). The potent anti-EGFR activity gave a reasonable rationale for testing vandetanib in cancers in which EGFR antagonists have been proven effective.

The clinical development so far was focused on NSCLC. First, the antitumor activity of vandetanib monotherapy or vandetanib with paclitaxel and carboplatin was compared with paclitaxel and carboplatin in previously untreated patients with NSCLC in a partially blinded, placebo-controlled, randomized Phase II study (Heymach et al. 2008). Patients were randomly assigned 2:1:1 to receive vandetanib alone, vandetanib plus chemotherapy, or chemotherapy alone. Interestingly, the risk of progression was reduced for patients receiving vandetanib plus chemotherapy ($n=56$) vs. chemotherapy alone ($n=52$; HR=0.76; $p=0.098$); but median PFS differed only by 1 week (24 vs. 23 weeks). The vandetanib monotherapy arm ($n=73$) was discontinued after a planned interim PFS analysis met the criterion for discontinuation. Also, the OS was not significantly different between groups. Rash, diarrhea, and hypertension were common adverse events. The authors concluded, that vandetanib could be safely administered to patients with NSCLC, including those with squamous cell histology and treated brain metastases. The slightly longer PFS for vandetanib met the prespecified study end point, but was not significant (Heymach et al. 2008).

The next set of studies focused on vandetanib in second-line therapy of NSCLC. Eligible patients had locally advanced or metastatic (stage IIIB/IV) NSCLC after failure of first-line platinum-based chemotherapy (Heymach et al. 2007). First, a randomized Phase II study was initiated comparing vandetanib (100 or 300 mg/day) plus docetaxel (75 mg/m^2 intravenous infusion every 21 days) vs. placebo plus docetaxel. After including 127 patients, median PFS was 18.7 weeks for vandetanib 100 mg plus docetaxel (n=42; HR=0.64; p=0.037); 17.0 weeks for vandetanib 300 mg plus docetaxel (n=44; HR=0.83; p=0.231); and 12 weeks for docetaxel (n=41). There was no statistically significant difference in OS among the three treatment arms. Common AEs included diarrhea, rash, and asymptomatic prolongation of corrected QT (QT$_C$) interval. At the time of publication, the authors concluded that the primary objective was achieved, with vandetanib 100 mg plus docetaxel demonstrating a significant prolongation of PFS compared with docetaxel in relation to the prespecified significance level. On the basis of these encouraging data, Phase III evaluation of vandetanib 100 mg plus docetaxel in second-line NSCLC (ZODIAC trial) was initiated in 2006. Until completion in September 2008, the study enrolled 1,391 patients previously treated with one prior anticancer therapy for advanced NSCLC. Median duration of follow-up was 12.8 months, with 87% patients progressed and 59% dead. Addition of vandetanib to docetaxel showed a statistically significant improvement in PFS versus docetaxel (HR 0.79, 97.58% CI 0.70-0.90; P<0.001). Significant advantages for vandetanib plus docetaxel were also seen for ORR (17% vs 10%, P<0.001). Overall survival showed a positive trend for vandetanib plus docetaxel that was not statistically significant (HR 0.91, 97.52% CI 0.78-1.07; P=0.196). The adverse event profile was consistent with that previously observed for vandetanib in NSCLC. Common AEs occurring more frequently in the vandetanib arm included diarrhea (42% vs 33%), rash (42% vs 24%) and neutropenia (32% vs 27%). (see Table 9.1).

Three other Phase III trials with vandetanib in second- and third-line therapy of NSCLC recently stopped recruiting patients and will complete data collection in 2009. The so-called ZEAL trial is a randomized, double-blind, placebo-controlled Phase III study evaluating the combination of vandetanib 100 mg with pemetrexed vs. pemetrexed alone. This study enrolled 534 patients previously treated with one prior anticancer therapy for advanced NSCLC. There were positive trends seen for vandetanib plus pemetrexed for both PFS (HR 0.86, 97.58% CI 0.69 -1.06; P=0.108) and OS (HR 0.86, 97.54% CI 0.65 -1.13; P=0.219). There was a statistically significant advantage for ORR (19.1% vs 7.9%, P<0.001) in the combination arm. The ZEST study also is a randomized, double-blind, Phase III study evaluating the efficacy of vandetanib 300 mg vs. erlotinib 150 mg, which enrolled 1,240 patients with locally advanced or metastatic NSCLC after failure of at least one prior anticancer therapy. There was no difference in PFS for patients treated with vandetanib versus erlotinib (HR 0.98, 95.22% CI 0.87 -1.10; P=0.721), and no difference in the secondary endpoints of OS (HR 1.01, 95.08% CI 0.89 -1.16; P=0.830) and ORR (both 12%). Finally, the ZEPHYR trial is a randomized Phase III study to assess the efficacy of vandetanib vs. best supportive care in patients with NSCLC (Stage IIIB-IV) after therapy with an EGFR inhibitor. This study is expected to enroll over 900 patients and data collection will be completed by April 2009.

At the time of writing this review, there was no active Phase III trial listed in the NCI's database, but 26 Phase II and 17 Phase I studies, including trials on medullary thyroid carcinoma, breast cancer, and glioma, were ongoing.

9.1.7
Vatalanib (PTK787/ZK222584)

Vatalanib (PTK787/ZK222584; Bayer Schering Pharma AG, Berlin; Novartis, East Hanover, NJ) is an oral multitargeted kinase inhibitor that acts on VEGFR-1, -2, -3, c-KIT, and PDGFR (Wood et al. 2000). After oral administration, vatalanib reaches peak concentration in 1.0–2.5 h and has a half-life of 4.5 h, with no evidence of accumulation at steady state following once-daily dosing. Vatalanib demonstrated clinical activity in patients with several types of human cancer (Drevs et al. 2000; Roboz et al. 2006; Sharma et al. 2009; Thomas et al. 2005; Thomas et al. 2007). For further clinical development, vatalanib was investigated in two multinational randomized phase III studies in first- (CONFIRM-1) and second-line (CONFIRM-2) metastatic CRC. In CONFIRM-2, 855 patients were randomized to FOLFOX4 chemotherapy plus vatalanib (1,250 mg/day) or placebo (Kohne et al. 2007). Eligibility included histologically documented metastatic CRC, pretreatment for metastatic disease with irinotecan-/fluoropyrimidine- based therapy, measurable disease by Response Evaluation Criteria In Solid Tumors (RECIST), good performance status, and adequate organ function. In both trials, toxicities were similar. In detail, for the CONFIRM-2 trial, grade 3–4 AEs were hypertension (21% for vatalanib vs. 5% for placebo), diarrhea (16 vs. 8%), fatigue (15 vs. 7%), nausea (11 vs. 5%), vomiting (9 vs. 5%), and dizziness (9 vs. 1%). Thrombotic and embolic events of all grades occurred in 6% of the vatalanib treated patients vs. 1% of the placebo group. At the time of interim analysis in July 2005, OS was 12.1 months in the vatalanib and 11.8 months in the placebo group (HR 0.94; $p=0.511$). PFS was significantly longer in the vatalanib arm (5.5 vs. 4.1 months; HR 0.83; $p=0.026$). Interestingly, Lactat dehydrogenase (LDH), a rather unspecific marker related to poor prognosis in CRC, was predictive for the outcome in the vatalanib group. Especially patients with high LDH gained improvement in PFS when treated with vatalanib (5.6 vs. 3.8 months; HR 0.63; $p<0.001$) and in OS (9.6 vs. 7.5 months; HR 0.78; $p=0.10$). For CONFIRM-1, 1,168 patients were randomized to receive FOLFOX-4 plus vatalanib (1250 mg/day) or FOLFOX-4 plus placebo. The addition of vatalanib did not result in differences in the response rate (42% for FOLFOX-4 plus vatalanib vs. 46% for FOLFOX-4 plus placebo) or PFS time (7.7 months for FOLFOX-4 plus vatalanib vs. 7.6 months for FOLFOX-4 plus placebo). Thus, it was concluded that significant clinical benefits for vatalanib treatment in CRC seems to be limited to LDH-high patients, the reason for this remains unclear (Hecht et al. 2005; Kohne et al. 2007).

Currently, no active Phase III studies with vatalanib are listed, but six Phase II and four Phase I studies for therapy of glioma, multiple myeloma, pancreatic cancer, and melanoma are active.

9.1.8
Endostatin (rh-Endostatin, YH-16, Endostar™)

Endostatin, a 20-kiloDalton (kDa) fragment of collagen XVIII, is a group member of endogenous antiangiogenic proteins activated by proteolytic processing (Ferreras et al. 2000). Endostatin was shown to inhibit endothelial cell proliferation, migration, invasion, and vascular sprouting (O'Reilly et al. 1997). The reduction in endothelial cell survival induced by endostatin has been proposed to involve binding to the fibronectin receptor $\alpha_5\beta_1$ (Sudhakar et al. 2003), interference with VEGF/VEGFR signaling (Hajitou et al. 2002; Kim et al. 2002b), inhibition of matrix metalloproteinases (MMP), e.g., MMP-2 (Kim et al. 2000), and downregulation of c-myc and cyclin-D1 (Hanai et al. 2002; Shichiri and Hirata 2001). Also, endostatin seems to downregulate a number of proteins essential to angiogenesis such as the Id1 and -3, HIF1-α and Ephrin B1 and B2 (Shichiri and Hirata 2001). Despite initial high hopes, the clinical development of endostatin came close to an unsuccessful end after treatment of about 160 cancer patients in Phase I and II studies when the sole manufacturer (EntreMed, Rockville, USA) announced the cease of production in 2003 due to lack of efficacy, difficult application scheme, and concerns about its production in yeast. Some years later, the Chinese protein chemist Luo may have solved the folding problem by adding nine amino acids to the endostatin molecule (Fu et al. 2008). This reformulation apparently made it possible to manufacture a soluble rh-endostatin (Endostar™, Simcere Pharmaceutical Co., Nanjing, China) using not yeast but bacteria and providing higher in vivo stability, now eligible for daily application once rather than twice. Phase I/II studies revealed that rh-endostatin was effective as single agent with good tolerance in clinical use. The first randomized study presented was designed to compare the response rate, median TTP, clinical benefit, and safety in patients with advanced NSCLC, treated with rh-endostatin (7.5 mg/m^2 on days 1–14) plus standard dose vinorelbine (25 mg/m^2 on day 1 and 5) and cisplatin (30 mg/m^2 on Days 2–4), or placebo plus chemotherapy (Sun et al. 2005). Altogether, 493 NSCLC patients in good performance status were recruited for this double-blind study (326 in the rh-endostatin group, 167 as control). Of the 486 assessable patients, overall response rates were 35.4% for rh-endostatin and 19.5% in the control group ($p=0.0003$). The median TTP were 6.3 and 3.6 months for rh-endostatin vs. control ($p<0.001$), yielding a clinical benefit rate of 73.3 vs. 64.0% respectively ($p=0.035$). Grade 3/4 neutropenia, anemia, nausea/vomiting were comparable in both arms. There was no data on OS reported. The authors concluded that the addition of rh-endostatin to standard chemotherapy resulted in significant improvement in response rate, median TTP, and clinical benefit rate compared with chemotherapy alone in advanced NSCLC patients (Sun et al. 2005). Subsequently, the national Food and Drug Administration of China approved Endostar™ for this setting. The currently listed Phase III studies involving rh-endostatin exclusively originate in China and enroll only NSCLC patients testing different combinations with chemotherapy or application in the adjuvant setting (see Table 9.1).

9.1.9
Thalidomide

One drug that exhibits an antiangiogenic effect by still not fully clarified mechanisms is thalidomide (D'Amato et al. 1994). Originally introduced as sedative and withdrawn due to deleterious side effects, today there is increasing evidence for the efficacy of thalidomide in cancer therapy. Thalidomide was developed in the 1950s and chiefly sold from 1957 to 1961 in almost 50 countries under at least 40 names to pregnant women, as an antiemetic to combat morning sickness and sleeping problems. Later, the teratogenic effects of thalidomide became clear when approximately 10,000 children mainly in Africa and Europe were born with severe malformations, including phocomelia in the late 1950s and early 1960s (Lenz 1967; Lenz and Knapp 1962). However, it was soon found that the teratogenicity caused by thalidomide was only associated with one particular optical isomer. Research continued, although the drug was not prescribed for decades, and finally the US FDA granted approval for treatment of erythema nodosum leprosum (ENL) in 1998. One year later, the first report was presented demonstrating activity of thalidomide in multiple myeloma (MM) tested in 180 patients with advanced disease (Singhal et al. 1999). Clinical development continued under strict regulations regarding the pregnancy status of patients and even their partners and finally the US FDA granted accelerated approval for thalidomide in combination with dexamethasone for the treatment of newly diagnosed MM in 2006. Since then, thalidomide was shown to be useful in a variety of tumors. Its mechanism of action in cancer is attributed to multiple, including direct cytotoxic, antiangiogenic, and antiinflammatory effects (Kumar 2006). The combination of temozolomide and thalidomide has shown promising activity in metastatic melanoma (Hwu et al. 2003), metastatic neuroendocrine

9

tumors (Kulke et al. 2006), and unresectable or metastatic leiomyosarcoma (Boyar et al. 2008). Recently, the surprising effects of thalidomide have led to the development of a series of immunomodulatory drugs (IMiDs) and selective cytokine inhibitory drugs (SELCIDs) with even higher antiangiogenic potency (Dredge et al. 2005; List et al. 2005). The modulation of the immune system consists of stimulation of T – cells and NK – cells (Chang et al. 2006). In our own studies, thalidomide demonstrated biological and clinical activity in myelodysplastic syndrome (MDS) and acute myeloid leukemia (AML) with ORR up to 56 and 25%, respectively (Steins et al. 2003; Steins et al. 2002). Responding patients experienced hematologic improvements including an increase in hemoglobin values and platelet counts. In four of 20 AML patients, a bone marrow blast clearance of at least 50% was achieved after treatment with thalidomide for at least 1 month (PR). Furthermore, we observed a long-term response in one AML patient of more than 20 months, subsequently meeting the criteria of complete remission. Interestingly, the decrease in leukemic blast infiltration in the bone marrow of responders was accompanied by a significant reduction of MVD. While it still remains unclear how exactly thalidomide inhibits angiogenesis, some data suggests a downregulation of VEGF as one possible mode of action (Komorowski et al. 2006; Li et al. 2003).

Currently, thalidomide and the subsequently developed IMiDs Revlimid™ (lenalidomide, CC-5013) and Actimid™ (CC-4047) are listed in 27 active Phase III trials in the NCI database. Apart from hematological malignancies, these substances are tested for treatment of poor liver function HCC and RCC (see Table 9.1).

9.1.10
Vascular Disrupting Agents

While classic inhibitors of tumor angiogenesis mostly compromise the formation of new blood vessels, occlusion of the existing tumor vasculature by inducing thrombosis or extensive endothelial damage leading to severe hemorrhagic necrosis is the main goal of the substances referred to as vascular disrupting agents (VDA). The largest group of VDAs already in clinical stage of development is the family of combretastatins, which act as microtubulin destabilizing drugs, and the structurally distinct flavonoid 5,6-dimethylxanthenone-4-acetic acid (DMXAA).

The first agent extensively studied was Combretastatin-4 (CA-4), which demonstrated rapid and extensive vascular disruption concomitant with hemorrhagic necrosis within the first hour of treatment in preclinical models (Dark et al. 1997). The fast onset of action is attributed to cytoskeletal shift changes including contraction of actinomyosin and the malformed assembly of stress fibers (see Fig. 9.2). Subsequently, this leads to disruption of the endothelial monolayer with increased permeability for macromolecules and shear-stress activation of platelets with intravascular thrombosis (Galbraith et al. 2001; Kanthou and Tozer 2002; Tozer et al. 1999). Finally, this endothelial disruption and platelet aggregation results in rapid almost complete vascular obstruction and tumor necrosis.

For the clinical setting, Combretastatin-A4P is developed by OXiGENE (Waltham, MA, USA) as Zybrestat™. In July 2007, the company initiated a 180-patient pivotal registration study with Zybrestat™ for the treatment of anaplastic thyroid cancer, under a Special Protocol Assessment (SPA) agreement with the US FDA. For this study, the FDA granted Zybrestat™ "Fast-Track" status as potential cancer therapy. This is a randomized open-label Phase II/III study in which the experimental drug is tested in combination with conventional chemotherapeutics carboplatin and paclitaxel (NCT00507429).

In a previous Phase II study with 18 patients suffering of advanced anaplastic thyroid cancer Zybrestat™ as monotherapy achieved a median

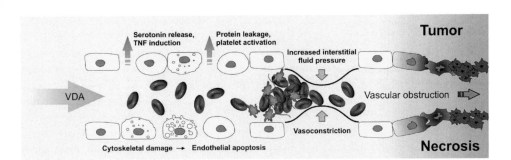

Fig. 9.2 *Proposed mechanism of vascular disrupting agents.* The lead compounds of this class, Combretastatin A-4 (Zybrestat™) or 5,6-dimethylxantheonone-4-acetic acid (DMXAA; ASA404) induce rapid vascular obstruction within the tumor by acting on the endothelial cytoskeleton. In detail, shape changes and intracellular damage is seen leading to subsequent disruption of the endothelial monolayer. Increased vascular permeability and high interstitial fluid pressure in the tumor adds up to vascular collapse and obstruction. Due to direct exposure of the basement membrane to blood cells, platelets and plasmatic coagulation are activated leading to rapid tumor vessel thrombosis within minutes of exposure

PFS of 7.4 weeks (range 2–84 weeks); with five patients remaining progression-free for more than 3 months (Cooney et al. 2006). The median OS in this study was approximately 20 weeks. Zybrestat™ also demonstrated activity in other Phase I studies for treatment of advanced solid neoplasms, such as NSCLC and ovarian cancer (Anderson et al. 2003; Bilenker et al. 2005; Dowlati et al. 2002; Rustin et al. 2003a; Stevenson et al. 2003). It is also the first VDA that has been clinically tested in combination with classic antiangiogenic drugs such as bevacizumab (Avastin™) (Nathan et al. 2008). In this study, 9 of 14 patients with advanced solid tumors experienced disease stabilization for more than 12 weeks. Three patients experienced SD for more than 24 weeks. Besides, DCE-MRI demonstrated statistically significant reductions in tumor perfusion. This effect rapidly reversed after Zybrestat™ alone, but was sustained following the combination of Zybrestat™ and BEV (Nathan et al. 2008). This observation and other preclinical evidence have prompted another randomized Phase II study in which the combination of carboplatin, paclitaxel, and BEV is evaluated with and without Zybrestat™ for patients with advanced NSCLC (Stadium IIIb and IV) as first-line therapy. Like in other studies involving antiangiogenic drugs, patients with predominant squamous cell histology are excluded. This study started in March 2008 and is aimed for enrollment of 60 patients until 2010 (NCT00653939).

The current lead compound of the structurally and mechanistically distinct flavonoids is DMXAA (AS1404, Antisoma Research Limited, London, UK) (Rewcastle et al. 1991). In contrast to combretastatins, cytoskeletal effects of DMXAA seem to be confined to actin assembly leaving interphase microtubules unharmed. In experimental models, DMXAA has been shown to enhance antitumor effects of melphalan and other cytotoxic agents as well as hyperthermia and radiation (Murata et al. 2001; Pruijn et al. 1997; Siim et al. 2003).

The first clinical Phase I study was presented in 2003 (Rustin et al. 2003b). DMXAA was applied to 46 patients for a total of 247 infusions of over 15 dose levels ranging from 6 to 4,900 mg/m². The MTD was reached at 3,700 mg/m² with DLTs observed in form of urinary incontinence, visual disturbance, and anxiety at the highest dose level (4,900 mg/m²). Dose-dependent increases in the serotonin metabolite 5-hydroxyindoleacetic acid were found at dose levels of 650 mg/m² and above. There was one unconfirmed PR at 1,300 mg/m².

Phase II studies have been published for ovarian cancer, NSCLC, and hormone refractory prostate cancer (HRPC). The first randomized study evaluated DMXAA in combination with carboplatin (AUC 6) and paclitaxel (175 mg/m²) in NSCLC with histologically confirmed stage IIIb or IV NSCLC previously untreated with chemotherapy (McKeage 2006). Until 2006, 77 patients were randomized to receive up to six cycles of carboplatin/paclitaxel with or without DMXAA (1,200 or 1,800 mg/m²). Thirty-five patients received chemotherapy alone, 36 chemotherapy plus 1,200 mg/m² DMXAA and 6 plus 1,800 mg/m² DMXAA. The safety profile in the control arm and DMXAA arm was comparable. Twenty-three of thirty patients in the control arm achieved disease control and seven progressed, for the 1,200 mg/m² DMXAA arm 28 of 33 patients reached disease control and five progressed. Finally, all six patients receiving 1,800 mg/m² DMXAA achieved disease control, with three confirmed PRs. The encouraging updated survival data was presented in 2008 (McKeage and Jameson 2008); median OS for chemotherapy alone being 8.8 months ($n = 36$), 14.0 months for chemotherapy plus 1,200 mg/m² DMXAA ($n = 34$) and 14.9 months for the 1,800 mg/m² DMXAA group ($n = 30$). It is noteworthy that in this trial, patients with squamous NSCLC were also benefited.

These data prompted the currently recruiting international multicenter, randomized Phase III trial ATTRACT-1 (Antivascular Targeted Therapy Researching ASA404 in Cancer Treatment; NCT00662597). Previously untreated patients with advanced NSCLC (St. IIIb or IV) are randomized to receive standard chemotherapy carboplatin/paclitaxel in combination with 1,800 mg/m² DMXAA (AS1404, now licensed to Novartis, Basel, Switzerland) or placebo. It is planned to recruit 1,200 patients with comparison of OS as primary objective. Safety data from the previous studies described earlier indicates a different toxicity profile in contrast to other antiangiogenic drugs. Typical vascular effects such as proteinuria, arterial hypertension and thrombosis, pulmonary hemorrhage, wound healing or other bleeding complications were almost not observed with DMXAA both in squamous and non-squamous histology. This allows also patients with predominant squamous histology to be recruited, a group that is usually ruled out in other trials involving most other antiangiogenic agents. Also, a second randomized Phase III study (ATTRACT-2) evaluating the efficacy of DMXAA in second-line therapy of NSCLC was initiated in late 2008 (see Table 9.1).

9.1.11
Accidental Antiangiogenesis Agents

Apart from the aforementioned agents, some already FDA-approved anticancer drugs were later to be shown to have antiangiogenic activity as well. For example, the FDA-approved EGFR antibodies cetuximab (Erbitux™; Merck) and panitumumab (Vectibix™; Amgen) as well as the EGFR antagonists erlotinib (Tarceva™; Genentech, OSI Pharmaceuticals in collaboration with Genentech and Roche) and gefitinib (ZD1839; Iressa™; AstraZeneca) were shown to inhibit tumor angiogenesis by partly blocking the VEGF receptor and downregulation of various pro-angiogenic factors such as VEGF (Ciardiello et al. 2001; Hoffmann et al. 2007; Huang et al. 2002; Perrotte et al. 1999; Pore et al. 2006), basic fibroblast growth factor (bFGF) (Albanell et al. 2001), HIF1-α (Li et al. 2008) and transforming growth factor- (TGF) (Pino et al. 2006). Also, the proteasome inhibitor bortezomib (Velcade™; Millennium Pharmaceuticals), approved for multiple myeloma, demonstrated potent antiangiogenic activity in clinical and preclinical models (Galimberti et al. 2008; Nawrocki et al. 2002; Williams et al. 2003). Even drugs like celecoxib (Celebrex™; Pfizer Inc.) originally approved not for therapy of malignant disease but for treatment of rheumatoid arthritis have been shown to increase production of endogenous angiogenesis inhibitors like endostatin and demonstrated clinical anticancer activity as well. Celecoxib is currently listed in four randomized Phase III trials for therapy of metastatic CRC, NSCLC, pancreatic, and prostate cancer (NCT00268476, NCT00295035, NCT00300729, NCT00486460). Also, the concept of metronomic chemotherapy was introduced meaning the inhibition of tumor angiogenesis by simply changing the dose and frequency of a cytotoxic chemotherapeutic agent like cyclophosphamide (Browder et al. 2000; Hanahan et al. 2000). Vice versa to these "accidental" antiangiogenic drugs, it became clear that "classic" antiangiogenic drugs affect not only endothelial but also tumor cells directly (Beaudry et al. 2008). Especially pancreatic and breast cancer cells were shown to express VEGFR-2 offering the possibility to directly target them with VEGF/VEGFR antagonists (Higgins et al. 2006a; Higgins et al. 2006b).

9.1.12
Conclusions and Future Perspectives

Taken together, the classic concept in cancer therapy that a drug is either directed exclusively against the tumor cell or against the vascular cell in tumor angiogenesis has been replaced by a far more complex model of tumor-stroma interactions. Thus, (multi-)targeted therapies against cancer have become more and more important. Up to date, numerous new substances were developed as angiogenesis inhibitors and evaluated in clinical trials for safety, tolerance, and efficacy. Yielding positive study results, some of these molecules have already been approved for clinical use as described earlier. Although the clinical benefit for patient groups studied is only in the range of few months, the benefit for single patients can be considerably more long-lasting. Treatment results begin to change even in diseases where no therapeutic advances could be made for decades. Today, the wide array of available agents offers the clinician multiple treatment choices.

However, the question of the optimal antiangiogenic approach is still an open debate and subject to a number of clinical studies described in this chapter; for example, which combinations for what tumors, treatment in early stage vs. advanced stage or maintenance?

In particular, the concept of tumor dormancy induced or maintained by angiogenesis inhibitors is widely discussed in the expert field. One intriguing observation for this model is the vast difference between the prevalence of clinically presenting cancer and unapparent malignant tumors found in autopsy studies. Besides, tumor dormancy may be a clinically relevant phenomenon in patients who have been treated for primary cancer and relapse after a long disease-free period (Demicheli et al. 2005; Uhr et al. 1997). Hypothetically, a small number of remaining malignant cells are able to re-activate their tumorigenic potential even years later. Most often, this phenomenon has been explained as consequence of a complex and poorly understood shift in the balance between host and tumor, the angiogenic switch. Historically, the failure to induce the angiogenic switch has been proposed as one of the mechanisms that may be responsible for tumor dormancy (Brem and Folkman 1975; Folkman and Kalluri 2004; Hanahan and Folkman 1996).

However, it is not clear whether a sustained production of angiogenic factors is required to finally break the balance or a short-term angiogenic burst may suffice to break dormancy. To this end, it is absolute speculative that the lower incidence of clinically apparent breast cancer in women with Down syndrome might be due to constant elevated serum values of endogenous angiogenesis inhibitor endostatin regulated on chromosome 21 (Retsky et al. 2009; Zorick et al. 2001). So far, it is still just an outlook into the future when hopefully our diagnostic tools are sensitive enough to detect recurrent disease before it leaves the dormant state and becomes symptomatic again or even better it might be possible to actively halt the tumor dormancy by antiangiogenic maintenance. However, the challenge for both basic researchers and clinicians will remain to integrate these numerous novel treatment approaches into existing protocols to eventually improve individual patient outcome.

Acknowledgment Supported by a grant of the Deutsche Forschungsgemeinschaft (SPP1190) and the Institute for Innovative Medical Research (IMF KE 110715; IMF LI 110633)

References

Abou-Alfa GK, Schwartz L, Ricci S, Amadori D, Santoro A, Figer A, De Greve J, Douillard JY, Lathia C, Schwartz B, Taylor I, Moscovici M, Saltz LB (2006) Phase II study of sorafenib in patients with advanced hepatocellular carcinoma. J Clin Oncol 24:4293–4300

Adnane L, Trail PA, Taylor I, Wilhelm SM (2006) Sorafenib (BAY 43–9006, Nexavar), a dual-action inhibitor that targets RAF/MEK/ERK pathway in tumor cells and tyrosine kinases VEGFR/PDGFR in tumor vasculature. Methods Enzymol 407:597–612

Albanell J, Codony-Servat J, Rojo F, Del Campo JM, Sauleda S, Anido J, Raspall G, Giralt J, Rosello J, Nicholson RI, Mendelsohn J, Baselga J (2001) Activated extracellular signal-regulated kinases: association with epidermal growth factor receptor/transforming growth factor alpha expression in head and neck squamous carcinoma and inhibition by anti-epidermal growth factor receptor trea. Cancer Res 61:6500–6510

Anderson HL, Yap JT, Miller MP, Robbins A, Jones T, Price PM (2003) Assessment of pharmacodynamic vascular response in a phase I trial of combretastatin A4 phosphate. J Clin Oncol 21: 2823–2830

Atkins M, Jones CA, Kirkpatrick P (2006) Sunitinib maleate. Nat Rev Drug Discov 5:279–280

Beaudry P, Nilsson M, Rioth M, Prox D, Poon D, Xu L, Zweidler-Mckay P, Ryan A, Folkman J, Ryeom S, Heymach J (2008) Potent antitumor effects of ZD6474 on neuroblastoma via dual targeting of tumor cells and tumor endothelium. Mol Cancer Ther 7:418–424

Bilenker JH, Flaherty KT, Rosen M, Davis L, Gallagher M, Stevenson JP, Sun W, Vaughn D, Giantonio B, Zimmer R, Schnall M, O'Dwyer PJ (2005) Phase I trial of combretastatin a-4 phosphate with carboplatin. Clin Cancer Res 11: 1527–1533

Boyar MS, Hesdorffer M, Keohan ML, Jin Z, Taub RN (2008) Phase II study of temozolomide and thalidomide in patients with unresectable or metastatic leiomyosarcoma. Sarcoma 2008:412503

Brem H, Folkman J (1975) Inhibition of tumor angiogenesis mediated by cartilage. J Exp Med 141:427–439

Browder T, Butterfield CE, Kraling BM, Shi B, Marshall B, O'Reilly MS, Folkman J (2000) Antiangiogenic scheduling of chemotherapy improves efficacy against experimental drug-resistant cancer. Cancer Res 60:1878–1886

Bukowski RM, Eisen T, Szczylik C, Stadler WM, Simantov R, Shan M, Elting J, Pena C, Escudier B (2007) Final results of the randomized phase III trial of sorafenib in advanced renal cell carcinoma: survival and biomarker analysis. J Clin Oncol 25(Suppl):5023 (abstract)

Cella D, Yount S, Du H, Dhanda R, Gondek K, Langefeld K, George J, Bro WP, Kelly C, Bukowski R (2006) Development and validation of the functional assessment of cancer therapy-kidney symptom index (FKSI). J Support Oncol 4:191–199

Chang DH, Liu N, Klimek V, Hassoun H, Mazumder A, Nimer SD, Jagannath S, Dhodapkar MV (2006) Enhancement of ligand-dependent activation of human natural killer T cells by lenalidomide: therapeutic implications. Blood 108:618–621

Ciardiello F, Caputo R, Bianco R, Damiano V, Fontanini G, Cuccato S, De Placido S, Bianco AR, Tortora G (2001) Inhibition of growth factor production and angiogenesis in human cancer cells by ZD1839 (Iressa), a selective epidermal growth factor receptor tyrosine kinase inhibitor. Clin Cancer Res 7:1459–1465

Cooney MM, Savvides P, Agarwala S, Wang D, Flick S, Bergant S, Bhakta S, Lavertu P, Ortiz J, Remick SC (2006) Phase II study of combretastatin A4 phosphate (CA4P) in patients with advanced anaplastic thyroid carcinoma (ATC). J Clin Oncol 24(Suppl):5580 (abstract)

D'Amato RJ, Loughnan MS, Flynn E, Folkman J (1994) Thalidomide is an inhibitor of angiogenesis. Proc Natl Acad Sci USA 91:4082–4085

Dark GG, Hill SA, Prise VE, Tozer GM, Pettit GR, Chaplin DJ (1997) Combretastatin A-4, an agent that displays potent and selective toxicity toward tumor vasculature. Cancer Res 57:1829–1834

Demetri GD, Huang X, Garrett CR, Schoeffski P, Blackstein ME, Shah MH, Verweij J, Tassell V, Baum CM, Casali PG (2008) Novel statistical analysis of long-term survival to account for crossover in a phase III trial of sunitinib (SU) vs. placebo (PL) in advanced GIST after imatinib (IM) failure. J Clin Oncol 26(Suppl):10524 (abstract)

De Boer R, Arrieta O, Gottfried M, Blackhall FH, Raats J, Yang CH, Langmuir P, Milenkova T, Read J, Vansteenkiste J (2009) Vandetanib plus pemetrexed versus pemetrexed as second-line therapy in patients with advanced non-small cell lung cancer (NSCLC): A randomized, double-blind phase III trial (ZEAL). J Clin Oncol 27: 8010

Demetri GD, van Oosterom AT, Garrett CR, Blackstein ME, Shah MH, Verweij J, McArthur G, Judson IR, Heinrich MC, Morgan JA, Desai J, Fletcher CD, George S, Bello CL, Huang X, Baum CM, Casali PG (2006) Efficacy and safety of sunitinib in patients with advanced gastrointestinal stromal tumour after failure of imatinib: a randomised controlled trial. Lancet 368: 1329–1338

Demicheli R, Miceli R, Moliterni A, Zambetti M, Hrushesky WJ, Retsky MW, Valagussa P, Bonadonna G (2005) Breast cancer recurrence dynamics following adjuvant CMF is consistent with tumor dormancy and mastectomy-driven acceleration of the metastatic process. Ann Oncol 16:1449–1457

Dowlati A, Robertson K, Cooney M, Petros WP, Stratford M, Jesberger J, Rafie N, Overmoyer B, Makkar V, Stambler B, Taylor A, Waas J, Lewin JS, McCrae KR, Remick SC (2002) A phase I pharmacokinetic and translational study of the novel vascular targeting agent combretastatin a-4 phosphate on a single-dose intravenous schedule in patients with advanced cancer. Cancer Res 62: 3408–3416

Dredge K, Horsfall R, Robinson SP, Zhang LH, Lu L, Tang Y, Shirley MA, Muller G, Schafer P, Stirling D, Dalgleish AG, Bartlett JB (2005) Orally administered lenalidomide (CC-5013) is anti-angiogenic in vivo and inhibits endothelial cell migration and Akt phosphorylation in vitro. Microvasc Res 69:56–63

Drevs J, Hofmann I, Hugenschmidt H, Wittig C, Madjar H, Muller M, Wood J, Martiny-Baron G, Unger C, Marme D (2000) Effects of PTK787/ ZK 222584, a specific inhibitor of vascular endothelial growth factor receptor tyrosine kinases, on primary tumor, metastasis, vessel density, and blood flow in a murine renal cell carcinoma model. Cancer Res 60:4819–4824

Drevs J, Siegert P, Medinger M, Mross K, Strecker R, Zirrgiebel U, Harder J, Blum H, Robertson J, Jurgensmeier JM, Puchalski TA, Young H, Saunders O, Unger C (2007) Phase I clinical study of AZD2171, an oral vascular endothelial growth factor signaling inhibitor, in patients with advanced solid tumors. J Clin Oncol 25:3045–3054

Dutcher JP, Wilding G, Hudes GR, Stadler WM, Kim S, Tarazi JC, Rosbrook B, Rini BI (2008) Sequential axitinib (AG-013736) therapy of patients (pts) with metastatic clear cell renal cell cancer (RCC) refractory to sunitinib and sorafenib, cytokines and sorafenib, or sorafenib alone. J Clin Oncol 26(Suppl):5127 (abstract)

Escudier B, Pluzanska A, Koralewski P, Ravaud A, Bracarda S, Szczylik C, Chevreau C, Filipek M, Melichar B, Bajetta E, Gorbunova V, Bay JO, Bodrogi I, Jagiello-Gruszfeld A, Moore N (2007a) Bevacizumab plus interferon alfa-2a for treatment of metastatic renal cell carcinoma: a randomised, double-blind phase III trial. Lancet 370: 2103–2111

Escudier B, Eisen T, Stadler WM, Szczylik C, Oudard S, Siebels M, Negrier S, Chevreau C, Solska E, Desai AA, Rolland F, Demkow T, Hutson TE, Gore M, Freeman S, Schwartz B, Shan M, Simantov R, Bukowski RM (2007b) Sorafenib in advanced clear-cell renal-cell carcinoma. N Engl J Med 356:125–134

Faivre S, Demetri G, Sargent W, Raymond E (2007) Molecular basis for sunitinib efficacy and future clinical development. Nat Rev Drug Discov 6:734–745

Ferrara N, Gerber HP, LeCouter J (2003) The biology of VEGF and its receptors. Nat Med 9:669–676

Ferrara N, Hillan KJ, Gerber HP, Novotny W (2004) Discovery and development of bevacizumab, an anti-VEGF antibody for treating cancer. Nat Rev Drug Discov 3:391–400

Ferreras M, Felbor U, Lenhard T, Olsen BR, Delaisse J (2000) Generation and degradation of human endostatin proteins by various proteinases. FEBS Lett 486:247–251

Figlin RA, Hutson TE, Tomczak P, Michaelson MD, Bukowski RM, Negrier S, Huang J, Kim ST, Chen I, Motzer RJ (2008) Overall survival with sunitinib versus interferon (IFN)-alfa as first-line treatment of metastatic renal cell carcinoma (mRCC). J Clin Oncol 26(Suppl):5024 (abstract)

Flaherty KT, Rosen MA, Heitjan DF, Gallagher ML, Schwartz B, Schnall MD, O'Dwyer PJ (2008) Pilot study of DCE-MRI to predict progression-free survival with sorafenib therapy in renal cell carcinoma. Cancer Biol Ther 7:496–501

Folkman J, Kalluri R (2004) Cancer without disease. Nature 427:787

Fu Y, Wu X, Han Q, Liang Y, He Y, Luo Y (2008) Sulfate stabilizes the folding intermediate more than the native structure of endostatin. Arch Biochem Biophys 471:232–239

Furuse J, Ishii H, Nakachi K, Suzuki E, Shimizu S, Nakajima K (2008) Phase I study of sorafenib in Japanese patients with hepatocellular carcinoma. Cancer Sci 99:159–165

Galbraith SM, Chaplin DJ, Lee F, Stratford MR, Locke RJ, Vojnovic B, Tozer GM (2001) Effects of combretastatin A4 phosphate on endothelial cell morphology in vitro and relationship to tumour vascular targeting activity in vivo. Anticancer Res 21:93–102

Galimberti S, Canestaro M, Ciancia E, Fazzi R, Marasca R, Petrini M (2008) Bortezomib is able to reduce angiogenesis in half of patients affected by idiopathic myelofibrosis: an ex vivo study. Leuk Res 32:1324–1325

Giantonio BJ, Catalano PJ, Meropol NJ, O'Dwyer PJ, Mitchell EP, Alberts SR, Schwartz MA, Benson AB 3rd (2007) Bevacizumab in combination with oxaliplatin, fluorouracil, and leucovorin (FOLFOX4) for previously treated metastatic colorectal cancer: results from the Eastern Cooperative Oncology Group Study E3200. J Clin Oncol 25:1539–1544

Gollob JA, Rathmell WK, Richmond TM, Marino CB, Miller EK, Grigson G, Watkins C, Gu L, Peterson BL, Wright JJ (2007) Phase II trial of sorafenib plus interferon alfa-2b as first- or second-line therapy in patients with metastatic renal cell cancer. J Clin Oncol 25:3288–3295

Goodman VL, Rock EP, Dagher R, Ramchandani RP, Abraham S, Gobburu JV, Booth BP, Verbois SL, Morse DE, Liang CY, Chidambaram N, Jiang JX, Tang S, Mahjoob K, Justice R, Pazdur R (2007) Approval summary: sunitinib for the treatment of imatinib refractory or intolerant gastrointestinal stromal tumors and advanced renal cell carcinoma. Clin Cancer Res 13: 1367–1373

Hajitou A, Grignet C, Devy L, Berndt S, Blacher S, Deroanne CF, Bajou K, Fong T, Chiang Y, Foidart JM,

Noel A (2002) The antitumoral effect of endostatin and angiostatin is associated with a down-regulation of vascular endothelial growth factor expression in tumor cells. FASEB J 16:1802–1804

Hanahan D, Folkman J (1996) Patterns and emerging mechanisms of the angiogenic switch during tumorigenesis. Cell 86:353–364

Hanahan D, Bergers G, Bergsland E (2000) Less is more, regularly: metronomic dosing of cytotoxic drugs can target tumor angiogenesis in mice. J Clin Invest 105:1045–1047

Hanai J, Dhanabal M, Karumanchi SA, Albanese C, Waterman M, Chan B, Ramchandran R, Pestell R, and Sukhatme VP (2002) Endostatin causes G1 arrest of endothelial cells through inhibition of cyclin D1. J Biol Chem 277: 16464–16469

Hecht JR, Trarbach T, Jaeger E, Hainsworth J, Wolff R, Lloyd K, Bodoky G, Borner M, Laurent D, Jacques C (2005) A randomized, double-blind, placebo-controlled, phase III study in patients (Pts) with metastatic adenocarcinoma of the colon or rectum receiving first-line chemotherapy with oxaliplatin/5-fluorouracil/leucovorin and PTK787/ZK 222584 or placebo (CONFIRM-1). J Clin Oncol 23(Suppl):3 (abstract)

Heinrich MC, Maki RG, Corless CL, Antonescu CR, Harlow A, Griffith D, Town A, McKinley A, Ou WB, Fletcher JA, Fletcher CD, Huang X, Cohen DP, Baum CM, Demetri GD (2008) Primary and secondary kinase genotypes correlate with the biological and clinical activity of sunitinib in imatinib-resistant gastrointestinal stromal tumor. J Clin Oncol 26:5352–5359

Herbst RS, Heymach JV, O'Reilly MS, Onn A, Ryan AJ (2007) Vandetanib (ZD6474): an orally available receptor tyrosine kinase inhibitor that selectively targets pathways critical for tumor growth and angiogenesis. Expert Opin Investig Drugs 16:239–249

Herbst RS, Sun Y, Korfee S, Germonpre P, Saijo N, Zhou C, Wang J, Langmuir P, Kennedy SJ, Johnson BE (2009) Vandetanib plus docetaxel versus docetaxel as second-line treatment for patients with advanced non-small cell lung cancer (NSCLC): A randomized, double-blind phase III trial (ZODIAC). J Clin Oncol 27: CRA8003

Heymach JV, Johnson BE, Prager D, Csada E, Roubec J, Pesek M, Spasova I, Belani CP, Bodrogi I, Gadgeel S, Kennedy SJ, Hou J, Herbst RS (2007) Randomized, placebo-controlled phase II study of vandetanib plus docetaxel in previously treated non small-cell lung cancer. J Clin Oncol 25:4270–4277

Heymach JV, Paz-Ares L, De Braud F, Sebastian M, Stewart DJ, Eberhardt WE, Ranade AA, Cohen G, Trigo JM, Sandler AB, Bonomi PD, Herbst RS, Krebs AD, Vasselli J, Johnson BE (2008) Randomized phase II study of vandetanib alone or with paclitaxel and carboplatin as first-line treatment for advanced non-small-cell lung cancer. J Clin Oncol 26:5407–5415

Higgins KJ, Abdelrahim M, Liu S, Yoon K, Safe S (2006a) Regulation of vascular endothelial growth factor receptor-2 expression in pancreatic cancer cells by Sp proteins. Biochem Biophys Res Commun 345:292–301

Higgins KJ, Liu S, Abdelrahim M, Yoon K, Vanderlaag K, Porter W, Metz RP, Safe S (2006b) Vascular endothelial growth factor receptor-2 expression is induced by 17beta-estradiol in ZR-75 breast cancer cells by estrogen receptor alpha/Sp proteins. Endocrinology 147:3285–3295

Hirte HW, Vidal L, Fleming GF, Sugimoto AK, Morgan RJ, Biagi JJ, Wang L, McGill S, Ivy SP, Oza AM (2008) A phase II study of cediranib (AZD2171) in recurrent or persistent ovarian, peritoneal or fallopian tube cancer: final results of a PMH, Chicago and California consortia trial. J Clin Oncol 26:5521 (abstract)

Hoffmann S, Burchert A, Wunderlich A, Wang Y, Lingelbach S, Hofbauer LC, Rothmund M, Zielke A (2007) Differential effects of cetuximab and AEE 788 on epidermal growth factor receptor (EGF-R) and vascular endothelial growth factor receptor (VEGF-R) in thyroid cancer cell lines. Endocrine 31:105–113

Holash J, Davis S, Papadopoulos N, Croll SD, Ho L, Russell M, Boland P, Leidich R, Hylton D, Burova E, Ioffe E, Huang T, Radziejewski C, Bailey K, Fandl JP, Daly T, Wiegand SJ, Yancopoulos GD, Rudge JS (2002) VEGF-Trap: a VEGF blocker with potent antitumor effects. Proc Natl Acad Sci USA 99:11393–11398

Huang SM, Li J, Armstrong EA, Harari PM (2002) Modulation of radiation response and tumor-induced angiogenesis after epidermal growth factor receptor inhibition by ZD1839 (Iressa). Cancer Res 62:4300–4306

Hurwitz H, Fehrenbacher L, Novotny W, Cartwright T, Hainsworth J, Heim W, Berlin J, Baron A, Griffing S, Holmgren E, Ferrara N, Fyfe G, Rogers B, Ross R, Kabbinavar F (2004) Bevacizumab plus irinotecan, fluorouracil, and leucovorin for metastatic colorectal cancer. N Engl J Med 350:2335–2342

Hwu WJ, Krown SE, Menell JH, Panageas KS, Merrell J, Lamb LA, Williams LJ, Quinn CJ, Foster T, Chapman PB, Livingston PO, Wolchok JD, Houghton AN (2003) Phase II study of temozolomide plus thalidomide for the treatment of metastatic melanoma. J Clin Oncol 21:3351–3356

Inai T, Mancuso M, Hashizume H, Baffert F, Haskell A, Baluk P, Hu-Lowe DD, Shalinsky DR, Thurston G, Yancopoulos GD, McDonald DM (2004) Inhibition of vascular endothelial growth factor (VEGF) signaling in cancer causes loss of endothelial fenestrations, regression of tumor vessels, and appearance of basement membrane ghosts. Am J Pathol 165:35–52

Johnson DH, Fehrenbacher L, Novotny WF, Herbst RS, Nemunaitis JJ, Jablons DM, Langer CJ, DeVore RF 3rd, Gaudreault J, Damico LA, Holmgren E, Kabbinavar F (2004) Randomized phase II trial comparing bevacizumab plus carboplatin and paclitaxel with carboplatin and paclitaxel alone in previously untreated locally advanced or metastatic non-small-cell lung cancer. J Clin Oncol 22:2184–2191

Kane RC, Farrell AT, Saber H, Tang S, Williams G, Jee JM, Liang C, Booth B, Chidambaram N, Morse D, Sridhara R, Garvey P, Justice R, Pazdur R (2006) Sorafenib for the treatment of advanced renal cell carcinoma. Clin Cancer Res 12:7271–7278

Kanthou C, Tozer GM (2002) The tumor vascular targeting agent combretastatin A-4-phosphate induces reorganization of the actin cytoskeleton and early membrane blebbing in human endothelial cells. Blood 99:2060–2069

Kim ES, Serur A, Huang J, Manley CA, McCrudden KW, Frischer JS, Soffer SZ, Ring L, New T, Zabski S, Rudge JS, Holash J, Yancopoulos GD, Kandel JJ, Yamashiro DJ (2002a) Potent VEGF blockade causes regression of coopted vessels in a model of neuroblastoma. Proc Natl Acad Sci USA 99:11399–11404

Kim YM, Hwang S, Pyun BJ, Kim TY, Lee ST, Gho YS, Kwon YG (2002b) Endostatin blocks vascular endothelial growth factor-mediated signaling via direct interaction with KDR/Flk-1. J Biol Chem 277:27872–27879

Kim YM, Jang JW, Lee OH, Yeon J, Choi EY, Kim KW, Lee ST, Kwon YG (2000) Endostatin inhibits endothelial and tumor cellular invasion by blocking the activation and catalytic activity of matrix metalloproteinase. Cancer Res 60: 5410–5413

Kohne C, Bajetta E, Lin E, Valle JW, Van Cutsem E, Hecht JR, Moore MJ, Germond CJ, Meinhardt G, Jacques C (2007) Final results of CONFIRM 2: a multinational, randomized, double-blind, phase III study in 2nd line patients (pts) with metastatic colorectal cancer (mCRC) receiving FOLFOX4 and PTK787/ZK 222584 (PTK/ZK) or placebo. J Clin Oncol 25(Suppl):4033 (abstract)

Komorowski J, Jerczynska H, Siejka A, Baranska P, Lawnicka H, Pawlowska Z, Stepien H (2006) Effect of thalidomide affecting VEGF secretion, cell migration, adhesion and capillary tube formation of human endothelial EA.hy 926 cells. Life Sci 78:2558–2563

Kulke MH, Stuart K, Enzinger PC, Ryan DP, Clark JW, Muzikansky A, Vincitore M, Michelini A, Fuchs CS (2006) Phase II study of temozolomide and thalidomide in patients with metastatic neuroendocrine tumors. J Clin Oncol 24:401–406

Kumar S (2006) Progress in the treatment of multiple myeloma. Lancet 367:791–792

Laurie SA, Arnold A, Gauthier I, Chen E, Goss G, Ellis PM, Shepherd FA, Matthews S, Robertson J, Seymour L (2006) Final results of a phase I study of daily oral AZD2171, an inhibitor of vascular endothelial growth factor receptors (VEGFR), in combination with carboplatin (C)+paclitaxel (T) in patients with advanced non-small cell lung cancer (NSCLC): a study of the National Cancer Institute of Canada Clinical Trials Group (NCIC CTG). J Clin Oncol 24:3054 (abstract)

Laurie SA, Gauthier I, Arnold A, Shepherd FA, Ellis PM, Chen E, Goss G, Powers J, Walsh W, Tu D, Robertson J, Puchalski TA, Seymour L (2008) Phase I and pharmacokinetic study of daily oral AZD2171, an inhibitor of vascular endothelial growth factor tyrosine kinases, in combination with carboplatin and paclitaxel in patients with advanced non-small-cell lung cancer: the National Cancer Institute of Canada clinical trials group. J Clin Oncol 26:1871–1878

Lenz W (1967) Perthes-like changes in thalidomide children. Lancet 2:562

Lenz W, Knapp K (1962) Thalidomide embryopathy. Arch Environ Health 5:100–105

Li X, Lu Y, Liang K, Pan T, Mendelsohn J, Fan Z (2008) Requirement of hypoxia-inducible factor-1alpha down-regulation in mediating the antitumor activity of the anti-epidermal growth factor receptor monoclonal antibody cetuximab. Mol Cancer Ther 7:1207–1217

Li X, Liu X, Wang J, Wang Z, Jiang W, Reed E, Zhang Y, Liu Y, Li QQ (2003) Thalidomide down-regulates the expression of VEGF and bFGF in cisplatin-resistant human lung carcinoma cells. Anticancer Res 23:2481–2487

Liegl B, Kepten I, Le C, Zhu M, Demetri GD, Heinrich MC, Fletcher CD, Corless CL, Fletcher JA (2008) Heterogeneity of kinase inhibitor resistance mechanisms in GIST. J Pathol 216:64–74

List A, Kurtin S, Roe DJ, Buresh A, Mahadevan D, Fuchs D, Rimsza L, Heaton R, Knight R, Zeldis JB (2005) Efficacy of lenalidomide in myelodysplastic syndromes. N Engl J Med 352:549–557

Llovet J, Ricci S, Mazzaferro V, Hilgard P, Raoul J, Zeuzem S, Poulin-Costello M, Moscovici M, Voliotis D, Bruix J (2007) Sorafenib improves survival in advanced hepatocellular carcinoma (HCC): results of a phase III randomized placebo-controlled trial (SHARP trial). J Clin Oncol 25(18 S):LBA1 (abstract)

McKeage M (2006) Phase Ib/II study of DMXAA combined with carboplatin and paclitaxel in non-small cell lung cancer (NSCLC). J Clin Oncol 24(suppl):7102 (abstract)

McKeage MJ, and Jameson MB (2008) Comparison of safety and efficacy between squamous and non-squamous non-small cell lung cancer (NSCLC) patients in phase II studies of DMXAA (ASA404). J Clin Oncol 26(suppl):8072 (abstract)

Miller K, Wang M, Gralow J, Dickler M, Cobleigh M, Perez EA, Shenkier T, Cella D, Davidson NE (2007) Paclitaxel plus bevacizumab versus paclitaxel alone for metastatic breast cancer. N Engl J Med 357:2666–2676

Motzer RJ, Hutson TE, Tomczak P, Michaelson MD, Bukowski RM, Rixe O, Oudard S, Negrier S, Szczylik C, Kim ST, Chen I, Bycott PW, Baum CM, Figlin RA (2007) Sunitinib versus interferon alfa in metastatic renal-cell carcinoma. N Engl J Med 356:115–124

Motzer RJ, Rini BI, Bukowski RM, Curti BD, George DJ, Hudes GR, Redman BG, Margolin KA, Merchan JR, Wilding G, Ginsberg MS, Bacik J, Kim ST, Baum CM, Michaelson MD (2006a) Sunitinib in patients with metastatic renal cell carcinoma. JAMA 295:2516–2524

Motzer RJ, Michaelson MD, Redman BG, Hudes GR, Wilding G, Figlin RA, Ginsberg MS, Kim ST,

Baum CM, DePrimo SE, Li JZ, Bello CL, Theuer CP, George DJ, Rini BI (2006b) Activity of SU11248, a multitargeted inhibitor of vascular endothelial growth factor receptor and platelet-derived growth factor receptor, in patients with metastatic renal cell carcinoma. J Clin Oncol 24: 16–24

Murata R, Siemann DW, Overgaard J, Horsman MR (2001) Improved tumor response by combining radiation and the vascular-damaging drug 5, 6-dimethylxanthenone-4-acetic acid. Radiat Res 156:503–509

Natale RB, Thongprasert S, Greco FA, Thomas M, Tsai CM, Sunpaweravong P, Ferry D, Langmuir P, Rowbottom JA, Goss GD (2009) Vandetanib versus erlotinib in patients with advanced non-small cell lung cancer (NSCLC) after failure of at least one prior cytotoxic chemotherapy: A randomized, double-blind phase III trial (ZEST). J Clin Oncol 27: 8009

Nathan PD, Judson I, Padhani AR, Harris A, Carden CP, Smythe J, Collins D, Leach M, Walicke P, Rustin GJ (2008) A phase I study of combretastatin A4 phosphate (CA4P) and bevacizumab in subjects with advanced solid tumors. J Clin Oncol 26(Suppl):3550 (abstract)

Nawrocki ST, Bruns CJ, Harbison MT, Bold RJ, Gotsch BS, Abbruzzese JL, Elliott P, Adams J, McConkey DJ (2002) Effects of the proteasome inhibitor PS-341 on apoptosis and angiogenesis in orthotopic human pancreatic tumor xenografts. Mol Cancer Ther 1:1243–1253

O'Reilly MS, Boehm T, Shing Y, Fukai N, Vasios G, Lane WS, Flynn E, Birkhead JR, Olsen BR, Folkman J (1997) Endostatin: an endogenous inhibitor of angiogenesis and tumor growth. Cell 88:277–285

Perrotte P, Matsumoto T, Inoue K, Kuniyasu H, Eve BY, Hicklin DJ, Radinsky R, Dinney CP (1999) Anti-epidermal growth factor receptor antibody C225 inhibits angiogenesis in human transitional cell carcinoma growing orthotopically in nude mice. Clin Cancer Res 5:257–265

Pino MS, Shrader M, Baker CH, Cognetti F, Xiong HQ, Abbruzzese JL, McConkey DJ (2006) Transforming growth factor alpha expression drives constitutive epidermal growth factor receptor pathway activation and sensitivity to gefitinib (Iressa) in human pancreatic cancer cell lines. Cancer Res 66:3802–3812

Pore N, Jiang Z, Gupta A, Cerniglia G, Kao GD, Maity A (2006) EGFR tyrosine kinase inhibitors decrease VEGF expression by both hypoxia-inducible factor (HIF)-1-independent and HIF-1-dependent mechanisms. Cancer Res 66:3197–3204

Pruijn FB, van Daalen M, Holford NH, Wilson WR (1997) Mechanisms of enhancement of the antitumour activity of melphalan by the tumour-blood-flow inhibitor 5, 6-dimethylxanthenone-4-acetic acid. Cancer Chemother Pharmacol 39:541–546

Ratain MJ, Eisen T, Stadler WM, Flaherty KT, Kaye SB, Rosner GL, Gore M, Desai AA, Patnaik A, Xiong HQ, Rowinsky E, Abbruzzese JL, Xia C, Simantov R, Schwartz B, O'Dwyer PJ (2006) Phase II placebo-controlled randomized discontinuation trial of sorafenib in patients with metastatic renal cell carcinoma. J Clin Oncol 24: 2505–2512

Retsky MW, Hrushesky WJ, Gukas ID (2009) Hypothesis: primary antiangiogenic method proposed to treat early stage breast cancer. BMC Cancer 9:7

Rewcastle GW, Atwell GJ, Li ZA, Baguley BC, Denny WA (1991) Potential antitumor agents. 61. Structure-activity relationships for in vivo colon 38 activity among disubstituted 9-oxo-9H-xanthene-4-acetic acids. J Med Chem 34: 217–222

Richly H, Schultheis B, Adamietz IA, Kupsch P, Grubert M, Hilger RA, Ludwig M, Brendel E, Christensen O, Strumberg D (2009) Combination of sorafenib and doxorubicin in patients with advanced hepatocellular carcinoma: results from a phase I extension trial. Eur J Cancer 45(4): 579–587

Richly H, Henning BF, Kupsch P, Passarge K, Grubert M, Hilger RA, Christensen O, Brendel E, Schwartz B, Ludwig M, Flashar C, Voigtmann R, Scheulen ME, Seeber S, Strumberg D (2006) Results of a phase I trial of sorafenib (BAY 43–9006) in combination with doxorubicin in patients with refractory solid tumors. Ann Oncol 17:866–873

Roboz GJ, Giles FJ, List AF, Cortes JE, Carlin R, Kowalski M, Bilic S, Masson E, Rosamilia M, Schuster MW, Laurent D, Feldman EJ (2006) Phase 1 study of PTK787/ZK 222584, a small molecule tyrosine kinase receptor inhibitor, for the treatment of acute myeloid leukemia and myelodysplastic syndrome. Leukemia 20:952–957

Roskoski R Jr (2007) Sunitinib: a VEGF and PDGF receptor protein kinase and angiogenesis inhibitor. Biochem Biophys Res Commun 356:323–328

Rugo HS, Herbst RS, Liu G, Park JW, Kies MS, Steinfeldt HM, Pithavala YK, Reich SD,

Freddo JL, Wilding G (2005) Phase I trial of the oral antiangiogenesis agent AG-013736 in patients with advanced solid tumors: pharmacokinetic and clinical results. J Clin Oncol 23: 5474–5483

Rustin GJ, Galbraith SM, Anderson H, Stratford M, Folkes LK, Sena L, Gumbrell L, Price PM (2003a) Phase I clinical trial of weekly combretastatin A4 phosphate: clinical and pharmacokinetic results. J Clin Oncol 21:2815–2822

Rustin GJ, Bradley C, Galbraith S, Stratford M, Loadman P, Waller S, Bellenger K, Gumbrell L, Folkes L, Halbert G, PIITCoCR UK (2003b) 5, 6-dimethylxanthenone-4-acetic acid (DMXAA), a novel antivascular agent: phase I clinical and pharmacokinetic study. Br J Cancer 88:1160–1167

Sandler A, Gray R, Perry MC, Brahmer J, Schiller JH, Dowlati A, Lilenbaum R, Johnson DH (2006) Paclitaxel-carboplatin alone or with bevacizumab for non-small-cell lung cancer. N Engl J Med 355:2542–2550

Sharma S, Freeman B, Turner J, Symanowski J, Manno P, Berg W, Vogelzang N (2009) A phase I trial of PTK787/ZK222584 in combination with pemetrexed and cisplatin in patients with advanced solid tumors. Invest New Drugs 27:63–65

Shichiri M, Hirata Y (2001) Antiangiogenesis signals by endostatin. FASEB J 15:1044–1053

Siim BG, Lee AE, Shalal-Zwain S, Pruijn FB, McKeage MJ, Wilson WR (2003) Marked potentiation of the antitumour activity of chemotherapeutic drugs by the antivascular agent 5, 6-dimethylxanthenone-4-acetic acid (DMXAA). Cancer Chemother Pharmacol 51:43–52

Singhal S, Mehta J, Desikan R, Ayers D, Roberson P, Eddlemon P, Munshi N, Anaissie E, Wilson C, Dhodapkar M, Zeddis J, Barlogie B (1999) Antitumor activity of thalidomide in refractory multiple myeloma. N Engl J Med 341:1565–1571

Siu LL, Awada A, Takimoto CH, Piccart M, Schwartz B, Giannaris T, Lathia C, Petrenciuc O, Moore MJ (2006) Phase I trial of sorafenib and gemcitabine in advanced solid tumors with an expanded cohort in advanced pancreatic cancer. Clin Cancer Res 12:144–151

Spano J, Chodkiewicz C, Maurel J, Wong RP, Wasan HS, Pithavala YK, Bycott PW, Liau KF, Kim S, Rixe O (2008) A randomized phase II study of axitinib (AG-013736) and gemcitabine versus gemcitabine in advanced pancreatic cancer, preceded by a phase I component. J Clin Oncol 25:4551 (abstract)

Steins MB, Bieker R, Padro T, Kessler T, Kienast J, Berdel WE, Mesters RM (2003) Thalidomide for the treatment of acute myeloid leukemia. Leuk Lymphoma 44:1489–1493

Steins MB, Padro T, Bieker R, Ruiz S, Kropff M, Kienast J, Kessler T, Buechner T, Berdel WE, Mesters RM (2002) Efficacy and safety of thalidomide in patients with acute myeloid leukemia. Blood 99:834–839

Stevenson JP, Rosen M, Sun W, Gallagher M, Haller DG, Vaughn D, Giantonio B, Zimmer R, Petros WP, Stratford M, Chaplin D, Young SL, Schnall M, O'Dwyer PJ (2003) Phase I trial of the antivascular agent combretastatin A4 phosphate on a 5-day schedule to patients with cancer: magnetic resonance imaging evidence for altered tumor blood flow. J Clin Oncol 21:4428–4438

Strumberg D (2005) Preclinical and clinical development of the oral multikinase inhibitor sorafenib in cancer treatment. Drugs Today (Barc) 41: 773–784

Strumberg D, Awada A, Hirte H, Clark JW, Seeber S, Piccart P, Hofstra E, Voliotis D, Christensen O, Brueckner A, Schwartz B (2006) Pooled safety analysis of BAY 43–9006 (sorafenib) monotherapy in patients with advanced solid tumours: is rash associated with treatment outcome? Eur J Cancer 42:548–556

Sudhakar A, Sugimoto H, Yang C, Lively J, Zeisberg M, Kalluri R (2003) Human tumstatin and human endostatin exhibit distinct antiangiogenic activities mediated by alpha v beta 3 and alpha 5 beta 1 integrins. Proc Natl Acad Sci USA 100:4766–4771

Sun Y, Wang J, Liu Y, Song X, Zhang Y, Li K, Zhu Y, Zhou Q, You L, Yao C (2005) Results of phase III trial of endostarTM (rh-endostatin, YH-16) in advanced non-small cell lung cancer (NSCLC) patients. J Clin Oncol 23:7138 (abstract)

Tang P, Cohen SJ, Bjarnason GA, Kollmannsberger C, Virik K, MacKenzie MJ, Brown J, Wang L, Chen AP, Moore MJ (2008) Phase II trial of aflibercept (VEGF Trap) in previously treated patients with metastatic colorectal cancer (MCRC): a PMH phase II consortium trial. J Clin Oncol 26: 4027 (abstract)

Thomas AL, Morgan B, Horsfield MA, Higginson A, Kay A, Lee L, Masson E, Puccio-Pick M, Laurent D, Steward WP (2005) Phase I study of the safety, tolerability, pharmacokinetics, and pharmacodynamics of PTK787/ZK 222584 administered twice daily in patients with advanced cancer. J Clin Oncol 23:4162–4171

Thomas AL, Trarbach T, Bartel C, Laurent D, Henry A, Poethig M, Wang J, Masson E, Steward W, Vanhoefer U, Wiedenmann B (2007) A phase IB, open-label dose-escalating study of the oral angiogenesis inhibitor PTK787/ZK 222584 (PTK/ZK), in combination with FOLFOX4 chemotherapy in patients with advanced colorectal cancer. Ann Oncol 18:782–788

Tozer GM, Prise VE, Wilson J, Locke RJ, Vojnovic B, Stratford MR, Dennis MF, Chaplin DJ (1999) Combretastatin A-4 phosphate as a tumor vascular-targeting agent: early effects in tumors and normal tissues. Cancer Res 59:1626–1634

Uhr JW, Scheuermann RH, Street NE, Vitetta ES (1997) Cancer dormancy: opportunities for new therapeutic approaches. Nat Med 3:505–509

Wedge SR, Kendrew J, Hennequin LF, Valentine PJ, Barry ST, Brave SR, Smith NR, James NH, Dukes M, Curwen JO, Chester R, Jackson JA, Boffey SJ, Kilburn LL, Barnett S, Richmond GH, Wadsworth PF, Walker M, Bigley AL, Taylor ST, Cooper L, Beck S, Jurgensmeier JM, Ogilvie DJ (2005) AZD2171: a highly potent, orally bio-available, vascular endothelial growth factor receptor-2 tyrosine kinase inhibitor for the treatment of cancer. Cancer Res 65:4389–4400

Wilhelm S, Carter C, Lynch M, Lowinger T, Dumas J, Smith RA, Schwartz B, Simantov R, Kelley S (2006) Discovery and development of sorafenib: a multikinase inhibitor for treating cancer. Nat Rev Drug Discov 5:835–844

Williams S, Pettaway C, Song R, Papandreou C, Logothetis C, McConkey DJ (2003) Differential effects of the proteasome inhibitor bortezomib on apoptosis and angiogenesis in human prostate tumor xenografts. Mol Cancer Ther 2: 835–843

Wood JM, Bold G, Buchdunger E, Cozens R, Ferrari S, Frei J, Hofmann F, Mestan J, Mett H, O'Reilly T, Persohn E, Rosel J, Schnell C, Stover D, Theuer A, Towbin H, Wenger F, Woods-Cook K, Menrad A, Siemeister G, Schirner M, Thierauch KH, Schneider MR, Drevs J, Martiny-Baron G, Totzke F (2000) PTK787/ZK 222584, a novel and potent inhibitor of vascular endothelial growth factor receptor tyrosine kinases, impairs vascular endothelial growth factor-induced responses and tumor growth after oral administration. Cancer Res 60: 2178–2189

Zorick TS, Mustacchi Z, Bando SY, Zatz M, Moreira-Filho CA, Olsen B, Passos-Bueno MR (2001) High serum endostatin levels in Down syndrome: implications for improved treatment and prevention of solid tumours. Eur J Hum Genet 9:811–814

Metronomic Chemotherapy: Principles and Lessons Learned from Applications in the Treatment of Metastatic Prostate Cancer

10

Urban Emmenegger, Giulio Francia, Yuval Shaked, and Robert S. Kerbel

Abstract By frequent and protracted administration of conventional cytotoxic drugs without prolonged interruptions, the primary treatment target shifts from the tumor cell population to the tumor vasculature. This "metronomic" way of chemotherapy administration results in antivascular effects, the mechanistic basis of which remains to be fully elucidated. We outline the basic aspects of the metronomic concept, describe the results of clinical applications of such chemotherapy by focusing on studies in metastatic prostate cancer, and discuss certain shortcomings. Based on preclinical findings, we finally point to the possible ways to address these shortcomings in order to bring this novel and promising use of conventional anticancer agents to full fruition.

U. Emmenegger (✉)
Department of Medicine, Division of Medical Oncology, and Department of Medical Biophysics, Division of Molecular and Cellular Biology, Sunnybrook Health Sciences Centre, University of Toronto, 2075, Bayview Avenue, Toronto, ON, Canada, M4N3M5
e-mail: urban.emmenegger@sri.utoronto.ca

10.1
Introduction

The concept of using antiangiogenic therapies as an anticancer strategy was formulated in 1971 by Folkman (1971) and clinically validated three decades later with the first successful application of an antiangiogenic agent, that is, the vascular endothelial growth factor (VEGF) targeting monoclonal antibody bevacizumab (Hurwitz et al. 2004). During this period, a sometimes tortuous path of discoveries led to an ever-increasing understanding of the complex process of tumor angiogenesis (Kerbel 2000). At present, the use of antiangiogenic agents is considered (part of) the standard of care for the treatment of colorectal, nonsmall cell lung, breast, kidney, and hepatocellular cancer, and involves the use of drugs such as bevacizumab and the antiangiogenic small molecule receptor tyrosine kinase inhibitors sunitinib and sorafenib (Kerbel 2006; Zhu 2008).

One interesting finding of the development of antiangiogenic therapies was that some targeted agents that were originally not developed as antiangiogenic drugs have been found to have "accidental" antiangiogenic properties (Kerbel et al. 2000). Furthermore, most conventional cytotoxic drugs can exert significant

R. Liersch et al. (eds.), *Angiogenesis Inhibition,* Recent Results in Cancer Research,
DOI: 10.1007/978-3-540-78281-0_10, © Springer Verlag Berlin Heidelberg 2010

antiangiogenic effects (Miller et al. 2001). However, when chemotherapeutics are used in a conventional manner (i.e., bolus drug administration followed by a 3–4-week drug-free period to allow the host to recover from the adverse side effects), the vascular damage inflicted by the cytotoxic drug(s) is thought to be rapidly repaired during the recovery period, thus negating any significant overall antiangiogenic effects. Conversely, Browder et al. showed that by shortening the drug-free break period between individual chemotherapy administrations, the net antiangiogenic effects of conventional cytotoxic drugs can be largely augmented (Browder et al. 2000). In addition, we showed that this form of antiangiogenic chemotherapy, commonly referred to as metronomic chemotherapy (Hanahan et al. 2000), is more potent when combined with targeted antiangiogenic agents, especially drugs that interfere with the endothelial cell survival activity of VEGF (Klement et al. 2000). As summarized by Kerbel and Kamen (2004), metronomic chemotherapy protocols are generally characterized by:

- Frequent (dose-dense) and regular (metronomic) – often daily – chemotherapy administration without any prolonged interruptions.
- Absence of a dose-escalation up to the maximal tolerated dose (MTD).
- Absence of the need for hematopoietic growth factor support.
- Preference for oral, outpatient regimens by using drugs such as cyclophosphamide (CPA).
- Low incidence or absence of treatment-related side effects.
- Potential for delayed emergence of resistance.

Because of mostly inconsequential side effects, metronomic regimens can be coadministered with targeted therapies for prolonged periods of time. Furthermore, the use of inexpensive, off-patent drugs such as CPA results in reduced costs compared to many MTD chemotherapy regimens (Bocci et al. 2005).

The feasibility and clinical benefits of this novel use of conventional cytotoxic drugs have been shown in various Phase II trials involving diverse tumor types such as breast, prostate, and ovarian cancer as well as non-Hodgkin's lymphomas among others (Colleoni et al. 2002; Glode et al. 2003; Burstein et al. 2005; Bottini et al. 2006; Buckstein et al. 2006; Colleoni et al. 2006; Young et al. 2006; Lord et al. 2007; Garcia et al. 2008). These findings remain to be confirmed in Phase III trials. Furthermore, important questions remain to be addressed such as the optimal dose and most effective dosing interval, improved monitoring of the antiangiogenic effects, the choice of cytotoxic drugs used for a given tumor type, and the most efficacious way to integrate metronomic chemotherapy into standard therapy protocols.

We provide an overview of the molecular mechanisms behind the antivascular effects of metronomic chemotherapy, and discuss clinical results as well as some shortcomings of the metronomic concept by focusing on published applications for the treatment of metastatic castration-resistant prostate cancer (CRPC). Finally, we discuss the potential future role of metronomic as compared to conventional MTD chemotherapy.

10.2
Mechanisms of Action of Metronomic Chemotherapy

Experimental evidence that chemotherapy administered in a condensed schedule slows down the repair of the drug-induced damage to the tumor vasculature was first reported in 2000. Browder et al. showed that CPA administered every 6 days produced more sustained antiangiogenic effects compared to conventional every 3-week MTD CPA administration (Browder et al. 2000). Intriguingly, CPA was even effective in tumors that had been made resistant in vivo to a conventional CPA regimen, further suggesting that mechanisms other than direct antitumor effects are the basis of the antitumor effects seen with metronomic protocols. In addition, when mice bearing large, established human neuroblastoma xenografts were treated by Klement et al. with twice weekly metronomic administrations of vinblastine combined with DC101, a monoclonal antibody blocking the murine vascular endothelial cell growth factor receptor 2 (VEGFR2), this combination therapy resulted in a significant therapeutic benefit (Klement et al. 2000). Tumors completely regressed over time and did not relapse during a 7-month period of uninterrupted therapy. Both studies suggest that metronomic regimens act largely by inhibiting tumor angiogenesis.

10.2.1
Preferential Antiproliferative Effects of Metronomic Chemotherapy Toward Endothelial Cells

In vitro studies indicated that a 6-day continuous exposure of human micro- and macrovascular endothelial cells to low concentrations of chemotherapy drugs such as paclitaxel or the CPA precursor 4-hydroperoxy-CPA resulted in preferential endothelial cell growth inhibition compared to other cell types, for example, human fibroblast and breast cancer cells (Bocci et al. 2002). These results provided further evidence that metronomic regimens using various chemotherapy drugs may have a highly selective effect against rapidly dividing vascular endothelial cells.

Subsequently, we reported that protracted in vitro exposure of endothelial cells to low concentrations of several cytotoxic agents causes a marked induction in the expression of thrombospondin-1 (TSP-1) at the mRNA and protein level (Bocci et al. 2003). TSP-1 is a potent endogenous inhibitor of angiogenesis, which acts primarily by binding to endothelial cells

expressing the CD36 receptor, resulting in the induction of endothelial cell death (Volpert et al. 2002; Yap et al. 2005). TSP-1 also exerts indirect antiangiogenic effects by binding and sequestering VEGF (Gupta et al. 1999). With regard to metronomic chemotherapy in vivo, induction of circulating TSP-1 plasma levels was observed in mice bearing human xenografts that were treated with metronomic CPA (Bocci et al. 2003). Further evidence for the role of TSP-1 was obtained by administering metronomic CPA to TSP-1 knockout mice bearing Lewis lung carcinoma. Compared to wild-type mice, the metronomic regimen lost its antitumor activity in the knockout mice. However, when CPA was administered at the MTD, retention of the antitumor effects in both wild-type and TSP-1 deficient mice was observed. Similar results were obtained by another group when CPA was administered on a weekly basis to TSP-1 knock-out mice bearing B16 mouse melanoma, and others (Hamano et al. 2004; Damber et al. 2006; Ma and Waxman 2007; Ma and Waxman 2008). Interestingly, the antitumor effects of metronomic regimens were retained in mice that were unable to produce either endostatin or tumstatin, both of which are other endogenous inhibitors of angiogenesis (Hamano et al. 2004). Taken together, these results suggested that TSP-1 is a mediator of the antiangiogenic effects of at least some metronomic regimens and confers endothelial cell specificity.

10.2.2
Circulating Bone Marrow-Derived Endothelial Precursor Cells as Targets of Metronomic Chemotherapy

In addition to *angiogenesis* mediated by local sprouting of rapidly dividing endothelial cells from pre-existing capillaries, the tumor vasculature also depends on *vasculogenesis* mediated by circulating endothelial precursor cells (CEPs) originating from the bone marrow. Following mobilization, CEPs enter the blood circulation and subsequently home to sites of active angiogenesis, where they differentiate and incorporate into the lumen of growing blood vessels and proliferate (Bertolini et al. 2006). A number of preclinical studies suggest that certain tumors are highly dependent on this vasculogenic support, namely lymphomas, Ewing's sarcomas, and inflammatory carcinomas of the breast (Bertolini et al. 2003; de Bont et al. 2001; Bolontrade et al. 2002; Shirakawa et al. 2002). For example, using NOD SCID mice bearing Namalwa or Granta 519 human lymphomas, Bertolini et al. demonstrated that shortly after the administration of an intensive MTD course of CPA, levels of CEPs were substantially reduced for the first few days, followed by a marked rebound during the drug-free break period. This rebound and its timing are reminiscent of the process of hematopoietic recovery after myelosuppressive therapy (Bertolini et al. 2003). In contrast, when CPA was administered in a metronomic regimen, that is, either injected i.p. every 6 days (Browder et al. 2000) or continuously via drinking water (Man et al. 2002), levels of CEPs gradually declined and remained suppressed during the entire treatment period. The degree of mobilization of CEPs and their viability during treatment with MTD versus metronomic CPA is depicted in Fig. 10.1.

Interestingly, we reported a similar or even more important CEP rebound after treatment with vascular disrupting agents (VDAs) (Shaked et al. 2006). As opposed to antiangiogenic agents, this class of drugs causes an acute occlusion of tumor blood vessels, which subsequently results in tumor cell death. However, some remaining viable tumor tissue is usually observed at the rim, from which tumor growth rapidly resumes. We have shown that CEPs can be mobilized from the bone marrow in a matter of hours of treatment with a VDA, and subsequently home to the viable tumor rim. CEPs then incorporate into the tumor blood vessels and promote angiogenesis, which results in rapid tumor repopulation. Taken together, the surge of CEPs following MTD chemotherapy or treatment with a VDA could contribute to the vascular repair process referred to by Browder et al. (2000). Conversely, the metronomic administration of cytotoxic drugs may inhibit the CEP rebound phenomenon and promote the antiangiogenic effects of such chemotherapy. Suppression of the CEP surge is one of the mechanisms that might account for the beneficial effects seen when metronomic or other antiangiogenic therapies are combined with MTD chemotherapy (Kerbel 2006).

10.2.2.1 Benefit of Combined Bolus and Metronomic Chemotherapy Administration

One aspect of the aforementioned study by Bertolini et al. (2003) was whether the combination of metronomic with intermittent bolus dose chemotherapy administration could be effective as a long-term antitumor treatment strategy. We hypothesized that the metronomic regimen might inhibit the CEP rebound following bolus chemotherapy administration. Using three different tumor models, that is, human prostate cancer xenografts (PC-3), Friend virus-induced murine erythroleukemia, and murine breast cancer (EMT-6), we demonstrated that the combination of bolus dose CPA (in our case one-third of the conventional MTD administered every 3 or 6 weeks) plus metronomic CPA was more effective than MTD or metronomic monotherapy (Shaked et al. 2005b). Importantly, the levels of CEPs remained suppressed despite bolus CPA administration. In another study, Pietras and Hanahan reported similar findings. Briefly, a "chemo-switch" regimen (defined by upfront MTD CPA, followed by metronomic CPA combined with targeted antiangiogenic agents) produced significant antitumor responses and survival benefits in a mouse pancreatic cancer model (Pietras and Hanahan 2005).

Fig. 10.1 The effect of metronomic and MTD chemotherapy regimens on CEP levels. Human Namalwa lymphoma bearing NOD/SCID mice were treated with CPA administered either at the MTD for this mouse strain, i.e., 75 mg/kg i.p. injection every other day for three doses per cycle (*purple arrows*), or as a metronomic regimen, i.e., 170 mg/kg i.p. injection every 6 days (*black arrows*). Tumor volumes (*upper graph*) and levels of CEPs detected in peripheral blood (*lower graph*) were monitored regularly (adopted with minor modifications from Bertolini et al. 2003, with permission from the publisher)

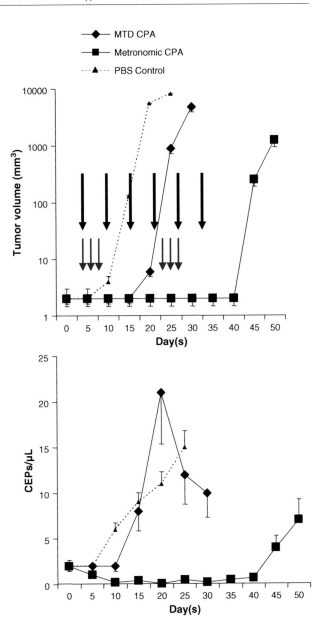

10.2.2.2
CEPs and Optimal Biological Dose of Antiangiogenic Agents

Evidence for antivasculogenic effects of metronomic chemotherapy was also reported in our study that sought to determine whether CEPs can serve as a pharmacodynamic biomarker to determine the optimal biological (=antiangiogenic) dose of antiangiogenic drugs or treatment strategies. The fact that CEPs gradually declined after treatment with metronomic CPA

(Bertolini et al. 2003) led us to investigate whether the levels of such circulating cells may reflect the level of antivascular activity in mice. A previous study had demonstrated that various mouse strains exhibit different levels of angiogenic responsiveness as measured by the corneal micropocket assay (Rohan et al. 2000). The angiogenic stimulus, that is, basic fibroblast growth factor (bFGF), was implanted into the corneas of different mouse strains and vessel growth/sprouting was evaluated. Strains such as C57Bl/6 exhibited a low number of sprouting vessels (indicating a low level of angiogenic responsiveness), whereas others strains, for example, BALB/c or 129, showed a very strong angiogenic response. In our studies, we evaluated the baseline CEP levels in different mouse strains and found a striking correlation between the number of such cells in peripheral blood and the angiogenic responsiveness previously determined for the same strains with the corneal micropocket assay (Shaked et al. 2005a). These results suggest that CEPs might be used as a biomarker to determine the level of angiogenic activity in mice. Subsequently, CEP levels were measured 1 week after treatment with antiangiogenic drugs such as DC101 or ABT-510, a TSP-1 mimetic peptide (Shaked et al. 2005a). In both cases, we found that the drug doses producing maximum antitumor activity also caused the greatest decline in viable CEPs. Similar results were obtained with metronomic regimens using various chemotherapy drugs, for example, CPA, vinblastine, vinorelbine, cisplatinum, ABI-007 (Abraxane®, a cremophor-free nanoparticle paclitaxel preparation), and UFT (Uftoral®, tegafur-uracil), administered to mice bearing various human tumor xenografts (Shaked et al. 2005c; Munoz et al. 2006; Ng et al. 2006). In fact, after a single week of treatment we found a striking correlation between the metronomic drug dose resulting in maximal antitumor activity without overt toxicity and the greatest decline in CEP levels in peripheral blood (Shaked et al. 2005c).

10.2.3
Mechanisms of Action Summarized

Figure 10.2 demonstrates some of the possible mechanisms of action of metronomic chemotherapy regimens. Thus far, such regimens have mostly been investigated with respect to their antivascular effects involving the inhibition of both the locally dividing activated endothelial cells and the systemic vasculogenic process mediated by CEPs. However, much needs to be learned about the effects of metronomic therapy on other bone marrow cell types that might promote angiogenesis or tumor growth via different mechanisms, possible direct effects of metronomic regimens on tumor cells, potential immunomodulatory activities of drugs like CPA, in particular when used in a protracted manner (Ghiringhelli et al. 2007), and possible adverse side effects (Fig. 10.3).

10.3
Metronomic Chemotherapy for the Treatment of Metastatic Castration-Resistant Prostate Cancer

Protracted cytotoxic drug administration was studied as early as in the 1970s (Vogelzang 1984). However, such chemotherapy regimens often included regular treatment-free breaks and the dosing was oriented toward maximizing the cytototoxic effects. Since the first preclinical descriptions in 2000 (Browder et al. 2000; Klement et al. 2000), the results of more than 50 clinical trials embracing the metronomic concept have been published. Breast and prostate cancer are among the best studied tumor types in this respect (Colleoni et al. 2002; Glode et al. 2003; Burstein et al. 2005; Bottini et al. 2006; Colleoni et al. 2006; Lord et al. 2007).

CRPC is particularly well suited for a metronomic chemotherapy type of treatment strategy. The role of angiogenesis in prostate cancer in

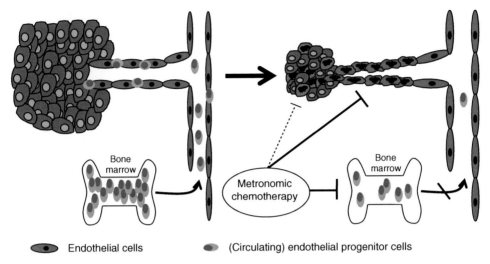

Endothelial cells   (Circulating) endothelial progenitor cells

Fig. 10.2 Antivascular effects of metronomic chemotherapy. Metronomic chemotherapy affects dividing, activated tumor endothelial cells and inhibits the mobilization and/or the viability of bone marrow derived CEPs, which can contribute to tumor neoangiogenesis. Furthermore, drugs like CPA used in a protracted, low-dose manner might also exert immunomodulatory effects. Direct anti-tumor effects seem not to play a major role in most instances when chemotherapy is given in a metronomic manner (modified from Shaked et al. 2005c, with permission from the publisher)

Fig. 10.3 Hypothetical dose-response curves of various metronomic CPA effects. When given at the optimal biological dose, metronomic CPA results in antiangiogenic and possibly also immunostimulatory effects. Higher CPA doses increase the risk of immuno/myelosuppression, likely without added benefit as far as antiangiogenic effects are concerned

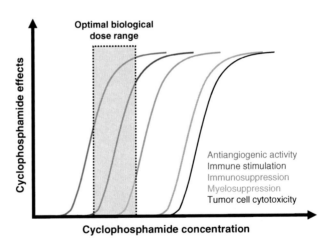

general, and in the castration-resistant stage in particular, is well documented (Nicholson and Theodorescu 2004). Furthermore, CRPC is mainly a disease of the elderly where treatment-related adverse effects may limit the use of overly toxic approaches (Pienta and Smith 2005). Historically, the focus on quality of life aspects rather than improving overall survival has been a necessity in the treatment of CRPC in the absence of therapies impacting on the latter (Tannock et al. 1996). The current standard MTD chemotherapy approach, that is, 3-weekly administration of docetaxel-based chemotherapy (Petrylak et al. 2004; Tannock et al. 2004), results in prolonged overall survival, improved pain control, and better quality of life. However, the impact on survival is only a modest 2–3 month increase compared to the former standard therapy of mitoxantrone/prednisone (Tannock et al. 1996). Thus, there is a clear need for novel strategies in patients that are not considered suitable for docetaxel chemotherapy or those that develop severe docetaxel-related side effects. In addition, there is an unmet need for new approaches in the maintenance setting following maximal response to docetaxel (Lin et al. 2007). Metronomic and other antiangiogenic therapies might meet these needs and are also an interesting option in early CRPC, where the possible benefits of conventional cytotoxic therapy do not outweigh the risk of adverse side-effects and their potential impact on the quality of life.

10.3.1
From Bench to Bedside

Given the lack of feasible metastatic prostate cancer models, the benefit of using metronomic chemotherapy in advanced metastatic disease has thus far been studied preclinically in spontaneous metastatic breast cancer and melanoma models (Munoz et al. 2006; Cruz-Munoz et al. 2008). An unexpected lesson from such studies is that the primary tumor response is not necessarily indicative of the effects of metronomic treatment strategies against metastatic disease. Briefly, breast cancer xenografts were allowed to grow in mice as primary, orthotopically implanted tumors, or to develop (following surgical removal of primary tumors) into visceral metastatic disease. Both primary tumors and metastases were then treated with metronomic CPA and UFT, administered as monotherapies or in combination. The results showed that the combination of CPA and UFT did not improve primary tumor response compared to CPA alone. However, the same combination was

highly efficacious against metastatic disease involving multiple organs. Similar results were obtained with vinblastine and CPA in a metastatic melanoma model (Cruz-Munoz, Man and Kerbel, unpublished observations). Thus, had the analysis been carried out only on a primary tumor model, it would likely have suggested the erroneous interpretation that UFT (or vinblastine) was ineffective in improving the anticancer benefits of metronomic CPA monotherapy. These results highlight the importance of consideration that is needed to identify new metronomic combinations, and the importance of assessing them in appropriate disease models including metastatic cancer. Restricting studies to primary tumors may result in novel metronomic regimens being erroneously discarded as ineffective. For the same reason, it is therefore important that better metastatic prostate cancer models be developed to carry out similar studies in prostate cancer.

In attempting to develop improved metronomic therapies and compare them to conventional chemotherapy administration, another factor might be relatively overlooked, that is, the lack of significant observable host toxicity resulting from metronomic regimens, particularly when compared to conventional MTD chemotherapy. The limited preclinical studies of metronomic regimens against metastatic disease have thus far confirmed this finding. The toxicity aspect has hitherto been little appreciated because host toxicity is seldom a limiting factor in the design and execution of preclinical studies involving primary tumor xenografts. If the impact of treatment-related toxicity is not considered, the benefit of metronomic treatment on survival in preclinical metastatic disease might be underappreciated when compared to standard MTD regimens. Although this assumption remains yet to be formally tested in metastatic models, there already is confirmatory evidence from long-term therapy studies involving metronomic vs. MTD dosing in primary tumor models by du Manoir et al. and Shaked et al. (2005b; du

Manoir et al. 2006). Thus du Manoir et al. treated a human breast cancer model with trastuzumab (Herceptin®) plus CPA, where the alkylating agent was administered either metronomically or in a MTD fashion. Shaked et al. described a detailed comparison of MTD CPA with a metronomic CPA regimen that included interspersed bolus administrations of CPA at one third of the MTD in order to minimize toxicity. Both studies showed tumor responses that are schematically shown in Figs.10.4a, b. When tumor volume measurements were analyzed, there was indication that MTD CPA therapy was more effective against primary tumor growth than the metronomic-based regimen, particularly over a short treatment period (e.g., less than 50 days). This is important since currently most preclinical studies are completed within a relatively short time frame in which it is not unusual for the treatment

to involve only one or two cycles of MTD therapy. However, over a longer treatment period, the mice on the MTD therapy had to be sacrificed. This was not because of complications arising from tumor growth, but because of overt toxicity, exemplified by weight loss (Fig. 10.4c). When the toxicity and tumor response were jointly considered in a Kaplan–Meier analysis, as done by du Manoir et al. (du Manoir et al. 2006), MTD CPA therapy did not show as significant an advantage over the metronomic-based regimen. Indeed, the fact that the mice on the MTD-based regimen died after three cycles of MTD actually made the metronomic regimen look better in the Kaplan–Meier plot comparison (Fig. 10.4d). On the other hand, in the study by Shaked et al. it was noted that mice on the MTD CPA regimen bearing human prostate cancer xenografts died after nine treatment cycles

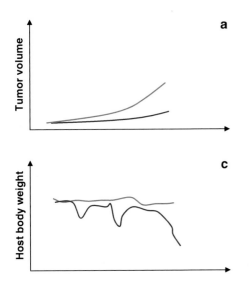

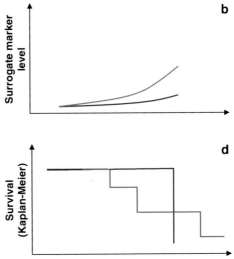

Fig. 10.4 Potential pitfalls in the design and interpretation of preclinical studies in mice using metronomic regimens. A number of studies have shown that in some cases, particularly over short periods of time, MTD (*blue lines*) can be more effective than metronomic (*red lines*) chemotherapy. This is something that would be assessed by (caliper based) tumor measurements (**a**), or surrogate marker analysis (**b**). However, such studies risk failing assessment of the relative impact of host toxicity which may only appear after a number of cycles of MTD administration, e.g., exemplified by progressive weight loss (**c**). This can be appreciated in a Kaplan–Meier plot (**d**), in which both toxicity and tumor growth are taken into account

due to toxicity (Shaked et al. 2005b). This is in sharp contrast to the metronomic CPA monotherapy regimen, which did not give rise to toxicity in the same mouse strain, even after several months of drug administration (Emmenegger et al. 2004; Emmenegger et al. 2006). Future preclinical metastasis studies reporting tumor size parameters and Kaplan–Meier plots will better define the contrast between MTD and metronomic dosing.

In clinical trials, parallel considerations may arise if a metronomic regimen proves equally effective to an MTD regimen in terms of survival, yet without the degree of toxicity that is often associated with MTD dosing (Rivera et al. 2008). To date, a number of clinical trials have reported the low incidence of high-grade toxic side effects with metronomic regimens (Colleoni et al. 2002; Bottini et al. 2006; Colleoni et al. 2006; Lord et al. 2007). Thus, one interesting possibility which would conceivably emerge is that metronomic chemotherapy protocols may be established as a valid alternative to MTD regimens, not because they are superior in prolonging survival, but because of an improved overall therapeutic benefit.

10.3.2
Key Findings of Metronomic Trials in Castration-Resistant Prostate Cancer and Emerging Questions

Table 10.1 summarizes the key findings of published metronomic CRPC trials (Nishimura et al. 2001; Glode et al. 2003; Nicolini et al. 2004; Di Lorenzo et al. 2007; Lord et al. 2007). With the exception of the study by Lord et al. (2007), many of the study subjects enrolled onto these trials had been previously exposed to conventional cytotoxic therapy. One of the drugs administered in all these studies is CPA, an agent that has been commonly used in the past for the treatment of CRPC using various nonmetronomic intravenous and oral regimens

(Mike et al. 2006; Winquist et al. 2006). The applied CPA dose varied from 50 mg/day – the dose most commonly used in metronomic trials involving CPA (Kerbel and Kamen 2004; Gille et al. 2005) – to alternating 100/150 mg/day (Nicolini et al. 2004). Although PSA responses of >50% were typically rare, clinical benefit in the form of either minor PSA responses <50% or PSA stabilization were commonly seen and maintained for several months.

Toxicity has not been a major issue in metronomic trials for CRPC. In fact, grade 3–4 side effects are rare, the only exception being G3 lymphopenias seen in one-third of the patients in the study by Lord et al. (2007). The rather high daily CPA dose of 50 mg/m^2 used by these authors (representing ~100 mg/day for most patients) might be an explanation for this unexpected high rate of lymphopenia. However, it is reassuring that the lymphopenias described did not result in opportunistic infections. Although lymphopenias have been described as a consequence of metronomic CPA therapy in mice at the optimal biological dose (Emmenegger et al. 2004), the commonly used CPA dose in metronomic clinical trials of 50 mg/day seems to be devoid of this side-effect despite clear evidence of clinical activity (Colleoni et al. 2002; Glode et al. 2003; Burstein et al. 2005; Bottini et al. 2006; Buckstein et al. 2006; Colleoni et al. 2006; Garcia et al. 2008).

In the study by Lord et al., 22 patients received fewer than 8 weeks of CPA therapy. Most of them had to be removed from the study because of rapid disease progression (Lord et al. 2007). This is a reminder that this type of therapy needs to be used with caution in patients with rapidly progressive disease. An alternative might be to consider an initial intravenous bolus dose of CPA (or another cytotoxic agent) before commencing metronomic scheduling (Fontana et al. 2007).

In summary, metronomic studies in CRPC show reasonable clinical activity combined with a very appealing toxicity profile, findings that need to be confirmed in Phase III trials. Similarly,

Table 10.1 Metronomic Chemotherapy Trials in CRPC

Reference	Lord et al. 2007	Glode et al. 2003	Nishimura et al. 2001	Di Lorenzo et al. 2007	Nicolini et al. 2004
CRPC stage	*Early*	*Early-advanced*	*Early-advanced*	*Advanced*	*Early-advanced*
N= (evaluable)	80(58)	34(32)	21(21)	16(16)	8(8)
Treatment	CPA 50 mg/m² o.d.	CPA 50 mg o.d. Dexamethasone 1 mg o.d.	CPA 50 mg b.i.d UFT 200 mg b.i.d. EMP 280 mg b.i.d	CPA 50 mg o.d. THD 100 or 200 mg o.d.	CPA alternating 100 or 150 mg o.d. Mesna 400 mg p.o. 3/4 weeks
PSA response (%)	3	69	57	15	25
PSA stabilization (%)	N/A	6	24	8	37.5
Clinical benefit (%)	45	75	81	23	62.5
Grade 3–4 toxicities	Lymphopenia G3 32.8% Neutropenia G3 1.7% Anemia G3 1.7%	N/A	Leucopenia G3 14% Hemorrhagic cystitis G3 3.5% G3.5%	Neutropenia 20% Anemia 10%	N/A
Median response duration (range)	7.5 months (3–18)	8 months (95% CI: 4–10)	7 months (2–15)	Median survival 15 weeks (9–19)	9 months (8–31)
Comments	22 patients did not finish at least two treatment cycles (8 weeks) and were not included in the analysis	Retrospective analysis; treatment interruption in four patients (mainly for hematological toxicity); CPA withdrawn in 1 patient (gastro-intestinal symptoms)		All patients post two lines of cytotoxic therapy; only combined G3/G4 toxicity data presented	Best PSA response 3, 5, 7, 8, and 31 months after treatment initiation

CRPC castration-resistant prostate cancer; *N* number of patients; *CPA* cyclophosphamide; *UFT* tegafur-uracil; *EMP* estramustine phosphate; *THD* thalidomide; *N/A* not available; *clinical benefit* = complete response + partial response + stable disease positive observations have been reported with other tumor types (Bottini et al. 2006; Buckstein et al. 2006; Colleoni et al. 2006; Garcia et al. 2008). However, these studies also raise many questions such as: What is the best choice of drug(s) used in such regimens? What is the optimal biological dose of a given drug? What are the most efficacious drugs or drug combinations to be used in metronomic protocols? How can metronomic regimens be integrated into current standards of practice?

10.3.2.1
Choice of Cytotoxic Drugs Used in Metronomic Regimens

CPA is an obvious choice for metronomic use in CRPC in that (a) the beneficial effects of metronomic CPA are well documented (pre)clinically (Man et al. 2002; Emmenegger et al. 2006), (b) the potential (long-term) side effects of CPA are well known from immunosuppressive protocols using CPA, albeit at higher daily doses than typically applied in metronomic regimens (Hoffman et al. 1992; Haubitz et al. 1998), and (c) CPA is available in an oral form. Furthermore, CPA has been used in the past for the treatment of CRPC, either orally or administered intravenously, albeit applying more conventional dosing schedules (Mike et al. 2006; Winquist et al. 2006). Interestingly, cytotoxic drugs successfully used in a conventional manner for a certain tumor type often also show clinical activity in metronomic protocols for the same tumor type. It remains to be seen whether this reflects certain tumor-related characteristics or whether it is rather a bias dictated by the experience of the prescribing oncologists. In fact, it is currently not known whether certain agents are more active in certain tumor types when used metronomically. Similarly, further study is needed to define whether the sequential use of cytotoxic drugs in metronomic regimens might be able to delay or overcome resistance (Kieran et al. 2005).

There is limited evidence that cytotoxics are not interchangeable when used as antiangiogenics. In fact, while inhibition of proliferation of endothelial cells seems to be likely a universal consequence of the metronomic use of chemotherapeutic agents (Bocci et al. 2002; Wang et al. 2003), other biological effects might be more drug-specific, such as the (a) TSP-1 induction by CPA and various microtubule inhibitors (Bocci et al. 2003; Hamano et al. 2004), (b) anti-Hif-1α activities of topoisomerase I inhibitors and microtubule inhibitors (Rapisarda et al. 2004; Escuin et al. 2005), and (c) the induction of CD95 on endothelial cells by agents such as doxorubicin and CPA (Quesada et al. 2005; Yap et al. 2005). Furthermore, pharmacokinetic characteristics might make certain chemotherapeutics drugs more or less suitable for metronomic use (Hahnfeldt et al. 2003).

Besides the question of which drug to use, it is also important to define patient and/or tumor characteristics that predict prolonged benefit from metronomic therapies. As an example, Orlando et al. have described advanced breast cancer patients receiving metronomic CPA/methotrexate with a median time to progression of almost 2 years (Orlando et al. 2006). In this study, patients achieving remissions or stable disease for 12 months or more comprised 15.7% of the entire study population.

10.3.2.2
Optimal Biological Dose

Preclinically, metronomic dosing often implies the frequent administration of ~1/3rd to 1/10th of the MTD of a given cytotoxic drug (Kerbel and Kamen 2004; Gille et al. 2005; Lam et al. 2006). More recently, a less empirical way to characterize the optimal biological dose was determined preclinically, that is, the dose with maximal CEP suppression in the absence of significant toxicity such as myelosuppression and body weight loss, as described earlier

(Shaked et al. 2005c). Unfortunately, the use of CEP levels for individual dosing is hampered in humans because of the lower number of such cells compared to mice (Bertolini et al. 2007).

Takahashi proposed the concept of the *individualized maximum repeatable dose* (Takahashi et al. 2005). Briefly, the weekly dose of gemcitabine was titrated to a dose resulting in stable Grade 1 toxicity despite prolonged gemcitabine use. As appealing as such an approach might be, it would likely be restricted to situations of metronomic monotherapy. As an alternative, the assessment of pharmacokinetic and/or pharmacodynamic parameters might become a way to tailor individual dosing in the future (Kamen et al. 2006; Emmenegger et al. 2007). However, despite major efforts there continues to be a lack of validated pharmacodynamic surrogate markers for antiangiogenic activity (Jubb et al. 2006).

Even when more sophisticated metronomic dosing might become feasible in the future, practical aspects need to be considered as well. As an example, in the metronomic clinical trial by Colleoni et al. in metastatic breast cancer, a daily CPA dose of 50 and 2.5 mg of methotrexate b.i.d. on Day 1 and 2 of every week were administered (Colleoni et al. 2002). The choice of these doses was driven by practical considerations such as available tablet size, and was assumed to facilitate a high level of patient compliance.

10.3.2.3
Combination Therapies

High levels of proangiogenic cytokines can confer endothelial cell resistance to the effects of cytotoxic drugs (Tran et al. 2002). Therefore, by combination with targeted antiangiogenic agents such as inhibitors of the VEGF pathway, the effects of metronomic chemotherapy can be augmented and vice versa (Klement et al. 2000; Burstein et al. 2005; Pietras and Hanahan 2005). In contrast to combinations involving MTD chemotherapy, which are generally limited to 6–10 continuous cycles, protocols involving targeted antiangiogenics combined with metronomic chemotherapy might be used for prolonged periods of time, given the excellent safety profile of such regimens (Bottini et al. 2006; Buckstein et al. 2006; Colleoni et al. 2006; Garcia et al. 2008). However, much needs to be learned about what type of drugs should be combined. For example, the combination of metronomic chemotherapy (CPA/methotrexate and CPA/vinblastine) with thalidomide or minocycline, respectively, two agents known to inhibit angiogenesis, seem not to be superior to metronomic chemotherapy alone (Colleoni et al. 2006; Young et al. 2006). On the other hand, the combination of bevacizumab with metronomic CPA has yielded very promising results in breast and ovarian cancer (Burstein et al. 2005; Garcia et al. 2008). Indeed, in the randomized Phase II trial of advanced breast cancer by Burstein et al. the bevacizumab plus metronomic CPA/methothrexate arm was superior compared to CPA/methotrexate therapy alone in terms of response rate and median time to progression (Burstein et al. 2005).

Besides doublet metronomic chemotherapy involving CPA and methotrexate, combinations of CPA and fluorinated pyrimidines are also showing promising clinical activity. The combination of metronomic CPA and UFT was clearly superior to monotherapy with either CPA or UFT in a preclinical model of advanced metastatic breast cancer (Munoz et al. 2006). A similar metronomic doublet of CPA and capecitabine combined with bevacizumab has been successfully applied for the treatment of advanced breast cancer, and seems to confirm the preclincial findings of Munoz et al. (2006). As far as the treatment of CRPC is concerned, Nishimura et al. successfully combined CPA with UFT and estramustine in a nonrandomized Phase II trial (Table 10.1) (Nishimura et al. 2001).

10.3.3
Integration of Metronomic Chemotherapy into Current Standards of Practice for Prostate Cancer

Metronomic chemotherapy has been generally studied in situations of advanced disease stages, with metastatic CRPC being a typical example (Kerbel and Kamen 2004; Gille et al. 2005). Such applications will likely continue to dominate in the near future. However, the results of a few studies suggest other indications worthy to be pursued.

For instance, metronomic chemotherapy might be considered as an adjunct to docetaxel chemotherapy, similar to other clinical trials which are comparing docetaxel monotherapy with docetaxel plus various antiangiogenics as first-line therapy in CRPC (Ryan et al. 2006). In fact, concomitant conventional and metronomic chemotherapy administration has shown to be beneficial preclinically (Shaked et al. 2005b) and clinically (Ellis et al. 2002; Casanova et al. 2004). As far as clinical results are concerned, the pilot study by Casanova et al. demonstrated the feasibility and activity of MTD vinorelbine and daily oral CPA in children with refractory or recurrent sarcomas. Furthermore, Ellis et al. described the use of continuous CPA combined with dose-dense doxorubicin in the adjuvant therapy of node-positive breast cancer patients, a promising regimen that is being further pursued in a Phase III trial.

An alternative to concomitant administration is the sequential use of MTD and metronomic chemotherapy, as preclinically described by Pietras and Hanahan (2005). Indeed, maintenance strategies following initial tumor debulking are actively studied in CRPC (Lin et al. 2007). Metronomic chemotherapy is an interesting treatment option in this respect, besides the use of various targeted agents.

Finally, beneficial effects of metronomic temozolomide combined with radiation therapy have been described for pediatric brain tumors (Sterba et al. 2002). Similarly, metronomic therapy might find a place in the CRPC setting when given concomitantly with radiation therapy.

Earlier stages of prostate cancer could also be considered for metronomic chemotherapy applications. While a metronomic combination of CPA and methotrexate is being studied in the adjuvant setting involving patients with ER- and PR-negative breast cancer (IBCSG 22-00, www.ibcsg.org), no such studies are yet underway for locally advanced prostate cancer following definite local therapy. Interestingly, adjuvant androgen deprivation therapy (ADT), the standard therapy in this setting, seems to act through antiangiogenic mechanisms (Nicholson and Theodorescu 2004). Thus, a strategy of combined ADT plus metronomic chemotherapy might be an interesting alternative to other approaches currently being studied which involve MTD chemotherapy (Glode 2006). For similar reasons, metronomic chemotherapy might also become an option for the treatment of hormone-sensitive prostate cancer, either concomitant with ADT or sequentially (in ADT-free intervals) when intermittent ADT is applied.

10.4
Conclusions and Perspectives

Over the last few years, beneficial effects of antiangiogenic tumor therapies have been described in several tumor types (Ferrara and Kerbel 2005). It also became increasingly clear that by changing the way of administration, the primary cellular target of cytotoxic drugs can shift from the tumor cell population to the tumor neovasculature, representing a potent antiangiogenic treatment approach. Metronomic chemotherapy is unlikely to replace conventional MTD chemotherapy administration when rapid tumor cell killing is needed. However, given the particular mode of action and the beneficial safety profile, it is likely to become a valuable alternative in combination therapies involving targeted (antiangiogenic) agents and in the palliative setting. Because many aspects of the metronomic approach remain empirical, major efforts are still needed to bring this novel and emerging concept to full fruition. Furthermore, the long-term administration of oral drugs involves new challenges such as treatment adherence and possibly an increased risk of interference with comedications (Emmenegger et al. 2007). Despite these drawbacks, metronomic chemotherapy has already come a long way from its description less than 10 years ago. It is hoped that the exciting Phase II trial results will be confirmed in future Phase III trials.

Acknowledgments   The work summarized in this review was supported by grants from the National Cancer Institute of Canada, the Canadian Institutes for Health Research, and the National Institutes of Health, USA, to Robert S. Kerbel, and by sponsored research agreements with ImClone Systems, New York, and Taiho Pharmaceuticals, Japan. Urban Emmenegger is supported by the Ontario Institute for Cancer Research through funding provided by the Province of Ontario. We thank Cassandra Cheng for her excellent secretarial assistance.

References

Bertolini F, Mancuso P, Shaked Y, Kerbel RS (2007) Molecular and cellular biomarkers for angiogenesis in clinical oncology. Drug Discov Today 12:806–812

Bertolini F, Paul S, Mancuso P, Monestiroli S, Gobbi A, Shaked Y, Kerbel RS (2003) Maximum tolerable dose and low-dose metronomic chemotherapy have opposite effects on the mobilization and viability of circulating endothelial progenitor cells. Cancer Res 63:4342–4346

Bertolini F, Shaked Y, Mancuso P, Kerbel RS (2006) The multifaceted circulating endothelial cell in cancer: towards marker and target identification. Nat Rev Cancer 6:835–845

Bocci G, Francia G, Man S, Lawler J, Kerbel RS (2003) Thrombospondin 1, a mediator of the antiangiogenic effects of low-dose metronomic chemotherapy. Proc Natl Acad Sci U S A 100: 12917–12922

Bocci G, Nicolaou KC, Kerbel RS (2002) Protracted low-dose effects on human endothelial cell proliferation and survival in vitro reveal a selective antiangiogenic window for various chemotherapeutic drugs. Cancer Res 62:6938–6943

Bocci G, Tuccori M, Emmenegger U, Liguori V, Falcone A, Kerbel RS, Del Tacca M (2005) Cyclophosphamide-methotrexate 'metronomic' chemotherapy for the palliative treatment of metastatic breast cancer. A comparative pharmacoeconomic evaluation. Ann Oncol 16:1243–1252

Bolontrade MF, Zhou RR, Kleinerman ES (2002) Vasculogenesis plays a role in the growth of Ewing's sarcoma in vivo. Clin Cancer Res 8: 3622–3627

Bottini A, Generali D, Brizzi MP, Fox SB, Bersiga A, Bonardi S, Allevi G, Aguggini S, Bodini G, Milani M, Dionisio R, Bernardi C, Montruccoli A, Bruzzi P, Harris AL, Dogliotti L, Berruti A (2006) Randomized phase II trial of letrozole and letrozole plus low-dose metronomic oral cyclophosphamide as primary systemic treatment in elderly breast cancer patients. J Clin Oncol 24: 3623–3628

Browder T, Butterfield CE, Kraling BM, Shi B, Marshall B, O'Reilly MS, Folkman J (2000) Antiangiogenic scheduling of chemotherapy improves efficacy against experimental drug-resistant cancer. Cancer Res 60:1878–1886

Buckstein R, Kerbel RS, Shaked Y, Nayar R, Foden C, Turner R, Lee CR, Taylor D, Zhang L, Man S, Baruchel S, Stempak D, Bertolini F, Crump M (2006) High-dose celecoxib and metronomic "low-dose" cyclophosphamide is an effective and safe therapy in patients with relapsed and refractory aggressive histology non-Hodgkin's lymphoma. Clin Cancer Res 12:5190–5198

Burstein HJ, Spigel D, Kindsvogel K, Parker LM, Bunnel CA, Partridge AH, Come SE, Ryan PD, Gelman R, Winer EP (2005) Metronomic chemotherapy with and without bevacizumab for advanced breast cancer: a randomized phase II study. In: San Antonio Breast Cancer Symposium. Breast Cancer Res Treat 94(Suppl 1):S6, Abstract 4

Casanova M, Ferrari A, Bisogno G, Merks JH, De Salvo GL, Meazza C, Tettoni K, Provenzi M, Mazzarino I, Carli M (2004) Vinorelbine and low-dose cyclophosphamide in the treatment of pediatric sarcomas: pilot study for the upcoming European Rhabdomyosarcoma Protocol. Cancer 101:1664–1671

Colleoni M, Orlando L, Sanna G, Rocca A, Maisonneuve P, Peruzzotti G, Ghisini R, Sandri MT, Zorzino L, Nole F, Viale G, Goldhirsch A (2006) Metronomic low-dose oral cyclophosphamide and methotrexate plus or minus thalidomide in metastatic breast cancer: antitumor activity and biological effects. Ann Oncol 17: 232–238

Colleoni M, Rocca A, Sandri MT, Zorzino L, Masci G, Nole F, Peruzzotti G, Robertson C, Orlando L, Cinieri S, de BF, Viale G, Goldhirsch A (2002) Low-dose oral methotrexate and cyclophosphamide in metastatic breast cancer: antitumor activity and correlation with vascular endothelial growth factor levels. Ann Oncol 13:73–80

Cruz-Munoz W, Man S, Kerbel RS. Effective Treatment of Advanced Human Melanoma Metastasis in Immunodeficient Mice Using Combination Metronomic Chemotherapy Regimens. Clin Cancer Res. 2009 Jul 21. [Epub ahead of print]

Cruz-Munoz W, Man S, Xu P, Kerbel RS (2008) Development of a preclinical model of spontaneous human melanoma CNS metastasis. Cancer Res 68(12):4500–4505

Damber JE, Vallbo C, Albertsson P, Lennernas B, Norrby K (2006) The anti-tumour effect of low-dose continuous chemotherapy may partly be mediated by thrombospondin. Cancer Chemother Pharmacol 58:354–360

de Bont ES, Guikema JE, Scherpen F, Meeuwsen T, Kamps WA, Vellenga E, Bos NA (2001) Mobilized human CD34+ hematopoietic stem cells enhance tumor growth in a nonobese diabetic/severe combined immunodeficient mouse model of human non-Hodgkin's lymphoma. Cancer Res 61:7654–7659

Dellapasqua S, Bertolini F, Bagnardi V, Campagnoli E, Scarano E, Torrisi R, Shaked Y, Mancuso P, Goldhirsch A, Rocca A, Pietri E, Colleoni M. Metronomic cyclophosphamide and capecitabine combined with bevacizumab in advanced breast cancer. J Clin Oncol. 2008;26:4899-905

Di Lorenzo G, Autorino R, De Laurentiis M, Forestieri V, Romano C, Prudente A, Giugliano F, Imbimbo C, Mirone V, De Placido S (2007) Thalidomide in combination with oral daily cyclophosphamide in patients with pretreated hormone refractory prostate cancer: a phase I clinical trial. Cancer Biol Ther 6:313–317

du Manoir JM, Francia G, Man S, Mossoba M, Medin JA, Viloria-Petit A, Hicklin DJ, Emmenegger U, Kerbel RS (2006) Strategies for delaying or treating in vivo acquired resistance to trastuzumab in human breast cancer xenografts. Clin Cancer Res 12:904–916

Ellis GK, Livingston RB, Gralow JR, Green SJ, Thompson T (2002) Dose-dense anthracycline-based chemotherapy for node-positive breast cancer. J Clin Oncol 20:3637–3643

Emmenegger U, Man S, Shaked Y, Francia G, Wong JW, Hicklin DJ, Kerbel RS (2004) A comparative analysis of low-dose metronomic cyclophosphamide reveals absent or low-grade toxicity on tissues highly sensitive to the toxic effects of maximum tolerated dose regimens. Cancer Res 64:3994–4000

Emmenegger U, Morton GC, Francia G, Shaked Y, Franco M, Weinerman A, Man S, Kerbel RS (2006) Low-dose metronomic daily cyclophosphamide and weekly tirapazamine: a well-tolerated combination regimen with enhanced efficacy that exploits tumor hypoxia. Cancer Res 66:1664–1674

Emmenegger U, Shaked Y, Man S, Bocci G, Spasojevic I, Francia G, Kouri A, Coke R, Cruz-Munoz W, Ludeman SM, Colvin OM, Kerbel RS (2007) Pharmacodynamic and pharmacokinetic study of chronic low-dose metronomic cyclophosphamide therapy in mice. Mol Cancer Ther 6:2280–2289

Escuin D, Kline ER, Giannakakou P (2005) Both microtubule-stabilizing and microtubule-destabilizing drugs inhibit hypoxia-inducible factor-1alpha accumulation and activity by disrupting microtubule function. Cancer Res 65:9021–9028

Ferrara N, Kerbel RS (2005) Angiogenesis as a therapeutic target. Nature 438:967–974

Folkman J (1971) Tumor angiogenesis: therapeutic implications. N Engl J Med 285:1182–1186

Fontana A, Bocci G, Galli L, Fontana E, Galli C, Landi L, Fioravanti A, Orlandi P, Del Tacca M, Falcone A (2007) Low-dose metronomic cyclophosphamide (CTX) plus celecoxib (C) and dexamethasone (DEX) in advanced hormone-refractory prostate cancer (HRPC): A phase II clinical trial with evaluation of clinical and pharmacodynamic effects of the combination. In: ASCO GU Proceedings 2007, abstract 215

Garcia AA, Hirte H, Fleming G, Yang D, Tsao-Wei DD, Roman L, Groshen S, Swenson S, Markland F, Gandara D, Scudder S, Morgan R, Chen H, Lenz HJ, Oza AM (2008) Phase II clinical trial of bevacizumab and low-dose metronomic oral cyclophosphamide in recurrent ovarian cancer: a trial of the California, Chicago, and Princess Margaret Hospital phase II consortia. J Clin Oncol 26:76–82

Ghiringhelli F, Menard C, Puig PE, Ladoire S, Roux S, Martin F, Solary E, Le Cesne A, Zitvogel L, Chauffert B (2007) Metronomic cyclophosphamide regimen selectively depletes CD4(+)CD25 (+) regulatory T cells and restores T and NK effector functions in end stage cancer patients. Cancer Immunol Immunother 56: 641–648

Gille J, Spieth K, Kaufmann R (2005) Metronomic low-dose chemotherapy as antiangiogenic therapeutic strategy for cancer. J Dtsch Dermatol Ges 3:26–32

Glode LM (2006) The case for adjuvant therapy for prostate cancer. J Urol 176:S30–S33

Glode LM, Barqawi A, Crighton F, Crawford ED, Kerbel R (2003) Metronomic therapy with cyclophosphamide and dexamethasone for prostate carcinoma. Cancer 98:1643–1648

Gupta K, Gupta P, Wild R, Ramakrishnan S, Hebbel RP (1999) Binding and displacement of vascular endothelial growth factor (VEGF) by thrombospondin: effect on human microvascular endothelial cell proliferation and angiogenesis. Angiogenesis 3:147–158

Hahnfeldt P, Folkman J, Hlatky L (2003) Minimizing long-term tumor burden: the logic for metronomic chemotherapeutic dosing and its antiangiogenic basis. J Theor Biol 220:545–554

Hamano Y, Sugimoto H, Soubasakos MA, Kieran M, Olsen BR, Lawler J, Sudhakar A, Kalluri R (2004) Thrombospondin-1 associated with tumor microenvironment contributes to low-dose cyclophosphamide-mediated endothelial cell apoptosis and tumor growth suppression. Cancer Res 64:1570–1574

Hanahan D, Bergers G, Bergsland E (2000) Less is more, regularly: metronomic dosing of cytotoxic drugs can target tumor angiogenesis in mice. J Clin Invest 105:1045–1047

Haubitz M, Schellong S, Gobel U, Schurek HJ, Schaumann D, Koch KM, Brunkhorst R (1998) Intravenous pulse administration of cyclophosphamide versus daily oral treatment in patients with antineutrophil cytoplasmic antibody-associated vasculitis and renal involvement: a prospective, randomized study. Arthritis Rheum 41: 1835–1844

Hoffman GS, Kerr GS, Leavitt RY, Hallahan CW, Lebovics RS, Travis WD, Rottem M, Fauci AS (1992) Wegener granulomatosis: an analysis of 158 patients. Ann Intern Med 116:488–498

Hurwitz H, Fehrenbacher L, Novotny W, Cartwright T, Hainsworth J, Heim W, Berlin J, Baron A, Griffing S, Holmgren E, Ferrara N, Fyfe G, Rogers B, Ross R, Kabbinavar F (2004) Bevacizumab plus irinotecan, fluorouracil, and leucovorin for metastatic colorectal cancer. N Engl J Med 350: 2335–2342

Jubb AM, Oates AJ, Holden S, Koeppen H (2006) Predicting benefit from anti-angiogenic agents in malignancy. Nat Rev Cancer 6:626–635

Kamen BA, Glod J, Cole PD (2006) Metronomic therapy from a pharmacologist's view. J Pediatr Hematol Oncol 28:325–327

Kerbel RS (2000) Tumor angiogenesis: past, present and the near future. Carcinogenesis 21: 505–515

Kerbel RS (2006) Antiangiogenic therapy: a universal chemosensitization strategy for cancer? Science 312:1171–1175

Kerbel RS, Kamen BA (2004) The anti-angiogenic basis of metronomic chemotherapy. Nat Rev Cancer 4:423–436

Kerbel RS, Viloria-Petit A, Klement G, Rak J (2000) 'Accidental' anti-angiogenic drugs. anti-oncogene directed signal transduction inhibitors and conventional chemotherapeutic agents as examples. Eur J Cancer 36:1248–1257

Kieran MW, Turner CD, Rubin JB, Chi SN, Zimmerman MA, Chordas C, Klement G, Laforme A, Gordon A, Thomas A, Neuberg D, Browder T, Folkman J (2005) A feasibility trial of antiangiogenic (metronomic) chemotherapy in pediatric patients with recurrent or progressive cancer. J Pediatr Hematol Oncol 27:573–581

Klement G, Baruchel S, Rak J, Man S, Clark K, Hicklin DJ, Bohlen P, Kerbel RS (2000) Continuous low-dose therapy with vinblastine and VEGF receptor-2 antibody induces sustained tumor regression without overt toxicity. J Clin Invest 105:R15–R24

Lam T, Hetherington JW, Greenman J, Maraveyas A (2006) From total empiricism to a rational design of metronomic chemotherapy phase I dosing trials. Anticancer Drugs 17:113–121

Lin AM, Ryan CJ, Small EJ (2007) Intermittent chemotherapy for metastatic hormone refractory

prostate cancer. Crit Rev Oncol Hematol 61:
243–254

Lord R, Nair S, Schache A, Spicer J, Somaihah N,
Khoo V, Pandha H (2007) Low dose metronomic
oral cyclophosphamide for hormone resistant
prostate cancer: a phase II study. J Urol 177:
2136–2140; discussion 2140

Ma J, Waxman DJ (2007) Collaboration between
hepatic and intratumoral prodrug activation in a
P450 prodrug-activation gene therapy model for
cancer treatment. Mol Cancer Ther 6:2879–2890

Ma J, Waxman DJ (2008) Modulation of the antitumor activity of metronomic cyclophosphamide
by the angiogenesis inhibitor axitinib. Mol
Cancer Ther 7:79–89

Man S, Bocci G, Francia G, Green SK, Jothy S,
Hanahan D, Bohlen P, Hicklin DJ, Bergers G,
Kerbel RS (2002) Antitumor effects in mice of
low-dose (metronomic) cyclophosphamide admin-
istered continuously through the drinking water.
Cancer Res 62:2731–2735

Mike S, Harrison C, Coles B, Staffurth J, Wilt TJ,
Mason MD (2006) Chemotherapy for hormone-
refractory prostate cancer. Cochrane Database
Syst Rev: CD005247

Miller KD, Sweeney CJ, Sledge GW Jr (2001)
Redefining the target: chemotherapeutics as
antiangiogenics. J Clin Oncol 19:1195–1206

Munoz R, Man S, Shaked Y, Lee CR, Wong J,
Francia G, Kerbel RS (2006) Highly efficacious
nontoxic preclinical treatment for advanced metastatic breast cancer using combination oral
UFT-cyclophosphamide metronomic chemotherapy. Cancer Res 66:3386–3391

Ng SS, Sparreboom A, Shaked Y, Lee C, Man S,
Desai N, Soon-Shiong P, Figg WD, Kerbel RS
(2006) Influence of formulation vehicle on metronomic taxane chemotherapy: albumin-bound
versus cremophor EL-based paclitaxel. Clin
Cancer Res 12:4331–4338

Nicholson B, Theodorescu D (2004) Angiogenesis
and prostate cancer tumor growth. J Cell
Biochem 91:125–150

Nicolini A, Mancini P, Ferrari P, Anselmi L, Tartarelli
G, Bonazzi V, Carpi A, Giardino R (2004) Oral
low-dose cyclophosphamide in metastatic hormone refractory prostate cancer (MHRPC).
Biomed Pharmacother 58:447–450

Nishimura K, Nonomura N, Ono Y, Nozawa M,
Fukui T, Harada Y, Imazu T, Takaha N, Sugao H,
Miki T, Okuyama A (2001) Oral combination of

cyclophosphamide, uracil plus tegafur and estramustine for hormone-refractory prostate cancer.
Oncology 60:49–54

Orlando L, Cardillo A, Rocca A, Balduzzi A,
Ghisini R, Peruzzotti G, Goldhirsch A,
D'Alessandro C, Cinieri S, Preda L, Colleoni M
(2006) Prolonged clinical benefit with metronomic chemotherapy in patients with metastatic
breast cancer. Anticancer Drugs 17:961–967

Petrylak DP, Tangen CM, Hussain MH, Lara PN Jr,
Jones JA, Taplin ME, Burch PA, Berry D,
Moinpour C, Kohli M, Benson MC, Small EJ,
Raghavan D, Crawford ED (2004) Docetaxel
and estramustine compared with mitoxantrone
and prednisone for advanced refractory prostate
cancer. N Engl J Med 351:1513–1520

Pienta KJ, Smith DC (2005) Advances in prostate
cancer chemotherapy: a new era begins. CA
Cancer J Clin 55: 300–318; quiz 323–305

Pietras K, Hanahan D (2005) A multitargeted, metronomic, and maximum-tolerated dose "chemo-
switch" regimen is antiangiogenic, producing
objective responses and survival benefit in a
mouse model of cancer. J Clin Oncol 23:
939–952

Quesada AJ, Nelius T, Yap R, Zaichuk TA,
Alfranca A, Filleur S, Volpert OV, Redondo JM
(2005) In vivo upregulation of CD95 and CD95L
causes synergistic inhibition of angiogenesis by
TSP1 peptide and metronomic doxorubicin treatment. Cell Death Differ 12:649–658

Rapisarda A, Zalek J, Hollingshead M,
Braunschweig T, Uranchimeg B, Bonomi CA,
Borgel SD, Carter JP, Hewitt SM, Shoemaker RH,
Melillo G (2004) Schedule-dependent inhibition
of hypoxia-inducible factor-1alpha protein accu-
mulation, angiogenesis, and tumor growth by
topotecan in U251-HRE glioblastoma xenografts.
Cancer Res 64:6845–6848

Rivera E, Mejia JA, Arun BK, Adinin RB,
Walters RS, Brewster A, Broglio KR, Yin G,
Esmaeli B, Hortobagyi GN, Valero V (2008)
Phase 3 study comparing the use of docetaxel
on an every-3-week versus weekly schedule in
the treatment of metastatic breast cancer.
Cancer 112:1455–1461

Rocca A, Dellapasqua A, Pietri E, Dettori M,
D'Alessandro C, Ghisini R, Colombo A,
Goldhirsch A, Colleoni M (2007) Metronomic
chemotherapy with capecitabine and oral cyclophosphamide in combination with bevacizumab

in metastatic breast cancer (mbc): evidence of activity of an antiangiogenic treatment. In: ASCO Annual Meeting Proceedings Part I. J Clin Oncol 25(18S): abstract 11501

Rohan RM, Fernandez A, Udagawa T, Yuan J, D'Amato RJ (2000) Genetic heterogeneity of angiogenesis in mice. Faseb J 14:871–876

Ryan CJ, Lin AM, Small EJ (2006) Angiogenesis inhibition plus chemotherapy for metastatic hormone refractory prostate cancer: history and rationale. Urol Oncol 24:250–253

Shaked Y, Bertolini F, Man S, Rogers MS, Cervi D, Foutz T, Rawn K, Voskas D, Dumont DJ, Ben-David Y, Lawler J, Henkin J, Huber J, Hicklin DJ, D'Amato RJ, Kerbel RS (2005a) Genetic heterogeneity of the vasculogenic phenotype parallels angiogenesis; Implications for cellular surrogate marker analysis of antiangiogenesis. Cancer Cell 7:101–111

Shaked Y, Ciarrocchi A, Franco M, Lee CR, Man S, Cheung AM, Hicklin DJ, Chaplin D, Foster FS, Benezra R, Kerbel RS (2006) Therapy-induced acute recruitment of circulating endothelial progenitor cells to tumors. Science 313:1785–1787

Shaked Y, Emmenegger U, Francia G, Chen L, Lee CR, Man S, Paraghamian A, Ben-David Y, Kerbel RS (2005b) Low-dose metronomic combined with intermittent bolus-dose cyclophosphamide is an effective long-term chemotherapy treatment strategy. Cancer Res 65:7045–7051

Shaked Y, Emmenegger U, Man S, Cervi D, Bertolini F, Ben-David Y, Kerbel RS (2005c) Optimal biologic dose of metronomic chemotherapy regimens is associated with maximum antiangiogenic activity. Blood 106:3058–3061

Shirakawa K, Furuhata S, Watanabe I, Hayase H, Shimizu A, Ikarashi Y, Yoshida T, Terada M, Hashimoto D, Wakasugi H (2002) Induction of vasculogenesis in breast cancer models. Br J Cancer 87:1454–1461

Sterba J, Pavelka Z, Slampa P (2002) Concomitant radiotherapy and metronomic temozolomide in pediatric high-risk brain tumors. Neoplasma 49: 117–120

Takahashi Y, Mai M, Sawabu N, Nishioka K (2005) A pilot study of individualized maximum repeatable dose (iMRD), a new dose finding system, of weekly gemcitabine for patients with metastatic pancreas cancer. Pancreas 30:206–210

Tannock IF, de Wit R, Berry WR, Horti J, Pluzanska A, Chi KN, Oudard S, Theodore C, James ND, Turesson I, Rosenthal MA, Eisenberger MA (2004) Docetaxel plus prednisone or mitoxantrone plus prednisone for advanced prostate cancer. N Engl J Med 351:1502–1512

Tannock IF, Osoba D, Stockler MR, Ernst DS, Neville AJ, Moore MJ, Armitage GR, Wilson JJ, Venner PM, Coppin CM, Murphy KC (1996) Chemotherapy with mitoxantrone plus prednisone or prednisone alone for symptomatic hormone-resistant prostate cancer: a Canadian randomized trial with palliative end points. J Clin Oncol 14:1756–1764

Tran J, Master Z, Yu JL, Rak J, Dumont DJ, Kerbel RS (2002) A role for survivin in chemoresistance of endothelial cells mediated by VEGF. Proc Natl Acad Sci U S A 99:4349–4354

Vogelzang NJ (1984) Continuous infusion chemotherapy: a critical review. J Clin Oncol 2:1289–1304

Volpert OV, Zaichuk T, Zhou W, Reiher F, Ferguson TA, Stuart PM, Amin M, Bouck NP (2002) Inducer-stimulated Fas targets activated endothelium for destruction by anti-angiogenic thrombospondin-1 and pigment epithelium-derived factor. Nat Med 8:349–357

Wang J, Lou P, Lesniewski R, Henkin J (2003) Paclitaxel at ultra low concentrations inhibits angiogenesis without affecting cellular microtubule assembly. Anticancer Drugs 14:13–19

Winquist E, Waldron T, Berry S, Ernst DS, Hotte S, Lukka H (2006) Non-hormonal systemic therapy in men with hormone-refractory prostate cancer and metastases: a systematic review from the Cancer Care Ontario Program in Evidence-based Care's Genitourinary Cancer Disease Site Group. BMC Cancer 6:112

Yap R, Veliceasa D, Emmenegger U, Kerbel RS, McKay LM, Henkin J, Volpert OV (2005) Metronomic low-dose chemotherapy boosts CD95-dependent antiangiogenic effect of the thrombospondin peptide ABT-510: a complementation antiangiogenic strategy. Clin Cancer Res 11: 6678–6685

Young SD, Whissell M, Noble JC, Cano PO, Lopez PG, Germond CJ (2006) Phase II clinical trial results involving treatment with low-dose daily oral cyclophosphamide, weekly vinblastine, and rofecoxib in patients with advanced solid tumors. Clin Cancer Res 12:3092–3098

Zhu AX (2008) Development of sorafenib and other molecularly targeted agents in hepatocellular carcinoma. Cancer 112:250–259

Targeting Inflammatory Cells to Improve Anti-VEGF Therapies in Oncology

11

Hans-Peter Gerber, Ezogelin Olazoglu, and Iqbal S. Grewal

Abstract Vascular endothelial growth factor A (VEGF-A) is a well-characterized regulator of physiological and pathological angiogenesis. Multiple therapeutic compounds interfering with VEGF-A-regulated signal transduction pathways are currently being developed for the treatment of neoplasias and other malignancies associated with pathological angiogenesis. A major challenge in developing anti-VEGF therapies are tumor intrinsic refractoriness and the emergence of treatment-induced resistance. A variety of molecular and cellular mechanisms contribute to tumor angiogenesis, including the recruitment of bone marrow (BM)-derived endothelial cell progenitors (EPCs) and inflammatory cells to the tumor mass. Among the latter, two types of tumor infiltrating, inflammatory cells were recently identified to mediate refractoriness to anti-VEGF treatment: CD11b + Gr1+ myeloid derived suppressor cells (MDSC) and tumor-associated macrophages (TAMs). In this chapter, we review some of the inflammatory components regulating tumor angiogenesis and their roles in mediating refractoriness toward anti-VEGF treatment. In addition, we discuss poten-tial therapeutic strategies targeting angiogenic pathways regulated by inflammatory cells. A better understanding of the biological and molecular events involved in mediating refractoriness to anti-VEGF treatment may help to further improve therapeutic strategies targeting tumor angiogenesis.

11.1
Role of Bone Marrow-Derived Tumor Infiltrating Cells in Tumor Angiogenesis

Traditionally, tumor cells were recognized as the major source of angiogenic factors, and therapeutic compounds targeting tumor-derived growth factors or signaling pathways regulated by these factors induced tumor growth inhibition in preclinical and clinical studies. More recently, it has become apparent that cancer development largely depends on the ability of tumor cells to engage and exploit normal physiological processes of the host, including the recruitment and activation of untransformed stromal cells. Many of the stromal cells that were shown to play important roles during tissue regeneration were also found to regulate tumor angiogenesis and to contribute to the development of refractoriness toward anti-VEGF therapy. Primary inducers of recruitment

H. P. Gerber (✉)
Sr Dir Discovery Tumor Prog,
Pharma, Research & Development, Pearl River, NY,
e-mail: gerberh@wyeth.com

R. Liersch et al. (eds.), *Angiogenesis Inhibition,* Recent Results in Cancer Research,
DOI: 10.1007/978-3-540-78281-0_11, © Springer Verlag Berlin Heidelberg 2010

of inflammatory cells to sites of tissue injury are ischemia, hypoglycemia, and tissue necrosis. Many of these conditions are also part of the pathophysiological changes observed in tumors treated with anti-VEGF (Gerber and Ferrara 2005). Therefore, it is tempting to speculate that anti-VEGF refractoriness may be caused by misguided inflammatory cells responding to stress signals induced by anti-VEGF treatment, initiating physiological changes associated with tissue regeneration (Dvorak 1986).

The production of angiogenic activities by tumor infiltrating stromal cells was attributed to fibroblasts (Dong et al. 2004; Orimo et al. 2005), endothelial progenitor cells (EPCs) (Asahara et al. 1997; Nolan et al. 2007; Shi et al. 1998), mesenchymal stem cells (MSCs) (Kanehira et al. 2007), and leukocytes (reviewed by (de Visser and Coussens 2006)). Hematopoietic cells exerting angiogenic functions include tumor-associated macrophages (TAMs) (De Palma et al. 2005; Yang et al. 2004), T- and B-lymphocytes (Freeman et al. 1995), vascular leukocytes (Conejo-Garcia et al. 2005), dendritic cells (Conejo-Garcia et al. 2004), neutrophils (Coussens et al. 2000), mast-cells (Coussens et al. 1999), and myeloid cells (Shojaei et al. 2007a; Yang et al. 2004) (Fig. 11.1). Such tumor-infiltrating leukocytes are variably loaded with chemokines, cytokines, cytotoxic mediators including reactive oxygen species (ROS), serine-cysteines and metalloproteases, membrane performing agents, interleukins, and interferons (Tlsty and Coussens 2006). Many of these factors were shown to be either pro- or anti-angiogenic, depending on the experimental model employed. Recent preclinical studies conducted with compounds interfering with VEGF signaling identified a novel role for tumor-infiltrating leukocytes in mediating refractoriness to anti-VEGF treatment (Fischer et al. 2007; Shojaei et al. 2007a; Shojaei et al. 2007b). The identification of a key role of inflammatory cells in mediating refractoriness toward anti-VEGF treatment validates these cells as potential targets for tumor therapy. Despite the important contributions of

inflammatory cells to tumor angiogenesis identified in various preclinical studies, their overall role for tumor development in cancer patients remains controversial (reviewed in (Coussens and Werb 2002)). Here, we review some of the key features associated with tumor-infiltrating leukocytes and the preclinical and clinical evidence in support of their potential role during tumor angiogenesis and escape from anti-VEGF treatment.

11.2
Endothelial Progenitor Cells (EPCs) and Circulatory Endothelial Progenitor Cells (CEPs)

Studies conducted with a large variety of experimental tumors in mice demonstrated that BM-derived EPCs are important for blood vessel formation through a process known as vasculogenesis (reviewed in Rafii et al. 2002). In this process, EPCs are mobilized to the peripheral circulation, from where they home as circulatory endothelial cells (CEPs) to distal sites of neovascularization, followed by their in situ differentiation to mature endothelial cells. Vasculogenesis does not only contribute to tumor angiogenesis, but also to tissue revascularization and regeneration in preclinical models of wound healing, hind-limb ischemia, postmyocardial infarction, atherosclerosis, and retinal and lymphoid organ neovascularization (reviewed in Rafii and Lyden 2003).

EPCs and CEPs were originally defined as cells expressing the hematopoietic stem cell markers CD34, CD133 and the endothelial marker VEGF receptor-2 (VEGFR-2). Studies with such triple positive EPCs demonstrated that their recruitment to the tumor vasculature is required for vascularization of certain experimental tumors (Table 11.1, (Asahara et al. 1997; Shi et al. 1998)). Initial preclinical studies demonstrating the requirement of EPCs for tumor angiogenesis were conducted in Id-mutant mice, which failed to generate CEPs and did not support tumor

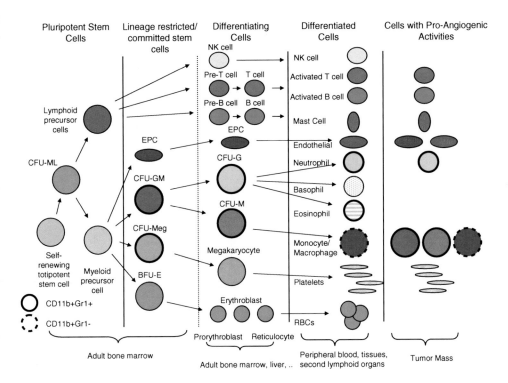

Fig. 11.1 Differentiation of hematopoietic lineages. Self-renewing totipotent stem cells in the bone marrow give rise to cells of the immune system. Colony-forming unit-myeloid-lymphoid (CFU-ML) precursor cells divide to produce two types of stem cells: Lymphoid precursor cells giving rise to NK cell, T cells and B cells, and myeloid precursor cells give rise to CFU-GM, CFU-Meg and BFU-E which eventually differentiates to granulocytes/monocytes, megakaryocytes producing platelets and erythrocytes, respectively. After encounter with an antigen, T cells become activated and differentiate to effector cells while B cells differentiate into antibody-secreting plasma cells. CFU-GM are the precursor cells giving rise to CFU-M and CFU-G, which are phenotypically CD11b+Gr-1+. CFU-M differentiates to monocytes that travel to the blood and eventually become macrophages in the tissue, these cells are phenotypically CD11b+Gr-1-. While monocytes are in the bone marrow, they are CD11b+, whereas Gr-1 is expressed only transiently. CFU-G is the precursor that eventually differentiates to neutrophils, basophils and eosinophils. They are termed granulocytes due to cytoplasmic granules and irregular shape of nuclei and they maintain CD11b+ and Gr-1+ on their cell surface. Mast cells arise from an unknown precursor and complete their maturation in the tissues and are known to be CD11b+, the expression of Gr-1 on these cells has not been assessed

angiogenesis and growth (Lyden et al. 2001). The consensus marker expression for EPCs in men and mice is defined as CD133+CD34+VEGFR2+ cells, which facilitates the direct comparisons between their angiogenic activities when tested in different experimental models (Urbich and Dimmeler 2004). In general, failure of EPCs to migrate from the BM to the tumor vasculature resulted in reduced tumor angiogenesis and growth (reviewed in (Luttun et al. 2002b)). The frequencies of EPCs within the vasculature of experimental tumors varies significantly, ranging from 0–100%, depending on the type of tumor, host, and stage of tumor growth (Lyden et al. 2001; Natori et al. 2002; Peters et al. 2005; Shaked et al. 2005). Despite the important roles

Table 11.1 Potential therapeutic targets to interfere with anti-VEGF refractoriness of solid tumors

Cell type targeted	Migration from bone marrow to circulation	Homing to tumors	Tumor mass
TAMs		CD51, CCL2, CCL3, CCL4,CCL5, CCL8, VEGF-A	PlGF, VEGF-A, bFGF, TNF-α, IL-8, MMP-2, MMP-7, MMP-9, MMP12, Cox2, uPA
EPCs	VEGF-A, PlGF, SDF-1α, GM-CSF, Ang1, elastase, cathepsin G, MMPs, Kit-ligand, e-NOS	MMP-9, integrin, αvβ3 and αvβ5, E-and P-selectin, glycoprotein ligand-1	
Neutrophils			VEGF-A, IL-8, MMP-2, MMP-9, elastase
CD11b + Gr1 + MDSCs	Gr1	Gr1	Bv8, Gr1
Mast cell and lymphocytes		CD20	CD20, VEGF, bFGF, IL-8 and TNF-α

of EPCs for growth of experimental tumors in mice, the frequencies of EPCs in advanced stage tumors in patients are low, ranging from 1 to 12% and averaged 4.9% (Peters et al. 2005). Some of the discrepancies between the frequencies of EPCs in the tumor vasculature between clinical and preclinical studies may be caused by the rapid kinetics of EPC recruitment to tumor vasculature, with maximum levels during the first couple of days post tumor implantation in animals. In contrast, the patient tumors analyzed in various studies represent mostly advanced-stage tumors.

The molecular mechanisms regulating the mobilization of EPCs from the BM to peripheral circulation are only incompletely understood. Initial experiments revealed that distinct classes of genes and environmental factors contribute to this process (reviewed in (Papayannopoulou 2004; Urbich and Dimmeler 2004)). Among them, local tissue ischemia is considered a predominant signal-inducing event, leading to mobilization of EPCs to sites of tissue injury or tumors (Akita et al. 2003) (reviewed in (Kawamoto et al. 2002)). Local hypoxia was shown to induce EPC-mobilizing cytokines within tumors, including VEGF-A, PlGF, SDF-1α (Yamaguchi et al. 2003), granulocyte macrophage colony-stimulating factor

(GM-CSF) (Rehman et al. 2003), and angiopoietin-1 (Hattori et al. 2001). In addition, activation of proteinases such as elastase, cathepsin G, matrix metalloproteinases (MMPs), cleavage of Kit ligand (Heissig et al. 2002), and expression of endothelial-nitric oxide synthetase (e-NOS) (Aicher et al. 2003; Ii et al. 2005; Wassmann et al. 2006) was also associated with the mobilization of EPCs from the BM to the peripheral circulation.

Homing of CEPs is initiated in specific "hotspot" regions within the tumor microvasculature, followed by their extravasation into the tumor interstitium and the formation of multicellular clusters, ultimately giving rise to functional vascular networks (Vajkoczy et al. 2003). Several genes that were found upregulated on the tumor vasculature are associated with the regulation of circulatory EPCs (cEPCs) homing and extravasation, including MMP-9, integrins $\alpha_v\beta_3$ and $\alpha_v\beta_5$, E-and P-selectin and glycoprotein ligand-1 (Urbich and Dimmeler 2004). Many of these genes were independently identified as downstream targets of VEGF signaling in endothelial cells (Hesser et al. 2004).

The relevance of EPCs to anti-VEGF refractoriness was investigated by using VEGF blocking compounds and experimental models employing genetically marked BM progenitor cells. Nolan et al. demonstrated critical roles for these cells during the early stages of tumor development. At later stages, however, vessels consisting of BM-derived EPCs became diluted with non-BM-derived vessels from the periphery (Nolan et al. 2007). Importantly, selective ablation of EPCs shortly after tumor implantation resulted in a marked tumor growth delay, suggesting that targeting EPC during early stages, but not at later stages of tumor progression, may be most beneficial. Lack of BM-derived EPCs in the tumor vasculature during later stages of tumor growth was confirmed independently by Shojaei et al., who investigated the recruitment of EPCs to tumor vasculature in mice treated with an VEGF-A selective antibody (G6-23), or a compound blocking VEGF-A, PlGF, and VEGF-B combined by using Flt-IgG. When assessed between Days 14 and 18 post tumor cell implantation, the frequencies of EPCs were low, and no differences in the numbers of EPCs in the vasculature of anti-VEGF sensitive and refractory tumors were discernable, irrespective of the treatment modality (Shojaei et al. 2007a). Combined, these finding suggest that recruitment of BM derived EPCs may not contribute significantly to refractoriness of late stage tumors to anti-VEGF treatment. These observations may help to enhance our understanding of some of the controversial reports regarding the frequencies and functional relevance of EPCs for tumor angiogenesis reported for different experimental models.

11.3
Tumor-Associated Macrophages

Macrophages are derived from CD34+ BM progenitors, which shed their progeny into the blood stream as promonocytes. They then develop into monocytes and extravasate to tissues where they differentiate into specific types of resident tissue macrophages, with marked phenotypic differences between different tissues. Resident macrophages share a set of common functions, including the defense against microbial infections, the regulation of normal cell turnover and tissue remodeling, and repair at sites of injury. Recruitment of macrophages to sites of tissue injury or tumor growth is a well- documented phenomenon, and environmental conditions including hypoxia, lack of nutrients, inflammation, and cell death were described as key stimulators of macrophage recruitment (Leek et al. 1999; Leek et al. 1996; Negus et al. 1997; Ohno et al. 2004). TAMs secrete a variety of cytokines and proteolytic enzymes that are capable of promoting tumor progression by stimulating tumor-cell proliferation, angiogenesis and by inducing alterations in the extracellular matrix favorable for tumor growth (reviewed in Knowles et al. 2004). Despite the angiogenic functions of macrophages identified in various preclinical models, the role of tumor-associated macrophages in cancer patients remains controversial (Bingle et al. 2002; Ohno et al. 2003). A positive correlation between the relative numbers of TAMs in breast, prostate, and kidney tumors and clinical prognosis was inferred from clinical studies. While a few reports correlated high TAM numbers with good prognosis, such as in the case of stomach, colorectal, and melanoma tumors, the majority of the clinical studies linked high TAM numbers with reduced patient survival (Lewis and Pollard 2006). In most human tumors studied, infiltration of high numbers of macrophages correlated with increased angiogenesis (Leek et al. 1996; Lin and Pollard 2007), and poor prognosis (Bingle et al. 2002). Combined, these findings led to the proposal to consider cytokine blockades as a potential strategy to modulate angiogenesis during inflammation and in cancer (Crivellato and Ribatti 2005). However, other preclinical studies associated inhibitory activities on tumor growth with increased levels of macrophages within tumors (reviewed in Kohchi et al. 2004). Thus, depending on the specific type of inflammatory cells recruited to tumors, immune cell infiltration may either antagonize tumor formation and growth (Dunn et al. 2004; Lin and Pollard 2004) or promote tumor growth by stimulating angiogenesis and tumor-cell proliferation (Coussens and Werb 2002; de Visser et al. 2005).

In the context of solid tumors, circulating monocytes are shown to be recruited to the tumor vicinity by a number of tumor-derived chemoattractants, including colony-stimulating factor-1 (CSF-1), CC chemokines such as CCL2, CCL3, CCL4, CCL5, CCL8, and VEGF (Murdoch et al. 2004; Sica et al. 2006) . TAMs were described as a significant source of proangiogenic activities in solid tumors and they play important roles in mediating tumor angiogenesis. TAMs release potent proangiogenic cytokines and growth factors, including VEGF-A, bFGF, TNF-α, and IL-8 (Lewis et al. 1995; Mantovani et al. 2002; Sunderkotter et al. 1991). They also upregulate other genes associated with the regulation of angiogenesis, including MMP- 2, MMP-7, MMP-9, MMP-12, and cyclooxygenase-2 (Cox-2, reviewed in (Lewis and Pollard 2006)). To sum up, the many proangiogenic activities produced by TAMs render them likely candidates for mediating escape from anti-VEGF treatment.

One of the key problems in defining the role of TAMs during tumor development is the lack of a common definition for their phenotypic markers or functional properties. TAMs have been characterized inconsistently by low expression levels of differentiation-associated macrophage antigens, carboxypeptidase M and CD51, high constitutive expression of interleukin (IL)-1, IL-6 and low expression of TNF-α, and the presence of the myeloid marker F4/80 in mice or CD68 in humans (Bingle et al. 2002). Macrophages derived from experimental or human tumors display greatly reduced immuno-stimmulatory activities on cytotoxic T-cells and NK cells. It was suggested that this may be the result of their exposure to IL-4 and IL-10 within the tumors, inducing TAMs to develop into polarized Type II or M2 macrophages (Mantovani et al. 2004).

Early macrophage ablation studies provided experimental evidence that TAMs are essential for the growth of certain experimental tumors in mice (Polverini and Leibovich 1987). Based on these findings, a model was proposed, wherein macrophages are capable of modulating angiogenesis (Sunderkotter et al. 1991). From studies conducted in a genetic model of mammary tumor, a correlation between the recruitment of TAMs to premalignant lesions before the onset of angiogenesis and transition to malignancy was identified. Depletion of macrophages in this model was associated with a significant reduction in vessel formation and an increase in hypoxic and necrotic areas in the tumors (Lewis and Pollard 2006).

More recently, a novel role for TAMs in the development of refractoriness toward treatment with anti-VEGF compounds was reported. When comparing the antitumor effects of therapeutic compounds blocking either PlGF selectively, or PlGF and VEGF-A combined with other antineoplastic agents, improved antitumor activity for the anti-PlGF selective compound was noted. The improved antitumor activity observed for the combination treatment correlated with a similar fold reduction in the numbers of tumor associated, F4/80 positive macrophages in anti-PlGF treated mice when compared to anti-VEGF treatment alone. Importantly, compounds blocking VEGFR-2 signaling induced different pharmacodynamic alterations, and gene expression analysis of tumors treated with anti-VEGF compounds revealed a shift toward a proangiogenic rescue/ antiangiogenesis escape signature. In contrast, anti-PlGF treatment did not induce such escape signature, providing an advantage of anti-PLGF compounds by potentially circumventing the development of refractoriness to antiangiogenic treatment (Fischer et al. 2007). In conclusion, the effects of blocking VEGF in combination with compounds targeting TAMs will be of relevance for future clinical development of anti-VEGF compounds.

11.4
CD11b+ Gr1+ Myeloid-Derived Suppressor Cells

CD11b+ Gr1+ myeloid cells, also termed myeloid suppressor cells (MSCs) or myeloid-derived suppressor cells (MDSC, (Gabrilovich et al. 2001)), were originally described based on their immuno-suppressive characteristics, enabling tumors to escape from immune surveillance (reviewed in Vieweg et al. 2007). Recently, preclinical studies identified potent proangiogenic activities by CD11b+Gr1+ cells in the context of experimental tumor models, enabling refractoriness toward anti-VEGF treatment (Shojaei et al. 2007a; Shojaei et al. 2007b). MDSC were investigated intensively within the context of their anti-inflammatory activities. MDSCs can exert immunosuppressive functions within the tumor environment by inhibiting the activation of CD4+ and CD8+ T-cells. Several other immunosuppressive mechanisms are employed by MDSCs, including the inhibition of antigen-specific T-cell functions via CD80 or B7-H1 expression, nitric oxide production, or the L-arginine metabolism. Thus, in addition to providing proangiogenic stimuli, the presence of MDSCs within solid tumors may significantly inhibit desirable antitumor adaptive immune responses. By definition, MDSCs express Gr1 and CD11b, which are typical markers of the myeloid precursor derived lineages, MDSCs display reduced expression on mature myeloid cells such as monocytes or macrophages, which differentiates these cells from TAMs described earlier (Fig. 11.1). When analyzed in BM cell isolates, most of the cells within the CD11b+Gr1+ population belong to the class of neutrophils and only a minority are representing monocytic lineages (Shojaei et al. 2007a; Shojaei et al. 2007b). Thus, MDSCs are rather heterogeneous and variable in their phenotype and functional properties. The precise nature of MDSCs depends on the tumor-type and the nature of the tumor-derived factors. Therefore, different tumor-types may contain MDSCs expressing different phenotypic markers and exerting different functional potencies. Given the difficulties in determining the nature of MDSCs, a proposal was made to standardize the phenotypic markers to CD11b+Gr1+ cells. Such consensus phenotype allows for the direct comparison between different experimental models and facilitates the use of a common term of "myeloid derived suppressor cells" (MDSCs) to describe these cells (Gabrilovich et al. 2007).

Importantly, ablation of CD11b+Gr1+ cells by means of an antibody binding to Gr1 resulted in improved antitumor effects when tested in combination with anti-VEGF compounds, compared to the antitumor effects obtained for single-agent treatments. These studies validated MDSCs as therapeutic targets for combination treatments with anti-VEGF in solid tumors (Shojaei et al. 2007a). In the clinic, accumulation of immature myeloid suppressor cells in peripheral blood of cancer patients was observed (Almasri et al. 2004; Serafini et al. 2004). Therefore, quantification of circulatory MDSCs in the peripheral blood of cancer patients and analysis of potential correlations with response to anti-VEGF therapy may represent a valuable diagnostic approach to identify patients with optimal responses. Lastly, the methods and cell surface makers used to identify TAMs in experimental or patient tumors frequently overlap with the phenotypic markers used to define MDSCs. Therefore, some of the activities reported for TAMs may be attributable to MDSCs, and vice versa. Further investigations regarding the identity of MDSCs and TAMs may help to better understand some of the similarities in the biological functions reported for these cell types.

11.5
Lymphocytes and Mast Cells (MCs)

Experiments conducted in genetic models of cancer in mice demonstrated that T- and/or B-cell deficiency is associated with significant alterations in tumor growth rates compared to tumors grown in immune-competent mice. Activation of the adaptive immune system identified CD8+ T cells to be necessary for the improvement of the antitumor immune responses in mice (Zitvogel et al. 2006). However, cancer burden, incidence, and angiogenesis of tumors developing in the skin and cervix were variable and dependent on the location and genetic background of the tumors (reviewed in de Visser et al. 2006). In a genetic model of mouse squamous cell carcinoma of the skin, B- and T-cell deficiency was associated with a marked decrease in the infiltration of innate immune cells and a decrease in tumor formation and progression. Transfer of B-cells or serum from immuno-competent, tumor-bearing mice was sufficient to restore tumorigenicity, demonstrating that soluble mediators derived from B-cells are critical for the stimulation of tumor growth (de Visser et al. 2005). In contrast, adoptive transfer of tumor-associated B-cells yielded opposite effects, stimulating tumor invasion and metastasis through antibody–antigen complex-mediated granulocye and macrophage induction (Barbera-Guillem et al. 1999). Thus, different elements of the adaptive immune-system can introduce confounding effects on tumor growth, depending on the tumor type and the model used. Importantly, the potential of B- and T-cells to mediate refractoriness toward anti-VEGF treatment has been addressed experimentally in SCID beige mice, which are deficient in B- and T-cell lineages and have low granulocytes. Tumor-growth experiments in these mice implanted with either anti-VEGF refractory or sensitive tumor cell lines revealed that anti-VEGF refractoriness is T- or B-cell independent (Shojaei et al. 2007a).

The presence of tumor-infiltrating mast cells (MCs) was described in a variety of human cancers, including breast carcinomas (Kankkunen et al. 1997), colorectal cancer (Lachter et al. 1995), basal cell carcinomas (Yamamoto et al. 1997), nonsmall cell lung cancer (Shijubo et al. 2003),

and pulmonary adenocarcinomas (Imada et al. 2000). Experiments in preclinical tumor models revealed important roles for MCs in the induction of tumor angiogenesis (Hiromatsu and Toda 2003; Toda et al. 2000). Activated MCs represent a source for many known angiogenic factors, including VEGF-A, bFGF, IL-8, and TNF-α. In addition, histamine and heparin stored in the secretory granules of MCs were shown to stimulate endothelial cell proliferation. The angiogenic potential of the granules of MCs was significantly reduced in presence of neutralizing compounds targeting VEGF-A or bFGF. Genetic depletion of MCs in mice resulted in reduced tumor angiogenesis of subcutaneously grown, syngeneic mouse tumors (Starkey et al. 1988), and reduced progression of malignant squamous cell carcinomas. Depletion of MCs was associated with diminished premalignant angiogenesis and reduced carcinoma incidence in a skin carcinoma model (Coussens et al. 1999; Coussens et al. 2000). Combined, these studies identified a critical role for the adaptive immune system, specifically B-cells, in the development of angiogenic responses in tumors. However, the role of MCs in mediating refractoriness to anti-VEGF treatment has not been addressed experimentally.

11.6
Neutrophils

Neutrophils play an active role in enhancing tumor angiogenesis, either directly via the release of vesicle-stored growth factors, cytokines such as VEGF-A or IL-8 (Schaider et al. 2003) and proteolytic activities, including matrix metalloproteinases (MMP-2) (Masson et al. 2005), MMP-9 (Coussens et al. 2000) and elastases (Iwatsuki et al. 2000). In general, neutrophil recruitment precedes the induction of angiogenesis in several preclinical tumor models, including genetic models (Coussens et al.

2000) or heterotransplant models of human cancers in nude mice (Gutschalk et al. 2006; Obermueller et al. 2004). The release of VEGF-A by neutrophils appears to be a key mechanism underlying the angiogenesis-promoting capacity of neutrophils, as depletion of neutrophils abrogated the angiogenic response to stimulation with CXCL1/MIP-2 in vivo (Scapini et al. 2004). Importantly, the angiogenic activities of MMP-9 positive neutrophils were potently suppressed by anti-VEGF compounds, indicating that these cells may not be part of the mechanism inducing refractoriness toward anti-VEGF treatment (Vosseler et al. 2005). The essential role of neutrophils during tumor angiogenesis was further supported by studies conducted with the Rip-Tag2 model of pancreatic islet carcinogenesis. In this model, transient depletion of neutrophils reduced the frequency of the angiogenic switch in dysplastic islets (Nozawa et al. 2006). Most of the proangiogenic activity produced by neutrophils was mediated by MMP-9, which releases matrix bound VEGF-A from the ECM and promotes VEGF-A binding and activation of VEGFR-2 on the tumor vasculature. In addition to the regulation of proangiogenic activities, an important role of neutrophils in the modulation of the phenotypes of TAMs was described (Gutschalk et al. 2006; Obermueller et al. 2004). Combined, these findings clearly demonstrated VEGF-dependent regulation of angiogenesis by neutrophils.

monocytic colonies in BM colony formation assays in vitro (LeCouter et al. 2003; LeCouter et al. 2004). Several human tumor-cell lines implanted into nude mice are infiltrated with CD11b+Gr1+ myeloid cells expressing high levels of Bv8. Pharmacological studies blocking Bv8 along with VEGF-A revealed improved antitumor effects. An increase in CD11b+Gr1+ cells could be observed within anti-VEGF treated tumors, which correlated with the onset of central tumor necrosis. These findings suggested that the pathophysiological changes induced by anti-VEGF treatment, including local hypoxia and/or necrosis of the tumor, increases Bv8 production and induces resistance to anti-VEGF treatment. In contrast, anti-VEGF treatment in syngeneic tumor models in mice did not increase the numbers of CD11b+ Gr1+ cells in the tumors. These finding suggest that tumor intrinsic refractoriness and treatment-induced resistance to anti-VEGF may be the result of the differences in the experimental models used. Alternatively, the differences between intrinsic versus and treatment-induced refractoriness may indicate that upregulation of Bv8 is treatment induced, whereas the recruitment of inflammatory cells to the tumor is tumor intrinsic. In conclusion, these studies demonstrated that blocking proangiogenic factors produced by tumor infiltrating, BM-derived CD11b+Gr1+ myeloid cells improved antiangiogenic therapy.

11.7
Therapeutic Targets to Overcome Anti-VEGF Refractoriness

11.7.1
Bv8

Bv8 is an endothelial cell mitogen that also induces haematopoietic cell mobilization and increases the production of granulocytic and

11.8
VEGF-B, -C, -D, and PlGF

VEGF-A, a member of the platelet-derived growth factor family, is among the most potent angiogenic factors described so far. Other family members are VEGF-B, VEGF-C, VEGF-D, VEGF-E, and placental growth factor (PlGF). VEGF-A promotes angiogenesis by binding to two receptor tyrosine-kinases, VEGFR-1 and

VEGFR-2, found predominantly on the surface of vascular endothelial cells. Studies show, however, that VEGFR-2, not VEGFR-1, is the principle receptor for VEGF signaling (reviewed in (Ferrara 2004)). VEGF-A and PlGF exhibit additional regulatory functions on nonendothelial cells, including the stimulation of hematopoietic stem cell survival (Gerber et al. 2002) and EPC recruitment to the circulation (Hattori et al. 2001; Hattori et al. 2002). Increased expression of VEGFR-1, VEGF-A, VEGF-B, and PlGF was reported in different models of tumor growth (Autiero et al. 2003b; Lyden et al. 2001). Studies using VEGFR-1 blocking antibodies also identified a critical role for VEGFR-1 in EPC recruitment to peripheral circulation (Autiero et al. 2003a; Autiero et al. 2003b; Lyden et al. 2001). Blocking PlGF was shown to be anti-inflammatory, consistent with the fact that PlGF is a chemoattractant for VEGFR-1+ macrophages (Luttun et al. 2002a; Pipp et al. 2003). The efficacy of VEGFR-1 blockade during tumor growth in mice, however, is variable (Luttun et al. 2002c), and was most pronounced in tumors expressing high endogenous or ectopic levels of ligands activating VEGFR-1 (Stefanik et al. 2001).

To investigate the roles of different VEGF family members in the recruitment of myeloid cells to experimental tumors, the effects of anti-VEGF compounds blocking either VEGF-A along (G6-23-IgG), or combined with VEGF-B and PlGF (mFlt(1–3)-IgG) were determined in syngeneic tumors or human tumor xenografts grown in mice (Shojaei et al. 2007a; Shojaei et al. 2007b). Both compounds induced comparable tumor growth delays in mice implanted with anti-VEGF-sensitive or refractory tumors, suggesting that endogenous levels of PlGF and VEGF-B are redundant during VEGF-A blockade. However, these observations did not exclude the possibility that PlGF or VEGF-B may potentially contribute to EPC recruitment in conditions when VEGF-A is not neutralized.

The effects of a neutralizing antibody selectively blocking PlGF were tested in experimental tumor models in mice, when administered either alone or in combination with anti-VEGF or cytotoxic agents (Fischer et al. 2007). Improved therapeutic effects were noted when the anti-PlGF antibody was combined with anti-VEGF compounds or chemotherapy, relative to single agent treatment groups. Interestingly, such increase in efficacy inversely correlated with the frequency of TAMs in treated tumors. Moreover, treatment with the anti-VEGF compound induced a set of angiogenic factors, which was not observed in anti-PlGF treated tumors (Fischer et al. 2007). Combined, these findings suggest that PlGF not only represents an important regulator of EPC recruitment to pathologic vasculature, but is also a key regulator of TAM recruitment to anti-VEGF resistant tumors. Therefore, compounds blocking PlGF may have therapeutic utility for the treatment of carcinomas.

11.9
Targeting MDSCs and TAMs

Recent experiments demonstrated a critical role of MDSCs and TAMs in mediating refractoriness to anti-VEGF treatment. These experiments were conducted with compounds inducing either systemic ablation of inflammatory cells or blocking of specific angiogenic activities produced by these cells. However, gene knock-out or pharmacological experiments demonstrated that prolonged ablation of more differentiated monocytes or macrophage lineages in mice resulted in severe toxicity and mortality due to secondary infections. Therefore, identification of therapeutic targets that interfere selectively with a subset of tumor-associated monocytic cells or with proangiogenic activities produced by these cells may be required to circumvent these limitations (Table 11.1).

11.10
Targeting EPCs

Blocking of the genes involved in the homing of EPCs to tumor vasculature carries the potential to improve antiangiogenic and antitumor effects. However, due to rapid kinetics of EPC recruitment to tumor vasculature, EPCs may represent promising targets in prevention type anticancer treatment strategies, which are initiated during the earliest stages of tumor development. Due to the low incidents of EPCs in advanced tumors, targeting EPCs in already established tumors may induce only limited antiangiogenic effects.

11.11
Conclusions

The identification of tumor-infiltrating inflammatory cells as key mediators of refractoriness to anti-VEGF treatment validates MDSCs and TAMs as potential targets for therapeutic intervention in combination with anti-VEGF modalities and eventually other antineoplastic agents. Conceptually, interference with tumor-associated inflammatory cells can occur at three stages during leukocyte differentiation and development: (1) interference with migration of progenitors from the BM to the peripheral circulation. (2) Interference with endothelial cell transmigration of leukocytes from the peripheral circulation to tumors. (3) Interference with proangiogenic functions of leukocytes within tumors.

Several therapeutic strategies targeting different subsets of inflammatory cells for the treatment of autoimmune and inflammatory diseases are currently undergoing clinical development and some have gained approval. Targeting inflammatory cells has revealed some challenges. For example, prolonged treatment with compounds inducing systemic leukopenia or neutropenia frequently leads to discontinuation of treatment due to secondary infections. On the other hand, chronic use of anti-inflammatory agents, specifically COX-2 inhibitors, induced promising antitumor effects in preclinical and clinical studies (Clevers 2004; Turini and DuBois 2002). Pharmacological studies targeting COX-2 provided evidence that targeting inflammatory processes in cancer can be beneficial. Inflammatory cells display a remarkable plasticity with regard to their surface marker expression and functional potencies, and the specific type of cells and the expression of phenotypic marker of inflammatory cells is largely dependent on the tumor type and the environment. Thus, careful selection of the most relevant inflammatory cell type and/or molecular targets for each cancer indication will be critical to optimize the therapeutic benefit.

References

Aicher A, Heeschen C, Mildner-Rihm C, Urbich C, Ihling C, Technau-Ihling K, Zeiher AM, Dimmeler S (2003) Essential role of endothelial nitric oxide synthase for mobilization of stem and progenitor cells. Nat Med 9:1370–1376

Akita T, Murohara T, Ikeda H, Sasaki K, Shimada T, Egami K, Imaizumi T (2003) Hypoxic preconditioning augments efficacy of human endothelial progenitor cells for therapeutic neovascularization. Lab Invest 83:65–73

Almasri NM, Habashneh MA, Khalidi HS (2004) Non-Hodgkin lymphoma in Jordan. Types and patterns of 111 cases classified according to the WHO classification of hematological malignancies. Saudi Med J 25:609–614

Asahara T, Murohara T, Sullivan A, Silver M, van der Zee R, Li T, Witzenbichler B, Schatteman G, Isner JM (1997) Isolation of putative progenitor endothelial cells for angiogenesis. Science 275: 964–967

Autiero M, Luttun A, Tjwa M, Carmeliet P (2003a) Placental growth factor and its receptor, vascular endothelial growth factor receptor-1: novel targets for stimulation of ischemic tissue revascularization and inhibition of angiogenic and inflammatory disorders. J Thromb Haemost 1: 1356–1370

Autiero M, Waltenberger J, Communi D, Kranz A, Moons L, Lambrechts D, Kroll J, Plaisance S, De Mol M, Bono F et al (2003b) Role of PlGF in the intra- and intermolecular cross talk between the VEGF receptors Flt1 and Flk1. Nat Med 9: 936–943

Barbera-Guillem E, May KF Jr, Nyhus JK, Nelson MB (1999) Promotion of tumor invasion by cooperation of granulocytes and macrophages activated by anti-tumor antibodies. Neoplasia 1:453–460

Bingle L, Brown NJ, Lewis CE (2002) The role of tumour-associated macrophages in tumour progression: implications for new anticancer therapies. J Pathol 196:254–265

Clevers H (2004) At the crossroads of inflammation and cancer. Cell 118:671–674

Conejo-Garcia JR, Benencia F, Courreges MC, Kang E, Mohamed-Hadley A, Buckanovich RJ, Holtz DO, Jenkins A, Na H, Zhang L et al (2004) Tumor-infiltrating dendritic cell precursors recruited by a beta-defensin contribute to vasculogenesis under the influence of Vegf-A. Nat Med 10:950–958

Conejo-Garcia JR, Buckanovich RJ, Benencia F, Courreges MC, Rubin SC, Carroll RG, Coukos G (2005) Vascular leukocytes contribute to tumor vascularization. Blood 105:679–681

Coussens LM, Raymond WW, Bergers G, Laig-Webster M, Behrendtsen O, Werb Z, Caughey GH, Hanahan D (1999) Inflammatory mast cells up-regulate angiogenesis during squamous epithelial carcinogenesis. Genes Dev 13:1382–1397

Coussens LM, Tinkle CL, Hanahan D, Werb Z (2000) MMP-9 supplied by bone marrow-derived cells contributes to skin carcinogenesis. Cell 103: 481–490

Coussens LM, Werb Z (2002) Inflammation and cancer. Nature 420:860–867

Crivellato E, Ribatti D (2005) Involvement of mast cells in angiogenesis and chronic inflammation. Curr Drug Targets Inflamm Allergy 4:9–11

De Palma M, Venneri MA, Galli R, Sergi Sergi L, Politi LS, Sampaolesi M, Naldini L (2005) Tie2 identifies a hematopoietic lineage of proangiogenic monocytes required for tumor vessel formation and a mesenchymal population of pericyte progenitors. Cancer Cell 8:211–226

de Visser KE, Coussens LM (2006) The inflammatory tumor microenvironment and its impact on cancer development. Contrib Microbiol 13:118–137

de Visser KE, Eichten A, Coussens LM (2006) Paradoxical roles of the immune system during cancer development. Nat Rev Cancer 6:24–37

de Visser KE, Korets LV, Coussens LM (2005) De novo carcinogenesis promoted by chronic inflammation is B lymphocyte dependent. Cancer Cell 7:411–423

Dong J, Grunstein J, Tejada M, Peale F, Frantz G, Liang WC, Bai W, Yu L, Kowalski J, Liang X et al (2004) VEGF-null cells require PDGFR alpha signaling-mediated stromal fibroblast recruitment for tumorigenesis. Embo J 23:2800–2810

Dunn GP, Old LJ, Schreiber RD (2004) The immuno-biology of cancer immunosurveillance and immunoediting. Immunity 21:137–148

Dvorak HF (1986) Tumors: wounds that do not heal. Similarities between tumor stroma generation and wound healing. N Engl J Med 315: 1650–1659

Ferrara N (2004) Vascular endothelial growth factor as a target for anticancer therapy. Oncologist 9(Suppl 1):2–10

Fischer C, Jonckx B, Mazzone M, Zacchigna S, Loges S, Pattarini L, Chorianopoulos E, Liesenborghs L, Koch M, De Mol M et al (2007) Anti-PlGF inhibits growth of VEGF(R)-inhibitor-resistant tumors without affecting healthy vessels. Cell 131: 463–475

Freeman MR, Schneck FX, Gagnon ML, Corless C, Soker S, Niknejad K, Peoples GE, Klagsbrun M (1995) Peripheral blood T lymphocytes and lymphocytes infiltrating human cancers express vascular endothelial growth factor: a potential role for T cells in angiogenesis. Cancer Res 55:4140–4145

Gabrilovich DI, Bronte V, Chen SH, Colombo MP, Ochoa A, Ostrand-Rosenberg S, Schreiber H (2007) The terminology issue for myeloid-derived suppressor cells. Cancer Res 67:425; author reply:426

Gabrilovich DI, Velders MP, Sotomayor EM, Kast WM (2001) Mechanism of immune dysfunction in cancer mediated by immature Gr-1+ myeloid cells. J Immunol 166:5398–5406

Gerber HP, Ferrara N (2005) Pharmacology and pharmacodynamics of bevacizumab as monotherapy or in combination with cytotoxic therapy in preclinical studies. Cancer Res 65:671–680

Gerber HP, Malik AK, Solar GP, Sherman D, Liang XH, Meng G, Hong K, Marsters JC, Ferrara N (2002) VEGF regulates haematopoietic stem cell survival by an internal autocrine loop mechanism. Nature 417:954–958

Gutschalk CM, Herold-Mende CC, Fusenig NE, Mueller MM (2006) Granulocyte colony-stimulating factor and granulocyte-macrophage colony-stimulating factor promote malignant growth of cells from head and neck squamous cell carcinomas in vivo. Cancer Res 66:8026–8036

Hattori K, Dias S, Heissig B, Hackett NR, Lyden D, Tateno M, Hicklin DJ, Zhu Z, Witte L, Crystal RG et al (2001) Vascular endothelial growth factor and angiopoietin-1 stimulate postnatal hematopoiesis by recruitment of vasculogenic and hematopoietic stem cells. J Exp Med 193:1005–1014

Hattori K, Heissig B, Wu Y, Dias S, Tejada R, Ferris B, Hicklin DJ, Zhu Z, Bohlen P, Witte L et al (2002) Placental growth factor reconstitutes hematopoiesis by recruiting VEGFR1(+) stem cells from bone-marrow microenvironment. Nat Med 8:841–849

Heissig B, Hattori K, Dias S, Friedrich M, Ferris B, Hackett NR, Crystal RG, Besmer P, Lyden D, Moore MA et al (2002) Recruitment of stem and progenitor cells from the bone marrow niche requires MMP-9 mediated release of kit-ligand. Cell 109:625–637

Hesser BA, Liang XH, Camenisch G, Yang S, Lewin DA, Scheller R, Ferrara N, Gerber HP (2004) Down syndrome critical region protein 1 (DSCR1), a novel VEGF target gene that regulates expression of inflammatory markers on activated endothelial cells. Blood 104:149–158

Hiromatsu Y, Toda S (2003) Mast cells and angiogenesis. Microsc Res Tech 60:64–69

Ii M, Nishimura H, Iwakura A, Wecker A, Eaton E, Asahara T, Losordo DW (2005) Endothelial progenitor cells are rapidly recruited to myocardium and mediate protective effect of ischemic preconditioning via "imported" nitric oxide synthase activity. Circulation 111:1114–1120

Imada A, Shijubo N, Kojima H, Abe S (2000) Mast cells correlate with angiogenesis and poor outcome in stage I lung adenocarcinoma. Eur Respir J 15:1087–1093

Iwatsuki K, Kumara E, Yoshimine T, Nakagawa H, Sato M, Hayakawa T (2000) Elastase expression by infiltrating neutrophils in gliomas. Neurol Res 22:465–468

Kanehira M, Xin H, Hoshino K, Maemondo M, Mizuguchi H, Hayakawa T, Matsumoto K, Nakamura T, Nukiwa T, Saijo Y (2007) Targeted delivery of NK4 to multiple lung tumors by bone marrow-derived mesenchymal stem cells. Cancer Gene Ther 14: 894–903

Kankkunen JP, Harvima IT, Naukkarinen A (1997) Quantitative analysis of tryptase and chymase

containing mast cells in benign and malignant breast lesions. Int J Cancer 72:385–388

Kawamoto A, Asahara T, Losordo DW (2002) Transplantation of endothelial progenitor cells for therapeutic neovascularization. Cardiovasc Radiat Med 3:221–225

Knowles H, Leek R, Harris AL (2004) Macrophage infiltration and angiogenesis in human malignancy. Novartis Found Symp 256:189–200; discussion 200–204, 259–269

Kohchi C, Inagawa H, Hino M, Oda M, Nakata K, Yoshida A, Hori H, Terada H, Makino K, Takiguchi K, Soma G (2004) Utilization of macrophages in anticancer therapy: the macrophage network theory. Anticancer Res 24:3311–3320

Lachter J, Stein M, Lichtig C, Eidelman S, Munichor M (1995) Mast cells in colorectal neoplasias and premalignant disorders. Dis Colon Rectum 38: 290–293

LeCouter J, Lin R, Tejada M, Frantz G, Peale F, Hillan KJ, Ferrara N (2003) The endocrine-gland-derived VEGF homologue Bv8 promotes angiogenesis in the testis: Localization of Bv8 receptors to endothelial cells. Proc Natl Acad Sci U S A 100:2685–2690

LeCouter J, Zlot C, Tejada M, Peale F, Ferrara N (2004) Bv8 and endocrine gland-derived vascular endothelial growth factor stimulate hematopoiesis and hematopoietic cell mobilization. Proc Natl Acad Sci U S A 101:16813–16818

Leek RD, Landers RJ, Harris AL, Lewis CE (1999) Necrosis correlates with high vascular density and focal macrophage infiltration in invasive carcinoma of the breast. Br J Cancer 79:991–995

Leek RD, Lewis CE, Whitehouse R, Greenall M, Clarke J, Harris AL (1996) Association of macrophage infiltration with angiogenesis and prognosis in invasive breast carcinoma. Cancer Res 56:4625–4629

Lewis CE, Leek R, Harris A, McGee JO (1995) Cytokine regulation of angiogenesis in breast cancer: the role of tumor-associated macrophages. J Leukoc Biol 57:747–751

Lewis CE, Pollard JW (2006) Distinct role of macrophages in different tumor microenvironments. Cancer Res 66:605–612

Lin EY, Pollard JW (2004) Role of infiltrated leucocytes in tumour growth and spread. Br J Cancer 90:2053–2058

Lin EY, Pollard JW (2007) Tumor-associated macrophages press the angiogenic switch in breast cancer. Cancer Res 67:5064–5066

Luttun A, Brusselmans K, Fukao H, Tjwa M, Ueshima S, Herbert JM, Matsuo O, Collen D, Carmeliet P, Moons L (2002a) Loss of placental growth factor protects mice against vascular permeability in pathological conditions. Biochem Biophys Res Commun 295:428–434

Luttun A, Carmeliet G, Carmeliet P (2002b) Vascular progenitors: from biology to treatment. Trends Cardiovasc Med 12:88–96

Luttun A, Tjwa M, Moons L, Wu Y, Angelillo-Scherrer A, Liao F, Nagy JA, Hooper A, Priller J, De Klerck B et al (2002c) Revascularization of ischemic tissues by PlGF treatment, and inhibition of tumor angiogenesis, arthritis and atherosclerosis by anti-Flt1. Nat Med 8:831–840

Lyden D, Hattori K, Dias S, Costa C, Blaikie P, Butros L, Chadburn A, Heissig B, Marks W, Witte L et al (2001) Impaired recruitment of bone-marrow-derived endothelial and hematopoietic precursor cells blocks tumor angiogenesis and growth. Nat Med 7:1194–1201

Mantovani A, Allavena P, Sica A (2004) Tumour-associated macrophages as a prototypic type II polarised phagocyte population: role in tumour progression. Eur J Cancer 40:1660–1667

Mantovani A, Sozzani S, Locati M, Allavena P, Sica A (2002) Macrophage polarization: tumor-associated macrophages as a paradigm for polarized M2 mononuclear phagocytes. Trends Immunol 23: 549–555

Masson V, de la Ballina LR, Munaut C, Wielockx B, Jost M, Maillard C, Blacher S, Bajou K, Itoh T, Itohara S et al (2005) Contribution of host MMP-2 and MMP-9 to promote tumor vascularization and invasion of malignant keratinocytes. FASEB J 19:234–236

Murdoch C, Giannoudis A, Lewis CE (2004) Mechanisms regulating the recruitment of macrophages into hypoxic areas of tumors and other ischemic tissues. Blood 104:2224–2234

Natori T, Sata M, Washida M, Hirata Y, Nagai R, Makuuchi M (2002) G-CSF stimulates angiogenesis and promotes tumor growth: potential contribution of bone marrow-derived endothelial progenitor cells. Biochem Biophys Res Commun 297:1058–1061

Negus RP, Stamp GW, Hadley J, Balkwill FR (1997) Quantitative assessment of the leukocyte infiltrate in ovarian cancer and its relationship to the expression of C-C chemokines. Am J Pathol 150:1723–1734

Nolan DJ, Ciarrocchi A, Mellick AS, Jaggi JS, Bambino K, Gupta S, Heikamp E, McDevitt MR, Scheinberg DA, Benezra R, Mittal V (2007) Bone marrow-derived endothelial progenitor cells are a major determinant of nascent tumor neovascularization. Genes Dev 21:1546–1558

Nozawa H, Chiu C, Hanahan D (2006) Infiltrating neutrophils mediate the initial angiogenic switch in a mouse model of multistage carcinogenesis. Proc Natl Acad Sci U S A 103:12493–12498

Obermueller E, Vosseler S, Fusenig NE, Mueller MM (2004) Cooperative autocrine and paracrine functions of granulocyte colony-stimulating factor and granulocyte-macrophage colony-stimulating factor in the progression of skin carcinoma cells. Cancer Res 64:7801–7812

Ohno S, Ohno Y, Suzuki N, Kamei T, Koike K, Inagawa H, Kohchi C, Soma G, Inoue M (2004) Correlation of histological localization of tumor-associated macrophages with clinicopathological features in endometrial cancer. Anticancer Res 24:3335–3342

Ohno S, Suzuki N, Ohno Y, Inagawa H, Soma G, Inoue M (2003) Tumor-associated macrophages: foe or accomplice of tumors? Anticancer Res 23: 4395–4409

Orimo A, Gupta PB, Sgroi DC, Arenzana-Seisdedos F, Delaunay T, Naeem R, Carey VJ, Richardson AL, Weinberg RA (2005) Stromal fibroblasts present in invasive human breast carcinomas promote tumor growth and angiogenesis through elevated SDF-1/CXCL12 secretion. Cell 121:335–348

Papayannopoulou T (2004) Current mechanistic scenarios in hematopoietic stem/progenitor cell mobilization. Blood 103:1580–1585

Peters BA, Diaz LA, Polyak K, Meszler L, Romans K, Guinan EC, Antin JH, Myerson D, Hamilton SR, Vogelstein B et al (2005) Contribution of bone marrow-derived endothelial cells to human tumor vasculature. Nat Med 11: 261–262

Pipp F, Heil M, Issbrucker K, Ziegelhoeffer T, Martin S, van den Heuvel J, Weich H, Fernandez B, Golomb G, Carmeliet P et al (2003) VEGFR-1-selective VEGF homologue PlGF is arteriogenic: evidence for a monocyte-mediated mechanism. Circ Res 92:378–385

Polverini PJ, Leibovich SJ (1987) Effect of macrophage depletion on growth and neovascularization of hamster buccal pouch carcinomas. J Oral Pathol 16:436–441

Rafii S, Lyden D (2003) Therapeutic stem and progenitor cell transplantation for organ vascularization and regeneration. Nat Med 9:702–712

Rafii S, Lyden D, Benezra R, Hattori K, Heissig B (2002) Vascular and haematopoietic stem cells: novel targets for anti-angiogenesis therapy? Nat Rev Cancer 2:826–835

Rehman J, Li J, Orschell CM, March KL (2003) Peripheral blood "endothelial progenitor cells" are derived from monocyte/macrophages and secrete angiogenic growth factors. Circulation 107: 1164–1169

Scapini P, Morini M, Tecchio C, Minghelli S, Di Carlo E, Tanghetti E, Albini A, Lowell C, Berton G, Noonan DM, Cassatella MA (2004) CXCL1/macrophage inflammatory protein-2-induced angiogenesis in vivo is mediated by neutrophil-derived vascular endothelial growth factor-A. J Immunol 172:5034–5040

Schaider H, Oka M, Bogenrieder T, Nesbit M, Satyamoorthy K, Berking C, Matsushima K, Herlyn M (2003) Differential response of primary and metastatic melanomas to neutrophils attracted by IL-8. Int J Cancer 103:335–343

Serafini P, De Santo C, Marigo I, Cingarlini S, Dolcetti L, Gallina G, Zanovello P, Bronte V (2004) Derangement of immune responses by myeloid suppressor cells. Cancer Immunol Immunother 53: 64–72

Shaked Y, Bertolini F, Man S, Rogers MS, Cervi D, Foutz T, Rawn K, Voskas D, Dumont DJ, Ben-David Y et al (2005) Genetic heterogeneity of the vasculogenic phenotype parallels angiogenesis; Implications for cellular surrogate marker analysis of antiangiogenesis. Cancer Cell 7: 101–111

Shi Q, Rafii S, Wu MH, Wijelath ES, Yu C, Ishida A, Fujita Y, Kothari S, Mohle R, Sauvage LR et al (1998) Evidence for circulating bone marrow-derived endothelial cells. Blood 92:362–367

Shijubo N, Kojima H, Nagata M, Ohchi T, Suzuki A, Abe S, Sato N (2003) Tumor angiogenesis of non-small cell lung cancer. Microsc Res Tech 60: 186–198

Shojaei F, Wu X, Malik AK, Zhong C, Baldwin ME, Schanz S, Fuh G, Gerber HP, Ferrara N (2007a) Tumor refractoriness to anti-VEGF treatment is mediated by CD11b+Gr1+ myeloid cells. Nat Biotechnol 25:911–920

Shojaei F, Wu X, Zhong C, Yu L, Liang XH, Yao J, Blanchard D, Bais C, Peale FV, van Bruggen N et al (2007b) Bv8 regulates myeloid-cell-dependent tumour angiogenesis. Nature 450:825–831

Sica A, Schioppa T, Mantovani A, Allavena P (2006) Tumour-associated macrophages are a distinct M2 polarised population promoting tumour progression: potential targets of anti-cancer therapy. Eur J Cancer 42:717–727

Starkey JR, Crowle PK, Taubenberger S (1988) Mast-cell-deficient W/Wv mice exhibit a decreased rate of tumor angiogenesis. Int J Cancer 42:48–52

Stefanik DF, Fellows WK, Rizkalla LR, Rizkalla WM, Stefanik PP, Deleo AB, Welch WC (2001) Monoclonal antibodies to vascular endothelial growth factor (VEGF) and the VEGF receptor, FLT-1, inhibit the growth of C6 glioma in a mouse xenograft. J Neurooncol 55:91–100

Sunderkotter C, Goebeler M, Schulze-Osthoff K, Bhardwaj R, Sorg C (1991) Macrophage-derived angiogenesis factors. Pharmacol Ther 51: 195–216

Tlsty TD, Coussens LM (2006) Tumor stroma and regulation of cancer development. Annu Rev Pathol 1:119–150

Toda S, Tokuda Y, Koike N, Yonemitsu N, Watanabe K, Koike K, Fujitani N, Hiromatsu Y, Sugihara H (2000) Growth factor-expressing mast cells accumulate at the thyroid tissue-regenerative site of subacute thyroiditis. Thyroid 10:381–386

Turini ME, DuBois RN (2002) Cyclooxygenase-2: a therapeutic target. Annu Rev Med 53:35–57

Urbich C, Dimmeler S (2004) Endothelial progenitor cells: characterization and role in vascular biology. Circ Res 95:343–353

Vajkoczy P, Blum S, Lamparter M, Mailhammer R, Erber R, Engelhardt B, Vestweber D, Hatzopoulos AK (2003) Multistep nature of microvascular recruitment of ex vivo-expanded embryonic endothelial progenitor cells during tumor angiogenesis. J Exp Med 197:1755–1765

Vieweg J, Su Z, Dahm P, Kusmartsev S (2007) Reversal of tumor-mediated immunosuppression. Clin Cancer Res 13:727s–732s

Vosseler S, Mirancea N, Bohlen P, Mueller MM, Fusenig NE (2005) Angiogenesis inhibition by vascular endothelial growth factor receptor-2 blockade reduces stromal matrix metalloproteinase expression, normalizes stromal tissue, and reverts epithelial tumor phenotype in surface heterotransplants. Cancer Res 65:1294–1305

Wassmann S, Werner N, Czech T, Nickenig G (2006) Improvement of endothelial function by systemic transfusion of vascular progenitor cells. Circ Res 99:e74–e83

Yamaguchi J, Kusano KF, Masuo O, Kawamoto A, Silver M, Murasawa S, Bosch-Marce M, Masuda H, Losordo DW, Isner JM, Asahara T (2003) Stromal

11

cell-derived factor-1 effects on ex vivo expanded endothelial progenitor cell recruitment for ischemic neovascularization. Circulation 107:1322–1328

Yamamoto T, Katayama I, Nishioka K (1997) Expression of stem cell factor in basal cell carcinoma. Br J Dermatol 137:709–713

Yang L, DeBusk LM, Fukuda K, Fingleton B, Green-Jarvis B, Shyr Y, Matrisian LM, Carbone DP, Lin PC (2004) Expansion of myeloid immune suppressor Gr+CD11b+ cells in tumor-bearing host directly promotes tumor angiogenesis. Cancer Cell 6:409–421

Zitvogel L, Tesniere A, Kroemer G (2006) Cancer despite immunosurveillance: immunoselection and immunosubversion. Nat Rev Immunol 6: 715–727

Antibody-Based Vascular Tumor Targeting

12

Christoph Schliemann and Dario Neri

Abstract The inhibition of angiogenesis represents a major step toward a more selective and better-tolerated therapy of cancer. An alternative way to take advantage of a tumor's absolute dependence on a functional neovasculature is illustrated by the strategy of "antibody-based vascular tumor targeting." This technology aims at the selective delivery of bioactive molecules to the tumor site by their conjugation to a carrier antibody reactive with a tumor-associated vascular antigen. A number of high-affinity monoclonal antibodies are nowadays available which have demonstrated a remarkable ability to selectively localize to the tumor vasculature. Indeed, some of them have already progressed from preclinical animal experiments to clinical studies in patients with cancer, acting as vehicles for the site-specific pharmacodelivery of proinflammatory cytokines or radionuclides.

In this chapter, we present a selection of well-characterized markers of angiogenesis which have proven to be suitable targets for antibody-based vascular targeting approaches. Furthermore,

different transcriptomic and proteomic methodologies for the discovery of novel vascular tumor markers are described. In the last two sections, we focus on the discussion of antibody-based vascular tumor targeting strategies for imaging and therapy applications in oncology.

12.1
Concept and Definitions

Conventional pharmaceuticals currently in use for the treatment of cancer often suffer from a lack of specificity, leading to the unintentional exposure of normal tissues and – in some cases – life-threatening side effects. The development of more selective and better-tolerated cancer therapeutics is possibly one of the most important goals in modern oncology. As we have seen in the previous chapters, the inhibition of critical angiogenic pathways may represent an attractive therapeutic approach without the disadvantages of classical cytotoxic cancer therapies. Alternatively, one may prefer to target the tumoral neovasculature by the development of monoclonal antibodies, which are able to discriminate between a mature blood vessel and a tumor blood vessel, thus potentially acting as "delivery vehicles." This approach is generally termed "antibody-based vascular

D. Neri (✉)
Institute of Pharmaceutical Sciences,
Department of Chemistry and Applied Biosciences,
Swiss Federal Institute of Technology Zürich,
Wolfgang-Pauli-Strasse 10, CH-8093, Zürich,
Switzerland
e-mail: dario.neri@pharma.ethz.ch

R. Liersch et al. (eds.), *Angiogenesis Inhibition,* Recent Results in Cancer Research,
DOI: 10.1007/978-3-540-78281-0_12, © Springer Verlag Berlin Heidelberg 2010

12

tumor targeting" and involves the selective delivery of bioactive agents to the tumor site by their conjugation to an antibody specific to a tumor-associated vascular antigen. The targeting to the tumor vasculature results in increased local concentrations of the delivered compound in the tumor tissue, while minimizing side effects to healthy organs. Indeed, the favorable toxicity profile of site-specific vascular-targeted therapeutics may open new avenues in the treatment of cancer, allowing the systemic administration of highly potent and promising agents, such as interleukin-12, whose clinical application has been to date compromised by unacceptable toxicities when administered in a nontargeted fashion (Cohen 1995; Halin et al. 2002b).

In principle, ligand-based tumor targeting applications fundamentally rely on good-quality markers of pathology, which allow a clear-cut discrimination between tumor and healthy tissues. It is not surprising at first sight that most efforts in the field have been made using targets expressed on the surface of cancer cells. However, targeting of antigens on tumor cells is a complex task and associated with a number of physical and kinetic barriers such as interstitial hypertension, long diffusion distances, or antigen heterogeneity, all significantly hindering deep-tissue penetration (Heldin et al. 2004; Jain 1999). Considering these obstacles, target molecules expressed in tumor-associated blood vessels seem particularly attractive in view of their inherent accessibility for blood-borne agents, their selective, abundant and stable expression, and their wide range of therapeutic options that they allow, from the recruitment of immune effector cells to intraluminal blood coagulation. Furthermore, as angiogenesis is a common feature of virtually all malignant tumors, including hematological malignancies, a single vascular targeting compound should, in principle, be applicable to a number of different tumor entities.

In this chapter, we refer to "vascular tumor targeting" as the targeted delivery of a bioactive agent (the effector molecule, typically a cytokine, procoagulant factor, drug, radionuclide or toxin) or an imaging molecule to the tumor site using an antibody specific for a tumor-associated vascular marker (the target molecule, either expressed on the surface of endothelial cells or in the subendothelial extracellular matrix). It is of significance that there is a fundamental conceptual difference between the targeted inhibition of an angiogenesis-related signaling pathway and the concept of vascular targeting as defined here. While the first strategy aims at the inhibition of target molecules involved in the process of new vessel development, the latter takes advantage of the target molecule as an easily accessible binding site for specific ligands capable of delivering bioactive molecules to the tumor site. The difference between both concepts becomes more obvious in light of the fact that the pathophysiological function of some well-characterized target molecules, proven to be excellently suitable for vascular targeting applications, is still largely unclear and possibly redundant (e.g., the extra domains of fibronectin). Depending on the properties of the selected effector function, the main therapeutic effect of a vascular targeting compound can be primarily directed either against the tumor cells themselves (whenever a vascular targeting approach is used to improve the therapeutic index of an otherwise less specific pharmaceutical) or against the endothelial cells of the vasculature (to destroy the tumor's blood supply). An example for the first scenario would be the delivery of immunostimulatory cytokines to the tumor environment. The latter scenario is illustrated by the targeted delivery of a toxin to the tumor vascular endothelium as reported in a proof-of-principle study by Burrows and Thorpe (1993) or by the delivery of an α-particle emitting radionuclide with a near-acting range to a target on the luminal aspect of endothelial cells (Singh Jaggi et al. 2007). Of note, many effector molecules such as β-emitters exert overlapping actions against both cell types, thereby combining vascular disruption with direct cytotoxicity against tumor cells.

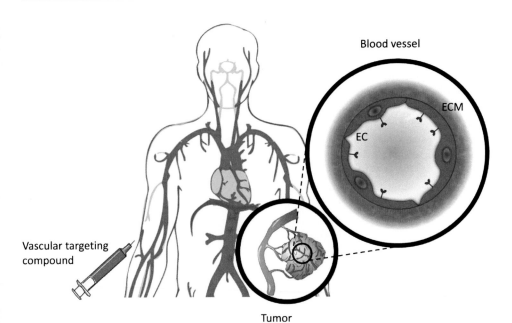

Fig. 12.1 *Concept of antibody-based vascular tumor targeting.* The vascular targeting agent, consisting of an antibody as a carrier molecule and an effector molecule, is administered systemically and homes to the tumor-specific vascular antigen, leading to the accumulation of the delivered pharmaceutical at the tumor site. As shown in the close-up, vascular antigens can be expressed on the luminal aspect of vascular endothelial cells (EC) or in the subendothelial extracellular matrix (ECM)

The general concept of antibody-based vascular tumor targeting is illustrated in Fig. 12.1.

12.2
Discovery of Novel Vascular Targets

Until recently, most efforts for the identification of novel tumor-associated vascular antigens were based on the study of in vitro cultures of endothelial cells, exposed to culture conditions which would mimic cell proliferation or quiescence. Another popular strategy has been to use endothelial cultures for the generation of antibodies either by immunization or phage display approaches. Major advances have arisen in the last years with the accessibility of full genome transcriptomic technologies, in particular, serial analyzes of gene expression (SAGE) in combination with bioinformatics, and, more recently, with perfusion-based proteomic technologies.

- The SAGE approach is based on the serial sequencing of short tags that are unique to each and every gene. These gene-specific tags are produced by a series of molecular biological manipulations and concatenated for automated sequencing. St. Croix and colleagues constructed SAGE libraries using isolated endothelial cells derived from normal and tumoral tissues and identified a number of genes that were specifically upregulated in the tumor endothelium, leading to the identification of several novel tumor endothelial markers (TEMs) (St Croix et al. 2000; Velculescu et al. 1995). Since target accessibility from the bloodstream is of fundamental

12

importance for vascular targeting approaches, further work has focused on those genes that encode proteins with predicted transmembrane domains. In a recent analysis, a SAGE approach revealed differences in gene expression patterns in endothelial cells derived from physiological and pathological angiogenic events (Seaman et al. 2007). Interestingly, 13 transcripts were identified in tumor-derived endothelial cells that were undetectable in the angiogenic endothelium of normal, regenerating tissue. One of the most promising tumor-specific endothelial markers was CD276.

- The increasing availability of transcriptome databanks has facilitated the *in silico* search for novel endothelial cell-specific tumor markers by comparative bioinformatics. One such approach applied a subtractive algorithm to the sequence tag expression data available in public databases and identified magic roundabout (Robo4) and an endothelial-specific protein disulfide isomerase (EndoPDI) as potential TEMs (Huminiecki and Bicknell 2000).

In general, transcriptomic analyzes are able to provide precise information on the quality and quantity of messenger RNAs that are expressed in the cell types and tissues of interest. However, a subsequent validation of the findings is of particular importance, since endothelium-associated targets identified in transcriptomic analyzes are not necessarily equally expressed at the protein level and surface-accessible for targeting agents. Thus, the most direct way to identify novel vascular antigens would involve the in vivo labeling of vascular structures, followed by the isolation and comparative proteomic analysis of proteins.

- Schnitzer and coworkers have demonstrated the use of colloidal silica for the in vivo coating of the vasculature, allowing the isolation of silica-coated luminal endothelial plasma membranes by subcellular fractionation, which are then analyzed by two-dimensional gel electrophoresis or multidimensional mass spectrometry techniques to produce high-resolution protein maps (Durr et al. 2004; Jacobson et al. 1992; Oh et al. 2004). Differential spot analysis, mass spectrometry of tryptic peptides, database searching and immunoblotting then allow the characterization of differentially expressed proteins. As an example, annexin A1 was found to be preferentially expressed on the surface of tumor-endothelial cells and was demonstrated to be suitable marker for antibody-based targeting applications (see below).

- More recently, a technology for the in vivo chemical labeling of vascular proteins based on the terminal perfusion of tumor-bearing animals with reactive derivatives of biotin has been described (Roesli et al. 2006; Rybak et al. 2005). This approach allows the biotinylation of proteins on the surface of endothelial cells or in the vessel-associated subendothelial matrix, which are readily accessible from the bloodstream. The purification of biotinylated proteins on a streptavidin column and comparative proteomic analyses based on LC-MS/MS methodologies subsequently permit the identification of hundreds of accessible vascular proteins and are able to reveal both quantitative and qualitative differences in the recovery of biotinylated antigens between the tumor and normal organs. Recently, this approach has been extended to the ex vivo perfusion of surgically resected human organs with tumors. The biotinylation of resected human kidneys bearing renal cell carcinomas led to the identification of a total of 637 proteins, 184 of which were exclusively expressed in the tumor vasculature, such as isoforms of periostin, versican, annexin A4 or MG50 (Castronovo et al. 2006).

12.3
Validated Markers of the Tumor Vasculature

In principle, vascular antigens can be either expressed on the surface of endothelial cells or in the subendothelial extracellular matrix (ECM)

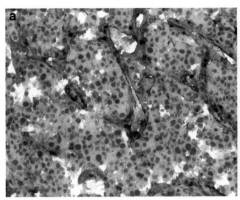
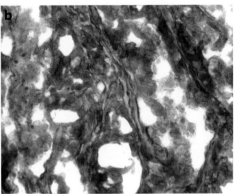

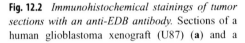

Fig. 12.2 *Immunohistochemical stainings of tumor sections with an anti-EDB antibody.* Sections of a human glioblastoma xenograft (U87) (**a**) and a human colorectal carcinoma (**b**) were stained with L19. Expression of extra domain B (EDB) fibronectin clearly associates with tumor vascular structures

of tumor blood vessels. The intuitive impression that antigens expressed on the luminal aspect of endothelial cells may be superior for targeting applications may not be valid in general. Indeed, luminal markers are easily reached from the circulation, but may carry the disadvantage of a relatively low abundance, precluding the accumulation of large quantities of the vascular targeting compound. In contrast, antigens expressed in the remodeled perivascular matrix offer the convenience of a typically more abundant and stable expression. Although they might seem less accessible, extravasation enables the ligand to bind to its antigen. In this section, we will discuss a selection of well-characterized targets of the tumor vasculature.

12.3.1
Extra Domains of Fibronectin

The extra domain B (EDB) is a type III homology domain of fibronectin which is not present in the fibronectin molecule under physiological, quiescent conditions but becomes inserted during tissue remodeling and angiogenesis by alternative splicing (Zardi et al. 1987). EDB fibronectin is virtually absent in normal adult tissues (exception made for the endometrium in

the proliferative phase and some vessels in the ovary), but is highly abundant in the subendothelial matrix of the neovasculature of many aggressive tumors (Fig. 12.2) (Birchler et al. 2003; Carnemolla et al. 1989; Castellani et al. 1994; Khan et al. 2005). The EDB sequence is completely identical in mouse, rat, rabbit, monkey and man. This feature facilitates animal experiments in immunocompetent syngeneic settings, but has, so far, prevented the generation of antibodies using hybridoma technology. However, synthetic human antibody phage libraries have allowed the isolation of specific EDB-antibodies (Carnemolla et al. 1996; Neri et al. 1997). These include the high-affinity antibody L19, which has been shown to efficiently localize to tumor-associated angiogenic blood vessels in various animal models (Borsi et al. 2002; Tarli et al. 1999) and in patients with cancer (Birchler et al. 2007; Santimaria et al. 2003). Among more than 30 L19-based fusion proteins that have been developed and investigated in animal models, L19 fused to interleukin-2 (L19-IL2), L19 fused to tumor necrosis factor (L19-TNF) and L19 in small immunoprotein format (SIP) labeled with ^{131}I are three therapeutic derivatives of the L19 antibody that have moved to clinical trials in patients with different types of cancer (Menrad and Menssen 2005).

Recently, the extra domain A (EDA) of fibronectin has been identified as a marker of primary tumors and metastatic lesions using a combination of in vivo vascular biotinylation and mass spectrometry (Rybak et al. 2007a). The human monoclonal antibody F8, directed against EDA, exhibited an impressive preferential localization at the tumor site, comparable to the targeting performance of L19 in the tumor models and antibody formats analyzed so far (Villa et al. 2008). Further comparative studies will assess which fibronectin antibody is the best suited targeting agent for a given tumor type, based on antigen expression data and quantitative biodistribution analyses.

12.3.2
Large Isoforms of Tenascin C

Tenascin C is a high molecular mass glycoprotein of the extracellular matrix. Alternative splicing generates several isoforms by insertion of additional domains (Siri et al. 1991). Although not completely absent from normal tissues, these large isoforms of tenascin C exhibit a more restricted pattern of expression as compared to the isoforms without extra domains (Borsi et al. 1992). Radiolabeled derivatives of monoclonal antibodies specific to the domains A1 and D have been used for imaging and radioimmunotherapy in patients with cancer for over a decade (Paganelli et al. 1999; Reardon et al. 2006; Riva et al. 1999). Among all domains, the C domain of tenascin C features the most restricted expression: while being essentially undetectable in normal human tissues, it is highly abundant in high grade astrocytomas and lung cancer. The tumor-targeting performance of the human high-affinity antibody G11, specific to the domain C of tenascin C, has been demonstrated in an orthotopic rat glioma model (Silacci et al. 2006). Similarly, the recently described human monoclonal antibody F16, specific to the domain A1 of tenascin C, exhibited an excellent tumor-targeting performance in

quantitative biodistribution experiments (Brack et al. 2006). A F16-based immunocytokine ("F16-IL2") has entered clinical trials for the treatment of metastatic breast, ovarian and lung cancer in combination with chemotherapy.

12.3.3
Phosphatidylserine

Phosphatidylserine (PS), an anionic phospholipid, is an essential component of the cell membrane, which is preferentially found in the inner leaflet of the lipid bilayer under normal conditions. Under conditions such as cellular stress, apoptosis, and proliferation, PS becomes exposed on the outer surface of the plasma membrane of angiogenic endothelial cells, rendering it accessible for targeting agents (Ran et al. 2002). Targeting experiments using monoclonal antibodies specific to PS have confirmed the accessibility of the antigen on the external surface of vascular endothelial cells in tumors (Ran et al. 2002, 2005). The PS-antibody 3G4 has been shown to exhibit potent single-agent activity as a naked antibody (by antibody-dependent cellular cytotoxicity against endothelial cells) (Ran et al. 2005) and to enhance the efficacy of chemotherapy in rodent models of cancer (Huang et al. 2005). Recently, the plasma protein β-2-glycoprotein 1, a member of the complement control protein family, has been identified as a critical cofactor mediating the interaction between 3G4 and surface-exposed PS (Luster et al. 2006). A chimeric version of 3G4, Bavituximab, is currently being investigated in Phase II clinical studies (Peregrine Pharmaceuticals, Inc.).

12.3.4
Annexin A1

Annexins are cytosolic proteins that can associate with plasma membranes in a calcium-dependent manner. Some annexins translocate the lipid bilayer to the outer cell surface. Using the methodology described above, Schnitzer and coworkers discovered annexin A1 as a target for vascular targeting applications (Oh et al. 2004). A monoclonal antibody to this antigen has been successfully used for the radioimmunoscintigraphic detection of solid tumors in a rat model. Furthermore, relatively low doses of the antibody labeled with ^{125}I (50 μCi as a single injection) showed therapeutic efficacy in the same animal model.

12.3.5
Prostate-Specific Membrane Antigen (PSMA)

PSMA, a membrane glycoprotein with proteolytic activity, has been originally found to be overexpressed in prostate cancer. However, several studies have documented that PSMA is also expressed in the neovasculature of several solid tumors (Chang et al. 1999; Liu et al. 1997; Silver et al. 1997), whereas its expression in healthy tissues appears to be restricted to prostatic, duodenal and breast epithelium and renal tubules. Of particular importance for vascular targeting strategies, it is virtually absent in normal blood vessels. The monoclonal-PSMA antibody J591 labeled with different radionuclides has demonstrated promising targeting efficacy in patients not only with prostate cancer but also with solid tumors in general (Bander et al. 2005; Milowsky et al. 2007; Morris et al. 2007).

12.3.6
Endoglin

Endoglin (CD105) is a homodimeric transmembrane glycoprotein which is overexpressed in neovascular endothelial cells of various solid tumors (Burrows et al. 1995; Wang et al. 1993). Although immunohistochemical studies revealed that endoglin is also significantly

detectable in normal organs (Balza et al. 2001; Minhajat et al. 2006), monoclonal anti-endoglin antibodies have been used in biodistribution studies and for imaging and therapy purposes in rodent and dog models of cancer (Bredow et al. 2000; Fonsatti et al. 2000; Korpanty et al. 2007; Matsuno et al. 1999).

12.3.7
Integrins

Integrins represent a class of cell-surface proteins which are critically involved in endothelial cell adhesion to the ECM or cellular receptor proteins. Due to their significant involvement in angiogenesis events, integrins have gained significant attention as targets for the pharmacological inhibition of angiogenesis (for details see Chap. 6).

In addition, integrins have been proposed as targets for the ligand-based delivery of therapeutic agents to the tumoral neovasculature. A murine antibody specific to the integrin $\alpha_v\beta_3$ (LM609), selectively labeled neovessels in a breast cancer model and was shown to localize at the tumor site in a magnetic resonance imaging setup in rabbits (Sipkins et al. 1998). A humanized and affinity-matured version of LM609, the high-affinity antibody Abegrin (Medi-522, MedImmune, Inc.), has completed Phase II clinical trials as an antiangiogenic agent (McNeel et al. 2005; Mulgrew et al. 2006). However, when used as a ligand for antibody-based targeting applications, only moderate targeting results have been observed using ^{64}Cu-labeled Abegrin in quantitative biodistribution experiments in an orthotopic mouse model of human breast cancer (Cai et al. 2006). As an alternative ligand for α_v integrins, the peptide RGD has been isolated by in vivo phage display (Pasqualini et al. 1997) and a variety of RGD derivatives have been evaluated both for imaging and therapy applications (Temming et al. 2005).

12.3.8
Vascular Endothelial Growth Factors (VEGFs) and Receptors

As key mediators in the regulation of pathological angiogenesis, VEGFs have been successfully exploited for antiangiogenesis approaches. In addition, the VEGF/VEGFR signaling system is also being recognized as a potential target for vascular targeting approaches. The in vivo localization of monoclonal antibodies to VEGF-A, VEGF receptor 2, and the VEGF/VEGFR-2 complex has been studied. However, the absolute amounts of antibodies accumulating at the tumor site were often only modest, which possibly reflects kinetic limitations in the targeting of antigens of low abundance, even though they are easily accessible from the bloodstream (Cooke et al. 2001; Jayson et al. 2002; Stollman et al. 2008). Interestingly, in a very recent study using radiolabeled preparations of the anti-VEGF monoclonal antibody bevacizumab, an inverse correlation between the administered dose of radiolabeled antibody and the tumor targeting performance was observed (Stollman et al. 2008). The highest tumor uptake (as expressed in percent injected dose per gram of tissue) and the highest tumor-to-blood ratios were observed at protein doses as low as 1–3 µg (20–25% ID/g), while at doses exceeding 100 µg the absolute tumor uptake was lower than 3% ID/g.

12.3.9
Nucleolin

Porkka and coworkers discovered a synthetic 31-amino acid peptide (F3) which may be suitable for the targeted delivery of therapeutic effector molecules into tumors, because it is internalized into tumor-associated endothelial cells and tumor cells upon binding to the cell surface (Porkka et al. 2002). Later, the receptor protein which is recognized by F3 was identified as nucleolin. Originally described as a nuclear protein involved in the regulation of cell proliferation and nucleogenesis, nucleolin is also expressed on the surface of proliferating endothelial cells but restricted to the nucleus in resting endothelium (Christian et al. 2003). However, although nucleolin seems to feature a restricted expression pattern and the ability to internalize binding molecules, quantitative biodistribution studies using antibodies specific to nucleolin have not been reported yet.

12.4
Vascular Tumor Targeting: Imaging Applications

As we have seen in the previous sections, a number of high-affinity monoclonal antibodies are nowadays available, which selectively localize to angiogenic blood vessels upon systemic administration and allow a clear-cut discrimination between proliferating and quiescent vasculature. In principle, these antibodies may represent valuable tools for the macroscopic imaging of active angiogenesis in vivo, not only for the diagnosis and staging of cancer but also for monitoring response to therapy, especially with angiogenesis inhibitors. From a theoretical point of view, two essential requirements for the successful visualization of a ligand homing to neovascular structures are necessary:

- a suitable chemical modification strategy which makes the ligand visible for the corresponding physical detection system;
- a target molecule which is abundant enough to compensate the small contribution of the vasculature to the overall tumor mass.

In practice, the ability of radiolabeled antibodies to image tumors in vivo using SPECT or PET or methodologies is very well established (Verel et al. 2005). Furthermore, antibodies conjugated with near-infrared fluorophores have been shown to be suitable for in vivo and ex vivo photodetection procedures in both animal models and patients with cancer (Bremer et al. 2003; Neri et al. 1997; Pelegrin et al. 1991). However, while yielding high resolutions in the detection of superficial lesions and transparent structures of the body (e.g., for angiogenesis-related ocular disorders), fluorescence-based imaging techniques are limited in the detection of deeper lesions, even when diffuse optical tomography procedures are used. In both cases, the antibody label (a radionuclide or a fluorophore) is relatively small and does not significantly influence the pharmacokinetic properties of the antibody. As long as antigens expressed on the luminal aspect of endothelial serve as targets, also larger structures such as microbubbles or paramagnetic nanoparticles for contrast-enhanced ultrasound or MRI imaging can be used for in vivo molecular imaging (Korpanty et al. 2007; Sipkins et al. 1998). However, it is not obvious at the time whether antibodies equipped with microbubbles, magnetic nanoparticles or luminescent quantum dots can efficiently bind to targets "behind" the endothelial cell layer, particularly in light of experiences of our group suggesting that antibody derivatives >250 kDa or with extreme pI values lose their tumor targeting ability in vivo, while retaining the antigen binding properties of the parental antibody in vitro (Halin et al. 2002a, 2003; Melkko et al. 2002; Niesner et al. 2002). In contrast to our observations, anti-PSMA antibodies labeled with encapsulated quantum dots have been suggested as suitable compounds for the direct in vivo imaging of PSMA-positive prostate cancer cells (Gao et al. 2004). In this study, the accumulation of antibody-quantum dot conjugates at the tumor site was primarily attributed to the active targeting of cancer cells. However, as no convincing microscopic analyzes have been reported that the conjugate was able to extravasate and reach the tumor cells in vivo, the expression of PSMA on vascular endothelial cells (see above) may have contributed to the

promising targeting performance as seen in the macroscopic imaging experiments. Thus, the issue remains controversial and it may well be possible that vascular-targeted imaging applications based on larger antibody labels may only be feasible with antibodies specific to antigens which are expressed on the inner surface of vascular structures.

12.5
Vascular Tumor Targeting: Therapeutic Applications

The selective localization of a targeting agent onto neovascular structures at the site of disease is an essential feature for the development of superior biopharmaceuticals, but it does not elicit a therapeutic response *per se*. Most often, ligands need to be coupled to suitable bioactive molecules, in order to mediate a therapeutic action. Before discussing the various therapeutic strategies which have been conceived and implemented experimentally over the years, it is useful to consider a few pharmacokinetic aspects related to vascular targeting.

After intravenous injection, a vascular targeting antibody (or antibody derivative) rapidly distributes in the body, while mainly remaining confined to vascular structures. The rates of elimination from blood greatly differ among the various molecular formats which can be considered. Two extreme cases may be represented by full immunoglobulins in IgG formats (which may remain in circulation for several weeks) and by the small scFv antibody fragments (for which the alpha phase accounts for over 95% of the biphasic clearance profile, with a typical half-life of 15–20 min) (Borsi et al. 2002). Similarly, clearance routes highly depend on the molecular features of the vascular targeting agent. While antibody derivatives with size below 60 kDa are rapidly filtered through the kidneys, larger antibody derivatives are typically eliminated via the hepatobiliary route. Also intact IgGs, which display long serum half-lives as a result of FcRn-mediated recirculation properties, are eventually cleared via the liver. Similar long circulatory half-lives can be obtained by PEG-modification of biopharmaceuticals, by their covalent fusion with serum albumin, or by a suitable modification with albumin-binding molecules (Dennis et al. 2007; Dumelin et al. 2008). For good quality tumor-associated vascular targets, high-affinity antibody derivatives display increasingly favorable tumor-to-blood and tumor-to-organ ratios at later time points after injection (Neri and Bicknell 2005). These ratios may be greater at early time points for small biopharmaceuticals, but the absolute amount delivered to tumoral lesions is typically larger for biopharmaceuticals which display longer circulatory half-lives (Adams et al. 2006; Borsi et al. 2002; Wu and Senter 2005). These considerations

should not be forgotten when planning a therapeutic strategy. Certain antibody derivatives start mediating toxic events immediately after injection (e.g., radiolabeled antibodies) when the biopharmaceutical has distributed to all tissues, and only gradually gain in selectivity, as the agent clears from all organs except tumors. By contrast, other strategies appear to be ideally suited for matching the slow build-up of a preferential antibody accumulation at the tumor site. For example, antibody-drug conjugates with suitable cleavable linkers may continue releasing the drug at the tumor site for a long time period, while most of the biopharmaceutical has cleared from blood and normal tissues. In most cases, special care will have to be devoted to the minimization of the toxic effects to the organs responsible for clearance (e.g., liver or kidney).

Figure 12.3 summarizes some of the antibody modification strategies which have been

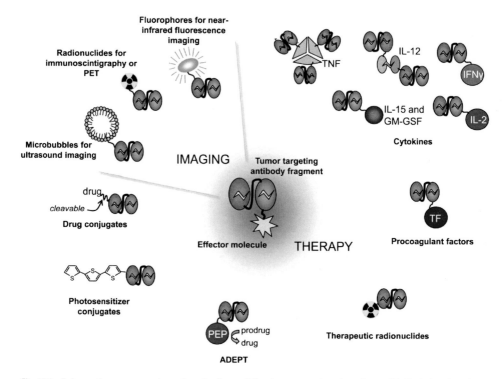

Fig. 12.3 *Schematic representation of antibody modification strategies.* A variety of L19-derivatives have been produced and investigated in animal models of cancer and clinical studies

considered for the development of targeted bio-pharmaceuticals. Many of these strategies have been experimentally implemented with the L19 antibody, specific to the EDB domain of fibronectin, thus allowing a direct comparison of the relative advantages and drawbacks of the different strategies. Such strategies are descri-bed in detail elsewhere (Rybak et al. 2007b; Schliemann and Neri 2007) and will only be briefly analyzed here.

Radiolabeled antibodies for cancer radioim-munotherapy represent a class of therapeutic agents of special interest, in light of the fact that their performance can be predicted on the basis of biodistribution and/or imaging data. It is generally believed that solid tumors may be cured if they receive a radiation dose of at least 50 Gy delivered by the radionuclide ^{131}I, while the bone marrow can tolerate at most 2.5 Gy. A systematic analysis of various antibody for-mats revealed that mini-antibodies are ideally suited for radioimmunotherapeutic applications (Berndorff et al. 2005; Hu et al. 1996; Tijink et al. 2006). By contrast, smaller fragments (e.g., scFv fragments) are rapidly cleared via the renal route and deliver excessive radiation doses to the kidneys, while the performance of radiola-beled IgG is often suboptimal, due to their long circulation time in the blood. The L19 antibody, in mini-antibody format and labeled with ^{131}I, is currently being investigated in Phase I/II clini-cal trials for the radioimmunotherapy of cancer. In animal models, this agent has shown a thera-peutic activity both in monotherapy and in com-bination with Erbitux (Tijink et al. 2006).

Immunocytokines represent a second class of considerable therapeutic potential. The targeted delivery of certain proinflammatory cytokines (e.g., IL-2, TNF, IL-12, IL-15, GM-CSF) has been shown to mediate superior therapeutic effects compared to the nontargeted version of the same cytokine (Borsi et al. 2003; Carnemolla et al. 2002; Ebbinghaus et al. 2005; Halin et al. 2002b, 2003; Kaspar et al. 2007). Indeed, L19-IL2 and L19-TNF are currently being investigated in clinical trials in patients with

cancer. It is worth mentioning that, upon fusion to certain cytokines or growth factors, vascular targeting antibodies may display a reduced tumor uptake. For example, fusion to interferon-γ was shown to reduce the tumor targeting per-formance of the L19 antibody. However, the tumor targeting potential could be restored in mice in which the interferon-γ receptor had been knocked out (Ebbinghaus et al. 2005). Similarly, fusion of the L19 antibody to murine VEGF-164 (but not VEGF-120) or to other highly charged polypeptides abrogates tumor targeting (Halin et al. 2002a; Melkko et al. 2002; Niesner et al. 2002). While our group has always preferred to construct immunocytokines by sequential gene fusion with scFv fragments, other groups have favored to append cytokines at the C-terminal end of antibodies in IgG format (Dela Cruz et al. 2004; Schrama et al. 2006).

A third class of therapeutic antibody deriva-tives of particular interest is represented by anti-body-drug conjugates with cleavable linkers (Chari 2008; Doronina et al. 2003). Most groups have so far used this technology with antibodies capable of selective internalization on tumor cells, but it would be conceivable to deliver potent drugs to the tumor neovasculature by means of antibodies which remain in the extra-cellular space and slowly release a drug as a con-sequence of hydrolytic processes. Considering the difference in molecular weight between anti-bodies and cytotoxic drugs, the availability of chemotherapeutic agents which are active at nano- or picomolar concentration and which can be coupled to antibodies will greatly facilitate progress in this area, thus leading to a new gen-eration of armed monoclonal antibodies.

Finally, it is worth mentioning that intact IgGs continue to represent an important segment of pharmaceutical biotechnology. In general, they display a low toxicity profile which makes them ideally suited for combination therapy. It is becoming increasingly clear that even IgGs spe-cific to tumor cell antigens are often confined to the perivascular space, as a result of the high interstitial pressure in the tumor environment

12

and of capture by antigen in stoichiometric excess immediately after extravasation (Adams et al. 2001; Dennis et al. 2007). Modern research in protein engineering aims at potentiating the IgG-mediated cytotoxic activity (ADCC) by increasing the affinity between the antibody Fc portion and the corresponding FcγRIII receptor, either by glycosylation engineering (Umana et al. 1999) or by introducing mutations in the Fc fragment (Lazar et al. 2006).

Acknowledgments Financial support from the Swiss National Science Foundation, the Gebert-Ruef Foundation, the Schweizer Krebsliga, the ETH Zurich and the European Union projects STROMA, FLUORMMPI and IMMUNOPDT is gratefully acknowledged. C.S. is recipient of a postdoctoral scholarship from the Deutsche Krebshilfe.

References

Adams GP, Schier R, McCall AM, Simmons HH, Horak EM, Alpaugh RK, Marks JD, Weiner LM (2001) High affinity restricts the localization and tumor penetration of single-chain fv antibody molecules. Cancer Res 61:4750–4755

Adams GP, Tai MS, McCartney JE, Marks JD, Stafford WF 3rd, Houston LL, Huston JS, Weiner LM (2006) Avidity-mediated enhancement of in vivo tumor targeting by single-chain Fv dimers. Clin Cancer Res 12:1599–1605

Balza E, Castellani P, Zijlstra A, Neri D, Zardi L, Siri A (2001) Lack of specificity of endoglin expression for tumor blood vessels. Int J Cancer 94:579–585

Bander NH, Milowsky MI, Nanus DM, Kostakoglu L, Vallabhajosula S, Goldsmith SJ (2005) Phase I trial of 177lutetium-labeled J591, a monoclonal antibody to prostate-specific membrane antigen, in patients with androgen-independent prostate cancer. J Clin Oncol 23:4591–4601

Berndorff D, Borkowski S, Sieger S, Rother A, Friebe M, Viti F, Hilger CS, Cyr JE, Dinkelborg LM (2005) Radioimmunotherapy of solid tumors by targeting extra domain B fibronectin: identification of the best-suited radioimmunoconjugate. Clin Cancer Res 11:7053s–7063s

Birchler MT, Milisavljevic D, Pfaltz M, Neri D, Odermatt B, Schmid S, Stoeckli SJ (2003)

Expression of the extra domain B of fibronectin, a marker of angiogenesis, in head and neck tumors. Laryngoscope 113:1231–1237

Birchler MT, Thuerl C, Schmid D, Neri D, Waibel R, Schubiger A, Stoeckli SJ, Schmid S, Goerres GW (2007) Immunoscintigraphy of patients with head and neck carcinomas, with an anti-angiogenetic antibody fragment. Otolaryngol Head Neck Surg 136:543–548

Borsi L, Carnemolla B, Nicolo G, Spina B, Tanara G, Zardi L (1992) Expression of different tenascin isoforms in normal, hyperplastic and neoplastic human breast tissues. Int J Cancer 52:688–692

Borsi L, Balza E, Bestagno M, Castellani P, Carnemolla B, Biro A, Leprini A, Sepulveda J, Burrone O, Neri D, Zardi L (2002) Selective targeting of tumoral vasculature: comparison of different formats of an antibody (L19) to the ED-B domain of fibronectin. Int J Cancer 102: 75–85

Borsi L, Balza E, Carnemolla B, Sassi F, Castellani P, Berndt A, Kosmehl H, Biro A, Siri A, Orecchia P, Grassi J, Neri D, Zardi L (2003) Selective targeted delivery of TNFalpha to tumor blood vessels. Blood 102:4384–4392

Brack SS, Silacci M, Birchler M, Neri D (2006) Tumor-targeting properties of novel antibodies specific to the large isoform of tenascin-C. Clin Cancer Res 12:3200–3208

Bredow S, Lewin M, Hofmann B, Marecos E, Weissleder R (2000) Imaging of tumour neovasculature by targeting the TGF-beta binding receptor endoglin. Eur J Cancer 36:675–681

Bremer C, Ntziachristos V, Weissleder R (2003) Optical-based molecular imaging: contrast agents and potential medical applications. Eur Radiol 13:231–243

Burrows FJ, Thorpe PE (1993) Eradication of large solid tumors in mice with an immunotoxin directed against tumor vasculature. Proc Natl Acad Sci USA 90:8996–9000

Burrows FJ, Derbyshire EJ, Tazzari PL, Amlot P, Gazdar AF, King SW, Letarte M, Vitetta ES, Thorpe PE (1995) Up-regulation of endoglin on vascular endothelial cells in human solid tumors: implications for diagnosis and therapy. Clin Cancer Res 1:1623–1634

Cai W, Wu Y, Chen K, Cao Q, Tice DA, Chen X (2006) In vitro and in vivo characterization of 64cu-labeled abegrintm, a humanized monoclonal antibody against integrin {alpha}v{beta}3. Cancer Res 66:9673–9681

Carnemolla B, Balza E, Siri A, Zardi L, Nicotra MR, Bigotti A, Natali PG (1989) A tumor-associated fibronectin isoform generated by alternative splicing of messenger RNA precursors. J Cell Biol 108:1139–1148

Carnemolla B, Neri D, Castellani P, Leprini A, Neri G, Pini A, Winter G, Zardi L (1996) Phage antibodies with pan-species recognition of the oncofoetal angiogenesis marker fibronectin ED-B domain. Int J Cancer 68:397–405

Carnemolla B, Borsi L, Balza E, Castellani P, Meazza R, Berndt A, Ferrini S, Kosmehl H, Neri D, Zardi L (2002) Enhancement of the antitumor properties of interleukin-2 by its targeted delivery to the tumor blood vessel extracellular matrix. Blood 99:1659–1665

Castellani P, Viale G, Dorcaratto A, Nicolo G, Kaczmarek J, Querze G, Zardi L (1994) The fibronectin isoform containing the ED-B oncofetal domain: a marker of angiogenesis. Int J Cancer 59:612–618

Castronovo V, Waltregny D, Kischel P, Roesli C, Elia G, Rybak JN, Neri D (2006) A chemical proteomics approach for the identification of accessible antigens expressed in human kidney cancer. Mol Cell Proteomics 5:2083–2091

Chang SS, O'Keefe DS, Bacich DJ, Reuter VE, Heston WD, Gaudin PB (1999) Prostate-specific membrane antigen is produced in tumor-associated neovasculature. Clin Cancer Res 5: 2674–2681

Chari RV (2008) Targeted cancer therapy: conferring specificity to cytotoxic drugs. Acc Chem Res 41:98–107

Christian S, Pilch J, Akerman ME, Porkka K, Laakkonen P, Ruoslahti E (2003) Nucleolin expressed at the cell surface is a marker of endothelial cells in angiogenic blood vessels. J Cell Biol 163:871–878

Cohen J (1995) IL-12 deaths: explanation and a puzzle. Science 270:908

Cooke SP, Boxer GM, Lawrence L, Pedley RB, Spencer DI, Begent RH, Chester KA (2001) A strategy for antitumor vascular therapy by targeting the vascular endothelial growth factor: receptor complex. Cancer Res 61:3653–3659

Dela Cruz JS, Huang TH, Penichet ML, Morrison SL (2004) Antibody-cytokine fusion proteins: innovative weapons in the war against cancer. Clin Exp Med 4:57–64

Dennis MS, Jin H, Dugger D, Yang R, McFarland L, Ogasawara A, Williams S, Cole MJ, Ross S, Schwall R (2007) Imaging tumors with an albumin-binding Fab, a novel tumor-targeting agent. Cancer Res 67:254–261

Doronina SO, Toki BE, Torgov MY, Mendelsohn BA, Cerveny CG, Chace DF, DeBlanc RL, Gearing RP, Bovee TD, Siegall CB, Francisco JA, Wahl AF, Meyer DL, Senter PD (2003) Development of potent monoclonal antibody auristatin conjugates for cancer therapy. Nat Biotechnol 21:778–784

Dumelin CE, Trüssel S, Buller F, Trachsel E, Bootz F, Zhang Y, Manocci L, Beck SC, Drumea-Mirancea M, Seeliger MWP, Baltes C, Müggler TP, Kranz FP, Rudin MP, Melkko S, Scheuermann JP, Neri D (2008) Discovery and applications of a portable albumin binder from a DNA-encoded chemical library. Angew Chem Int Ed Eng 47(17):3196–3201

Durr E, Yu J, Krasinska KM, Carver LA, Yates JR, Testa JE, Oh P, Schnitzer JE (2004) Direct proteomic mapping of the lung microvascular endothelial cell surface in vivo and in cell culture. Nat Biotechnol 22:985–992

Ebbinghaus C, Ronca R, Kaspar M, Grabulovski D, Berndt A, Kosmehl H, Zardi L, Neri D (2005) Engineered vascular-targeting antibody-interferon-gamma fusion protein for cancer therapy. Int J Cancer 116:304–313

Fonsatti E, Jekunen AP, Kairemo KJ, Coral S, Snellman M, Nicotra MR, Natali PG, Altomonte M, Maio M (2000) Endoglin is a suitable target for efficient imaging of solid tumors: in vivo evidence in a canine mammary carcinoma model. Clin Cancer Res 6:2037–2043

Gao X, Cui Y, Levenson RM, Chung LW, Nie S (2004) In vivo cancer targeting and imaging with semiconductor quantum dots. Nat Biotechnol 22:969–976

Halin C, Niesner U, Villani ME, Zardi L, Neri D (2002a) Tumor-targeting properties of antibody-vascular endothelial growth factor fusion proteins. Int J Cancer 102:109–116

Halin C, Rondini S, Nilsson F, Berndt A, Kosmehl H, Zardi L, Neri D (2002b) Enhancement of the antitumor activity of interleukin-12 by targeted delivery to neovasculature. Nat Biotechnol 20:264–269

Halin C, Gafner V, Villani ME, Borsi L, Berndt A, Kosmehl H, Zardi L, Neri D (2003) Synergistic therapeutic effects of a tumor targeting antibody fragment, fused to interleukin 12 and to tumor necrosis factor alpha. Cancer Res 63: 3202–3210

Heldin CH, Rubin K, Pietras K, Ostman A (2004) High interstitial fluid pressure - an obstacle in cancer therapy. Nat Rev Cancer 4:806–813

Hu S, Shively L, Raubitschek A, Sherman M, Williams LE, Wong JY, Shively JE, Wu AM (1996) Minibody: A novel engineered anti-carcinoembryonic antigen antibody fragment (single-chain Fv-CH3) which exhibits rapid, high-level targeting of xenografts. Cancer Res 56:3055–3061

Huang X, Bennett M, Thorpe PE (2005) A monoclonal antibody that binds anionic phospholipids on tumor blood vessels enhances the antitumor effect of docetaxel on human breast tumors in mice. Cancer Res 65:4408–4416

Huminiecki L, Bicknell R (2000) In silico cloning of novel endothelial-specific genes. Genome Res 10:1796–1806

Jacobson BS, Schnitzer JE, McCaffery M, Palade GE (1992) Isolation and partial characterization of the luminal plasmalemma of microvascular endothelium from rat lungs. Eur J Cell Biol 58: 296–306

Jain RK (1999) Transport of molecules, particles, and cells in solid tumors. Annu Rev Biomed Eng 1:241–263

Jayson GC, Zweit J, Jackson A, Mulatero C, Julyan P, Ranson M, Broughton L, Wagstaff J, Hakannson L, Groenewegen G, Bailey J, Smith N, Hastings D, Lawrance J, Haroon H, Ward T, McGown AT, Tang M, Levitt D, Marreaud S, Lehmann FF, Herold M, Zwierzina H (2002) Molecular imaging and biological evaluation of HuMV833 anti-VEGF antibody: implications for trial design of antiangiogenic antibodies. J Natl Cancer Inst 94: 1484–1493

Kaspar M, Trachsel E, Neri D (2007) The antibody-mediated targeted delivery of interleukin-15 and GM-CSF to the tumor neovasculature inhibits tumor growth and metastasis. Cancer Res 67: 4940–4948

Khan ZA, Caurtero J, Barbin YP, Chan BM, Uniyal S, Chakrabarti S (2005) ED-B fibronectin in non-small cell lung carcinoma. Exp Lung Res 31: 701–711

Korpanty G, Carbon JG, Grayburn PA, Fleming JB, Brekken RA (2007) Monitoring response to anti-cancer therapy by targeting microbubbles to tumor vasculature. Clin Cancer Res 13:323–330

Lazar GA, Dang W, Karki S, Vafa O, Peng JS, Hyun L, Chan C, Chung HS, Eivazi A, Yoder SC,

Vielmetter J, Carmichael DF, Hayes RJ, Dahiyat BI (2006) Engineered antibody Fc variants with enhanced effector function. Proc Natl Acad Sci USA 103:4005–4010

Liu H, Moy P, Kim S, Xia Y, Rajasekaran A, Navarro V, Knudsen B, Bander NH (1997) Monoclonal antibodies to the extracellular domain of prostate-specific membrane antigen also react with tumor vascular endothelium. Cancer Res 57:3629–3634

Luster TA, He J, Huang X, Maiti SN, Schroit AJ, de Groot PG, Thorpe PE (2006) Plasma protein beta-2-glycoprotein 1 mediates interaction between the anti-tumor monoclonal antibody 3G4 and anionic phospholipids on endothelial cells. J Biol Chem 281:29863–29871

Matsuno F, Haruta Y, Kondo M, Tsai H, Barcos M, Seon BK (1999) Induction of lasting complete regression of preformed distinct solid tumors by targeting the tumor vasculature using two new anti-endoglin monoclonal antibodies. Clin Cancer Res 5:371–382

McNeel DG, Eickhoff J, Lee FT, King DM, Alberti D, Thomas JP, Friedl A, Kolesar J, Marnocha R, Volkman J, Zhang J, Hammershaimb L, Zwiebel JA, Wilding G (2005) Phase I trial of a monoclonal antibody specific for alphavbeta3 integrin (MEDI-522) in patients with advanced malignancies, including an assessment of effect on tumor perfusion. Clin Cancer Res 11:7851–7860

Melkko S, Halin C, Borsi L, Zardi L, Neri D (2002) An antibody-calmodulin fusion protein reveals a functional dependence between macromolecular isoelectric point and tumor targeting performance. Int J Radiat Oncol Biol Phys 54: 1485–1490

Menrad A, Menssen HD (2005) ED-B fibronectin as a target for antibody-based cancer treatments. Expert Opin Ther Targets 9:491–500

Milowsky MI, Nanus DM, Kostakoglu L, Sheehan CE, Vallabhajosula S, Goldsmith SJ, Ross JS, Bander NH (2007) Vascular targeted therapy with anti-prostate-specific membrane antigen monoclonal antibody J591 in advanced solid tumors. J Clin Oncol 25:540–547

Minhajat R, Mori D, Yamasaki F, Sugita Y, Satoh T, Tokunaga O (2006) Organ-specific endoglin (CD105) expression in the angiogenesis of human cancers. Pathol Int 56:717–723

Morris MJ, Pandit-Taskar N, Divgi CR, Bender S, O'Donoghue JA, Nacca A, Smith-Jones P,

Schwartz L, Slovin S, Finn R, Larson S, Scher HI (2007) Phase I evaluation of J591 as a vascular targeting agent in progressive solid tumors. Clin Cancer Res 13:2707–2713

Mulgrew K, Kinneer K, Yao XT, Ward BK, Damschroder MM, Walsh B, Mao SY, Gao C, Kiener PA, Coats S, Kinch MS, Tice DA (2006) Direct targeting of alphavbeta3 integrin on tumor cells with a monoclonal antibody, Abegrin. Mol Cancer Ther 5:3122–3129

Neri D, Carnemolla B, Nissim A, Leprini A, Querze G, Balza E, Pini A, Tarli L, Halin C, Neri P, Zardi L, Winter G (1997) Targeting by affinity-matured recombinant antibody fragments of an angiogenesis associated fibronectin isoform. Nat Biotechnol 15:1271–1275

Neri D, Bicknell R (2005) Tumour vascular targeting. Nat Rev Cancer 5:436–446

Niesner U, Halin C, Lozzi L, Gunthert M, Neri P, Wunderli-Allenspach H, Zardi L, Neri D (2002) Quantitation of the tumor-targeting properties of antibody fragments conjugated to cell-permeating HIV-1 TAT peptides. Bioconjug Chem 13:729–736

Oh P, Li Y, Yu J, Durr E, Krasinska KM, Carver LA, Testa JE, Schnitzer JE (2004) Subtractive proteomic mapping of the endothelial surface in lung and solid tumours for tissue-specific therapy. Nature 429:629–635

Paganelli G, Grana C, Chinol M, Cremonesi M, De Cicco C, De Braud F, Robertson C, Zurrida S, Casadio C, Zoboli S, Siccardi AG, Veronesi U (1999) Antibody-guided three-step therapy for high grade glioma with yttrium-90 biotin. Eur J Nucl Med 26:348–357

Pasqualini R, Koivunen E, Ruoslahti E (1997) Alpha v integrins as receptors for tumor targeting by circulating ligands. Nat Biotechnol 15:542–546

Pelegrin A, Folli S, Buchegger F, Mach JP, Wagnieres G, van den Bergh H (1991) Antibody-fluorescein conjugates for photoimmunodiagnosis of human colon carcinoma in nude mice. Cancer 67:2529–2537

Porkka K, Laakkonen P, Hoffman JA, Bernasconi M, Ruoslahti E (2002) A fragment of the HMGN2 protein homes to the nuclei of tumor cells and tumor endothelial cells in vivo. Proc Natl Acad Sci USA 99:7444–7449

Ran S, Downes A, Thorpe PE (2002) Increased exposure of anionic phospholipids on the surface of tumor blood vessels. Cancer Res 62:6132–6140

Ran S, He J, Huang X, Soares M, Scothorn D, Thorpe PE (2005) Antitumor effects of a monoclonal antibody that binds anionic phospholipids on the surface of tumor blood vessels in mice. Clin Cancer Res 11:1551–1562

Reardon DA, Akabani G, Coleman RE, Friedman AH, Friedman HS, Herndon JE 2nd, McLendon RE, Pegram CN, Provenzale JM, Quinn JA, Rich JN, Vredenburgh JJ, Desjardins A, Gururangan S, Badruddoja M, Dowell JM, Wong TZ, Zhao XG, Zalutsky MR, Bigner DD (2006) Salvage radioimmunotherapy with murine iodine-131-labeled antitenascin monoclonal antibody 81C6 for patients with recurrent primary and metastatic malignant brain tumors: phase II study results. J Clin Oncol 24:115–122

Riva P, Franceschi G, Frattarelli M, Lazzari S, Riva N, Giuliani G, Casi M, Sarti G, Guiducci G, Giorgetti G, Gentile R, Santimaria M, Jermann E, Maeke HR (1999) Loco-regional radioimmunotherapy of high-grade malignant gliomas using specific monoclonal antibodies labeled with 90Y: a phase I study. Clin Cancer Res 5:3275s–3280s

Roesli C, Neri D, Rybak JN (2006) In vivo protein biotinylation and sample preparation for the proteomic identification of organ- and disease-specific antigens accessible from the vasculature. Nat Protoc 1:192–199

Rybak JN, Ettorre A, Kaissling B, Giavazzi R, Neri D, Elia G (2005) In vivo protein biotinylation for identification of organ-specific antigens accessible from the vasculature. Nat Methods 2:291–298

Rybak JN, Roesli C, Kaspar M, Villa A, Neri D (2007a) The extra-domain A of fibronectin is a vascular marker of solid tumors and metastases. Cancer Res 67:10948–10957

Rybak JN, Trachsel E, Scheuermann J, Neri D (2007b) Ligand-based vascular targeting of disease. ChemMedChem 2:22–40

Santimaria M, Moscatelli G, Viale GL, Giovannoni L, Neri G, Viti F, Leprini A, Borsi L, Castellani P, Zardi L, Neri D, Riva P (2003) Immunoscintigraphic detection of the ED-B domain of fibronectin, a marker of angiogenesis, in patients with cancer. Clin Cancer Res 9:571–579

Schliemann C, Neri D (2007) Antibody-based targeting of the tumor vasculature. Biochim Biophys Acta 1776:175–192

Schrama D, Reisfeld RA, Becker JC (2006) Antibody targeted drugs as cancer therapeutics. Nat Rev Drug Discov 5:147–159

12

Seaman S, Stevens J, Yang MY, Logsdon D, Graff-Cherry C, St Croix B (2007) Genes that Distinguish Physiological and Pathological Angiogenesis. Cancer Cell 11:539–554

Silacci M, Brack SS, Spath N, Buck A, Hillinger S, Arni S, Weder W, Zardi L, Neri D (2006) Human monoclonal antibodies to domain C of tenascin-C selectively target solid tumors in vivo. Protein Eng Des Sel 19:471–478

Silver DA, Pellicer I, Fair WR, Heston WD, Cordon-Cardo C (1997) Prostate-specific membrane antigen expression in normal and malignant human tissues. Clin Cancer Res 3:81–85

Singh Jaggi J, Henke E, Seshan SV, Kappel BJ, Chattopadhyay D, May C, McDevitt MR, Nolan D, Mittal V, Benezra R, Scheinberg DA (2007) Selective alpha-particle mediated depletion of tumor vasculature with vascular normalization. PLoS ONE 2:e267

Sipkins DA, Cheresh DA, Kazemi MR, Nevin LM, Bednarski MD, Li KC (1998) Detection of tumor angiogenesis in vivo by alphaVbeta3-targeted magnetic resonance imaging. Nat Med 4:623–626

Siri A, Carnemolla B, Saginati M, Leprini A, Casari G, Baralle F, Zardi L (1991) Human tenascin: primary structure, pre-mRNA splicing patterns and localization of the epitopes recognized by two monoclonal antibodies. Nucleic Acids Res 19:525–531

St Croix B, Rago C, Velculescu V, Traverso G, Romans KE, Montgomery E, Lal A, Riggins GJ, Lengauer C, Vogelstein B, Kinzler KW (2000) Genes expressed in human tumor endothelium. Science 289:1197–1202

Stollman TH, Scheer MGW, Leenders WPJ, Verrijp CN, Soede AC, Oyen WJG, Ruers TJM, Boerman OC (2008) Specific imaging of VEFG-A expression with radiolabeled anti-VEGF monoclonal antibody. Int J Cancer 122(10):2310–2314

Tarli L, Balza E, Viti F, Borsi L, Castellani P, Berndorff D, Dinkelborg L, Neri D, Zardi L (1999) A high-affinity human antibody that targets tumoral blood vessels. Blood 94:192–198

Temming K, Schiffelers RM, Molema G, Kok RJ (2005) RGD-based strategies for selective delivery of therapeutics and imaging agents to the tumour vasculature. Drug Resist Updat 8:381–402

Tijink BM, Neri D, Leemans CR, Budde M, Dinkelborg LM, Stigter-van Walsum M, Zardi L, van Dongen GA (2006) Radioimmunotherapy of head and neck cancer xenografts using 131I-labeled antibody L19-SIP for selective targeting of tumor vasculature. J Nucl Med 47:1127–1135

Umana P, Jean-Mairet J, Moudry R, Amstutz H, Bailey JE (1999) Engineered glycoforms of an antineuroblastoma IgG1 with optimized antibody-dependent cellular cytotoxic activity. Nat Biotechnol 17:176–180

Velculescu VE, Zhang L, Vogelstein B, Kinzler KW (1995) Serial analysis of gene expression. Science 270:484–487

Verel I, Visser GW, van Dongen GA (2005) The promise of immuno-PET in radioimmunotherapy. J Nucl Med 46(Suppl 1):164S–171S

Villa A, Trachsel E, Kaspar M, Schliemann C, Sommavilla R, Rybak J, Rösli C, Borsi L, Zardi L, Neri D (2008) A high-affinity human monoclonal antibody specific to the alternatively-spliced EDA domain of fibronectin efficiently targets tumor neo-vasculature in vivo. Int J Cancer 122:2405–2413

Wang JM, Kumar S, Pye D, van Agthoven AJ, Krupinski J, Hunter RD (1993) A monoclonal antibody detects heterogeneity in vascular endothelium of tumours and normal tissues. Int J Cancer 54:363–370

Wu AM, Senter PD (2005) Arming antibodies: prospects and challenges for immunoconjugates. Nat Biotechnol 23:1137–1146

Zardi L, Carnemolla B, Siri A, Petersen TE, Paolella G, Sebastio G, Baralle FE (1987) Transformed human cells produce a new fibronectin isoform by preferential alternative splicing of a previously unobserved exon. Embo J 6:2337–2342

Caveolae and Cancer

13

Kerri A. Massey and Jan E. Schnitzer

Abstract All blood vessels are lined by a layer of endothelial cells that help to control vascular permeability. The luminal surface of vascular endothelial cells is studded with transport vesicles called caveolae that are directly in contact with the blood and can transport molecules into and across the endothelium. The vasculature within distinct tissue types expresses a unique array of proteins that can be used to target intravenously injected antibodies directly to that tissue. When the tissue-specific proteins are concentrated in caveolae, the antibodies can be rapidly pumped out of the blood and into the tissue. Tumors appear to be a distinct tissue type with their own unique marker proteins. Targeting accessible proteins at the surface of tumor vasculature with radiolabeled antibodies destroys tumors and drastically increases animal survival. One day, it may be possible to specifically pump targeted molecules into tumors. This could increase therapeutic efficacy and decrease side effects because most of the drug would accumulate specifically in the tumor. Thus, targeting caveolae may provide a universal portal to pump drugs, imaging agents, and gene vectors out of the blood and into underlying tissue.

J. E. Schnitzer (✉)

Proteogenomics Research Institute for Systems Medicine, 11107 Roselle St, San Diego, CA 92121, USA

e-mail: jschnitzer@prism-sd.org

13.1
Vascular Endothelium

All blood vessels are lined by a monolayer of endothelial cells called the endothelium that helps to control vascular permeability. To serve the specific needs of the underlying organs, vascular endothelial cells show molecular and functional variation, depending on their location in the body (Gumkowski et al. 1987; Janzer and Raff 1987; Aird et al. 1997). Three major types of endothelium have been identified based on structural differences. Sinusoidal endothelium lacks a basement membrane and is characterized by large intercellular gaps between endothelial cells. Thus, this endothelium is minimally restrictive and allows rapid and relatively nonselective flow from the blood into the tissue. Liver, spleen, and bone marrow all have sinusoidal endothelia. Fenestrated endothelium exhibits fenestrae, 60–80 nm circular transcellular openings. This endothelium is generally found in organs that need to rapidly exchange small molecules, such as the kidney, endocrine glands, and intestine. Continuous endothelium forms the most restrictive barrier via a monolayer of attenuated cells linked by intercellular junctions with various degrees of tightness (Jennings and Florey 1967).

Molecules can pass through the endothelial barrier via both passive and active mechanisms.

R. Liersch et al. (eds.), *Angiogenesis Inhibition,* Recent Results in Cancer Research,
DOI: 10.1007/978-3-540-78281-0_13, © Springer Verlag Berlin Heidelberg 2010

Generally, water, solutes, and other small molecules may be passively transported by diffusion and convection through intracellular junctions, fenestrae, or transendothelial channels (Wagner and Chen 1991). Larger molecules may require active transport to move into the endothelial cell (endocytosis) or across the endothelial cell barrier (transcytosis).

13.2
Caveolae Structure

Two major forms of active transport are clathrin-coated vesicles and caveolae. Caveolae are 60 nm omega-shaped invaginations found at the plasma membrane in most continuous endothelia that may mediate both endocytosis and transcytosis (Palade 1953; Ghitescu et al. 1986; Milici et al. 1987; Ghitescu and Bendayan 1992; Ghinea et al. 1994; Schnitzer et al. 1994; Jacobson et al. 1996). Caveolae are abundant structures at the endothelial surface, occupying up to 50–70% of the surface plasma membrane and 10–15% of the total cell volume (about 500–600 vesicles/μm^3) (Bruns and Palade 1968; Simionescu et al. 1974; Johansson 1979). Caveolae are most abundant in the microvascular endothelia of the lung, skeletal muscle, and heart; relatively rare in the highly restrictive microvascular endothelia of brain, retina, and testes; and largely absent in passively leaky vessels with sinusoidal endothelia (Ogi et al. 2003), such as in liver.

Electron microscopy reveals that caveolae are structurally distinct from clathrin-coated vesicles, which have a thick, electron-dense coat. Instead, caveolae have bipolar oriented, thin striations that are formed by the oligomerization of the structural coat protein caveolin (Peters et al. 1985; Rothberg et al. 1992). The mammalian caveolin gene family has three members. Caveolin-1 is a 21 kDa integral membrane protein with two isoforms produced by alternative initiation, α and β, and which oligomerize to form the structural coat of the caveolar bulb (Monier et al. 1995; Sargiacomo et al. 1995). Caveolin-1 is both necessary and apparently sufficient to drive formation of caveolae in vitro and in vivo (Fra et al. 1994; Parolini et al. 1999; Drab et al. 2001; Razani et al. 2002a). Additionally, caveolae are lost from the cell surface when caveolin-1 mRNA expression is reduced with antisense oligonucleotides (Griffoni et al. 2000). Caveolin-2 is a 20 kDa protein that can form stable hetero-oligomeric complexes with caveolin-1 (Scherer et al. 1997) and is co-expressed with caveolin-1 in some endothelial cells, adipocytes, epithelial cells, smooth muscle cells, and fibroblasts (Scherer et al. 1997). Caveolin-2 requires caveolin-1 for proper membrane targeting and protein stability (Mora et al. 1999; Parolini et al. 1999), but caveolin-1 appears to be able to localize to the plasma membrane and influence caveolae formation without caveolin-2. Yet, the co-expression of both caveolin-1 and caveolin-2 appears necessary for the formation of stable, deep, plasma membrane-attached caveolae (Razani et al. 2002b; Sowa et al. 2003). Caveolin-3 appears to be expressed mainly in muscle cells, including smooth, skeletal, and cardiac myocytes (Tang et al. 1996).

13.3
Isolation of Caveolae

Early attempts to isolate caveolae relied on detergent-resistance and/or buoyant density after cell fragmentation. These isolates were often contaminated with significant amounts of low-density, detergent-resistant membranes derived from other intracellular organelles, such as nuclei, Golgi, and endoplasmic reticulum, as well as other membrane domains, such as lipid rafts (Smart et al. 1995; Oh and Schnitzer 1999). Alternative methods to isolate caveolae, especially in vivo, have been recently developed to isolate purer populations. In one method, a solution of colloidal silica nanoparticles is per-fused through the blood vessels to selectively coat the luminal surface of endothelial cells. After tissue homogenization, the denser, silica-coated plasma membranes can be isolated away from the rest of the tissue by ultracentrifugation through a high-density media gradient. This effectively isolates luminal plasma membranes of endothelial cells, as can be seen by electron microscopy and western analysis. Known endothelial cell surface markers are highly enriched (>15-fold) while markers of blood, other tissue cells, and subcellular organelles are markedly depleted (15-fold).

The silica coat stabilizes the surface membrane but silica nanoparticles are too large to readily enter the caveolae. Caveolae can be separated from endothelium by mechanical force (Schnitzer et al. 1995c). GTP can also cause caveolae to bud through activation of dynamin (Schnitzer et al. 1996; Oh and Schnitzer 1998), allowing a more physiologically induced separation for isolation. Once separated from the endothelial cell membrane, caveolae can be isolated by flotation using a sucrose density gradient. Electron micrographs of the isolated membranes showed a homogeneous population of 60–80 nm vesicles. Caveolae markers such as caveolin are highly enriched whereas markers for other subcellular organelles are markedly depleted. Additionally, using beads conjugated to caveolin antibodies to further isolate caveolae showed that the population was highly pure (>95%) (Oh and Schnitzer 1999). These methods are especially valuable to separate caveolae from lipid rafts. Though lipid rafts are functionally distinct, they are difficult to isolate away from caveolae because both domains have a similar density. As lipid rafts are flat domains at the surface, they are coated by silica and retained with the rest of the plasma membrane when caveolae are separated (Schnitzer et al. 1995c). The proportion of lipid rafts to caveolae appears quite low in vivo, unlike in vitro where caveolae abundance decreases 50–100-fold in cultured endothelial cells and lipid rafts appear far more prevalent in the isolated detergent-resistant membrane.

13.4 Caveolae in Signal Transduction

By selectively isolating caveolae, the molecular and functional aspects of these structures can be studied with greater confidence. In the past few decades, significant research has accumulated showing that caveolae participate in signal trans-duction, either by directly transducing signals themselves or by concentrating and organizing signaling complexes (Carver and Schnitzer 2007b). The vascular endothelium is directly exposed to the blood and constantly subjected to mechanical forces, including shear forces and pressure. One of the major roles of the endothelium is to rapidly respond to changes in mechanical stressors to prevent damage. Caveolae themselves may be acute mechanosensing organelles (Oh and Schnitzer 1996; Liu et al. 1997; Rizzo et al. 1998b; Rizzo et al. 1998a; Oh and Schnitzer 2001).

Caveolae are responsive to changes in pressure or shear stress both in vitro and in vivo. In cultured endothelial cells, increasing flow rates increases the amount of caveolin and the number of caveolae at the luminal cell surface (Park et al. 2000; Boyd et al. 2003; Rizzo et al. 2003). In high-pressure conditions in vivo (Lee and Schmid-Schonbein 1995), caveolae are distorted and can even disappear or "pop." Caveolin may play a central role in signal transduction through caveolae. Caveolin oligomerizes to form a shell around caveolae that may allow these structures to directly transduce changes in mechanical stress by acting as tension-bearing springs (Rizzo et al. 1998a). Caveolin may also serve as a mechano-sensitive scaffold, concentrating and inhibiting key signaling molecules in caveolae. Molecular mapping studies show that caveolae are enriched in various signaling molecules including specific

G-proteins, select nonreceptor tyrosine kinases, Ras, Raf, and eNOS (Rizzo et al. 1998b; Rizzo et al. 1998a; Oh and Schnitzer 2001; Rizzo et al. 2003). Many of these are enriched in caveolae under basal conditions and may be inhibited by interaction with caveolin (Li et al. 1995; Li et al. 1996; Song et al. 1996). Increasing hemodynamic stressors rapidly activates signaling pathways. Specific pathways, such as ERK, are dependent on both cholesterol and caveolin-1 for activation (Park et al. 1998; Park et al. 2000; Boyd et al. 2003). Proteins concentrated within caveolae are often tyrosine-phosphorylated in responses to changes in mechanical stress (Rizzo et al. 1998a), which can alter functional interactions. Caveolin interacts with eNOS and inhibits activity. Increased flow in situ rapidly dissociates eNOS from caveolin, freeing eNOS to associate with positive modulators such as calmodulin (Rizzo et al. 1998b; Feron and Balligand 2006). Conversely, overexpression of caveolin decreases activation of select mechanotransduction pathways, including the p42/44 MAPK pathway (Engelman et al. 1998). Also, mice lacking caveolin-1 have impaired mechanotransduction, showing a decreased ability to regulate blood vessel diameter in response to changes in flow rates, as well as a decreased activation of eNOS (Yu et al. 2006).

13.5
Caveolae as Active Transport Vesicles

Since caveolae were first identified in 1953 (Palade 1953); researchers have debated over whether these membrane invaginations might play a role in transport (Severs 1988). Over 50 years of evidence has accumulated to suggest that caveolae can indeed function as active transport vesicles. Cultured endothelial cells have been used to show that caveolae are dynamic vesicular carriers. Caveolae appear to traffic select ligands, such as cholera toxin and albumin-gold

complexes, to specific locations within the cell, such as endosomes and lysosomes (Tran et al. 1987; Schnitzer et al. 1988a; Parton et al. 1994). Caveolae may also provide a route of entry for SV40 (Norkin 1999; Pelkmans et al. 2001), ebolavirus (Empig and Goldsmith 2002), and polyomavirus (Mackay and Consigli 1976; Richterova et al. 2001). Furthermore, cholesterol-binding agents, such as filipin, reduce caveolae number and significantly decrease caveolae-mediated cellular trafficking of such molecules as albumin (Schnitzer and Oh 1994; Orlandi and Fishman 1998).

The discovery that caveolae contain proteins classically associated with transport vesicles, including v-SNARES, NSF, and SNAP, suggested that caveolae might function as transport vesicles. Additionally, several GTPases known to play roles in vesicle budding have been found within caveolae (Schnitzer et al. 1995a). These proteins are found in caveolae under basal conditions; no activation is necessary to translocate the necessary machinery to the caveolae. This suggests that caveolae are ready to bud under basal conditions and may be primed for rapid transport. Like other vesicular pathways, caveolae-mediated endocytosis is sensitive to N-ethylmaleimide (NEM), a thioalkylating agent that inhibits the fusion of vesicles to target membranes (Goda and Pfeffer 1991; Schnitzer et al. 1995b).

More recently, isolated endothelial cell plasma membranes were used to show that caveolae can bud and form free vesicles. When GTP and ATP are added to isolated plasma membranes, caveolae budding is induced. Caveolae separate from the membrane and the budded caveolae can be isolated. This reconstituted, cell-free, in vitro assay was used to identify dynamin as the GTPase mediating this fission. Dynamin forms a ring around the neck of caveolae, likely acting as a pinchase to form free vesicles (Oh and Schnitzer 1996; Oh et al. 1998) This was subsequently confirmed in hepatocytes (Henley et al. 1998) which have readily apparent caveolae in cell culture but interestingly, have very few to no caveolae natively in liver tissue in vivo.

Caveolae appear to function in vesicular transport in vivo as well. Normally, albumin can be endo- or transcytosed by caveolae through interaction with caveolar proteins, even when conjugated to gold particles (Ghitescu et al. 1986; Milici et al. 1987; Schnitzer et al. 1988b; Schnitzer et al. 1992). In caveolin-1 knockout mice, the caveolae in microvascular endothelium are absent and this transport pathway is lost (Razani et al. 2001). Although albumin-gold particles bound to the endothelial cell surface in vivo, they were not transported into or across endothelial cells. Because caveolin-knockout mice are viable, other mechanisms must mediate the transport of essential nutrients and other molecules to underlying tissue cells. Indeed, these animals demonstrate increased paracellular transport. They have an overall increased microvascular permeability in vivo (Drab et al. 2001; Razani et al. 2001), resulting in rapid, nonselective transvascular transport of both large and small molecules from the bloodstream, apparently due to significant changes to intercellular junctions between the endothelial cells (Schubert et al. 2002).

13.6
Vascular Targeting

Caveolae are found at the luminal surface of most endothelium and may underlie transport to many different organs and even solid tumors. Many tumors, especially malignant ones, are highly vascularized. Without the ability to rapidly recruit new blood vessels, tumors must rely on passive diffusion to receive nutrients and are thus limited in size (1–2 mm) and localized to their primary site (Nicolson 1988; Blood and Zetter 1990). Tumor blood vessels differ significantly from blood vessels in normal tissue. Tumor blood vessels are usually disorganized and dilated with reduced basement membranes (Workman 2001; Anzick and Trent 2002). They also lack some normal endothelial cell markers, suggesting that they may express a unique array of proteins (Schlingemann et al. 1991). Because tumor growth depends on neovascularization, many investigators have suggested that both the process of angiogenesis and the vasculature itself are potential targets for tumor therapy (Dvorak et al. 1991; Drews 2000; Lindsay 2003).

A major part of recent anti-cancer research has focused on using antibodies to target treatments to the tumor cells themselves. These treatments have been successful in vitro, but the vast majority has failed when used in humans, probably because the endothelium limits movement into the tumors (Dvorak et al. 1991; Huang et al. 1997). Unlike antibodies, chemotherapeutic drugs are small molecules that can readily enter all tissues. As a result, these agents are rapidly diluted, cleared from the blood, and excreted. For both large antibodies and small chemotherapeutics, it appears that only a small portion of the injected dose actually reaches the inside of the tumor where it can be effective. Thus, higher doses must be administered to reach effective levels within the tumor, often leading to severe systemic side effects (Vitetta 2000). The vascular surface and its caveolae are a promising alternative target. Though targeting antibodies passively cross the endothelium of many organs very poorly, they may be transported more readily and rapidly across the endothelial cell barrier via caveolae.

To be effective, vascular targeting depends on the specific and unique expression of target proteins in different tissues and disease states. Multiple methods have been developed over the years to identify differential gene and protein expression. Initial work was performed in vitro, where large quantities of endothelial cells could be grown and analyzed. These early studies in culture revolutionized the study of vascular biology by providing both a pure population of cells to study and by identifying endothelial specific markers (for review see Jaffe 1987). Even in culture, endothelial cells are responsive to components of the environment, including mechanical forces such as shear stress and chemical factors such as chemokines (Malek and Izumo 1995), suggesting that it is vital to study these cells in the native environment.

Both in vitro and in vivo, endothelial cells from different vascular beds are unique (Auerbach et al. 1985; Kallmann et al. 2002; Durr et al. 2004; Oh et al. 2007). However, once in culture, endothelial cells rapidly de-differentiate into a more common phenotype (Madri and Williams 1983; Schnitzer 1997; Thum et al. 2000). Many tissue-specific proteins are no longer expressed and the number of caveolae decreases up to 100-fold (Schnitzer 1997). In spite of these changes, endothelial cells derived from different organs express different genes and proteins. Differences between different vascular beds and the rapid de-differentiation seen in culture strongly suggest that tissue microenvironment can profoundly influence the structure and function of endothelial cells. Recent mass spectrometry analysis shows that approximately 40% of the proteins expressed in vivo are not found in cultured endothelial cells (Durr et al. 2004). Cultured cells lack a normal microenvironment, including circulating blood, the basement membrane, perivascular cells, the tissue parenchyma, and hemodynamic forces (Rizzo et al. 2003), all of which can alter protein expression, structure, and function of endothelial cells. Therefore, experiments seeking to identify tissue-specific vascular targets must be performed, or at the very least, validated in vivo.

13.7
Phage Display Libraries

The idea of phage display libraries was first introduced by George Smith in 1985 (Smith 1985). He suggested that filamentous bacteriophages could be used to display proteins or antibody fragments by fusing a protein of interest to the coat protein of the bacteriophage. In 1991, he showed that these phage could be used to display vast amounts of short peptides (Smith 1991). These peptides were expressed on the surface of the bacteriophage and could bind to antibodies or other proteins. It is also possible to express larger proteins, such as antibody fragments, which are expressed in their native configuration on the outer surface of the phage. Because each bacteriophage expresses one protein of interest, huge libraries of random peptides can be rapidly screened for the ability to bind proteins, antibodies, or even tissue. Because the approach can use a large, random library, it is unbiased and unknown targets can be identified. In a process called panning, unbound phage are washed away, and the bound phage are isolated and amplified. This process is repeated until the phage that bind tightly are separated from those that bind non-specifically. Phage that bind to available proteins can be purified and used as probes themselves to isolate the binding partner for identification (Pasqualini and Ruoslahti 1996; Rajotte et al. 1998).

Phage can also be injected intravenously. Presumably, these phage circulate and bind to the endothelial surface in vivo if the protein targets are available. Then they can be isolated from each organ or tissue of interest. Several iterations create the opportunity for selection of specific peptides or antibodies with defined tissue tropism. However, phage are rapidly scavenged from the blood by the liver and spleen, preventing sufficient equilibrium to bind to endothelial cell surface proteins in vivo. Additionally, short peptides can lack specificity and may bind a large range of proteins in a multitude of organs, requiring additional ex vivo validation. Problems with in vivo targeting can be partially overcome by using phage that recognize specific proteins on endothelial cell extracts to create antibody-like fusion proteins. These can successfully immunotarget in vivo (Valadon et al. 1998). Though phage display libraries have revealed some promising targets, it seems particularly challenging for this approach on its own to be used in a high throughput manner to identify selective tissue-targeting probes, as well as their molecular targets.

13.8
Large-Scale Approaches

Comprehensively defining all the genes or proteins in an organ, cell type, or disease state can help to define the function of these cells, as well as identify therapeutic targets and biomarkers. Additionally, diseases such as cancer are extremely heterogeneous; tumors can differ widely within the same patient or even within the same tumor. Accordingly, tumors show marked variability in invasiveness, metastatic potential, and response to therapy. Comprehensively identifying the changes in gene or protein expression in an individual tumor may better predict the clinical outcome and allow more effective, personalized therapy. It is likely that hundreds of genes or proteins must be identified in order to successfully classify tumors, which demands rapid, high throughput methods.

Genomic approaches theoretically provide a means to identify gene expression in tissues or disease states and identify differences among samples in a relatively rapid manner (Huber 2003; Lindsay 2003). Thus genomic analysis can be used to compare global changes in gene expression. Large changes are needed to detect differences and to differentiate real changes. Even so, thousands of possible targets are often identified, requiring laborious in vivo validation. Additionally, changes in gene expression do not always correlate with changes in protein expression and proteins can be altered in subtler ways. Moving from the cell membrane to an intracellular compartment can render a protein at the endothelial cell surface inaccessible. Additionally, posttranslational modifications can rapidly alter protein function. To truly define the proteins present at the endothelial cell luminal surface, protein expression itself must be characterized.

Several methods allow for identification of proteins within a sample. Two-dimensional (2D) gels are a simple and rapid way to visualize differences between samples. By separating proteins based on multiple characteristics, these gels provide better separation between proteins. Spots that are unique to one tissue can be isolated; known proteins can be identified with antibodies and unknown proteins can be identified with mass spectrometry. For these approaches, successful identification of proteins requires that the proteins migrate onto the gel. Many proteins, especially integral membrane proteins, simply do not separate well on such gels and can be underrepresented or lost altogether. Mass spectrometry-based techniques can identify proteins based on the presence of digested peptides. Similar to genomics approaches, mass spectrometry allows relatively rapid analysis of large numbers of proteins. Because highly complex samples are difficult to separate, samples are often prefractionated before analysis. This has traditionally been done by 2D gels; however, analyzing each distinct spot can be prohibitively time consuming. An attractive alternative uses 2D liquid chromatography to further separate proteins before they are analyzed by the mass spectrometer (Washburn et al. 2001). Samples are separated on a column and directly fed into the mass spectrometer, decreasing handling time. A third alternative, protein arrays, uses antibodies or peptides to identify the proteins present in the sample, but is limited by affinity of the probes and the complexity of the sample. A detailed description of this field has recently been reported (Carver and Schnitzer 2007a).

13.9
Reducing Complexity

Each of these methods is limited by the complexity of the starting sample. Sample complexity can be reduced by focusing on subsets of cells or even subdomains of cells. Proteins at the surface of endothelial cells are directly exposed to the blood and can be labeled by perfusion with radiolabeled or biotinylated compounds. Radiolabeling has most often been used to verify the presence of known proteins because the fact that there is no simple way to separate and identify radiolabeled proteins significantly limited the utility of this approach. In contrast, in vivo biotinylation chemically labels proteins at the luminal surface of vascular endothelial cells and the strong interaction between biotin and avidin can be used to purify biotinylated proteins which can be identified with mass spectrometry (Rybak et al. 2005; Scheurer et al. 2005) or antibodies (Sargiacomo et al. 1989; Fujimoto et al. 1992). Though this method indeed labels a subset of endothelial cell-surface proteins (De La Fuente et al. 1997), some surface proteins may be missed or the small biotin compounds may permeate throughout the tissue and identify proteins beyond the endothelial surface. Labeling other cell types can effectively dilute the pool and increase the false-positive discovery rate of endothelial surface targets considerably.

As discussed earlier, using silica-based nanoparticles can selectively coat the luminal surface of endothelial cells in vivo, allowing this surface to be isolated from the rest of the tissue and further subfractionated to yield a pure population of caveolae. Though far simpler than total tissue homogenate, the membrane isolate is still a complex mixture of proteins. Further separation can be provided by linking 2D chromatography to mass-spectrometry (MudPIT). In MudPIT, proteins are solubilized and digested, then separated by both hydrophobicity and charge. Even with these extra separation steps, each mass spectrometry measurement only identifies a portion of the proteins present in a sample. Identifying new tissue-specific proteins requires comprehensive analysis of the proteins present in different tissues. Five to ten replicates are needed to identify approximately 95% of the proteins identifiable by a single method (Durr et al. 2004).

Additionally, combining multiple mass spectrometry-based methods can increase the number of proteins identified. Recently, traditional 2D mass spectrometry methods such as MudPIT were compared with first separating peptides by size on SDS-PAGE gels followed by analysis by mass spectrometry. These experiments showed that gel prefractionation preserved many membrane proteins that do not re-solubilize after the sample preparation steps required for traditional mass spectrometry. Each technique identified unique peptides; therefore, combining multiple techniques dramatically increased sensitivity, especially for integral membrane proteins. Previous analysis of the plasma membranes identified 450 proteins (Durr et al. 2004). Using the combination of methodologies described earlier identified 1834 proteins were (Y. Li et al. 2009).

Though replicate measurements and multiple methods appear necessary to comprehensively map all proteins present in a sample, intrinsic variability between measurements and methodologies makes it difficult to compare the levels of peptides found with different techniques. New, label-free methods offer a way to overcome these limitations by normalizing and quantifying mass spectrometry data using intrinsic properties of the data. By normalizing data around a Spectral Index that takes peptide number, spectral count, peak precursor ion intensities, and protein length into account, this method reduces the variance between replicates and across a dynamic range of protein loads. Such quantification and normalization of the data is essential for mapping the proteome of endothelium and its caveolae and to identifying tissue or disease-specific targets.

13.10
Tissue-Specific Targets

When samples of the luminal surface of vascular endothelial cells from the lung were analyzed by mass spectrometry, nearly 2000 proteins were identified (Y. Li et al. 2009). Though further analysis must be undertaken to fully map proteins found within subdomains such as the caveolae, this analysis provides the first step in identifying tissue-specific targets.

Endothelial cells depend on the tissue microenvironment to maintain both structure and protein expression. Different vascular beds or even diseases such as cancer can lead to changes in the structure, function, and protein complement of the endothelial cells. Therefore, proteins that are expressed both in vivo and in culture may also be expressed universally across different vascular beds or disease states. Similarly, if protein expression is lost when endothelial cells are grown in culture, this could indicate that expression is dependent upon a specific tissue microenvironment. Thus, eliminating proteins found in culture focuses attention on those proteins that might be more selectively expressed. Only endothelial cell surface proteins that extend into the blood are readily accessible to circulating antibodies. By analyzing the sequences of identified proteins, those likely to have extracellular domains can be identified. Of the 450 proteins identified at the luminal surface of lung endothelium at that time, and of the 187 proteins that were not detected in lung endothelial cells grown in culture, only APP and OX-45 were both specific to lung and likely to extend into the luminal space (Durr et al. 2004; Oh et al. 2004).

Further analysis showed that APP is concentrated in caveolae and accessible to circulating antibodies (Oh et al. 2007). Electron microscopy studies showed that antibodies against APP collected in endothelial caveolae in lung tissue and were internalized and transcytosed across the endothelial cell layer (McIntosh et al. 2002; Oh et al. 2007). When APP antibodies were imaged with dynamic intravital microscopy, this trafficking proved to be extraordinarily rapid. Fluorescently labeled APP antibodies bound to the lung microvascular endothelium within 10 s after intravenous injection and were detected within 15 s outside the endothelium in the perivascular space and interstitium of the tissue. Within minutes, the antibody was cleared from the blood (>80%) as it rapidly accumulated in the lungs. This transcytotic trafficking was

specific, active, and dependent on caveolae. Antibodies were actually pumped out of the blood and across the endothelial cell barrier to accumulate at higher concentration in the tissue than the blood. The antibody rapidly filled the entire lung tissue but did not extend beyond this tissue, nor did fluorescent control IgG leak from the vasculature into the tissue (Oh et al. 2004).

Target enrichment in caveolae may be necessary for rapid transport. Antibodies targeted against proteins found outside of the caveolae still bound to the vasculature but were not pumped into the tissue. If caveolae were depleted by reducing expression levels of the structural protein caveolin, APP antibodies could still bind to the endothelium but were not transported out of the vessels and into tissue. Whole-body imaging as well as biodistribution analysis showed that APP antibodies also target the lungs within minutes in the context of the whole animal. Radiolabeled antibody rapidly accumulated in the lungs and was maintained in the tissue for several days (Oh et al. 2004; Oh et al. 2007).

13.11
Tumor-Specific Targets

Though APP antibodies readily traffic to the lungs, these antibodies do not target lung tumors. When injected into rats bearing lung tumors, APP antibodies were concentrated in the tumor-free lung tissue. When the luminal endothelial surface of vasculature from lung tumors was isolated and run on a 2D blot, a distinct pattern of proteins was seen, suggesting that the solid tumors might form a distinct type of tissue. Analyzing this extract with mass spectrometry confirmed that APP expression was lost in tumor vasculature. Instead, several known cancer markers were upregulated. Surprisingly, a novel protein was induced at the endothelial cell surface. AnnexinA1 (AnnA1) is reported to be expressed in select cells, normally intracellularly; but AnnA1 could be detected at the luminal endothelial cell surface in tumor tissue. AnnA1 expression is also found in blood vessels of many types of human solid tumors (prostate, liver, breast, lung), but is lacking from healthy tissue (Oh et al. 2004).

The AnnA1 found on vascular endothelial cells in tumors was accessible to the blood. Intravenously injected AnnA1 antibodies specifically targeted tumor vasculature and provided excellent imaging with single photon emission computed tomography (SPECT) of lung tumors in the rat. Tumor-bearing rats that received injections of radiolabeled IgG died several days after the injection. When rats were instead injected with radiolabeled AnnA1 antibodies, the vast majority survived, even with just one treatment (Oh et al. 2004). It still remains to be determined which, if any, tumor-induced endothelial proteins exist concentrated in caveolae.

13.12
Clinical Implications

Targeting drugs directly to the caveolae may provide a universal route into underlying tissue. Tumor-specific delivery and transcytosis of drugs and imaging agents could increase efficacy and decrease harmful side by effectively concentrating drugs in the target tissue. Active pumping of antibodies across the endothelial cell layer and into tissue may increase the therapeutic potential (Oh et al. 2007; Red-Horse and Ferrara 2007). Additionally, targeted anti-angiogenic compounds can be used to specifically destroy vasculature, effectively destroying all the cells fed by that vasculature. Such targeting could also revitalize older drugs that failed in clinical testing due to severe side effects. These drugs could be retargeted to the diseased tissues, thus significantly decreasing systemic side effects.

Comprehensive analysis of the vascular proteome is absolutely essential to identify tissue-specific protein expression and to identify differences between normal and diseased tissue. Identifying unique markers may allow the targeting of gene therapy, drugs, and imaging agents. Comprehensive mapping of the proteins in both healthy and tumor tissue may identify additional targets and extend the utility of targeted delivery. Drugs could theoretically be targeted to the endothelial surface, to the endothelial cell itself, or to the underlying tissue, depending on the nature of the target and the processing of the antibody once bound. Additionally, understanding the functional changes in the endothelial cell plasma membrane between tissues and between healthy tissue and disease states provides insight into the needs of each tissue and the changes that develop with disease.

Developing animal models of tumors that better represent human disease is essential not only for identifying targets, but also for testing the efficacy of targeted drugs. Most current models rely on subcutaneous tumors grown directly on the skin. These tumors lack the native tissue microenvironment and may differ from tumors grown on orthotopic tissue. Indeed, most new drugs are tested in subcutaneous tumor models. Efficacy in these models rarely reflects efficacy in human trials. Many genetic models of tumors currently exist. However, these spontaneous tumors do not, so far, fully recapitulation human disease, are often difficult to image, and are rarely used for preclinical testing. Clearly, reliable models are needed to bridge the gap between laboratory experiments and success in human patients.

The possibilities of caveolar targeting go well beyond the delivery of drugs to cancer cells. Tissue-specific markers for the lung itself have been identified and validated in vivo (Oh et al. 2007). Such markers could target drugs, imaging agents, nanoparticles, or even genetic material to a specific organ. Additionally, caveolae are rich in signaling molecules, and targeted small molecules, siRNAs, peptides, or nanoparticles could be used to activate or inhibit specific pathways. Pumping agents into a specific tissue may open the door not only to new molecular therapies but also to more effective experimentation in vivo, including molecular and functional imaging.

References

Aird WC, Edelberg JM, Weiler-Guettler H, Simmons WW, Smith TW, Rosenberg RD (1997) Vascular bed-specific expression of an endothelial cell gene is programmed by the tissue microenvironment. J Cell Biol 138:1117–1124

Anzick SL, Trent JM (2002) Role of genomics in identifying new targets for cancer therapy. Oncology (Huntingt) 16:7–13

Auerbach R, Alby L, Morrissey LW, Tu M, Joseph J (1985) Expression of organ-specific antigens on capillary endothelial cells. Microvasc Res 29:401–411

Blood CH, Zetter BR (1990) Tumor interaction with the vasculature: angiogenesis and tumor metastasis. Biochim Biophys Acta 1032:89–118

Boyd NL, Park H, Yi H, Boo YC, Sorescu GP, Sykes M, Jo H (2003) Chronic shear induces caveolae formation and alters ERK and Akt responses in endothelial cells. Am J Physiol Heart Circ Physiol 285:H1113–H1122

Bruns RR, Palade GE (1968) Studies on blood capillaries. I. General organization of blood capillaries in muscle. J Cell Biol 37:244–276

Carver LA, Schnitzer JE (2007a) Proteomic mapping of endothelium and vascular targeting in vivo. In: Aird WC (ed) Endothelial biomedicine. Cambridge University Press, New york, pp 881–898

Carver LA, Schnitzer JE (2007b) Multiple functions and clinical uses of caveolae in endothelium. In: Aird WC (ed) Endothelial biomedicine. Cambridge University Press, New york, pp 664–678

De La Fuente EK, Dawson CA, Nelin LD, Bongard RD, McAuliffe TL, Merker MP (1997) Biotinylation of membrane proteins accessible via the pulmonary circulation in normal and hyperoxic rats. Am J Physiol 272:L461–L470

Drab M, Verkade P, Elger M, Kasper M, Lohn M, Lauterbach B, Menne J, Lindschau C, Mende F, Luft FC, Schedl A, Haller H, Kurzchalia TV (2001) Loss of caveolae, vascular dysfunction, and pulmonary defects in caveolin-1 gene-disrupted mice. Science 293:2449–2452

Drews J (2000) Drug discovery: a historical perspective. Science 287:1960–1964

Durr E, Yu J, Krasinska KM, Carver LA, Yates JRI, Testa JE, Oh P, Schnitzer JE (2004) Direct proteomic mapping of the lung microvascular endothelial cell surface in vivo and in cell culture. Nat Biotechnol 22:985–992

Dvorak HF, Nagy JA, Dvorak AM (1991) Structure of solid tumors and their vasculature: implications for therapy with monoclonal antibodies. Cancer Cells 3:77–85

Empig CJ, Goldsmith MA (2002) Association of the caveola vesicular system with cellular entry by filoviruses. J Virol 76:5266–5270

Engelman JA, Chu C, Lin A, Jo H, Ikezu T, Okamoto T, Kohtz DS, Lisanti MP (1998) Caveolin-mediated regulation of signaling along the p42/44 MAP kinase cascade in vivo. A role for the caveolin-scaffolding domain. FEBS Lett 428:205–211

Feron O, Balligand JL (2006) Caveolins and the regulation of endothelial nitric oxide synthase in the heart. Cardiovasc Res 69:788–797

Fra AM, Williamson E, Simons K, Parton RG (1994) Detergent-insoluble glycolipid microdomains in lymphocytes in the absence of caveolae. J Biol Chem 269:30745–30748

Fujimoto T, Nakade S, Miyawaki A, Mikoshiba K, Ogawa K (1992) Localization of inositol 1, 4, 5-trisphosphate receptor-like protein in plasmalemmal caveolae. J Cell Biol 119:1507–1513

Ghinea N, Mai TV, Groyer-Picard MT, Milgrom E (1994) How protein hormones reach their target cells. Receptor-mediated transcytosis of hCG through endothelial cells. J Cell Biol 125:87–97

Ghitescu L, Bendayan M (1992) Transendothelial transport of serum albumin: a quantitative immunocytochemical study. J Cell Biol 117:745–755

Ghitescu L, Fixman A, Simionescu M, Simionescu N (1986) Specific binding sites for albumin restricted to plasmalemmal vesicles of continuous capillary endothelium: receptor-mediated transcytosis. J Cell Biol 102:1304–1311

Goda Y, Pfeffer SR (1991) Identification of a novel, N-ethylmaleimide-sensitive cytosolic factor required for vesicular transport from endosomes to the trans-golgi network in vitro. J Cell Biol 112:823–831

Griffoni C, Spisni E, Santi S, Riccio M, Guarnieri T, Tomasi V (2000) Knockdown of caveolin-1 by antisense oligonucleotides impairs angiogenesis in vitro and in vivo. Biochem Biophys Res Commun 276:756–761

Gumkowski F, Kaminska G, Kaminski M, Morrissey LW, Auerbach R (1987) Heterogeneity of mouse vascular endothelium. Blood Vessels 24:11–23

Henley JR, Krueger EW, Oswald BJ, McNiven MA (1998) Dynamin-mediated internalization of caveolae. J Cell Biol 141:85–99

Huang X, Molema G, King S, Watkins L, Edgington TS, Thorpe PE (1997) Tumor infraction in mice by antibody-directed targeting of tissue factor to tumor vasculature. Science 275:547–550

Huber LA (2003) Is proteomics heading in the wrong direction? Nat Rev Mol Cell Biol 4:74–80

Jacobson BS, Stolz DB, Schnitzer JE (1996) Identification of endothelial cell-surface proteins as targets for diagnosis and treatment of disease. Nat Med 2:482–484

Jaffe EA (1987) Cell biology of endothelial cells. Hum Pathol 18:234–239

Janzer RC, Raff MC (1987) Astrocytes induce blood-brain barrier properties in endothelial cells. Nature 325:253–257

Jennings MA, Florey L (1967) An investigation of some properties of endothelium related to capillary permeability. Proc R Soc Lond B Biol Sci 167:39–63

Johansson BR (1979) Size and distribution of endothelial plasmalemmal vesicles in consecutive segments of the microvasculature in cat skeletal muscle. Microvasc Res 17:107–117

Kallmann BA, Wagner S, Hummel V, Buttmann M, Bayas A, Tonn JC, Rieckmann P (2002) Characteristic gene expression profile of primary human cerebral endothelial cells. FASEB J 16:589–591

Lee J, Schmid-Schonbein GW (1995) Biomechanics of skeletal muscle capillaries: hemodynamic resistance, endothelial distensibility and pseudopod formation. Ann Biomed Eng 23:226–246

Li S, Okamoto T, Chun M, Sargiacomo M, Casanova JE, Hansen SH, Nishimoto I, Lisanti MP (1995) Evidence for a regulated interaction between heterotrimeric G proteins and caveolin. J Biol Chem 270:15693–15701

Li S, Seitz R, Lisanti MP (1996) Phosphorylation of caveolin by src tyrosine kinases. The alpha-isoform of caveolin is selectively phosphorylated by v-Src in vivo. J Biol Chem 271:3863–3868

Li Y, Yu J, Wang YZ, Griffin NM, Long F, Shore S, Oh P, Schnitzer JE (2009) Enhancing identifications of lipid-embedded proteins by mass spectrometry for improved mapping of endothelial plasma membranes in vivo. Mol Cell Proteomics 8(6):1219–1235

Lindsay MA (2003) Target discovery. Nat Rev Drug Discov 2:831–838

Liu J, Oh P, Horner T, Rogers RA, Schnitzer J (1997) Organized cell surface signal transduction in caveolae distinct from GPI-anchored protein microdomains. J Biol Chem 272:7211–7222

Mackay RL, Consigli RA (1976) Early events in polyoma virus infection: attachment, penetration, and nuclear entry. J Virol 19:620–636

Madri JA, Williams SK (1983) Capillary endothelial cell culture: phenotype modulation by matrix components. J Cell Biol 97:153–165

Malek AM, Izumo S (1995) Control of endothelial cell gene expression by flow. J Biomech 28:1515–1528

McIntosh DP, Tan X-Y, Oh P, Schnitzer JE (2002) Targeting endothelium and its dynamic caveolae for tissue-specific transcytosis in vivo: a pathway to overcome cell barriers to drug and gene delivery. Proc Natl Acad Sci USA 99:1996–2001

Milici AJ, Watrous NE, Stukenbrok H, Palade GE (1987) Transcytosis of albumin in capillary endothelium. J Cell Biol 105:2603–2612

Monier S, Parton RG, Vogel F, Behlke J, Henske A, Kurzchalia TV (1995) VIP21-caveolin, a membrane protein constituent of the caveolar coat, oligomerizes in vivo and in vitro. Mol Biol Cell 6:911–927

Mora R, Bonilha VL, Marmorstein A, Scherer PE, Brown D, Lisanti MP, Rodriguez-Boulan E (1999) Caveolin-2 localizes to the golgi complex but redistributes to plasma membrane, caveolae, and rafts when co-expressed with caveolin-1. J Biol Chem 274:25708–25717

Nicolson GL (1988) Cancer metastasis: tumor cell and host organ properties important in metastasis to specific secondary sites. Biochim Biophys Acta 948:175–224

Norkin LC (1999) Simian virus 40 infection via MHC class I molecules and caveolae. Immunol Rev 168:13–22

Ogi M, Yokomori H, Oda M, Yoshimura K, Nomura M, Ohshima S, Akita M, Toda K, Ishii H (2003) Distribution and localization of caveolin-1 in sinusoidal cells in rat liver. Med Electron Microsc 36:33–40

Oh P, Schnitzer JE (1996) Dynamin-mediated fission of caveolae from plasma membranes. Mol Biol Cell 7:83a

Oh P, Schnitzer JE (1998) solation and subfractionation of plasma membranes to purify caveolae separately from glycosyl-phospatidylinositol-anchored protein microdomains. In: Celis J (ed) Cell biology: a laboratory handbook. Academic Press, New York, pp 34–46

Oh P, Schnitzer JE (1999) Immunoisolation of caveolae with high affinity antibody binding to the oligomeric caveolin cage. Toward understanding the basis of purification. J Biol Chem 274: 23144–23154

Oh P, Schnitzer JE (2001) Segregation of heterotrimeric G proteins in cell surface microdomains: Gq binds caveolin to concentrate in caveolae whereas Gi and Gs target lipid rafts by default. Mol Biol Cell 12:685–698

Oh P, McIntosh DP, Schnitzer JE (1998) Dynamin at the neck of caveolae mediates their budding to form transport vesicles by GTP-driven fission from the plasma membrane of endothelium. J Cell Biol 141:101–114

Oh P, Li Y, Yu J, Durr E, Krasinska KM, Carver LA, Testa JE, Schnitzer JE (2004) Subtractive proteomic mapping of the endothelial surface in lung and solid tumours for tissue-specific therapy. Nature 429:629–635

Oh P, Borgstrom P, Witkiewicz H, Li Y, Borgstrom BJ, Chrastina A, Iwata K, Zinn KR, Baldwin R, Testa JE, Schnitzer JE (2007) Live dynamic imaging of caveolae pumping targeted antibody rapidly and specifically across endothelium in the lung. Nat Biotechnol 25:327–337

Orlandi PA, Fishman PH (1998) Filipin-dependent inhibition of cholera toxin: evidence for toxin internalization and activation through caveolae-like domains. J Cell Biol 141:905–915

Palade GE (1953) Fine structure of blood capillaries. J Appl Phys 24:1424

Park H, Go YM, St John PL, Maland MC, Lisanti MP, Abrahamson DR, Jo H (1998) Plasma membrane cholesterol is a key molecule in shear stress-dependent activation of extracellular signal-regulated kinase. J Biol Chem 273: 32304–32311

Park H, Go YM, Darji R, Choi JW, Lisanti MP, Maland MC, Jo H (2000) Caveolin-1 regulates shear stress-dependent activation of extracellular signal-regulated kinase. Am J Physiol Heart Circ Physiol 278:H1285–H1293

Parolini I, Topa S, Sorice M, Pace A, Ceddia P, Montesoro E, Pavan A, Lisanti MP, Peschle C, Sargiacomo M (1999) Phorbol ester-induced disruption of the CD4-Lck complex occurs within a detergent-resistant microdomain of the plasma membrane. Involvement of the translocation of activated protein kinase C isoforms. J Biol Chem 274:14176–14187

Parton RG, Joggerst B, Simons K (1994) Regulated internalization of caveolae. J Cell Biol 127: 1199–1215

Pasqualini R, Ruoslahti E (1996) Organ targeting in vivo using phage display peptide libraries. Nature 380:364–366

Pelkmans L, Kartenback J, Helenius A (2001) Caveolar endocytosis of Simian virus 40 reveals a novel two-step vesicular transport pathway to the ER. Nat Cell Biol 3:473–483

Peters KR, Carley WW, Palade GE (1985) Endothelial plasmalemmal vesicles have a characteristic striped bipolar surface structure. J Cell Biol 101:2233–2238

Rajotte D, Arap W, Hagedorn M, Koivunen E, Pasqualini R, Ruoslahti E (1998) Molecular heterogeneity of the vascular endothelium revealed by in vivo phage display. J Clin Invest 102: 430–437

Razani B, Engelman JA, Wang XB, Schubert W, Zhang XL, Marks CB, Macaluso F, Russell RG, Li M, Pestell RG, Di Vizio D, Hou H Jr, Kneitz B, Lagaud G, Christ GJ, Edelmann W, Lisanti MP (2001) Caveolin-1 null mice are viable but show evidence of hyperproliferative and vascular abnormalities. J Biol Chem 276:38121–38138

Razani B, Woodman SE, Lisanti MP (2002a) Caveolae: from cell biology to animal physiology. Pharmacol Rev 54:431–467

Razani B, Wang XB, Engelman JA, Battista M, Lagaud G, Zhang XL, Kneitz B, Hou H Jr, Christ GJ, Edelmann W, Lisanti MP (2002b) Caveolin-2-deficient mice show evidence of severe pulmonary dysfunction without disruption of caveolae. Mol Cell Biol 22:2329–2344

Red-Horse K, Ferrara N (2007) Vascular targeting via caveolae. Nat Biotechnol 25:431–432

Richterova Z, Liebl D, Horak M, Palkova Z, Stokrova J, Hozak P, Korb J, Forstova J (2001) Caveolae are involved in the trafficking of mouse polyomavirus virions and artificial VP1 pseudocapsids toward cell nuclei. J Virol 75:10880–10891

Rizzo V, Sung A, Oh P, Schnitzer JE (1998a) Rapid mechanotransduction in situ at the luminal cell surface of vascular endothelium and its caveolae. J Biol Chem 273:26323–26329

Rizzo V, McIntosh DP, Oh P, Schnitzer JE (1998b) In situ flow activates endothelial nitric oxide

13

synthase in luminal caveolae of endothelium with rapid caveolin dissociation and calmodulin association. J Biol Chem 273:34724–34729

Rizzo V, Morton C, DePaola N, Schnitzer JE, Davies PF (2003) Recruitment of endothelial caveolae into mechanotransduction pathways by flow conditioning in vitro. Am J Physiol Heart Circ Physiol 285:H1720–H1729

Rothberg KG, Heuser JE, Donzell WC, Ying YS, Glenney JR, Anderson RG (1992) Caveolin, a protein component of caveolae membrane coats. Cell 68:673–682

Rybak JN, Ettorre A, Kaissling B, Giavazzi R, Neri D, Elia G (2005) In vivo protein biotinylation for identification of organ-specific antigens accessible from the vasculature. Nat Methods 2:291–298

Sargiacomo M, Lisanti M, Graeve L, Le Bivic A, Rodriguez-Boulan E (1989) Integral and peripheral protein composition of the apical and basolateral membrane domains in MDCK cells. J Membr Biol 107:277–286

Sargiacomo M, Scherer PE, Tang Z, Kubler E, Song KS, Sanders MC, Lisanti MP (1995) Oligomeric structure of caveolin: implications for caveolae membrane organization. Proc Natl Acad Sci U S A 92:9407–9411

Scherer PE, Lewis RY, Volonte D, Engelman JA, Galbiati F, Couet J, Kohtz DS, van Donselaar E, Peters P, Lisanti MP (1997) Cell-type and tissue-specific expression of caveolin-2. Caveolins 1 and 2 co-localize and form a stable hetero-oligomeric complex in vivo. J Biol Chem 272: 29337–29346

Scheurer SB, Roesli C, Neri D, Elia G (2005) A comparison of different biotinylation reagents, tryptic digestion procedures, and mass spectrometric techniques for 2-D peptide mapping of membrane proteins. Proteomics 5:3035–3039

Schlingemann RO, Rietveld FJ, Kwaspen F, van de Kerkhof PC, de Waal RM, Ruiter DJ (1991) Differential expression of markers for endothelial cells, pericytes, and basal lamina in the microvasculature of tumors and granulation tissue. Am J Pathol 138:1335–1347

Schnitzer JE (1997) Vascular endothelium: physiology, pathology and therapeutic opportunities. In: Born GVR, Schwartz CJ (eds) The endothelial cell surface and caveolae in health and disease. Schattauer, Stuttgart, pp 77–95

Schnitzer JE, Oh P (1994) Albondin-mediated capillary permeability to albumin. Differential role of receptors in endothelial transcytosis and endocytosis of native and modified albumins. J Biol Chem 269: 6072–6082

Schnitzer JE, Carley WW, Palade GE (1988a) Specific albumin binding to microvascular endothelium in culture. Am J Physiol 254:H425–H437

Schnitzer JE, Carley WW, Palade GE (1988b) Albumin interacts specifically with a 60-kDa microvascular endothelial glycoprotein. Proc Natl Acad Sci U S A 85:6773–6777

Schnitzer JE, Bravo J, Sung A, Pinney E (1992) Non-coated caveolae-mediated endocytosis of modified proteins via novel scavenger receptors, gp30 and gp18. Mol Biol Cell 3:59a

Schnitzer JE, Oh P, Jacobson BS, Dvorak AM (1994) Caveolin-enriched caveolae purified from endothelium in situ are transport vesicles for albondin-mediateed transcytosis of albumin. Mol Biol Cell 5:A75

Schnitzer JE, Liu J, Oh P (1995a) Endothelial caveolae have the molecular transport machinery for vesicle budding, docking, and fusion including VAMP, NSF, SNAP, annexins, and GTPases. J Biol Chem 270:14399–14404

Schnitzer JE, Allard J, Oh P (1995b) NEM inhibits transcytosis, endocytosis, and capillary permeability: implication of caveolae fusion in endothelia. Am J Physiol 268:H48–H55

Schnitzer JE, McIntosh DP, Dvorak AM, Liu J, Oh P (1995c) Separation of caveolae from associated microdomains of GPI-anchored proteins [see comments]. Science 269:1435–1439

Schnitzer JE, Oh P, McIntosh DP (1996) Role of GTP hydrolysis in fission of caveolae directly from plasma membranes [publisher's erratum appears in Science 1996 Nov 15;274(5290):1069]. Science 274:239–242

Schubert W, Frank PG, Woodman SE, Hyogo H, Cohen DE, Chow CW, Lisanti MP (2002) Microvascular hyperpermeability in caveolin-1 (-/-) knock-out mice. Treatment with a specific nitric-oxide synthase inhibitor, L-name, restores normal microvascular permeability in Cav-1 null mice. J Biol Chem 277:40091–40098

Severs NJ (1988) Caveolae: static inpocketings of the plasma membrane, dynamic vesicles or plain artifact? J Cell Sci 90:341–348

Simionescu M, Simionescu N, Palade GE (1974) Morphometric data on the endothelium of blood capillaries. J Cell Biol 60:128–152

Smart EJ, Ying YS, Mineo C, Anderson RG (1995) A detergent-free method for purifying caveolae membrane from tissue culture cells. Proc Natl Acad Sci U S A 92:10104–10108

Smith GP (1985) Filamentous fusion phage: novel expression vectors that display cloned antigens on the virion surface. Science 228:1315–1317

Smith GP (1991) Surface presentation of protein epitopes using bacteriophage expression systems. Curr Opin Biotechnol 2:668–673

Song KS, Li S, Okamoto T, Quilliam LA, Sargiacomo M, Lisanti MP (1996) Co-purification and direct interaction of Ras with caveolin, an integral membrane protein of caveolae microdomains. Detergent-free purification of caveolae microdomains. J Biol Chem 271:9690–9697

Sowa G, Pypaert M, Fulton D, Sessa WC (2003) The phosphorylation of caveolin-2 on serines 23 and 36 modulates caveolin-1-dependent caveolae formation. Proc Natl Acad Sci U S A 100: 6511–6516

Tang Z, Scherer PE, Okamoto T, Song K, Chu C, Kohtz DS, Nishimoto I, Lodish HF, Lisanti MP (1996) Molecular cloning of caveolin-3, a novel member of the caveolin gene family expressed predominantly in muscle. J Biol Chem 271: 2255–2261

Thum T, Haverich A, Borlak J (2000) Cellular dedifferentiation of endothelium is linked to activation and silencing of certain nuclear transcription factors: implications for endothelial dysfunction and vascular biology. FASEB J 14:740–751

Tran D, Carpentier JL, Sawano F, Gorden P, Orci L (1987) Ligands internalized through coated or noncoated invaginations follow a common intracellular pathway. Proc Natl Acad Sci U S A 84: 7957–7961

Valadon P, Nussbaum G, Oh J, Scharff MD (1998) Aspects of antigen mimicry revealed by immunization with a peptide mimetic of *Cryptococcus neoformans* polysaccharide. J Immunol 161: 1829–1836

Vitetta ES (2000) Immunotoxins and vascular leak syndrome. Cancer J 6(Suppl 3):S218–S224

Wagner RC, Chen S-C (1991) Transcapillary transport of solute by the endothelial vesicular system: evidence from thin serial section analysis. Microvasc Res 42:139–150

Washburn MP, Wolters D, Yates JR III (2001) Large-scale analysis of the yeast proteome by multidimensional protein identification technology. Nat Biotechnol 19:242–247

Workman P (2001) New drug targets for genomic cancer therapy: successes, limitations, opportunities and future challenges. Curr Cancer Drug Targets 1:33–47

Yu J, Bergaya S, Murata T, Alp IF, Bauer MP, Lin MI, Drab M, Kurzchalia TV, Stan RV, Sessa WC (2006) Direct evidence for the role of caveolin-1 and caveolae in mechanotransduction and remodeling of blood vessels. J Clin Invest 116:1284–1291